1004

$20

The Brandons and Others

The Brandons
and Others

BY

ANGELA THIRKELL

HAMISH HAMILTON
LONDON

This Edition first published in Great Britain, 1968
by Hamish Hamilton Ltd
90 Great Russell Street, London W.C.1
Copyright © 1968 Angela Thirkell Estate

The Brandons and *Before Lunch* were first published in 1939
Cheerfulness Breaks In was first published in 1940

SET BY GLOUCESTER TYPESETTING CO. LTD.
PRINTED IN GREAT BRITAIN
BY CLARE, SON AND CO., LTD., WELLS, SOMERSET ENGLAND

Contents

THE BRANDONS

THE BRANDONS

BREAKFAST AT STORIES

'I WONDER who this is from,' said Mrs. Brandon, picking a letter out of the heap that lay by her plate and holding it at arm's length upside down. 'It is quite extraordinary how I can't see without my spectacles. It makes me laugh sometimes because it is so ridiculous.'

In proof of this assertion she laughed very pleasantly. Her son and daughter, who were already eating their breakfast, exchanged pitying glances but said nothing.

'It doesn't look like a handwriting that I know,' said Mrs. Brandon, putting her large horn-rimmed spectacles on and turning the letter the right way up. 'More like a handwriting that I *don't* know. The postmark is all smudgy so I can't see where it comes from.'

'You might steam it open and see who it's from,' said her son Francis, 'and then shut it up again and guess.'

'But if I *saw* who it was from I'd *know*,' said Mrs. Brandon plaintively. 'In France and places people write their name and address across the back of the envelope so that you know who it is.'

'And then you needn't open it at all if you don't like them,' said Francis, 'though I believe they really only do it to put spies from other places off the scent. I mean if Aunt Sissie wanted to write to you she would put someone else's name and address on the flap, and then you would open it instead of very rightly putting it straight into the waste-paper basket.'

'You don't think it's from Aunt Sissie, do you?' said Mrs. Brandon. 'Whenever I get a letter I hope it isn't from her; but mostly' she added, reverting to her original grievance, 'one knows at once by the handwriting who it's from.'

'If it's Aunt Sissie,' said her daughter Delia, 'it will be all about being offended because we haven't been to see her since Easter.'

'Well, we couldn't,' said Mrs. Brandon. 'Francis hasn't had a holiday since Easter, and you were abroad and if I go alone she is only annoyed. Besides she is more your aunt than mine. She is no relation of mine at all. That she is a relation of yours you have to thank your father.'

Francis and Delia again exchanged glances. It was a habit of their

9

mother's to make them entirely responsible for any difficulties brought into the family by the late Mr. Brandon, saying the words 'your father' in a voice that implied a sinister collaboration between that gentleman and the powers of darkness for which her children were somehow to blame. As for Mr. Brandon's merits, which consisted chiefly in having been an uninterested husband and father for some six or seven years and then dying and leaving his widow quite well off, no one thought of them.

'Well, after all, Mother, father was as much your father as ours,' said Francis, who while holding no brief for a parent whom he could barely remember, felt that men must stick together, 'at least *you* brought him into the family, and that makes you really responsible for Aunt Sissie. And,' he hurriedly added, seeing in his mother's eye what she was about to say, 'it's no good your saying father wouldn't have liked to hear me speak to you like that, darling, because that's just what we can't tell. Can I have some more coffee?'

Mrs. Brandon, who had been collecting her forces to take rather belated offence at her son's remarks, was so delighted to fuss over his coffee that she entirely forgot her husband's possible views on how young men should address their mothers and saw herself very happily as a still not unattractive woman spoiling a handsome and devoted son. That Francis's looks were inherited from his father was a fact she chose to ignore, except if his hair was more than usually untidy, when she was apt to say reproachfully, 'Of course that is your father's hair, Francis,' or even more loftily and annoyingly to no one in particular, 'His father's hair all over again.'

Peace being restored over the coffee, Mrs. Brandon ate her own breakfast and read her letters. Francis and Delia were discussing a plan for a picnic with some friends in the neighbourhood, when their mother interrupted them by remarking defiantly that she had said so.

A small confusion took place.

'No, no,' said Mrs. Brandon, 'nothing to do with hard-boiled eggs or cucumber sandwiches. It is is your Aunt Sissie.'

By the tone of the word 'your' her children realized that they were about to be in disgrace for thinking of picnics at such an hour.

'Then it *was* Aunt Sissie,' said Delia. 'What is the worst, Mother? Does she want us to go over?'

'Wait,' said Mrs. Brandon. 'It isn't Aunt Sissie. At least not exactly. It is dictated. I will read it to you. And that,' said Mrs. Brandon laying the letter aside, 'is why I couldn't tell who it was from. It is written by someone called Ella Morris with Miss in brackets, so as none of the maids are called Morris it must be a new companion.'

'Heaven help her,' said Francis, 'and that isn't swearing, darling, and I am sure father would have said it too. Give me the letter or we shall never know what is in it. Delia, the blow has fallen. Ella Morris,

Miss, writes at the wish of Miss Brandon to say that she, Miss Brandon, hereinafter to be known as Aunt Sissie, is at a loss to understand why all her relations have forsaken her and she is an ailing old woman and expects us all to come over on Wednesday to lunch or be cut out of her will. Mother, who gets Aunt Sissie's money if she disinherits us?'

Mrs. Brandon said that was not the way to talk.

After half an hour's detailed consideration of the question the Brandon family left the breakfast table, not that the subject was in any way exhausted, but Rose the parlourmaid had begun to hover in an unnerving and tyrannical way. Francis said he must write some letters, Delia went to do the telephoning which she and her friends found a necessary part of daily life, while Mrs. Brandon went into the garden to get fresh flowers, choosing with great cunning the moment when the gardener was having a mysterious second breakfast. Certainly anyone who had met her coming furtively and hurriedly but triumphantly in by the drawing-room window, her arms full of the gardener's flowers, would entirely have agreed with her own opinion of herself and found her still not unattractive, or possibly felt that a woman with so enchanting an expression could not have been more charming even in her youth. Mrs. Brandon herself, in one of her moods of devastating truthfulness, had explained her own appearance as the result of a long and happy widowhood, and as, after a little sincere grief at the loss of a husband to whom she had become quite accustomed, she had had nothing of consequence to trouble her, it is probable that she was right. Her house and garden were pretty, comfortable, and of a manageable size, her servants stayed with her, Francis had been one of those lucky, even-tempered boys that go through school with the good-will of all, if with no special distinction, and then fallen straight into a good job.

As for Delia, she combined unconcealed scorn for her mother with a genuine affection and an honest wish to improve her and bring her up to date. Mrs. Brandon thought her daughter a darling, and had gladly given up any attempt at control years ago. The only fault she could find with her children was that they didn't laugh at the same jokes as she did, but finding that all their friends were equally humourless, she accepted it placidly, seeing herself as a spirit of laughter born out of its time.

But human nature cannot be content on a diet of honey and if there is nothing in one's life that requires pity, one must invent it; for to go through life unpitied would be an unthinkable loss. Mrs. Brandon, quite unconsciously, had made of her uninteresting husband a mild bogey, allowing her friends, especially those who had not known him, to imagine a slightly sinister figure that had cast a becoming shadow over his charming widow's life. Many of her acquaintances said sympathetically they really could not imagine why she had married such a man. To them Mrs. Brandon would reply wistfully that she had not been very happy as a girl and no one else had asked her, thus giving the impression that she had in her innocence seized an opportunity to escape from loveless home to what proved a loveless marriage. The truth, ever so little twisted in the right direction by her ingenious mind, was that Mr. Brandon had proposed to her when she was not quite twenty. Being a kind-hearted girl who hated to say no, she had at once fallen in love, because if one's heart is not otherwise engaged there seems to be nothing else to do. Her parents had made no difficulties, Mr. Brandon had made a very handsome will and taken his wife to Stories, his charming early Georgian house at Pomfret Madrigal in the Barchester country. Francis was born before she was twenty-one, a deed which filled her with secret pride, though no one else would have guessed it from her usual plaintive and ambiguous statement, 'of course my first baby was born almost at once,' a statement which had made more than one of her hearers silently add the word Brute to Mr. Brandon's epitaph.

Delia was born four years later, and Mrs. Brandon, wrapped up in her nursery, was only beginning to feel ruffled by her husband's dullness when death with kindly care removed him through the agency of pneumonia. As it was a cold spring Mrs. Brandon was able to go into black, and the ensuing summer being a particularly hot one gave her an excuse for mourning in white, though she always wore a heavy necklace of old jet to show goodwill.

It was during that summer that Mr. Brandon's Aunt Sissie, hitherto an almost mythical figure, had made her first terrifying appearance at Stories. Mrs. Brandon was sitting in the ex-library, now called her sitting-room, writing to her parents, when the largest Rolls Royce she had ever seen came circling round the gravel sweep. As it drew up she saw that there were two chauffeurs on the front seat. The man who was driving remained at his post to restrain the ardour of his machine while the second got out and rang the front door bell. The bonnet was facing Mrs. Brandon and she could not see who was inside the car without making herself too visible at the window, so she had to wait till Rose, then only a young parlourmaid, but older than her mistress and already a budding tyrant, came in.

'Miss Brandon, madam,' she announced, 'and I've put her in the drawing-room.'

'Miss Brandon?' said her mistress. 'Oh, that must be Mr. Brandon's aunt. What shall I do?'

'I've put her in the drawing-room, madam,' Rose repeated, speaking patiently as to a mental defective, 'and she said the chauffeurs was to have some tea, madam, so Cook is looking after them.'

'Then I suppose I must,' said Mrs. Brandon, and went into the drawing-room.

It was here that for the first and only time she felt a faint doubt as to the propriety of mourning in white, for her aunt by marriage was wearing such a panoply of black silk dress, black cashmere mantle, black ostrich feather boa and unbelievably a black bonnet trimmed with black velvet and black cherries, that Mrs. Brandon wondered giddily whether spinsters could be honorary widows.

'When once I have sat down I don't get up again easily,' said Miss Brandon, holding out a black-gloved, podgy hand.

'Oh, please don't,' said Mrs. Brandon vaguely, taking her aunt's lifeless hand. 'How do you do, Miss Brandon. Henry will be so sorry to miss you — I mean he was always talking about you and saying we must take the children to see you.'

'I had practically forbidden him the house for some years,' said Miss Brandon.

To this there appeared to be no answer except Why? a question Mrs. Brandon had not the courage to ask.

'But I would certainly have come to the funeral,' Miss Brandon continued, 'had it not been my Day in Bed. I take one day a week in bed, an excellent plan at my age. Later I shall take two days, and probably spend the last years of my life entirely in bed. My grandfather, my mother and my elder half-sister were all bed-ridden for the last ten years of their lives and all lived to be over ninety.'

Again it was difficult to find an answer. Mrs. Brandon murmured something about how splendid and felt it was hardly adequate.

'But I went into mourning for my nephew Henry at once,' said Miss Brandon, ignoring her niece's remark, 'as you see. I have practically not been out of mourning for fifteen years, what with one death and another. A posthumous child?' she added with sudden interest, looking piercingly at her niece's white dress.

'Oh, no,' said Mrs. Brandon. 'Mamma and papa are still alive.'

'Tut, tut, not you,' said Miss Brandon. 'What is your name?'

Mrs. Brandon said apologetically that it was Lavinia.

'A pretty name,' said Miss Brandon. 'When last I saw your husband Henry Brandon, he mentioned you to me as Pet. It was before his marriage and he was spending a week-end with me. I had to say to him, "Henry Brandon, a man who can call his future wife Pet and speak of the Government as you have spoken can hardly make a good husband and is certainly not a good nephew." I suppose he made you suffer a good deal.'

Here if ever was an opportunity for Mrs. Brandon to indulge in an orgy of sentiment, but her underlying sense of fairness suddenly choked any complaint she could truthfully have made.

'No, I don't think so,' she said, looking straight at her husband's aunt. 'He was very nice to the children when he noticed them, and he liked me to be nicely dressed, and we were always very comfortable. Would you like to see the children, Miss Brandon?'

She rang the bell and asked Rose to ask Nurse to bring the children down.

'I see you are determined not to give Henry away,' said Miss Brandon, not disapprovingly. 'But when is it? I see no other reason for wearing white so soon.'

Her gaze was again so meaningly fixed upon her niece's white dress that Mrs. Brandon began to blush violently.

'I don't think I understand,' she faltered, 'but if that is what you mean of course it isn't. I just thought white was less depressing for the children.'

'I am glad to hear it. That I could *not* have forgiven Henry,' said the disconcerting Miss Brandon, and then the children were brought down, approved, and taken away again.

'Now you can ring for my second chauffeur, Lavinia,' said Miss Brandon. 'He always comes with me to help me in and out of the car. I prefer to have the first chauffeur remain at the wheel, for one never knows.'

She then expounded to Mrs. Brandon in the hall, unmoved by the presence of her chauffeur and the parlourmaid, her plans for the disposal of her affairs. As far as Mrs. Brandon, shaken by Rose's presence, could understand, Francis and Delia were to be the heirs of their aunt's large fortune, unless she saw fit to leave it to a cousin whom she had never seen. She was then hoisted into her car, the second chauffeur got into his place, the first chauffeur put in the clutch and the equipage moved away. Mrs. Brandon, much the worse for her aunt's visit, declined Rose's suggestion of an early cup of tea and went up to the nursery for comfort. Here she found Francis and Delia already having tea. Francis was sitting on a nursery chair with a fat cushion on it. He was wearing a green linen suit with a green linen feeder tied round his neck, and was covered with apricot jam from his large smiling mouth to the roots of his yellow hair. Delia, in a yellow muslin frock with a feeder of yellow towelling, and a yellow ribbon in her brown curls was being fed with strips of bread and butter by Nurse.

'Don't move, Nurse,' said Mrs. Brandon, as Nurse sketched the gesture of one who has no intention of getting up. 'Can I have tea with you?'

'If we had known mummie was coming, we'd have had our clean pinny on,' said Nurse severely to Delia.

'Pinny,' said Delia.

'You'd hardly believe the words she picks up, madam,' said Nurse with quite unjustifiable pride considering how many times a day the words clean pinny were said by her. 'We'll get another cup and saucer out of the cupboard, won't we, baby, a nice cup and saucer with a duck on it for mummie. Would you like the duck, madam, or the moo-cow?'

Mrs. Brandon expressed a preference for the moo-cow, on hearing which Delia, who was holding a mug of milk to her mouth with both hands, said 'Moo-cow,' into it. The milk spluttered all over her face, Francis began to laugh and choked on a piece of bread and butter and jam, Nurse dashed with first aid from one to another, and Mrs. Brandon found herself laughing till suddenly she was crying and couldn't stop. Her children, deeply interested, stopped choking to stare.

'I don't know what's the matter, Nurse,' said Mrs. Brandon through her sobs. 'An aunt of Mr. Brandon's came to call and it was very upsetting.'

'I don't wonder, madam,' said Nurse, deeply approving her mistress's show of feeling as suitable to a young widow. 'Suppose you go and lie down and I'll bring you the tea in your room. We'll give mummie the nice moo-cow cup of tea, won't we baby? Francis, wipe your mouth on your feeder and say your grace and get down and Nurse will come and wash your hands as soon as she has taken mummie some tea.'

Thanks to the tea and a rest Mrs. Brandon quite soon recovered from her mild hysterics, but the affair was not at an end. On Thursdays, which this day happened to be, the nursery maid had her half-day out; by a great oversight the kitchenmaid who took Nurse's supper tray up when the nursery maid was out, had been given special leave to go and see her married sister who had had triplets. On any ordinary occasion Nurse would have gone supperless sooner than condescend to go downstairs, just as the second housemaid would sooner have lost her place than deputized for the kitchenmaid, but the urgent need of communicating gossip drove both sides into some semblance of humanity. As soon as Francis and Delia were asleep Nurse went down to the kitchen and there found the second housemaid talking to Rose.

'Well, Nurse,' said the second housemaid, 'I was just going to take your tray up as Gladys is out.'

'Thanks, Grace,' said Nurse with the courtesy that a superior should always show to an inferior, 'that is very obliging of you, but I hardly feel like touching a thing. Just the bread and butter and that bloater paste and a bit of cheese and a cup of tea.'

She assumed an interesting pallor and smiled faintly.

'Rose feels just like you do, Nurse,' said Grace. 'It's all that upset this afternoon.'

'Madam did mention that she was upset,' said Nurse, exploring the ground, but careful to give nothing away.

'I couldn't hardly touch my own tea,' said Rose. 'That Miss Brandon talking of making her will with Mr. Brandon only four months buried and all. No wonder madam didn't fancy her tea after that.'

Cook, who had come in as Rose was speaking, said those chauffeurs were nice young fellers and the young one with the little moustache had worked in the works where her brother was, and there were twenty indoors and out at Miss Brandon's place, and didn't Nurse want a bit of that cold pork.

'Thanks, Cook, ever so,' said Nurse, 'but it would go against my feelings. It gave me quite a turn seeing madam so upset. Seeing Master Francis and baby having their tea seemed to bring it all home as you might say. So I said to madam, If you was to have a nice lay down, madam, you'd feel much better.'

She paused.

'No wonder she was upset,' said Rose. 'I knew she was reel upset because I said If you was to have a cup of tea, madam, now, it would do you good, because it was only half-past four and drawing-room tea isn't till five.'

'My nursery kettle was just on the boil,' said Nurse airily, 'so I took madam a cup of tea and she seemed ever so much better when she'd drunk it.'

This was an appalling piece of provocation on Nurse's part, carefully led up to and deliberately uttered. Between her and Rose there was an unspoken rivalry for the possession of their mistress. Rose had been with Mrs. Brandon since her marriage and was therefore the senior, besides holding the important position of unofficial lady's maid, but Nurse had through the children an unassailable hold over the household. Rose might be able to bully her mistress about the hour for tea, or the evening dress she should wear, but it was with Nurse that Mrs. Brandon spent an hour or two in the nursery or the garden every day, Nurse that she allowed to help her to get flowers for the church, or to finish the half-dozen hideous and badly cut flannelette nightgowns that were her forced contribution to a thing called Personal Service that levied blackmail on the gentry. Rose knew in her heart that if it came to a showdown Nurse would win, for Mrs. Brandon as a mother was as incapable as she was adoring, and this did not improve her feelings. Nurse, equally conscious of this vital fact, was more polite to Rose than anyone could be expected to bear. To-day she had made an incursion into the enemy's territory that would not easily be forgiven. If Mrs. Brandon chose to demean herself to have tea in the nursery, Rose could but pity her, while admitting that she had a perfect right to have tea with her own children. But that her mistress should refuse the cup of tea she had so kindly offered and then accept the offering from Nurse, not even in the nursery but in her own room, sacred to Rose's ministrations, that was an insult Rose would not readily forget, and for which she chose to put the entire blame on her rival. So she said, in a general way, that Indian tea wasn't no good for the headache.

Nurse said in an equally general and equally offensive way that so long as tea was made with *boiling* water, it didn't matter if it was Indian or China.

Cook said she found a good dose was the best thing for the headache, but it must be a *good* dose, to which both housemaids added a graphic description of the effect a good dose had on (*a*) a bed-ridden aunt, and (*b*) a cousin who had fits.

Rose said to Cook it was no wonder madam didn't have no appetite for her dinner, poor thing, to which Nurse was just preparing a barbed reply when to everyone's mingled disappointment and relief the kitchenmaid suddenly appeared, and by sitting down and bursting into tears at once became the centre of interest. Cook at once provided a cup of very strong tea and while drinking it the kitchenmaid explained with sobs and gulps that two of the triplets were dead and looked that beautiful that you wouldn't credit it. Everyone applauded her display of feeling and a delightful conversation took place about similar events in everyone's own family circle. Nurse, who only recognized the children of the gentry, circles in which triplets are for some obscure social or economic reason practically unknown, came off poorly in this contest and retired quietly with her tray.

But from that day the silent struggle for the soul of the unconscious Mrs. Brandon became the ruling passion in Nurse and Rose. If Nurse brushed and twisted Delia's curls with absent-minded ferocity, or Rose cleaned the silver ornaments in the drawing-room till they were severely dented and had to go to Barchester to be repaired, they were not thinking of their respective charges, but of an enemy above and below stairs. When Francis went to school and Delia had a French governess, Rose's hopes soared high. Mrs. Brandon had intended to give Nurse notice, with a huge tip and glowing recommendations, but from day to day she found that she dared not do it, from month to month Nurse's position became stronger, and from year to year Nurse stayed on, partly as maid to Delia, partly as general utility, always in a state of armed neutrality towards Rose.

After this terrifying visit, nearly seventeen years ago, Miss Brandon had never visited Stories again, but from time to time had summoned her niece and her children to Brandon Abbey. These visits seemed to Mrs. Brandon to have been the inevitable occasion for some outburst from her offspring. It was here that Francis had fallen through a hot-house roof, where he had no business to be, cutting his leg to the bone and bringing down the best grape vine in his fall; here that he had laboriously baled all the water out of the small lily-pond with one of the best copper preserving pans, abstracted no one ever discovered how from the kitchen regions, leaving all the high-bred goldfish to die in the mud. Here it was that Delia, usually so good, had been found in Miss Brandon's dressing-room, that Holy of Holies, peacocking before the glass in her great-aunt's mantle and bonnet. Here it was that Francis, at a later age, had learnt to drive a car with the connivance of the second chauffeur and run over one of Miss Brandon's peacocks, while on the same ill-omened visit Delia had broken the jug and basin in the best spare bedroom where she had been sent to wash her hands, and flooded the Turkey carpet.

Miss Brandon had made very little comment on these misfortunes, but her niece noticed that after each of them she had talked a good deal about the cousin she had never seen, the possible inheritor of her money. Mrs. Brandon, who did not care in the least what her aunt's plans might be, but was genuinely sorry for the indomitable old lady, yearly becoming more bed-ridden as she had predicted, was at last goaded into a mild remonstrance, pointing out to Miss Brandon that if it had not been for her nephew Henry, the children would never have existed, to which Miss Brandon had replied cryptically that it took two to make a quarrel.

Thinking of all this and of her aunt's letter, Mrs. Brandon carried her flowers into the little room known as the flower room, along one wall of which ran a long marble slab with four basins in it, relics of a former Brandon with four gardening daughters. She then fetched yesterday's flowers from the hall and living-rooms, refilled the vases, and began to arrange her flowers. This she always called 'my housekeeping', adding that it took more time than all her other duties put together, but she couldn't bear anyone else to do it, thus giving the impression of one who was a martyr to her feeling for beauty. As a matter of fact she spoke no more than the truth, for Cook arranged the menus, and Nurse looked after the linen and did all the sewing and darning, so that Mrs. Brandon would have been hard put to it to find anything useful to do.

Presently Delia's voice at the telephone in the hall penetrated her consciousness, and she called her daughter's name.

'Oh, bother,' said Delia's voice to her unknown correspondent, 'mummie's yelling for me. Hang on a moment. What is it, Mummie?' she inquired, looking into the flower room.

'It's about Aunt Sissie, darling. She said Wednesday, so don't arrange the picnic that day.'

'Oh, Mother, any day would do for Aunt Sissie. We must have Wednesday for the picnic or the Morlands can't come.'

'I can't help it,' said Mrs. Brandon, massing sweet peas in a bowl. 'We haven't been for ages and she's all alone, poor old thing.'

'Don't be so mercenary, Mother,' said Delia. 'Here Francis, come here a moment.'

Francis, who was passing through the hall came to the flower room door and asked what the matter was.

'It's mummie, going all horse-leechy,' said Delia. 'Wednesday's the only possible day for the picnic and now mummie says we must go and be dutiful to Aunt Sissie. I wish Aunt Sissie would give all her money to that cousin of hers straight away and leave us in peace. Oh, Mummie, *do* be sensible.'

'I am,' said Mrs. Brandon, 'and I don't see why we shouldn't be kind to poor Aunt Sissie even if she *is* rich. If I were very old and alone and spent most of my time in bed, I would be very glad when people visited me.'

At this both her children laughed loudly.

Nurse, on her way upstairs with an armful of sewing, stopped to interfere.

'Oh, Nurse — —' said all three at once.

'I want you, Miss Delia, so I can try on your tennis frock,' said she. 'Come up with me now.'

'Oh, Nurse, any time will do. I'm telephoning now. Be an angel and I'll come up presently. Mummie wants us to go over to Aunt Sissie on Wednesday, and that's the only good day for the picnic.'

'Nonsense, Miss Delia,' said Nurse. 'There's plenty of other days in the week. Now come straight up with me and try that dress on.'

Delia followed her old Nurse mutinously upstairs, making faces, till Nurse, who appeared to have, as she had often told the children when they were small thus frightening them horribly, eyes in the back of her head, said sharply that that was enough, and so they vanished.

'Francis, darling,' said Mrs. Brandon, who had collected another great bunch of sweet peas and was holding them thoughtfully to her face, 'we *must* go to Aunt Sissie on Wednesday.'

'Yes, I think we must,' said Francis. 'Anyone who didn't know you would think you were mercenary, darling, but I know you haven't the wits to concentrate. You've got a kind heart though, and anyone who looked at you sympathizing with people would think you really cared. Give me a smell of those sweet peas.'

Mrs. Brandon held up the flowers and Francis sniffed them violently.

'There are few pleasures like really burrowing one's nose into sweet peas,' he said, much refreshed. 'You're a bit like them, darling, all soft pinky-purply colours and a nice smell. Do you want your tall hand-some son to help you to take the flowers to the church? It will look so well if we go together, and everyone will say what a comfort I am to you and what a wonderful mother you have been.'

Mrs. Brandon laughed with a great good humour and gave Francis a long basket to fill with tall flowers. Then they walked across the garden, up a lane, past the Cow and Sickle, and so into the churchyard by the side gate.

Mrs. Brandon could never be thankful enough that her husband had died at Cannes and been decently buried in the English cemetery. If he had been buried in Pomfret Madrigal church she would have had to keep his grave and memory decorated with flowers. If she had undertaken this pious duty herself she would certainly have forgotten it and left the flowers, a wet mush of decay, to scandalize the village. If she had told Turpin the gardener to look after it, not only would the village have been scandalized, but he would have chosen the stiffest asters and dahlias like rosettes, bedded out begonias, even cultivated immortelles for the purpose, and given the little plot the air of a County Council Park. The only alternative Mrs. Brandon could imagine was to have what might be called an all-weather grave, sprinkled with chips from the stone-mason's yard, or battened down under a granite slab, and to do this to the unconscious Mr. Brandon would have seemed to his widow a little unkind. So Mr. Brandon reposed at Cannes and a sum of money was paid yearly to keep his memory as green as the climate allowed, while a neat tablet in Pomfret Madrigal church bore witness in excellent lettering to the dates of his birth and death.

Pomfret Madrigal church was of great antiquity, being the remains of the former Abbey of that name. Part of it was supposed to date from the reign of King John, but as that particular part was considered by archaeologists to be buried in the thick chancel walls, everyone was at liberty to have his own opinion. A few years previously the Vicar, Mr. Miller, a newcomer and an ardent enthusiast for his new church, had discovered faint traces of colour in a very dark corner high up on the south wall. Mrs. Brandon, always pleased to give pleasure, had made a handsome contribution towards a fund for church restoration, a learned professor famed for extracting mural paintings from apparently blank walls had visited the church, and the work had been put in hand. After several months' slow, careful, and to the Vicar maddeningly exciting work, Professor Lancelot had brought to light two square feet of what might have been a patterned border, and a figure, apparently standing on its head, which was variously identified as Lucifer, Fulke de Pomfret who had impounded some of the Abbey pigs in revenge for alleged depredations on his lady's herb garden, and Bishop Wyckens who had made himself extremely unpopular with the Abbey about the matter of some waste land over at Starveacres. However, all these differences of opinion were drowned and forgotten in Professor Lancelot's supreme discovery that the fragment of border might almost with certainty be attributed to Nicholas de Hogpen, an extremely prolific artist practically none of whose work was known. Others supported the view that the work should stand to the credit of an unknown monk whose work in Northumberland was described in an imperfect MS. which the owner, Mr. Amery P. Otis of Brookline, Mass., would not allow anyone to see. The correspondence on this subject, beginning in the *Journal of the Society of Barsetshire Archaeologists*, had overflowed into the *Sunday Times* and *Observer*, causing several correspondents to write to the Editor about yellow-backed tits who had nested near mural paintings, or the fact that their great-great-grandfather had as a child sat on the knee of a very old man whose grandfather said he remembered someone who said he had heard of the Reformation. The Vicar read every word of correspondence and pasted all the cuttings into an album, as also a photograph from the *Daily Spectrum* with the caption 'Rector of Pomfret Madrigal says Mural Paintings unique,' and an inset called The Rev. Milker.

Since these eventful doings the paintings had gradually receded into the walls and were now invisible except to the eye of faith, which could often be found in the tourist season, guide book in hand, twisting itself almost upside down in its efforts to make out the inverted figure.

The July morning was now very hot. The little churchyard, on a slope facing the south, was shimmering with heat, and the flowers in the jam jars and Canadian salmon tins on the poorer graves were already wilting. In spite of her shady hat and her parasol of a most becoming shade of pink, Mrs. Brandon was glad to get into the coolness of the little church. She slipped into a pew, knelt for a moment, and then emerged, apparently spiritually much refreshed.

'What *do* you say, darling, when you do that?' asked Francis. 'I've often wondered.'

Mrs. Brandon looked guilty.

'I never quite know,' she said. 'I try to concentrate, but the only way I can concentrate is to hold my breath very hard, and that stops me thinking. And when I shut my eyes I see all sorts of spokes and fireworks. I always mean to ask to be nicer and kinder, but things like Rose wanting to change her afternoon out, or Aunt Sissie's letter, come into my mind at once. But I did have one very good idea, which was that if Rose changes her afternoon we could have the picnic that day and kill two birds with one stone.'

'People have been excommunicated for less than that,' said Francis. 'Pull yourself together, darling; here comes Mr. Miller.'

Mr. Miller, in the cassock and biretta that were the joy of his life and that no one grudged him, came up.

'Good morning, good morning,' he said, not so much in a spirit of vain repetition as in double greeting.

'I always feel I ought to ask you to bless me,' said Mrs. Brandon taking his hand and looking up at him.

'My dear lady!' said Mr. Miller, much embarrassed, and only just stopping himself saying 'It is rather you who should bless me.'

'Come off it, mamma,' said Francis kindly but firmly. 'Don't you know my mamma well enough yet, Mr. Miller, to realize that she is a prey to saying what she thinks most effective?'

'I don't think you ought to talk like that in church, Francis,' said his mother severely. 'Come along, the altar is waiting for us.'

At this Francis exploded in a reverent guffaw and handed the basket of flowers to the Vicar, saying that he would fill the watering can at the tap in the churchyard and bring it in. So Mr. Miller found himself alone with Mrs. Brandon and an armful of flowers, and didn't know if he ought to stay with her or visit the poor, who were always kind to him but at the same time gave him the impression that they had just stopped a deeply absorbing conversation, probably about himself, and were only waiting till his back was turned to continue it. Mr. Miller was about Mrs. Brandon's age and having never met anyone that he felt like marrying had romantic views on celibacy. His richer parishioners like him and he dined out a good deal, while the poorer part of his flock accepted him with good-humoured tolerance and always put off the christenings till he had come back from his yearly holiday. Funerals unfortunately could not so be postponed, though it was considered distinctly bad taste in Old Turpin, Mrs. Brandon's gardener's uncle, to have died four days before the Vicar's return, in particularly hot weather. Weddings were also postponed so that the contracting parties could have the benefit of their own priest, but since the sexton's daughter had produced a fine pair of twins owing to her insistence on waiting to celebrate the nuptials till Mr. Miller came back from Switzerland, he had been very firm on the subject.

As was inevitable, he was romantically in love with Mrs. Brandon, but luckily for his own peace of mind he did not recognize the symptoms which he mistook for respect and admiration, though why these respectable qualities should make one give at the knees and become damp in the hands, he did not inquire.

Now Francis came back with the watering can and the vestry wastepaper basket for the dead flowers, and Mrs. Brandon arranged sheaves of gladioli to her own satisfaction. All three walked down the church together and emerged blinking into the hot noonday glare. Mrs. Brandon slowly put up her parasol, looking so angelic that Francis felt obliged to ask his mother what she was thinking about.

'I was wondering,' said she, 'if one *ought* to bring a watering can into the church. Wouldn't it look better to bring the vases outside and fill them at the tap?'

'My mother is the most truthful woman I know,' said Francis to Mr. Miller, 'except when she isn't.'

Mr. Miller wanted to say that Mrs. Brandon's touch would sanctify even a watering can and that Francis ought not to speak lightly of such a thing as Truth, but was overcome by nervousness and said nothing. Francis said, Well, they must be getting along, and Mr. Miller was inspired by desperation to ask them into the Vicarage to look at the new wall-paper in his study. Accordingly they walked through the little gate into the Vicarage garden and up by the yew hedge to the sixteenth-century stone Vicarage which was basking in the sun. The new wall-paper, which turned out to be that part of the wall where the damp patch used to be, freshly distempered, was duly admired.

'One does feel,' said Mrs. Brandon, sinking elegantly into a very comfortable leather armchair, 'that this house needs a woman.'

Francis, alarmed by his mother's fresh outburst of truthfulness, made gestures behind Mr. Miller's back, designed to convey to his mother that the Vicar's cassock and biretta made such a suggestion very un-becoming. Mr. Miller felt that if Mrs. Brandon were always sitting in that chair on a hot summer morning in the subdued light that filtered through the outside blinds, holding the broken head of a white gladiolus in her gloved hand, the parish would be much easier to manage.

'It really needs a good housekeeper,' said Mrs. Brandon, continuing the train of her own thoughts. 'Turpin's Hettie is a nice girl, but she is much too kind to insects. She has never killed a spider in her life. Look!'

And she pointed the gladiolus accusingly at a corner where a fat spider was dealing with a daddy-long-legs.

'Oh dear!' said Mr. Miller, in despair.

'I'll hoick her down,' said Francis, looking round for something that would reach the ceiling. 'Can I take one of your oars, Mr. Miller?'

Without waiting for permission he took down from the wall the oar with which Mr. Miller had stroked Lazarus to victory in Eights Week, and made a pat at the spider. The spider was dislodged, but with great presence of mind clung to the end of the blade with all her arms and legs.

'Get off,' said Francis, waving the oar. 'Help, Mr. Miller, she is laying hold with her hands or whatever it says. It's more in your line than mine.'

On hearing this suggestion of clerical interference the spider ran down the oar in a threatening way. Mr. Miller flapped feebly at her with his biretta, which caused her, or so Francis subsequently asserted, to bare her fangs and snarl. Mrs. Brandon got up and enveloped the spider in her handkerchief, which she then threw out of the window into the heliotrope.

'Thank you, darling,' said Francis, putting the oar back on the wall. 'It takes a woman to fight a woman.'

'I wonder why spiders should be female?' said Mr. Miller, so over-wrought by his narrow escape that he hardly knew what he was saying.

'I suppose it's because they eat their husbands,' said Mrs. Brandon.

'Mamma darling, *don't*,' said Francis, 'not in the Vicarage,' thus completing Mr. Miller's confusion.

'Please rescue my handkerchief, Francis,' said Mrs. Brandon, 'only see that the spider has really gone.'

Francis leant his long form over the window sill, picked up the hand-kerchief, shook it and returned it to his mother. Mr. Miller, who had had a wild thought of keeping the handkerchief for himself, realized that his chance was lost.

'It smells so deliciously of heliotrope now,' said Mrs. Brandon, hold-ing it to her face. This delightful gesture gave a little comfort to her host, who would be able to reflect that his flowers had furnished the scent that pleased his guest.

Just as the good-byes were getting under way, the study door opened and a dark young man of poetic and pale appearance came in, and seeing company began to back out.

'Wait a moment, Hilary,' said Mr. Miller. 'Mrs. Brandon, this is Mr. Grant who is reading with me. He only arrived last night. And this is Francis Brandon, Hilary Grant.'

Further handshaking took place and it seemed that the visit had really come to an end, when on the doorstep Mrs. Brandon suddenly stopped.

'I was thinking,' she said, 'that it would be so nice, Mr. Miller, if you would dine with us next Wednesday. It will only be a kind of cold meal, but if you care to come we'd love to have you. And would Mr. Grant perhaps come too?'

Mr. Miller accepted for himself and his pupil and the Brandons went away.

'Really, Mamma,' Francis expostulated, 'I didn't think you had it in you to be so mean!'

'I know quite well what you are hinting,' said his mother, with distant dignity. 'But it isn't my fault if Rose changes her afternoon out, and I have been meaning to ask Mr. Miller for some time, and it isn't as if being a clergyman made one not able to eat cold supper. And now I must answer Aunt Sissie's letter. I cannot think how it is that one never has time to do *anything*.'

'Because you never have anything to do, darling,' said Francis. 'You take yourself in, but you can't take in your tall, handsome son. Come along or we shall be late for lunch and Rose will lower.'

II

BRANDON ABBEY

IN spite of Delia's mild sulks the picnic was put off till Friday and Miss Brandon's invitation, or command, obeyed. The weather remained set fair and as the Brandon family got into the car at twelve o'clock, Francis puffed loudly and said it was worse than a third-class railway carriage that had been standing in a siding. The road to Brandon Abbey was through some of the loveliest scenery in Barsetshire. Leaving Pomfret Madrigal it went through Little Misfit, with a glimpse of the hideous pinnacles of Pomfret Towers in the distance, and then followed for several miles the winding course of the Rising, among water meadows that looked greener than ever in contrast with the sun-parched country. At the Mellings Arms there was a choice of ways. One went through

Barchester, the other, marked as a second-class road, went up and over the downs, as straight as the Romans had built it, skirted Rushwater by the beech avenue and so by the Fever Hospital to Brandon Abbey.

As the Mellings Arms came in sight, Mrs. Brandon leant forward and tapped on the glass. Francis, who was by the chauffeur, slid the window back and poked his face through.

'Tell Curwen, darling, that we'll go by the downs,' said Mrs. Brandon.

Her clear voice carried well and Curwen's back visibly took offence. Francis exchanged a few words with him and turned back to his mother and sister.

'He says there's a bad patch near the top and he doesn't think the springs will stand up to it,' he said.

Mrs. Brandon made a face of resignation.

'Don't let that stop us,' said Francis. 'I'm all for the downs myself, aren't you, Delia?'

'Rather,' said Delia. 'We might see the place where the motor char-à-banc was on fire last week.'

Francis shut the window and spoke to Curwen again. That harbinger of misfortune listened with a stony face and turned the motor's head towards the downs. To Delia's great pleasure the burnt out corpse of the motor char-à-banc was still by the roadside, and Curwen so far unbent as to inform his mistress, via her son, that there was one of the bodies burnt so bad they couldn't identify it, after which he devoted his attention to driving with quite maddening care over the stony patches, wincing at each little jolt as if a pin had been stuck into him.

At twenty minutes past one the gloomy lodge of Brandon Abbey was reached. Miss Brandon always kept her gates shut to mark her disapproval of things in general, and as the lodge-keeper was deaf and usually working in his back garden, Curwen had to get out and go and find him, which he did with the gloomy satisfaction of a prophet whose warnings have been disregarded. Another five minutes' driving down the gloomy avenue which wound its way downwards to the hole in which the house was situated, brought them to the front door.

'Welcome to the abode of joy,' said Francis, politely opening the door of the car for his mother and sister. 'I'll ring the front door bell, but I don't suppose anyone will come. No wonder Aunt Sissie spends her time in bed. I would if I lived here.'

Certainly Brandon Abbey was not an encouraging place. The house, a striking example of Scotch baronial, spouting pepper-pot turrets at every angle, had been built in the 'sixties by Miss Brandon's father, an extremely wealthy jute merchant, on the site of a ruined religious house. The locality though favourable for stewponds and contemplation was damp and gloomy in the extreme. Mushrooms sprouted freely in the cellars, damp spread in patches on the bedroom walls, the flooring of the servants' hall was from time to time lifted by unknown fungoid growths. The trees which Mr. Brandon had planted far too thickly and far too near the house had thriven unchecked, and screened the house from all but the direct rays of the midday summer sun, which then made the servants' bedrooms under a lead roof intolerably hot. On the mossy stones of the terrace the peacocks walked up and down, believing according to the fashion of their kind that everyone was admiring the tail feathers which they had moulted some time ago.

'Nightmare Abbey,' said Francis, after they had waited some time, and rang the bell again. Even as he rang it and said the words, the door was opened by Miss Brandon's permanently disapproving butler, who said Miss Brandon was very sorry she couldn't come down to luncheon, but would like to see Mrs. Brandon afterwards. He then showed the family into the drawing-room and left them to meditate till lunch was ready.

'Bother,' said Delia, after hunting in her bag, 'I've left my looking-glass at home.'

She looked round for one, but on the walls, thickly hung with the real masterpieces, the blatant fakes, and, incredibly, the china plates in red velvet frames that Mr. Brandon's catholic and personal taste had bought, there was not a mirror to be seen.

'Try the overmantel or what not,' suggested Francis, pointing to the fireplace, above which towered a massive, yet fanciful superstructure of fretwork. Shelves with ball and fringe edgings, turned pillars, Moorish arches, Gothic niches, were among the least of its glories, while here and there were inserted round or diamond shaped mirrors, hand-painted with sprays of plum blossom, forget-me-not, and other natural products.

By standing on tiptoe on the heavy marble fender Delia could just see her face among some painted bulrushes, and behind it a reflection of the room. In the reflection she saw the door open and a young man come in. Excited by the unexpected apparition she hastily put away her powder puff, turned, knocked down the polished steel fire irons with a frightful crash and stood transfixed with shame. To her great surprise the young man took no notice of the noise, but stood gazing at her mother who was apparently half asleep. Francis was the first to recognize the newcomer as Mr. Miller's pupil and though surprised to see him here, had enough presence of mind to say 'Hullo, Grant.'

'Oh, hullo,' said Mr. Grant, inquiringly.

'Francis Brandon,' said Francis, 'you remember meeting me at Mr. Miller's last week.'

'Of course, I'm so sorry,' said Mr. Grant, his eyes still wavering towards Mrs. Brandon. 'I mean how do you do.'

'Nicely, thank you,' said Francis. 'This is my sister Delia, and mamma will come to in a minute. Mamma, here is Mr. Grant that you met at the Vicarage.'

Mrs. Brandon, who had succumbed for a few seconds to the heat and ante-lunch exhaustion, opened her eyes and gave Mr. Grant her hand with a smile. Francis was rather afraid that the shock of waking up might prompt her to one of her worse indiscretions, but luckily lunch was announced, and they all went into the dining-room. This impressive apartment was lined with pitch pine and adorned with pictures by deceased R.A.'s, pictures which, as Mr. Brandon had informed every visitor, had all been hung on the line. The lofty ceiling was decorated with strips of pitch pine crossing each other diagonally and at each intersection was fixed a naked electric light in a copper lotus. The dado and the panels of the door were of the finest Lincrusta Walton and the bronze clock on the mantelpiece represented a Knight Templar, with the clock face under his horse's stomach.

From the very beginning of lunch it was obvious to Francis and Delia that Mr. Grant was in their language a case, and they had the great pleasure of kicking each other under the table whenever he looked at their mother. They were used to her rapid and entirely unconscious conquests, which Francis regarded with malicious enjoyment and Delia with good-humoured contempt. Delia's heart was so far untouched except by the heroes, whether villain or detective, of thrillers and American gangster films, and as Mr. Grant, apart from a pair of horn-rimmed spectacles, had nothing in common with these supermen, she mentally labelled him Not Wanted.

Conversation during lunch was of a disjointed nature. Francis and Delia were consumed with curiosity as to why Mr. Miller's pupil should be lunching at Brandon Abbey. On ordinary occasions they would have had no inhibitions about asking him what he was doing in their aunt's house, but the presence of the disapproving butler, who never left the room for a moment, not to speak of the two footmen, cramped their style a little. Their mother would have been capable of any indiscretion, but, as her children well saw, she had not yet recovered from her slumber before lunch and although she had grasped the fact that she had met Mr. Grant at the Vicarage, she appeared to be under the impression that he was going to be a curate, and was industriously and ignorantly talking on church subjects. Mr. Grant was doing his best to second her, but was hampered by an ignorance equal to her own and a tendency to look at her rather than listen to her. Altogether it was a relief to everyone when the butler, as soon as dessert was set on the table, told Mrs. Brandon that Miss Brandon would be glad if she would come up and have coffee in her room. Mrs. Brandon made a face at her children, sympathetically answered by hideous faces from them, and got up from the table, dropping a pale pink handkerchief as she rose. Mr. Grant, who had stood up with her, was about to rescue it when a footman, at a sign from the butler, picked it up and gave it to his superior, who put it on a silver salver and handed it to its owner.

Mrs. Brandon looked at the handkerchief, then looked in her bag, and finding that her handkerchief was not there, seemed surprised.

'I must have dropped it,' she said, taking it from the salver. 'Thank you so much.'

She was then wafted away by the butler, and the three young people were left alone with Miss Brandon's glasshouse peaches and grapes, besides the less rare products of the kitchen garden. Francis, approaching his subject cautiously, asked Mr. Grant what he was reading with old Miller.

'Classics,' said Mr. Grant.

'Is that to go to Oxford, or something?' asked Francis.

'No, I'm afraid I'm through Oxford,' said Mr. Grant apologetically. 'Mother thought I'd better read for the bar, and as I did history my classics were a bit sticky, so she sent me here to rub them up. Were you a history man?'

'No, I'm afraid I'm only an Old School Tie,' said Francis in his turn apologetic. 'I wasn't very brainy at school and when a good job turned up in Barchester I jumped at it. I rather wish I'd let mamma send me to a University now, but anyway it's about five years too late.'

'I think you're jolly lucky,' said Mr. Grant. 'I wanted to go into a publisher's office when I left school, but I'd got a mouldy kind of scholarship by mistake so they made me take it up, and then mother made me go abroad, and here I am at twenty-three only just beginning.'

'That's exactly as old as Francis,' said Delia. 'When's your birthday?'

Mr. Grant said March.

'Well I'm February and Francis is April,' said Delia, 'so that's rather funny. Do you go to the movies much? There's not a bad cinema at Barchester.'

Mr. Grant said he didn't go very much, but he had seen *Descente de lit* in which Zizi Pavois was superb, and *Menschen ohne Knochen* which, even allowing for propaganda, was an astoundingly moving affair.

Delia said she meant *films* and there was going to be an awfully good one at Barchester next week called *Going for a Ride* with Garstin Hermon as the villain and she had been told it was absolutely *ghastly*. As she said these words her pretty brown eyes sparkled, her cheeks flushed in a most becoming way and her hair seemed to curl even more than usual. Mr. Grant looked at these phenomena with an historian's appraising eye and thought how much lovelier gentle blue eyes were than bold brown, how preferable was a soft pale skin to the rude glow of health, and how infinitely more touching were loose waves of hair, a little touched with grey, than a mop of corkscrews. Thinking these chivalrous thoughts he said, with the annoyingly tolerant manner that Oxford is apt to stamp upon her sons, that it sounded very exciting.

'Look here, Delia, that's your fourth peach,' said Francis. 'You'll be sick. Let's come out in the garden.'

Accordingly the three young people strolled out into the terrace and sat on the broad balustrade, looking at the foolish peacocks. At the end of the yew avenue the former stewpond, now a formal basin, gleamed among the leaves of the water lilies. The one white peacock, white by courtesy but really looking rather grey, posed self-consciously against the yews. It was all very peaceful and for a time no one had anything to say.

'I'm afraid my aunt's in rather a bad mood to-day,' said Mr. Grant at last. 'I do hope she isn't giving Mrs. Brandon a bad time.'

'Your aunt?' said Delia.

'Aunt Sissie. She's an aunt of yours too, isn't she?'

'Good Lord,' said Francis, 'you are our long-lost rival. I'm jolly glad to meet you. Aunt Sissie is always ramming you down our throats and I thought you were an old man with a beard. And I jolly well hope you do get this foul Abbey — I mean if you'd like it.'

Mr. Grant looked so uncomfortable that even Delia felt that her brother might have been more tactful.

'You see, Aunt Sissie is a bit of a bully,' she said, 'and she thinks she can frighten us by saying she'll leave the money to you, but we really don't care two hoots.'

Mr. Grant looked more uncomfortable than ever after this explanation.

'Sorry,' said Francis, vaguely feeling that some reparation was necessary.

'It's all right,' said Mr. Grant. 'But it's rather a shock. I knew practically nothing about Aunt Sissie till father died, and then she wrote to mother and said she was a very old woman whose relatives neglected her and would I come and visit her. She didn't say anything about leaving this place or anything. I only came over here yesterday afternoon and I had an awful night in a four-poster stuffed with knobs, and there was a marble bath with a mahogany surround about three hundred yards down the passage, and Aunt Sissie was rather unpleasant, and thank goodness I'm going back to the Vicarage. If I hadn't promised Aunt Sissie I'd stay to tea I'd go at once. I can't stand this.'

He spoke with such vehemence that his hearers were surprised, not understanding that in his mind's eye he saw himself depriving that wonderful Mrs. Brandon of her birthright and turning her out into the snow while he lived among peacocks and butlers.

'All right,' said Francis. 'If I get it I'll give it to you and if you get it you give it to me. If I had it I'd sell it for a lunatic asylum. Anyhow it's almost one now.'

'If it were mine I'd burn the damned thing down,' said Mr. Grant, toying with the idea of handing over the insurance money to Mrs. Brandon anonymously.

Warming to the theme the two heirs, ably supported by Delia, began to alter the house according to their individual tastes, turning the pond into a swimming pool, the enormous servants' hall into a squash court, and the drawing-room into a dance room with bar. By the time they had decided to make their aunt's room into a Chamber of Horrors, charging half a crown for admission, they were all laughing so much that even when Delia suddenly uttered one of her celebrated screams, it was hardly heard above the noise the men were making. Her shriek was merely a prelude to the announcement that if Aunt Sissie was everybody's aunt they must be Hilary's cousins, adding that she hoped he didn't mind her calling him Hilary, but she always did. On inquiry it turned out that Mr. Grant's father and the Brandons' father were connected with Miss Brandon's family on quite different sides and no relationship existed, but it was agreed that a state of cousinship should be established.

When Mrs. Brandon left the dining-room she found Miss Brandon's maid waiting for her in the hall.

'Good afternoon, Sparks,' said Mrs. Brandon. 'How is Miss Brandon to-day?'

'Thank you, madam, a little on the edge,' said Sparks. 'Young Mr. Grant's visit seemed to upset her a good deal, being as he reminded her of her brother, Captain Brandon, the one that was killed by a pig in India, madam.'

At any other moment Mrs. Brandon might have wondered why Mr. Miller's pupil should remind her Aunt Sissie of Captain Frederick Brandon who was killed while pig-sticking in Jubilee year, but her whole attention was concentrated on getting upstairs. The great stair-case at Brandon Abbey, square, made of solid oak, had been taken from an Elizabethan house that was being demolished. Mr. Brandon, after taking one look at its rich natural colour, had decided that it did not look worth the considerable sum he had given for it, so he dismissed his architect who had advised the purchase and had the whole staircase painted and grained to resemble the oak of which it was made. Having done this he admired the result so much that, with a taste far in advance of his time, he left it bare, instead of covering it as the hall and corridors were covered with a layer of felt, a rich Kidderminster carpet, and a drugget above all. He then gave orders that it was to be waxed and polished twice a week, which had been faithfully carried out ever since, even after Mr. Brandon had slipped and broken his ankle and a second footman (who should have been using the back stairs and was at once dismissed) had crashed down the final flight carrying six empty brass water cans.

Knowing the dangers, Mrs. Brandon clung to the banisters and went slowly upstairs. Safely arrived on the landing she followed Sparks along the gloomy corridor to the door that led to Miss Brandon's sitting-room. This door was guarded by two life-size and highly varnished black wooden statues of gorillas, wearing hats and holding out trays for visiting cards, which images had been the terror of Francis and Delia's childhood. Delia always the bolder of the two, had only suspected that they would claw her as she went into her aunt's room, but Francis knew, with the deadly certainty of childhood, that they came over the downs to Stories every Friday night, when Nurse was out, and got under his bed. Perhaps the happiest day of his life was when he was taken to Brandon Abbey in his first prep school holidays, and fresh from a world of men suddenly realized that the gorillas were nothing but very hideous wooden figures, which knowledge he imparted to Delia in a lofty and offhand way, as one who had always known the truth but had not troubled to mention it.

Sparks left Mrs. Brandon in the sitting-room while she went to prepare her mistress. Mrs. Brandon walked about the room, idly looking at the many faded photographs of old Mr. and Mrs. Brandon at all stages, of Captain Brandon with military moustache and whiskers, of Miss Brandon from a plump, pretty child with ringlets to a well-corseted young woman in a bustle, after which epoch she had apparently never been photographed again. She wondered idly, not for the first time, what Amelia Brandon's life had been, what secrets her heart might have held, before she became the immense, terrifying old lady whom she had always known. These unprofitable reflections were interrupted by the door into Miss Brandon's room being opened and Mrs. Brandon, turning to face Sparks, saw a stranger. It was a woman no longer young, with greying hair and a rather worn face, neatly dressed in dark blue silk.

'Mrs. Brandon?' said the stranger. 'I am Ella Morris, Miss Brandon's companion.'

Mrs. Brandon found Miss Morris's voice very pleasant.

'Oh, how do you do,' said she, shaking hands. 'Thank you so much for writing for Aunt Sissie and I do hope you aren't having a dreadful time.'

'Nothing to what I have had with my other old ladies,' said Miss Morris composedly. 'I was so sorry not to be down when you came, but Miss Brandon wanted me to read some old letters to her. I hope everything was all right at lunch.'

'Perfect,' said Mrs. Brandon. 'And forgive my asking, but knowing Aunt Sissie as I do, have *you* had any lunch.'

'Oh, no,' said Miss Morris as composedly as ever. 'Miss Brandon likes me to read to her while she is lunching. She has a remarkably good appetite. I shall have mine now. Will you come in?'

'How many days a week is she in bed now?' Mrs. Brandon asked softly, as they approached the door.

'Six and half, since Whitsun when I came,' said Miss Morris. 'She gets up on Tuesday for the afternoon, and that is why she is always a little fatigued on Wednesday.'

With these ominous words she opened the door, saying, 'Miss Brandon, here is Mrs. Brandon.' She then went away and Sparks, who had been keeping guard at the bedside, got up and followed her.

In the huge room, hung with dark tapestries, filled with heavy mahogany furniture, there was very little light. The blinds were drawn against the westering sun and Mrs. Brandon, dazzled by the gloom, could only advance slowly towards the fourposter with its embroidered canopy, below which her husband's aunt lay propped upon pillows.

Miss Brandon in a state of nature bore a striking resemblance, with her almost bald head and her massive jowl, to the more decadent of the Roman Emperors. To conceal her baldness she had taken of late years to a rather cheap wig, whose canvas parting was of absorbing interest to the young Brandons as they grew tall enough to look down on it, but when in bed she preferred to discard the wig, and wore white bonnets, exquisitely hand-sewn by Sparks, frilled, plaited and goffered, in which she looked like an elderly Caligula disguised as Elizabeth Fry. Round her shoulders she had a white Cashmere shawl, fine enough to draw through a wedding ring, and about her throat swathes of rich, yellowing lace, pinned with hideous and valuable diamond brooches. Diamonds, rubies, sapphires, emeralds sparkled in the creases of her swollen fingers, and in the watch pocket above her head was the cheap steel-framed watch that her father had bought as a young man with his first earnings.

'Stand still and shut your eyes for a moment,' commanded Miss Brandon's voice from the bed, 'and then you'll be able to see. I can't have the blinds up. My eyes are bad.'

Mrs. Brandon obediently halted, shut her eyes, and presently opened them again. The gloom was now less dense to her sight and without difficulty she reached the chair placed by the bedside.

'How are you, Aunt Sissie,' she said, taking her aunt's unresponsive hand, and then sat down.

Miss Brandon said that her legs were more swollen than ever and it was only a question of Time. Her niece, she added, could look at them if she liked.

'Oh, thank you *very* much, Aunt Sissie, but I don't think I could *bear* it,' said Mrs. Brandon truthfully.

'You don't have much to bear, Lavinia,' said her aunt grimly, 'and I think you might take a little interest in my sufferings. Even my father's legs weren't as bad as mine. But all you young people are selfish. Hilary wouldn't look at them. What do you think of him?'

'Oh whom?' Mrs. Brandon asked, a little bewildered.

'Hilary Grant. My nephew. First cousin once removed to be exact, as his father was a son of my youngest aunt. Same relation your children are.'

'Do you mean Mr. Grant?' faltered Mrs. Brandon. 'I thought he was going to be a clergyman.'

Miss Brandon almost reared in bed.

'I have always been sorry for you, Lavinia, as Henry's wife,' she announced, 'but I am beginning to be sorry for Henry. Have you *no* intelligence?'

'Not much,' said her niece meekly.

'None of you have,' said the invalid. 'Four people having lunch together and can't find out who they are. Why didn't Miss Morris tell you?'

'I didn't see her, Aunt Sissie. She was reading to you, she said, when we got here.'

'Oh, that's what she said, is it,' said Miss Brandon. 'Well, as a matter of fact she is perfectly correct. She was reading some of Fred's letters from India to me. I would like you to read me some, Lavinia. Take a chair nearer the window and pull up the blind a little. Here they are.'

She handed her niece a large sachet, worked in cross-stitch with a regimental crest, containing a bundle of yellowing letters. Mrs. Brandon went towards the window and could not resist saying as she went,

'Is it the cousin you sometimes talk about?'

'His son. I didn't like the father and the mother is a fool, but luckily she lives in Italy a good deal. I like young Hilary.'

She said this with such meaning that Mrs. Brandon was almost goaded into saying that she wished her aunt would leave everything to Mr. Grant at once, and then they needn't ever come to Brandon Abbey again. But when she looked at her aunt's helpless bulk, and thought of her legs, and the years of pain and loneliness she had had and might have to come, she felt so sorry that she said nothing, pulled up the blind a little, sat down and opened the sachet. A marker of perforated cardboard sewn with blue silk onto a faded blue ribbon and stitched with the initials F. B., showed the place where Miss Morris had left off.

'Shall I read straight on?' she asked.

Receiving no reply, she began to read. But Captain Brandon's writing had never been his strong point, the ink was pale with age, the letters were heavily crossed. And as they consisted almost entirely of references to fellows in the regiment, or the places where they had been quartered or in camp, she found herself floundering hopelessly.

'You'd better stop, Lavinia,' said her aunt's voice after a time, though not unkindly. 'Miss Morris can do it far better than you can. I think of Fred as if it were only yesterday. He was twelve years older than I was. Sissie was his pet name for me; he didn't like Amelia. When he was a lieutenant he used to let me ride on his knee and pull his moustaches. He was a very fine figure of a man. My father made an eldest son of him, and sent him into the Army and gave him every advantage. And all the end of it was that Fred was killed. And now I am all that is left. Hilary reminded me of Fred. I should like to think of someone like Fred living here when I am gone.'

Mrs. Brandon understood that her aunt was talking to herself and without malice. Neither did she feel any resentment herself at the old lady's outspoken preference for her new nephew. For many years she had felt that the prospect of an inheritance might be bad for Francis. Luckily he had hitherto treated the whole subject as a joke and worked just as hard as if he had no expectations from his aunt and no allowance from his mother. But if by any chance Miss Brandon did bequeath him the Abbey and even a part of her fortune, Mrs. Brandon saw no end to the trouble that such a white elephant would bring. What the amount of Miss Brandon's estate might be she had no idea, but she thought the death duties would effectually keep the inheritor from improving or even keeping up the place. Never in fact had the mother of a possible legatee been less grateful. It was almost without knowing that she was speaking that she said, 'I hope that he will then, Aunt Sissie.'

'What?' said Miss Brandon sharply.

Mrs. Brandon found what she had just said too difficult to repeat and was silent.

'Read me some of *The Times*,' said Miss Brandon. 'The cricket news. My father was very fond of cricket and I used to know all the names of the county players. It is a poor game now. Go on.'

Mrs. Brandon read the descriptions of the chief matches for some time, looking occasionally at the bed to see if her aunt was listening. Gradually she let her voice tail away into a murmur, then gently got up and was tip-toeing towards the door to call Sparks, when a sharp voice from the bed said, 'Lavinia!'

'I'm so sorry,' said Mrs. Brandon, returning to the bedside, 'I thought you were asleep.'

'You've never thought in your life,' said Miss Brandon. 'Come here.'

Mrs. Brandon approached the bed.

'You are a silly woman, Lavinia,' said her aunt, 'but there's a lot of good in you. I heard what you said quite well. It was no business of yours, but I daresay you are right. I'm going to give you something. It is the diamond Fred brought back from India the last time he came on leave. I always wore it till my hands began to swell, and I wouldn't have it altered because it was set just as Fred gave it to me. If you don't get anything else, you'll get that.'

She took a little case from beside her bed and handed it to her niece, who opened it and saw a diamond ring in an open setting of very thin gold, a store of a thousand lights and twinklings.

'Put it on,' said Miss Brandon. 'That's right. It looks better on you than it ever looked on me. You have a lady's hands. Mine are like my father's, workman's hands. Go away now and send Sparks to me.'

She shut her eyes so determinedly that Mrs. Brandon did not dare to thank her, so she kissed the swollen, bejewelled hand very gently and went out of the room. In the sitting-room she found Miss Morris writing letters and told her that Miss Brandon wanted Sparks. Miss Morris rang the bell.

'I hope very much to see you before you go,' she said. 'Miss Brandon has her tea about half-past four and I have ordered tea for you at five if that suits you and then I can come down. Five to seven is my off time. I hope you found Miss Brandon pretty well. She has been looking forward to your visit very much indeed.'

'I never knew anyone who could show their pleasure at seeing one less than Aunt Sissie,' said Mrs. Brandon, 'but she was very kind and gave me this ring.'

She held out her left hand on which the diamond was sparkling. Mrs. Brandon had exquisite hands and though she was by no means puffed up she might sometimes be found gazing at them with a frank and pensive admiration that amused her best friends. She wore no rings except her wedding ring, having secretly sold her ugly diamond half-hoop engagement ring many years ago. Captain Brandon's Indian diamond now shone in its place.

'It looks perfect on your hand,' said Miss Morris in a matter of fact voice that yet somehow conveyed to Mrs. Brandon that her hands were admired and the gift approved. 'I think your son and daughter are in the garden with Mr. Grant. Or would you rather rest?'

Again Miss Morris's pleasant voice conveyed an unmistakable meaning, and Mrs. Brandon went downstairs feeling rather like a child that has been told it may get down from table. In the hall she picked up her parasol and gloves and went out into the shimmering afternoon. To young Mr. Grant, sitting on the edge of the lily-pond, while Francis and Delia tried to tickle for goldfish, it seemed that never had a goddess been more apparent in her approach. Being in private a poet he tried to think of a suitable description, rejected the words swimming, floating, gliding, light-footed, winged, and several others, and finally as she came near delivered his soul in the words, 'Oh, Mrs. Brandon,' standing up and straightening his tie as he did so.

'Hullo, mamma,' said Francis. 'Don't come any nearer or you will frighten my goldfish. Hilary, take mamma away or she will want to look, and if there's one thing goldfish can't bear it's people looking. There are millions of seats about.'

He waved his hand comprehensively at a stretch of green turf and dark walls of yew and bent himself again to his tickling. Mrs. Brandon smiled indulgently and turning to Mr. Grant said,

'I think we must be cousins by marriage.'

This statement, which when previously made by Delia had caused Mr. Grant no emotion at all, suddenly assumed a totally different aspect. To be Mrs. Brandon's cousin was like suddenly becoming a member of the Royal Family, or being asked to tea by the Captain of the Eleven; or like going to Heaven. In a state of unspeakable nervous exaltation he began to explain the relationship, but one half of his mind, and that, if the expression may be permitted, by far the larger half, was trying to visualize the Tables of Affinity in the beginning of the Prayer Book and to remember whether a man might marry his father's aunt's nephew's on another side's wife, or rather widow. So he stammered and repeated himself and wished he had shaved more carefully that morning. When he had stammered himself into silence, Mrs. Brandon said she thought there was a seat under the tulip tree, so they walked there; and there were two deck chairs, just as if it had been meant.

'Now,' said Mrs. Brandon, settling herself comfortably, 'tell me about yourself.'

This kind suggestion naturally threw Mr. Grant into a state of even more acute palsy and paralysis, but to please the goddess he explained, in a not very intelligible way, that his father had died some time ago and his mother was rather Italian.

'Have you Italian blood then?' asked Mrs. Brandon, interested.

Not like that, Mr. Grant explained, but he meant his mother lived mostly in Italy and had got rather Italian, at least, he added in a burst of confidence, the kind of Italian that English people do get.

'I know,' said Mrs. Brandon. 'She talks about Marcheses and would like you to kiss people's hands.'

So confounded was Mr. Grant by this proof of semimiraculous understanding, and at the same time so overcome by the idea that he might perhaps be allowed to kiss Mrs. Brandon's hand, that he forgot all the hard words he had been about to utter concerning his mother, and wished she had forced him from earliest youth to kiss the hand of every delightful woman he met. Mrs. Brandon said she thought the custom of kissing hands was so charming, which inspired Mr. Grant's heart with fresh ardour, but that she thought Englishmen could never do it well, at which his heart sank and he thought more unkindly than ever of his mother.

Mrs. Brandon pulled off her gloves and looked thoughtfully at her hands.

'Aunt Sissie gave me this ring to-day,' she said. 'Isn't it beautiful?'

She held out her hand. Mr. Grant, put his own hand very respectfully beneath it and raised it a little. He looked intently at the diamond and the elegant fingers and imagined himself gently pressing his lips upon them. He then, entirely against his own will, found himself withdrawing his own hand and saying the ring was lovely. This would have been a good moment to add that the hand it adorned was lovelier still, but his voice refused its office and flames consumed his marrow. By the time he came to, Mrs. Brandon was telling him about the wall paintings in the church.

'I liked them awfully,' said Mr. Grant, 'and all the monuments and things.'

'I suppose you saw my husband's memorial stone,' said Mrs. Brandon, assuming quite unconsciously a most intriguing air of melancholy.

'No, I'm awfully sorry I didn't,' said Mr. Grant. 'Is it a good one – I mean sculpture or anything?'

'Oh, no; quite simple,' said Mrs. Brandon, in a voice that made Mr. Grant feel how moving simplicity was, compared with sculpture. 'Just the dates of his birth and death. He died at Cannes, you know, so he couldn't be buried here.'

Mr. Grant said again he was awfully sorry.

'That is very sweet of you,' said Mrs. Brandon, turning grave blue eyes upon him. 'I don't think much about it. I wasn't very happy. There are things one is glad to forget.'

If Mr. Grant's guardian angel had been there he would have been perfectly within his rights to take Mrs. Brandon by the shoulders and shake her. Mr. Grant, deeply moved by this touching confidence, saw his exquisite new friend in the power of a sadist, a drunkard, a dope fiend, nay Worse, though why it should be worse he didn't quite know, and in his agitation got up and began to walk about.

'Yes, I suppose it is nearly tea-time,' said Mrs. Brandon. 'Let's find the children. And you won't mind if I call you Hilary, will you? If we are cousins it seems ridiculous to say Mr. Grant.'

'I'd love it,' said Mr. Grant.

'And you must call me Lavinia,' said Mrs. Brandon, putting her parasol up again as they walked back across the lawn to the pond.

'There is one name I would like to call you,' said Mr. Grant, in a low, croaking voice.

Mrs. Brandon stopped and looked interested.

'I would like to call you my friend,' said Mr. Grant.

'Of course,' said Mrs. Brandon, laughing gently, 'that goes without saying. But if you feel I am too old for Christian names, never mind.'

Mr. Grant felt that this misunderstanding was so awful that it would be no good trying to explain it. They collected Francis and Delia, who had by now tired of the goldfish, and all four went back to the house for tea. Here Miss Morris was waiting for them at the head of the dining-room table, which was loaded with scones, sandwiches, cakes of all sorts and sizes, sweets and fruit. Mr. Grant had not yet arrived at the stage when love makes one resent the sight of food, and all three young people made a very hearty meal. When Miss Morris had finished pouring out the tea she asked Mrs. Brandon if it would be inconvenient for her to take Mr. Grant back in her car.

'I had ordered Miss Brandon's car to take Mr. Grant back,' she said, 'but as he is almost next door to you I thought you wouldn't mind.'

'Of course not,' said Mrs. Brandon. 'And now I come to think of it, you are having supper with us to-night, aren't you Hilary, so it all fits in.'

Mr. Grant on hearing those lips speak his name lost his senses and said, Oh, of course, he had quite forgotten, and again felt that it was no good trying to explain. Ever since the invitation had been issued on the previous Saturday he had been living for that evening, but in the unexpected joy of seeing Mrs. Brandon again at the Abbey, and the whirlpool of emotion into which he had been thrown by finding her even more exquisite than he thought, only the present had existed for him, and so drowned was he in the moment that he had truly and completely forgotten about the evening.

'Well, it's no good forgetting now,' said Francis, 'if you're coming back with us. No need to bother about changing to-night. When Rose is out we relax a little. And anyway there's not much sense in telling old Miller to change because you can hardly tell the difference. He ought to be allowed to dress like a monk or something for dinner; he'd get an awful kick out of it.'

While the young members were loudly discussing suitable evening dress for Mr. Miller, Mrs. Brandon turned to Miss Morris and pressed cake upon her. Miss Morris refused it.

'You are too tired to eat,' said Mrs. Brandon accusingly. 'You have had nothing for tea, and I'm sure you didn't have enough lunch. Was it a poached egg?'

'Oh, no. Just what you had. Cold salmon, grilled cutlets. I order the meals for Miss Brandon and I make a point of tasting everything. One must keep the servants up to the mark.'

'Yes, tasting,' said Mrs. Brandon severely. 'Three grains of rice and a mouthful of cutlet.'

Miss Morris said nothing. Her mouth tightened, but her eyes looked at Mrs. Brandon for a moment as if appealing for help.

'I know *exactly* what you feel like,' said Mrs. Brandon untruthfully, 'but it's no good going on like that. You need a holiday.'

'I have only been with Miss Brandon since Whitsun, Mrs. Brandon.'

'And have you once been outside the grounds? or had a day to yourself? or gone to bed before one o'clock?'

'I really could get out if I wanted to,' said Miss Morris, 'but there's nowhere particular to go, and the motor bus doesn't come any nearer than Pomfret Abbas. And I don't mind going to bed late at all. I used to read to my father a great deal at night.'

'Now what I want you to do,' said Mrs. Brandon, 'is to come for a picnic with us on Friday. Francis has a little car and he can come and fetch you and take you back. We are going to the Wishing Well over beyond Southbridge and you will like it very much.'

'How good of you,' said Miss Morris. 'But I can't.'

Her mouth set into a hard line again, but Mrs. Brandon saw it tremble and took a secret resolution.

'Miss Brandon sent her love,' said Miss Morris, deliberately changing the subject and speaking for the whole table to hear, 'and she is very sorry that she doesn't feel up to seeing Mr. Brandon, or Miss Brandon — —'

'Bountiful Jehovah!' said Francis, piously grateful.

' — or Mr. Grant, but she would like you to come up before you go, Mrs. Brandon.'

Mrs. Brandon said she would come at once then, as they must be getting home, and went upstairs with Miss Morris, saying no more about the picnic.

Miss Brandon was propped up on her pillows, finishing what looked like the remains of a tea that would have fed several people.

'Well,' said she to her niece, 'so you are going. I can't see those young people. They tire me. I suppose they have been getting into mischief as usual.'

'No, Aunt Sissie. Just sitting in the garden.'

'Idling as usual,' said Miss Brandon. 'My father never idled, nor did I.'

Mrs. Brandon, suppressing an impulse to say And look at you both now, thanked her aunt for a pleasant visit, at which her aged relative grunted.

'I wanted Miss Morris to come for a picnic with us on Friday,' she said.

'Well, she can't,' said the invalid, who seemed to be imbibing fresh strength as she dipped plum cake into her tea and mumbled it.

'But she said she wouldn't,' Mrs. Brandon continued, with great cunning.

'She *wouldn't*!' said Miss Brandon. 'I don't know why girls are so ungrateful now. I never could stand a proud stomach. I suppose you wanted her to help with the sandwiches, Lavinia. Something for nothing.'

Having thus satisfactorily attributed the lowest of motives to her niece and her companion, Miss Brandon drank the rest of her tea and rang the handbell violently. Sparks appeared and was ordered to fetch Miss Morris, while Miss Brandon ate lumps of sugar in a state of mental abstraction which her niece thought it better not to disturb.

'I want you to go with Mrs. Brandon on Friday and help with the sandwiches,' said the invalid, as soon as Miss Morris appeared. 'The car will take you, and tell Simmonds to put up some of her potted salmon and crab apple jelly and make some cakes. And you'd better take some of the marsala. You can read to me all Friday evening to make up. Good-bye, Lavinia.'

'Good-bye, Aunt Sissie, and thank you very much for the ring. It is the loveliest diamond I've ever seen,' said Mrs. Brandon.

'Fred liked pretty women to have jewellery,' said Miss Brandon with a surprising chuckle. 'It was the diamond bracelet he gave to Mrs. Colonel Arbuthnot that made him have to exchange – that was at Poona in seventy-six. I was only a young woman then, but Fred told me everything. Come again, soon, but I don't want to see all those young people. Come alone, and I'll show you my legs.'

Taking this as permission to retire, and seeing no means of reaching her aunt across the tea-things, Mrs. Brandon repeated her farewell and went out, followed by Miss Morris.

'Is it all right for Miss Brandon to eat so much?' she inquired as they went downstairs. 'I thought she was on a diet.'

'So she is, but she doesn't take any notice of it. She told Dr. Ford last time he came that she was going to die in her own way and he needn't come again if he didn't like it, so he just comes and talks to her occasionally. She likes it. Mrs. Brandon, I can't thank you enough, but do you really want me?'

At this slavish question, which no one should ever ask, Mrs. Brandon almost felt she didn't. But she looked at Miss Morris's thin shoulders and her worn face and decided that she did.

'I do want you,' she said, 'but I'm not sure if I really want Aunt Sissie's car. Anyway Francis shall drive you back.'

Then they all got into the car. Curwen asked with long-suffering if he should go by the downs, and on receiving the order to go by Barchester managed to express by the set of his shoulders his opinion of employers, their children, and their guest. Francis chose to ride inside, so he and Delia continued their plans for remaking Brandon Abbey, while Mrs. Brandon thought of nothing in particular and Mr. Grant felt that he now knew what true religion was like. As they approached Pomfret Madrigal, Mrs. Brandon told Curwen to drive first to the Vicarage. Francis protested that there was no need to change, and Hilary might as well come straight to Stories and have a singles with him before dinner. But Mr. Grant, increasingly unconscious of his unsuccessful shave that morning, said he would really like to go to the Vicarage first if nobody minded, and, as an afterthought, that he might as well change. Mrs. Brandon smiled approval, Mr. Grant was decanted at the Vicarage, the car rolled away and darkness fell on the world.

III

UNDER THE SPANISH CHESTNUT

THE darkness which had covered the universe was not apparent to anyone else. The Vicarage cook was sitting at the kitchen door in the sunshine, knitting a jacket for her married sister's latest; Hettie, the friend of spiders, was in the pantry reading a very nice book in a two-penny edition called *Pure as the Lily*, with the sun glancing on her spectacles, while Mr. Miller, reclining in a deck chair under the beech on the lawn, was reading the Bishop of Barchester's pastoral charge, bathed in the late afternoon light. Cook shouted to Hettie that she didn't remember a summer like that, not since her aunt died; Hettie yelled back to Cook that she must hurry up with her voyle for the Feet, it was that hot, a statement which Cook rightly interpreted as a wise decision of Hettie's to get her new cotton voile dress finished before the annual Church Fête, which took place, with Mr. Miller's resigned permission, in the Vicarage grounds; while Mr. Miller thought that if there were a hotter place than his garden he wished the Bishop were in it. Seeing his pupil approach he dashed his Bishop's letter to the ground and asked Mr. Grant how he had got on at Brandon Abbey.

Quite well, said Mr. Grant. His aunt was a peculiar old lady, but quite kind, only he did wish she wouldn't make hints about leaving things to him, because the Abbey was a ghastly place and he would hate to have anything to do with it. Her companion, Miss Morris, was very nice too. And, he added, speaking with some difficulty, Mrs. Brandon was there.

'Mrs. Brandon. Ah, yes,' said Mr. Miller.

There was a silence.

'It's a most extraordinary thing,' said Mr. Grant, 'but she is a sort of cousin of mine. I never knew about it till to-day.'

Mr. Miller found himself indulging in the sin of envy. To be Mrs. Brandon's cousin must be in itself a state of grace to be envied by any-one. Then he rebuked himself, and concentrated on thinking how glad he was that his pupil, whom he already liked, should have this great happiness.

Silence fell again, till Mr. Miller, hearing the church clock strike seven, said he supposed they must be thinking of dressing. So they thought about it very comfortably till half-past and then there was rather a scurry. Mr. Grant, getting into his white shirt, was for the sixth or seventh time suddenly struck hot with shame and remorse as he remembered the various bricks he had dropped that afternoon. His stud fell from his nerveless hands, rolled across the sloping oak floor and disappeared in the gap under the skirting board. Mr. Grant knew he had another stud somewhere, but where he couldn't think. After untidying all his drawers he went down the passage and knocked at Mr. Miller's door.

'I say, I'm awfully sorry, Mr. Miller,' he said, putting his head in, 'but one of my studs has got down a hole in the wall and I can't find my spare one. Could you possibly lend me one? It's only an ordinary gold one.'

'The worst of my profession is that one doesn't have much to do with studs,' said Mr. Miller, who was in his trousers and vest and preparing to put his collar on. 'Wait a minute and I'll see."

He hunted in a box and found a stud which was just sufficiently unlike Mr. Grant's to make that young gentleman conscious of it for the whole evening. He handed it to Mr. Grant, and seeing him look with furtive curiosity at his clerical collar, kindly offered to show him how it did up.

'Oh, thanks most awfully,' said Mr. Grant. 'I've always wanted to know how that gadget worked. I say, that's awfully interesting. Thanks most awfully.'

He dashed back to his bedroom, hated his own face, hair and tie, wondered if Mrs. Brandon would notice a small spot of grease on one of the lapels of his dinner jacket, wished his evening shoes were newer, and hurried downstairs and into Mr. Miller's little open car, in which his tutor was already waiting.

'You will enjoy dining at Stories,' said Mr. Miller, as they drove along the lane. 'The house is a delightful example of early Georgian; about 1720 I think.'

Mr. Grant said that would be awfully jolly and wished his throat were not so dry, nor his heart banging so absurdly against his ribs.

'And Mrs. Brandon is a most charming hostess,' Mr. Miller continued.

This understatement could only be met with silence, and nothing more was said till they drew up at the front door.

When Mrs. Brandon got home she went upstairs to rest a little before dinner. Not that she was in need of rest, but she vastly enjoyed the ritual of leisurely bath, lying on her sofa in a becoming wrap, and slowly dressing. Francis and Delia went off to play tennis before their skimpier toilets, and their fraternal yells came sweetly to her ears from beyond the walled garden. She took off her hat and rang.

'Did you ring, madam?' said Rose, appearing with great celerity.

'My bath please, Rose, and I'll wear that old pink thing,' said Mrs. Brandon, recognizing with some trepidation that Rose had a grievance, and suddenly realizing that she shouldn't have been there at all, as it was her afternoon out.

'I thought you would prefer the black, or the mauve to-night, madam,' said Rose, so meaningly that her mistress had to ask her why.

'You wore the pink if you remember, madam, the last time Sir Edmund dined here.'

'Sir Edmund? But he isn't coming here to-night.'

'I am sorry, I am sure, madam, but understanding from Nurse that Sir Edmund had rung up I thought I had better stay in and take My Afternoon on Friday. If I had taken the message, madam, I should have written it down on the pad, but of course with Nurse taking it I did not wish to interfere, not being any business of mine.'

Without giving her mistress time to answer she disappeared into the bathroom and drowned all attempts at conversation in a roaring of taps, so that she did not hear a knock on the bedroom door.

'Come in,' cried Mrs. Brandon, shutting the bathroom door to lessen the noise.

Nurse came in.

'It's about Miss Delia's tennis frock, madam,' she began. 'I'm sure I am ready to work at it all night if need be, but I can't finish it without a fitting, and Miss Delia is playing tennis.'

'Then you'd better tell her to come up to you before she dresses for dinner,' said Mrs. Brandon, knowing well that Delia always obeyed Nurse and that this complaint was but a preface to further wrongs.

'Just as you say, madam,' said Nurse, 'and I am sure I am sorry if I have stepped out of my place, but when the telephone rings for quite three minutes, as I said to Cook, being downstairs at the moment, and the other girls upstairs tidying themselves after lunch, and it being Rose's afternoon off and she happened to pass the remark quite distinctly before lunch that she was going to Southbridge on her bike as soon as she had set the dinner table, it is hardly to be surprized at that I went to the phone. Let me take your stockings off, madam, I'm sure you are tired.'

'What *is* all this about the telephone?' asked Mrs. Brandon, sinking into a chair.

'Sir Edmund, madam,' replied Nurse, suddenly becoming brisk and business-like. 'He rang up to ask if he could come to dinner and I said you were out all day, madam, so he said he would come at eight and hoped it was all right.'

'Oh well, I suppose he must,' said Mrs. Brandon. 'Thanks, Nurse.'

At this minute Rose emerged from the steaming bathroom and saw her rival in the act of putting the bedroom slippers on her mistress's feet. She controlled herself very well, merely saying in an icy voice that she supposed there was nothing more.

'Yes, my old pink dress,' said Mrs. Brandon, goaded to defiance. 'Thanks, Nurse. You'd better go and catch Miss Delia before dinner. Now Rose, what is this about Sir Edmund?'

'I understood, madam, from something Nurse let slip,' said Rose coldly, 'that Sir Edmund was coming to dinner, so not being sure what you wished I changed My Afternoon back to Friday.'

In face of this revolting and quite unnecessary self-sacrifice Mrs.

Brandon could say nothing. She escaped into the bathroom, but not before she had seen Rose pick up the stockings that Nurse had folded and carry them ostentatiously away to be washed. In the bath her spirits revived a good deal. The worst of the interview with Rose and Nurse was over, and she understood her staff well enough to know that they would mobilize and rise to a crisis, and that she could count upon a good dinner. So she finished dressing with a fairly light heart and came downstairs. For a moment she thought of asking Rose if she had remembered the special port for Sir Edmund, but feeling that she could better face her guest's disappointment than her parlourmaid's displeasure she refrained.

Sir Edmund Pridham was an old friend of the Brandons', Mrs. Brandon's trustee, and one of those useful middle-aged men who appear to have no particular business but do a hundred unpaid jobs with no thought of the sacrifice of their own time and strength. The Pridhams had lived at Pomfret Madrigal for at least two hundred years, always doing their duty to their tenants, to the church, being Justices of the Peace, sitting on and controlling local committees, once or twice sitting unwillingly but efficiently in Parliament because no one else would contest the seat. The present baronet, a childless widower, had commanded the Barsetshire Yeomanry for two years of the War and when he was invalided with a permanently crippled leg had run the whole county, even bullying the Matron of the Barchester War Hospital and the terrifying head of the Waacs. He knew the country and the people almost as well as old Lord Pomfret, and was entirely unmoved by their affection or dislike. His relations with Mrs. Brandon as trustee had always been very pleasant, as he managed her affairs with the same diligence that he applied to everything else and she always signed everything he told her to without asking why. Of late he had insisted that Francis should go thoroughly into his mother's money matters and the two had got on well together.

Of course the county had married him to Mrs. Brandon again and again in the last eighteen years or so, but nothing was further from their thoughts. Sir Edmund looked upon Mrs. Brandon as what a woman should be, goodlooking, docile, not too intelligent, always charming. Her flashes of insight he completely ignored, but he saw through all her self-deceptions with a ruthless though admiring eye, and never missed an opportunity of pointing them out to her. Mrs. Brandon liked him very much, accepted his homage and his scorn with equal placidity, consulted him about everything, and except on money matters, rarely took his advice.

Presently Rose, her voice divided between the deference due to a baronet and the resentment she was still feeling against Nurse and in a lesser degree against her innocent mistress, announced Sir Edmund. At the sight of his tall figure, which almost filled the drawing-room door,

Mrs. Brandon felt very comfortable. For years his broad shoulders, straining to the uttermost stitch the well-cut coats that he would not take the trouble to renew, his red neck rigidly confined by a stiff collar and overlapping a little behind, his close-cropped sandy-grizzling hair and moustache, his angry but equitable blue eyes, had represented the safe background of her life. After outraging Rose by asking after her mother's leg, Sir Edmund bore down upon his hostess, who rose to greet him.

'Out to kill, Lavinia,' said Sir Edmund, eyeing her dress with interest. 'Who is it this time?'

'Mr. Miller is coming to dinner,' said Mrs. Brandon, ignoring her guest's question, 'and Mr. Grant who is a cousin of ours, at least he seems to be a cousin of Henry's and a cousin of Miss Brandon's. We met him there to-day and he is delightful.'

'A cousin of Amelia Brandon's?' said Sir Edmund, who prided himself on knowing the genealogies of the whole county. Grant, eh? Now, let's see. Old Mrs. Brandon's sister — Mortons they were from Cheshire and a good family, Miss Morton was considered to have thrown herself away on Brandon, till he made all his money — married a man called Grant in the Barsetshire Regiment, met him at the Barsetshire Hunt Ball when she was down here staying with her sister at Brandon Abbey. Their son was born the year Lord Pomfret was made Lord Lieutenant, now what the devil was his name? Edward. That's it. Called after someone — can't think who at the moment. Edward married a damn silly woman and this must be their boy. Hope you've got a good dinner, Lavinia. I'm hungry. Been out all day about those drains.'

'Have some sherry then,' said Mrs. Brandon, going to the table where Rose had put the decanter. She certainly looked very agreeable in the old pink rag, what she herself called a soft elderly pink, and no wonder that Mr. Grant, looking from his considerable height over Mr. Miller's shoulder as they came in, was again transfixed by arrows of very respectful desire.

'Well, Miller,' said Sir Edmund, who was Vicar's Churchwarden, read the lessons on Sundays and while supporting all the Vicar's doings in public, bullied him a good deal in private, 'everything all right, eh?'

To this comprehensive question Mr. Miller could but answer weakly that it was. Mr. Grant bowed rather low over Mrs. Brandon's hand, thus affording exquisite pleasure to Francis and Delia who followed hard upon him, and was introduced to Sir Edmund.

'So you are Edward's son,' said Sir Edmund, shaking hands. 'What's your name? Robert?'

Mr. Grant, feeling that an apology was necessary said he was sorry but his name was Hilary.

'Hilary, eh? Oh, well, nothing wrong with that. There was a saint called Hilary, a bishop; more in Miller's line than mine. But I should have thought your father would have called you Robert, after your grandfather,' said Sir Edmund, more in sorrow than in anger.

Luckily dinner was coldly announced by Rose and the party drifted into the dining-room. Sir Edmund, lingering behind with his hostess, remarked, in a voice of whose carrying powers he was quite unconscious, that he was sorry he had told young Grant that he thought he should have been called Robert, because he remembered now that there had been the deuce of a row between young Grant's father and grandfather on the occasion of young Grant's father's marriage.

'Here, Grant,' he called, 'what's the name of that woman your father married? The dark one?'

Mr. Grant looked round, startled.

'My mother, do you mean, sir?' he asked.

'That's right, your mother, you know what I mean. Never mind the name,' said Sir Edmund, who had evidently satisfied himself on the subject.

Conversation at dinner was led by Delia, who had been reading the local weekly and had come across a delightful report of the coroner's inquest on the bodies of the people who were burned in the motor bus.

'It must have been simply *ghastly*, Sir Edmund,' she said with relish. 'The doors and windows got jammed and the ones that got out simply *trampled* on the others and got all cut to bits on the broken glass, and it took two days to sort the others out, and there was one of them that there was so little of him left that they didn't know who he was, and even with the false teeth they couldn't tell because there was another man that died afterwards in the Barchester Infirmary and all he would say was "My teeth, my teeth," only they couldn't understand for ages because he hadn't got any teeth, and you know the way having no teeth makes people so difficult to understand, but anyway one of the nurses who had false teeth herself had a brain wave and said she expected he wanted to know where his false teeth were, because when she was in a car accident once that was the first thing she thought of when she came to, and so they fetched the teeth from the refrigerator or wherever the coroner keeps the bodies, but he was dead then and couldn't identify them. I think they ought to have buried them with him, like Ur and Vikings and all that sort of thing, but they kept them in case anyone could identify them. I'd have put them in the Barchester Museum.'

'In which department?' asked Mr. Grant, interested in Delia's maiden fancies.

'Oh, anywhere. Fossils or War Souvenirs or something. I mean then if anyone wanted them they'd always be there.'

'And what happened to the one they couldn't identify?' said Francis.

'Oh, he got buried. It's a pity we couldn't have had him buried here. It would have been *ghastly*. I mean seeing a coffin and knowing there was really nothing to speak of inside. Is it all right to bury people in the churchyard, Mr. Miller, when there really isn't any of them to bury except the burnt bits? I mean would the Bishop mind?'

'I have luckily never been faced with such a contingency,' said Mr. Miller, who was very fond of Delia, but had not her strength of mind. 'It is all rather horrible to think of.'

Sir Edmund, who owing to the excellent soup and fish had only been a listener to the foregoing conversation, now spoke as the representative of law and order.

'We all know you'd do your duty, Miller,' he said, wiping his moustache with his table napkin crumpled into a ball. 'But better to marry than to be burnt, eh?'

He then applied himself to the next course. Mr. Grant and Francis, catching one another's eye, fell into wild suppressed giggles, and Mrs. Brandon applied herself to soothing Mr. Miller, which she did so well that the whole dinner was held up while he hung upon her lips and Rose, preferring not to demean herself by making her presence known, stood silently at his elbow with the sweet, till Delia jogged him.

'I say, Mr. Miller, it's an ice,' she said earnestly. 'It's an ice, so do hurry up or my bit will go all to squelch. I say, Mother, let's have coffee under the chestnut.'

'We might,' said Mrs. Brandon doubtfully. 'Rose, do you think we could have the little table out there? Mr. Francis would help you with it.'

But Rose had as yet neither forgotten nor forgiven and said, with a manner that froze the blood, that she could manage the table quite well by herself.

'Very well,' said Mrs. Brandon, again driven by persecution and injustice to rebel, 'we'll have dessert and coffee and the liqueurs outside, and the port if no one minds.'

Rose, who had a secret passion for anything that savoured of theatre, gave her outwardly grudging consent to this plan, and with the help of one of the housemaids arranged the fruit and wine under the tree and brought her mistress a black lace scarf. Sir Edmund, Mr. Miller and Mr. Grant took out chairs, while Francis and Delia triumphantly bore silver candlesticks with shaded candles through the dusk. There was not a breath of air and the candles burnt steadily under the great Spanish chestnut. Rose, contemplating the scene from the front door, said to the housemaid that madam really looked quite the thing tonight in her pink, and it was just like the scene in *Moonlight Passion*, the one she saw at the Barchester Odeon last week, where the Italian count gives the feet for Princess Alix. Princess Alix, she added, was taken by Glamora Tudor, the one that they called in Hollywood 'The Woman who Cannot Love', but madam reely looked every inch as good-looking, and if people who answered the telephone would only write down the messages it would save a lot of trouble to other people she could mention and standing there wouldn't get the dining-room table cleared nor the washing up done. So she vanished, and the yellow path of light from the front door was suddenly obscured, and in the gathering gloom the radiance of the rising moon could now be seen through the branches.

'The full moon is rising,' Mrs. Brandon breathed.

At the sound of her low voice uttering these words Mr. Grant nearly fainted.

'Nonsense, Lavinia,' said Sir Edmund, lighting a cigar. 'Full moon doesn't rise till much later. Two or three days off the full. Any child knows that.'

'But I'm not a child,' murmured Mrs. Brandon.

At these words Mr. Grant's soul took flight and assuming the form of a bird, perched in the chestnut tree, tuning its notes to the music of the spheres which sang 'Mrs. Brandon, Mrs. Brandon,' leaning its breast against a thorn regardless of botany, embracing in its vision the whole universe, for what worlds could exist outside the pool of candle-light below the leaves? It saw Mrs. Brandon, a shadowy goddess, draped in the rose light of evening, veiled in the black lace of tattered clouds, a diamond flashing like a star on her finger. It saw the rest of the party, privileged beyond their knowledge, beyond their worth, laughing and talking in that sacred presence; Sir Edmund pulling at his cigar, Francis and Delia eating more peaches than it would have thought anyone could eat who had already had so many at lunch, Mr. Miller, to him alone was vouchsafed a glimpse of the true light, gazing from the shadow at the foundress of the feast. It saw the diamond sparkle and flash again with a thousand fires, growing in size till all earths, all seas, all heavens were included in its bounds, a burning rose at the core. Spreading its wings it flew through an infinity of time and space towards that fiery centre, burning to immolate itself on such a pyre and rise again transfigured to the skies.

'Of course you aren't a child, Lavinia,' said Sir Edmund. 'Can't call a woman of your age a child. What I said was, A child would have more sense.'

Mr. Grant's soul returned suddenly to his body, but as no one had noticed its absence in the interval between Mrs. Brandon's words and Sir Edmund's reply, its return passed unobserved. Its owner, a little dizzy, helped himself to port. There was a silence in which Mrs. Brandon drew her mantilla round her with one hand and gazed meditatively upon the other with its gleaming ring.

'What's that you're wearing, Lavinia?' said Sir Edmund suddenly.

'Only my old pink,' said Mrs. Brandon, 'and the Spanish lace shawl that Henry brought from Toledo.'

'No, no, don't be dense. I can see perfectly well what you have on. The ring I mean. Haven't seen that before.'

'It is a diamond. Miss Brandon gave it to me to-day. Isn't it lovely?'

She held out her hand to Sir Edmund.

'A good one,' said he, looking at the ring, but not troubling to raise or support her hand, for which Mr. Grant could have killed him. 'Worth a round two hundred, I should say. I'd better have it insured with your other things. Remind me to take it into Barchester next time I go. Queer thing if Amelia Brandon is giving anything away. She must be breaking up. Never knew her give anything to anyone — except charities, of course. Always go to her if we want anything for the hospital. By the way, Lavinia, does she ever mention her will?'

At this appalling frankness everyone was struck dumb.

'I don't think one ought to talk about things like that,' said Mrs. Brandon, 'do you, Mr. Miller?'

'Now never mind Miller, Lavinia,' said Sir Edmund. 'He knows what's what. Render unto Caesar, eh, Miller?'

'Yes, yes, indeed, Sir Edmund,' said Mr. Miller hastily, not wishing to offend his churchwarden, but doubtful as to the applicability or relevance of his statement.

Francis came to the rescue and said Aunt Sissie was always trying to frighten someone by saying she'd leave something to someone else, but no one wanted that awful Abbey and if he or Hilary got it they were going to give it to each other or turn it into a lunatic asylum. Mr. Grant corroborated this statement by saying, Rather. On hearing these subversive remarks Sir Edmund nearly burst. To treat the sacred rights of property as a joke was something almost beyond his comprehension, almost worse than robbing the poor box or shooting foxes. If Amelia Brandon left the Abbey, as he had always understood she might, to Lavinia's boy, it would be a big responsibility, but Francis would have to take it on and do the best he could for the place and the tenants, and he would give help and advice if Francis needed it and would take it. If the old lady was going to leave it to this new nephew, who seemed a harmless enough young man for one whose mother was a damn silly woman, that was entirely her affair and no one would grudge it to him. But to talk of a stake in the country, and more especially in Barsetshire, as if it were a shuttlecock to be thrown to and fro or dropped, was worse than Bolshevism, worse than Communism, or Germany, or Italy, or Spain, or Russia, or the United States, or the Labour Party, or any of numerous nations, sects or parties which Sir Edmund found unworthy of his approval.

Filling his glass again, he addressed the two young men on the subject of the rights of property, fixing them with a choleric blue eye that they could not and dared not avoid. Delia melted away and was presently heard playing the gramophone to herself in the drawing-room. A moth fluttered round the candles. Mrs. Brandon exclaimed, Mr. Miller blew them out, but Sir Edmund's voice rumbled on in the leaf-chequered moonlight. Presently Rose's white apron was seen coming from the house, to the young men a welcome diversion, to Mrs. Brandon a vague source of uneasiness. Kindly reluctant to interrupt the gentry in their talk, Rose stood on the outskirts of the group emanating an atmosphere of such condescending tolerance that even Sir Edmund became conscious that something was wrong, and was checked in his flow of speech.

'Yes, Rose?' said Mrs. Brandon.

'Curwen would wish to speak to you, madam, if it is convenient,' said Rose.

'It isn't really,' said Mrs. Brandon helplessly, 'but I suppose he'll have to. Where is he?'

Rose stepped dramatically aside, revealing the hitherto unsuspected form of Curwen.

'I'm sure I didn't wish to trouble you, madam,' Curwen began, an ill-concealed triumph in his voice.

'Can't hear a word you say. Come up here. Bad enough not seeing anything, without not hearing anything,' barked Sir Edmund, in his orderly-room voice. Curwen, an old soldier, automatically moved forward and stood to attention.

'It was going over the downs done it, madam,' he announced with gloomy relish.

'Did what?' asked Sir Edmund. 'Why the devil can't your man speak plainly, Lavinia?'

'Done it in, Sir Edmund,' said Curwen.

Delia, tired of her gramophone, had drifted back again and wanted to know who was done in and if Curwen had seen the body, and if so if she could see it too.

'That's *enough*, Delia,' said Sir Edmund in a state of exasperation. 'Let the man get on with whatever he is trying to say. Carry on, Curwen.'

Curwen, looking straight in front of him, embarked on a long un-punctuated statement from which it appeared that owing to his employer's complete disregard for and want of sympathy with the sensitive works of the car, he had been forced to drive her, by which he meant the car and not his employer, over roads which the County Council had deliberately made to afford employment to garages, the proprietors and employees of which places would, in his opinion, be all the better for six months in the trenches, that he had said at the time what would happen and was therefore guiltless, but that at the same time he would always hold it against himself what had happened. He had taken her, he continued, straight down to Wheeler's the minute he found it and Wheeler, who was an honest sort of chap himself, though that young Bert and Harry couldn't be trusted even to oil her, couldn't possibly get it done before Friday.

'Well, come clean, Curwen; what is it?' said Francis. 'Springs gone? I thought I felt an awful bump when we went over the level crossing.'

'It *might* have been the springs, Mr. Francis,' said Curwen regretfully, 'but it happened to be the shock absorber.'

'That's a bit of an anti-climax,' said Francis cheerfully, 'but it dishes the picnic, doesn't it? Can't Wheeler get it done by to-morrow night?'

'Not with the Thursday half-holiday, sir,' said Curwen cheered by the thought. 'That young Bert and Harry are going to Barchester to the cricket.'

'Good thing, cricket,' said Sir Edmund, who was tired of the conversation. 'Not what it was though. Well, Lavinia. I must be getting along. Glad to have met you, Grant. Where are you staying? With Miller? That's right. Mensa, eh? They pronounce it all wrong now. Latin's not what it was in my time.'

With which unfounded aspersion on the classics Sir Edmund heaved himself up to go.

'I suppose you wouldn't care to come to our picnic on Friday?' said Mrs. Brandon, taking his hand in farewell.

'No, Lavinia. And what's more you can't have my car. My chauffeur is having his holiday and I'm driving myself over to Rushwater about a bull. You know I never go to picnics. Wasps and jam sandwiches. Good night, Miller.'

He kissed Delia. The whole party moved to the front door. Sir Edmund, assisted by Francis, got into his little car and drove away.

While Francis was dispensing farewell drinks in the drawing-room a complicated discussion took place about the picnic on Friday. Mrs. Brandon was in favour of putting it off till her car was back, but her children protested so loudly that she had to give in, though to drive in Francis's little runabout was not any pleasure to her. Mr. Miller then offered his car which was gratefully accepted, but as it was very small and uncomfortable and everyone insisted on his coming too, matters were not much more forward till Delia remembered Miss Brandon's offer.

'Look here, Mother,' she said. 'Let's telephone to Aunt Sissie and ask if Miss Morris can come and pick you up and you can go comfortably, and then Francis and I can go in the runabout and we'll go round by Starveacres and see where they're dragging for the gipsy that was drowned below the hatches on Monday night, at least Turpin says they think he was, and then Mr. Miller and Hilary can come in Mr. Miller's car. You're coming, Hilary, aren't you?'

'Of course Hilary is coming,' said Mrs. Brandon. So the matter was left, pending a telephone call to Brandon Abbey on the following morning, and good nights were said. Mrs. Brandon, not unconscious of the becoming frame that her black mantilla made for her head, came out to see the Vicarage party into their car.

'Come up for tennis some time to-morrow, Hilary,' she said, laying her hands on the door of the car. For all answer Mr. Grant, pot-valiant with the moon, the candles, the port, the hot still night, raised it to his lips.

'I was thinking, Mr. Miller,' said the goddess, when Mr. Grant had finished with her hand, 'that if Hettie would let us have some of her parsnip wine on Friday it would be so nice. Of course we shall bring everything else.'

Mr. Miller said Indeed, indeed, yes, and urged his little car homewards. Mrs. Brandon went upstairs, thinking not of moonlight, candlelight or the hot scented night air, but of how nice it was to go to bed, however nice a party had been. Rose had left everything exactly as she liked it and just as she was settling to sleep a light tap came at the door. Nurse put her face round it with a caution that would have woken the heaviest sleeper.

'Excuse me, I'm sure, madam,' said Nurse, 'but I saw the light under your door, so I thought it would be all right.'

'Yes?'

'I'd thought you'd just like to know, madam, that Rose and I have had quite an explanation. It is always so unpleasant when there is an unpleasantness of any sort, and much more pleasant when things are explained, as they could easily have been in the first place.'

'Yes, it is,' said Mrs. Brandon sleepily. 'That's all right then. Good night, Nurse.'

Outside their bedroom doors Francis and Delia exchanged a few words on life, with special reference to Mr. Grant's too visible passion for their mother, which Delia characterized as a bit slooshy if Francis knew what she meant.

'Perhaps it is a bit slooshy,' said Francis, 'but it doesn't look bad, this hand-kissing business. Rather like the Prisoner of Zenda and that sort of thing. I wish mamma had brought up her tall handsome son to kiss her hand. I think I'll take to it.'

His sister murmured the word potty, adding that she dared him to. Francis at once accepted the dare, they rubbed the tips of their noses together, relic of a nursery superstition connected with the binding powers of a dare, and separated for the night.

*

In the Vicarage Mr. Miller and his pupil found it difficult to go to bed. There was a very sacred subject on which both would have liked to speak, while both felt a very creditable diffidence in embarking upon it. Although there were more than twenty years between them, they were both at that ingenuous stage of a first love which makes it necessary for the sufferer to celebrate aloud the beauties and virtues of the adored. Later may come doubts, torments, secrecies, jealousies; but in the first golden days the young lover, whether young in years or in experience, far from wishing to conceal the beloved in some unsuspected isle in far-off seas, is more inclined to stand at the cross roads and challenge anyone to mortal combat who denies her charms, or to sing those charms with all comers in the alternate verses beloved of the Muses.

So it was with Mr. Miller and Mr. Grant, but being English gentlemen they found the approach to these mysteries singularly difficult.

'Well, we really must be turning in,' said Mr. Miller, when he and
Mr. Grant had consumed respectively a glass of orange juice and a
lemon squash and said nothing for three-quarters of an hour.

'Yes, I suppose we must,' said Mr. Grant. 'It was an awfully nice
evening.'

'Yes, it was delightful to sit out after dinner. There are so few evenings in an English summer when one can comfortably sit out,' said
Mr. Miller.

Mr. Grant agreed, adding that it was often too cool to sit out comfortably. Also, he said, the light often attracted moths.

Both men thought how a moth had fluttered into the candle under
the chestnut, and how Mrs. Brandon had exclaimed against it. Both
would willingly have celebrated her enchanting childlike terrors,
the sweetness of her voice, but neither found himself capable of beginning.

'Well,' said Mr. Grant, 'I suppose we ought to be turning in.'

By dint of repeating this comfortable phrase often enough they
managed to get themselves upstairs. On the landing they paused.

'Well, we really ought to be in bed,' said Mr. Miller. 'Good night,
Hilary.'

'Good night,' said Mr. Grant. 'And thanks awfully for a splendid
evening.'

'Oh, that's all right,' said Mr. Miller. 'We really ought to thank
Mrs. Brandon,' he added in a voice singularly unlike his own.

'Oh yes, Mrs. Brandon,' croaked Mr. Grant. And having let loose
this word of power both were overcome with confusion and separated
abruptly. Mr. Grant took off his dinner jacket and waistcoat and gazed
into the night. Unfortunately his window looked in exactly the opposite
direction from Stories, but this presented no obstacle to his mind's eye,
which ran lightly up the side of the house like Dracula, scaled the
beautiful stone roof, perched on the chimney, and thence with extensive
view surveyed the landscape. It was during this trance that Mr. Grant
was suddenly smitten with an idea for a poem, totally new in conception and treatment, containing in itself the finest elements of all previous
poetry, yet of an epoch-making originality. Pushing aside the books
upon which he had been working earlier in the day, or rather on the
preceding day, for it was now well after twelve, he sat down, twisted
his legs round the front legs of his chair, tilted the chair forwards, and
plunged into literary composition.

An hour or so later he heard a light tap at his door. His tutor, also
without coat or clerical waistcoat, entered the room. Mr. Grant, drunk
with his own written words, gazed at him stupidly.

'I couldn't go to sleep,' said Mr. Miller, though his dress afforded no indication of his having tried to do so, 'and I wondered if you had that stud of mine.'

It seemed to Mr. Grant in his present demented state of mind eminently reasonable that Mr. Miller should want an assurance of the safety of his stud at one in the morning. Wrenching it from his shirt front he handed it to its owner in silence.

'Thanks,' said Mr. Miller, apparently much relieved. 'I just wanted to be quite sure, that was all. Are you working?'

'Yes,' said Mr. Grant, 'I mean no. At least yes, but not exactly working. Just writing. An idea I had.'

'Oh,' said Mr. Miller, interested, but not liking to ask.

'Just an idea,' Mr. Grant repeated, longing for a sympathetic audience, but not liking to ask.

'Well,' said Mr. Miller, 'I suppose I ought to be turning in. Thanks for the stud. I hope I didn't disturb you.'

'Oh, rather not,' said Mr. Grant. 'It was just an idea I had — a sort of idea,' he explained.

Mr. Miller, hearing the appeal in Mr. Grant's voice, said he didn't suppose he would care to let him look at it. Mr. Grant, who wanted nothing more, said he didn't suppose there was anything in it, but if Mr. Miller really *cared* — He then pushed a sheet of paper towards his host, saying that it was only an idea.

'Poetry,' said Mr. Miller. 'If you don't mind, Hilary, I'll read it aloud to myself. I can't ever quite get the feeling of poetry unless I read it aloud. Let me see,' he added, looking at the various rough drafts and erasures, 'where exactly does it begin? Oh, yes, I see.

> Methinks most like a god is he
> Who in Lavinia's company
> Amazed can sit, and gaze the while
> On the enchantment of her smile.
>
> But when I, wretched, see my saint,
> My tongue is held, my senses faint,
> My eyes are darkened with desire
> And all my veins consumed with fire.

An imitation of Catullus, I see,' said Mr. Miller, suddenly becoming professional, 'but free, very free. In a way I think you are right to compress your rendering. It is a more general fault to expand from the original. But you will have to work at it a good deal, Hilary.'

'I never thought of Catullus,' said Mr. Grant miserably, his golden vision of a totally original poem dashed to the dust.

'My dear boy, you only have to look at that first line,' said Mr. Miller. 'By the way, why Lavinia? Surely Lesbia is good enough?'

Mr. Grant said it didn't seem to fit in.

'Lavinia,' said Mr. Miller, speaking aloud to himself, 'is Mrs. Brandon's name.'

'I know,' said Mr. Grant defiantly. 'That's why.'

Mr. Miller looked at his pupil, who returned his gaze.

'I think,' said Mr. Miller, very kindly, 'that you had better finish undressing and go to bed.'

'I suppose I had. I only once went to bed in my trousers, after a bump supper it was: no, it can't have been that time because they took all my trousers away. Anyway it was jolly uncomfortable,' said Mr. Grant yawning. 'Good night, sir, and thanks awfully.'

He tore the paper into fragments, put them in an ash tray, struck a match and watched them burn.

'Good night,' said Mr. Miller and went away.

Mr. Grant was in bed in two minutes and such is human frailty and such is youth that he was asleep in two minutes more, and slept soundly till long after breakfast time.

IV

A VISIT TO THE WISHING WELL

AFTER a good deal of telephoning, complicated by Miss Brandon's butler's total inability to understand or take any message and Miss Brandon's refusal to let her companion go to the telephone, the use of her car was obtained for the day. It was to come at twelve with Miss Morris, the crab apple jelly, the potted salmon, the cakes and the marsala, and be at Mrs. Brandon's disposition as long as she needed it, a concession which would have made Sir Edmund even more unhopeful of Miss Brandon's mental and physical condition.

At half-past eleven on the Friday morning, as Mrs. Brandon was thinking of getting ready, Mr. Grant came in with a face of such dire portent that even his hostess noticed that something was wrong and asked what it was.

'It's the most ghastly thing,' said Mr. Grant. 'My mother is here from Italy. I never knew she was coming. She turned up last night quite late, in a taxi from Barchester, and she has taken a room at the Cow and Sickle.'

'I'm afraid she won't be very comfortable there,' said Mrs. Brandon. 'They *will* not have that window in the bedroom made to open and if it did open the pigstye is just outside. But it will be nice for you to have her.'

'It won't,' said Mr. Grant, in such anguish that he contradicted his hostess flatly. 'She has come to see how I'm getting on, and it's too awful, because she won't leave me alone and she wants to come to the picnic. It's all my fault. I let out we were going. I did think perhaps Francis would take her, because there's room for three in his car, but I found he'd gone already. Mr. Miller will have to take her, that's all, and I'll stay at home and swot, but I thought I must tell you. I simply *loathe* missing the picnic, but there it is. I daresay she won't stay long, because she has a ghastly friend called Lady Norton she is going on to, but I wish to goodness she'd stayed in Italy.'

'She could come with me and Miss Morris in Miss Brandon's car,' said Mrs. Brandon kindly. 'Would that help?'

'I say, that *is* kind of you,' said Mr. Grant. 'Don't you really mind?'

'There's heaps of room,' said Mrs. Brandon, 'and it will be perfectly easy. Do tell her that I will call at the Cow soon after twelve. We shall have a delightful day. My friend Mrs. Morland who writes books is joining us and her boy who is at Southbridge school, and some young friends of my children, and I hope Dr. Ford will look in if he has time. I am so glad you let me know about your mother.'

Thus cheered Mr. Grant sped back to the Cow and Sickle, while Mrs. Brandon put on some very special cream and powder to protect her from the sun, a shady hat, the pinky-purply scarf that Francis had approved, and long gloves. Being thus prepared for a country expedition she read the newspaper in the drawing-room till Miss Brandon's car arrived. Miss Morris got out of it with a huge bunch of flowers.

'Miss Brandon sent you these,' she said, as her hostess met her in the hall. 'She thought you wouldn't have enough in your garden.'

'They are lovely,' said Mrs. Brandon, touching them gently. 'You look tired. Were you up late?'

'Rather late,' said Miss Morris. 'But I'm used to that. What rather alarmed me was the drive here. Miss Brandon ordered the second chauffeur to drive, and as he never gets a real chance he asked me if I would mind if he let her out a bit, to use his own expression. We seem to have taken every corner in Barsetshire at seventy miles an hour on the wrong side of the road.'

Mrs. Brandon sympathised warmly.

'Miss Brandon was rather upset this morning,' continued Miss Morris, 'by a letter from Mrs. Grant, Mr. Grant's mother. It seems that she has come over quite unexpectedly from Italy and is going to stay somewhere in the neighbourhood, but she didn't give any address. Miss Brandon has some kind of prejudice against her and is determined not to see her, so Sparks and the butler have the strictest orders not to open the front door at all to-day. She was so worried that I hardly thought I would get away.'

'I'm so glad you did,' said Mrs. Brandon.

'Nothing would have stopped me,' said Miss Morris, 'after you were so kind in asking me.'

'But,' said Mrs. Brandon as they got into the car, continuing the train of her own thoughts, 'I must tell you what a dreadful thing has happened. Poor Hilary came up here this morning quite distracted. His mother is here, at the Cow and Sickle, which is a very uncomfortable little inn with roses on the front, and she is coming to the picnic. Now did Rose put the fruit in? Yes, I see it in the corner, so that is all right. I don't know what she is like, but I daresay she is quite nice. You will like our Vicar, Mr. Miller, who is coming, and my friend Laura Morland who writes books and several young friends of my children. I never know who they are, but they are all very intelligent and know all about the ballet, and here we are at the Cow.'

Miss Brandon's second chauffeur drew up, a little contemptuously, as near the Cow and Sickle as the immense dray of Messrs. Pilward and Sons Entire, which was disgorging casks and bottles at the front door would allow. The two enormous grey cart horses which Messrs. Pilward and Sons used with some ostentation for deliveries in the neighbourhood of Barchester, were eating their lunch from modern, laboursaving nosebags hung from the front of the pole; every inch of their glossy coats shone with grooming, every boss of brasswork on their complicated harness glittered, the paintwork of the great dray was spotless in red and black; the draymen, in the scarlet linen coats and black leggings over which the A.U.H.P.B.C. (Amalgamated Union of Horse Propelled Beer Conveyancers) had nearly split, (some saying What about Red Spain, others What about the Blackshirts, both parties agreeing in passing a resolution which called upon the Government to reduce taxation, increase the Air Force, abolish militarism, fight everybody, and establish a thirty hour week with pensions for everyone at fifty) looked like superior if eccentric hunt servants, and Miss Brandon's large, powerful, expensive car was entirely put out of countenance.

Mrs. Brandon got out and went to the door.

'Good morning, Spindler,' she said to the proprietor, who was the uncle of the Vicar's cook. 'I've come to fetch a Mrs. Grant who is staying here.'

Mr. Spindler, a stout gentleman of few words, nodded in the direction of the dray horses. At the head of the nearer horse, so that she had not been visible as the car drove up from behind, was standing what Mrs. Brandon at once recognized as an Englishwoman Abroad. Her shoes were sensible, her stockings of lisle thread, her light grey homespun skirt dipped slightly at the back, her jumper was of an orange hue, a green handkerchief was round her neck, a grey felt hat was jammed onto her head, on one arm she carried her homespun jacket. With her free hand in its washleather gauntlet she was offering the horse some sugar on her outspread palm. The horse took its face out of its nosebag, looked at the sugar, blew at it several times, decided in its favour, and in rather a slobbery way mouthed it up, then producing a loud champing, roaring, tearing sound, more appropriate to an engineering works on overtime than to a peaceful Beer Conveyancer eating a blameless lump or two of sugar.

'Excuse me,' said Mrs. Brandon advancing, 'but are you Mrs. Grant? I am Mrs. Brandon.'

Mrs. Grant turned. Mrs. Brandon saw a handsome face, wavy hair, bobbed and going grey, and a multitude of necklaces of amber, coral and other semi-precious stones, which rattled as their wearer moved.

'That is very kind of you,' said Mrs. Grant, holding out her gloved hand which was fresh with a greenish slime from the horse's blowings and mouthings.

Mrs. Brandon offered her own white-gloved hand as a sacrifice without flinching, reflecting how glad she was that she had told Rose to put a spare pair in the car.

'I'm so glad you can come to the picnic,' said Mrs. Brandon. 'Hilary came up to tell me this morning. Are you ready?'

'I will just get my mackintosh,' said Mrs. Grant.

'Oh, I don't think you'll need it,' said Mrs. Brandon, thinking that Mrs. Grant was already far too warmly and sensibly clad for so hot a day.

'One cannot trust the English climate,' said Mrs. Grant, and striding into the hotel she reappeared shortly with a raincoat and a stout walking stick. Miss Morris had already installed herself on one of the folding seats, introductions took place, the usual polite argument about seats was held, Miss Morris was firm, and the car with Mrs. Brandon and Mrs. Grant on the back seat drove on towards Southbridge.

'What lovely horses those were,' said Miss Morris.

'You are treating animals much better in England,' said Mrs. Grant. 'One hardly ever sees an ill-treated or broken-down horse now.'

'I suppose you see lots in Italy,' said Mrs. Brandon, rather resenting the aspersion on English humanity.

'Oh no,' said Mrs. Grant pityingly. 'Mussolini has stopped all that. Italians *adore* animals now. Wherever I go in Italy I always ask the peasants if they are kind to their animals and their delightful expressive faces simply light up. After St. Francis, Mussolini is the greatest animal lover the world has known. I put them together, don't you?'

'I don't quite know. I never actually *met* Mussolini,' said Mrs. Brandon cautiously, and somehow implying that she had at some period been introduced to St. Francis.

'Of course you wouldn't,' said Mrs. Grant. 'No one does. But going everywhere as I do, among very intellectual people in Rome and Florence and among the most illiterate peasants of Calabria, I hear a great deal.'

This statement Mrs. Brandon found it impossible to contradict, though it seemed to have no particular relevance to Mrs. Grant's argument, and she could not help imagining that both intellectuals and illiterates stood a poor chance of expressing their own views in Mrs. Grant's presence. That lady, her necklaces rattling with her enthusiasm, conversed with unceasing fluency on the joys of Italy all through the half-hour's drive to Southbridge, while Mrs. Brandon, throwing in a polite interjection from time to time thought of a good way of having her pink evening frock renovated by Nurse's clever fingers and wondered if she would get a black velvet for the autumn.

From every side the picnic party was now converging upon the Wishing Well, a little bubbling spring pleasantly situated in the beech woods above Southbridge. When Mrs. Brandon's party arrived, they found Mrs. Morland from High Rising already there. Mrs. Brandon greeted her affectionately and introduced her guests.

'And where is Tony?' she asked.

Mrs. Morland pointed to a pair of grey flannel legs stretched on the ground below a leafy bank.

'You can't see the rest of him,' she said, 'because it is in the Wishing Well. He wanted to see if he could stop the spring by putting his arm into the place where the water bubbles up. Tony! Here is Mrs. Brandon.'

The legs made a convulsive movement, clearly signifying 'Bother,' and reared themselves up, together with the body belonging to them. Their owner, his blue short-sleeved shirt soaked with water, his arms muddy to the shoulders, advanced unwillingly upon the group, with an expression of abstracted dislike and resentment.

'This is my youngest boy,' said Mrs. Morland to Mrs. Grant and Miss Morris. 'He is in his last year at school. I'm afraid he is too dirty to shake hands.'

'I always shake hands,' said Mrs. Grant, advancing on Tony with outstretched hand. 'Mother Earth has no terrors for me. The Italian peasants, who never wash, are among the cleanest of God's creatures.'

'It's more Mother Mud,' said Tony, taking Mrs. Grant's proffered hand. 'I say, Mother, I can't think how the water comes up so clean. That hole is absolutely stinking.'

Miss Morris said How do you do, but made no attempt to shake hands. Tony made a very slight inclination towards her and appeared to be favourably impressed, immediately inviting her to come and see the hole where the stinking mud was. Miss Morris accepted his offer and the two went off to the Wishing Well.

'What a splendid young animal!' said Mrs. Grant enthusiastically. 'He reminds me of a young fisherman who used to bring me fresh frutta di mare at a little seaside village in Calabria. Your boy is fairer of course, but he and Tonio might have been twins.'

'Perhaps twins that had a different father,' said Laura Morland, who always tried to sympathise, 'which would account. And my boy is Tony too.'

'And there are people who do not believe in the transmigration of souls!' exclaimed Mrs. Grant.

'Is your fisherman dead then?' inquired Mrs. Morland. 'Because Tony is seventeen, so your man would have had to transmigrate a good while ago, and I don't remember anything particular happening.'

'Non ragioniam di lor,' said Mrs. Grant, finding the philosophical level more than she had bargained for.

'No, indeed,' said Mrs. Morland. 'And now, Lavinia, where shall we put the food? It is bound to be uncomfortable wherever we sit, but thank heaven it isn't damp.'

Mrs. Brandon had brought in the car two folding tables on which she proposed to spread the feast and let everyone help him or herself. These were set up by Miss Brandon's chauffeur, and the three ladies unpacked and arranged the huge store of food provided from High Rising, Brandon Abbey and Stories. While they were thus occupied Mr. Miller's little open car came chunking up and its two occupants joined the company, each bearing a large stone jar.

'Good morning, good morning, or rather good afternoon,' said Mr. Miller. 'And here is the parsnip wine, Mrs. Brandon, to which Hettie insisted on adding some of her dandelion wine. Both are excellent.'

'Thank you so very much,' said Mrs. Brandon. 'Have you met Mrs. Grant yet?'

Mr. Miller expressed his pleasure at meeting his pupil's mother and hoped she would be staying in the neighbourhood for some time, at which Mr. Grant groaned almost audibly. Then five or six pleasant young men and women, friends of the young Brandons, arrived; all, as Mrs. Brandon had complained, very intelligent, bursting with information about the ballet, and practically indistinguishable, the girls being in trousers and the men a little long in the hair.

'How are you all?' said Mrs. Brandon. 'Francis and Delia haven't come yet. They were going to see the place where the gipsy was drowned.'

One of the young men said What energy. One of the young women, apparently called Betty, said they had passed a crowd near the river, ackcherly, as they came along, and they all began to talk cryptically among themselves. Tony, returning from the Wishing Well with Miss Morris, who had miraculously persuaded him to clean the mud off his arms, cast a look of withering contempt on the little group and drifted away towards Miss Brandon's chauffeur, with whom he was soon deep in technical conversation. Mrs. Brandon introduced Mr. Miller to Miss Morris and had an uneasy feeling that they were not going to take to each other, when much to her relief Francis's car came up, and he and Delia completed the party. Francis, in pursuance of a plan which he and Delia had been perfecting, approached his mother, took her hand, and bowing low over it, kissed it respectfully, saying as he straightened up, 'How charming you look this morning, mamma.'

Mrs. Brandon, accepting with tolerance all Francis's whims, said she thought she looked much the same as at breakfast, and had he said how do you do to Mrs. Grant. Francis, turning to give the customary careless handshake, was horrified to find a far from clean washleather glove rising towards his face. Rapidly though unwillingly grasping what was expected of him, he bent over it, avoided touching it with his lips, and restored it courteously to its owner.

'Mi piace tanto,' said Mrs. Grant in a loud voice to Mrs. Brandon, 'to find a young man with manners. All the Italians, high and low, have such exquisite natural manners. I only wish Hilary had profited by his year abroad. Any Italian who came into my house and did not kiss my hand would never be invited again.'

'Serves you right,' said Delia to her brother, making a hideous face, and various of his young friends asked what had bitten him, the girl called Betty adding that it was the first time she had seen anyone kiss anyone's hand, ackcherly, except on the flicks.

'I say,' said Francis who had been examining the feast, 'what about marsala? Is that Aunt Sissie's contribution? When does one drink it, Miss Morris?'

Miss Morris didn't know, so Francis said they would have it as a cocktail and served it round in gaily-coloured tumblers made of some composition.

'Bless Uncle Woolworth for these pretty gauds,' he said, 'even if they are made of high explosives.'

'Ackcherly,' said Betty, 'they're made of milk, because I know a man that told me. They do something to the milk and make things of it.'

'It's a much more elaborate process,' said Tony, who had come back at the sight of food, 'but you wouldn't understand if I told you. Oh, Mother, potted salmon! Can I take some to Hooper?'

'Who is Hooper?' inquired Mrs. Morland.

'Miss Brandon's chauffeur,' said Miss Morris. 'Yes, please do take him some lunch, Tony.'

Tony made a selection of tempting food and drink and took it to Hooper, but soon returned with his gifts and the depressing intelligence that Hooper was a teetotaller and had brought what he fancied for his own lunch.

'Great bleeding slices of cold beef and a bottle of pickles,' he said with gleaming eyes, 'and a huge chunk of cold plum pudding and some green cheese and some cold tea. Oh Mother, can I have lunch with Hooper?'

'No, have lunch here,' said Mrs. Morland, 'and you can talk to Hooper afterwards.'

Her son's face, still soft and gently rounded in spite of his years, though faint hollows were just beginning to show below his cheek bones, clouded slightly, but at the sight of sausage rolls and meringues he recovered his spirits and explained at length to the uninterested Betty the methods by which milk was transformed to a bright blue tumbler.

'But how do they get plum pudding in the height of summer?' said Francis to Miss Morris.

'If you lived at Brandon Abbey you wouldn't ask,' said Miss Morris. 'Like Mrs. Herbert Pocket's servants, they allow a very liberal table.'

'Oh, heaven bless you, Miss Morris,' said Francis fervently, lifting his marsala towards her. 'And how is Aunt Sissie?'

Miss Morris said pretty well.

'I've been thinking,' said Francis, 'about what Sir Edmund said the other night. You remember, Hilary, about responsibilities and all that.'

'Well?' said Mr. Grant.

'Well, I was thinking that perhaps we oughtn't to turn the Abbey into a lunatic asylum. I mean it would be a bit hard on the servants and the gardeners and what not. I thought perhaps you and I could club together and have a sort of what's its name — you know what I mean.'

'You mean a sort of home for old retainers?' asked Mr. Grant.

'No, you great ass, they'll all get pensioned off all right. I say, Miss Morris, I'm awfully sorry. I mean I didn't mean anything, I only meant Sparks and that lot,' said Francis crimsoning violently.

'It is quite all right,' said Miss Morris composedly. 'I'd like to hear your ideas for the Abbey.'

'Would you really?' said Francis, much cheered. 'Well, I meant a sort of thing rather like a monastery, only that isn't the word.'

'Ackcherly one can't be a monk in England,' said Betty.

'I never said monk,' said Francis with some heat, 'and anyway one can, because there are a whole lot somewhere in Somerset and they make honey in little cardboard pots.'

'Oh, *those*,' said Betty scornfully.

Her friends then all contributed their views on the subject of monks, appearing to have founded their theories largely on the Ingoldsby Legends. Suddenly Francis's voice dominated the tumult with the word 'Phalanx.'

'That's what I meant, phalanx,' he repeated.

'Phalanstère I expect you mean,' said Tony Morland courteously, managing at the same time to put half a meringue away in one cheek like a monkey in his desire to impart information. 'The theory of the phalanstère was begun and put into practice by Fourier, about 1832, but it was never much of a success. He wanted to organize society into bodies called phalanges, who were to live in phalanstères which were a square league. There is a lot more but you wouldn't understand it. I know about it all because we did it last term.'

'I never heard about him ackcherly,' said Betty.

'It isn't phalan whatever you said,' said one of the young men, who had but imperfectly followed the foregoing conversation. 'Phalangist is what you mean. God! if only the Government had enough planes to bomb them all!'

'Well, they're increasing the Air Force ackcherly,' said Betty.

'The *Spanish* Government,' the young man almost spat at her.

Mr. Miller said that Civil Strife was very dreadful.

'Well, anyway you know what I mean,' said Francis. 'And if Hilary and I get the Abbey we'll jolly well not have any politics there. I say, let's go and wish at the Wishing Well.'

This suggestion was received with universal pleasure; by the younger members because it would mean that they needn't help with the clearing up; by the older members because they would be able to clear up in peace without the young; and by Tony Morland because he saw a chance of escaping to his friend Hooper and explaining to him the general outline of European politics in the years after the Congress of Vienna.

It did not take the grown-ups long to tidy away the food and pack up the baskets, and when they had finished Mrs. Brandon suggested a visit to the Wishing Well.

'I think we could manage,' she said doubtfully, looking at the fifty yards that separated them from the Well, and putting up her parasol. Escorted by Mr. Miller and followed by Mrs. Morland, Mrs. Grant and Miss Morris, she walked to the green, beech-crowned bank under which the springing water for ever troubled a little pool.

'It is so lovely,' she said. 'If we had a rug we could sit down.'

Mr. Miller sprang away, seized a rug from Hooper who was putting it into the car, and was back in an instant. Mrs. Grant compared him favourably with several of her Italian acquaintance, who she said, were useless out of doors, though delightful in the drawing-room, and sat down resolutely upon her mackintosh.

'I do hope, Mr. Miller,' she said, 'that Hilary is going to do well with you. He is a difficult nature, with a certain morbidezza that English people cannot readily understand.'

'I must say I have found him—' Mr. Miller began, but found he might as well spare his breath, for Mrs. Grant, merely lowering her voice to a more powerful diapason continued, 'Like me he adores beauty, but unfortunately he must work. He is a devoted son, mio figlio, but I do not wish him to be tied to my apron strings. There is a charming proverb in Calabria which runs—but you would not understand it in dialect; I will translate roughly, though of course it does not give the fuoco of the original—the ass that stays at home will never learn to roam. My husband was always under his mother's domination, ma! una donna prepotente! and what was the result? My life made me what I am.'

'I do think you are so right,' said Mrs. Morland, giving some of her heavy back hair an extra twist and ramming the hairpins into it. 'Boys *always* ought to get away from their mothers. I hardly ever see my three eldest, whom I adore; the eldest is secretary to an American explorer and is always somewhere where he can't send any news, John is doing very well in Burma, and Dick has just rejoined his ship at Malta. Of course Tony is a little different. He is enough to drive anyone mad, because I never know if he is going to be a mentally defective child of five or a man of the world of thirty, but all the same he does need me, and I really don't think he despises me as much as he pretends to,' said Mrs. Morland proudly. 'Of course it is a pity that he hasn't a father, but my husband wasn't really very much use, so I daresay we have got on just as well and I think we shall go on getting on well so long as he doesn't tell me anything. Confidences between people are such a mistake and if he does what he wants to do and doesn't tell me, it's all right, like the time he went through the railway tunnel at Southbridge which is half a mile long and *entirely* forbidden and a train came through when he was there, but most luckily I didn't discover it till a year afterwards.'

'I am really very lucky with Francis,' said Mrs. Brandon, taking off one glove and looking at her hand, 'because he tells me nothing at all ever and is never rude. If my husband had lived I am sure he would have wanted to be a father to Francis, and that wouldn't have done at all.'

If the enthralled reader will imagine that these three speeches not only followed rapidly upon one another, but were to a certain extent superimposed, he will have a fair idea of how much the ladies were enjoying themselves and how very much out of it Miss Morris and Mr. Miller felt. But they didn't turn to each other for relief and Mrs. Brandon still felt, with all the delicate perception of a nature that hopes everything will always be comfortable, that they weren't going to hate each other at sight.

'I have only just thought of it!' Mrs. Morland suddenly exclaimed in her impressive voice, pushing her hair and her hat wildly back from her forehead with both hands. 'We are all widows!'

'So we are,' said Mrs. Brandon, looking round distractedly as if she might see a few more somewhere, 'but not what I would *call* widows.'

'I suppose,' said Mrs. Morland, 'the longer one is a widow, the less one *is* a widow. Or is it that one just has it in one or else one hasn't?'

To this entrancing philosophical problem no one was capable of giving an immediate answer, and then Francis and Mr. Grant reappeared, saying that the conversation of the others was too intellectual for them.

'Let's all wish,' said Francis. 'You drop a pin or a piece of money into the well and wish and don't tell anybody, and then it comes true. The trouble is one never knows what to wish. Don't let's.'

Mrs. Grant said Hilary must get his hair cut and there was a delightful old custom in Calabria by which young men and maidens spent the night under a tree on the night of the full moon and drew lots with the bristles of a hog who had died a natural death, and whoever drew the longest bristle died in childbirth within the year. She then quoted in support of this interesting piece of folk lore several verses of a very old song in an archaic dialect, which she did not, she said, herself fully understand.

'And just as well, probably,' said Francis to Miss Morris in an undertone.

'Io t'amo o pio bove,' said Mrs. Brandon suddenly, contemplating her ringed hand.

At this startling statement everyone looked at her.

'My dear mamma, you mustn't say things like that,' said Francis.

'I can't think why it came into my head,' said Mrs. Brandon apologetically. 'I suppose it was hearing all that Italian. It's something I had to learn by heart once.'

'A little learning is a dangerous thing,' said Francis sententiously, 'talking of which how glad you ought to be to have a son who gets his quotations right. I say, Mr. Miller, did you know that they've got chicken pox down at Grumper's End? The postman told me when he brought up the cat's bit of liver this morning with the letters to save the butcher's boy an extra journey.'

'Indeed? I am sorry to hear it,' said Mr. Miller. 'I must go and see them. That means that Jimmy Thatcher won't be able to carry out his duties on Sunday.'

'Jimmy is an enchanting little boy,' Mrs. Brandon explained to Miss Morris, 'who helps Mr. Miller with the service in a kind of surplice with a frill round his neck. He is very ambitious and wants to be a dentist when he grows up. You would love him, wouldn't she, Mr. Miller?'

'I think,' said Miss Morris, her pale cheeks flushing, 'that there is no need for me to tell Mr. Miller what I think of such arrangements as he may see fit to make for the celebration of his services.'

There was no mistaking the open hostility in her voice.

'I had hoped, Miss Morris,' Mr. Miller began in a low tone, but Miss Morris got up and walked away. Everyone felt uncomfortable and each member of the party tried to cover the awkwardness by dashing into an artificial normality of manner. Mrs. Morland and Mrs. Grant discovered a very dull common acquaintance who lived on the Riviera and discussed her with zeal. Francis plied Mr. Miller with details about the chicken pox at Grumper's End, some gathered from the postman, some invented on the spur of the moment, and Mrs. Brandon asked Mr. Grant if he would like to have a wish, at the same time stretching out her hand that he might help her to rise.

'How is your work, Hilary?' Mrs. Brandon inquired.

'How did you know about it?' Mr. Grant asked, going rather pink.

'Well, you are doing classics with Mr. Miller, aren't you?' asked Mrs. Brandon, puzzled.

'Oh yes, of course. But that's only a sort of lessons. I'm really trying to write a book at least I don't know if it will ever be a real book, but anyway a sort of article about a French poet called Jehan le Capet, at least his real name was Eugène Duval, but he was a Romantic so he had to have a name that sounded better. No one knows much about him, but I somehow got interested and dug up quite a lot of stuff.'

'Do tell me about him,' said Mrs. Brandon, in a voice whose warm interest would not have deceived Sir Edmund or her son Francis for a moment.

'Well, there's not very much,' said Mr. Grant, beginning to stammer a little in his excitement at discussing his great work with a goddess. 'He was a Satanist and died very young of absinthe and only published one very small volume called *Belphégor*. All his other work was destroyed by his mistress,' said Mr. Grant, rapidly slurring over a word which he suddenly felt might sully the goddess's ethereal atmosphere, 'who was really called Angèle Potin, but was known as Nini Le Poumon because she had only one lung because of consumption,' he continued, stammering more than ever as he found his interest in his chosen study involving him in an explanation which must, he felt, be highly offensive to his divinity, 'because she was jealous.'

'Of whom?' asked Mrs. Brandon.

'Oh, just jealous,' said Mr. Grant vaguely, feeling that a detailed description of Mimi la Salope, Jehanne de Valois, and the other ladies who disputed the unhappy ci-devant Eugène Duval's attentions while alive and his literary remains when dead, were hardly fit offerings to lay on Mrs. Brandon's altar.

'It sounds enchanting,' said Mrs. Brandon. 'Will you read me some of it one day?'

'Would you really like me to?' asked Mr. Grant, incredulous.

'I'd love it,' said Mrs. Brandon. 'When are you going to publish it?'

Mr. Grant had to confess that he hadn't got as far as a publisher yet. Mrs. Brandon said Mrs. Morland had a very nice one who she was sure would do and had Hilary a halfpenny to put into the Wishing Well. He had not, but was able to express his devotion by dropping a shining new sixpence to which he was rather attached into the clear, moving water. Mrs. Brandon, a practical woman, said it would do for them both and now they must wish.

'Only I find it so difficult to wish,' she said plaintively. 'It's like concentrating. I have to hold my breath and shut my eyes tight, and then I go red in the face and can't think of anything at all. Oh, I know what I've wished. I wished — —'

'But you mustn't say what you wished,' said Mr. Grant. 'You don't get it if you do.'

'Don't you?' said Mrs. Brandon. 'What did *you* wish?'

'I can't tell you,' said Mr. Grant; and truly; for his incoherent and jumbled wish had been entirely a prayer to be allowed to die some violent and heroic death while saving Mrs. Brandon from something or somebody, to have her holding his chill hand, and perhaps letting her cheek rest for a moment against his as his gallant spirit fled, all with a kind of unspoken understanding that he should not be really hurt and should somehow go on living very comfortably in spite of being heroically dead. 'I wouldn't get my wish if I did.'

'Of course, and I do want you to get it,' said Mrs. Brandon, melting Mr. Grant's marrow with a smile. 'Laura, have you wished?' she asked, as Mrs. Morland and Mrs. Grant came strolling up to them, followed by Francis and Mr. Miller.

'It is a splendid well,' said Mrs. Morland. 'Once when Tony was smaller we came here for a picnic, and he was showing off on his bicycle and frightened me dreadfully and I wished the bicycle would somehow get put out of action without hurting him, and it did. I know what I'll wish. I'm frightfully stuck in a serial I've *got* to have ready by September, so I'll wish — —'

'You mustn't tell,' broke in Mrs. Brandon. 'You won't get it if you do.'

'I think that is what Tony used to call supersistious,' said Mrs. Morland severely. 'Don't you, Mr. Miller?'

'One might of course condemn the whole ritual as superstitious and highly pagan,' said Mr. Miller, 'but all the same I do not propose to tell my wish.' Upon which he dropped a halfpenny into the well and wished with heathen fervour that Jimmy Thatcher might not get chicken pox.

'Oh, do you write?' Mrs. Grant asked Mrs. Morland.

'Only to earn my living,' said Mrs. Morland apologetically, for although her stories about Madame Koska's dressmaking establishment, where spies, Grand Dukes, drug-smugglers and C.I.D. officers flourished yearly, had a large sale, and she had arrived at the happy point where her public simply asked for 'the new Mrs. Morland', instead of mentioning the name of the book, she thought quite poorly of her own hard-working talent and greatly admired people who wrote what she called real books.

'I expect you know my book about Calabria,' said Mrs. Grant.

Mrs. Morland said the libraries were so stupid and never had the books one wanted.

'I do wish mother wouldn't,' said Mr. Grant in a low and unfilial voice to Francis. 'It isn't a book, it's only a sort of little thing in paper covers that she had printed by a very good-looking, bounderish sort of printer somewhere she was staying in Italy, and she behaves as if it were the Encyclopaedia Britannica. What do you think was the matter with Miss Morris?'

Francis said he couldn't think, and he supposed it was something someone had said, but why talking about the chicken pox at Grumper's End should send anyone off their rocker he couldn't imagine. Mr. Grant said perhaps someone she was very fond of had died of chicken pox and anyway she was a very good sort, but so was Mr. Miller.

Mrs. Grant, all her necklaces clashing together, now knelt at the pool and dropping a coin into it moved her lips as if in prayer. Everyone looked on in interest, and her son in weary disgust.

'If only mother wouldn't be so confoundedly in the spirit of the thing,' he complained to Francis. 'I never knew anyone adapt themselves to local customs as she does. She used to make me awfully uncomfortable in Italy, putting little offerings on shrines and things and everyone thought her necklaces were rosaries and it was all frightfully embarrassing, and she would help herself to holy water in the country churches because she didn't like to be out of it.'

'That was a little prayer that the inhabitants of a village on the south coast of Calabria address to the presiding spirit of wells,' she said. 'An invocation from time immemorial. The peasants drink the water and repeat the words that their fathers have taught them.'

So saying she scooped up a handful of water and put it to her lips.

'Don't drink it, Mrs. Grant,' cried Mr. Miller in great alarm. 'The water is not fit for human consumption. The Medical Officer of Health condemned it as thoroughly infected from the sewage farm at Southbridge.'

Everyone waited anxiously to see Mrs. Grant burst, or come out all over spots, but she rose, her homespun skirt rather baggy at the knees and smiling with tolerance said she believed with St. Francis that water was her sister and could do her no harm.

'A lot your mother knows about sisters,' said Francis aside to Mr. Grant. 'Wait till she's seen Delia in a temper.'

Mrs. Brandon, anxious to change a difficult and controversial subject, said to Mrs. Morland that Mr. Grant was looking for a publisher and what about her man.

'I think you'd like Adrian Coates very much, Mr. Grant,' said Mrs. Morland earnestly. 'He is the son-in-law of my old friend George Knox, the one who writes biographies, and his wife is a perfect darling and they have two delightful babies. The elder is called Laura, after me, and the little boy, who will be a year old in March, is called Richard, though after whom I don't know.'

Having given these eminently satisfactory testimonials to her publisher's business capacity, she pushed one or two loose hairpins into their place and said it must be nearly tea-time. A general move was made to the picnic place, where they found Miss Morris, outwardly as composed as ever, laying out the tea-things with Tony's help. Everyone recognized with annoyance that it would be impossible to find out what was wrong between Mr. Miller and Miss Morris until one or other of them could be got at alone, and this in the communal atmosphere of a picnic tea was going to be very difficult.

Mr. Grant, though annoyed that his mother should have heard of his publishing plans, about which he knew she would Ask Questions, could not resist talking about himself to a real author, and shaking himself temporarily free from the shackles of Venus transferred his homage to the Muses in the person of Mrs. Morland. Her he found kind and communicative but singularly unhelpful, as she did not seem to know anything about the ways of publishers.

'You see,' she said in her impressive voice, 'I have only got one publisher and I was really very lucky because I really met him quite by accident and we have always got on very well. He always gives me a bit more for every book, and if I need anything doing in town, like flowers being ordered for someone's funeral or birthday, or finding out if the name I want to call my new book has been used by someone else, he always gets it done for me at his office. And he plays golf very well, I believe, though I know nothing about the game myself. And Tony likes him,' she added, looking with dislike and adoration at her youngest son, who was helping Betty and Delia to kill wasps by cutting them in two.

'Do you think he would like my book when it is finished?' said Mr. Grant.

'What kind of book?'

Mr. Grant described to her, with more freedom than he had cared to use when speaking to Mrs. Brandon, parts of the career of that unfortunate Satanist, M. Eugène Duval, which made Mrs. Morland laugh so much that she had to get several spare hairpins out of her bag and pin herself together.

'As a matter of fact,' she said, when she had stopped laughing, 'Adrian Coates mostly does either rather bad novels like mine or frightfully dull stuff by journalists about all the European crises and the private lives of dictators, which people somehow like to read I can't think why, but he's always on the look-out for something fresh and I must say your book sounds very funny.'

Mr. Grant then had to explain to Mrs. Morland that it wasn't really a funny book, and when this was thoroughly grasped Mrs. Morland became serious again and asked what *Belphégor* was like.

'Rather wonderful,' said Mr. Grant. 'He had a special theory of punctuation. He believed in commas, but not in any other sort of stops. In *Belphégor* you sometimes find a comma after every word. He used to say "La virgule vaut bien la particule." '

'That was just snobbishness, wasn't it, sir?' said Tony Morland, who scenting an intellectual discussion had suddenly deserted the wasp-hunters and come over to his mother. 'He knew he couldn't be an aristocrat, so he pretended to despise them. I know all about him because our French master, Mr. Knight, who is a very good man on his job, did the Romantics in the upper Sixth last term. He hasn't got a frightfully good accent, but he knows all about French literature and absolutely hundreds of useful idioms. If I had my notebook here I'd tell you some of them. When I went to France with mother at Easter I used heaps of idioms and surprized people very much. I expect you've heard of Mallarmé, sir,' said Tony kindly, 'well he was just the opposite of your man because he didn't believe in stops at all.'

'What have you read of his?' asked Mr. Grant, amused.

'I haven't exactly *read* anything,' said Tony, 'but we did him with Mr. Knight, and Mr. Knight read us some of the *Après midi d'un Faune*.'

'What you mean Après midi d'un Faune?' asked Betty, who also an intellectual, and subjugated by Tony's free and easy manner of dealing with wasps, had followed him slavishly. 'You can't *read* it. Ackcherly it's a ballet.'

Before Tony could collect his forces for a withering reply, the whole of the younger set, hearing the word ballet, burst into the argument without knowing what it was about, intoxicating themselves by the names of their favourite dancers, Russian and English. Tony quickly recovered himself and plunged headlong into the fray, managing to give the impression of one who had lived in the coulisses from earliest childhood, and ogled the legs of Taglioni. Mrs. Morland, who knew that her youngest son had not been more than three or four times to the ballet, marvelled humbly at his grasp of the subject.

'Sadler's Wells!' said Tony scornfully. 'What I call Empire ballet. People don't even dress for it. I'd rather not go to ballet at all if I couldn't go to decent seats at Covent Garden and wear my dinner jacket.'

'Better men than you haven't been ashamed to go in tails,' said the voice of a newcomer whose approach over the grass had not been heard among the warring voices. 'Shut up, Tony and get me some tea,' said Dr. Ford, Laura Morland's old friend and physician, the friend of half the county, and at present the medical attendant of Miss Brandon.

Tony collapsed and Dr. Ford folded his long legs up and sat down by Mrs. Morland, who introduced him to Mrs. Grant and her son.

'And I can't think why Tony is so uppish about the ballet,' she said plaintively. 'Adrian Coates has taken him once or twice, and his dinner jacket suit was too small and there was such a gap between his waistcoat and trousers that he had to crouch instead of standing up, to hide it, but I said I simply would not get him a new suit just for one evening, when he couldn't be needing it again till the Christmas holidays and I could get it in the sales.'

'Quite right too,' said Dr. Ford. 'Thanks, Tony, that's a nice selection of cakes. And now go away and play with your young friends.'

Tony, who had never yet managed to assert himself against Dr. Ford, gave one soft, sullen look at the group of grown-ups and strolled away ostentatiously in the direction of Hooper, hoping that everyone would see him not playing with the young friends.

Mrs. Grant began to ask Dr. Ford about Miss Brandon's health in a far from tactful way, and his cool parrying of her questions amused all the onlookers so much that Miss Morris, who had been quietly waiting for this chance, was able to speak aside to Mrs. Brandon.

'Could we walk to the Wishing Well again, Mrs. Brandon?' she asked. 'I forgot to wish.'

Mrs. Brandon willingly got up and accompanied her. When they had reached the well Miss Morris opened her bag, took out a penny and dropped it into the water.

'I really ought to wish for a better temper,' she said. 'I can't tell you, Mrs. Brandon, how sorry and ashamed I am for the way I behaved just now. If you knew the reasons — but I don't want to justify myself, only to apologize and beg you to forgive me.'

'It was nothing,' Mrs. Brandon hastened to reassure her. 'And Mr. Miller is a little trying sometimes with his enthusiasm.'

'My father was a clergyman,' said Miss Morris violently.

Mrs. Brandon, recognizing from long experience the voice of one who was determined to confess, was torn between a wish not to receive Miss Morris's confidences and the natural lazy kindness that made her so good a listener. Her kindness got the upper hand and she suggested that they should take a little stroll among the beeches. For a few moments they walked in silence, and then Miss Morris said,

'He took pupils. Mr. Miller came to him a good many years ago, before he got his theological degree. My father liked him very much and spoke highly of his gifts, but he was horrified to find in him a strong tendency to the doctrines of Rome.'

'Like Cardinal Newman,' said Mrs. Brandon sympathetically.

'Thank God he did not go so far. But it caused the deepest grief to my father, and I am afraid high words passed between them. Mr. Miller left us very suddenly and my father never mentioned his name again. I have often thought of him,' said Miss Morris simply, 'and prayed that he might be forgiven for the grief he gave my dear father. I didn't know he was Vicar here, and when I met him and found that he had not changed his ways of belief I thought of my father and lost my self-control. I am very, very sorry.'

Mrs. Brandon's mind was by now such a jumble of pity, mild curiosity about the Reverend Mr. Morris, and a private feeling that it was all a fuss about nothing, that she could find nothing better to say than 'I *am* so sorry,' but Miss Morris seemed comforted by these words, and much to Mrs. Brandon's relief did not, as most women would have done, burst out into a great flood of confidences. Mrs. Brandon asked her a little about her father. The Reverend Justin Morris, even as described by his daughter in whose eyes he was perfect, seemed to have combined in himself all the less agreeable qualities of the fanatic, the priest, and the parent. Mrs. Brandon gathered from her companion's artless words that Mr. Morris had worked his wife to death and done his best to kill his daughter. For the last years of his life he had been almost blind and Miss Morris had acted as working housekeeper, sometimes with a village girl to help her, sometimes alone, secretary, nurse, and companion, reading aloud to him far into the night. On his death it was found that he had sunk the whole of his little fortune in an annuity, and Miss Morris had been thankful to get, through the interest of various old pupils, for he had been an excellent theological scholar and coach for those whose beliefs were like his own, a position as companion to one elderly lady after another. Her practical sense and her almost entire self-effacement had made her invaluable to her employers, and when she had worn herself out in tending one old lady, another was always waiting to snap her up after the funeral. Her present position with Miss Brandon was, she said, far happier than any she had yet held, and to read aloud to her employer till one and two in the morning was no more than she had done for her father.

'And it is so pleasant to see young people from time to time,' said Miss Morris. 'I can't tell you how much good your visit with your children did me, and having Mr. Grant for the night. And then your kindness in getting Miss Brandon to let me come to the picnic to-day. I have so much to be thankful for, and I do hope you will forget my disgraceful show of temper though I shan't.'

Mrs. Brandon, saying vague reassuring things in her pleasant voice, led Miss Morris gradually back to the picnic. Dr. Ford seemed to have been looking for them, for as soon as he caught sight of them he got up and came in their direction.

'I didn't want to tell you this in public, Miss Morris,' he said, 'but I looked in at the Abbey this afternoon and found Miss Brandon convinced that she was going to die. She has had a good row with Sparks, but it isn't half so much fun bullying a maid as it is bullying a lady. I don't think there is any danger, but she is quite capable of working herself into a fit, which wouldn't do her heart any good, so I said I would bring you home if I could find you. When I left,' said Dr. Ford with grim relish, 'Miss Brandon had the head housemaid, who was scared stiff, to sit by her, and Sparks was having hysterics in the housekeeper's room. You are a marvel, Miss Morris, to stand that lunatic asylum.'

'Then I suppose I'd better go back,' said Miss Morris, with no sign of regret for cutting her holiday so short. 'But what about the car? You'll need it to go home, Mrs. Brandon.'

'That's all right,' said Dr. Ford. 'Sparks told me all about the car, and I told Miss Brandon she couldn't have you and the car as well. Hooper is to take Mrs. Brandon home and I'll run you back to the Abbey in my car whenever you like.'

Miss Morris thanked him and said she would go at once if it suited him. She then said good-bye to such guests as were still on the picnic ground and was just going to thank Mrs. Brandon for her treat when Mrs. Grant came up.

'Do I hear,' said Mrs. Grant, 'that Miss Brandon is ill?'

'Not a bit,' said Dr. Ford. 'Only temper.'

'I feel it is my duty to see her,' said Mrs. Grant, eyeing Dr. Ford suspiciously. 'I may not be down here long, and as my husband was one of her nearest relations I certainly ought to pay her a visit. If you are going back, Miss Morris, I will come with you.'

Miss Morris said quietly that she was afraid Miss Brandon could see no one just at present, but if Mrs. Grant would write, Miss Brandon would be glad to hear from her. Mrs. Grant, who evidently suspected Miss Morris of spending all her time making her employer alter her will in her favour, uttered a Calabrian exclamation of annoyance, whose tone was singularly like that of a similar English exclamation. Just as Dr. Ford was starting up his disgraceful little car, Tony Morland appeared.

'Oh, good-bye, Miss Morris,' he said. 'If I write you a letter will you answer it? Most of my friends are awfully bad at answering letters. I have about seven letters not answered this week. I simply shan't write to them if they don't answer.'

'Of course I will,' said Miss Morris. 'I always answer letters by return of post and I love getting them.'

An expression of mystic satisfaction spread over Tony's face. He made a vague suggestion of a courtly bow somewhere in Miss Morris's direction, returned to Hooper, who said he wouldn't be in Miss Morris's shoes for something, and took up his exposition of European history from 1848, the point at which he had been interrupted by tea, but barely had he outlined to Hooper the downfall of Metternich when a summons came for the car. The younger members had suddenly recollected a cocktail party on the other side of Barchester and were anxious to be off, and the grown-ups were quite ready to go home. After a tremendous amount of arguing and organizing Francis and Delia went off in Francis's car with their friends, taking Mr. Grant with them. Mrs. Brandon and Mrs. Grant were to return in Miss Brandon's car, leaving Mr. Miller to drive home by himself.

'Could I come round and see you before dinner?' said Mr. Miller urgently to Mrs. Brandon as she was getting into the car. 'Oh, dear, oh, dear, the parsnip wine has been in the sun and the cork has blown out. So has the dandelion wine,' he added, gazing helplessly at the wreckage.

Mrs. Brandon saw more confidences ahead, but was too kind to say no, though she felt the beginnings of a headache, which Mrs. Grant's ceaseless conversation on the way back did not improve. At the Cow and Sickle she deposited Mrs. Grant, promising to make an arrangement to meet again soon, and was thankful to find Rose in an excellent temper.

'My bath at once, please Rose,' she said, 'and Mr. Miller is coming to see me before dinner, so you might put the sherry out. Mr. Francis and Miss Delia have gone to a cocktail party so they'll probably be late.'

When Mr. Miller arrived he found his hostess, robed in filmy black, lying back in the most comfortable armchair, her feet on a low pouf.

'Forgive me if I don't get up,' she said, giving him her hand. 'I'm really rather tired after such a long day and so many people.'

If this was a hint Mr. Miller was determined, in spite of his deep admiration, not to take it.

'It is indeed thoughtless of me to intrude my own affairs upon you,' he said, sitting down near her, 'but you are kindness itself and I know you will forgive me.'

Instead of throwing the ink at him and saying she had a headache, as she would dearly like to have done, Mrs. Brandon said of course she would, and could she help him at all. It was obvious to the meanest intelligence that Mr. Miller was bursting to say something, but hadn't the faintest idea how to begin, and he maundered on about the beauty of the flowers in the drawing-room till Mrs. Brandon felt someone more competent must take the matter in hand.

'The flowers came from Brandon Abbey,' she said. 'Miss Morris brought them over this morning. What a very nice person she is. My children like her very much and so does Hilary, and Tony Morland took to her at once.'

Mr. Miller said she was a lady for whom he had a very deep respect and then lost his voice and his wits.

'She seems to have had a very difficult father,' said Mrs. Brandon, wondering if she would have to ask Mr. Miller to stay to dinner.

'I do not wish to speak ill of any minister of the gospel,' said Mr. Miller, who evidently did, 'but Mr. Morris, in narrowness, bitterness and entire want of charity, was as near a Personal Devil as any man I have known.'

'Miss Morris seems to have been very fond of him,' said Mrs. Brandon, her kind heart compelling her to stand up for the absent.

'Miss Morris has a very fine sense of duty,' said Mr. Miller, 'but I was for some time an inmate of the family, as a pupil of Mr. Morris, and can speak with authority on what I saw. I doubt whether even the present Bishop of Barchester would have tolerated his views on church discipline. Miss Morris naturally—whether rightly or not it is hardly for me to say—took her father's side, and there was an unhappy but unavoidable breach.'

Mrs. Brandon who knew that the Bishop was very Low Church, began dimly to apprehend that what she had romantically hoped to be an old romance between Mr. Miller and Miss Morris was only a squabble about doctrine, but wisely kept this regrettable point of view to herself.

'I am very sorry,' she said. 'It is so uncomfortable when one's friends don't like each other.'

'Pray, pray, dear lady, do not mistake me,' cried Mr. Miller. 'It is not that I dislike Miss Morris, for whom, as I said, I have a very deep respect, but to judge from what passed at the picnic to-day, she evidently still dislikes and misjudges me. I cannot tell you how sorry I am that so ungracious an incident should have marred our delightful outing. If any of the fault was mine I apologize most sincerely.'

Mrs. Brandon assured Mr. Miller that no one had blamed him for a moment, told him how handsomely Miss Morris had expressed her regret, and embroidered a little on Miss Morris's mention of her friendly remembrance of Mr. Miller before the break. She did not tell him that Miss Morris prayed for him to be forgiven, feeling that this was a liberty which even a clergyman might resent. Mr. Miller was so overcome by Mrs. Brandon's angelic sweetness that he again lost his voice.

'Do have some sherry,' said Mrs. Brandon, waving her hand at the decanter. 'No, not for me thank you, but help yourself.'

Mr. Miller filled and sipped and spoke again.

'But that,' he said, 'wasn't really what I wanted to see you about. It was, rather selfishly, about my own affairs.'

This did not at all surprise his hostess, who never expected her friends to come to her about anything else, and she begged him to go on.

'I may have mentioned to you,' said Mr. Miller, coughing, 'that I have been working at a little book on Donne — whom I *cannot*,' he added in a burst of confidence, 'bring myself to call Dunne.'

Mrs. Brandon said she should think so, she meant she should think not, and wasn't he the one with his head tied up like a turnip in St. Paul's. Mr. Miller, at once recognizing by her description the well-known statue of the Dean with his grave-clothes done up in a top knot, said indeed, indeed, that was he. His opusculum, he said, was now practically finished, but before sending the typescript to the publishers who had commissioned it, he had a request to make. Might he again trespass on Mrs. Brandon's perpetual kindness to allow him to read some of it aloud to her. Nothing was so helpful in forming an estimate of one's own work as to read it aloud to someone whose delicate perception and critical sense would at once detect any flaw.

'How stupid I am,' said Mrs. Brandon with great candour. 'I thought it was Miss Morris you wanted to talk about, but it was your book.'

'Miss Morris?' exclaimed Mr. Miller. 'Indeed I had hardly thought of her except in so far as the few moments' awkwardness this afternoon might have affected *you*. May I hope you will with your usual kindness forgive my egoism and allow me to bring my little work for your critical approval?'

'Yes, please do,' said Mrs. Brandon, casting a sidelong despairing look at the clock which said a quarter to eight. 'I suppose you don't mean now?'

'Well, I have by chance,' said Mr. Miller most untruthfully, 'the first chapter of the typescript upon me, if you would care to hear it.'

He produced a folded sheaf of typescript from his coat pocket and lovingly turned its pages.

'I would simply have adored it,' said Mrs. Brandon, throwing all the conviction she could into her voice, 'but I have such a stupid head to-night. I think it was the sun, or the long day, or Mrs. Grant.'

'How thoughtless, how inconsiderate I am,' said Mr. Miller getting up. 'You spend yourself for others, and we selfishly take advantage of you. Forgive me, dear friend, if I may use that word.'

In the middle of the night, thinking sleepily of Hilary Grant's wish to call her friend rather than trespass upon her Christian name, a thought had come to Mrs. Brandon, an answer so perfect that she fell into despair at having missed her chance of using it. Now heaven had sent her another chance and she was determined not to let it slip.

'I think I feel about that word rather as Shelley did about the word love,' said Mrs. Brandon, her voice sounding to Mr. Miller like a distant golden bell,

> "One word is too often profaned
> For me to profane it." '

Exhausted (though satisfied) by this sentimental and literary effort she shut her eyes. Mr. Miller touched her hand with his finger tips and went quietly away, marvelling at the deep sensitiveness of her nature.

If her son Francis had been there he would certainly have felt justified in his remark that his mother was a prey to saying what she thought would be most effective.

V

READING ALOUD

ACCORDING to telephone advice received from Brandon Abbey Miss Brandon had not died, nor had she worked herself into a fit. Mr. Grant worked hard at his classics with Mr. Miller, though sorely tried by his mother who was for ever demanding his company to make a piccolo giro and openly shamed him by alluding to Mr. Miller as the parroco. Francis went back to work, but as he didn't have to leave Stories till a quarter to nine and was usually back by soon after six, no one much noticed the difference. Delia had several skirmishes with Nurse in which she came off second best and saw the labourer who had been gored by a bull being carried on a hurdle to the Barchester ambulance. The weather got hotter and hotter and Mrs. Grant, tramping the countryside in her homespuns, lamented the cold English climate and pined for the sun of Calabria till everyone wished it had never been invented. The chicken pox at Grumper's End dragged on from child to child, and though Jimmy Thatcher didn't get it, he was in quarantine from school and from his religious duties and never had such a happy summer in his life.

Mr. Miller had not forgotten that Mrs. Brandon wished to hear him read his book about Donne, for such he had persuaded himself was her desire, and gradually wore her down to the point of settling a day for the first reading. The hour was to be between tea and dinner and when Mr. Miller, all eagerness, arrived with his typescript at half-past five, he found Mrs. Brandon seated under the Spanish chestnut.

'I have been looking forward so much to this,' she said. 'I have been reading some of Donne's poetry, which I only knew in anthologies before. I always thought he was the same as George Herbert and mixed them both up with Vaughan and Crashaw, but that,' she said with a proud simplicity, 'was chiefly ignorance. Now that I have read his poems I shall always know exactly who Donne is.'

Mr. Miller found this imbecility quite beautiful and could hardly refrain from saying so.

'Shall I begin with the preface, or go straight to the first chapter?' he asked, settling himself near his hostess.

'Oh, the preface; or do you think the first chapter would be nicer?' she asked. 'But here comes Rose to clear away the tea-things. We had better wait till she has finished. I never asked you if you had had any tea. Rose, please bring some fresh tea for Mr. Miller.'

In vain did Mr. Miller protest not that he had already had tea, for that would have been a lie, but that he didn't really want tea and often went without it altogether.

'Well, this isn't Friday,' said Mrs. Brandon, whose ideas on fasting were very sketchy, 'so it will do you good. Yes, Rose, please get fresh tea. It is extraordinary,' she said, as Rose went away, 'how long it always takes to make fresh tea. I believe they fill the largest kettle with cold water and put it on a slow fire. I am always telling Rose that a small kettle boils faster than a big one, but it is hopeless.'

'I might begin the first chapter while the kettle is boiling,' said Mr. Miller.

'You look so tired,' said Mrs. Brandon. 'Rest a few moments first. It is the heat, and I'm sure you've been down at Grumper's End. Have the Thatchers got it yet?'

Mr. Miller said so far they hadn't and that Jimmy would be out of quarantine next week. Mrs. Brandon then related several anecdotes of her children's infantile ailments and in time Rose came back with the fresh tea.

'That is perfect,' said Mrs. Brandon. 'They have made it with really boiling water, which they so seldom do.'

As Mr. Miller preferred his tea without milk or even lemon, its extreme hotness could not be modified. He wished he dared pour it backwards and forwards from cup to saucer and saucer to cup, but this was unthinkable, so he tried to drink it scalding, hurt himself and had to put his cup down. Mrs. Brandon, viewing his plight with sympathy, said she believed that putting a silver teaspoon in the cup drew off some of the heat, at least if you put a spoon in a glass when you wanted to pour boiling water into it, it usually didn't crack, though, even so, it often did. Grateful for this kindness Mr. Miller put his spoon in his cup, left it there for a moment, and tried to drink. The tea appeared to be as hot as ever, and the spoon, by now at white heat, slid round against his face, causing him considerable anguish.

'I think one ought to take it out first,' said Mrs. Brandon, and picking up the spoon with her handkerchief she dropped it into the slop basin.

Mr. Miller said he would try a little milk and though he disliked the mixture excessively he was able to swallow enough tea to satisfy his hostess. Refusing a second cup, though she assured him earnestly that it would be cooler this time, he produced his typescript and prepared to begin.

'This is lovely,' sighed Mrs. Brandon comfortably. 'Will you just give me that cushion, Mr. Miller, and then I shall be able to listen perfectly.'

Mr. Miller got up, fetched the cushion, put it reverently at Mrs. Brandon's back, sat down again and opened the typescript.

'Drummond of Hawthornden, in his Notes of Ben Jonson's Conversation, on the occasion of Jonson's famous visit to him in 1618,' he began, and then, overcome by the pride of authorship and the excitement of reading aloud to one who, in an earthly way, was perfection itself, choked a little and had to drink the remains of his tepid, milky tea.

'You have clergyman's throat,' said Mrs. Brandon in a voice of angelic sympathy. 'Have a little rest before you go on.'

Mr. Miller bravely said it was nothing and he was not at all tired.

'I think it is wonderful how you can speak for so long in church,' said Mrs. Brandon admiringly. 'If I had to read the service and preach I should be quite voiceless, besides making all sorts of mistakes.'

Mr. Miller looked at his saint with an instant's doubt, recovered himself and began again.

'Drummond of Hawthornden, in his Notes of Ben Jonson's Conversation, on the occasion of Jonson's famous visit to him in 1618, reports Jonson —' he began, when a lawn mower, whose distant whirr had sounded not unpleasantly across the garden, came roaring nearer and nearer and began to move backwards and forwards with hideous recurring crescendo and diminuendo just behind the tree. Mr. Miller stopped.

'Do go on,' said Mrs. Brandon, but finding her own words almost inaudible, she sat up and looked round.

'That must be Turpin,' she said, while the lawn mower was at the furthest point of its beat. 'I have said again and again that he *must* get the lawns mown before lunch. Do call him, Mr. Miller.'

Mr. Miller laid down his typescript and went towards the lawn mower, but as the gardener was deaf, and the noise of the machine deafening, and Turpin's eyes were glued to the delicate watered pattern on the grass that he must follow, Mr. Miller had to walk the whole length of the lawn beside him before he could get his attention. When Turpin saw who his visitor was he stopped and touched his cap, pleased at the attention, for Hettie gave her employer an excellent character as one who did not too closely inquire into matters of dusting and sweeping, provided his hours of study were not disturbed. Thinking, though erroneously, that his Vicar had come to discuss the weather with him, Turpin gave it as his opinion that this drought wouldn't break for a long time yet, but the gardens were doing wonderful well considering and he had a nice big marrow saving up for the Harvest Festival. He well remembered, he added with a chuckle, the year he had that great whopper of a marrow, and when he came to pick it he found Miss Delia had cut a comic face on the under side with her new pocket knife. At this point Mr. Miller, seizing his chance, managed to convey to Turpin by a combination of shouting and pantomime that his mistress wanted to see him.

'Please take the lawn mower right away, Turpin,' said Mrs. Brandon, whose gentle voice appeared to be perfectly audible to her gardener. 'You know I will *not* have the lawns done on this side of the house after lunch.'

The substance of Turpin's reply was that Mrs. Brandon well knew he always got the lawns done before his dinner now, but if people's cars would splutter the new gravel off the drive onto the grass edge, he couldn't help it if stones got in the machine and Curwen had said he'd run her down in the car to the blacksmith to have the blades re-set, but being as the car was wanted to take Miss Delia over to Rushwater he had to send the garden boy down with her on the barrow, and she was only just back and running so beautiful it seemed a shame not to use her while the weather lasted.

Mrs. Brandon replied that the weather would last for a long time and he could do the lawn to-morrow, upon which Turpin touched his cap and departed, the vengeful noise of his machine growing fainter and fainter, till the silence of golden afternoon enfolded the garden.

'How lovely the silence is,' said Mrs. Brandon.

'Shall I go on now?' asked Mr. Miller.

'Yes *do*,' said Mrs. Brandon. 'And begin right at the beginning again, so that I shall miss nothing. Oh, I am so sorry, but could you just pick up that cushion again?'

Mr. Miller got up, fetched the cushion, put it with reverence slightly tinged by impatience at Mrs. Brandon's back, sat down again and opened the typescript.

'Drummond of Hawthornden,' he began, 'in his Notes of Ben Jonson's Conversation, on the occasion of Jonson's famous visit to him in 1618, reports Jonson as declaring that "He esteemeth John Donne —" '

'Excuse me one moment,' said Mrs. Brandon. 'It is Rose. What is it, Rose?'

'Only the tea-things, madam,' said Rose in an aggrieved voice, 'but I can leave them till later if you wish.'

'No, you can take them,' said Mrs. Brandon.

'And Nurse wishes to speak to you, madam,' said Rose. 'Seeing Mr. Miller was here she didn't like to trouble you, but it's about Miss Delia.'

'Well, tell Nurse to come and tell me what it is,' said Mrs. Brandon. 'I'm sure you won't mind,' she added, turning to Mr. Miller. 'It won't take a moment and then Rose will have finished clearing away and we can be quite peaceful.'

Mr. Miller could but acquiesce.

'I'm sorry to disturb you, madam,' said Nurse, 'but I thought I'd better speak to you. It's about Miss Delia's knickers,' she continued, after a glance at the Vicar and a rapid decision that his cloth protected him. 'She really hasn't a pair fit to wear, not if she goes away to stay anywhere. I really don't know what she does to them. So I thought if you didn't need those three yards of that double width pink crêpe de chine you got in the sales I could start on some at once. I'd just run down to the village on my bike before the shop shuts and see if Miss Thatcher can match me up some pink sewing silk.'

'Yes do, Nurse,' said Mrs. Brandon. 'And tell Rose to bring me out my spectacles.'

Nurse went off and was almost immediately seen running to the village on her bicycle.

'Just one moment till I have my spectacles,' said Mrs. Brandon to her Vicar. 'I don't really need them, but I like to know where they are. Thank you, Rose. Now, Mr. Miller, go on where we stopped. I *am* so sorry for these interruptions, but now we can be perfectly quiet.'

Mr. Miller said he thought he had better go back to the beginning again, rather than pick up the thread in the middle of a sentence. He opened his typescript and began:

'Drummond of Hawthornden, in his Notes of Ben Jonson's Conversation, on the occasion of Jonson's famous visit to him in 1618, reports Jonson as declaring that "He esteemeth John Donne as the first poet in the world for some things." But Jonson also asserted that "Donne . . ."'

He read on, sometimes stumbling over a word when he raised his eyes and saw Mrs. Brandon's face brooding in quiet beauty on his words. It was difficult to decide, Mrs. Brandon reflected, whether she had better get Nurse to alter that apricot slip which she had felt at the time she bought it to be a mistake, or simply cut her losses and give it away. On the whole, give it away, she thought, and having decided this, so exquisite a light of peace and contentment irradiated her face that Mr. Miller, turning over the second page, felt that so must angels look.

'That is like Sir Edmund's car,' said Mrs. Brandon, a distinct interest in her voice. 'I do hope he won't spoil our reading, Mr. Miller. I daresay it is only a message about something and as soon as he has gone we will begin again. I'm glad to see he has his chauffeur back. He drives so badly himself and with his lame leg one never knows what might happen.'

Sir Edmund was seen at the front door holding a short colloquy with Rose, who pointed out to him the party under the chestnut tree, towards whom he then directed his steps.

'Well, Lavinia, out here, eh?' said Sir Edmund. 'Afternoon Miller. Phew! it's hot.'

'You would like some fresh tea,' said Mrs. Brandon.

'No, I wouldn't,' said Sir Edmund. 'Poison to me, Lavinia, as you well know. But if that girl of yours would bring me a brandy and soda, I wouldn't say no.'

'*Would* you mind, Mr. Miller,' said Mrs. Brandon, 'going to the house and asking Rose to bring out the brandy and a siphon and some glasses, and she might as well bring the sherry too, as Francis will soon be back.'

Mr. Miller rose, laid his typescript on his chair, and went to the house. When he got back he found Sir Edmund telling Mrs. Brandon about the new drains in a piece of land over near Starveacres.

'Thank you so much, Mr. Miller,' said Mrs. Brandon. 'Mr. Miller was reading aloud to me, Sir Edmund.'

'Bible, eh?' said Sir Edmund.

'No, no. I'm not *ill*,' said his hostess. 'It was a book of his own, all about Donne.'

'Didn't know you were keen on cricket,' said Sir Edmund.

'I was once twelfth man for my college third eleven,' said Mr. Miller, 'but I'm afraid I can claim no special knowledge of the subject.'

'What's all this about a book about Bradman then?' asked Sir Edmund.

'I didn't say Bradman, I said Donne,' said Mrs. Brandon.

'Well, it's all one,' said Sir Edmund. 'Fine fellows those Australians. I must get that book. What's it called, eh?'

'No, not that kind of Don,' said Mrs. Brandon, sticking to her point.

'Don Juan then, eh?' said Sir Edmund with a loud laugh which made Mr. Miller want to excommunicate him.

'Don't be dense, Sir Edmund,' said Mrs. Brandon severely. 'It is a book about *Donne*, the clergyman that has his head tied up in St. Paul's.'

Before Sir Edmund could burst with mystification, Mr. Miller, concealing his mortification very well, explained that he was reading to Mrs. Brandon the first chapters of a small book on John Donne, Dean of St. Paul's from 1621 to 1631, and author of a number of poems, religious and erotic.

'Religious and – well, I suppose you know best, Miller, but it sounds a bit queer to me,' said Sir Edmund, whose chivalry very properly took alarm at the word erotic used in front of a lady. 'Go on, go on, never mind me.'

'I think if you went back to the beginning it would be better,' said Mrs. Brandon. 'Then Sir Edmund wouldn't miss anything.'

'That's right. Always do things thoroughly,' said Sir Edmund, composing himself to listen.

Mr. Miller turned back to the first page of the typescript and began, a little nervously,

'Drummond of Hawthornden –'

'Just a moment,' said Mrs. Brandon. 'Thanks, Rose. Sir Edmund, will you help yourself. Do have a glass of sherry, Mr. Miller, or would you rather have brandy and soda?'

Mr. Miller politely refused both and waiting till Sir Edmund had filled his glass, prepared to begin again.

'That *stupid* cushion again,' said Mrs. Brandon. 'Oh, thank you so much, Mr. Miller. Now, we will have a really cosy time.'

It did cross Mr. Miller's mind that cosy was not perhaps the mot juste for the author of his choice, but he resolutely put the thought from him as savouring of criticism of his hostess, and took up the typescript.

'Drummond of Hawthornden, in his Notes of Ben Jonson's Conversation –'

'Sorry to interrupt you, Miller,' said Sir Edmund, 'but the name Drummond reminds me that old Mrs. Perkins down at Grumper's End has sciatica again badly. We'll have to get her into the infirmary, but she's a devilish obstinate old woman. Just thought I'd mention it while it was in my mind. Carry on.'

' — on the occasion of Jonson's famous visit to him in 1618 — ' continued Mr. Miller, determined not to go back to the beginning again.

'Sixteen eighteen, eh?' said Sir Edmund. 'That's a deuce of a long time ago, eh? Wonderful old fellows they were.'

At this Mr. Miller threw up the sponge, folded his typescript and was wondering whether he could make his excuses without betraying the annoyance in his voice, when Francis's car rushed up the drive, halted, and disgorged Francis and Delia.

'Mother, mother,' shrieked Delia, 'oh, how do you do, Mr. Miller, hullo, Sir Edmund, what do you think? Francis came to fetch me from the tennis party and as we were coming down the Southbridge Hill a car came out of Patcher's Lane and a motor bike ran slap into it and the man went right through the windscreen. He wasn't a bit hurt but he was bleeding like anything, so the people in the car took him straight to the Nutfield Cottage Hospital and Dr. Ford was there and he put ten stitches in, and the bike is absolutely smashed to bits.'

'If I had my way those hazels at the corner of Patcher's Lane would be cut back,' said Sir Edmund angrily. 'That corner's a perfect death trap. I've told the County Council about it again and again. When someone is killed perhaps they'll take some notice. Well, Lavinia, I must be off. Can I give you a lift, Miller? Early to bed and early to rise, you know.'

Mr. Miller, hearing the church clock strike seven, accepted the offer and said good-bye to Mrs. Brandon with a shade of stiffness which she noticed but could not account for.

'It was lovely to hear your book,' she said, holding Mr. Miller's hand in both her own. 'You must come again and we will have another long reading, that is if you are sure it doesn't tire you,' she added with deep affectionate interest in her voice.

Mr. Miller truthfully said that he could have read twice as much to her without being tired and with a look of respectful adoration went away.

'At it again, darling?' said Francis to his mother as the visitors left. 'Seducing the clergy.'

Mrs. Brandon said he oughtn't to say things like that and she was going in to have her bath.

* * *

Dinner passed off peacefully enough except for Delia's lamentations that Dr. Ford would not let her see the stitches put in. It was too bad, she said, that she took all the trouble to pass that rotten First Aid exam and now she wasn't allowed to do anything. Even when Sid, the garden boy, had that huge boil on his neck they wouldn't let her see it burst.

'No, I'll say it for you, darling,' said Francis, anticipating his mother. 'Delia, one oughtn't to say things like that. It's enough to take a hard-working young man's appetite away. Oh, I brought out some new dance records. There's an awfully good one called "I'm all of a muddle when I cuddle, cuddle, cuddle." It's played by Cash Campo and his Symposium Boys.'

Accordingly Delia opened the gramophone and Francis turned back a couple of rugs, and he and Delia slid up and down the drawing-room to the glutinous sentiment of 'I'm all of a muddle' and the other records that Francis had brought. Mrs. Brandon, at the far end of the room, sat under a shaded light by the window with her embroidery, pleased to see her nice, good-looking offspring enjoying themselves.

Gradually she became conscious of an alien presence, and looking up saw Mr. Grant standing outside the open window. She smiled at him.

'Oh,' said Mr. Grant, 'I just happened to be passing and I happened to see you. Could I come in?'

The thought did just trouble Mrs. Brandon's consciousness that people did not come up the drive, which led nowhere except to her front door, by accident, but as she was quite pleased to see a visitor she invited Mr. Grant to join them.

Instead of going round to the front door Mr. Grant stood on one leg and then came nearer to the window.

'It was that book of mine you said you'd like me to read to you,' he said, leaning his elbows on the window sill.

'I always hope the sash cord won't break when people do that,' said Mrs. Brandon. 'One of them did break once, and the window came down with such a crash that two panes were broken, but most luckily no one was under it at the time.'

'I just happened to have the manuscript with me if you'd care to hear it,' said Mr. Grant, standing up.

'I'd love to,' said Mrs. Brandon, 'but I don't see how you could possibly read to me here with the gramophone. I'll tell Rose to take you to my sitting-room. Ring the front door bell and I'll catch her in the hall.'

Mr. Grant continued his journey, rang the front door bell and was shown by Rose into Mrs. Brandon's sitting-room. From the drawing-room beyond came the wail of Cash Campo and his Symposium Boys. The door which led into the drawing-room was opened, the wail rose to a nostalgic shriek, Mrs. Brandon, carrying an armful of tapestry work and trailing embroidery wool, came in and shut the door behind her. Mr. Grant found himself alone with the most exquisite woman in the world and dropped his manuscript, which fluttered down and lay strewn on the floor.

'Oh, dear,' said Mrs. Brandon sympathetically, as she sat down, shedding her scissors, her gold thimble and several skeins of wool.

'I'll pick them up,' said Mr. Grant with eager devotion, and leaving his manuscript to its fate he pursued the thimble under a table, retrieved

it, collected the scissors and wools, and still on his knees presented them
to their owner.

'Hullo, Hilary,' said Francis, looking in. 'What are you doing? Don't
propose to mamma, because I've sworn an oath that no home will hold
me and a stepfather and I'd hate to turn you out. I say, mamma, do
you know where that record of "The Surprise in your Eyes" has got to?'

'I think Nurse borrowed it to play on her little gramophone,' said
Mrs. Brandon, 'and don't be so silly. And shut the door, darling,
because Hilary is going to read to me.'

Francis looked with avuncular tolerance at his young friend and
went away. Mr. Grant sorted his manuscript and put on his spectacles.

'Are yours for long sight or short sight?' asked Mrs. Brandon.

'Astigmatism,' said Mr. Grant. 'I squint with one eye and not with
the other, or something of the sort. My man says I'll get over it if I wear
glasses for a few years.'

'Mine are for short sight,' said Mrs. Brandon proudly. 'I can see
anything, absolutely anything at a distance, but close to my eyes are
quite useless to me.'

Mr. Grant found the thought of Mrs. Brandon's blue eyes, endowed
with the eagle's sight for ranging over the great free distances but
betraying their owner for the level of every day's most quiet needs, so
moving that he sat silent. Divine poetry alone could, he felt, deal
adequately with the theme, but as the only line which immediately
presented itself was 'Eyeless at Gaza in the mill with slaves,' which even
he recognized to be inappropriate, he gave up the search.

'Now, I am longing to hear about Robert le Diable,' said Mrs.
Brandon.

'Jehan le Capet,' Mr. Grant corrected her.

'Of course, how silly of me. Tell me, was Laura Morland able to help
you about a publisher?'

Mr. Grant said her publisher, Mr. Coates, sounded very nice, but he
was afraid no one would really want his book very much. He had, he
said, a frightful inferiority complex, which came from the way his
mother had brought him up.

'Which reminds me,' said Mrs. Brandon, 'that I have never asked
your mother to dinner yet. What with one thing coming after another
and the days following each other as they do I seem to have got
behindhand. I hope she won't think it rude of me.'

'Of course she won't. And anyway she's only been at the Cow a week
and I think she is going on to Lady Norton to-morrow. But she's bound
to come back again,' said Mr. Grant gloomily, 'and spoil everything as
usual. I mean she was never unkind to me or anything, but I have
never had a real chance. When I was at school and my father was alive
we always went to Frinton for the Easter and summer holidays and
stayed at home for Christmas, to please father. Then when he died and

I went to Oxford, mother took to going to Italy and made me spend all my holidays there, so you see it really never gave me a chance at all.'

Mrs. Brandon did not quite follow Mr. Grant's argument, but said soothingly that she was sure he would get his book published at once, and that she for one had never noticed his inferiority complex.

Mr. Grant said in a hushed voice that was just like her. He felt, he added, quite, quite different when he was with her. He had very few *real* friends, he said, but with the real friends whom he loved he could be himself.

Mrs. Brandon, interested in philosophical discussion, said it was extraordinary how one felt quite different with different people and was going on to instance some of the different people that she felt different with, but Mr. Grant, though he adored her and was still quite hot and damp from having mentioned that there were a few real friends whom he loved, alternately hoping and fearing that she would have seized his meaning, took the opportunity of a second's pause to enlarge upon the abstract theme of how different one felt with different people, which he did for seven or eight minutes.

'When I met you at Miss Brandon's I was wishing I had never been born,' said Mr. Grant Byronically, 'but now everything is different.'

There was a short silence.

'Now, do read me your book,' said Mrs. Brandon, 'and I will fill in some of my background and then I can listen beautifully.'

'You always listen beautifully,' said Mr. Grant in a hoarse voice, but Mrs. Brandon was trying to match some wool and either did not hear or took no notice.

'My great difficulty,' said Mr. Grant, 'was to know how to approach my subject. As practically nothing is known about le Capet I thought of treating him fictionally, but I thought that treatment would hardly do.'

He paused, evidently anxious for an opinion. Mrs. Brandon said No, of course it wouldn't do.

'On the other hand,' continued Mr. Grant, 'one doesn't want to be too prosaic and dry, so I have used a method which I think will combine the best elements of both. If you don't mind, I'll begin at the beginning.'

Without waiting for the goddess's consent to this novel manner of reading a book he plunged recklessly into his first chapter, reading in a quick, unnatural, high-pitched voice and stammering violently, his face very red with mingled emotions. Mrs. Brandon, occasionally detaching her thoughts from the apricot slip, a new carpet for the servants' sitting-room, and other weighty affairs, gathered that le Capet's chief claim to immortality was that he had just missed meeting everyone of note in Paris and was in bed with a cold on the first night of *Hernani*. From an altered tone in her young admirer's voice she presently realized that he was reading some of le Capet's verses aloud, tried to anchor her drifting attention and just caught the last line of a poem ending

Sirène, fange, boue, immondices, ordure.

'It's fine,' said Mr. Grant, his voice now itself again, 'to be able to say that about the woman you love.'

'I don't think everyone would like it,' said Mrs. Brandon with surprising firmness.

Mr. Grant came to earth with a bang, and realizing that he had grossly insulted and offended his hostess, got up and said he must go.

'Oh, don't go,' said Mrs. Brandon.

Mr. Grant sat down again.

'I simply loved it,' said Mrs. Brandon. 'I am sure it is going to be an enormous success. Let us go and watch Francis and Delia and you must have a drink. You must be thirsty.'

Mr. Grant got up again, moved beyond speech by these exquisite words, and they went into the drawing-room, where Francis dispensed drinks. Mrs. Brandon said she was going to bed and held out her hand to Mr. Grant who grasped it with fervour.

'Tut, tut,' said Francis; and bending low over his mother's hand he kissed it, while Delia giggled.

'Headache, darling?' he said as he escorted his mother to the door.

'A little,' said Mrs. Brandon. 'I find being read aloud to is very exhausting. Mr. Miller read to me all afternoon and Hilary all evening and they never seem to get anywhere.'

'You shouldn't let them,' said Francis. 'It's only vanity that makes you so kind, because you think how nice you look when you listen. I say, what a ripping title for a fox-trot. Good night, mamma. Now, Hilary, stop being my stepfather and be a man. I'll do the gramophone and you dance with Delia.'

Mr. Grant did as he was told and enjoyed himself very much, winding up with a tremendous wrestling match with Francis and a race down the drive. Not till the following morning did he remember, with a sense of guilt, that he had not thought of Mrs. Brandon for quite nine hours, for eight and a half of which he had been asleep.

VI

BRANDON ABBEY AGAIN

ON THE following day, much to everyone's relief, Mrs. Grant left the Cow and Sickle to go and stay with her dull friend Lady Norton, for

the last two years a widow whose jointure was the despair of the
nephew who inherited the title. Mrs. Brandon went to say good-bye to
her and hoped she had been comfortable.

'Comfortable really means nothing to me,' said Mrs. Grant. 'In
Calabria I have often slept on a sack stuffed with chestnut husks.'

'The mattresses at the Cow are pretty uncomfortable, but I don't
think there are husks in them,' said Mrs. Brandon apologetically. 'Did
you manage to get the bedroom window to open?'

'I sleep so well that I hardly notice whether the window is open or
shut. In Calabria none of the peasants open their windows. It is an old
superstition that evil spirits suck the blood of sleepers if the window is
open. Besides they are out all day. There is a proverb which roughly
runs in English, "Do not draw the curtain till the sun's rays are certain."
That does not of course give the real meaning at all.'

'Well, I hope you will have a very nice time with Lady Norton,' said
Mrs. Brandon. 'I believe her garden is beautiful. And we will all take
care of Hilary for you. What a nice boy he is.'

'He is absolutely devoted to me,' said Mrs. Grant, toying with her
heavy amber necklace. 'Sometimes I almost wish he were less devoted.
He never made friends at school and preferred to spend his holidays
with me – and his father of course – at Frinton or at home. I always
hoped that when he went to Oxford he would make a circle for himself,
but he came out to me in Italy every vacation. I loved having him, but
he does not understand the Italian mind and cannot get on with my
beloved peasants. If only he would marry some nice English girl I
should be quite happy, so long as I wasn't expected to take any interest
in my grandchildren.'

'I think I should like grandchildren,' said Mrs. Brandon. 'They
would make me feel important. How are you going to Lady Norton?'

'She is sending the car for me. She is very fond of driving, and while
I am with her I shall get her to take me over to Brandon Abbey. My
husband was anxious for me to see his Aunt Amelia again, and I feel
I ought to go while she is still alive.'

In this sentiment Mrs. Brandon fully acquiesced, feeling that a visit
after Miss Brandon's death would not be the same thing. She wondered
whether she ought to hint at Miss Brandon's disinclination to see her
niece by marriage, but came to the conclusion that she had better not
interfere. Lady Norton's car then arrived and Mrs. Grant's rather
shameful luggage, consisting largely of gaily striped bags and baskets,
was indignantly put into it by the chauffeur.

'No, no, put my things inside,' said Mrs. Grant, coming out to
superintend. 'I will go in front with you. They are all human, if we
treat them as human beings,' she added in far too audible an aside to
Mrs. Brandon, who made no comment, knowing well that Lady
Norton's chauffeur would die sooner than be human.

Mrs. Grant bade embarrassingly affectionate farewells to the staff of the Cow and Sickle, bestowing handsome largesse at the same time, and got up beside the unwilling chauffeur, whose face of rigid disapproval boded ill for human relationships. Mrs. Brandon walked homewards, considering the matter of the apricot slip. It had come to her in a flash while doing her hair that morning that perhaps Miss Morris would like it and she was determined to leave no stone unturned, although she knew that Nurse, who wanted the slip for Delia, would strongly disapprove. Accordingly she wrote to Miss Morris to ask if the gift would be acceptable. Two or three days passed without an answer, and she was beginning to wonder whether Miss Morris was offended, when after lunch Rose announced a telephone call from Brandon Abbey. It was Miss Morris herself, who told Mrs. Brandon that her aunt was not at all well and had expressed a desire to see her.

'She wants to know,' said Miss Morris, 'if you will come over to-morrow afternoon and bring your son and Mr. Grant. I understand that her solicitor is also coming, and I can't tell you anything more, because I don't know anything. And I would simply love to have the apricot slip. It is too good of you to think of me.'

'It all sounds extremely uncomfortable,' said Mrs. Brandon, 'but of course I'll come if she really wants me, though if it is business I simply cannot understand it ever. I'll bring Hilary and I'll see if Francis can get off work early. How are you?'

Miss Morris said she was quite well, thanked Mrs. Brandon again for the slip, and rang off.

As soon as Francis came back his mother told him what Miss Morris had said and they agreed that if the solicitor was coming it must be something to do with legal matters. Francis was at first extremely unwilling to go, feeling that the whole affair savoured of fortune-hunting, and when his mother pressed the point he suggested that they should walk over to the Vicarage and see Mr. Grant, who was equally involved.

Mrs. Brandon, though she was as disinterested as anyone can possibly be when a large inheritance is in question, did feel that it would not only be unkind to her old aunt, but a really foolish flying in the face of Providence if this invitation were neglected, and said so with unusual energy. When they got to the Vicarage they found Mr. Grant playing tennis with his coach and looked on till the set was finished. Mr. Miller, who looked much nicer in flannels than in his clerical garb, or so Mrs. Brandon privately thought, came and sat beside her, while Mr. Grant and Francis had a little horseplay, but finding it too hot, soon came and sat down on the grass. Mr. Grant complained bitterly that Mr. Miller always beat him. Mr. Miller looked gratified, remembered that pride is sinful, and said he hoped it would be fine for the Harvest Festival. Francis said he was all with them there except that they wanted a little rain at Stories to bring their giant gooseberry on that they were saving

up to decorate the font. Mrs. Brandon said Francis oughtn't to say
things like that, and it was something quite different that she had come
to talk about, something that Hilary ought to know. On hearing this
Mr. Miller offered to go away, but Mrs. Brandon begged him not to,
saying that his advice would be of the greatest value, and that though
luckily Francis and Delia would be quite comfortably off when she
was dead, that was no reason for not being polite to people. To this, as
a general axiom, Mr. Miller gave his approval and asked if she would
tell him what the circumstances were that called for his advice; advice,
he added, which was ever at her disposal if it could be of any service.

'But I told you,' said Mrs. Brandon plaintively, 'about Miss Brandon.
After all she *is* a relation.'

'Well, you know darling,' said Francis, 'that listening is your strong
suit, not explaining. Leave this to your able and businesslike son.'

He then told Mr. Grant about Miss Morris's telephone message and
said it was all extraordinarily uncomfortable, but he thought they
ought to go. It might look like fortune-hunting if they did, but it would
be rude and unkind to an old lady if they didn't, and what did Hilary
think. Mr. Grant said with some vehemence that he loathed the Abbey
and never wanted to hear of it again, but if Mrs. Brandon thought he
ought to go, he would.

'Well, she *is* our relation,' said Mrs. Brandon, sticking firmly to her
original point. 'What do you think, Mr. Miller?'

Mr. Miller, who was not quite sure whether he was being appealed
to as pastor or neighbour, said visiting the sick was undoubtedly one
of the duties laid upon us, a duty from which no material considerations
should deter us, and he was sure Mrs. Brandon would judge for the best.

'Well, I really hardly come into it, because Cousin Amelia never
threatened to leave *me* anything,' said Mrs. Brandon with great candour, 'but it would be very silly of Hilary and Francis not to go, and
very inconsiderate. And the solicitor may be coming about something
quite different, like drains, or the kitchen chimney,' said Mrs. Brandon,
who appeared to confuse solicitors with plumbers and builders. 'You
never know.'

'Well, thank you very much for helping, Mr. Miller,' said Francis,
'and now that mamma has decided to do what she always meant to do,
we can go home again. How's the book, Mr. Miller?'

Mr. Miller, slightly self-conscious, said it had gone to his publishers.

'Oh, shan't I hear any more of it then?' asked Mrs. Brandon.

'I was going to ask you a favour, a very great favour,' said Mr. Miller
in a lower voice, hitching his chair nearer hers. 'Will you think me
presumptuous if I ask you to allow me to dedicate my little work to you?'

'To me?' exclaimed Mrs. Brandon, in genuine astonishment and
delight.

'To whom else?' asked Mr. Miller.

'Well, lots of people,' said Mrs. Brandon, thinking of the Archbishop of Canterbury and Mrs. Miller's old stepmother at Harrogate. 'But to me! Oh, Mr. Miller, how enchanting of you. I have never had a book dedicated to me before. I couldn't think of anything nicer happening to me. Thank you so very much.'

She looked so pleased and happy, like a child with a new toy as Mr. Miller in a flight of fancy afterwards put it to himself, that the author really felt for a moment as if he were doing a kindness rather than receiving one.

'And what exactly will you put in the beginning?' asked Mrs. Brandon.

Mr. Miller, who had not actually thought of anything except one or two extremely unsuitable lines from Donne's works, hesitated.

'Why not just "To the Listener"?' said Mr. Grant.

'You might as well say "To the Daily Telegraph",' said Francis. 'Pull yourself together, my boy. What about a spot of Latin, Mr. Miller?'

'I think simply "To L. B. in gratitude",' said Mr. Miller.

Mrs. Brandon's face assumed such a beatific expression that Mr. Miller felt he was already well repaid.

'I was thinking how nice L. B. looked on my dressing case when I was married,' she explained. 'My initials used to be L. O., Lavinia Oliver—Francis's second name is Oliver, you know—and they looked so silly and the girls at school would make jokes about them. L. B. looks much nicer.'

Having stemmed romance by this piece of reminiscence, she said good-bye to Mr. Miller.

'Come to lunch to-morrow, Hilary,' she said as she left, 'and we'll go to the Abbey together. Francis is coming separately, from Barchester, and I'm sure it will be most uncomfortable.'

Mr. Grant and Mr. Miller, finding as usual that speech on the one subject of which their hearts and minds were full was difficult, returned to their tennis, where so fired was Mr. Grant by the thought of the morrow that he served eight double faults running and lost two of the new balls among the laurestinus. All evening, when he should have been working at Cicero, he was thinking with envy of Mr. Miller, who had really finished a book commissioned by a real publisher, and was going to dedicate it to Mrs. Brandon. An idea began to float about in his mind and by the time he came down to breakfast next day it had almost assumed the nature of a resolve. If Mr. Miller had not been thinking about the Church Fête and how he could, in a spirit consistent with Christianity, keep his parishioners away from the little rock garden which he sometimes felt to be a stumbling block in the way of complete humility, he would have noticed that his pupil was strangely silent and was jotting down notes on a piece of paper in the manner of one who hopes someone will ask him what he is doing.

The morning passed all too slowly for Mr. Grant. At half-past twelve he could contain his impatience no longer and set out for Stories, hoping against hope that by walking slowly he could make the journey last till half-past one, which was Mrs. Brandon's lunch-time. By twenty minutes to one he was at the front gate and in despair sat down on the grassy side of the road to die. Before kindly death could ease his pains Delia came up the road on her bicycle. When she saw Mr. Grant she stopped and got off.

'Good morning,' said Mr. Grant.

'Hullo, Hilary. Feeling sick?' asked Delia.

'Oh, no. I was a bit early for lunch, that's all.'

'I should think you were,' said Delia, 'it's only a quarter to one, but I can easily find some biscuits if you're hungry.'

'It's not that,' said Mr. Grant moodily.

'Well, if you are sick, say so,' said Delia, mistaking the moodiness for nausea. 'I'd love to hold your head.'

Mr. Grant looked up anxiously. The gleam of the Born Nurse was in Delia's eye and he felt that sooner than forgo her prey she would hypnotise him into feeling ill, so he got up and shook the odds and ends of dry grass and dust off his trousers.

'You'd better come up to the house,' said Delia, accommodating her pace to the invalid's. 'We can eat gooseberries if you're sure you're all right.'

As eating gooseberries appeared to be as good a way as another of passing the time till lunch, Mr. Grant accompanied Delia to the kitchen garden where, bent double under the gooseberry nets, torn by the thorny gooseberry bushes, the hot noontide sun beating upon them, they enjoyed a hearty meal of unripe fruit.

'I say,' said Delia, 'are you really writing a book?'

'Damn,' said Mr. Grant, as a large and unexpectedly ripe red gooseberry exploded in his hand. 'Sorry, I mean yes.'

'Mother said you read it to her,' said Delia. 'Try this bush, it's a bit riper. All about absinthe and things, isn't it?'

Mr. Grant said rather stiffly that it was about a French poet, who had indeed hastened his end by over-indulgence in absinthe, but had produced some very remarkable work.

'There's a man at Nutfield,' said Delia, 'who drinks methylated spirits and power alcohol. Dr. Ford says he'll have spontaneous combustion some day. I'd like to be there. It must be marvellous to see anyone spontaneously combusting. You can't do anything to stop them and there's nothing left but a black sticky sort of mess. It must be even more difficult to collect enough to bury than it was with the man who got burned in the motor char-à-banc. Anyway I hope your book will be a best seller. I shall give it to all my friends for Christmas if it isn't more than three and sixpence.'

Touched by this kind interest Mr. Grant shyly said he had been thinking of dedicating it to her mother.

'Good idea,' said Delia. 'Mother will love it. What will you put?'

Mr. Grant said he didn't know. Something Latin perhaps.

'Oh, I wouldn't do that,' said Delia. 'It puts people off buying if they see Latin. Why don't you say To Cousin Lavinia with Love from Hilary?'

At this brutal suggestion Mr. Grant felt a gulf opening between himself and his cousin Delia which only time could bridge. The gong sounded.

'There; now we'll be late,' said Delia. 'If you are too early for a thing you nearly always get too late. Come on. Careful with that net.'

Her words came too late. Mr. Grant, rather indignantly extricating himself from the gooseberries, found one of his buttons inextricably tangled in the net, wrenched impatiently at it and tore the button together with a strip of grey flannel from his coat. Delia said Now he had done it and they'd better find Nurse. Before he could protest she had hustled him in by the garden door and driven him up two flights of stairs, calling 'Nurse, Nurse' at the top of her voice.

'I'm not deaf, Miss Delia,' said Nurse, appearing at the top of the stairs. 'Why aren't you at lunch?'

'Oh, you know Hilary Grant,' said Delia, leading the way into Nurse's sitting-room, 'the one I told you about that's a sort of cousin. He was eating gooseberries and got his button off. Can you sew it on?'

'And you've got a great ladder in your stocking, Miss Delia,' said Nurse. 'You know what I said about those gooseberry bushes. Why can't you wait till Turpin picks them for the table? Go and change them at once.'

Delia said she hadn't a pair to wear except her good ones. Nurse with conscious magnanimity pointed to a pile of stockings on her table and said they were all mended and quite good enough for the garden. Delia, to Mr. Grant's embarrassment, immediately stripped off her stockings and, sitting on the table, put one one of the mended pairs, while, to his even greater embarrassment, Nurse, addressing him as Mr. — or possibly, he thought but couldn't be certain of it, Master — Hilary, told him to take his coat off.

'I'll get you one of Mr. Francis's to wear,' she said, 'and when you've finished lunch I'll have this nice and ready for you. You can wash in the bathroom here and there's a nail-brush on the shelf.'

With these humiliating words she drove Mr. Grant into a bathroom, doled him out a clean towel, and left him in such a state of terror that he spent two long minutes sitting on the side of the bath in case Nurse should think he wasn't having a thorough wash. When at last he ventured out he found Delia waiting for him with one of Francis's coats, and they ran downstairs together.

'Sorry we're late, Mother,' said Delia. 'Hilary felt sick, and we ate such a lot of gooseberries his buttons came off, so Nurse is mending them.'

Much to Mr. Grant's relief his hostess took no notice of this misleading statement and asked after his mother. As Mr. Grant had not heard from her since she went to Lady Norton this subject dropped at once.

'I say, Mother,' said Delia, 'you know that book Hilary was reading to you? Who do you think he's going to dedicate it to?'

On hearing this blatant exposition of his heart's secret, Mr. Grant went cold with anger and looked at Delia in a way intended to express his disapproval. Delia, a past mistress owing to long practice with her brother Francis in the art of making faces, took his look as a sign of friendliness and made a hideous face back at him.

'I can't think,' said Mrs. Brandon.

In despair Mr. Grant kicked Delia under the table, forming at the same time the word 'No' with his lips. Delia, realizing at last what he meant, said with great presence of mind that it was a deadly secret.

'Then I won't ask,' said Mrs. Brandon, including Mr. Grant in a motherly tolerance that made him wince. 'You must read some more to me, Hilary, as soon as we have a free evening.'

After lunch Mrs. Brandon went to rest, leaving Mr. Grant a prey to Delia, who challenged him to play croquet with some balls she had found in an old set of bowls, and they both laughed so much that Mr. Grant quite forgot literature and his consuming passion. Delia, while assuming airs of authority over him in ordinary life, showed a respect for his position as an author which made him feel delightfully grown-up, and he was almost sorry when the car came.

'Aren't you coming?' he asked her.

Delia said she loathed the old Abbey and hoped they'd have a jolly time. Mr. Grant was getting into the car where Mrs. Brandon was already seated, when Nurse came to the front door.

'Your coat, Mr. Hilary,' she said reproachfully.

'You'll hardly want another coat,' said Mrs. Brandon. 'It's such a hot day.'

Mr. Grant then had to explain that he had torn the button off his coat on the gooseberry bushes, and had furthermore to humiliate himself by getting out of the car, taking off Francis's coat and appearing in his shirt sleeves before his hostess and putting his own coat on again with Nurse's kind help.

'Thanks awfully,' he said, backing away from Nurse, who might, he felt, want to look at his nails, and got back into the car, all his grown-up self-confidence crushed. Mrs. Brandon, who was still sleepy after her rest, didn't talk much, and her unhappy young cousin, taking her silence for scorn, wished he were in the Foreign Legion.

When they got to Brandon Abbey they found Miss Morris in the drawing-room giving tea to a stranger whom she introduced as Mr. Merton.

'I've heard about you so much from the Keiths,' said Mrs. Brandon. 'Isn't Lydia rather a friend of yours? How is she?'

'Very well, I believe,' said Mr. Merton. 'I was down there for Kate's wedding, and Lydia trod on her own dress in church and ripped a large piece out of it just as the blessing was being given.'

'What happened?' asked Mrs. Brandon.

'Kate nearly didn't get married at all,' said Mr. Merton, 'because she heard the noise and knew what had happened and wanted to mend it, but luckily she was kneeling down and it all passed over.'

'I wish I had been there,' said Mrs. Brandon, 'but I was away. I adore weddings. They always make me cry.'

'Lydia cried like anything,' said Mr. Merton proudly. 'In fact she cried so much that I had to take her to see the Barchester Amateur Dramatic Society act *Ghosts*, and that cheered her up.'

While this innocent conversation was going on, Mr. Grant was a prey to black fury and despair. Here was a man, not more than a few years older than himself, talking away on terms of friendly intimacy to Mrs. Brandon, all because he knew some people called Keith, while he was despised and ignored and treated as a child. Probably this Mr. Merton, or whatever his name was, had come down to persuade Miss Brandon to make a new will leaving everything away from her niece, or to embezzle her money, or fraudulently convert, or one of those things that solicitors were always being had up for doing.

'Are you making a new will for Aunt Sissie?' asked Mrs. Brandon, with superb disregard of professional feeling. 'You are a lawyer, aren't you?'

'Only a barrister unfortunately,' said Mr. Merton, 'and as such not entitled to make people's wills. No, Miss Brandon is an old friend of my father's who is a solicitor, and has an annoying way of summoning me to give her advice that she never takes. What she wants me for this time I don't know. I'm staying with the Dean at Barchester. I hope she won't want to keep me long as I have to get back for tennis at six. How is the old lady?'

Mrs. Brandon appealed to Miss Morris, who said Miss Brandon had not been at all well, but seemed better to-day and would like to see Mr. Merton as soon as he had had tea.

'It seems very rude to keep you waiting, Mrs. Brandon,' she said, 'but Dr. Ford said she must be humoured as much as possible.'

Mrs. Brandon said she was in no hurry and as Francis had not yet come she would wait comfortably. So Miss Morris took Mr. Merton upstairs and Mrs. Brandon, lulled by tea and the hot afternoon, relapsed into a state of semi-consciousness, while the unhappy Mr. Grant, torn by hatred of Mr. Merton, looked at several large books illustrated by the late Gustave Doré, wishing for the first time in his life that he were an artist, so that he might express his feelings about his rival in an adequate manner. Presently Francis arrived and his mother partially woke up to tell him about Mr. Merton. Francis said he remembered him quite well at the Keiths, a very decent sort of fellow.

'And I hope he'll make Aunt Sissie leave everything to the Cats' Home,' he said, 'and serve us all right. What's that you're reading, Hilary? Doré? Those books used to frighten me out of my wits when I was small. There's a lovely one of Arachne turning into a spider with legs simply sprouting out of her. Let's look!'

'Do you remember that spider at Mr. Miller's?' said his mother, suddenly regaining complete consciousness.

'A fine British matron she was, too,' said Francis. 'I wonder what happened to her when you threw her out of the window. I expect she walked up the drain pipe and is lurking in your bedroom, Hilary. If she lets herself down from the ceiling onto your face one night, blame mamma.'

'That was the day we first met you, Hilary,' said Mrs. Brandon, turning her eyes upon her young relative, who could hardly restrain himself from crying aloud 'God bless you, Mrs. Brandon, for remembering that day.' But as Francis was in the room he did restrain himself, though for many days to come the mention of the word spider sent the blood coursing wildly through his veins.

'I can't think what Aunt Sissie wants to talk to Mr. Merton about,' said Mrs. Brandon.

'You aren't meant to, darling,' said Francis. 'That's why she had Merton to herself instead of having us all in the room at once. You can ask him if you like, but you won't get much change. Hullo, Merton,' he said, as that gentleman came in, 'here you are again. My dear mamma wants to know what devil's work you've been up to with the old lady.'

'Francis, you mustn't say things like that,' said his mother, roused and indignant.

'I am sure that Mrs. Brandon hasn't the faintest curiosity about our interview,' said Mr. Merton, with a kind of gallantry as from a man of the world to a woman of the world, over the heads of the youngsters, which Mr. Grant found inexpressibly galling. 'It was a small matter of business. Mrs. Brandon, I am so sorry to have to say good-bye, but I must go back to the Deanery.'

Mrs. Brandon shook hands and expressed the hope that Mr. Merton would come over and see her one day, an invitation which Mr. Grant considered, though showing a divine charity and tolerance, to be entirely misplaced.

'Yes, do,' said Francis. 'We can give you some fairly decent tennis.'

Mr. Merton said he would love to and would write to Mrs. Brandon, and so took himself off. Mrs. Brandon said to Francis what a charming person that Mr. Merton was and no wonder all the Keiths liked him so much. Francis quite agreed and Mr. Grant gave a hollow mockery of assent. Mrs. Brandon then wondered once more why Aunt Sissie wanted them all, yawned and gave it up. By the time that Francis and Mr. Grant had exhausted the pleasures of Doré Miss Morris came down again.

'Miss Brandon would be very glad if you could all come up now,' she said, 'and could I speak to you for a moment, Mrs. Brandon.'

Mrs. Brandon said she would come up with Miss Morris to the sitting-room and asked Francis to show Mr. Grant old Mr. Brandon's cabinet of dried seaweed and come upstairs in ten minutes.

'No, darling, not the seaweed,' said Francis. 'Hilary doesn't look strong enough. I'll show him the photographs of Venice in the red plush album. They have practically faded altogether so it won't be a tax on the intellect.'

When the ladies reached the sitting-room it was obvious to Mrs. Brandon that Miss Morris didn't know how to begin what she wanted to say. It seemed to Mrs. Brandon that every friend she had needed winding up before conversation became possible and she kindly applied herself to the task of winding Miss Morris up by asking whether her aunt had been more troublesome than usual. Miss Morris said, No, began to say something else, and stopped.

'Well, what is it?' asked Mrs. Brandon in desperation. 'Can I help you at all?'

'It seems a shame to trouble you when you have been so very, very kind to me,' said Miss Morris, 'but I couldn't bear you to misunderstand.'

Visions of Nurse, of Rose, of various holiday governesses, French, German and English, flitted through Mrs. Brandon's mind. All had adored her, all had made her life extremely uncomfortable by being jealous of each other and imagining that they had offended her by mistake, or that she was deliberately neglecting them. Nurse and Rose were made of sterner stuff, but all the governesses had cried and had orgies of reconciliation, and Mrs. Brandon had once in a fit of exasperation told Sir Edmund that she intended to go into a monastery. Sir Edmund had said he supposed she meant a nunnery and not to talk nonsense, but the idea of a world without women had often charmed her mind, not of course counting sensible women like herself and Mrs. Morland and the Dean's wife and a good many more. In Miss Morris she now recognized the stereotyped beginnings of a scene of unnecessary self-abasement which would leave the abased refreshed and strengthened and probably drive herself into a headache as bad as those brought on by being read aloud to.

But she looked at Miss Morris and thought of her dull life, her selfish old father, her poverty, and the really unselfish devotion she had shown to a very tyrannical, self-indulgent, bed-ridden old lady, and her kind heart melted.

'It wouldn't be a trouble at all,' she said, wondering whether she would be called upon to compose a misunderstanding between Miss Morris and the butler or the housekeeper, or whether Miss Brandon had for once been more outrageously rude than even a paid companion could bear.

'I don't know what you thought when you found Mr. Merton here,' said Miss Morris nervously, 'but I can assure you that I didn't know till this morning that he was coming. I usually write Miss Brandon's letters for her, but she must have written to him herself and given it to Sparks to post.'

'It was very nice to see Mr. Merton. I have always heard about him from the Keiths at Southbridge and wanted to meet him.'

'But I mean, I hope you didn't think that I had anything to do with his coming.'

If Mrs. Brandon had spoken the truth she would have said that she hadn't thought about it at all, but this would have implied an indifference to her anxious companion which she felt would at once be misinterpreted, so she said she was sure Miss Morris had known nothing about it.

Miss Morris looked grateful, said she couldn't bear to be misjudged, and stopped short, evidently in need of winding up again. Mrs. Brandon looked out of the window. The heat of the long summer afternoon had turned to an oppressive sultriness. The deep unclouded blue of the sky had changed to a fierce copper and though the sun was shining as brightly as ever the sunlight looked baleful. The great trees that surrounded the Abbey and clothed the rising ground before it stood out with unnatural clearness and above them a heavy mass of cloud was slowly rising. A spirit of wind, come and gone in the twinkling of an eye, troubled the tops of the high beeches, and Mrs. Brandon wondered whether that was a shiver of lightning that ran through the sky, just above the massing clouds. It appeared to her that storm outside and inside the house was to be expected, and with her instinct for making things as pleasant as possible she left the elements, which she could not control, to look after themselves, and turned to Miss Morris.

'This is quite an uncomfortable day for everyone,' she said, 'and I expect Aunt Sissie will make it even more uncomfortable, but it is a great comfort to have you here and we are all so grateful to you for being so good to Aunt Sissie.'

This, she hoped, would be enough to stem Miss Morris's uneasy desire to grovel, but Miss Morris, with a woman's passion for saying what is far better not put into words, could not be restrained.

'Of course I don't know why Miss Brandon wanted to see Mr.

Merton,' she said, 'but I do know that his father is her lawyer, and I couldn't bear it if you imagined – people in my position are exposed to all sorts of imaginings – it has happened before when my old ladies have been ill and relations are anxious about things – but I couldn't bear you to think anything like that.'

'But I don't,' said Mrs. Brandon, concealing her irritation quite heroically. 'I am perfectly sure that Aunt Sissie will always do exactly what she likes, and in any case what she does is her own affair and none of us will mind in the least what it is. If,' she continued, plunging to the heart of the subject as she heard the voices of the young men in the corridor, 'Aunt Sissie had just made a will and left the Abbey to you, or the Dean of Barchester, or the Salvation Army, we should be perfectly happy.'

'Of course Miss Brandon wouldn't do that,' said Miss Morris, flushing, 'but I did want you to feel that if she did consult Mr. Merton about any kind of change in her arrangements I knew nothing about it.'

'No one ever has known anything about Aunt Sissie's wills,' said Mrs. Brandon, 'if that is what you mean by arrangements, and I don't suppose they ever will. And now we will forget all about it.'

'I shan't forget your kindness,' said Miss Morris, and was so obviously about to say again that she couldn't bear Mrs. Brandon to think what she wasn't thinking, that it was a great relief when Francis and Mr. Grant came in. Miss Morris cast one look of slavish devotion towards Mrs. Brandon and disappeared into Miss Brandon's room.

'Hilary and I have been admiring the gorillas,' said Francis. 'They wear remarkably well. Do you remember when I put Aunt Sissie's Sunday hat on one of them and how furious she was? She ought to have one of them put up over her tomb; it would look very handsome. And don't tell me not to say that, mamma, because I have said it.'

'There is going to be a storm,' said Mrs. Brandon, looking again at the uneasy sky.

'Not just yet,' said Francis. 'It may even be one of those affairs that go rumble-bumbling all round the hills and then go off and blast an oak at the other end of the county and never come here at all. When does the fun begin?'

'If you mean Aunt Sissie, I don't suppose it will be very funny,' said Mrs. Brandon. 'From the state of poor Miss Morris's nerves I should think Aunt Sissie was in one of her bad moods. I only hope we shall get away before the storm, because I do hate noise.'

Miss Morris now reappeared and said Miss Brandon would like to see them, so they passed into the next room. As usual the blinds were lowered and the curtains half drawn, but Mrs. Brandon could see, even in that dim light, that her aunt was greatly changed. The old lady looked as indomitable as ever, but the marks of pain were very evident on her face and she was making an effort to sit up among her pillows.

Mrs. Brandon took her aunt's hand which lay cold and unresponsive in her own, and said how do you do.

'How do you expect me to do at my age?' said Miss Brandon. 'No, don't go away, Miss Morris. Didn't you hear me say I wanted you. Who is that there? Don't all stand where I can't see you. Oh, Francis. You get more like your father every time I see you, and a poor creature he was. And who is that? Here, young man, which of them are you?'

Mr. Grant, struck by the beauty of Mrs. Brandon's child-like fear of storms, had been plunged in an exquisite reverie, in the course of which he had been protecting his goddess from the bolts of Jove and she had hidden her lovely face against his shoulder as the thunder crackled and boomed around them. Just as he was saying to her, 'You have nothing to fear, Mrs. Brandon, while I am here,' he was rudely awoken by his cousin Francis hitting him in the ribs with his elbow and saying, 'It's Hilary, Aunt Sissie,' and in a lower voice, 'Wake up, you chump.'

'Hilary?' said the old lady. 'Edward Grant's son. Your mother has been writing to me, Hilary. She wants to come and see me. Tell her I won't see her. All I want is to die in peace, and you all come crowding into my bedroom.'

Each of Miss Brandon's visitors felt that this remark was very unfair. They had come at her summons, unwillingly, to satisfy the whim of an ill, lonely aunt, and to be accused of crowding her bedroom was hard to bear.

'I don't very well see how Hilary can tell his mother that,' said Mrs. Brandon. 'Let him say that you aren't well.'

'I was never better in my life,' said Miss Brandon angrily. 'I suppose the boy is frightened of his mother. Why don't you all sit down.'

Mrs. Brandon took an armchair near her redoubtable aunt's bed and the young men sat a little further away. Francis amused and already a little bored, Mr. Grant in a very uncomfortable turmoil of emotions. His aunt's words had gone too near the mark to be pleasant. If he dared to face facts he had to admit this, his mother had more power over him than he liked.

It was not that she made any very unreasonable demands, but her whole attitude to him was that any work he was doing was unimportant and he never felt safe from her unless she were abroad. His visits to Italy were a sacrifice, for he knew that he would never be allowed to work in peace, but with the good-nature that he inherited from his easy-going father he gave in to his mother's exigencies and managed to get his reading done early in the morning and late at night, and took a very tolerable degree. There had been one moment, at the memory of which he still was shaken with fear, when Mrs. Grant, after a quarrel with some Italian authorities, had thought of settling in Oxford, imagining that Hilary could live with her and as it were do his homework under her eye. Luckily this scheme had come to nothing and she had remained abroad, but in her short visit to Pomfret Madrigal she had managed to devastate his working hours with her demands that Hilary should walk with her, give her advice that she never took on her Italian affairs, tell her all about what he was reading, and worst of all dine with her at the Cow and Sickle and sit talking or rather being talked to, till the small hours of the morning. He had managed to get through these evenings by withdrawing his mind into itself and indulging in dreams of Mrs. Brandon, but he could not master the growing irritation that assailed him whenever he heard the clash of his mother's necklaces, or her voice calling gaily from the garden below his window with some caressing Italian diminutive, which would, he was sure, afford far too much pleasure to Mr. Miller's staff.

Again and again he blamed himself for these feelings of irritation, for ingratitude towards a mother who was very fond of him and supported him in comfort; repeatedly did he make good resolutions of patience and forbearance and self-control which broke down as soon as they were made. By the end of the week that his mother spent at the Cow and Sickle he was barely able to control his annoyance and had indeed so far forgotten himself once or twice as to give a snappy or sulky answer, which had caused him subsequent agonies of remorse and even indigestion. To all these emotions his mother was sublimely unconscious, and had now gone off to Lady Norton with the happy assurance that she had cheered up her son in his dull country retreat. As for his Aunt Sissie's remark he could only hope that neither of the Brandons would notice it, and went hot with shame and misery in the darkened room.

'Well,' continued the old lady, 'I suppose you all want to know why I sent for Noel Merton.'

Mr. Grant was too far sunk in misery to care. Francis said under his breath that he was damned if he did. Mrs. Brandon, with some vague, amorphous idea of saving the situation, was the only one with courage to answer.

'I have never met Mr. Merton before, Aunt Sissie,' she said, 'but I had heard about him a great deal from the Keiths at Southbridge. Young Colin Keith is reading law with him, and he was down there for Kate Keith's wedding. He was very amusing about Lydia. He really seems very delightful and I have asked him to come to Stories next time he is at the Deanery.'

During this quite unnecessary speech Miss Brandon had been eyeing her niece by marriage with a stony intensity that penetrated even Mrs. Brandon's placid mind. Her voice faltered and trailed away and she sat silent.

'I have said before and shall say it again,' said Miss Brandon, 'that you are one of the silliest women I know, Lavinia, and if Henry were here I should say there were a couple of you. I didn't send for you to hear about the wedding of some young woman in whom I have no interest at all. I have something to tell you and propose to tell it without further interruption.' She picked up some papers from the table by her bed and began sorting them. 'I can't see,' she said angrily. 'Pull the blind up, Miss Morris. How do you expect me to see in the dark?'

Miss Morris began to walk round the great bed to get to the window, but Francis, who was sitting near it, got up and pulled the blind cord.

'Not too much,' said his aunt warningly.

'Of course not, Aunt Sissie,' he said kindly. 'I think just like this will be enough for you. Hullo, there's a car at the front door.'

'A car?' said the invalid. 'Whose car? No one has any business to bring cars here.'

'I can't see whose, Aunt Sissie,' said Francis, 'except that it's a Rolls, but the county is rather well off in Rollses, so it might be anyone. I think cars ought to have the names of their owners painted very large on the roof so that one could see who is there and not open the front door.'

'Don't talk nonsense,' said the old lady. 'Cars indeed! When I was younger we knew all our friends' carriages by sight, and their horses and their coachmen and footmen. Go and see whose car it is, Miss Morris. I will not have cars in my drive.'

Miss Morris again started on her errand, but again was interrupted. There was a knock at the door and Sparks came in.

'Who is that?' said Miss Brandon. 'Oh, you, Sparks. Well, go and see what all this fuss is about a car at the front door. I will not have strange cars at the front door.'

'It is Lady Norton, miss,' said Sparks, 'and she wants to know how you are, and would like to come up and see you.'

'Tell her I'm quite well and seeing nobody,' said the invalid.

'I did, miss,' said Sparks, 'but there was another lady with her, miss, and she must see you because she wasn't in England for long.'

Mr. Grant knew that Providence had now reached the end of its tether. Nothing it chose to do to him in the future would have the slightest effect. Let it heap thunders, cataracts, mountains, whirlwinds on his devoted head, he would stand erect, shrug his shoulders and simply say 'Ha-ha.' Meanwhile he greatly wished that he could get under the bed or into a wardrobe, and become practically unconscious. Francis murmured 'Golly' in tones of deep appreciation and prepared himself to enjoy the scene.

'Tell Mrs. Grant I can't see anyone. I am very ill,' said Miss Brandon. 'Tell her at once, Sparks, and don't be a fool.'

Sparks looked nervously over her shoulder, opened her mouth, but never got as far as speech, for a noise was heard in the sitting-room, the door was opened, a voice said, 'I have come to see how you are, Amelia,' and in came a tall middle-aged woman in black, with the face

of a distinguished horse and the unmistakable air of authority that the
best garden in the county gives. Mrs. Brandon recognized Lady Norton
and felt that events were entirely out of control.

'Well, here I am, a dying old woman, Victoria,' said Miss Brandon,
'and now you can go away again.'

'Nonsense,' said Lady Norton. 'You need cheering up, Amelia. I see
you have some visitors. That's very sensible. And I have brought one
of my visitors over to see you; Felicia Grant, poor Edward's widow.'

Mrs. Grant, who had been almost hidden behind Lady Norton's
imposing bulk, came forward with a rattle of coral and amber.

'I have been looking forward to seeing you for a long time, Cousin
Sissie,' she said. 'Edward always wanted me to. So when Lady Norton
offered to bring me over, I came.'

The noble simplicity of this remark did not appear to affect Miss
Brandon, who very disconcertingly shut her eyes and made no reply.

'I was so glad that Hilary had been to see you,' Mrs. Grant continued,
'and what luck it is to find him here to-day, and Mrs. Brandon and
Francis.'

'I said I didn't want to see you,' said Miss Brandon, her eyes still
tightly shut, 'and I don't, and what's more I won't.'

'Come, come, Amelia,' said Lady Norton, who had been talking to
Mrs. Brandon, but the invalid remained silent and blind, merely expressing her dislike of her visitors by playing five finger exercises on her
sheet. Mrs. Brandon and Lady Norton tried to make a little conversation, but the weight of Miss Brandon's disapproval was too heavy and
their voices died away.

'Good-bye,' said Miss Brandon very distinctly.

Lady Norton said she supposed they had better be going. It was useless to try to shake hands with a hostess who was drumming on the
bedclothes with her eyes shut, so Lady Norton, not without dignity,
made her farewells to Mrs. Brandon and Francis, expressed pleasure at
having met Hilary, and retreated in good order, carrying Mrs. Grant
with her.

'See them out, Sparks,' said Miss Brandon, and Sparks followed the
visitors, shutting the door behind them.

'And now what have you all to say for yourselves?' said Miss Brandon,
opening her eyes and folding her bejewelled hands.

'Well, nothing, Aunt Sissie,' said Mrs. Brandon truthfully. 'We came
because you asked us to, and here we are. I expect you feel a little
tired now, so perhaps we'd better go.'

'Wait a moment,' said Miss Brandon. 'Put my pillows a little higher,
Miss Morris.'

Miss Morris came forward, re-arranged the pillows, and helped her
employer to raise her unwieldy bulk. The effort obviously cost Miss
Brandon a good deal of pain, but for once she made no complaint.

Only when the move was accomplished did she utter a kind of grunt and told Miss Morris to get the brandy quickly. Miss Morris measured a tablespoon in a medicine glass and gave it to Miss Brandon.

'And now,' said Miss Brandon, handing the glass back to Miss Morris, 'if you want to know why I asked you to come here it doesn't matter. Noel Merton knows what I had to say, and that's quite enough. I'm an ill old woman and if Victoria Norton sees fit to let fools come into my room and upset me, I can't be blamed for the consequences. Why poor Edward Grant married that woman I never could imagine. A pretentious, selfish woman if ever there was one. I told her I wouldn't see her and I didn't. You can blame your fool of a mother, Hilary Grant, for anything that happens now.'

Mr. Grant had been wishing that his mother had never been born, or were a thousand leagues away, but trying as she was, she was still his mother and all the chivalry in him was roused. It was not easy to defend what he secretly felt to be almost indefensible, or to hold his own against a domineering old lady who was quite capable of deliberately having a fit if crossed, and who had also expressed some liking for him. He longed for Francis's easy assurance, which might have turned the whole thing off as a joke and restored their aunt to some kind of good humour. A thousand years of fright, misery, indecision, seemed to him to have passed before he replied with the slight stammer that nervousness always made him produce.

'I'm sorry, Aunt Sissie, if mother coming upset you, but I expect she is pretty upset, too, and I'm going to see if she needs me, so good-bye.'

'I said the boy was frightened of his mother,' said Miss Brandon.

If an unseen enemy had suddenly hit Mr. Grant in the face he could hardly have suffered more. The knowledge that what his aunt said was partly true, his loyalty to his mother, the extreme distastefulness of the whole scene, the unreality of this half lighted room, the helpless, venomous old lady in the great bed, the consciousness that Mrs. Brandon and Francis and Miss Morris were spectators, however unwillingly, of his humiliation, even the increasing sultriness in the atmosphere outside, all were arrayed against him. As he spoke he was facing the window through which Francis had seen Lady Norton's car. The blind was still drawn up. Mrs. Brandon saw him turn so pale and then flush so deeply that she was afraid.

'Good-bye, Aunt Sissie,' he said again, and made a step towards the door, but Mrs. Brandon said 'Hilary' and slipped her arm through his, so that he had to stand still.

'Really, Aunt Sissie,' she said, 'Mrs. Grant may be a little trying, but after all if Lady Norton brought her she couldn't very well help it, and she is just as much a relation of yours as I am. It was nothing to do with Hilary at all. In fact it was really more Lady Norton's fault. So perhaps we had better all go now.'

No one in the room could quite appreciate the heroism underlying this unnecessary, muddle-headed and on the whole quite unhelpful speech. Francis thought, with amusement, that mother was trying to see everything in as pleasant a light as possible by burying her head in the sand. Mr. Grant, wishing that he could have a whole bottle of champagne, or mercifully faint, was only conscious that Mrs. Brandon was trying to defend him, and despised himself more than ever. Miss Morris was divided between anxiety for her difficult employer and nervousness at finding herself assisting at a family scene and it is probable that Miss Brandon herself was the only member of the party to appreciate her niece's courage, though she had no intention of admitting it.

'Don't be a fool, Lavinia,' she said sharply. 'Hilary is quite old enough to look after himself. He doesn't need a woman old enough to be his mother hanging round his neck.'

At these words Mr. Grant felt the hand that was laid on his arm tremble, though ever so slightly. He took it, pressed it in gratitude, and let Mrs. Brandon withdraw it. There was a moment's tense, uncomfortable silence, not improved by a sudden, aimless flash of lightning from the livid sky. Then Francis in a detached voice that barely concealed a white-hot fury said,

'I had better take mother home, Aunt Sissie, and I think it will be better if none of us come here again for the present. Do you agree, Hilary?'

Mr. Grant uttered a strangled Yes.

'Good-bye, Aunt Sissie,' said Francis. 'Good-bye, Miss Morris,' and he herded his mother and his cousin out of the room.

'Oh, Miss Morris, I left the apricot slip in a parcel on the hall table,' said Mrs. Brandon, turning in the doorway. 'It might just need taking up a little on the shoulders, but I do hope you'll like it.'

Miss Morris made a step towards Mrs. Brandon but a call from her employer stopped her, and Francis hustled his mother out and shut the door.

'Help me to lie down again,' said Miss Brandon.

With some difficulty the old lady was rearranged in bed.

'Pull that blind down again,' she said to her companion, 'and read to me for a little.'

Miss Morris took up the book on which they were engaged and began to read. Her employer lay very still and Miss Morris hoped she might be sleeping. When she came to the end of a chapter she paused. Miss Brandon still lay quiet and Miss Morris was assailed by a sudden fear that she might be in a faint, or even dying, after the conditions of the afternoon.

'I suppose you think I am a wicked old woman,' said Miss Brandon, without heat.

'I am afraid Mrs. Brandon will be very unhappy,' said Miss Morris.

'Not she,' said Miss Brandon. 'She has a mind like a feather-bed, always had. I wish I could think Edward's wife would be unhappy. What a conceited fool that woman is. I feel really sorry for Hilary.'

'Mr. Grant is very nice,' said Miss Morris non-committally, 'and so is Mr. Francis Brandon.'

'Oh, you are taking sides too, are you,' said Miss Brandon. 'Well, you can think what you like, but I have spoken my mind to Noel Merton and that's the end. Shut the window and turn the lights on. I can't bear thunder.'

Miss Morris did as she was told and came back to the bed. Her employer, her frilled nightcap a little askew, looked at her with an expression that she could not fathom, a compound of secrecy, amusement, and a tolerance that she was not used to.

'So you stick up for the Brandons, do you?' said the old lady. 'Very well, very well. You're not the first one that has liked Lavinia Brandon, though she is nearly as big a fool as Edward's wife. Fred would have liked Lavinia. That's why I gave her his diamond ring. She is like Mrs. Colonel Arbuthnot that Fred got into such hot water over. She was a fool too, but as pretty as they make them. Yes, Fred would have liked her to have the ring and a good deal more besides,' said Miss Brandon with a chuckle of terrifying archness. 'Go on reading. It keeps the thunder out of my head. Fred wouldn't have looked at you.'

'No, I suppose not,' said Miss Morris.

'But someone else might,' said Miss Brandon, 'when I'm dead. Go on with the book. I think I shall fancy my dinner to-night.'

Miss Morris, puzzled, but resigned to the ways of her old ladies, went on reading. Outside the lightning leapt, the thunder crackled and boomed, the rain came down in torrents.

The Brandons and Mr. Grant found speech extremely difficult as they went downstairs and into the drawing-room. Mrs. Brandon didn't really mind being called a fool, a name which her aunt freely bestowed upon her on various occasions, and confessed very simply in her own heart that she was one. But to see poor Hilary, who was already so nervous that one often couldn't quite make out what he was saying, and stammered so much over reading his book aloud that one often thought of other things, so baited and badgered, was more than one could bear. Aunt Sissie calling one old enough to be his mother didn't matter, because one was, and the statement was perfectly reasonable, but that he should hear himself accused of sheltering behind her and feeling it with all his sensitiveness made her really angry. In fact when Aunt Sissie let loose those words she had been so shaken by sudden anger that it took Hilary's kind pressure of her hand to make her control herself. Such fresh annoyance surged up in her that she felt she would like to be very cross with someone, a feeling very alien to her gentle nature.

Nor was Mr. Grant less furious. His mother had been insulted, not but what she jolly well deserved it for coming meddling with everyone and he wished fervently for the hundredth time that she had stayed in Calabria, but still she was his mother. And far, far worse, Mrs. Brandon had been insulted. She had tried to prevent his leaving his aunt in anger, she had taken his arm, she had said 'Hilary,' enduring his name with a magic that he had never before known it to possess, she had tried to protect him, she, an exquisite delicate creature, unfitted for harshness and brutal words. When Miss Brandon called her a fool, he had felt her hand tremble. Good God! that such a woman should be tortured on his account. Blast Aunt Sissie! Blast his mother for bringing shame on him and shame on the woman he respectfully adored! Blast everything! He kicked violently at a hassock, which hit a hideous vase that stood against the wall with peacocks' feathers in it and knocked it over.

'Here, look out,' said Francis sharply, for in spite of his assurance he was still fuming with suppressed rage at his aunt's rudeness to his mother and ready to fall foul of anyone. 'Look out. You needn't break Aunt Sissie's things, even if she is an old devil. Yes, Mother, I said devil and I meant it, and if you don't like it I can't help it.'

'Oh, all right, all right,' said Mr. Grant. 'I haven't broken the beastly thing and I don't want to. I wouldn't touch anything in this house with a barge pole.'

'Well, no one asked you to,' said Francis, and then the heavens suddenly opened and the thunder resounded from the roof-tree, the lightning looked as if it were going to shrivel every tree in the garden, and rain came down hissing and bubbling and steaming.

'Shall we have to drive home through this?' asked Mrs. Brandon.

'Well, there isn't any other way,' said Francis, 'and I'm not going to stop in this house if I were paid for it. Isn't Curwen round with the car? I told them to tell him.'

He rang the bell impatiently and repeated his inquiry. It was then revealed by the butler that Curwen had understood Mr. Francis to say he was going to drive Mrs. Brandon and Mr. Grant back in his own car, and so had taken Mrs. Brandon's car home.

'All right,' said Francis. 'Of course the roof leaks and I haven't got a spare tyre, but that's all part of the fun. Come along, Mother.'

Mr. Grant rushed into the hall, wildly hoping to put a coat about Mrs. Brandon and shelter her from the storm as she went down the steps, or perish in the attempt, but was immediately frustrated by the butler, who produced an enormous carriage umbrella and held it over her head.

'You'd better get in behind, Mother,' said Francis, 'it doesn't leak so much there. You come in front, Hilary, and keep the windscreen wiper going, because it usually sticks.'

Luckily the temperature had not dropped with the rising storm and Mrs. Brandon in the back seat of the car, where the leak was barely perceptible, was warm enough, and would have been quite comfortable had not her jangled nerves decided that Francis was driving too fast and taking unnecessary risks. In a crescendo of hysteria she gave instructions to her son which though they drove him nearly mad he bore very well. Even Mr. Grant, occupied as he was in pushing the reluctant windscreen wiper to do its duty, in avoiding the steady drip that fell onto the seat between him and Francis, felt a slight irritation mingle with his adoration. By the time they had got through Barchester, skidding on the tram lines, both young men were with difficulty restraining their temper. At Stories Mr. Grant got quickly out and ran round to open the car door, but again was thwarted by Rose, who descended, umbrella and raincoat in hand and assisted her mistress into the house.

'I don't suppose you mind if I don't drive you home,' said Francis. 'I want to put my car away and blow Curwen up. I'm sopped as it is. Why you couldn't catch some of that drip in your hat or something I don't know. And mother cackling like a hen all the time. She's as bad as yours.'

Without a word Mr. Grant turned away and walked into the rainy evening, with such thoughts in his mind as he did not care to examine. He found that Mr. Miller was dining at the Deanery and Cook, misunderstanding his instructions, had let the kitchen fire out, and Hettie had gone home. Mr. Grant said he didn't want any dinner and banged out of the house again. Cook with kindly tolerance put the cold ham and loaf and butter in the dining-room, and when Mr. Grant came in a little later, defeated by the weather and wetter than ever, he was glad to partake of it. When Mr. Miller came back at eleven o'clock he found his pupil so hard at work that he very kindly didn't tell him how he had put the Dean down on a quotation from St. Augustine, and went rather disappointed to bed, hoping that his unselfishness might be counted to him for righteousness and then reproaching himself for the hope.

Meanwhile Francis, having failed to find Curwen, who was at the Cow and Sickle playing darts with Mr. Spindler and Wheeler from the garage, dressed very crossly for dinner, at which meal Delia appeared with red eyes and a swollen face. She had, she explained, been over to Grumper's End to see how the chicken pox was getting on, and on the way back a field mouse had somehow got under her bicycle and been killed. First Aid was of no avail for a squashed mouse, and she said, and indeed looked it, that she had been crying ever since. Mrs. Brandon was very sorry about the mouse, but felt compelled to speak to her son Francis again about his driving, thus causing Francis, who hardly ever lost his temper, to have the sulks. Any discussion of the dreadful afternoon they had gone through became impossible and when after dinner Delia, to show her grief, put on all the most depressing crooners' records, it seemed a suitable end to a very unsuccessful day. About half-past nine Sir Edmund looked in and Delia was told to stop playing the gramophone.

'Well Lavinia,' said Sir Edmund, 'had a good day, eh? How's Amelia Brandon?'

To the best of her ability Mrs. Brandon described the scene in Miss Brandon's bedroom and expressed the view that if Miss Brandon ever was going to leave anyone anything she now wouldn't, and that she, Mrs. Brandon, would be very glad if the Abbey and all the money went to the Salvation Army, so long as she might never hear of it again.

'Mustn't say that, Lavinia. Not the way to talk at all,' said Sir Edmund. 'And what's the matter with Delia, eh? Got a cold? Nasty things colds at this time of year.'

Mrs. Brandon was just going to explain what had happened when Nurse appeared at the door. Seeing Sir Edmund she prepared to withdraw with such ostentatious discretion that her mistress was obliged to ask what the matter was.

'It's only Miss Delia's knickers, madam,' said Nurse in a stage whisper. 'I'd be glad if she could come and try them on before she goes to bed so that I can finish them to-night.'

'Go along then, darling,' said Mrs. Brandon, 'and perhaps you'd better not come down again if you are too unhappy.'

Delia, sniffing loudly, left the room in Nurse's wake.

'Well, I won't be staying,' said Sir Edmund, not enjoying this depressing domestic atmosphere. 'Good night, Lavinia.'

'Need you go?' said Mrs. Brandon, stretching out a hand towards Sir Edmund.

'Now don't try your tricks on me, Lavinia,' said Sir Edmund. 'See you again soon. Good night. Good night, Francis.'

Francis took Sir Edmund to the door. When he got back to the drawing-room he met Rose leaving it with an expression of injured but triumphant virtue.

'Anything up with Rose?' he asked his mother.

'Yes. Nurse's sewing machine has gone wrong, and she asked Rose to lend her the kitchen machine and Rose says she supposes Nurse must have it.'

'That's all right then,' said Francis.

'Yes, but Nurse won't come down and fetch it, and Rose won't carry it up, and the housemaids are out till half-past ten.'

Francis looked at his mother. Then, for the first time since they left Miss Brandon's room, he began to laugh. His mother began to laugh too.

'Well, to hell with old Mother Grant for all the trouble she has brought on us to-day,' said Francis. 'Go along to bed, darling, and I'll put the lights out. What a day! What a day!'

VII

BAD NEWS AT STORIES

BY THE following morning the storm had rumbled itself away and the weather was as brilliant and hot as ever, though with a pleasant rain-washed freshness. Francis, strolling into the garden before breakfast, was seized by Turpin and taken to admire the giant marrow which had apparently put on several pounds in the night. Turpin expressed the opinion that by the day of the Harvest Festival she would be a whopper.

'When is the Festival?' Francis asked.

Turpin told him the date, a few weeks ahead, and said he also intended to send up some flowers and garden produce for the Feet.

'Good Lord, yes, the Feet,' said Francis. 'That's Saturday week, isn't it? I must lay in some threepences for the coconuts and whatnots.'

Turpin said he didn't hold with them new threepennies, characterizing them as mucky.

'Hardly the mot juste for a nice new shining three-pence,' said Francis, 'but never mind. Good luck with the marrow.'

He went back to the house. His mother was having breakfast in her room and he was able to tell Delia, now happily recovered from the death of the field mouse, all about the scene at the Abbey. Delia listened with great interest.

'I wish I'd been there,' she said. 'I'd have asked to look at Aunt Sissie's legs. That would have calmed her down all right. You haven't seen them, have you?'

Francis shudderingly said he hadn't, and didn't wish to discuss the matter at breakfast.

'It was the time I went alone with mother, when you were in France. They were simply *ghastly*,' said Delia with simple enthusiasm, 'and she was ever so bucked at my seeing them. But she had no business to come down on Hilary. If I'd been there I'd have stopped it.'

'Poor old Hilary,' said Francis. 'It was tough luck to be told you are frightened of one woman and sheltering behind another. He looked pretty rotten.'

'Poor Hilary,' Delia echoed, with almost as much compassion as she had shown for the mouse.

'But mother stood up for him like a Trojan,' said Francis. 'I really thought he might be going to faint or something, he looked so queer. He doesn't know Aunt Sissie as well as we do. I must say I got annoyed myself when she started letting off at mother. Next time Aunt Sissie wants to be rude she can just be rude to old Sparks, or Miss Morris. I'm not going there again. Well, I must be off.'

He kissed the top of his sister's head and went off to Barchester.

Delia remained at the breakfast table, considering what Francis had said. The thought of Aunt Sissie bullying Hilary made her unaccountably angry. He was so obviously the sort that couldn't look after himself. People who wrote books might be brainy, but they were never quite all there in Delia's opinion, and needed someone with some sense to look after them. It had been just like mother to try to help anyone who was in trouble, but Delia felt that if she had been there she would not only have protected Hilary just as well, but have carried the war into the enemy's country and routed Aunt Sissie thoroughly.

As she was thinking these thoughts she looked up and saw Mr. Grant walking about in the drive.

'Hullo, Hilary,' she yelled out of the window. 'Hang on a moment and I'll come out.'

She bolted the rest of her toast and marmalade, took two peaches and went into the garden.

'Have a peach,' she said, handing one to Mr. Grant. 'You'd better put your face well forward while you eat it, or it'll run all down your front.'

Mr. Grant took her advice and the peaches were eaten.

'Francis was telling me about Aunt Sissie,' said Delia. 'What a beast she must have been. Francis said he thought you were going to pass out.'

'I simply couldn't bear her being so rude to your mother,' said Mr. Grant.

'Oh, mother's all right,' said Delia, with the fine confidence of the young that their elders have no feelings at all. 'She never much notices what Aunt Sissie says.'

Mr. Grant felt sorry that Mrs. Brandon's daughter should be so entirely destitute of sensibility.

'I'll tell you what I wish,' said Delia. 'I wish Aunt Sissie had thrown her stick at you and broken your arm or your leg. Then they'd have had to send for Dr. Ford to set it, and I'd have come and helped him. I'm awfully good at that sort of thing. And then I'd have told Aunt Sissie exactly what we all thought of her.'

She gazed at her cousin with an intensity which made him feel that she might rush at him and fracture one of his limbs for the sheer pleasure of helping Dr. Ford to set it.

'When Herb Thatcher, that's Jimmy Thatcher's brother down at Grumper's End, broke his arm, I was there and made a splint till the doctor came. It was splendid. But it wasn't Dr. Ford, and the other man set it wrong and I got Mrs. Thatcher to let Dr. Ford see it, and they had to take Herb to the Barchester Hospital and break it again and re-set it, and they wouldn't let me come and see,' said Delia with sad indignation.

'Do you think your mother is in?' said Mr. Grant.

'Of course,' said Delia, not at all surprised that her cousin wanted her mother rather than herself. 'I expect she's up now. Come and look.'

She led the way into the hall. Mrs. Brandon was just hanging up the telephone receiver. There was on her face a peculiar expression of self-consciousness and amusement and a little pride which Mr. Grant couldn't understand, but which if Sir Edmund had been there, he would infallibly have diagnosed as Lavinia up to her tricks again.

'Good morning, Hilary,' she said. 'I do hope you didn't get wet last night.'

'Not a bit,' said Mr. Grant untruthfully.

'That was Mr. Merton, that we met at the Abbey,' said Mrs. Brandon. 'He rang up to say how sorry he was he couldn't get over to see us, but he wants to come next time he is at the Deanery or the Keiths. You'd like him Delia.'

'Well, I think I'd better go back and do some work,' said Mr. Grant, hating people who rang people up and said they would come and see them.

'Oh, must you?' said Mrs. Brandon. 'I thought perhaps you were going to read to me.'

'Well, I had got a few pages on me,' said Mr. Grant, going scarlet. 'I was just walking about a bit and saw Delia, so I came in. I hope you don't mind.'

'Always come in,' said Mrs. Brandon. 'I've got to see Cook and do a few things, but do read to Delia, and then I'll join you later.'

So saying she drifted away to her sitting-room, still wearing her peculiar happy, mischievous smile. Mr. Grant gazed longingly after her.

'Will you really read me some of your book?' asked Delia humbly.

'Would you really like it?' asked Mr. Grant, with almost equal diffidence.

'Rather. I've never had a real book read to me,' said Delia, apparently thinking that manuscript made a book more real than print.

'Well, it isn't exactly a *real* book,' said Mr. Grant. 'I mean it hasn't been published or anything and I daresay it never will be.'

'Of course it will,' said Delia. 'All books get published. Just look what loads there are of them.'

On hearing these encouraging words Mr. Grant's opinion of his cousin rose considerably, and accompanying her to a bench in the garden he began reading. Curiously enough it seemed easier to read to Delia than to her mother. Although he missed Mrs. Brandon's inspiration he found that it was pleasant not to be interrupted and pleasant to have an audience that paid attention to what one was reading. He also discovered that Delia, who had spent a year in Paris with a family, had read a great deal of the romantic school of poetry and actually knew one poem of Jehan le Capet's which was in an anthology. All this was balm to an author and disposed him to regard his cousin even more favourably.

Delia, flattered beyond words at Hilary's condescension, drank in every sentence, admired Hilary's French accent, which was indeed very good, and secretly determined to boast to her friend Lydia Keith when next they met of how her cousin who was an author had read aloud a real book to her that no one else had heard.

'Shall I go on?' asked Mr. Grant when he had come to the end of the third chapter.

'I'd love it, but I don't think I could *bear* it,' said Delia, who was nearly bursting with admiration of the writing and sentimental pity for le Capet, whose fourth mistress had just abandoned him for an elderly commis voyageur, taking with her his mother's portrait and ninety francs. And Mr. Grant not only understood this peculiar tribute, but was pleased by it.

'It is a bit powerful,' he admitted. 'Perhaps a bit too powerful. I wonder if the public will stand it. But one must tell the truth at all costs.'

Delia said one must, and both young people fell silent, reflecting upon the beauty of this axiom, till Mrs. Brandon drifted out to them and asked if the reading had begun. On hearing that it was over she sat down on the bench and said how nice and wouldn't they like to get some gooseberries.

Mr. Grant was just elaborating in his mind a plan for picking a dozen of the largest and ripest gooseberries and bringing them to Mrs. Brandon on a particularly fine rhubarb leaf, when Rose came out to say that Dr. Ford wanted to speak to Mrs. Brandon. She was closely followed by Dr. Ford himself, whose determination to go and find Mrs. Brandon in the rose garden was as great as Rose's determination to keep the flag of convention flying by announcing him properly.

'Come and have some gooseberries, Dr. Ford,' said Delia. 'There are some lovely red ones that burst all over you.'

'No thanks,' said Dr. Ford. 'I've been at the Abbey this morning and as I had to go over to Southbridge I thought I'd look in and tell you I don't like the look of things.'

'Do you mean Aunt Sissie is worse?' asked Mrs. Brandon.

Dr. Ford said he had sent for a nurse and wouldn't be surprised if she didn't last out the night.

'How dreadful,' said Mrs. Brandon. 'You don't think we killed her, do you, Dr. Ford?'

'I shouldn't think so,' said Dr. Ford. 'Did you try to?'

'No, no,' said Mrs. Brandon, 'but we were there yesterday and she was very mysterious, and when Lady Norton and Mrs. Grant came it was really quite unpleasant, and Hilary really behaved very well, with the storm working up all the time, and I was afraid she might feel it.'

'I'm glad I'm not having to cross-examine you, Mrs. Brandon,' said Dr. Ford. 'Grant, you seem to have been there. Can you tell me what really happened?'

Mr. Grant explained that Miss Brandon had apparently been going to tell them something about her testamentary disposition when Lady Norton and his mother, for whom Miss Brandon had a strong dislike, had more or less forced their way in and been summarily ejected.

'And then Aunt Sissie was *beastly* to Hilary,' Delia broke in indignantly. 'Francis told me, and he said Hilary behaved splendidly.'

'You needn't be alarmed,' said Dr. Ford. 'The old lady thrives on rows, and one more or less wouldn't hurt her, in fact it probably bucked her up. Judging from what Miss Morris told me about the supper she insisted on eating last night I should say it was the effect of acute indigestion on a weak heart. I'm going to see her again this evening and I'll ring you up.'

He then departed as unceremoniously as he had arrived, followed by Rose's silent scorn.

The immediate and peculiar effect of this news was to make Mrs. Brandon suddenly become an invalid and the centre of attraction. Mr. Grant and Delia didn't know what to say, both secretly feeling the deep resentment of the young that their elders should do anything disturbing or unusual. This sentiment in Delia's case was complicated by a burning desire to be in at the death, if death there was to be, combined with a certain diffidence in mentioning her wish and the conviction that her mother would not allow it. The tension was broken by the arrival of Nurse, holding something pink.

'I'm sure I didn't know you weren't alone, madam,' she said, looking right through Mr. Grant in a disconcerting way, 'or I wouldn't have come out. I saw Dr. Ford with you and I said to myself I won't go down just now as Dr. Ford is with madam and then I saw him go so I said Well now madam is alone it will be a good chance to show her Miss Delia's —'

'Dr. Ford brought some very upsetting news, Nurse,' said Mrs. Brandon, automatically drooping like the flower which the rough ploughshare had touched. 'Miss Brandon is very ill again and he is afraid she won't last out the night.'

'Oh dear, I *am* shocked about that,' said Nurse, in intense enjoyment. 'Shall I get you a cushion, madam?'

'Thank you so much, Nurse,' said Mrs. Brandon in a dying voice.

'Couldn't I go and get it?' asked Mr. Grant, longing to be of some use and atone for his share in yesterday's crime.

'No, I'll look after madam,' said Nurse in her most nursish voice. 'You and Miss Delia go along now, Mr. Hilary. There's some nice gooseberries ripe under the nets.'

Not otherwise had Mr. Grant been addressed in his early youth by his own Nannie when she told him not to bother her asking questions but run along and play. Bitterly did he resent the implication that he was worse than useless in a moment of crisis, but realizing that the rites of the Bona Dea were about to be accomplished he felt he would be safer elsewhere and looked at Delia for help.

'You can just stay here a minute while I get a cushion,' said Nurse, and sped away to the house.

'I say, I'm awfully sorry,' said Mr. Grant.

Mrs. Brandon closed her eyes, looking, as Mr. Grant put it to himself, like a martyred saint, and murmured:

'Come and see me this afternoon, Hilary. I shan't be so silly then.'

At these beautiful and unselfish words Mr. Grant's heart swelled to such an extent that he was nearly choked, but Nurse's return dispelled romance and he gladly followed Delia to the gooseberry nets.

'It seems so sudden,' said Mrs. Brandon. 'Thank you, Nurse, that cushion is just what I wanted.'

As her aunt had been bed-ridden with a weak heart and might have died at any moment for several years, this remark was a tribute rather to her own imagination than to any actual fact, but Nurse thoroughly agreed with her, adding that her own stepsister, who was thirty years older than she was, had been taken just like that.

'I'd like to get you some sherry or something, madam,' said Nurse, 'but I don't like to leave you.'

Mrs. Brandon with rare heroism said she was all right and only needed to pull herself together and get over it, when by a heaven-sent chance Cook came into the garden to speak to her mistress about making some gooseberry jam.

'Oh, Cook,' said Nurse, who was surveying her cushion-supported mistress with the air of an artist, 'I'm so glad you're come. Dr. Ford had some shocking news. It seems poor Miss Brandon is taken worse and they don't expect she'll last the night. I was just going to ask Rose to get a glass of sherry for madam, but I didn't like to leave her.'

'Well, I am sorry, mum,' said Cook, who had never seen Miss Brandon and only heard of her as a paragon of bad temper. 'The poor old lady. That's what my tea-leaves meant last night. You remember, Nurse, when you was in the kitchen about Rose's machine, I said there was a funeral in my cup.'

Nurse said she well remembered, and how it had given her quite a funny feeling, for which she could not at the moment account, but which in the light of subsequent events was all too clear, and that they did say the tea-leaves never lied. But there she was standing chattering, she exclaimed, suddenly taking on the bright air of the professional nurse, when what madam needed was a glass of sherry.

'I couldn't touch sherry,' said Mrs. Brandon weakly. 'Do you think, Cook, I could have a cup of tea?'

Cook, seeing the chance of a lifetime to get in first with a really exciting piece of news, said she would have the kettle boiling in a moment and tell Rose to get the tray ready. She had left the kettle, she

said, nearly on the boil, because she was going to scald the tomatoes for
the salad which was much the easiest way to get their skins off, so if she
ran back it would be just on the boil, only she must hurry, because when
a kettle had come to the boil the water wasn't the same and she wouldn't
like to keep madam waiting while she filled the kettle and brought it
up to the boil again. Nurse, who had been torn between a wish to be
the first to bear the glad tidings to the kitchen and a feeling that she
would have scored heavily against Rose by being the first to succour her
mistress, decided to keep her position of vantage, and encouraged Cook
to go back and get the tea as soon as possible. The kettle must have been
exactly on the boil, for in an incredibly short space of time Rose
appeared, carrying a tray. Sinking their differences in the face of the
common danger, she and Nurse united in tending their mistress, sparing
her every effort except that of actually swallowing the tea. Mrs. Brandon,
who was very much enjoying the fuss and feeling extremely well, then
dismissed her attendants and went back to the house. Both the hand-
maids besought her to have a nice lay down before lunch, but finding
her obdurate they retired to the kitchen, loud in praise of her courage.
Class distinctions were for once entirely broken down and the whole
staff discussed the enthralling news over cups of tea and jam tarts. The
general opinion was that Mrs. Brandon would immediately inherit a
sum varying from two to twenty millions and go to live at the Abbey. If
this happened, said Cook, she would give notice, because there were no
buses within half a mile and they said the bedrooms were shocking. The
kitchenmaid said she had heard that if you hadn't any near relations the
Government took it all, but otherwise no untoward incident marred
the general excitement and content till a quarter past twelve, when
Cook said What about her lunch and what a mercy it was cutlets.

Mrs. Brandon and her daughter were alone at lunch. Delia suggested
in an off hand way that it might be a tactful thing to go over and inquire
about Aunt Sissie, secretly hoping to see if not a corpse at least a death
agony, but receiving no encouragement she dropped the subject, and
she and her mother discussed the Fête, for which it was Mrs. Brandon's
custom to provide a stall with home-made cakes and jam and such
garden produce as Turpin saw fit to release.

Meanwhile, through the agency of every tradesman who came to the
kitchen door, through Turpin and the garden boy when they went
home to dinner, through Nurse having to run down on her bike to
match up some more pink sewing silk, through the Vicar's Hettie who
had no business to be in Mrs. Brandon's kitchen at all, the delightful
tidings were spread far and wide. Dr. Ford on his way to Southbridge
passed Sir Edmund, who was having words with a foreman about the
repairs to a cottage, and stopped for a moment to tell him the old lady was
sinking, and it was only by the special mercy of Providence that he missed
meeting Lady Norton in the chemist's at Southbridge by five minutes.

Owing to a report of midges in the garden Mrs. Brandon decided to have tea in the drawing-room. She had hardly begun when Rose brought Mr. Miller in, with the air of a junior priest leading the first sacrifice to the altar.

'I cannot tell you,' said Mr. Miller, holding her hand a little longer than was strictly necessary, 'how grieved I am by this news.'

'What news?' asked Mrs. Brandon, who had really forgotten about her aunt since lunch-time.

'I am not misinformed, I hope,' said Mr. Miller anxiously, and feeling even as he spoke that the phrase might have been more happily turned. 'Hilary told me at lunch that your aunt had been taken seriously ill.'

Such is the power of suggestion that Mrs. Brandon at once languished, thus causing Mr. Miller severely to blame himself for gross want of consideration.

'Poor Aunt Sissie,' she sighed. 'Tell me, Mr. Miller, do you think six of Cook's pound cakes and about six dozen of her cream puffs would do for the cake stall? I shall get the rest of the things from Barchester.'

'You always send exactly what is right,' said Mr. Miller, admiring the courage that could deal with daily life while an aunt lay danger-ously ill. 'Do you think I could be of the slightest use to Miss Brandon? I would not, of course, for the world interfere, but if I could be of any comfort I would willingly go over.'

'How nice of you,' said Mrs. Brandon, 'but I really don't think you could do much. Miss Morris is there, and Dr. Ford has sent a very good nurse, and he is looking in himself this evening.'

'I was speaking less as a friend than as a priest,' said Mr. Miller, and then wondered if he had been harsh.

'Oh, I see what you mean,' said Mrs. Brandon. 'That is very nice of you, but I'm afraid Aunt Sissie has a kind of feeling about clergymen. She has quarrelled with every rector and with the Bishop and even with the Dean who is so kind. But you will see us all at Church on Sunday as usual,' she added, by way of appeasing Mr. Miller.

Mr. Miller gave it up and ate chocolate cake.

'I don't know,' he said when he had finished, 'if it would interest you at all to hear a little more of my Donne. The typescript has gone to the publishers, but I have a carbon copy which is quite legible in parts. We all have our pet economies and I fear that one of mine is carbon paper, which I use far too long.'

'Mine is tissue paper,' said Mrs. Brandon, her face and voice assum-ing an animation hitherto lacking. 'I keep every scrap that comes in parcels, but even so I can hardly keep pace with Rose. She uses such a lot when she packs for me. But I have freed myself from the tyranny of string.'

'The tyranny of string?' the Vicar repeated.

'You know,' said Mrs. Brandon earnestly, 'how one keeps all the bits of string off parcels and puts it away in little circles that are always coming undone?'

The Vicar said indeed, indeed he did.

'Well, when I get a parcel now, I simply cut the string and throw the bits into the waste-paper basket,' said Mrs. Brandon proudly.

'And what do you do for string then?' asked Mr. Miller.

'I buy it,' said Mrs. Brandon, with a slight air of bravado. 'You just cut off what you want, and it lasts for quite a long time.'

Mr. Miller, much impressed, said he must try that, and was just going to re-introduce the subject of Donne when Delia came in with Mr. Grant.

'Oh, Mother,' said she, 'oh hullo, Mr. Miller, I met Hilary in the drive, so I brought him up to tea. Chocolate cake!'

'You said I might come this afternoon,' said Mr. Grant, noticing with pleasure that his hostess seemed to have recovered from the shock of Dr. Ford's news. But at the same moment she remembered it and assumed a stricken air that wrung Mr. Grant's withers.

'I say, Mother,' said Delia, who was cutting chocolate cake in a most unfair way, giving herself far more icing than her rightful share, 'Hilary read aloud some of his book to me this morning. It's ripping. I loved that poem, Hilary, about

> Proie sanglante d'une fière et mâle rage,
> Dieu châtré des chrétiens, je crache à ton visage.'

This couplet, delivered in excellent French with a fine melodramatic rendering, was hardly what one would in one's calmer moments choose to recite to one's Vicar, but Delia was assailed by no such scruples. Mr. Miller was wondering whether he ought to make a protest, or pretend, thus sacrificing his reputation as a scholar, that he hadn't understood, when Delia, pleased with her own voice, continued,

'When I was young and did that thing of Villon's about the Neiges d'Antan I always thought châtré meant punished. I suppose I was mixing it up with châtié, and no one ever told me. What a lot of words there are in French.'

This last remark gave the opportunity to her paralysed audience, all of whom remembered having made the same mistake and no one ever telling them, to change the subject. Hilary hastily said that Italian had an enormous number of words, and Mr. Miller extolled the vocabulary of the ancient Romans.

'I think German is the worst,' said Mrs. Brandon, 'not that I know any Latin. It is really nothing but words. If you try to read a German book you spend all your time looking up words, and there doesn't seem to be any special reason for them to mean anything and the minute you have looked them up you forget what they mean. And they all begin with a prefix or a suffix.'

'I hope the news of Aunt Sissie isn't any worse,' said Mr. Grant.

Mrs. Brandon, who was leaning back in her chair after the arduous duty of pouring out tea, suddenly sat up.

'If anything happened,' she said, impressively, 'I believe I haven't got a single thin black frock.'

'Oh, Mother,' said Delia. 'There's that one with the pleated skirt.'

'Delia darling, it is a *rag*. One couldn't wear that frock even in church. You know what I mean, don't you, Mr. Miller? And you haven't anything at all, Delia, except that coat and skirt. I must have a talk to Nurse. Oh dear!'

Both gentlemen felt a surge of resentment against Miss Brandon who by her illness was causing anxiety to so exquisite a creature. Conversation rippled spasmodically over hidden depths. What every person in the room wanted to discuss was whether Miss Brandon was going to die this time and what the contents of her will would be, but everyone felt that at such a time it would not be quite nice. Even Mrs. Brandon felt a slight constraint and asked Mr. Miller if he wouldn't read aloud to them. This chance was not to be neglected and drawing his typescript from his pocket, Mr. Miller cleared his throat.

'Will you go on from where we left off?' asked Mrs. Brandon.

Mr. Miller, who had altered one or two commas since the last reading and wanted to hear how they sounded, said it would perhaps be more interesting for Delia and Hilary if he went back to the beginning. This would have been all very well with the original typescript, but as the first few pages of the carbon copy happened to be particularly blurred, he made but little headway. He apologized for his halting delivery by explaining that he had used the same sheet of carbon which had already served for typing out notices of the Fête and by plunging back into his text just managed to stop Mrs. Brandon telling everyone what she did with tissue paper and string.

For at least three minutes the Vicar read happily if haltingly on. Mrs. Brandon with a rapt expression let free her inhibitions and thought of how Nurse could alter that pleated black frock. Mr. Grant, observing her expression, felt like a clod, while Delia thought how much nicer Hilary's book was than Mr. Miller's.

Francis, back from his office, came into the drawing-room unobserved and had a good look at this domestic scene, his mother reclining with the air of languor that always gently amused him in a woman who had no nerves to speak of and an excellent constitution, the rest of the party draped admiringly round her. It surprised him a little to see his cynical sister among the worshippers, but he could not know that she was thinking of Hilary Grant. His mother was the first to see him and welcome him with delight, not only because she was glad to see him, but as a good pretext for interrupting anything that was going on and doing a little fussing.

'Francis, darling,' she said. 'You will excuse us for a moment, won't

you, Mr. Miller? I'll just order some fresh tea for Francis and then you
will go on reading to us. Just ring, Francis.'

As soon as Rose had brought the tea, Mr. Miller said to Francis how
sorry he was about the news.

'What news?' asked Francis. 'Is the Bishop coming?'

Nothing could be worse than that, said Mr. Miller emphatically, and
why Barchester always had a Low Church, he would not say Evangelical
bishop, and always had since the days of Bishop Proudie, it was not for
him to inquire. No: he referred to the news about Miss Brandon.

'She isn't dead, is she?' said Francis.

'Francis, you shouldn't say things like that,' said his mother, 'especially when Mr. Miller is here. Dr. Ford came to see me this morning
and said she is much worse and he has sent a nurse to the Abbey and
will ring us up again to-night, so Mr. Miller was very kindly reading
aloud. Poor Aunt Sissie.'

'Well, that is very sad, but hardly surprizing after yesterday,' said
Francis. 'And so right of you, dear mamma, to lie there doing a sort of
couvade, and looking so nice.'

'I don't know what you mean,' said Mrs. Brandon, who knew perfectly well but was not going to admit it, and was pleased at being told
she looked nice.

'It is a sort of things the savages do,' said Delia, who liked to air her
knowledge. 'If one of them had a baby the husband makes an awful fuss
and pretends it's him.'

This lucid explanation of Mrs. Brandon's languishing and very becoming airs was too much for Francis and Mr. Grant, who burst into
ribald laughter. Mr. Miller looked at them over his eye-glasses in a
quelling manner, but said nothing. Mrs. Brandon, suddenly seeing the
joke against herself began to laugh too, and Delia was pleased by the
success of her remark.

'Poor Aunt Sissie,' said Francis. 'Well, if there's a funeral I'll have
to get my hair cut. I ought to have had it done to-day. Give me another
bit of cake, Delia.'

Again the conversation ran lightly over secret depths. Francis, for all
his careless ways and speech, could not bring himself to discuss openly
what must be in everyone's mind, and Mr. Miller began to rustle his
typescript ominously, so that everyone was glad when Sir Edmund
walked in.

'Well, Lavinia, anything wrong?' he said. 'Afternoon, Miller. Grass
is getting very long outside the north aisle. Pity we can't turn a few
sheep in. Afternoon, young people.'

'Not really wrong,' said Mrs. Brandon, 'but Dr. Ford brought me
some rather upsetting news this morning.'

'I met Ford down at the new cottages this morning. A nice mess they
are making of them too,' said Sir Edmund. 'Not even a damp-course. I

told the foreman I'd see the local health authorities and he wasn't to lay a brick till he'd heard from them. I'll get Pomfret's agent onto it, young Wicklow. He has a head on his shoulders. They aren't on Pomfret's land, but some of his people live there and he won't stand it. Thanks,' he said to Rose who had brought him a brandy and soda. 'Well, Lavinia, I'm sorry about Amelia Brandon, but that's no reason for you to behave like an invalid.'

'I really don't see what else I can do,' said Mrs. Brandon. 'She doesn't want to see me and she has Miss Morris and a nurse and all the servants.'

'Well, well, I daresay you're right,' said Sir Edmund. 'Question is: if Amelia Brandon dies, who does the property go to?'

A kind of silent sigh of relief rose from every breast. No one liked to make a suggestion, but there was a general feeling that Sir Edmund would do it for them.

'Must be practical, you know,' said Sir Edmund. 'Well, this is how we stand. Amelia Brandon must have made a will, but no one knows what's in it.'

There was a murmur of assent.

'Well, I look at it this way,' said Sir Edmund, assuming the voice he used on the bench, 'she must have left it to someone. She wouldn't split it up. I remember her telling me that her father had made the place and she meant to pass it on as he had left it. Now we get down to facts. Francis!'

'Yes, sir,' said Francis.

'The way I look at it is this. Either your Aunt Amelia — stupid name Sissie, never liked it — leaves you the property, or she doesn't. If she does, I'm always ready to give you a hand. If she doesn't, she doesn't.'

'Thank you, sir,' said Francis.

'As for Grant,' said Sir Edmund, staring at Mr. Grant, 'as I see it the facts are like this. If Amelia Brandon has left the place to him, there it is. If she hasn't, well there we are. Your mother wouldn't want to live there, would she?'

'I don't know,' said Mr. Grant. 'I hadn't thought about it. She mostly lives in Italy.'

'Good!' said Sir Edmund. 'Well then, that's that. Of course if she leaves it to someone else, that old uncle of Cedric Brandon's — you'd never have heard of him, he lives at Putney — or the cousin that lives in New Zealand, then of course that alters the state of affairs. That's all, I think.'

'Sir Edmund,' said Delia, 'if Aunt Sissie — well you know what I mean — if she does, what do you suppose will happen to Miss Morris?'

As it happened, no one in the room had thought of Miss Brandon's companion. Mr. Miller felt sorry for companions in general and suddenly felt very sorry for Miss Morris in particular.

'Happen, eh?' said Sir Edmund. 'I suppose she'll find another job. Plenty of old ladies about.'

'Yes, but Sir Edmund,' said Delia, 'I mean now, at once, if Aunt

Sissie is really as ill as Dr. Ford says. I mean it must be pretty ghastly for her to be in that awful Abbey alone.'

Mr. Miller made a violent effort.

'Delia is undoubtedly right,' he said. 'Miss Morris should not be left at the Abbey unless she wishes. It might perhaps be possible to find her lodgings in the village for the present. I know they have a furnished bedroom and sitting-room at the shop. If there were any difficulty of any kind,' he added diffidently, 'and a small contribution would help — —'

'Nonsense, Miller,' said Sir Edmund, who knew that the Vicar's income was not large and that much of it went in charity, 'nonsense. There are two rooms at Clematis Cottage and Mrs. Bevan is a very nice, clean, respectable woman and I'd see to all that.'

Mrs. Brandon had barely heard what her kind-hearted guests were saying. She remembered how worn Miss Morris looked, how patient she had been with the old lady, with what gratitude she had accepted so dull a treat as a picnic. She also remembered with less sympathy how Miss Morris had shown unmistakable signs of devotion to her, but put this away as selfishness. Here was Stories, with two spare bedrooms which were seldom used except at week-ends. The servants would enjoy having a guest in the house so fresh from the excitement of a funeral. Her duty seemed plain.

'I think, Sir Edmund, she had better come here,' she said. 'It is most kind of you and Mr. Miller, but I really think she would be better at Stories. She has had a most trying time with Aunt Sissie and looks as if she needed a good rest. I could easily have her for two or three weeks, or more if she doesn't find a new place. I like her and I think we'd get on quite well. Of course I hope this is only a false alarm and that Aunt Sissie will get well again, but if anything does happen I'll go over to the Abbey and fetch her.'

Sir Edmund and Mr. Miller expressed their approval of this scheme and Mr. Miller went so far as to say that it was just like her.

'Not a bit,' said Mrs. Brandon. 'As a matter of fact I hadn't thought about her at all till Delia mentioned her, which was very selfish and forgetful of me. It is really Delia's plan.'

Delia blushed and looked gratified. Sir Edmund and Mr. Miller took their leave. Mr. Grant lingered to speak to his hostess.

'I do think it is marvellous of you, Mrs. Brandon,' he said.

'I suppose you have to go on saying, Mrs. Brandon,' said she. 'I wish you would say Cousin Lavinia, or just Lavinia.'

'You know by what name I always think of you,' said Mr. Grant in a dark quivering voice.

'No,' said Mrs. Brandon, enjoying herself immensely. 'May I hear?'

Mr. Grant looked self-conscious, looked down, up, and wildly about him, and said in a hoarse croak:

'I did tell you once. In my mind I call you my friend.'

Having made this avowal he waited for Mrs. Brandon to dismiss him for ever from her sight. As she said nothing he dared to raise his eyes and look at her. Her charming face, a little tired, a little dark under the eyes after yesterday's scene, bore an expression as of one whose thoughts are fixed on a distant star.

'I feel,' said Mrs. Brandon, in a low, thrilling tone, 'about that word as Shelley felt about the word Love.'

She paused for a moment, to get it right. Mr. Grant, on hearing the word Love, a word which he had hardly dared to use even to himself, nearly lost consciousness, but recovered himself in time to hear the goddess's last words.

' "One word",' said Mrs. Brandon, ' "is too often profaned for me to profane it." '

Mr. Grant, while feeling that it was he rather than Mrs. Brandon who intended to profane the word, fully realized the exquisite quality of the rebuke, and mumbling good-bye, hastened after his coach.

Francis, who had frankly been eavesdropping, now approached his mother.

'Really, mamma!' he said.

Mrs. Brandon looked at him with the face of a saint and then broke into her mischievous amused smile.

'I couldn't help it,' she said.

'I know you couldn't, darling,' said Francis. 'But what you could have helped was saddling yourself with Miss Morris.'

'I had to,' said his mother. 'She seems to have no friends or relations and she has had a dreadful time with Aunt Sissie. If only she didn't have a slight passion for me, it would be all right. But I do hope Aunt Sissie will get better."

'So do I,' said Francis, 'if it means you being worn to the bone by Miss Morris's devotion. Perhaps we could interest her in church work.'

'I'm afraid she and Mr. Miller don't approve of each other,' said his mother, 'which makes it all more difficult.'

'All true Brandons thrive on difficulties, or else they make them for other people,' said Francis. 'I am an example of the first and Aunt Sissie of the second. To make matters smooth between Miss Morris and Mr. Miller shall be my life's work. Come and look at Turpin's marrow, mamma. You will find it has a soothing and inspiriting influence.'

VIII

THE LAST OF BRANDON ABBEY

THE more Mrs. Brandon thought about her kind offer to take Miss Morris in the event of 'anything happening' as everyone preferred euphemistically to put it, the more she wished she had not felt she must make it. Then she blamed herself and thought again of Miss Morris's position, and how horrid it must be to go from one old lady to another, with no home or background of her own. Dr. Ford's report next day was that Miss Brandon was still much the same, and he promised to let Stories know of any change. Mrs. Brandon asked if her aunt would like to see her and was greatly relieved to hear that the old lady did not want to see anyone but Sparks and Miss Morris. Her only pleasure, he said, was to hear Miss Morris read Captain Brandon's old letters aloud, when she was not in a semi-conscious condition.

Mrs. Brandon told her children the news. Francis went off to work and Delia, oppressed by a shadow that had never before overcast her young spirits, went over to Grumper's End to see how the chicken pox was. Mrs. Brandon went up to Nurse's room, where Nurse was pressing one of Delia's evening frocks.

'Dr. Ford has just rung up,' said Mrs. Brandon. 'He says Miss Brandon is much the same.'

'I'm sure I'm glad to hear that, madam,' said Nurse, who had been hoping for something much more exciting.

'If anything did happen,' said Mrs. Brandon, 'I am going to ask her companion, Miss Morris, here for a few weeks. She is a clergyman's daughter and very nice. And I was thinking about that black frock of mine with the pleated skirt. I haven't worn it since the winter, but I think if you took the gold belt off and put on a black one, and put some of that black lace that is in the carboard box with the flowers on it on the top shelf of my big cupboard round the neck, I could wear it quite nicely.'

As she spoke she looked Nurse firmly in the eye, as if challenging her to prove that the mention of the black frock was anything but a house-wife's careful attention to her wardrobe. Nanny, seconding admirably this pretence, said she would just run down and get the dress and see. She was back in a few moments carrying an armful of clothes which she laid on the table.

'I'd better turn the iron off,' said Nurse, 'or we'll be having an accident, like the time that nursery maid left the electric kettle on all afternoon and burnt the hearth rug. I brought up some frocks I thought you might like to go over, madam.'

'I had quite forgotten about that black and white foulard,' said Mrs. Brandon. 'It looks well with a black hat. You see what I mean about the pleated frock, Nurse.'

'Yes, madam,' said Nurse. 'It would look quite effective with a black belt and the lace, the way you said. And I brought up this black georg-ette. You did say it had got a little tight for you, but there didn't seem to be anything to let out, so I wondered if it might do for Miss Delia. I'll try it on her as soon as she gets back. I wish you'd speak to her, madam, about visiting Grumper's End. I know she's had chicken pox twice, but it isn't so much the chicken pox as Other Things she might get there.

'Yes, Nurse, I'll try to,' said Mrs. Brandon, absent-mindedly. 'Why did you bring up the pale green? I thought we were going to give it away.'

'It would dye nicely, madam, and if I sent it to Barchester to-day we'd have it back in two days if it's a special order, and it might come in quite handy.'

'Yes, do,' said Mrs. Brandon. 'And there's that lilac georgette.'

'You wouldn't have it *dyed*, madam,' said Nurse, shocked. 'It's all made on the cross and things on the cross do shrink up so when they are dyed. It would come in quite handy for later, madam. Really the two black frocks for you, the pleated one and the green one dyed, and your old black frock for Miss Delia would be quite enough. The black and white foulard and the lilac georgette would come in for afterwards, if the weather still keeps hot. I'll finish pressing this frock of Miss Delia's and then I'll send the pale green to be dyed and get on with altering the the belt.'

'Well, I think that's all,' said Mrs. Brandon and left Nurse to her ironing, both ladies perfectly satisfied by a conversation which had covered Miss Brandon's death, funeral, and the subsequent light mourning, without once mentioning an unpleasant word. On the landing Mrs. Brandon found Ethel, the upper housemaid, and paused to tell her that the Green Room might be wanted quite soon, as Miss Morris might be coming from Brandon Abbey if anything happened, and to see that there was clean paper in all the drawers, an order which filled the recipient with ghoulish joy. Thence proceeding to the ground floor she found Rose in the sitting-room, taking away the silver ornaments to clean them.

'Oh, Rose,' she said, 'Dr. Ford rang up just now. It seems that Miss Brandon is just the same.'

'Oh, dear, madam,' said Rose.

'Her companion, Miss Morris, has had a very hard time,' said Mrs. Brandon, 'and I thought if Miss Morris needed a rest I could have her over here for a fortnight. I told Ethel to see that the Green Room was ready. I was thinking she could use the little dressing-room as a sitting-room if we put a comfortable chair into it.'

Rose, understanding perfectly well the implications of these remarks, said the chair out of the Pink Room would go in nicely, and would Mrs. Brandon mention it to Ethel, as really she sometimes hardly liked to say anything to Ethel herself, and was always one for peace and quiet.

This matter adjusted, Mrs. Brandon passed on to the kitchen. Cook, who had already heard the news from Nurse and Ethel, said she really was sorry to hear Miss Brandon was no better and she was thinking of

making some beef tea and some calves' foot jelly, because it was as well
to be prepared and she always liked two clear days for her jellies, and if
people had had a shock there was nothing like it.

*

Meanwhile at Brandon Abbey old Miss Brandon's life was slowly ebb-
ing away. It had perhaps not been a very interesting life, or one which
contained much affection, but its owner had enjoyed it in her own way.
She had admired the father who made a fortune and built the Abbey,
and done her best to administer as he would have wished it the vast
fortune that he left her. 'Be just before you are generous' was her
guiding rule, and made her disliked, for the justice was kept for servants, tenants, tradespeople and such few friends as she had, while the
generosity was confined to large subscriptions and donations to various
charitable institutions, often appearing as anonymous gifts. The one
deep feeling of her life had been her affection, amounting to adoration,
for her scapegrace brother, Captain Brandon. To have been in his
regiment was a sure passport to her favour, and successive Colonels
could have told of help given to any of the regiment whose needs were
made known to her. In her younger days more than one officer, who as
a subaltern had known Captain Brandon, had come to her when in
difficulties with ladies of confirmed or brevet rank, and had been
rescued, the only price of his rescue being Miss Brandon's ribald
chuckle as she insisted on having the story retailed to her in every detail.

Now she lay half asleep for hours together, watched by Sparks and
Miss Morris by day, by the nurse at night, rousing herself from time to
time to order Miss Morris to read aloud Captain Brandon's old, yellow
letters, never tiring of those in which he described the unfortunate
entanglement with Mrs. Colonel Arbuthnot which had resulted in his
having to exchange.

Late in the afternoon a clerk from her solicitors, to whom Miss
Morris had written at her request on the previous day, arrived at
Brandon Abbey. The old lady summoning her energy insisted on seeing
him alone, except for Sparks, and he soon went away again. After
this her interest in the world lapsed altogether. At five o'clock next
morning the nurse tapped at Miss Morris's door. Miss Morris, who had
almost forgotten what a good night's sleep was like, was up and dressed
in a very short time and came into Miss Brandon's bedroom. Nurse had
drawn up the blind and the early sun was shining into the room, as it
had not been allowed to do for many years.

Miss Morris came near the bed. Her employer was lying back on the
pillows, her eyes shut, her heavy face in its frilled cap looking very tired
and old.

'She will notice you presently,' said the nurse. 'She was asking for
you.'

'Never could abide nurses. Meddling fools,' said the old lady in a weak but distinct voice, without opening her eyes.

'It's Miss Morris, Miss Brandon, you asked for her, you know,' said nurse in a voice of patient brightness that fully justified Miss Brandon's dislike.

'Come here,' said the old lady. 'Fred wouldn't have looked at you, but you'll find someone else will, before long. I'm sorry I couldn't fancy my supper last night. It's high time I was dead.'

These may be said to have been Miss Brandon's last sensible words. Miss Morris, who was sitting by her bed did indeed hear her mutter, 'Mrs. Colonel Arbuthnot' and give a ghostly chuckle, but otherwise she never spoke again. Presently Miss Morris and the nurse looked at each other. Then Miss Morris went and telephoned to Dr. Ford, and because there was nothing else to be done she went back to her room, vaguely wondered in what kind of bedroom she would find herself in her next place, and lay down, dressed as she was, on her bed.

By ten o'clock Mrs. Brandon was at the Abbey. When Dr. Ford rang her up Francis had offered to come, but as there would have been nothing for him to do she refused his kind offer. Poor Delia, after all her longing to see the last of her aunt, was suddenly overcome by the tender heart that she kept beneath her robust exterior and burst into tears, weeping for her disagreeable aunt as bitterly as if she had been a field mouse. So her mother left her to Nurse and started alone. At the drive gate Curwen suddenly pulled up, as a figure rose from the ditch where it had been sitting.

'Hilary!' exclaimed Mrs. Brandon.

'Dr. Ford rang Mr. Miller up,' said Mr. Grant. 'I had an idea you would be going, because of that very kind thing you said about Miss Morris. I didn't like to bother you, but I thought I'd wait here, and if you did come I wanted to ask if I could do anything to help.'

'Get in and come with me,' said Mrs. Brandon.

Mr. Grant did as he was told. As on a previous journey Mrs. Brandon spoke very little, but this time her companion did not take her silence for scorn. To his adoration there began to be added a cooler admiration for someone who was going to do a job that not everyone would have done, and was doing it without any fuss. When they got to the Abbey Mrs. Brandon suddenly became an efficient grown-up person and disappeared upstairs with a red-eyed Sparks, leaving Mr. Grant a prey to a sense of his own incompetence. The butler offered him sherry in so suitable a voice that Mr. Grant, though he disliked sherry early in the morning excessively, was afraid to refuse it, and under the butler's eye not only had to drink it, but also eat two small biscuits with caraway seeds in them, a form of refreshment that he loathed. When he had choked upon the second the butler hastened to refill his glass, and Mr. Grant wished Mrs. Brandon could see what he was suffering for her sake.

Accompanied by poor Sparks, who was bewailing her mistress as if she had been the kindest of employers. Mrs. Brandon visited the dead woman's room, laid on the bed the spray of flowering myrtle that she had brought with her, had a few words with the nurse, and came out again into the little sitting-room with relief that one part of her duty was done. She then set herself to comfort poor Sparks, who found real consolation in telling Mrs. Brandon of the various passages she had had with the nurse, even going so far as a dark hint that some nurses got a retaining fee from undertakers, but at this point Mrs. Brandon, with as much tact as possible, interrupted and asked where Miss Morris was. Sparks had to confess that she hadn't seen her that morning, but offered to go and look.

Mrs. Brandon, left alone, looked for the last time on the serried rows of photographs, wondering by what slow process the plump, pretty child with ringlets had been changed to the shapeless, bed-ridden old woman, feared or disliked by most of those who came in contact with her. Looking absent-mindedly at her own hands according to custom, Mrs. Brandon saw the diamond ring and wondered if Miss Brandon was even now meeting Captain Frederick Brandon and if so in what possible kind of heaven. Probably an Indian station, she thought, where Miss Amelia Brandon, keeping house for her gallant brother, would for ever look on his escapades with an indulgent eye and listen to his stories of pretty ladies. But realizing that these were irreligious thoughts, she pulled herself together. Sparks then returned with a face of pleasurable gloom to say that she had knocked at Miss Morris's door, but couldn't get any answer, and she didn't like to think what might have happened.

'She is asleep, I expect,' said Mrs. Brandon calmly. 'I had better go and see her. Where is her room?'

From her voice Sparks knew that Mrs. Brandon had now stopped being a sympathetic friend and had resumed her position as an employer. With sad resignation she took Mrs. Brandon up to Miss Morris's room. Mrs. Brandon knocked, received no answer, opened the door and went in. She saw what she expected, Miss Morris lying in an exhausted sleep. She told Sparks, who having been disappointed of seeing a bleeding corpse with its throat cut was hoping at least for a death by drugs, to go and make some tea and bring it up. To this she added a request for some nice bread and butter, knowing what magic the word nice has in the kitchen. She then sat down and waited.

As she waited she looked at the bedroom. One could not say it was a servant's bedroom, but neither could one call it a guest's room. The furniture obviously consisted of rejects from better bedrooms, the bedstead was of black japanned iron with brass knobs and rails from which all pretence of polish had long since departed, and Mrs. Brandon's housekeeping eye could see how the old-fashioned wire mattress sagged and she could imagine how noisy it would be whenever Miss Morris turned. The carpet had been good but was now faded to a nondescript colour, the dressing table had a mirror which had to be wedged with a piece of cardboard to prevent it from turning somersaults, the thin curtains would obviously keep out neither light nor cold.

When Sparks came back Mrs. Brandon told her to put the tray down and then go and get a nice cup of tea for herself, with which crumbs of comfort Sparks departed for the housekeeper's room, there to boast a good deal about what she had seen and heard.

Mrs. Brandon poured out a cup of tea, clinking the china as much as possible. Miss Morris stirred a little.

'Do you feel like a cup of tea?' asked Mrs. Brandon in her usual placid voice.

Miss Morris sat up, pushed her hair back, and looked wildly at the newcomer for a moment. Then she recovered herself and with almost her usual calm accepted the tea and thanked Mrs. Brandon.

'I am afraid I must have been asleep,' she said. 'What time is it?'

'Eleven,' said Mrs. Brandon. 'Didn't you have any breakfast?'

'I lay down for a few moments after I left Miss Brandon this morning. Oh, did you know?'

Mrs. Brandon said Dr. Ford had told her.

'I was rather tired, so I suppose I went to sleep,' said Miss Morris. 'I wonder what I could do now. I suppose I can stay on here for a little and be useful.'

Mrs. Brandon looked at Miss Morris, saw the dark circles under her eyes and the shaking of her hands as she held the cup and saucer, and determined to tell the staff what she thought of them for forgetting Miss Morris and never offering her breakfast. Then she determined to tell a lie and said,

'Dr. Ford wants you to come back with me to Stories.'

A look of intense relief came into Miss Morris's face and then the mask of the professional companion fell again.

'How very kind of you, Mrs. Brandon,' she said, 'but I ought to stay here. I expect I'll be needed.'

'There will be plenty of people to look after everything,' said Mrs. Brandon, not caring in the least whether there would be or not, 'and Dr. Ford said most particularly that I was to take you with me now. So if you will drink the rest of the tea and eat up that nice bread and butter, I will wait for you downstairs. I will send Sparks up to help you to pack.'

Without waiting for any possible protest she went down to the drawing-room, where Mr. Grant was sitting in a horrid atmosphere of sherry, and rang the bell, looking so determined that he dared not address her.

'Please send Sparks to me at once,' she said when the butler appeared.

In a few minutes Sparks came in, still chewing the remains of her nice cup of tea.

'Please go and help Miss Morris to pack,' said Mrs. Brandon. 'I'm taking her home with me. And I find that she had no breakfast this morning. How was that?'

Sparks said she supposed the third housemaid, who was supposed to take Miss Morris's breakfast up to her room was upset. They were all upset downstairs, she said, and she could hardly manage more than cocoa and a piece of cake herself.

'Then I'd better see the housekeeper. Please tell her I want to speak to her at once,' said Mrs. Brandon with a tone of cold finality that sent Sparks speechless from the room and made Mr. Grant cringe inside himself.

She then went to the dining-room, where Mr. Grant could hear her telephoning.

The housekeeper came and looked at Mr. Grant as if he were a beetle. She then said to no one in particular that she understood Mrs. Brandon wished to see her. Mrs. Brandon, coming back from the telephone, said she did, and that she wished to know why no one had taken up any breakfast to Miss Morris.

'I am sure I could hardly say, madam,' said the housekeeper.

'Then that is not much use,' said Mrs. Brandon with icy politeness. 'Miss Brandon's lawyers are going to send out someone to look after the house till suitable arrangements are made. The person who is sent will give you any orders that are necessary. That is all, thank you.'

If Mr. Grant could have got under a sofa, he would gladly have done so. The goddess armed with Jove's thunders was a formidable being whom he had never suspected, and he hardly knew whether to worship or to shut his ears and eyes. He did shut his eyes for a moment. When he opened them the housekeeper had gone, probably shrivelled into nothingness, and the kind goddess was once more apparent.

'I am going to ask you to do something for me, Hilary,' she said. 'I am going to take Miss Morris home with me now. Will you please stay here and see Mr. Merton? I managed to get him on the telephone at the Deanery and he is coming out with someone from the lawyers. Tell him how sorry I am I couldn't stay, and you could bring back any messages from him. I will send Curwen back to fetch you as soon as possible.'

Mr. Grant said of course he would.

Miss Morris then came downstairs with Sparks carrying her suitcase. Mr. Grant stood up respectfully.

'Give Miss Morris some sherry,' said Mrs. Brandon. 'Yes, of course you can drink it; it will do you good.'

Miss Morris obediently drank the sherry and thanked Mr. Grant. Mrs. Brandon then led her captive to the car and Mr. Grant was left

alone. His feelings were mixed. The foremost was a kind of anger that
Mr. Merton, that stranger who spoke with such ease and assurance to
Mrs. Brandon as if she were an ordinary person, should be coming to
the house at all. It was like his impudence to be staying at the Deanery
at such a time; even more like it to answer the telephone when Mrs.
Brandon rang him up; and most like it to be coming out with someone
who would give orders. On the other hand Mrs. Brandon was not waiting to see him, which made Mr. Grant smile a smile of grim satisfaction
that afforded him much pleasure till he suddenly saw his face in one of
the looking glasses on the overmantel and hastily recomposed it in case
any of the servants came in. But though his face now betrayed no
emotion, none the less did he inwardly exult. Mr. Merton, the man of
the world the gilded popinjay, the roué (for to such heights did Mr.
Grant's imagination in its flights now ascend) would arrive at the
Abbey, all expectation, to find the bird flown and in its place a coldly
courteous representative (bearing the form and lineaments of Mr.
Grant) who would give him any necessary information, hear anything
that he might have to say, and then rejoin the goddess, leaving Mr.
Merton to deal with graves and worms and epitaphs. Turning over in
his mind these agreeable thoughts he walked up and down the drawing-
room, when suddenly something dreadful occurred to him. It might be
that Mrs. Brandon was deliberately shunning Mr. Merton because she
wanted to see him. He had heard, and read in books, that women often
fled where they would most fain pursue; that Ravishers (for such Mr.
Merton was rapidly becoming in his mind) were more inflamed by the
fugitive nymph than by bold advances; and, as a happy afterthought,
that women were well known to have nothing but contempt for men
who were content to worship from afar.

Thus unpleasantly and unfruitfully meditating he did not hear a car
drive up. The first thing that attracted his attention was the sound of
voices in the hall, and the butler saying to Mr. Merton that he thought
the young gentleman that come with Mrs. Brandon was in the drawing-
room. Mr. Grant would have ground his teeth if he had known how to
do it. 'Young' forsooth, and 'gentleman' indeed! Then Mr. Merton
came in and said very pleasantly, 'Grant, isn't it? I think we met here
before. Mrs. Brandon has gone, I expect.'

Mr. Grant said he had, and had taken Miss Brandon's companion
away with her.

'Splendid,' said Mr. Merton. 'I have to get back to town to-day so
I haven't much time. I've brought a man from my father's office who
is used to this sort of thing and he will take over for the present. Are you
staying here?'

'No,' said Mr. Grant. 'I'm only waiting for Mrs. Brandon to send the
car back. She said you might have some messages to send her.'

'I don't think there will be anything special,' said Mr. Merton.

'They will let her know about the funeral from the offices of course. Simpson!'

A youngish middle-aged man who looked as if he spent his life carrying out instructions to the letter, came in.

'Mr. Simpson from the office, Mr. Grant,' said Mr. Merton. 'Now, Simpson, you might as well see the servants and I'll go up and see the nurse and then I must go. Well, good-bye, Grant. I hope we'll meet again. Tell Mrs. Brandon not to worry about anything and I hope very much to come over and see her when next I'm down.'

He went upstairs and Simpson went into the dining-room. Mr. Grant, consumed with envy of people who knew how things were done and could grapple with nurses, felt the house was no place for him and wandered into the garden, where he had the pleasure of tormenting himself by the remembrance of the afternoon he had spent there with Mrs. Brandon, and reflecting how he had then every opportunity of casting himself at her feet and saying 'Oh, Mrs Brandon,' but had not done so. A man like Mr. Merton, he felt, would not so basely have wasted his opportunities. In these unprofitable musings, he was surprised by Mr. Simpson, who came advancing over the grass with the staid yet cheerful step of an undertaker.

'Excuse me, sir,' said Mr. Simpson, 'but Mrs. Brandon's car is here.'

'Oh, thanks awfully,' said Mr. Grant. 'How did you know where I was?'

'Not at all, sir,' said Mr. Simpson, apparently in reply to the first of Mr. Grant's remarks, and leaving that young gentleman to marvel secretly at the powers of divination that had found him near the lily-pond. Mr. Simpson then insisted, much to Mr. Grant's discomfiture, on seeing him into the car and telling Curwen he would not be wanted again. Mr. Grant, who had already seen from Curwen's expression how deeply he resented having to do the journey to Brandon Abbey twice in a morning, feared that this final insult would cause him to overturn the car into a disused quarry, or into the River Rising, out of sheer spite, but Curwen found all the outlet he needed in the back of his neck, which expressive portion of the human body so paralysed Mr. Grant that he would have given anything to be allowed to get out and walk. When they got near Pomfret Madrigal Curwen further completed his discomfiture by suddenly opening the glass slide with one hand and asking through the corner of his mouth whether Mr. Grant wished to be taken to Stories or to the Vicarage. Thus challenged he dared not say Stories, and said he would get out at the Cow and Sickle and walk, which made Curwen despise him more than ever, as one who was not born to a car.

The Vicarage and its garden looked so peaceful in the sun that Mr. Grant found it difficult to believe that anything had really happened. Time seemed to have stopped since he got into Mrs. Brandon's car at her gate and he thought it was probably tea-time, when the church clock striking two made him realize that he was extremely hungry and very late for lunch. He hurried up the flagged path to the house, where he found Mr. Miller smoking a pipe over a book and the remains of lunch.

'Hullo,' said Mr. Miller. 'I thought you were out.'

'So I was,' said Mr. Grant.

'Well, here you are,' said his tutor. 'Had lunch?'

Mr. Grant said he hadn't and would awfully like some if it weren't a bother. Mr. Miller then rang for Hettie, who conferred with Cook and brought word that there was a nice piece of the beefsteak pie left that could be hotted up in a moment, so Mr. Grant sat down to wait and drank a whole glass of beer.

'Thirsty?' said Mr. Miller kindly.

'I was,' said Mr. Grant. 'I've been at Brandon Abbey. I happened to be passing Stories just as Mrs. Brandon was starting, and she asked me to come.'

'I suppose — —' said Mr. Miller.

'Oh yes, really dead,' said Mr. Grant, fully understanding that Dr. Ford's message was not in itself a death certificate.

'And Mrs. Brandon?' asked the Vicar.

'She was splendid, sir. She simply took charge of everything. Poor Miss Morris had been up for nights and not had any breakfast, and Mrs. Brandon simply pitched into the servants like anything. Oh, thanks awfully, Hettie, that looks splendid. I just stayed on a bit to look after things till Mr. Merton came. He is some kind of relation of Miss Brandon's lawyers.'

'That must be Noel Merton,' said Mr. Miller. 'A very brilliant barrister. I coached him one vacation. I must ask him down here some time. I like to keep up with my old pupils. Is your lunch all right, Hilary?'

'Rather, sir,' said Mr. Grant, his mouth full of beefsteak pie with the crust for which the Vicarage cook was doubtfully famous, mashed potatoes, french beans and gravy.

Mr. Miller went on with his book and his pipe, while Mr. Grant finished his pie and Hettie brought him gooseberry fool and cream with sponge fingers from the baker, and coffee. When Mr. Grant had finished, she cleared away, and all the time Mr. Grant had a feeling that his host was saving something up to say to him. When Hettie had gone back to the kitchen Mr. Miller put his pipe into his book to mark the place and looked confused.

'Is that a good book, sir?' asked Mr. Grant.

'Journalism, journalism,' said Mr. Miller, looking at *A Wastepaper Basket from Three Embassies* by Jefferson X. Root, who had never certainly set foot in any of them, but was well into his second hundred thousand, 'as practically everything is now,'

He paused again uncomfortably.

'I wonder,' said Mr. Grant to ease the tension, 'if the French think it funny that their chief classical authors are called Mr. Root and Mr. Crow.'

Mr. Miller stared for a moment and then laughed and said the Romans had some curious names themselves, and what about Naso and Locusta.

'By the way,' he continued quickly, before his courage could cool. 'I don't want to interfere of course, Hilary, but have you any idea whether your aunt's death will in any way affect you?'

Mr. Grant went bright red.

'Of course nothing is further from my mind than any wish to ask indiscreet questions,' Mr. Miller pursued, 'but if an older man's advice would at any time be of any use, I thought I would like you to know that it is entirely at your disposal.'

This was an act of truly disinterested kindness on Mr. Miller's part, as he had no capacity for or understanding of business at all, and except for the lucky fact that his private income was under a Trust would doubtless have been entirely dependent on his small stipend. As it was he always found himself in or out of pocket over any accounts in connection with church activities, and after the last Fête he had been obliged to make up a deficit of seventeen shillings and threepence from his own purse.

Mr. Grant, who didn't know this, was much touched, and thanked his coach warmly, after which he too fell into silent confusion.

'I cannot understand the appeal that this kind of book makes to the public,' said Mr. Miller, whose pipe was lying in page two hundred and seventy. 'It is like Dr. Johnson's mutton, ill-conceived, ill-written, ill-presented.'

Mr. Grant laughed a little too loudly.

'By the way,' he said, before his courage could cool, 'you've been so decent to me, sir, that I'd like to say something.'

By way of carrying out this resolution he suddenly stopped speaking and looked with intense interest at the photograph of the Lazarus Eight in 1912 with Mr. Miller looking incredibly young and round faced.

'Yes, my boy,' said Mr. Miller encouragingly, and then wishing he hadn't used this form of address.

'I only meant,' said Mr. Grant, still studying the photograph with an absorbed face, 'that if I did happen to get anything I wouldn't take it.'

Mr. Miller vaguely felt that there was some Scriptural precedent for this, but was too much surprised by his pupil's statement to run this fugitive thought to earth, so he made a deprecating kind of noise which might also be taken for agreement, sympathy, or a slight clearing of the throat.

'I think,' said Hilary, 'it would be jolly unfair if I got anything, considering Mrs. Brandon is Aunt Sissie's niece, and how jolly good she was to her, going to see her at that awful Abbey. I think I ought to do some work, sir, as I didn't do any this morning.'

He left the room abruptly and could be heard going up to his room. Mr. Miller gazed pensively into the garden thinking what fun it must be to be young, to have something to sacrifice for someone worthy of the renunciation. If he had anything he could sacrifice for Mrs. Brandon he would willingly have done so, but his oars and his little library, his most cherished possessions, would obviously be of no use to her. With a sigh he picked up his pipe and resumed Mr. Root's book at the point where the ingenious author would have seen Lenin, had he not been out of Moscow at the moment. If this sentence is a little ambiguous it must in fairness be said that whether it was Lenin or Mr. Root who was out of Moscow, the result would have been much the same and equally dull.

When Delia had finished crying about her Aunt Sissie her spirits began to rise again, and she had a very spirited argument with Nurse about the black georgette frock that was a little too tight for her mother. Nurse, who had an understandable if erroneous belief that Delia, her baby, was still in the nursery, said it made her look much too old and wished to shorten it. Delia, very conscious when it came to a question of good clothes, of her nineteen years, was enchanted by her own imposing appearance and peacocked up and down in front of the glass in her mother's room till Nurse nearly lost her temper, and told Delia to come along like a good girl and take it off.

'Well, if I do take it off,' said Delia, unwillingly beginning to pull the frock off over her head, 'will you swear to shorten it at once, Nurse, so that I can have it on when Miss Morris comes.'

'Certainly not, Miss Delia,' said Nurse, shocked. 'It wouldn't look at all nice to be all in black when poor Miss Morris comes, just as if you'd been Expecting it.'

Delia, now safely extricated from the georgette, said after all one couldn't help expecting it when everyone knew Aunt Sissie was about a hundred and Dr. Ford had told them she was very ill, but Nurse, suddenly assuming the position of an authority on etiquette, ignored Delia's protest and carried the dress off to be shortened. Delia got into her ordinary frock again and went into the garden to get flowers for Miss Morris's room.

'Good morning, Turpin,' she said to the gardener, who was tying up dahlias. 'Isn't it awful, Aunt Sissie is dead.'

'That's another of them gone,' said Turpin with gloomy relish. 'How old was she, miss?'

'Oh, I don't know. Eighty-something.'

'My father was ninety-three when Mr. Moffat—that was the Vicar before Mr. Lane, him as was before Mr. Miller — took and buried him,' said Turpin, leaving his hearer to understand that Mr. Turpin senior, if not forcibly interred, might have been alive yet. 'And his father, that was my grandfather in a manner of speaking, was nigh on a hundred and hadn't had a tooth in his head for forty years. Ah, they didn't need teeth in those days,' said Turpin, shaking his head over the degeneracy of modern times.

'Well, Aunt Sissie had false teeth and a wig,' said Delia, zealous for the honour of the family.

'What did she want with wigs at her age?' said Turpin. 'The Lord sends these things to try us and I don't hold with flying in his face with false hair and false teeth like them as are no better than they should be.'

With this cruel aspersion on a profession which, whatever its moral status, certainly does not depend on dentures or postiches for its attractions, Turpin pulled a length of bast from the tress that was tucked into his belt, and resumed his labours. Delia, seeing that further conversation was useless, moved away and began to pick carnations.

'Not them red ones, Miss Delia,' shouted Turpin, who had followed her actions with a suspicious eye. 'I want them for the Feet.'

'All right,' said Delia, now goaded beyond bearing, 'if you think I want red carnations for Miss Morris's room when Aunt Sissie is only just dead, I don't. I'm only getting white flowers.'

So saying she cut two tall white lilies almost viciously, and walked away with them before the outraged Turpin could protest.

'Buds and all!' he muttered, as Delia went off to another flower bed, and then applied himself afresh to his labours, comforting himself with the thought that one death often brought on another.

By this time Delia's blood was up. She stripped the garden of practically every white flower she could find and arranged them all in the Green Room, choosing several rather valuable white Chinese vases that were kept in a cabinet and never used. By the time she had decorated the dressing table, the writing table and the mantelpiece, and massed white phlox in the fender, the room with its pale green curtains and chintzes and its pale green walls, with the light filtering through the half-drawn white blinds, was like a dwelling under a glassy, cool, translucent wave, and Delia was filled with admiration for her own work.

Presently she heard the car come back, so she tidied away all the débris of stalks and leaves, washed her hands, and ran down to the drawing-room where she found her mother and Miss Morris seated in calm and amicable converse. Concealing her disappointment, for she, like Sparks, had hoped at least to see an almost inanimate corpse, she stood on one leg in the doorway.

'Come in, darling,' said her mother. 'You remember Delia, don't you, Miss Morris?'

Miss Morris said of course and shook hands. Then Mrs. Brandon said it was nearly lunch-time and she expected Miss Morris would like to see her room.

'Will you take Miss Morris up,' she said to Delia, 'while I write a couple of letters.'

Rather nervously Delia led the way, wondering if it was etiquette to talk about people who were dead, or if she ought to let Miss Morris do it first. She opened the door of the Green Room and stood outside for Miss Morris to go in. Her things were already unpacked and laid out, and Ethel was taking her suitcase away, having, as a matter of fact delayed to so do till she heard her coming upstairs, so that she might with her own highly favoured eyes gaze upon one who had so lately been near a death-bed and tell the kitchen about it. The account which she gave in the kitchen of Miss Morris looking as pale as chalk and obviously not long for this world was so much the product of her own film-fed mind that we need pay no attention to it, except to remark that it spurred Cook on in her kind preparation of beef tea and calves' foot jelly and so made lunch seven minutes late.

Miss Morris thanked Ethel and stood looking about her. It was perhaps the first time since she had embarked upon her life as a companion that she had been in any bedroom but such as were just too good for the servants. She knew it could not last, that she would probably wake up in a third floor back in Birmingham, or an attic at Droitwich, and hear a bell ringing to summon her to read aloud, or take a little dog for a walk, or pick up stitches in knitting, but until that waking came she was going to be perfectly happy.

'Is it all right?' said Delia anxiously.

'Those flowers!' said Miss Morris, almost with a gasp.

'I did them. Do you like them?' asked Delia, anxious for praise.

'I have never seen anything so lovely in my life,' said Miss Morris, with such sincerity that Delia felt a glow, that is not always given to benefactresses. 'They remind me of my father's garden at home.'

This was not strictly true, for Mr. Morris was interested in nothing but chrysanthemums, but Delia did not know this, and Miss Morris was seeing everything through a haze of grateful sentiment, so both were happy. Miss Morris then opened a very shabby little leather box and took out a photograph which she placed on the table, by her bed. Delia looked at it with interest. It was a middle-aged man in a clerical collar with a thin face, across which his mouth made a tight, hard line, drawn down at the corners.

'Is that your father?' Delia asked.

'Yes,' said Miss Morris. 'It was taken just before he became so ill. He always liked it and it was reproduced in the Parish Magazine after his death''

If it had been anyone else's father Delia would have thought it looked like a horrid old parson, but being Miss Morris's she looked at it respectfully, while Miss Morris put away her outdoor things and washed her hands in the green basin with green soap and dried them on a green towel. Then they went down and had lunch, which was duck and green peas and potato croquettes, followed by gooseberry fool and cream (which every house in Barsetshire was having that week because of not letting the gooseberries be wasted), and home-made sponge fingers. As Miss Morris ate her lunch and drank half a glass of white wine, Rose's opinion of her went down by leaps and bounds. If, she confided to Cook, *her* late mistress had been lying stiff, she was sure she would never have been able to touch a thing. But Cook darkly hinting at delayed shock, though in other words, never ceased in the preparation of calves' foot jelly.

After lunch Miss Morris, on Mrs. Brandon's instructions, had a rest in her room on the green chintz sofa, with a Shetland shawl on her feet and a very nice novel of Mrs. Morland's to read. She still found it impossible to believe that she was herself. Only a few hours ago she had been the companion, lying exhausted on an iron bedstead with a knobbly mattress, wondering how soon she would be adrift on the world again with a month's not very good wages. Now she was a guest, lying on a sofa in a room full of flowers, among kind, pleasant people whose one wish seemed to be to put her at her ease. She wished she had some pretty frocks to do them honour and some better underclothes to please the housemaid, but otherwise her cup was full to the brim with happiness. Companions must not cry, so Miss Morris shed no tears, but it was not quite easy to see some of the pages in Mrs. Morland's book.

She must have gone to sleep without knowing it for presently the light had crept round and was shining on the white lilies on the mantelpiece and Delia was standing by her side, looking at her with interest.

'I say,' said Delia, her eyes shining with the inspiration of a great plan, 'I thought I'd better tell you it's nearly tea-time.'

Miss Morris thanked her and got up.

'I say,' said Delia again, 'I don't know if you believe in wearing mourning or anything.'

'I suppose I shall have to if I go to the funeral,' said Miss Morris. 'I've got a black coat and skirt and I suppose that would do.'

'You'd be awfully hot in a coat and skirt,' said Delia. 'I've got an awfully good idea. There's a black frock of mother's that's a bit too tight for her and Nurse has been shortening it for me, but if you'd like it I'd awfully like you to have it. I mean you're smaller than I am, so if it's the right length for me it'll be about right for you, I mean the right sort of longness for a person — —'

'For someone of my age,' said Miss Morris, kindly finishing the sentence for her. 'Thank you very much, Miss Brandon. I would really be grateful.'

Delia heaved a sigh, partly of relief that her offer had not given offence, partly of regret for what she dearly loved and was only giving up after a severe mental struggle, and produced from behind her back the black frock.

'Could you try it on now!' she said.

Miss Morris was perfectly ready to do so.

'Hang on a minute and I'll get Nurse,' said Delia and rushed upstairs to drag Nurse down and explain the situation to her all in one breath, thus giving her no chance to grumble or expostulate.

'Here's Nurse,' she said, breathless.

'How do you do, Nurse,' said Miss Morris, coming forward and giving her hand with what Nurse considered exactly the right nuance of deference as from an unplaced companion to a pillar of the house, equality as from employee to employee, and proper condescension as from a clergyman's daughter to a children's nurse, which won her complete approval.

'I say, Nurse,' said Delia, 'be an angel and see if that dress fits Miss Morris.'

Nurse helped Miss Morris to take off her well-worn blue dress and slip on the georgette, and approved the result. Delia, fired by the pleasure of doing good and now quite reconciled to her sacrifice, insisted on adding a pair of very thin silk stockings to the toilet, and Miss Morris, accepting calmly and gratefully, really looked extremely distinguished, and promised to wear the dress that night. Nurse took it away to press, and on her way upstairs went down to the kitchen, nominally to ask if those pillow slips were back from the wash yet, but really to make easy allusion to what had just passed and to stamp Miss Morris with her official sanction, while Delia took her guest down to tea. Miss Morris, secretly intoxicated by the thought of a dress which she mentally (and correctly) priced at about twenty guineas when new, looked almost sparkling and made her hostess and Delia laugh by describing some of her experiences with old ladies. Mrs. Brandon, who had been a little nervous of gratitude, found to her relief that Miss Morris was not showing any symptoms of adoration and everything was going very well when Mr. Miller was announced.

Poor Mr. Miller had not at all wished to come to Stories that afternoon, but his conscience had told him that if there was anyone in sadness or trouble he ought to see if his help was wanted, so not stopping to consider whether Miss Morris was likely to be sad or troubled about the death of a very irritable old lady, he had put on his Panama and walked over. At his entrance Miss Morris stiffened and became the companion again.

'How are you, Mrs. Brandon,' said the caller. 'And Delia. I have just called to express my sincere sympathy Mrs. Brandon. And may I say how glad I am to see you among us, Miss Morris.'

Miss Morris said thank you in a correct, toneless voice. Conversation flagged and became so difficult that Mrs. Brandon was reduced to asking Mr. Miller when he was going to read some more of his book to her. Mr. Miller, in his really single-minded wish to do his duty by the afflicted, had given no thought to himself, and the typescript was in a drawer in his writing table. It had indeed been a source of inward conflict to him, for he had managed quite unnecessarily to persuade himself that to read it aloud to someone as delightful, cultivated and sympathetic as Mrs. Brandon, was perhaps in the nature of a sensual gratification and should be discouraged. While putting it away he had come upon a bundle of old papers, and going through them had wondered, as we all do, why on earth he had kept most of them and what practical, emotional, or spiritual value they could ever have had, and had put most of them into the waste-paper basket. Among them were two numbers of the Parish Magazine for 1913 edited by the Rev. Justin Morris, and these Mr. Miller had saved, because he thought Miss Morris might care to have them, and these he now took from his pocket.

'I was looking over some papers to-day,' he said to Miss Morris, thinking it better not to say throwing some papers away, 'and found these numbers of your Parish Magazine, which I thought you might care to see. There is a delightful contribution by Mr. Morris on some local customs, and a little article by myself which I thought good at the time, but now realize to be a very immature production. But setting that aside, I thought you might possibly care to have the magazines. They remind me of some very happy days in the past.'

It was evident that Mr. Miller was getting more and more nervous and talking without knowing really what he was saying. When he had come to an end, Miss Morris replied politely that she had a complete set of the Parish Magazine and would not like to deprive Mr. Miller of the numbers in which his own contributions appeared. Mrs. Brandon and Delia sat for a moment in horrified silence and then plunged simultaneously into an incoherent conversation about the forthcoming Fête. Mr. Miller tried to bear his part in this, but under Miss Morris's silence he became so uneasy that both his hostesses were extremely glad when he said he must go. With great courage he took Miss Morris's ungracious hand, begged her to let him know if he could ever do anything for her and got away.

'I think,' said Miss Morris, as Rose came in to clear away tea, 'I will go upstairs if you don't mind, Mrs. Brandon.'

'Yes, do,' said Mrs. Brandon, 'and have a good rest. And would you care for dinner in bed? It would be quite easy and perhaps you would be glad to be alone for a bit.'

'I am afraid I am a stupid sort of guest,' said Miss Morris, forcing a smile.

'Indeed you aren't,' said Mrs. Brandon warmly, hoping to fend off the attack of self-depreciation which she saw in her guest's eye. 'You must do just as you like about dinner. We shall love to see you if you do feel like coming down. If not, you shall have a tray in bed and be as quiet as you like.'

But Miss Morris was not to be baulked.

'I am afraid I behaved unpardonably just now,' she said. 'It was more than kind of Mr. Miller to come over, and I am sure his wish to give me those magazines was well meant, but you know what my feeling is about the way he hurt my dear father.'

'What did he do?' asked Delia eagerly, rather hoping for news of some bloody assault with a flat iron or a carving knife.

'Mr. Miller and Miss Morris's father did not agree on certain points,' said Mrs. Brandon in rather a hurried way. Delia recognized a danger signal, but did not see where the danger was coming from, so she stood by.

'There was no question of agreement. It was a matter of right or wrong,' said Miss Morris, her pale cheeks flushing.

'Well,' said the practical Delia, 'Mr. Miller did say that was a jolly good article of your father's and he said those were the good old times or something of the sort. He's awfully nice really, Miss Morris, and we never take any notice of him.'

Miss Morris with an incoherent apology left the room. Rose, who had cleared away as slowly as possible, had the intense pleasure of hearing her give a kind of dry sob as she went upstairs, and so was able to prepare the kitchen agreeably for the worst. Nor was it long before the worst occurred, for Nurse, taking the black dress to Miss Morris's room, knocked, had no answer, went in, and found her trying to take off her blue dress and shaking uncontrollably from head to foot. With the light of battle in her eye Nurse mobilized the household. Mrs. Brandon came hurrying upstairs with Delia just in time to receive the full blast of the breakdown which, to do Miss Morris justice, was no more than her due after the last weeks. Beyond kind words Mrs. Brandon could not do much, but Delia, well up in first aid, so bullied her patient, standing no nonsense of any sort, that within ten minutes Miss Morris had drunk sal volatile, cried, choked, drunk more sal volatile, somehow got undressed while crying violently all the time, and was in bed with a hot water bottle, in fact with two, as Nurse and Ethel each considered it her own special office. Delia then drove her not unwilling mother away, told Nurse and Ethel she didn't want them, and installed herself firmly by the patient.

When Dr. Ford, urgently summoned by Mrs. Brandon, arrived, he said there was nothing wrong with Miss Morris at all and a good fit of hysterics would do her good, left a sleeping draught to be taken with a light supper, and promised to look in next day. Just outside the gate of Stories he nearly ran over Mr. Grant and pulled up.

'Oh,' said Mr. Grant, 'I was just going to ask if Mrs. Brandon was all right.'

'I can't think why you want to know,' said Dr. Ford unsympathetically. 'Fit as a fiddle. Always is. Miss Morris has just been having hysterics. Do her all the good in the world. Funeral's the day after to-morrow.'

'It's awfully lucky that Miss Morris had Mrs. Brandon to look after her,' said Mr. Grant reverently.

'Mrs. Brandon is one of the most charming women I know,' said Dr. Ford, making a horrible noise with his gears, 'but no use in a sick room. Your little friend Delia is the one with a head on her shoulders. She handled that woman as if she had been born a nurse. See you at the funeral, I suppose.'

He clanked away, leaving Mr. Grant to consider his words. Deeply did he resent having Delia called his little friend, as if he were in knickerbockers. Deeply did he resent any suggestion that Mrs. Brandon was not perfect. The first seed of doubt as to the infallibility of his goddess was sown, and he found the feeling most uncomfortable. Broad-mindedly, he admitted that one might have a worse person than Delia to look after one in a crisis; he could quite see that she might be a tower of strength. But he didn't want towers of strength. For him an exquisite, shrinking, delicate woman, to whom he could say, 'Mrs. Brandon, I am here. Have no fear,' and embroidering on this delightful theme he went back to the Vicarage.

Cook felt it would go against her conscience to send up calves' foot jelly till it had stood twenty-four hours, but put her whole soul into the beef tea, and at seven o'clock a tray was ready. Delia annoyed the whole staff, though probably preventing bloodshed, by coming into the kitchen, seizing the tray, and taking it up herself. She then administered the sleeping draught and the beef tea, and when she came down to dinner was able to announce that the patient was dozing. As the drug took possession of her senses, Miss Morris thought of the day that was now ending, from the nurse's call in the early morning to the disgraceful but blessed fit of crying that had left her so relaxed and sleepy. Only one thing troubled her in her half-dreaming state and that was that her father and Mr. Miller had been arguing so fiercely about something. She knew her father was right, but Mr. Miller had such a pleasant face and such gentle ways that she felt sure he could not be wrong. Surely Mr. Miller had said something about those very happy days in the past. Yes, very happy they had been, above all in that summer when Mr. Miller was being coached by her father and the weather was so fine. So Miss Morris slid gently back into them, and when Delia came tiptoeing in after dinner, all she had to do was to switch off the reading light, before installing herself in the Green dressing-room where she most unnecessarily proposed to spend that evening and sleep the night.

IX

MISS MORRIS RELENTS

AFTER a good night's rest and a morning in bed, Miss Morris was much better. She thanked Delia warmly for her care, but it was sadly evident that the full force of her gratitude was reserved for Mrs. Brandon. When a reserved nature allows itself to show feeling, it does it with a vengeance, and Miss Morris's devotion began to loom alarmingly, taking the form of wanting to help Mrs. Brandon with the accounts and the flowers. Mrs. Brandon felt that she ought to be touched, but found herself irritated, for her accounts lived in a peculiar muddle which she felt unequal to explaining, and she liked fussing over the flowers herself. However, with real kindness she let Miss Morris help Nurse, who had constituted herself a kind of co-guardian with Delia of their guest's welfare, to go through the linen cupboard and mark some new sheets, which Miss Morris did with exquisitely fine embroidery. Miss Morris also offered to read aloud in the evening, but after one experience gave it up. Francis, alarmed, had made a pretext of work to do and left the room, Delia had slipped away to play the gramophone, and Mrs. Brandon had got into such a muddle of trying to get her tapestry right and look as if she were listening, that Miss Morris's sense of humour, almost buried alive by her old ladies, got loose, and she laughed quietly at herself and gave up the attempt. Her own future was going to be a matter of concern, but Mrs. Brandon had refused even to hear anything about it till after the funeral, and for a few days Miss Morris resigned herself to drift, enjoying the sunshine and the garden and her comfortable bedroom.

Miss Brandon's funeral took place at the little church of Pomfret Abbas, whose vicar had gone in fear of his patroness for many years, while deeply grateful for her subscriptions to his various charities. It was not expected that many people would be there, for all Miss Brandon's contemporaries were dead and she had few friends.

When the car from Stories arrived with the Brandons and Miss Morris, Sir Edmund was standing at the church porch counting the arrivals.

'Morning, Lavinia,' he said. 'Poor house. Very poor house. Not seen a worse once since old Potter was buried, you know, the man over near Rushwater who used to shoot foxes. Bad time of year for a funeral with nearly everyone away or abroad. Pomfret would have come but he's away on a cruise with the young Fosters. The Dean went to Finland yesterday. Can't think why he went to Finland. Palestine more in his line, I should have thought. Don't stand about in the sun. I've kept places for you inside.'

Francis made Delia giggle by saying *sotto voce* that they wouldn't have been much good outside, and they all followed Sir Edmund up the aisle. Mrs. Brandon looked like a ravishing widow in the black pleated frock, Miss Morris looked distinguished in the georgette, and Delia had compromised in her mother's black and white foulard with a black coat over it.

'I put you well up in front,' said Sir Edmund, taking no pains to moderate his voice. 'You are about the nearest relations poor Amelia had. Who'll be chief mourner, you know.'

So saying he herded them into the pew usually reserved on happier occasions for the bride's father and mother and went away to look for fresh prey.

Mrs. Brandon looked about her and saw a few familiar faces. Roddy Wicklow, Lord Pomfret's agent, evidently representing the family; Mr. Leslie from Rushwater House, who had often drawn on Miss Brandon's purse for various county charities; Lord Stoke, who never missed a funeral and had put off going to Aix on purpose to attend; Mr. and Mrs. Keith from Northbridge Manor. At the back of the church a number of tenants and all the indoor and outdoor servants from the Abbey made a fairly respectable show. Presently Sir Edmund came back with Mr. Miller and Mr. Grant whom he put into the front pew across the aisle.

'He's a relation too,' said Sir Edmund to Mrs. Brandon. 'Nice of Miller to come with him, but a bit awkward for the Vicar here. Must put you off your stroke a bit to see another professional looking at you.'

A rather majestic scuffling was now heard near the door. It was Lady Norton, more imposing then ever in gait and array, wearing a kind of plumed hussar's hat, carrying with her Mrs. Grant.

'Good God!' exclaimed Sir Edmund, far more loudly than the atmosphere of a sacred edifice warrants, 'it's Victoria Norton. Who's that with her?'

Mrs. Brandon looked round and saw Mrs. Grant, wearing her home-spun, but paying homage to the conventions by having substituted for her amber and coral beads a heavy jet necklace and jet earrings.

The sexton attempted to usher Lady Norton into an empty pew behind the Brandons, but her ladyship, who was used to sitting on the platform at public meetings, was not so to be put off.

Taking a good look through her lorgnon at the congregation, she spied out Mr. Miller and Mr. Grant and entered graciously into their pew, driving them up into the far corner.

'You will want to sit by your boy, Felicia,' she said to Mrs. Grant. 'Dear me, how he has grown since I saw him at Frinton ten years ago. If you will come on my other side, Mr. Miller, then Mrs. Grant can sit between me and Hilary.'

After a little confusion Mrs. Grant edged past Mr. Miller and sat

next to her unwilling son. It would not be true to say that he had forgotten about his mother, to whom he dutifully wrote every day at her
express desire, but he hoped so much that she would not descend on him
again for the present that he had managed to persuade himself that his
wish was a fact. Heroically keeping back the scowl which he would
willingly have bestowed upon her, he shook hands, not quite sure
whether kissing was permissible in church.

'Dear boy,' said Mrs. Grant. 'Come stai?'

'Oh, I'm all right,' said Mr. Grant, and then mercifully the har-
monium pealed and he was safe. That the whole congregation had
their eyes riveted on Lady Norton's funereal plumes and his mother's
swinging earrings he knew only too well.

The little service was soon over and Miss Brandon's coffin laid in the
hideous family grave consisting of a block of red granite weighing about
three tons with the words 'I am hiding in thee' picked out in black along
the edge, where her parents reposed. Mr. Simpson who had been
hovering usefully about, then came forward to suggest refreshments,
but no one wanted to go to the Abbey, and there was no one to be
offended if they didn't, so the offer was politely refused and Mr.
Simpson, entirely unmoved, vanishes from these pages for evermore.

Mrs. Brandon and the party exchanged a few civil words with Lady
Norton and hoped she was coming to their Church Fête on Saturday.
Lady Norton said she would certainly try to, and as Felicia Grant was
coming back to Pomfret Madrigal on Saturday, she could drive her
over and visit the Fête at the same time.

'I didn't know you were coming back to us so soon,' said Mrs.
Brandon to Mrs. Grant, to break the silence. She then felt she might
have put it better.

'Yes, yes, my little giro with Victoria is over,' said Mrs. Grant gaily,
'and I am coming back to see something of dear Hilary before I return
to Italy. I have got my little room at the Cow and Sickle with our good
Mr. Spindler.'

Mrs. Brandon knew that she ought to ask Mrs. Grant to Stories. She
had a spare bedroom and a very adequate staff and there was really no
excuse at all for not showing hospitality, but she felt that Miss Morris,
with her devotion and her willingness to help, was all she could bear,
so she delayed for a moment, fighting her lower but really more sensible
self.

Mr. Miller, with the better excuse of a small and not very competent
staff, was going through the same agony. What added to his perplexity
was that he knew his pupil would dislike above all things to have his
mother on the premises, but his strong sense of duty overpowered all
considerations of reason.

'I do hope, Mrs. Grant,' he said, 'that you will allow me to offer the
hospitality of the Vicarage. The Cow cannot be really comfortable and

I have a spare room at your disposal. If you would honour it, we should do our very best to make you comfortable.'

Mr. Grant could have martyred his coach with the greatest of pleasure. Yet into his fury crept a certain admiration, for he knew that in the rather scantily furnished house Mr. Miller had not room in his little bedroom for all his belongings and kept a good many of them in the cupboard in the spare room, and had to move them out whenever he had a guest.

'Mr. Miller has taken the words out of my mouth,' said Mrs. Brandon untruthfully. 'I don't want to interfere, Mr. Miller, but if Mrs. Grant cared to come to Stories I should be delighted and we are only a step from the Vicarage.'

At this Francis and Delia, who did not know that she was making amends to her own conscience by trying to give discomfort to every one else, could equally have murdered their mother.

'How kind you all are,' cried Mrs. Grant. 'What can I say? Even in Calabria I have never received such hospitality. Shall I do as I used to when all my dear peasants invited me to their huts, and spend a week in each?'

Francis said 'No' so loudly that it was almost audible, and Delia made a face at Mr. Grant which he answered with another face before he knew what he was doing. Mr. Miller ardently wished that he had not spoken first and Mrs. Brandon as ardently wished she had let well alone, and all the young people hated the grown-ups who had landed them in this unconscionable mess, when Lady Norton, for the first time in her life being of some real use, told Mrs. Grant to take her advice and go back to the Cow.

'You'll be a fool if you don't, Felicia,' she said. 'Mrs. Spindler was my kitchenmaid for three years and is a very nice woman. Go to her and you can do what you like, and she can cook vegetarian things, because Norton had to have them on account of his gastric trouble. And if you want to go folk-loring in the evening it won't matter if you are late for meals. Mrs. Brandon and Mr. Miller have guests already, so you'll only be a nuisance.'

'Well, I daresay you are right, Victoria,' said Mrs. Grant, enjoying this competition for her favours. 'And I left two trunks and a lot of Calabrian pottery at the Cow, so I might as well go back. But we will all meet often and merrily,' she added, jangling her earrings.

Mrs. Brandon and Mr. Miller, freed from this pressing terror, felt they didn't care how often or how merrily they met so long as Mrs. Grant was not staying under either of their roofs, and began feverishly to plan dinners and lunches for Mrs. Grant.

'Come along, Felicia,' said Lady Norton. 'Lunch will be waiting. Good-bye, Mrs. Brandon; good-bye, Mr. Miller. I shall certainly come over to the Fête on Saturday.'

After exchanging a few words with friends, largely it is to be feared with the intention of getting them to come to the Fête, Mrs. Brandon moved towards the car when a thought struck her. She paused, looked at Miss Morris, went on again and then stopped once more.

'I was thinking,' she said to Miss Morris, 'of asking Mr. Miller and Mr. Grant to come back to lunch, because I know it is his cook's day off. But if it would be at all uncomfortable for you — —'

Miss Morris hastened to say that she would of course like it very much.

'I can't tell you how ashamed I still am of my rudeness the other day,' she said. 'When I think how good you have been to me I feel I can never apologize enough. If only you knew how grateful I am for all your kindness.''

'Then that will be very nice,' said Mrs. Brandon, suppressing a desire to say that Miss Morris would give her great pleasure by never being grateful again. Then she issued her invitation to Mr. Miller, who said Indeed, indeed, they would be delighted to come.

Lunch passed off very pleasantly indeed. Mr. Miller was a little nervous at first, but Miss Morris was again the calm, competent woman that Mrs. Brandon had first met, and spoke to the Vicar as if he were any ordinary human being. While Rose was about, the conversation was general, though one thought was naturally uppermost in all minds, and when they were at last alone over coffee, Francis was the first to voice it.

'When does one know about people's wills?' he inquired of the company at large. 'Don't tell me not to say things like that, mamma. I thought we all came home to a feast after the funeral and had pork pie and ham and bottled beer and cheese and whisky and then the lawyer read the will aloud and everyone was disappointed.'

Delia, who had talked the matter over thoroughly with Francis and had read one or two Victorian novels, said yes, and another will would be found in a hat box and they would all have a million pounds and she would spend a lot of it at the Fête.

Francis said she was counting her chickens before they were hatched.

'Well, what really *does* happen?' said his mother. 'Mr. Miller, you are always having funerals. What do they do?'

Mr. Miller had to confess that he had never been present at one of those gatherings dear to the older novelists when the will is read over madeira and seedcake, but he said that judging from his own very small personal experience when his aunt left him two thousand pounds of worthless Brazilian stock, Miss Brandon's lawyers would write to anyone concerned as soon as possible.

'Then if we don't hear from her lawyers we don't get anything,' said Francis cheerfully. 'Come on, Hilary, I'll have a shilling with you on who gets the gorillas.'

Mr. Grant being agreeable, each gentleman made a note of the transaction and Francis asked Miss Morris to hold the stakes, which she obligingly consented to do.

Mr. Miller then said he must go, as a lot of notices for the Fête still had to be written, about teas and where to park bicycles, and the Assistant-Scoutmaster, Mr. Spindler's brother at Little Misfit, who had kindly offered to help him, nearly always got his 'N's' and 'S's' the wrong way round. Everyone felt they ought to help too.

Mr. Miller said lingeringly well he must be off. Everyone breathing again at the thought that help with the notices need not now be offered, said what a shame, with an undercurrent of relief which could only have passed unnoticed by one so simple and trusting as the Vicar. As he said good-bye to Miss Morris, she looked uneasy and then said, 'Mr. Miller.'

He stopped.

'I don't know if I could be of any help, said Miss Morris. 'I used to write out all my father's church notices — you probably wouldn't remember — and as I have nothing at all to do here, I thought I could perhaps be of assistance to you.'

'You are kind, very kind,' said Mr. Miller, humbly surprized and gratified. 'Indeed, indeed I remember your writing, a real work of art. But ought you to try yourself so much? You have had a severe shock and need rest.'

'Idleness does one no good,' said Miss Morris severely. 'And to make myself useful is my only way of thanking Mrs. Brandon for all her wonderful kindness.'

'She is indeed kindness itself,' said Mr. Miller, gratified by this praise of his hotess. 'Mrs. Brandon, one moment if I may trespass on your time — Miss Morris has kindly offered, most kindly, to help me with the notices for the Fête. While her assistance would be invaluable, for she does beautiful lettering, I feel she should not undertake too much at present.'

'I know,' said Mrs. Brandon, voicing her knowledge of her own thoughts rather than of Miss Morris's calligraphy. 'I know. You bring all your notices up here, Mr. Miller, and Miss Morris can have a table in the Green dressing-room, where no one will disturb her, and do just as much as she feels like.'

'Excellent, excellent,' cried Mr. Miller. 'But Miss Morris must not overtax her strength.'

'I won't let her,' said Mrs. Brandon, thus filling both her hearers with a passion of gratitude for her noble unselfishness.

Mr. Miller then took his leave, promising to be back within the hour with the necessary materials. Mrs. Brandon said not within the hour, because Miss Morris must have a rest, but perhaps at tea-time. Mr. Miller was overcome by a sense of guilt at his own selfishness and said doubtless he could do the notices himself, but Mrs. Brandon said, 'Tea-time then,' so firmly that he went away without another word.

'You think of nothing but others,' said Miss Morris to Mrs. Brandon, fervently. Mrs. Brandon smiled, sent her upstairs to rest till tea-time, and went back to the drawing-room where she sank, a little dramatically, onto the sofa.

'When you look at us all with that brave smile, it is obvious what has happened, darling,' said Francis. 'You have as usual been a prey to doing the effective thing and now you are going to pay for it by having Miss Morris be grateful and devoted all over you, and that will make you very tired.'

'I don't see what else I could do,' said Mrs. Brandon apologetically. 'If only she wouldn't be grateful she would be no trouble at all.'

'Well, she will be grateful,' said Francis, 'and if you aren't careful she'll stay here for ever and do the flowers. I wonder if we could get Sir Edmund to marry her. Coming to play tennis, Hilary?'

Mr. Grant said he was sorry but he must go back to the Vicarage and work.

'All right, I'll take Delia on,' said her brother. 'Come on, Silly-Dilly.'

They went off, leaving Mr. Grant with his hostess. Mr. Grant said he must be going. Mrs. Brandon felt that if anyone said again that he must be going and didn't go at once, she might scream, so she shut her eyes.

'I have tired you,' said Mr. Grant, all aglow to abase himself. 'Forgive me for being so selfish. I will go at once, without disturbing you.'

Mrs. Brandon felt pleasantly weak with self-pity and said nothing, hoping that her guest would go. Hearing no sound she cautiously opened her eyes again and saw that Mr. Grant, far from having gone without disturbing her, was gazing down at her with dark violence.

'You know I would do *anything* for you,' he stammered, and banging into a chair he left the room.

Mrs. Brandon shut her eyes again and dropped into a refreshing slumber, from which she was not disturbed till tea was brought in and Miss Morris came down. She was closely followed by Mr. Miller with a parcel.

'You see I have taken you at your word, Mrs. Brandon,' said Mr. Miller, 'and come to tea. And here are the materials, Miss Morris, if you are sure the effort will not tire you. I have cut all the notices to the right size and lightly pencilled upon them the words they should carry. The actual form of the lettering I leave of course entirely to you. I only beg you not to do more than you feel equal to. I fear we need rather a large number, two notices for the Bicycle Park, three of Teas, One Shilling, though of course the words One Shilling will be written in figures, one for the Ice Cream and Soft Drinks tent, and one or two saying This Way to the Fête, Admission Adults Sixpence, Children Twopence. These I shall have put up in the village to catch the unwary tourist. They will also,' said Mr. Miller, looking worried, 'require arrows on them, some pointing in one direction, some in another, if I make myself clear.'

'Perfectly,' said Miss Morris. 'You mean an arrow pointing one way on one notice and the other way on another so that people approaching the Vicarage from opposite directions may know which direction to take.'

'I see what you mean,' said Mrs. Brandon, who had not been able to concentrate before because of pouring out tea. 'If you are coming *up* the street from the Cow you want an arrow pointing towards the Vicarage; but if you were coming *down* the street from the shop, you'd need an arrow pointing to the Vicarage in the other direction.'

'You are sure it will not be too much for you?' said Mr. Miller, looking anxiously at Miss Morris.

'It will remind me of old days,' said Miss Morris. 'I still have the brushes with which I used to do my father's announcements, and with some Indian Ink I believe I could make quite a good effect.'

'Aha!' cried Mr. Miller. 'I thought I remembered that you preferred Indian Ink and brought some with me.'

Mrs. Brandon said she had a call to make in the village and went away.

'I do feel it indeed a privilege to have Mrs. Brandon as a neighbour,' said Mr. Miller, gazing at the drawing-room door through which she had just departed.

'I have never met anyone so genuinely kind,' said Miss Morris. 'I would do anything for her to show my gratitude, but unfortunately there is nothing I can do.'

'I am certain,' said Mr. Miller earnestly, 'that she feels being allowed to help you in this your hour of need is the greatest privilege she could have. Besides I am sure you are the greatest comfort to her in many ways.'

'I can do the flowers for her,' said Miss Morris, 'and I have offered to help with her accounts. I find that she has considerable difficulty in adding up figures.'

'She has my deepest sympathy,' said Mr. Miller. 'I assure you, Miss Morris, that any accounts connected with church or parish work cause me sleepless nights. For my own income that does not matter so much. When I have allotted a tenth part to my poorer brethren all I have to do is not to live outside the rest, and with the help of an occasional guest, such as Hilary Grant, that is quite possible. But on Saturday, for instance, with the Fête, I know, I positively know that I shall be confused. Last year, as I told Mrs. Brandon, I found myself seventeen shillings and threepence out of pocket. Not,' he added hastily, 'that I grudged the money, but suppose, which is equally probable, that I had found myself seventeen shillings and threepence to the good.

How unjust would have been my stewardship of money that is only in my hands in trust for others.'

He looked so wretched that Miss Morris felt here was someone she could help.

'I suppose you would not care to let me take over the merely technical side of the Fête accounts,' she said, not quite knowing what she meant by the word technical, but feeling that in using it she was being careful to distinguish between helping Mr. Miller as a man and as a priest.

'Your kindness – really, Miss Morris,' said the Vicar.

'It would really be a pleasure,' said Miss Morris, the spirit of a thoroughly competent daughter of the clergy beginning to shine in her eye. 'I did all my father's accounts, church and personal, and I have usually done the household accounts for my old ladies.'

'No, I cannot allow myself to trespass upon your kindness, Miss Morris,' said Mr. Miller firmly. 'Whatever muddles I have made this year are the outcome of my own stupidity and I must face the consequences. Next year – if it were not too much to ask – –'

'I don't know where I shall be next year,' said Miss Morris simply. 'I have to find another situation as soon as possible.'

'Forgive me,' said Mr. Miller, much distressed. 'My thoughtlessness is unpardonable. And to think that I should cast my burdens upon you at such a time.'

He made as though he would sweep all the cardboard and Indian Ink into his embrace and carry them off again, but Miss Morris, ignoring this gesture, said she would like to start work at once, so he said good-bye.

'Before you go, Mr. Miller, there is one thing I must say,' said Miss Morris. 'If I do not go to church with Mrs. Brandon on Sunday, I hope you will not misunderstand me. I know that my presence or absence could make no difference, but I would not like you to think me wanting in courtesy. I cannot so far ignore my dear father's wishes as to attend a form of worship that he disapproved. If there is, within walking distance, a place where worship is conducted as my father would have wished, I shall go to it.'

'I do respect your scruples,' said Mr. Miller earnestly. 'There is Tompion over at Little Misfit, two miles by the fields though, too far for you at present; and Carson at Nutfield who would, I am sure, suit you admirably, delightful fellows both, though we do not see eye to eye. But Nutfield is too far. What can be done?'

Miss Morris begged him not to trouble, as she was well used to looking after herself, and thanked Mr. Miller for his understanding.

'Your father and I could not, alas, agree to differ,' said Mr. Miller, with one of his very rare smiles, 'but I hope that you and I may agree on that, if on nothing else.'

Miss Morris took the cardboard and Indian Ink upstairs to the Green dressing-room and began her work.

*

Francis's idle words about making Sir Edmund marry Miss Morris at once bore fruit in his mother's fertile mind. Happening to meet Sir Edmund in the village she asked him to dine on the following night, and added Mr. Grant to the party to make up even numbers. By putting Miss Morris between Francis and Sir Edmund and explaining to Francis exactly the self-effacing role required of him, she hoped to precipitate matters considerably, but being no conspirator by nature she forgot to explain to her son the part he was to play. The result was that Francis and Miss Morris, who had a sort of understanding based on a kindly cynicism about human nature, talked to each other through most of dinner, while Sir Edmund fell a prey to Delia who had, as usual, some interesting local news to impart. A mentally defective labourer on Lord Pomfret's estate had killed the old uncle and aunt with whom he lodged by battering their heads in with a huge billet of wood. He had then knocked up his nearest neighbours, boasted gleefully of what he had done, gone home and thrown himself down the well. With what her family recognized as Delia's luck, she had passed the cottage on her bicycle just as the police were getting the body out. True, they had not allowed her to see it, nor to try artificial respiration, but she had had the intense pleasure of seeing Something with a blanket over it taken away, after which she had had a happy day with the otter hounds.

Sir Edmund said he had heard about it from his bailiff, and the Tiddens were always in trouble of some sort.

'Well, this was Horace Tidden,' said Delia. 'His father was always a bit dotty.'

'That would have been Ned Tidden,' said Sir Edmund, who had the intricate relationships of the countryside at his finger tips. 'He married his cousin, Lily Tidden. She was illegitimate of course. Ford sees her in the County Asylum from time to time. Since she nearly killed one of the nurses she has been quite happy and quiet.'

By these pleasant rural paths the conversation meandered to Grumper's End, where the chicken pox was still about. Delia said she hoped Jimmy Thatcher wasn't sickening, but he had a horrid cough.

Meanwhile Mrs. Brandon, thrown back on Mr. Grant's society, told him all about the pleated frock and the georgette that was a little too tight and the green frock that was dyed and the black and white foulard and the lilac georgette for afterwards, and Mr. Grant felt that he was the kind of man to whom exquisite ladies confided their secrets and could talk about really interesting things; rather like an abbé under the ancien régime.

After dinner Mrs. Brandon made another effort to get Sir Edmund into connection with Miss Morris.

'Do, Sir Edmund,' she said, making room for him on the sofa beside her, 'do have a little talk to Miss Morris. She is such a delightful person and such a help to me with the flowers.'

'Looks a sensible woman,' said Sir Edmund, glancing at Miss Morris who was examining gramophone records with the three young people. 'Not my style though. A bit too quiet. No life in her. Couldn't get a word out of her at dinner.'

'You didn't try as far as I could see,' said Mrs. Brandon.

'You couldn't see at all,' said Sir Edmund. 'Playing your tricks on that young Grant. I've got something I want to say to you, Lavinia.'

'What is it?' asked Mrs. Brandon, all flattering attention, hoping to bend Sir Edmund to her desires.

Sir Edmund pulled an envelope out of his pocket.

'You know that row I've been having about those new Council cottages,' he said. 'Well, I've written a pretty strong letter to the *Barchester Chronicle* about them and I'd like you to hear it before it goes. The average reader isn't very intelligent and I'd like to try it on you.'

Mrs. Brandon said she would love to hear it, and taking up her tapestry work prepared herself to attend.

'Don't fiddle with that embroidery, Lavinia,' said Sir Edmund. 'You can't do two things at once. No one can. I want you to listen.'

Mrs. Brandon, smiling angelically, wrapped her work up again in a silk handkerchief and looked intelligent.

'I'll just tell you exactly how the matter stands about those cottages,' said Sir Edmund, 'then you'll see the point of my letter."

As his précis of the affair included a description of every battle he had fought with the Barchester County Council during the last forty years, and exactly what he thought of all builders and contractors, Mrs. Brandon had plenty of time to construct a charming romance in which Sir Edmund and Miss Morris were married at Barchester Cathedral and she had a new dress for the wedding with one of those little hats with veils that were so becoming. Just as she was thinking how nice it would be if Mr. Miller could take part in the marriage ceremony, Sir Edmund said, 'I don't believe you've heard a word I've been saying, Lavinia.'

'Well, quite truthfully I haven't heard much,' said Mrs. Brandon. 'You see I was thinking about you so hard that I couldn't listen to you.'

'Don't talk nonsense, Lavinia,' said Sir Edmund, quite unmoved by this subtle flattery. 'I don't suppose you were thinking about me at all. Thinking about the new dress more likely.'

'Well, I was,' said Mrs. Brandon meekly. 'At least a dress that I'd had dyed. But what I *really* want to hear is your letter, not about the County Council. I think Miss Morris ought to hear it too. She is so practical. Miss Morris!' she called across the room, 'could you come here for a moment.'

Miss Morris came.

'Sir Edmund has a most interesting letter to read to us,' said Mrs. Brandon, 'and we are sure you can help. Do begin again from the beginning, Sir Edmund, and tell Miss Morris all about the cottages.'

Sir Edmund obligingly began all over again, fought all his battles with the County Council and the contractors, and finally read his letter aloud, though with some difficulty, owing to the number of corrections he had made.

'Pretty strong, I think,' he said approvingly when he had finished.

'If you will excuse me, Sir Edmund,' said Miss Morris, who had been listening with impartial intelligence, 'I would suggest —' and she made one or two very practical suggestions, which would have the double advantage of making the letter intelligible and alleviating the danger of three or four separate libel actions. Sir Edmund, recognizing the value of her remarks, wrote her wording over his own and then looked disconsolately upon the paper which had become a palimpsest several layers deep.

'I could easily type it out for you if you like, Sir Edmund,' said Miss Morris, 'with a copy, and it would reach the *Chronicle* offices in plenty of time. They don't go to press till Tuesday.'

At this point Mrs. Brandon, delighted at her success in throwing her two guests together, abstracted herself from their society and went over to the gramophone. Mr. Grant was waiting for Francis and Delia who had gone to look for some records that Francis had left in his car, and was enchanted to have his hostess to himself for a moment.

'I have hardly seen you this evening, Hilary,' said Mrs. Brandon in a most upsetting way, and apparently forgetting that he had been next to her for all the early part of the evening.

'I was so hoping to have a word with you,' said Mr. Grant, who might have been thought by an impartial observer to have had practically nothing else all through dinner. 'I don't know why, but you are the only person I can really talk to about myself.'

Having made this noble avowal Mr. Grant went bright red and gazed appealingly at Mrs. Brandon, who was enjoying herself immensely. The conversation would doubtless have proceeded along these interesting if well-worn lines had not Rose come in to say that Mr. Merton wished to speak to Mrs. Brandon on the phone. She was absent from the room for nearly ten minutes and when she came back Francis and Delia were with Mr. Grant.

'Who were you talking to, darling?' said Francis. 'You have your mysterious mischief face.'

'Mr. Merton rang me up,' said Mrs. Brandon, ignoring her son's last words. 'He is staying with the Keiths this week-end and is coming over

with them to the Fête to-morrow, and said he would like to come and
see us. So I said a glass of sherry about six. I couldn't say tea, because
we must have Tea, One Shilling to please Mr. Miller.'

Francis and Delia expressed loud approval of a visit from Mr.
Merton. Mr. Grant kept his disapproval to himself and christened Mrs.
Brandon the Belle Dame Sans Merci in his own mind.

'Well, Lavinia, I must be off,' said Sir Edmund, coming up. 'Miss
Morris is going to type that letter for me. I will make the Council sit up.
Quite a nice woman. She says she wants a job, secretary or something.
If I hear of anything I'll let you know.'

With this lover-like speech he said good-bye and the party broke up.

'I do hope you had a nice talk with Sir Edmund,' said Mrs. Brandon
to Miss Morris, when she took her to her room.

'Very nice,' said Miss Morris. 'He has kindly promised to let me
know if he hears of any work I could do.'

It was hardly the attitude of one whose heart was involved, and Mrs.
Brandon could only tell herself that everything must have a beginning.
When she had said good night and gone to her room, Miss Morris got
out her typewriter and made two fair copies of Sir Edmund's letter. It
was now eleven o'clock, but there was still work that her conscience
told her must be done. The cards with arrows and directions for reaching the Vicarage had only been sketched in pencil. Miss Morris got out
her Indian Ink and her brushes and sat down at the table in the Green
dressing-room. As she worked she felt that she was once more at home,
doing the notices for her father, and that their pleasant young guest
Mr. Miller would help to put them up to-morrow morning. It was
true that her bedroom at home was an attic, poorly furnished with
painted deal furniture and an iron bedstead, and that instead of a
shaded reading lamp she would have been working by a little oil lamp
while she waited for her father to call out for her to come and read to
him. But though so much was changed, one thing was unchanged. Mr.
Miller, who if he had not behaved so unkindly to her father would have
been the most agreeable pupil they had ever had, was in the Vicarage,
not far away, and would be putting up to-morrow morning the notices
that she was finishing now. There was yet another thing unchanged, but
Miss Morris did not notice it, because it was herself, and not being
given by temperament or training to introspection, it never occurred to
her to consider that Miss Morris, the homeless and penniless companion,
was only Ella Morris, the Vicar's daughter, in other circumstances and
surroundings. The gulf between her old life and the life of the last
twenty-five years was so great that she saw a stranger on the far side of
it, having little in common with herself. When she had finished she laid
down her brush and pondered on Ella Morris, who had once been so
angry with Mr. Miller for annoying her father that she could not even
pray for him. Then Miss Morris the companion put her work tidily

away, but before she lay down she knelt by her bed, as she had been taught to do and had always done, and prayed for Mr. Miller as heartily as if he were her enemy.

X

NEXT morning promised well for the Fête. As Mr. Grant looked out of his window he saw the valley still shrouded in a light mist which, by a beautiful and poetical flight of fancy, he compared to the filmy veils of sleep from which Mrs. Brandon would presently emerge, a goddess made manifest. He then remembered with some annoyance that his mother was coming that afternoon, but put the disagreeable thought resolutely away and went down to breakfast. Already in the Vicarage paddock stalls were being put up and helpers were getting in the way. A lorry came crashing past the front gate and turned into the field where it unloaded the marquee in which tea was to be served. The roundabout with its steam organ had arrived the night before and was partly erected. Two oily men were carrying boats, ostriches, aeroplane bodies, cocks, horses, swans and other usual methods of transit, from the van to the platform and fixing them to the brightly polished spiral brass poles which would carry them on their circular path. Mr. Miller came in, hot but not entirely without hope.

'Good morning, sir,' said Mr. Grant. 'It looks like a fine day for the Fête.'

'Indeed, indeed it does,' said Mr. Miller. 'I have just been putting up some of the Tea, One Shilling notices. I do hope we shall not have so much paper left about as last year. The schoolmaster has spoken about it to the children, and the Women's Institute and the Scouts are collaborating. Mr. Spindler has offered us the use of two large dustbins for rubbish of all sorts, and a party of Wolf Cubs are at this moment scrubbing them out. I shall put one near the Confectionery Stall and one near the Ice-Cream Stall. And I must have notices written for them. What would you put, Hilary? "Rubbish" or "Refuse" or simply "Waste Paper"?'

Mr. Grant thought Rubbish would do.

'I must ask Hettie if we have any old cardboard boxes,' said the Vicar. 'White ones of course, because ink doesn't show on brown, and then I must write the notices.'

'Couldn't I do it, sir?' asked Mr. Grant.

'That would indeed be kind,' said the Vicar. 'I will ask about some cardboard at once.'

But before he could ring, Hettie came in with a parcel.

'Please sir, Sid brought this over from Stories,' she said, 'and we was to be sure to be careful with it.'

'Thanks, Hettie,' said the Vicar. 'And do you think we have any pieces of carboard large enough to write Rubbish on?'

'I'm sure I don't know sir,' said Hettie. 'There's plenty of paper in your study, sir, if you wanted to write rubbish. There was that new lot from the Nutfield Co-op. come only a fortnight ago.'

'Mr. Miller means he wants to write Rubbish on a large piece of cardboard to put it up,' said Mr. Grant.

'Well, I daresay Cook or me could find something if he really wants to write rubbish,' said Hettie, obviously impressed by her master's determination thus to free his soul.

'Look, Hilary,' said Mr. Miller excitedly.

He had opened the parcel. In it were three exquisitely written notices of This Way to the Fête, complete with arrows, some pointing one way, some the other.

'Those are ripping, sir,' said Mr. Grant. 'And what's under them?'

Mr. Miller drew out a rather smaller package. He unwrapped it and took out three placards on which were emblazoned the words NO LITTER. KINDLY PUT ALL RUBBISH IN HERE.

'It is like an answer to prayer,' said Mr. Miller.

'And a jolly quick answer too,' said Mr. Grant, yielding to none in his admiration of an omniscient and evidently all-potent Providence. 'I mean you'd only just begun thinking about the rubbish, hadn't you, sir?'

'There are things that we do not understand,' said Mr. Miller, truthfully, and at the same time much abashing his pupil. 'But here is a letter which will doubtless explain. You may read it,' he added, pushing it towards Mr. Grant.

The letter was neatly typewritten and ran as follows:

DEAR MR. MILLER,

I am sending you the notices of the Fête. Mrs. Brandon is kindly allowing the garden boy to take them over as I am sure you will be early at work. You may remember that my father, who had a great dislike for disorder of any kind, always had receptacles for paper and other rubbish at any church functions. In case this thought has also occurred to you, I am also sending you three notices. If you have no special receptacles for litter, I might suggest that empty dustbins, well scrubbed out with a disinfectant, would answer the purpose. I always cleared the Vicarage dustbin myself for this purpose in old days.

With every good wish for the success of the Fête,

Yours sincerely,

ELLA MORRIS

'How marvellous of Mrs. Brandon to think of sending them over early,' said Mr. Grant in a reverent voice.

Mr. Miller began to busy himself in tidying the paper and string that were littering the end of the dining-room table. He suddenly remembered a summer morning more than twenty-five years ago and Mr. Morris's daughter in a check apron outside the kitchen door, carrying a pail of water and a scrubbing brush. Young Mr. Miller had offered to carry the pail, but Miss Morris had said she could quite well manage, but would he be kind enough to get the tin of Jeyes' Fluid off the scullery window sill, as she must clean out the dustbin for the Church Lads' Brigade tea and entertainment. The smell of disinfectant came nostalgically back to him across the years. He stopped smoothing and folding the papers and stood still.

'You look a bit tired, sir,' said Mr. Grant, with real concern. 'You haven't had breakfast yet. I'll clear that paper away.'

Mr. Miller, remembering that he must be hard at work all day and not fail his parishioners at any point, obediently sat down and made a fairly good breakfast.

'You had better make a good meal now, Hilary,' he said. 'Hettie and Cook always have the day off for the Fête and I'm afraid it will only be the sort of lunch they leave on the table. I sometimes wish that cold tongue and tomatoes had never been invented.'

When Miss Morris, who did not always get up for breakfast, came down about eleven o'clock she found her hostess slightly discomposed.

'I *cannot* make up my mind about this afternoon,' said Mrs. Brandon. 'I meant to wear the black and white foulard, the one I lent Delia for the funeral, but Nurse wants me to wear the lilac georgette and make Delia wear the foulard.'

'I think Nurse is right,' said Miss Morris gravely. 'With that pinkish hat and scarf of yours it would look very well.'

'I had thought of that,' said Mrs. Brandon. 'But I don't see how one could really count pink as mourning.'

Miss Morris said it was two days after the funeral.

'Yes, I have put it to myself that way,' said Mrs. Brandon with an air of broad-mindedness, 'but I somehow feel that one cannot quite go out of mourning on a Saturday. Monday would be all right, but I can't quite *feel* Saturday. But it is all very mixing, because if one goes on wearing mourning for Aunt Sissie it looks as if one were trying to influence her.'

Miss Morris pointed out that as Miss Brandon's will must necessarily have been made before her death, it was highly improbable that it could be in any way influenced by Mrs. Brandon's choice of a dress. Mrs. Brandon, while admitting the justice of this contention, said that she had a feeling about it. Having thus settled the question she asked Miss Morris what she meant to wear.

'My usual blue dress,' said Miss Morris.

'Wouldn't the black georgette be cooler?' said Mrs. Brandon. 'It's going to be frightfully hot. Or if you wouldn't mind the black and white foulard Delia would love not to wear it. She wants to wear a green dress and Nurse is making difficulties.'

'Thank you so much,' said Miss Morris, 'but I think my blue dress would be best. I haven't any reason to wear mourning and a long dress would not be very suitable for me. I thought Mr. Miller might need a little help during the afternoon, and if I take an apron with me I shall be quite prepared.'

'But you mustn't dream of helping,' said Mrs. Brandon, genuinely anxious about her protégée's health. 'You aren't up to it. You have no idea how stuffy everything gets, and all the children, and the noise of the roundabout. I am always exhausted after an hour of it.'

'I am quite used to that sort of thing,' said Miss Morris. 'I ran everything for my father when I was a girl and I always got on well with the children. Of course we couldn't afford the roundabout — it was a very poor parish — but we had the Temperance Silver Brass Band and the noise they made was quite dreadful.'

Mrs. Brandon gave in and with considerable heroism said she would wear the foulard, so that Delia would be free to wear her green frock.

'Lunch has to be at one to-day,' she said. 'I do hope you don't mind, but the maids all take it in turns to go down to the Fête, so it will be a kind of picnic.'

*

The picnic, which included veal cutlets and three vegetables and a chocolate soufflé and gooseberry fool (which was still tyrannizing over the countryside) with little freshly made almond fingers and cream cheese and several sorts of biscuits and coffee and a choice of lemonade, white wine and cider, was being repeated with differences all over the neighbourhood. At the Vicarage Mr. Miller and Mr. Grant were mildly depressed by slices of pressed beef from the Barchester Co-op. gently perspiring on a blue dish, three overripe tomatoes, and the remains of yesterday's stewed gooseberries put into a smaller dish. At Southbridge Mr. and Mrs. Keith, their unmarried daughter Lydia and their guest Mr. Merton had lunch at a quarter past one instead of half-past, so that the parlourmaid and the cook could catch the motor bus. Those excellent fellows Tompion at Little Misfit and Carson at Nutfield, found themselves condemned, by a kind of unwritten law one supposes, to the same pressed beef, tomatoes, and yesterday's stewed gooseberries as were being served at Pomfret Madrigal Vicarage. Mr. Tompion, who was famed for his bad luck, had the heel of one piece of pressed beef and the toe or beginning of another, because he had done the shopping himself in Barchester and was too humble to tell the young man at the

Co-op. to give him a quarter of a pound from a nice piece that was already in cut. Mr. Carson, on the other hand, had some nice fresh slices, personally chosen by his housekeeper who liked pressed beef herself, but the gooseberries, which she didn't like, were two days old and tasted of ferment, besides having one or two suspicious patches of fur, so that only fear of the housekeeper made Mr. Carson eat them at all. But everyone will be glad to know that both those gentlemen married within the year, Mr. Tompion in January a colonel's daughter from Leamington, and Mr. Carson at Easter a very nice widow from the midlands who stood no nonsense from servants, and both ladies treated their husbands extremely well.

At Norton Park Lady Norton said to Mrs. Grant that they would not have a glass of sherry before lunch, so that some of the servants could go in the estate Ford to the Fête, a piece of altruism which made her butler, who was not going, despise her. The only person who really picnicked was Sir Edmund, who disliked lunch and seized the opportunity of having sandwiches, which he ate in front of the council cottages in a manner highly disconcerting to his enemy the foreman, who felt nervously compelled to work right up to the legal time of knocking off.

Down at Grumper's End Jimmy Thatcher, who had a nasty cough and an obvious temperature, ate far too much pickled pork because his mother said if he didn't finish what was on his plate he could go to bed and stay there, and to hurry up about it.

By half-past two the first piercing blasts of the steam organ announced to the village, most of whom were already on the field, that the Fête had really begun. The gentry did not begin to turn up till later, among the first being the party from Stories. Mrs. Brandon had insisted on giving a ten shilling note to each of her party, to be spent at the various stalls. Francis and Delia gladly accepted the gift and Miss Morris's protests were overruled by all three Brandons, who pointed out that she was for the present one of the family. Her protestations were finally cut short by Francis, who with great foresight had laid in two pounds' worth of sixpences, threepenny bits and coppers at the bank in Barchester that morning, and offered to change everyone's notes for them.

'That is really practical,' said Miss Morris admiringly. 'I can't think why we never thought of that at our Fêtes. I remember what difficulty we always had about change, and as we always had the Fête on a Thursday, which was early closing day, the shop and the bank were shut.'

'Don't be extravagant, Miss Morris,' said Francis. 'And remember I have booked the first ride on the roundabout with you. I bag the cock, but if you don't like the ostrich you and Delia can go in an aeroplane.'

As they walked to the Vicarage Miss Morris's placards drew forth much admiration from the Brandon's who had not yet seen them, and

when a carful of obvious strangers was seen to slow down, look at the
notice, stop, consult, and turn the car towards the Vicarage gate,
Francis, whose relations with Miss Morris were now on much the same
gentlemanly and unemotional footing as those of Mr. Swiveller and
Miss Brass, hit her kindly on the back and said that meant at least ten
shillings in teas and side shows. Miss Morris smiled indulgently at
Francis and walked quietly on, but her whole being was seething with
an excitement she could hardly control. She had been brought up, as
the widower parson's daughter, on mothers' meetings, G.F.S. meetings,
sewing parties, Sunday School excursions, bazaars, fêtes, rummage
sales and the hundred activities of the Vicarage. She had given un-
grudgingly her time, thought and labour, and it was her secret pride
that no event for which she had been responsible had ever been a failure.
Under her management receipts had always exceeded expenses, even
if only by so narrow a margin as three and elevenpence halfpenny, teas
had been generous, no children had ever been lost or had accidents,
mothers had happily sat wedged in a motor coach for four hours, spent
one hour in the pouring rain at Weston-Super-Mare, and happily and
damply sung for four hours on the way home. Fractious children had
been quelled by her presence, and for all infantile diseases Miss Morris's
help and advice were infinitely preferred to those of the district nurse by
mothers and patients alike. She knew that there was nothing she could
not organize and carry through successfully, which gave her a sense of
power, very dear to her heart.

   With her father's death all this had come to an end. For twenty years
she had hidden herself under the mask of Miss Morris, rather a *reserved*
kind of woman, my dear, but quite trustworthy and nursed poor Aunt
Emma up to the end, and would do splendidly for your husband's
old sister, I am certain. It had been a life of severe self-repression. Not
as regarded her old ladies, for to them she felt on the whole a kindly and
unsentimental tolerance, but as regarded the arrangements of the
houses and hotels where they lived, the organization of service, the discipline of servants, the regulating of expenditure. But in dreams she
beheld a parish, every detail of which was under her hand and eye,
every relationship known to her, where she would collaborate with all
officials and at the same time protect her flock against them, where
everything would be a part of one smoothly-running machine of which
she was the centre. As for the actual spiritual leader of this parish, she
gave him no thought, for her imagination did not work on those lines.
If he existed at all it was as a conscientious if shadowy figure who came to
her for advice on every point and did not meddle. To-day for the first
time since her servitude had begun, she was to live for a few hours in the
familiar life, and though no one heard her, she was saying Ha-ha
loudly and exultingly.

   Admission Sixpence was paid by Mrs. Brandon for the whole party and they entered the field. Mr. Grant, who was helping with the coconut shies, had been looking out for them and came forward to meet them.

'I suppose you wouldn't care to try for a coconut, Mrs. Brandon,' he said.

Mrs. Brandon said she thought not and she would go and buy some things at the Produce Stall and the Fancy Stall and then perhaps sit in the Vicarage garden away from the noise.

'You all go and amuse yourselves,' she said to the three young people, 'and come and fetch me at four o'clock and we'll have tea in the marquee. It is rather horrible but one must. And Francis, ask whoever is in charge of the teas to keep me a table. I'll get the Keiths to join us and Mrs. Morland and your mother, Hilary, and Lady Norton if she stays, so we might be about a dozen. I know they have the two ping-pong tables from the British Legion club room, so do ask them to put them together and that will do nicely.'

'O.K. mamma,' said Francis. 'I go, I go, see how I go. Come with me, Miss Morris. I'm sure you can deal with tea-tents better than I can.'

Miss Morris said she would be very glad if she could be of any help and the two went off.

'And now,' said Mrs. Brandon to Delia, 'you won't want to go round the stalls, darling. I know what will happen. I shall have to buy Cook's jam and cake, and Ethel's knitted dish-cloths, and Nurse's baby woollies, and send them all to the hospital. Take Hilary on the roundabout.'

Mr. Grant was wounded to the quick by Mrs. Brandon's summary relegation of him to the rank of a young person, but Delia gave him no time to feel annoyance. Expressing a fear that someone might have bagged the ostrich, she urged her cousin Hilary rapidly in the direction of the roundabout. The boats and other conveyances were just slowing down and several people were getting off. Calling to Mr. Grant to follow her, Delia climbed onto the still moving platform and seized the ostrich onto which she leapt and sat side saddle with an expression of pride and contentment. Under her direction Mr. Grant took possession of the cock, whose orbit was within that of the ostrich, and mounted it astride. One of the oily men came round.

'I pay this one,' said Delia, 'and you pay the next, and so on. Two please.' And she held out four pennies.

'Threepence, miss,' said the oily man.

'It was twopence last year,' said Delia.

The oily man was understood to say that it was threepence this year because of the Government, and that even so it was a dead loss to the proprietor, Mr. Packer, who ran it on a purely philanthropic basis.

'All right,' said Delia. 'Here's half a crown, and tell Mr. Packer I'm going to have my rides at twopence a time. That's seven and a half rides each, and Mr. Grant will give you another half-crown and that makes fifteen rides each, or we may use some of them for friends.'

The oily man said he supposed that was all right and went off to collect the other fares.

'Cheek!' said Delia to Mr. Grant. 'It's always twopence a ride, and they know it.'

'Are you really going to have fifteen rides?' asked Mr. Grant.

'Of course. I adore roundabouts,' said Delia, and the steam organ gave a frightful screech, intended to warn laggards, and burst into 'The Honeysuckle and the Bee', the popular song of the year the organ first appeared in public. The platform began to revolve, Mr. Packer's face appeared for a moment above the machinery, even oilier than that of his subordinate, and the whole intoxicating equipage was in motion. To Delia the roundabout had represented since her youthful days the highest point of romance. Seated side saddle, her hair blown by the oil-scented breeze of the ostrich in its career, her elegant legs dangling, Delia felt herself to be d'Artagnan, Sir Lancelot, a Cavalier riding with dispatches to King Charles, a heroine doing something or other for someone she was in love with, Mazeppa, Cortes and several other people. At every flower show she spent most of her money and time, sometimes in a boat or aeroplane body but most often on a bird, and usually descended from her mount in a state of exaltation which lasted until after dinner and sometimes made her rather remote and disagreeable.

Mr. Grant, who did not understand his cousin's peculiar devotion to this form of mental stimulus, was ready enough to ride on a cock two or three times, but felt a distinct uneasiness at the thought of half a crown's worth of this exercise. However Delia looked so happy and so pretty, with the flush of excitement on her face, that he determined to endure as long as possible. As the second twopennyworth was coming to an end, he saw a large good-looking girl striding over the grass towards the roundabout, followed by Mr. Merton. The last revolution of the platform then carried him away, but as he came round again the girl called out 'Hoy' in piercing tones. Delia looked for the noise, saw it, and shrieked 'Lydia' at the top of her voice. The girl barely waiting for the ostrich to stop, mounted the platform.

'I knew it was you on the ostrich,' she said to Delia. 'I told Noel you'd be here, didn't I, Noel?' she added to Mr. Merton, who had climbed up after her. 'I say, someone's on my cock.'

'It's only my cousin Hilary,' said Delia. 'He won't mind changing, will you, Hilary. It's Lydia Keith that I was at Barchester High School with. Hullo, Mr. Merton.'

Mr. Grant, really quite glad of an excuse to dismount, offered his cock to Lydia, who immediately flung a leg over it, explaining that she had put on a frock with pleats on purpose, as she always felt sick if she rode sideways.

'You and Hilary can go in the swan boat behind us,' she shouted to

Mr. Merton. 'Sorry, I didn't meant to say Hilary, but Delia never said what your name was.'

'Grant,' said the gentleman addressed.

'Well, do you mind if I call you Hilary?' said Lydia. 'Hurry up and get into the swan.'

'We'd better,' said Mr. Merton to Mr. Grant, 'or Lydia is capable of riding all over the field after us on the cock.'

Accordingly the two gentlemen seated themselves face to face in a kind of canoe with a swan's head and shoulders growing out of its prow.

'It makes me feel a bit like Lohengrin,' said Mr. Merton, 'or half of him.'

'Now I know why he always arrives standing, however unbalanced,' said Mr. Grant, whose knees were hitting his chin. 'They never thought of people's legs when they made these boats.'

'It was a poor idea to have swans to drag one about anyway,' said Mr. Merton. 'I'd always be afraid they might turn round and hiss at me or bite.'

Mr. Grant said he didn't suppose Wagner had really worked it out. The steam organ burst into 'Farewell, my Bluebell', a romantic song of adieu familiar to an older generation, and the whole cavalcade was once more set in motion. The oily man came up for Mr. Merton's fare, but Mr. Grant explained that the two half-crowns were covering expenses for his shipmate and also for the young lady on the cock. The oily man, who by now couldn't hear himself speak, nodded understanding and went away.

As they slowed down again Mr. Grant, who found this circular travel very boring, asked Mr. Merton, whom much to his annoyance he still couldn't help liking, whether he thought they would have to stay much longer.

'Not if you are feeling as sick as I am,' said Mr. Merton, who had been travelling backwards and not liking it. 'Lydia and Miss Brandon will be talking about their old school for ages, and I know that once Lydia is on her cock nothing will get her off. I came here last year with the Keiths and she had thirteen rides.'

'Delia has paid for fifteen,' said Mr. Grant, with some pride in his cousin's spirit, 'and I'm supposed to be having fifteen too, but if we got off Miss Keith could use mine.'

'I'd willingly pay half a crown never to have got on the thing at all,' said Mr. Merton. 'It's stopping now. Hullo, there's Tony Morland.'

Mr. Grant had been aware, during the latter and slower revolutions of this particular twopennyworth, of someone in grey flannels standing near the roundabout and gazing with an expression of detached scorn upon the vagaries of mortals. This person he saw, as the machine came to a standstill, to be the same boy he had met at the picnic.

'I'm frightened of that boy,' he said to Mr. Merton as they staggered off the boat. 'He makes me feel I am twenty years his junior and slightly imbecile at that.'

'I know,' said Mr. Merton. 'He is a bit like the gentleman in Tennyson, holding no form of creed but contemplating all. But I believe he is human inside. At least his housemaster, who is rather a friend of mine and married Lydia's sister, seems to think so. Hullo, Tony,'

Tony Morland turned his head slightly and saw Mr. Merton and Mr. Grant.

'How do you do, sir,' he said, with a distant courtesy of manner, as from fallen royalty to one who was respectfully pretending not to see through his incognito. 'How do you do, Mr. Grant.'

Both gentlemen felt as if they had been talking in church. Mr. Merton was the first to recover himself and asked if Tony was going on the roundabout.

'Perhaps later,' said Tony. 'Did you get to the ballet last week, sir?'

'Not I,' said Mr. Merton. 'This is my holiday and I'm not going back to town till I must.'

'It's hardly worth seeing this year,' said Tony negligently. 'There is nothing new except Les Centaures et les Lapithes with Bolikoff's décor, and I'd hardly advise anyone to go unless they had read Vougeot's *Entrechats Gris*. The whole is a bit determinist, though there's one of the corps de ballet that really understands the pointes.'

'Do you *have* to talk like that?' asked Mr. Merton.

'Yes, sir,' said Tony, the faintest flicker of a smile passing over his face. 'You see I have a friend who talks like that and I have to copy his mannerisms at present. I'll grow out of it. It was much worse last holidays.'

Lydia Keith, swinging past them on the cock, now shouted a greeting at Tony and a command to join the roundabout.

'Aren't you coming, sir?' Tony said to Mr. Merton.

'No,' said Mr. Merton, casting a nauseated look at the swan boat. 'I'm going to find Mrs. Brandon. Do you know where she is?'

'With my mother, in the Vicarage garden when I last saw her,' said Tony, and leapt onto the moving platform.

Mr. Grant suddenly felt that if Mr. Merton was going to make himself pleasant to Mrs. Brandon, he, Mr. Grant, might as well emigrate, so he boarded the roundabout again as it stopped. Let Mr. Merton go and wanton in Mrs. Brandon's smiles. For him the free roving life of a Conquistador. He mounted the nearest steed, a dapple grey with a red saddle and bridle painted on it, and found to his surprise that Delia was riding abreast with him on a chestnut with violet trappings.

'I gave the ostrich to Tony,' she said, 'because Lydia wanted to talk to him. I say, Hilary, do you suppose we'll soon know about Aunt Sissie? I know it's rather beastly to say things like that, but I had an idea.'

'About something?' said Mr. Grant.

'Yes. Really as a matter of fact about if she did by mistake happen to have I mean if there was anything even if it was only a very little,' said Delia.

As she had stopped speaking Mr. Grant came to the conclusion that she had said what she wanted to say. The wording had been obscure in the extreme, but he guessed what she was driving at. He felt that she was in difficulties and decided that as Aunt Sissie's will was not a subject that could be indefinitely avoided, he might as well break the ice and save his cousin any further embarrassment.

'It does seem rather beastly,' he admitted, raising his voice as the steam organ broke again into 'The Honeysuckle and the Bee', 'but after all it's only business. I'll tell you what, Delia, but it's a secret, if I did get anything from Aunt Sissie I'm going to make a will and say if I die first your mother is to have it. I shan't use any of it myself.'

He could not hear through the blaring of the organ his young cousin's hero-worshipping, long-drawn 'Oh, Hilary,' but he read admiration and approval in her eyes and was not displeased.

'And now tell me yours,' he said, as soon as a pause in the sequence of melodies allowed him to make himself heard.

'Well,' said Delia, looking straight in front of her, 'if I did get anything, I don't mean me and Francis but only me, I thought I would give it to Miss Morris. She's had an absolutely rotten time. Do you suppose I could?'

A great many thoughts suddenly dashed into Mr. Grant's mind. Among the first was a feeling of shame that Delia and not himself should have been the first to think of this. He realized, with some mental discomfort, that his plan of giving up his potential inheritance to Mrs. Brandon, who didn't need it, was a thoroughly selfish piece of self-glorification. If he had been whoever it was who gave his lady his falcon for dinner there might conceivably have been some merit in the sacrifice, though he had always had private doubts as to the amount of eating on a falcon. But to give a quite rich person some money that he didn't need himself, simply to make himself a benefactor in her eyes and be charmingly thanked, was pure egoism. And considering Mrs. Brandon, he now saw how probable it was that she, who never thought of or valued money, because she had always had it, would have accepted his tribute with her usual charm, perhaps said 'Dear Hilary, this is too sweet of you,' and laid a hand on his arm, but would have felt no particular obligation, no deep gratitude, and quite likely have refused, lightly, to take it, treating him as a child who did not know what he was doing.

And here was Delia, to whom in his arrogance, absorbed as she was by his romantic devotion to her mother, he had paid little attention, except as a useful person for tennis, who had seen at once where help was needed and was prepared to give it. Perhaps she too was only expressing a devotion, the devotion of a generous nature to anything that had called out its powers of helping, but in the sacrifice she proposed to make there was at least something very practical. He wanted to give what he didn't need to someone who didn't need it, persuading himself that this was a sacrifice to — Well, to what? Thinking of Mrs. Brandon as he so often had since he met her, in the night, when he ought to be working, in the melting air of twilight, in the intoxicating warmth of high noon up on the downs, in church (where, he had decided, to think of her was exactly the same as paying attention to the service), in the early morning when the summer mists lay on the world, he had occasionally tried to give his feelings a name. Love, desire; delicious words to intoxicate himself with, but not what he meant. Passion, even with a very small p, would be a desecration of his thought. Adoration, devotion, was perhaps nearer the mark, but did not satisfy him. What human word could ever express one's feeling, at the same time worshipping and protecting, for so exquisite a creature, the child in the woman. As he thought of her in her sunlit, flowery drawing-room, or by candlelight below the chestnut tree, veiled in shadowy lace, her lovely eyes a little tired, her enchanting voice muted, listening to him as he read to her, or telling him about Nurse and Rose, he was suddenly so pierced and torn by whatever it was he felt, that he nearly fell off his dapple grey steed.

'I think your idea is very good too,' said the voice of Delia, who thought his silence might mean that he disapproved her own plan, 'and I expect mother would think it was awfully kind of you. You've got a pretty good crush on her, haven't you? Everyone has,' said Delia proudly.

At these words it would not be quite correct to say that the scales fell from Mr. Grant's eyes, for one's eyes are not as a rule opened to one's own peculiarities so quickly and finally. But the word crush, deeply as he disliked and resented it, seemed to fill a gap that no other word had filled. For a fleeting moment he wondered if he had been a little ridiculous. Then he put his doubt at the back of his mind and turned his attention to Delia.

'I think your plan is splendid,' he said, 'and I only wish I'd thought of it myself. It would be simply perfect to give Miss Morris something. I like her awfully, don't you?'

'She's all right,' said Delia tolerantly. 'Of course she will drive mother mad if she stays here long, because she will be humble and grateful. I'm going to see that she has a good rest and get her a bit fatter and then I was thinking Mr. Miller's stepmother at Harrogate might have her.'

'Does she want a companion?' asked Mr. Grant.

'I don't know,' said Delia, 'but that's no reason why she shouldn't. Mother has an idea of Sir Edmund marrying Miss Morris, but that's all sentiment. Mother is an angel, but she never sees things except the way she wants them, and that's the way things don't go. I say, how many rides have we had?'

Mr. Grant said he should think about ten, but would ask. The oily man when appealed to said it was nine for the young lady and four for the other young lady on the cock and three for the gentleman who had got off and seven for this young gentleman and three for the young gentleman on the ostrich.

'All right, that makes twenty-six,' said Delia. 'Four more to go. Oh, Lydia and Tony are getting off. Shall we do the other four Hilary?'

Mr. Grant said he would love to, and offered to stand his cousin as many more as she liked. So they continued their wild career, talking eagerly whenever the music allowed and enjoying their scheme of philanthropy for Miss Morris, till Mr. Grant noticed a sudden thinning of the crowd on the field and looking at his watch said it was four o'clock and they must go to the tea-tent.

'Had a nice ride, sir?' asked Mr. Packer, raising his dirty face from among the machinery as his customers dismounted.

'Splendid, thanks,' said Mr. Grant. 'We might come back after tea. That's an awfully good horse I've been riding.'

'That's Persimmon, sir. All called after Derby winners,' said Mr. Packer. 'He's getting on, but there's life in him yet. Needs a new tail, but we all have our troubles.'

Mr. Grant asked if a shilling would be of any assistance towards a new tail and on hearing that it would, he handed it over in trust to Mr. Packer, who thanked him warmly and said he would drink the young lady's health at the Cow and Sickle when he went to get his bit of supper before the evening rush. Old Persimmon, he added, seeing a slight shade of disappointment on Mr. Grant's face at this re-appropriation of the tail-money, wouldn't grudge a man his pint of beer, and to prevent any further argument on the subject disappeared into the machinery again.

'Don't say anything about my plan,' said Delia to her cousin Hilary, as they walked towards the tent. 'I want it all to be a surprise — I mean if anything did happen. And I won't say anything about your plan.'

'My plan is dead,' said Mr. Grant with sudden determination. 'If I did have anything, would you mind if I came into your plan? I don't want to shove in if you'd rather not, but I think your plan is so good that I'd like to be in it, if you don't mind.'

'O.K.,' said Delia, 'and it's very nice of you.'

*

Miss Lydia Keith and Mr. Anthony Morland, having left the roundabout, as we saw, some time earlier, had done the round of the various side shows pretty thoroughly. At the shooting gallery Tony with his

O.T.C. experience was an easy first, hitting a tin rabbit that bobbed up and down at various points on a landscape six times out of six and thus qualifying as the recipient of a small mug left over from the coronation of the summer before, while Lydia, who only fired a gun once a year at the Southbridge Flower Show, missed every time.

'Come on, let's try hitting the weight,' said Lydia, leading the way towards an upright plank with figures on it. As they approached, Mr. Spindler from the Cow took up a large blacksmith's hammer, whirled it round his head and brought it down vehemently on a kind of anvil at the base of the plank. A weight rushed about three-quarters of the way up and fell down again.

'Anyone could do that,' said Tony scornfully, and picking up the hammer he aimed a blow at the anvil. The hammer glanced off it and Tony nearly fell over.

'Here, that's not the way,' said Lydia, and wresting the hammer from his grasp she whirled it in the air with all the strength of her hockey-playing muscles. The weight flew up almost to the top and a large rent appeared in the armhole of her dress.

'You've split something,' said Tony with gloomy pleasure.

'Arm, I suppose,' said Lydia, trying to look over her own shoulder. 'Bother! I always split something. Do you remember that awful dress of Geraldine Birkett's that I split for her the summer before last, the one she was sick of? She's gone to college, as if school weren't bad enough. Let's try the coconuts.'

At the coconuts, for which Tony, chivalrously though ostentatiously insisted on paying, luck was fairly even, and they were awarded a coconut between them.

'You can have it,' said Tony. 'I've got the mug.'

Lydia held the prize up and looked critically at it.

'It's awfully like someone with a nasty face all close together. I know, it's like the Pettinger,' said Lydia, alluding to the headmistress of the Barchester High School. 'When I had to go into her study before I left and have a holy kind of talk, she looked just like that.'

'What did she say?' asked Tony.

'Oh, I don't know,' said Lydia indifferently. 'Something about an opportunity for something or other. I say, this coconut weighs about a ton.'

'Carry it in your hat,' said Tony.

This seemed to Lydia a good idea. She took off her hat which had a band of ribbon that went round the back of her head to moor it into place, put the coconut in the crown and carried it by the ribbon as if in a basket.

'Come on,' said Tony, 'it's nearly four and your mother said we were to meet her at the tea-tent.'

'What are you going to do with your mug?' asked Lydia, who rather coveted it.

'Give it to someone, I expect,' said Tony. 'As a matter of fact I'm going to give it to Miss Morris. I saw her when I came.'

Lydia asked who Miss Morris was.

'She was at a picnic Mrs. Brandon had,' said Tony, 'and she was rather decent. Mother said she was being a companion to Mrs. Brandon's aunt and had rather a dull time, so I went to the Wishing Well with her and I told her a lot about the early Christian church, because her father was a clergyman. I did early Christians in history last term, so I know them pretty well.'

'Gosh!' said Lydia. 'Her old lady was that Miss Brandon that father and mother went to the funeral of. I saw Miss Brandon once, like a great black hen with feathers in her hat being rude to people. I expect she Persecuted Miss Morris. I might give Miss Morris the coconut.'

'She'd never be able to open it,' said Tony. 'I'll tell you what. I'll open it at tea-time with the corkscrew in my knife, and we'll drink the juice, and then we'll smash the shell up with something and eat the inside.'

Lydia said she didn't like coconut to eat, because one kept on putting bits into one's mouth and chewing them, but they never seemed to get really chewed and then one had to spit them out. The ribbon of her hat then gave way and the coconut rolled to the ground, so she and Tony dribbled it among the feet of the crowd, right up to the entrance to the tea-tent.

Mrs. Brandon, after buying conscientiously all the things that were selling least well, and leaving her purchases in a heap at each stall to be fetched by Curwen later, drifted across to the Vicarage garden, where four deck chairs, six rush-bottomed chairs from the dining-room, four cane-bottomed chairs from the bedrooms and three hassocks, were disposed for visitors under the beech tree. Here she disposed herself gracefully in the safest looking of the deck chairs and gave herself up to contemplation. No sound came from the Vicarage, so Mrs. Brandon knew that Hettie and Cook were at the Fête. The sound of the steam organ came not unpleasantly from the far side of the field, filling Mrs. Brandon with a gentle sentiment for a childhood when those well-worn tunes had been popular favourites. Hot sunshine poured down, and as a faint breeze passed over the garden it brought to Mrs. Brandon the scent of Mr. Miller's heliotrope in the border beneath the study windows. It reminded her of the spider, which made her think again of Mr. Miller and how a woman was needed at the Vicarage. If Mr. Miller had a wife, she reflected, he could read his book aloud to her every night instead of having to come over to Stories. Ever since he had so kindly begun to read his Donne to her Mrs. Brandon had lived in apprehension of further readings, at some one of which she would, she knew, go to sleep, or hopelessly fail to grapple with some quotation, or otherwise disgrace herself. If only he and Miss Morris did not get on so badly one might have done some match-making in that direction, but though Miss Morris had so nicely come to the rescue and done the notices for the Fête, it was obvious to the meanest intelligence that it was rather a sentiment of duty towards the church that had inspired her than any personal feeling for the Vicar.

Neither had her encounter with Sir Edmund been wholly satisfactory. True she had offered to recast and type his letter to the *Barchester Chronicle*, but Mrs. Brandon could not conceal from herself that her secretarial conscience would have made her do the same by anyone who was going to make such a fool of himself as Sir Edmund. It would also, she felt, be unkind to force anyone into marriage with Sir Edmund, if it meant having to listen to his letters to the newspaper more than once a week. If no marriage could be arranged, she must bestir herself about finding a new job for Miss Morris, before her guest had quite overwhelmed and exhausted her with doing the flowers and being grateful. She ran through the other bachelors of her acquaintance mentally, but found none suitable. Francis and Hilary were out of the question. As for Hilary, she thought a wife would not be a bad plan for him either, if only to relieve her from having to listen to any more readings of his French poet, whom she found incomprehensible and faintly distasteful.

Then thoughts of Miss Brandon and that troublesome will, about which they surely must soon know some details, passed through her mind, naturally leading to thoughts of Mr. Merton, and at this moment Francis would certainly have observed that his mother had her mysterious mischief face. She had no intention of offering Mr. Merton as a husband to Miss Morris, for he seemed to her very amusing and an excellent player at that enchanting game of heartwhole flirtation which she so dearly loved and for which she found so few intelligent players. And as she remembered that Mr. Merton was coming over to the Fête with the Keiths and later to Stories for a drink, she did what in the nineties would have been described as dimpling.

'Lavinia,' said an impressive voice.

She looked up and saw Mrs. Morland, in a flowered frock and majestic kind of flowing cape which she wore apologetically.

'Darling Laura, I can't get out of this chair, but I am so glad to see you,' said Mrs. Brandon. 'Sit down. Have you been to the Fête?'

'No. Tony has gone off to the roundabout, but I saw that nice Miss Morris near the gate and she told me you might be at the Vicarage, so I came to look for you. Tony has really come to talk to Lydia Keith, who is such a nice girl, with no nonsense about her,' said Mrs. Morland, who evidently felt with Mr. Edmund Sparkler that this was a high recommendation. 'I didn't mean to come, because I'm all behindhand with a book as usual, but Tony hasn't got his driving licence yet, so I had to bring him.'

'Tell me about the book,' said Mrs. Brandon, obeying the law of her nature.

Mrs. Morland looked piercingly at her friend, pulled her hat impatiently down on her forehead and shook her head.

'It is very kind of you, Lavinia,' she said, 'and just like you, but certainly not. You know as well as I do that you only asked me to talk about my book because you like to be nice to people and for people to think how nice you are, and so you are, very nice, but you don't really want to hear things, except so that you can think about other things.'

'How clever you are, Laura,' said Mrs. Brandon admiringly. 'I suppose it comes of being a novelist. I don't know why it is, but I can't prevent people reading things aloud to me. Mr. Miller and Hilary Grant and Sir Edmund all do it, and it is so interesting but I simply *can't* attend, and it makes me so nervous in case I suddenly stop thinking of having my black frock altered or whatever it is and don't say the right thing.'

'I wish I had invented you,' said Mrs. Morland, in her turn gazing with admiration at her friend. 'No one would believe in you, but they'd all love you. What is that nice Miss Morris doing now? I did like her so much when you brought her to the picnic.'

Mrs. Brandon explained that Miss Morris was staying with her for a rest before looking for another job, but did not divulge her plans for Miss Morris's future.

'I simply love having her,' she said, 'if only she wouldn't be so grateful. It's bad enough when she will do the flowers for me, but when she thanks me it is very alarming.'

'I know,' said Mrs. Morland sagely. 'I know. I wonder if she would like to go to George Knox's old mother. The girl that was with her as companion has married a naval man and Mrs. Knox is looking out for someone. Shall I mention it to her?'

'Oh, do,' said Mrs. Brandon. 'I expect you will see her at tea. What time is it?'

But before Mrs. Morland could answer, the imposing form of Lady Norton swept into the garden, accompanied by Sir Edmund.

'Don't move, don't move,' said Lady Norton, who as the widow of an ex-Governor knew exactly how to put people at their ease. 'I have just brought Mrs. Grant over and left her at the Cow and Sickle with her luggage; and happening to see Sir Edmund I asked him where you were likely to be.'

'I didn't know where you were, Lavinia,' said Sir Edmund. 'Not my brother's keeper or anything of that sort, but I saw that Miss Morris of yours near the tea-tent and she said you might be up here. She's typed that letter deucedly well for me. I'd like you to see it, Lady Norton. It's about those council cottages.'

But Lady Norton was so much occupied in renewing her acquaintance with Mrs. Morland, for whose works she had a sincere if condescending admiration, that she did not hear.

'I always say to the girl at the library,' said her ladyship, ' "You simply must get me a copy of Mrs. Morland's latest book at once." I hope we shall have one for Christmas.'

'Well, not exactly Christmas, but Easter,' said Mrs. Morland, with the air of offering a suitable ecclesiastical alternative. 'Easter is early next year.'

'That is all the better for your readers,' said Lady Norton graciously. 'What were you saying, Sir Edmund?'

'You know those council houses near the cross roads,' said Sir Edmund. 'Disgraceful piece of jobbery that whole thing and not even a proper damp course. I've written a pretty stiff letter to the *Chronicle* about it and I'd like to read you what I said.'

Lady Norton, who enjoyed being consulted about things, inclined her head graciously.

'Don't tell me that you wrote that letter, Sir Edmund,' she said when he had finished.

'Not written it?' said Sir Edmund. 'Oh, I see what you mean. Not quite so strong as usual, eh? To tell the truth I had a little help. Miss Morris, a very nice quiet woman too, touched it up a bit and typed it for me. You know her, Lady Norton. Poor Amelia Brandon's companion or secretary or whatever you like to call it.'

'Oh, Miss Morris,' said her ladyship thoughtfully. 'Have you taken her on as secretary then?'

'Good Lord, no,' said Sir Edmund. 'She's staying with Lavinia here. Having a holiday, you know. Anyone would need a holiday after living with Amelia. De mortuis of course, but must face the facts.'

'I was thinking,' said Lady Norton, 'that my eldest niece, the one who lives in Cape Town, is needing a secretary. She does an enormous amount of work among diseased half-castes and writes to me that the life is most interesting. She cannot offer a salary, but the opportunities are unlimited. It might suit Miss Morris. I will write to my niece about it.'

All present felt that this was a plan which had absolutely nothing to recommend it, and comforted themselves by thinking that even with the Air Mail it would take some little time before Lady Norton could get a reply from her niece.

While this conversation was going on the sound of a bell had been heard two or three times. No one had taken any notice of it, but as it at last impinged on Mrs. Brandon's consciousness she realized that someone must be trying to get into the Vicarage by the front door.

'I wonder if we had better see what that is,' she said. 'Someone is ringing the front door bell, but I know Hettie and Cook are at the Fête.'

'I'll go and see,' said Sir Edmund. 'Bad plan, leaving a house empty. Miller ought to have a dog. Often told him so. Quis custodiet, you know.'

'Perhaps they'll go away if we do nothing,' said Mrs. Brandon hopefully, but at that moment Mrs. Grant came round the corner of the house. She had discarded her jet adornments and was again wearing coral and amber and had a wide sash of what are known as Roman stripes tied round a rather shapeless straw hat.

'Oh, there you are, Victoria,' she said, advancing upon the party. 'And Mrs. Brandon and Mrs. Morland and, che piacere! Sir Edmund, isn't it.'

'Haven't seen you since poor Edward died,' said Sir Edmund shaking hands.

'I never, never think of him,' said Mrs. Grant. 'What is gone is gone. I am afraid I am rather a pagan, but living so much as I do among the gracious rural deities of Calabria, the spirit of Greece beneath the Italian sun, one learns their laughing philosophy. Death comes graciously under that blue sky.'

'Died at Frinton, didn't he?' said Sir Edmund. 'Frinton's all right if you like it. I don't. Edward never looked well there.'

'I came to find Hilary,' said Mrs. Grant, 'but no one answered, so I gathered that the house was empty. Then I heard voices and eccomi!'

Mrs. Brandon got up and said it was nearly tea-time and she expected they would find Hilary and the others down at the tent, so they all walked across the garden and out through the little gate into the field.

XI

THE VICARAGE FÊTE (2)

FRANCIS and Miss Morris had gone as Mrs. Brandon told them to the tea-tent. Here they found Mrs. Spindler and several helpers arranging tables, dragging clothes onto the tables, and hurling crockery and cutlery onto the cloths. On each table Mrs. Spindler put a half-pint mug with too many dhalias crammed into it.

'Good afternoon, Mrs. Spindler,' said Francis. 'You seem pretty busy.'

'That's right, Mr. Francis,' said Mrs. Spindler. 'It never rains but it pours and we're two short. I'm sure I don't know how we'll manage.'

'I say, that's too bad,' said Francis sympathetically. 'I suppose you haven't got the ping-pong tables from the British Legion over here, have you?'

'I'm using them for the urns and cutting the bread-and-butter, Mr. Francis,' said Mrs. Spindler firmly.

'Mother rather wanted them for her party,' said Francis. 'We shall be about twelve, or fifteen, and she wanted to get everyone together.'

Mrs. Spindler said if there hadn't been that unpleasantness with Mrs. Wheeler over the matter of that cask, she would have sent some of the scouts down for the trestle table at the garage, but being as it was she didn't see what could be done.

Francis, who was something of a diplomatist, saw that Mrs. Spindler was not in a mood for concessions and determined to play his trump card.

'It's a pity about those ping-pong tables,' he said, 'because mother has got rather a special party. This is Miss Morris, old Miss Brandon's companion, who has been very ill. The shock of Miss Brandon's death was too much for her. I hear my aunt never spoke again.'

He paused to study the effect on Mrs. Spindler's expression.

'I'm sure Miss Morris would like to meet you,' he added carelessly.

'Well, I'm sure,' Mrs. Spindler began, wiping her hands on a cloth. Francis without waiting to hear what she was sure of darted across to Miss Morris, who had stood a little aside and was looking at the tea-urns with a professional eye.

'I say,' he said in a low voice, 'would you mind shaking hands with Mrs. Spindler. Her husband keeps the Cow and Sickle, and if she is placated she will let mother have the ping-pong tables for her tea-party. You wouldn't feel equal, would you,' he added as Miss Morris was moving towards Mrs. Spindler, 'to saying a few words about Aunt Sissie's death. They would go down awfully well. Mrs. Spindler, I want you to meet Miss Morris.'

'Pleased, Miss Morris, I'm sure,' said Mrs. Spindler, holding out a damp hand.

'I'm so glad to meet you, Mrs. Spindler,' said Miss Morris, shaking hands warmly.

'I'm sure I *am* sorry about poor Miss Brandon,' said Mrs. Spindler. 'Mr. Spindler read me the piece in the paper about how she was taken, and I passed the remark to him at tea-time that I was sorry for anyone that happened to be there. I lost my own aunt twelve years ago and to this day I don't like to think of it.'

'Thank you so much, Mrs. Spindler,' said Miss Morris. 'You must know exactly what I felt like. When the nurse told me all was over I lay down on my bed, just as I was, and never knew anything till Mrs. Brandon came in and woke me.'

This strictly truthful account gave Mrs. Spindler such pleasure that she relented about the ping-pong tables at once. Two scouts were sent to borrow some wooden cases from the Garden Produce tent. On these

Mrs. Spindler ordered her helpers to put the urns and the bread-and-butter, while Francis and Mr. Miller's Hettie, who had brought down some rockcakes from the Vicarage, put the ping-pong tables together and found a cloth for them.

'Now, I know what you want, Miss Morris,' said Mrs. Spindler. 'A nice cup of tea. I've just got the big urn on the boil, but what with being two short and behindhand with the bread-and-butter, I really hardly know where I am.'

'I would love a cup of tea, thank you,' said Miss Morris. 'That is most refreshing. I suppose I couldn't help you with the bread-and-butter?'

'Really, Miss Morris, you mustn't think of such a thing,' said Mrs. Spindler, shocked but gratified.

'You'd better let Miss Morris do her worst, Mrs. Spindler,' said Francis. 'Her father was a clergyman and what she doesn't know about parish teas isn't worth knowing. Up, Miss Morris, and at them!'

'Well, if Miss Morris doesn't mind,' said Mrs. Spindler.

Miss Morris finished her cup of tea and took out of her large sensible bag a neatly folded overall, which she explained she had brought in case. A moment later she was buttering and slicing tin loaves with a calm competence that overpowered Mrs. Spindler and the other helpers. Francis was so enchanted by the sight that he borrowed a clean glass-cloth from Mrs. Spindler, tied it round him like an apron, and devoted himself to cutting up enormous slabs of cake and making all Mrs. Spindler's assistants giggle. Here he was presently found by Noel Merton, who had been distracted from his search for Mrs. Brandon by a request from Mr. Miller to judge the sack-races. They had discovered, in the intervals of disqualifying boys who deliberately bumped into others, that Mrs. Brandon was known to them both.

'What a perfectly delightful woman Mrs. Brandon is,' said Mr. Merton. 'Isn't Miss Morris, Miss Brandon's companion, staying with her now? I am sure that boy with red hair isn't running under Queensberry rules. He has got one of his feet out of the sack.'

'Dear, dear, no,' said Mr. Miller. 'Teddy! Teddy Thatcher! Come here.'

Teddy shuffled up to him.

'Let me look at your sack,' said Mr. Miller. 'Now that won't do at all. Your foot is right out of the sack.'

'Please sir, it had a hole in it,' said Teddy.

'Nonsense,' said the Vicar sharply. 'I looked at all the sacks myself. Let me see.'

A closer examination showed that a hole had been cut in the corner and Teddy Thatcher was excommunicated.

'I'm always so glad the Scoutmaster isn't here when that sort of thing happens,' said the Vicar. 'He will talk about honour.'

'How dreadful,' said Mr. Merton sympathetically.

'It makes me hot and cold,' said Mr. Miller. 'What is it, Teddy? Oh, it was your new pocketknife, was it? Well, don't do it again. Run and get another sack and you can go in for the under fourteen race. Yes, Miss Morris is with Mrs. Brandon at present.'

'I thought she seemed a very pleasant, competent person when I once saw her at the Abbey,' said Mr. Merton.

'Very pleasant indeed. Her future is a source of considerable anxiety to me,' said Mr. Miller, struggling vainly to untie the sack from the neck of one of the young Turpins, who was convinced that he would have to spend the rest of his life in it, armless and legless. 'It's all right, Bobby, don't cry. There you are! Yes; the question of finding another situation arises. Mrs. Brandon and I have had a talk about it, but so far there is nothing definite in view.'

'Oh well, I expect it will be all right,' said Mr. Merton in what the Vicar felt to be rather a callous way. Then the Vicar blamed himself for imputing evil motives and by that time he was needed to judge the hat trimming competition, and Mr. Merton, gently abstracting himself from these joys, strolled in the direction of the tea-tent where, as we have already said, he found Francis and Miss Morris whom he entertained with small talk, refusing resolutely to cut cake or fill milk jugs.

At four o'clock all Mrs. Brandon's guests converged upon the tea-tent, including Lydia's parents, Mr. and Mrs. Keith, who are quite immaterial to the progress of this book, except in so far as they made the number up to fourteen, thus causing a good deal of distraction. Mrs. Brandon, in consultation with Mrs. Spindler, counted the party four times, getting a different result each time, partly because they never remembered if Miss Morris and Francis were guests or helpers.

'If we really are fourteen we can't possibly fit into the ping-pong tables,' said Mrs. Brandon. 'And I had forgotten Mr. Miller. If he joins us we shall be fifteen. Can we put another table up to these, Mrs. Spindler?'

'Don't trouble about me. I never take tea,' said Lady Norton, sitting down on one of the school chairs that had been lent for the occasion.

'Then that makes thirteen,' said Mrs. Brandon helplessly.

Mrs. Grant threw out her hand in what she explained was a Calabrian gesture, useful to ward off the evil eye.

'No, darling, it is fourteen all right,' said Francis. 'Lady Norton will be one of us, even if she doesn't have any refreshment. It's the spirit of the thing that counts. Couldn't we have that little table near the door, Mrs. Spindler?'

'Well, Mr. Francis, I did put it there because it's a bit uneven in the legs,' said Mrs. Spindler. 'Of course you *could* have it.'

'Well, if we could, we can,' said Francis. 'Will you get it, Tony.'

Tony Morland picked the table up, balanced it legs upwards on his head and so carried it across the tent to the loudly expressed terror of all the grown-ups and the even more loudly expressed admiration of Delia and Lydia.

'I often carry desks about the form room like that,' said Tony to the girls as he set the table down.

'What does your master say?' asked Delia, slightly incredulous.

'He doesn't say anything,' said Tony. 'I have them all well under my thumb except Mr. Carter. I do history with him and he gives us some jolly useful notes so I let him do what he likes. Come on, I'm going to eat twenty sandwiches.'

'Bravo!' cried Mrs. Grant. 'I shall come and sit with you and we will have great fun at our end of the table.'

Anyone else would have been put off by the mask of stolid indifference, thinly masking hatred and contempt, immediately assumed by the three young people, but Mrs. Grant was used to breaking down the barriers between herself and the unwilling peasantry of Calabria, and took her seat at the end of the table with Delia, Lydia and Tony.

'Mr. Merton, you must sit by me,' said Mrs. Brandon, 'and meet Lady Norton.'

Mr. Merton said he would love to. Mr. Grant, overhearing this, thought some very scornful thoughts about women and took refuge with Mrs. Morland who would, he felt, appreciate hearing a little more about Jehan le Capet. Francis and Miss Morris, removing their aprons, joined the party at the children's end as Mrs. Grant playfully called it. The conversation at the grown-up end was necessarily a little dull, including as it did Lady Norton and Mr. and Mrs. Keith, though Mr. Merton and Mrs. Brandon seemed to find it amusing enough.

'I hope,' said Mr. Merton, 'that having tea with you now is without prejudice to my having a glass of sherry with you later. I rather particularly want to see you.'

'Of course not,' said Mrs. Brandon. 'Won't Mr. and Mrs. Keith come too?'

'I think not,' said Mr. Merton firmly. 'I have got my own car with me and if you don't mind my bringing Lydia, who clings to me with very flattering affection, we will let the Keiths go home by themselves. In any case they wouldn't stay long, and I know Lydia won't be happy till she has done all the side shows.'

'What a nice girl she is,' said Mrs. Brandon. 'She and Delia were at Barchester High School and went to Paris when they left, but not to the same family.'

'She is one of the nicest girls I know,' said Mr. Merton, 'and wonderfully toned down since she went to Paris, though she doesn't seem to have learnt any French there.'

A hubbub from the far end of the table now attracted everyone's attention to the finished product of Paris who, together with Delia and

Tony Morland, was having a friendly discussion with Mrs. Grant about cruelty to animals. The conversation had begun by Mrs. Grant loudly lamenting the cruelty involved in allowing a small pony, property of the grocer, to be let out at threepence a ride for children.

'I know that pony,' said Lydia. 'He used to belong to the butcher at Southbridge. He was called Toby then, but the man who has him now didn't like Toby, so he called him Punch.'

'That is typically English,' said Mrs. Grant, 'not to allow an animal any right even in its own name. But if you know that animals' owner, Miss Keith, you should protest. I saw it with my own eyes, with no less than two children on its back at once, being beaten with a stick to make it trot up and down the field.'

'If that is Simpson's pony,' said Delia, joining in the fray, 'you have to beat him. I broke one of mother's parasols over his back two years ago when I had him in the old governess cart for fun.'

'I wish I'd been there,' said Tony, his eyes gleaming. 'I'd have stuck a pin into a stick and jabbed him, all very literary.'

'Have you ever heard of St. Francis?' said Mrs. Grant meaningly to Tony.

'Yes, I know all about him. We did him in some notes on the monastic orders last term,' said Tony negligently. 'If you want to find out anything about him I can give you the names of one or two really good books. I expect you only know the Brother Elderberry kind. I wrote a pretty good essay on the Influence of the Poverello on Contemporary Society.'

'And do you know what he called animals?' asked Mrs. Grant, almost threateningly.

Tony's face assumed a world-weary air which his mother, had she not been so immersed in le Capet, or Dr. Ford, had he been present, would at once have recognized as a preparation for showing off. But Lydia, who detested what she called rot, which meant broadly anything she didn't agree with, was ready with an answer before Tony could collect his forces.

'Of course he called them brother and sister and all that,' said she, dominating that end of the table by her powerful voice, 'but that's nothing to go by. I mean in Italian you call people anything. It's a very rich language, though I must say I don't know a frightful lot of it, but what's the use of learning a language if you aren't going there and there's nothing to read except things like Dante. But St. Francis lived in the twelfth century — oh, all right, Tony, thirteenth century then, twelve hundreds, it's all the same thing, and you could easily call people brothers and sisters because there weren't so many things to call. I mean it would be absolutely different now with aeroplanes and radio and gasmasks and all that. Anyway it was a pity St. Francis went off the deep end about animals like that, because it simply set the Italians

against animals for life and they've been doing cruelty to animals ever
since. It's the blood too of course. Look at the ancient Romans. Of
course Virgil had some quite modern ideas about kindness to bees in
the Georgics, but he tells you to pull their wings off all the same, and I
expect he'd have made some jolly good hexameters about beating
Simpson's pony if he'd known it. And calling people brothers and sisters
doesn't really mean anything.'

> ' "If hate killed men, brother Lawrence
>   God's blood, would not mine kill you?" '

said Tony approvingly.

'But Browning was speaking of a *Spanish* cloister,' said Mrs. Grant,
laughingly.

'That's the marvellous part of Browning,' said Lydia. 'I mean he sees
human nature everywhere, like Shakespeare, but the Italians haven't
got that. Of course St. Francis was perfectly marvellous, but he hadn't
that deep kind of understanding of people that Browning and Shakespeare have. Of course he was a good bit earlier and I daresay people
weren't so developed then.'

She looked round, pleased with herself.

'One only understands St. Francis after long study and suffering in
the stern school of life,' said Mrs. Grant with an annoying and tolerant
condescension. 'When you have lived in Italy as much as I have, Miss
Keith, you will understand how St. Francis's love of animals has
become part of daily life now.'

'I read a book about animals in Italy,' said Delia, her eyes gleaming
as Tony's had gleamed. 'It was by a clergyman who lived at Genoa or
somewhere and it was perfectly *ghastly*. What do you think he saw a
man do to a horse in Pisa? He had a great knife, and he − −'

'Delia,' said Miss Morris.

There was a tone in her voice, as of a very competent governess, that
made Delia much to everyone's relief stop short and say 'Yes, Miss
Morris,' exactly as if she had been at school.

'I think I see Mr. Miller looking for us,' said Miss Morris, 'and I can't
shout up the table at your mother. Could you rescue him?'

Delia, who was seated nearest the door of the tent, got up and rescued
Mr. Miller who, confused by the dimmer light of the tent after the glare
outside and all the noise of talk and crash of crockery, was peering
wretchedly about, unable to find his tea-party. Francis admired Miss
Morris's well-timed interruption and couldn't make up his mind
whether it was deliberate or not. Mr. Merton with the utmost good-
humour gave up his seat next to Mrs. Brandon to the Vicar and came
and sat by Lydia on a stool lent by the Badgers' Patrol of the Boy
Scouts.

It was very lucky for Mr. Grant that he had so kind an audience as

Mrs. Morland. That worthy creature had a trick of appearing deeply absorbed in what her friends said which was often her undoing, but for the moment she was genuinely amused by what Mr. Grant was telling her about his hero and neither of them took any notice of the argument between Lydia and Mrs. Grant, which was just as well, or Mr. Grant would have been more than usually ashamed of his mother.

'I think le Capet was a genius to have so many mistresses all at once,' said Mrs. Morland. 'How on earth did he manage it?'

'He needed them,' said Mr. Grant. 'No, I don't mean like that, but he was very poor and very extravagant and they were mostly pretty poor too, so it took several to support him. It was to them that he wrote his poem "Les mains qui donnent," which some people consider his best.'

It was then that Mrs. Morland, putting a stray piece of hair away behind her ear and frowning, made the suggestion that, as Mr. Grant subsequently said, changed his whole life.

'Why don't you make a novel of it, Mr. Grant,' she said. 'There's a lot of very good material, simply asking to be used. All that Vie de Bohéme stuff goes down very well and with a good jacket you ought to get real sales. I'll talk to my publisher, Adrian Coates, about it if you like.'

'I couldn't,' said Mr. Grant, shocked, yet agreeably flattered. 'So little is really known about him. In fact I believe I'm about the only person that has done any work on him.'

'Well, there you are,' said Mrs. Morland. 'If you are the only one that knows, you can write the book. If you called it something rather vulgar, like "A Poet of the Gutters", or "A Minstrel of Montmartre", it would be a help.'

Mr. Grant, throwing himself into the spirit of the thing, then suggested several extremely unsuitable titles which made him and Mrs. Morland laugh so much that three of her tortoiseshell hairpins fell under the table, and had to be rescued.

'Thank you so much,' said Mrs. Morland as Mr. Grant, rather red in the face, surged up again bearing the hairpins in triumph.

'Thank *you* as we say,' said Mr. Grant. 'You can't think what fun it is to talk to you. You are really the only person I can talk to about myself and my work.'

On hearing this frightful disloyalty to Mrs. Brandon the heavens should have sent a thunderbolt straight through the tent onto Mr. Grant's head, but they refrained.

'You ought to meet my old friend, George Knox, the biographer,' said Mrs. Morland. 'He talks about himself more than anyone I know, but he's very nice. Tony! I think we ought to be going.'

'Oh Mother, must we?' said her son. I've eaten twenty sandwiches and three slices of cherry cake and I promised Lydia I'd have a sixpenny ice.'

'Very well. After the ice,' said Mrs. Morland getting up.

A general move was now being made. Mrs. Morland said good-bye to her hostess and seized the opportunity of asking Miss Morris to come to see her at High Rising some day.

'I could easily come over and fetch you and take you back,' she said. 'And I would like you to meet my old friend, George Knox, the biographer you know. His mother who is French and very nice and has always been very kind to me lives alone, and her companion, Miss Grey, a very nice girl but a little peculiar, has just married a naval man after great exertions, and I know Mrs. Knox would be extremely grateful to anyone who would come and live with her. Of course I don't want to bother you, but if you did feel like Mrs. Knox and cared to talk to me and George Knox about it, it would be a real kindness.'

'That is very kind indeed of you, Mrs. Morland,' said Miss Morris. 'I have no plans at all for the moment, but I can't go on trespassing on Mrs. Brandon's kindness and shall be glad to find a place where I can be of use.'

'Then I'll ring you up in about a week, when George Knox is back from visiting his mother,' said Mrs. Morland, 'and you shall come to lunch and meet him. Now I have lost Tony. If you see him will you tell him that I have gone to get the car. There is such a jam in the car park.'

She shook Miss Morris warmly by the hand and hurried away. Lady Norton now advanced majestically upon Miss Morris.

'You must get Mrs. Brandon to bring you over to see my garden while you are staying with her,' said her ladyship.

Miss Morris, fully realizing that this was not only a royal command but a piece of benevolent condescension, made suitable acknowledgements.

'My eldest niece, who works among diseased half-castes at Cape Town, has written to me that she needs a secretary,' said Lady Norton. 'It is most interesting work, and hearing from Mrs. Brandon that you might be available for a new post, I thought it might interest you, especially as I understand that you have been used to parish work. Some of them are discharged lepers,' said Lady Norton by way of making the position sound more attractive.

Miss Morris, who had been offered just as unattractive jobs by people far less well-meaning than Lady Norton, again made suitable acknowledgements and her ladyship passed on. She was closely followed by Mr. and Mrs. Keith, lamenting the disappearance of their daughter Lydia.

'I think,' said Miss Morris, 'that she may have gone to the ice-cream tent with Mrs. Morland's son. They were talking about it.'

Even as she spoke the two reprobates came up.

'Lydia, what *have* you done to your dress?' said Mrs. Keith. 'She tears everything, Miss Morris, and now that her sister, my elder girl, is married we never seem to be able to keep her tidy.'

'It was only hitting the weight, Mother,' said Lydia, craning her neck as far round as possible and casting an approving eye on the ever-widening rent. 'And it's a foul dress anyway.'

'And where is your hat?' asked her mother helplessly.

'I don't know,' said Lydia indifferently. 'The ribbon got broken when I was carrying the coconut.'

'You were sitting on it at tea-time,' said Tony.

'Bother, so I was,' said Lydia, and went back to the tea table.

'Good-bye, Tony,' said Miss Morris.

Tony took her hand and bowed with an awkward young grace that suddenly touched her.

'If ever you come to Southbridge,' he said, looking up at her from under his dark lashes, 'please come and have tea in my study. I've got matron under my thumb and she'll let us have heaps of scones and things.'

Before Miss Morris could answer he had given her one more of his inscrutable, flickering looks and gone after his mother. Lydia returned from her quest, her hat a good deal the worse for wear in one hand, the coconut in the other.

'I thought you'd like this,' she announced, thrusting it at Miss Morris. 'Some people like the milk. I think it's beastly myself, but it isn't so bad if you smash it to bits and eat the white stuff, only I always spit it out when I've chewed it a bit because you don't seem to get any further.'

'Thank you so much,' said Miss Morris gratefully.

Mrs. Grant, who had just finished her good-byes to Lady Norton, inquired anxiously if Miss Morris really needed the coconut. If not, she said, she would gladly take it to the Cow and get Mr. Spindler to cut it in two and hang the halves up for St. Francis's little feathered brothers and sisters. Miss Morris, realizing that Lydia was about to say what she thought of feathered brothers and sisters having the coconut that she had bestowed upon a friend, hastened to assure Mrs. Grant that she had a peculiar affection for both the milk and the edible parts of that unwholesome fruit. Mrs. Grant smiled pityingly and passed on.

'Anyway St. Francis didn't have coconuts,' said Lydia scornfully. 'Good-bye, Miss Morris. Thanks awfully for having the coconut. Tony told me what a rotten time you'd had, and I wanted you to. I hope you'll have awfully good luck now.'

She hurt Miss Morris's hand, and banging into the canvas in a way that nearly shattered it left the marquee in search of her friend Noel Merton.

'I do apologise for Lydia,' said Mrs. Keith as she shook hands. 'I thought Paris would improve her.'

'She seems to me a delightful girl,' said Miss Morris warmly.

'Everyone likes her,' said Mrs. Keith, 'but I do wish she wouldn't split all her clothes. If you are staying on in this part of the country, I do wish you would come to us for a few days. I feel certain that Lydia would pay attention to you, and my husband never notices the guests much.'

Miss Morris, who secretly felt that Lydia was quite perfect in her own way, and did not in the least wish that ingenuous young lady to look upon her in the light of a mentor or improver, made some suitably civil remark, said good-bye to Mr. Keith, and found herself for a moment alone. She was a little dizzy after the hot tea in the tent and the unusual amount of company she had been seeing, not to speak of the kindness, whether suitable or not, that everyone had shown, and glad to sit on a packing case near the tea-urns and rest. Not one of the offers of posts that had been made to her was in the least what she wanted, yet she felt she ought to examine the possibility of them all. She could not live with Mrs. Brandon indefinitely. Every day that she spent in the easy, luxurious atmosphere of Stories seemed to her to be sapping her initiative. It was a fresh daily pleasure to have morning tea and often breakfast in bed, her own bath-room, towels, changed nearly every day, leisurely meals, a comfortable bed, lazy quiet afternoons and evenings. Independent as she was, she could not refuse the presents that Mrs. Brandon and Delia were always giving her, of stockings, scarves, underthings, a frock, a coat, all offered with such charming good-will that she could not bring herself to deny the affectionate givers the pleasure they took in giving. Every day she stayed was going to make it harder to go. To-day would make it harder than ever. For the first time for many years she had come into her own kingdom again and ruled part of a parish, if only for an afternoon. The blood of generations of vicarage ancestors sang in her veins as she looked upon the tea-urns, the tin loaves, the slabs of cake, the crockery, now all empty, destroyed, dirty but none the less a symbol. She thanked Mr. Miller in her heart for having had the Fête on a day when she could be there. Mrs. Spindler and her assistants were tidying and packing up. Miss Morris rose and went over to them.

'Thank you so much for letting me help, Mrs. Spindler,' she said. 'It has been a most enjoyable experience.'

'Thank *you*, miss, I'm sure,' said Mrs. Spindler, forgetting in her enthusiasm to assert her gentility by using Miss Morris's name. 'As I was saying to Mrs. Thatcher just now, it's a real pleasure to have a lady that knows how things should be done and what a pity, I said to Mrs. Thatcher, there isn't one at the Vicarage. The dirt and waste there you wouldn't believe, miss. Not that the girls mean anything, but it stands to reason you don't get things done the way you do with a good mistress over them. I was passing the remark to Mrs. Thatcher that I wouldn't be surprised if Mr. Miller hadn't had a drop of hot food to-day, with Cook and that Hettie down here since before lunch, wasn't I, Mrs. Thatcher?'

Mrs. Thatcher, a handsome draggled woman, the mother of Jimmy Thatcher and his four brothers and three sisters, said that was right, and she hoped Jimmy wasn't at the ice-cream stall, as he'd been sick to-day twice.

Miss Morris volunteered to go and look for him, an offer that Mrs. Thatcher accepted with embarrassed relief, begging her to tell Jimmy to come straight along to the tent like a good boy or he'd get the strap when his dad got back. Armed with a description of the afflicted Jimmy, Miss Morris went out of the stuffy marquee into the grounds. There the heat and noise were rather overpowering, but it was good to be in the fresh air again. She went over to the ice-cream stall. Here she found not Jimmy but Mr. Miller, giving pennies to small boys to buy a slice of frozen custard-powder and condensed milk between two synthetic wafers apparently made of compressed shavings.

'Excuse me, Mr. Miller,' said Miss Morris, 'but have you seen Jimmy Thatcher? His mother wants him.'

'I believe he is at the roundabout,' said Mr. Miller, bestowing his last penny. 'May I help you to find him ?'

'There is no need,' said Miss Morris, but quite kindly.

'Oh, but do let me,' said Mr. Miller. 'No, Herb, you've had one penny and so has Les.'

'Well, thank you very much,' said Miss Morris, remembering that it was the duty of young clergymen — for as such she still considered Mr. Miller — to assist vicars' daughters.

But just as Mr. Miller had freed himself from the last of the little boys, Mrs. Brandon accompanied by Sir Edmund came up.

'Oh, Mr. Miller,' she said, 'I did so want a word with you. Could you possibly spare a moment?'

'Would you excuse me, Miss Morris?' said Mr. Miller.

'It won't take long,' said Mrs. Brandon. 'Sir Edmund, you'll take care of Miss Morris while I talk to Mr. Miller, won't you?'

Without waiting for an answer she carried Mr. Miller off.

'I only wanted to consult you about church to-morrow,' she said. 'I had got a kind of idea that Miss Morris doesn't like our kind of service and I wondered if you knew what she does like. I suppose I oughtn't to ask you,' said Mrs. Brandon, suddenly showing a late-flowering tact, 'when it's your service, but somehow I always look upon you as a friend more than a vicar.'

With which quite idiotic remark she turned her blue eyes on him with such an air of confidence in his understanding and sympathy that he said, Of course, of course, and he had himself had a little talk with Miss Morris on the matter and had suggested that she should go to

Tompion at Little Misfit, or Carson at Nutfield, delightful fellows both, even if a little evangelical in their outlook.

'Then that's all right,' said Mrs. Brandon, evidently much relieved.

'I wish I could drive her over myself,' said Mr. Miller, quite sincerely, 'but the hours of our services make it impossible.'

Mrs. Brandon said he mustn't dream of suggesting such a thing and Curwen, who only went to an evening service at the Methodist chapel, could easily take her over.

'While we are on the subject, I should be glad to know if anything suitable has offered itself in the way of a post. Lady Norton kindly mentioned a niece of hers in Cape Town, but the work, largely among Unfortunates,' said Mr. Miller, hoping that Mrs. Brandon in her heavenly innocence would not know or ask what he meant, 'seems to me hardly suitable for a lady of Miss Morris's gifts, and in a hot climate.'

'Lady Norton is always busybodying about her nieces,' said Mrs. Brandon. 'I certainly shouldn't dream of letting Miss Morris go to South Africa, though I believe it is quite cold in winter, if one can call it winter when it happens in the summer. I hope very much to find something for her nearer home. That's partly why I left her with Sir Edmund. I know he particularly wants to speak to her about something, so I thought we might be tactful and keep away.'

Mrs. Brandon smiled mysteriously to herself. Though she had not been feeling very hopeful of Sir Edmund as a wooer for Miss Morris, it seemed to her that a suggestion of his, made to her at tea-time, that he should sound Miss Morris about taking over the secretaryship of the Barsetshire Benevolent Association (founded in 1783), of which he was President, contained the germs of possible romance.

'It would mean,' she continued, following her own train of thought and quite oblivious of the fact that she had not given the Vicar the slightest indication of what she was talking about, 'that she would be living not very far away, and even with her new duties we should be seeing quite a lot of her. Don't you think that would be very nice?'

Mr. Miller said indeed, indeed it would be delightful. And looking at it dispassionately what could be more delightful than that a gifted, attractive woman who had been through many years of poverty and self-suppression, should marry a man of quite suitable age, of excellent family and character, comfortably off, and from his house continue her career of beneficence on a larger scale. As a plan Mr. Miller could see no fault in it, which made him blame himself all the more for his unwarrantable dislike of the whole idea. Only a thoroughly selfish person could grudge Miss Morris so eminently desirable a marriage, and Mr. Miller suddenly knew that sooner or later he must confess to himself that he was that person. Too shy and too oppressed to ask Mrs. Brandon any more about the affair, he walked with her up and down the path under the Vicarage garden wall, looking at the Fête with unseeing eyes, hearing the steam organ without knowing what it was, fighting his own feelings, but fatally certain that in the night they would lie in ambush and fall upon him without pity.

Mrs. Brandon, walking beside him in the sun, reflected placidly upon life and whether the wedding, if she could bring it about, would take place in the winter or the spring. If in the winter, that blue angora frock with her fur coat and perhaps a new hat would do very well. If it was in the spring she really didn't know. But by that time she would be getting some new clothes. Then she considered what Miss Morris should wear as a bride and decided to take her to town herself and have her suitably dressed. A dark blue tailor-made always looked well, or possibly a wine-coloured dress with a coat to match and a felt hat. Five minutes or so had passed away in these pleasant reflections when Mr. Miller, resolutely shaking off the dark cloud that was oppressing him, said he had promised to guide Miss Morris to the roundabout and ought perhaps to be looking for her. Accordingly they went back to the ice-cream stall. Sir Edmund and Miss Morris were nowhere to be seen, but a small boy, who was picking up the uneaten points of larger boys' cones and making a hearty meal off them, said the lady had gone on the horses.

'I can't think that Miss Morris has really gone on the roundabout,' said Mrs. Brandon placidly, 'but we'll go and look.'

*

Sir Edmund, left alone with Miss Morris, lost no time in saying what he had to say. In a very few sentences he put the advantages and disadvantages of the Barsetshire Benevolent Association before Miss Morris, named the salary, the hours, the responsibilities, the opportunities for taking on other work of a similar nature and any other points he considered useful. Miss Morris, pleased with his kind business-like manner, listened attentively and promised to consider the matter and give him an answer as early as possible.

'I would like to mention it to Mrs. Brandon if I may,' she said. 'She has been so good to me and I would feel ungrateful if I concealed my plans from her.'

'Tell Lavinia by all means,' said Sir Edmund. 'Woman has less sense for her age than anyone I know, but she doesn't gabble.'

'I don't think you are quite fair to her, Sir Edmund,' said Miss Morris.

'Don't you?' said Sir Edmund. 'Well, look at her now.'

Miss Morris looked and saw nothing worse than Mrs. Brandon and Mr. Miller pacing up and down under the Vicarage wall.

'Miller's up at Stories pretty often,' said Sir Edmund. 'Nice fellow, but needs a firm hand. Not Lavinia's style at all. I've known her ever since she married. Brandon was a dull dog. Women don't seem to know what's what. What do you say, eh? Clever woman like you ought to notice things.'

Miss Morris, for perhaps the first time in her quiet competent life, was utterly flabbergasted. Any idea of a possible attachment between Mrs. Brandon and Mr. Miller had never entered her head. She had seen, as who could help seeing, that Mr. Miller found Mrs. Brandon's charm rather overpowering, but then she felt it herself and could fully sympathise. As for Mrs. Brandon, it would never have struck her that, beyond her real kindness to all around her and anyone in trouble, she was capable of any feelings stronger than, or indeed so strong as her complete absorption in her children, her house, and her clothes. The whole idea seemed to her so fantastic that she could not dismiss it as she would have done a more reasonable one, and it made her extremely ill at ease, she could not have said why.

'No, I don't notice anything,' she said pleasantly. 'Shall we go to the roundabout, Sir Edmund? I promised Mrs. Thatcher that I would send Jimmy to her. It seems he isn't well and oughtn't to go on the horses.'

Sir Edmund accompanied her to the roundabout, giving her as they went an account of the Thatcher family, their numbers, names, accidents and diseases. Miss Morris listened with professional interest, an interest which she found greatly increased when Sir Edmund mentioned how good Mr. Miller had been to them.

'Good Samaritan and all that, you know,' said Sir Edmund. 'Sat up with Thatcher for two nights in the last 'flu scare, so that Mrs. Thatcher and the children could get some sleep. Know for a fact he paid for an extra week's convalescence for Edna Thatcher, that's the one that had the illegitimate baby—no, that was in '36—it was Doris that had one in '37. Can't think why he wears those clothes though. No need to go about looking like an old woman, Miller, I say to him. There's Jimmy, Miss Morris. Doesn't look too fit, eh?'

To Miss Morris's practised eye Jimmy Thatcher looked indeed far from fit. Mounted on the ostrich he was swept past them at regular intervals, his face green and glistening with perspiration. Miss Morris didn't like the look of it at all, and as the music slowed down she walked quickly round to where Jimmy was convulsively clutching the ostrich's neck.

'Come along, Jimmy,' she said. 'Mother wants you.'

'I can't, miss,' said Jimmy hoarsely.

'Well, try,' said Miss Morris.

'I'll be sick if I do, miss, and it hurts so,' sobbed Jimmy.

Miss Morris put down Lydia's coconut, lifted Jimmy kindly and firmly off his ostrich and sat down on a chair hastily brought by the proprietress of the shooting gallery.

'Boy been eating too many sweets, eh?' said Sir Edmund. 'Better tell his mother. I'll run them home. She's been working in the tent all day.'

'I'm sorry, Sir Edmund,' said Miss Morris, 'but we ought to have a doctor. It's not my business, but it looks very like appendicitis. I've been with several cases. Is there a doctor?'

'Ford isn't here to-day,' said Sir Edmund, who knew everything, 'and Macfadden's away on holiday and I'm pretty sure I saw Horton driving over the other side of Barchester as I came. Better get him to the hospital. I've got the car here. Get his mother, one of you boys.'

But Mrs. Thatcher, already warned by swift-footed rumour that Jimmy had been taken bad, arrived as he spoke and burst into loud tears. At the same moment Mrs. Brandon and Mr. Miller came up and learnt what had happened. Mrs. Brandon immediately went to find her car where there was a rug, and Miss Morris followed carrying Jimmy. In a few moments they were packed into Sir Edmund's car, Jimmy greener than ever, too much in pain and fright even to cry. Just as they were starting, the proprietress of the shooting gallery came up with Miss Morris's coconut.

'Here's something you left behind, dearie,' she said, thrusting it at its owner.

Jimmy's eyes brightened for a moment.

'Be a good boy, Jimmy, and you can have my coconut,' said Miss Morris.

Jimmy's face assumed the expression of a martyr who sees the gates of heaven beyond the tormentors' swords, as he feebly clutched the prize.

'We'll telephone to you from Barchester, Mrs. Brandon,' said Sir Edmund. 'Can you manage, Miss Morris?'

Miss Morris said she thought so, and then caught sight of Delia.

'May Delia come, Mrs. Brandon?' she said. 'I'd be rather glad of someone that can keep her head.'

Delia did not wait for her mother's permission. Her face lighted at the idea of going to a hospital with a possible appendix patient, even as Jimmy's had lighted at the coconut. She got into the back seat with Miss Morris and the patient, and the car drove off.

'That was *ripping* of you,' she said to Miss Morris. 'Gosh, doesn't poor Jimmy look *ghastly*.'

There was in her voice and air a mixture of true compassion for the invalid and what almost might be called gloating over the illness, that convinced Miss Morris she couldn't have made a better choice of a companion, who would not only be a support to her, but derive infinite satisfaction from the circumstances of the journey.

'I say, Mrs. Thatcher was howling like anything,' said Delia, 'but Mr. Miller was awfully nice to her and he was taking her up to the

Vicarage to have a good cry and he said he'd keep her there till we telephoned. He's a good old sort for a parson.'

Miss Morris did not even think of chiding Delia for her language. She felt an unreasonable pride that her father's old pupil should have been so kind and thoughtful to the unhappy Mrs. Thatcher. Then she remembered what Sir Edmund had said about Mr. Miller and Mrs. Brandon and told herself that Mr. Miller deserved anything good, *anything* that heaven saw fit to send him. The journey to Barchester was soon over.

XII

MR. MERTON EXPLAINS

EVERYONE was agreeably excited by Jimmy's sudden appearance as News, some saying that they could see he would die on the way and the Panel ought to do something about it, others maintaining that he would be operated upon at once and die under the operation and the Government ought to do something about it. The crowd had now thinned and gone home to its tea, and the proprietors of the various shows were taking it easy till the evening rush began again about seven o'clock.

Mrs. Brandon collected Francis and went home, where she was soon joined by Mr. Merton and Lydia. Francis distributed sherry and the peace of Stories fell on the party.

'Excuse me, madam,' said Nurse, appearing in the doorway, 'but is Miss Delia back? I wanted her to try on that slip that I've been altering.'

'She's been taken to the Barchester Hospital,' said Francis.

'Don't be silly, Francis,' said his mother, and explained to Nurse the circumstance under which Delia had gone.

But even this delightful news did not appease Nurse, who said in a chilly way that she couldn't get on with the slip without Miss Delia, and then remained silent in the doorway like a hovering Nemesis.

'I'll tell you what, Nurse,' said Mrs. Brandon. 'Could you mend Miss Keith's frock? She tore it at the Fête and her mother was rather upset.'

'Oh, I say, don't bother,' said Lydia, backing. 'It's a foul frock anyway, Mrs. Brandon, and I always tear my things.'

'You *have* torn it, miss,' said Nurse, combining approval of the magnificence of the job on hand with deep disapproval of the frock's owner. 'If you come upstairs with me, miss, I'll stitch it up. You can't go back like that, and with a gentleman.'

As she spoke she cast a disapproving look at Noel Merton which made him feel that she probably regarded him as a professional seducer, who began his ravishing by tearing the sleeves of his victims' frocks. Lydia, her bold spirit for once outmatched, followed Nurse meekly from the room.

'That is a remarkable woman,' said Mr. Merton. 'I have never known anyone who had the faintest effect on Lydia before.'

'It's nothing to the effect she has on us,' said Francis. 'Have some more sherry?'

Mr. Merton said he would.

'When I accepted your kind invitation,' he said to Mrs. Brandon, 'I did so with the express intention of betraying a confidence, and propose to do so at once, before Lydia comes back and stuns us all. You know my father did Miss Brandon's business. Well he has told me something about her will and I propose to tell it to you because I know how pleased you will be. His professional letters about it are already in the post and everyone concerned will get them on Monday, so it isn't really a breach of confidence at all.'

'Well hurry up,' said Francis. 'I'm not a fortune hunter, but I would like to know the worst.'

But before Mr. Merton could begin to say whatever it was, Rose announced Mrs. Grant and Mr. Grant, who had never aroused such annoyance before.

'You will be quite surprised to see us again,' said Mrs. Grant, while Francis murmured to Mr. Grant that surprised wasn't the word and Mr. Grant looked miserable. 'I went up to the Vicarage with my Boy, but there was such confusione, a woman in tears, the parroco consoling her, so different from our dear Calabrian peasants who seek the confessional in the church, never in the presbiterio, that sono rimasta stupefatta. Hilary said you were having a little sherry party and I thought I might be allowed to accompany him as I shall not be here much longer.'

On hearing this delightful news everyone became almost cordial. Mrs. Grant refused sherry and asked for lemonade.

'And when do you really have to go?' asked Mrs. Brandon.

'Who knows?' replied Mrs. Grant. 'There is a proverb in Calabria which runs roughly, "To-morrow has also its own evil—"'

Francis said aloud to himself that to-day had it too and Mr. Merton exchanged a glance of sympathy with him.

'—and che sarà sarà. If I go to-morrow, I go; if not, it is for later,' said Mrs. Grant gaily. 'As long as my Boy needs me, I shall be here.'

'Well, I'm afraid I'll have to be getting back to Southbridge,' said Mr. Merton to his hostess in amused despair.

'Look here, Mr. Merton, it isn't fair to leave us all in this shattering state of suspense,' said Francis. 'After all, Hilary is just as much interested as we are.'

Mr. Grant, deeply oppressed by his mother's presence, looked incapable of interest in anything. Mrs. Brandon said Francis was perfectly right, though she wasn't sure if one ought to talk about these things.

'Anyway you can't go till Nurse releases Lydia, so you might as well come clean, if you'll excuse the revolting expression,' said Francis to Mr. Merton.

'I must explain,' said Mr. Merton to the Grants, 'that I was just going to tell Mrs. Brandon something about her aunt's will, that I know will interest you all. It will be common property on Monday, but I thought Mrs. Brandon would have a particular interest in knowing it now. By a codicil, made just before her death, Miss Brandon has left her companion Miss Morris ten thousand pounds, with some very appreciative remarks about her patience and kindness.'

He finished his sherry, with the consciousness of having made a good point.

'I am *very* glad,' said Mrs. Brandon with all the enthusiasm of her kind nature.

'Good old Aunt Sissie,' said Francis. 'Now I can propose to Miss Morris, unless it means cutting you out, Hilary.'

'Good luck,' said Mr. Grant, brightening up for the first time since his arrival. 'I'll be best man.'

These expressions of pleasure were genuine and unforced, but Mr. Merton, sensitive by nature and training to changes of voice and atmosphere, felt that something was wanting, though he couldn't tell what. Mrs. Brandon, Francis and Mr. Grant were indeed enchanted to find that Miss Morris had been remembered, but it was impossible for them not to wonder about the rest of the property. There was an uncomfortable pause and silence.

'There was another legacy that my father couldn't quite understand,' said Mr. Merton. 'May I help myself to some more sherry?'

'Oh, sorry,' said Francis getting up. 'Hilary?'

'No thanks,' said Mr. Grant.

'It was ten thousand pounds to a Captain Arbuthnot,' said Mr. Merton. 'He exists all right, but he doesn't seem to be any relation. All we know is that it's an Indian Army family.'

'No, not exactly a relation,' said Mrs. Brandon in an abstracted way, 'but there were very old family ties. What sort of age is he?'

'Oh quite young. Under thirty,' said Mr. Merton, who was still under forty. 'Do you think Lydia will soon be ready, Mrs. Brandon? We really ought to be getting back.'

'But who gets the Abbey?' said Mrs. Grant.

The rest of the company, while thinking poorly of such open curiosity, were greatly relieved that anyone had little enough fine feeling to ask

what by this time they were all burning to know. Burning is not perhaps quite the right word to express Mrs. Brandon's mild want of
interest, or the fact that Francis and Mr. Grant (as they found on
comparing notes afterwards) both suddenly felt slightly sick; but it will
serve.

'Oh, the Abbey and most of the property go as was always arranged,'
said Mr. Merton. 'Miss Brandon hadn't made a will since the year she
inherited her father's estate. She added one or two codicils, but nothing
that affects the disposition of the bulk of her property. Hullo Lydia, are
you mended now?'

'I say, Mrs. Brandon,' said Lydia, knocking a record which was
lying on the gramophone lid onto the floor, where it broke in half.

'Do bear your body more seeming, Lydia,' said Mr. Merton, picking
up the pieces. 'I apologise for her, Mrs. Brandon.'

'Ass!' said Lydia good-humouredly, giving her friend a violent hit
which he appeared to expect and indeed enjoy. 'I'm awfully sorry,
Mrs. Brandon. I say, Noel, what were you talking about codicils?'

'Only Miss Brandon's,' said Mr. Merton.

'Oh, the one mother and father went to the funeral of,' said Lydia.
'Who is going to live in the Abbey?'

'It was left in trust with most of the money to be a kind of home for
old people, specially anyone connected with certain regiments. I think
she had an uncle or a brother she was very fond of in the Army. But
what is really interesting, Lydia, is that Miss Morris is to have ten
thousand pounds.'

'That's fine!' said Lydia. 'And I gave her the coconut Tony got at
the shy. I say, Mrs. Brandon, your nurse is a tough guy. I'd like to see
her and the Pettinger have a go at each other. I'd back your nurse any
day.'

'Miss Pettinger was headmistress of the Barchester High School
where Lydia and Delia went,' Mrs. Brandon explained to Mrs. Grant.
'Well, good-bye, Mr. Merton, and thank you so much for telling us
about Miss Morris. I shan't say anything till Monday, when your
father's letter comes. I can't tell you how pleased we all are. Good-bye
Lydia. Never mind about the record. We are always breaking them.'

'Thanks awfully,' said Lydia. 'I do think your house is ripping.'

'So do I,' said Mr. Merton. 'Will you let me come and see it and you
again while I'm down here?'

'Yes, do,' said Mrs. Brandon, adding in a siren's voice, 'Ring me up
and come over some day when I am alone.'

Mr. Merton shook hands in a deliberately lingering way which made
Francis nudge Mr. Grant and say 'Mother at it again,' at which Mr.
Grant was just going to scowl when he realized to his own great surprise
that there was nothing to scowl about and smiled at Francis, thinking as
he did so that though Mrs. Brandon was still one of the nicest people in

the world, one looked for something more than charm in a woman; intellect and appreciation of one's work for instance.

'Well,' said Francis, when he returned from seeing the visitors off and had picked up the visiting cards that the whiff and wind of Lydia's progress through the hall had scattered from a table onto the floor. 'Well, there is an end of an old song; for auld sang I cannot nor will not say.'

'I daresay the Abbey will make a very nice home for old people,' said Mrs. Brandon, picking up her embroidery, 'that is if they don't mind the damp. After all, Aunt Sissie lived to be very old herself.'

Mrs. Grant, who had sat for some time with an expression of deep disapproval, got up and said she and Hilary must be going.

'Do come again, soon,' said Mrs. Brandon. 'Perhaps you and Hilary would dine with us next week.'

'I always believe in speaking the truth,' said Mrs. Grant.

'Yes, truth is so important,' said Mrs. Brandon, anxious as usual to agree. 'Would Wednesday suit you perhaps?'

'I feel I owe it to Miss Morris to tell her that I suspected her of trying to get Miss Brandon's property,' said Mrs. Grant earnestly.

'Oh I say, Mother,' said her son, surprised and horrified.

'I don't think it would really be a good plan,' said Mrs. Brandon. 'Mr. Merton says Aunt Sissie never altered her will since the one she made when her father died, so Miss Morris really has nothing to do with it at all, and after all ten thousand pounds is really nothing when you think how much money Aunt Sissie had.'

Even Francis had to admit that this was the most muddle-headed piece of special pleading that his dear mamma had ever achieved, but Mrs. Grant appeared to find it satisfactory.

'Yes, yes, I see what you mean,' she said with an alarmingly earnest gaze. 'You have intuition about these things.'

'I don't think so,' said Mrs. Brandon doubtfully, 'but I do hope you are free on Wednesday.'

This repetition of the invitation seemed to Francis simply asking for trouble, especially when Mrs. Grant, having freed her mind of Miss Morris, accepted it.

'Wednesday then will be delightful,' she said. 'We must go now, Hilary. I will go back to the Vicarage with you. It is really a comfort that all this affair of the Abbey is settled. Finito.'

She raised her long amber necklace with one hand and let it fall heavily on her coral necklace, her silver chain, and her coloured wooden beads, with a gesture of final doom. She then left, carrying her son, annoyed and speechless, with her.

'Well, darling, you said a mouthful asking that Original Gipsy Lee with all her clanking necklaces to dinner,' said Francis. 'I expect Hilary will cut his throat if she stays here much longer.'

'Francis, you shouldn't say things like that,' said his mother. 'Darling, you aren't at all sorry, are you?'

'About the Abbey? No, darling. Apart from the glamour of having the most revolting and inconvenient house in Barsetshire bar none, unless it's Pomfret Towers, and the joy of having a large fortune most of which would go in death duties and legacies to other people, I am really honestly quite happy, I may say relieved. And I'm sure Hilary feels exactly the same. By the way who is that Captain Arbuthnot? You seem to know about him.'

Mrs. Brandon paused for a moment before answering.

'Aunt Sissie's brother, Captain Brandon, had an entanglement with the wife of a Colonel Arbuthnot in India,' she said. 'He had to exchange his regiment because of it. Aunt Sissie was rather proud of the whole affair. She did say that I was a little like Mrs. Arbuthnot,' said Mrs. Brandon, looking pleased.

'Mamma, you shock me,' said Francis.

*

In spite of her son's attempts at dissuasion, Mrs. Grant insisted an accompanying him to the Vicarage. He knew that his mother would disgrace him and wished that she would do so at the Cow and Sickle rather than in the presence of Mr. Miller, who must be tired by the Fête and looking after Mrs. Thatcher. The Vicar was in the garden and Mr. Grant couldn't possibly warn him of the fate that was descending on him, so he said rather sulkily to his tutor, 'Here's mother sir,' and escaped into the house. Mrs. Grant established herself on the seat by the heliotrope border, and telling Mr. Miller that she had come to talk about her boy, proceeded to talk about herself. Mr. Miller was very tired. All that week he had been working for the Fête, in addition to his ordinary duties. Since breakfast-time he had been on duty, arranging, planning, judging, composing quarrels, adjusting differences, a buffer for every contending force. Just as he had hoped for a few words with Miss Morris, who had helped so splendidly in the tea-tent, she had been taken away from him by Sir Edmund; but he quickly put that thought away, though he couldn't help stopping to hope that Miss Morris would have everything good that life could give her. Then Jimmy Thatcher had been taken ill, and while he had done nothing, Sir Edmund and Miss Morris had taken the whole affair in hand with a competence which he hopelessly envied. He humbly thought of his own inefficiency. All he could do was to take charge of Mrs. Thatcher. After finding Edna, the eldest Miss Thatcher, she who had had an illegitimate baby in '36, and telling her to look after the other children, he had brought Mrs. Thatcher to the Vicarage and let her cry and talk in the study. There was no one in the house and Cook and Hettie were lost among the side shows, so he had been inspired to tell Mrs. Thatcher he felt like a cup of tea and introduce her to the kitchen. With loud but less despairing blubberings she had found the tea, milk and sugar, brought the kettle to the boil and produced for him the strongest, sweetest, nastiest cup of tea he had ever tasted. He had persuaded her to sit down with him at the kitchen table and share the odious drink, under whose influence she became as cheerful as circumstances permitted, giving him a graphic account of Thatcher's bad leg. After this he suggested that she should have a rest in Cook's armchair, found for her on the dresser what Cook called a nice book, being a twopenny work of fiction called *Her Dreams Came True*, and left her to herself, promising to tell her as soon as there was any news of Jimmy. He knew he ought to go back to the Fête, but was so tired with the long day and his own anxieties, that he sat for a little in his garden, and so fell a prey to Mrs. Grant.

While she talked he tried to listen, tried to focus his attention by looking at her beads and earrings, and then his mind wandered back to its preoccupation with Sir Edmund, till suddenly the name of Miss Morris brought his thoughts back with a jerk to what his guest was saying.

'Excuse me, I didn't quite catch what you said,' he said to Mrs. Grant. 'Do you mean that Miss Morris has been left something by Miss Brandon?'

'Not the Abbey, of course,' said Mrs. Grant. 'That was always left to some charity, so I understood from Mr. Merton, but she is to have ten thousand pounds. If you look on it as capital she will have an income for life if it is properly invested. Not much, but it makes a good background.'

Mr. Miller said to himself that even at three per cent one would have thirty pounds a year on a thousand pounds, and three hundred pounds on ten thousand pounds. Then there would be income tax, he supposed, but even so it would make a single woman a good deal better off than he was. So he expressed to Mrs. Grant his pleasure at this good news, saying he was sure no one deserved it more.

'By the way,' said Mrs. Grant, with a belated attack of conscience, 'Mrs. Brandon doesn't mean to tell Miss Morris, because she will hear about it in a lawyer's letter on Monday, but I feel sure she wouldn't mind my telling *you*. So don't give me away.'

Mr. Miller assured her that the confidence should be respected, and almost disliked her. So to make amends for this he asked her if she would stay and have a cold meal with him and her son.

'No, thank you,' said Mrs. Grant. 'I am going back to the Cow, where I have promised to teach Mrs. Spindler to prepare macaroni in the native fashion, that is as far as is possible when the macaroni itself is bought, not made at home. I shan't disturb Hilary, for I know how hard he has to work.'

In proof of this virtuous resolve she called up to her son's window in what Mr. Miller could only suppose to be an Italian way, till he put his face unsympathetically out and said good-bye.

When she had gone Mr. Miller knew he ought to call his pupil, have the cold tongue and tomatoes, and go back to the Fête, but an overpowering fatigue of mind and body so assailed him that he remained in the garden and was still there when Sir Edmund's car drove up. Mr. Miller went to the gate, but Sir Edmund was alone.

'Knew you'd want to know about the boy, Miller,' said Sir Edmund through the car window, 'so I came round this way after I'd dropped Miss Morris and Delia at Stories. It's appendicitis all right. Clever woman Miss Morris. They're going to operate at once. I had a good talk with Miss Morris on the way back, and we understand each other pretty well. Head on her shoulders. Heart too. Not on her shoulders — you know what I mean. I promised Jimmy I'd tell his mother he is all right. Plucky little fellow. Well, I must get along to Grumper's End.'

'Mrs. Thatcher is here,' said Mr. Miller. 'She was so upset that I thought some tea would do her good.'

Sir Edmund stared at his Vicar with respect and admiration, but made no comment.

'If you would ring me up as soon as there is news of Jimmy,' said the Vicar, 'I'll keep her here, and Cook or Hettie, can see her home.'

Sir Edmund nodded and drove off.

Mr. Miller and Mr. Grant then partook of supper, almost in silence. Mr. Grant, bitten by Mrs. Morland's idea of a novel, was in a state of literary frenzy. Mr. Miller was thinking of a happy future for an admirable, intelligent woman, an ideal companion, and at the same time telling himself that such thoughts were better left in an eternal shadow. At nine o'clock Cook and Hettie came back from the Fête and had the rest of the cold tongue and tomatoes with Mrs. Thatcher. At nine-fifteen Sir Edmund rang up to say that Jimmy Thatcher had been operated on successfully and was doing well, a piece of news received by Mrs. Thatcher with loud and thankful hysterics, by Cook and Hettie with pleasure mingled with a lasting regret that the operation had not delightfully proved fatal. At nine-thirty the Vicar sent Mrs. Thatcher home in charge of his servants and by ten o'clock Cook and Hettie were back and had gone to bed, and Mr. Grant had retired. Mr. Miller sat in his study in the summer darkness, long after the noise and lights of the Fête were over, till he fell asleep with heavy fatigue of mind, and in the unfriendly grey heralding of dawn he woke unrefreshed and went to bed.

*

Dinner at Stories consisted chiefly of a long and happy monologue from Delia, who had not only enjoyed every moment of the drive and insisted on having Jimmy on her lap, but had had the exquisite pleasure of seeing two operation cases being wheeled back from the operating theatre, looking like corpses. Her mother and brother, conspirators, said little and Miss Morris was rather tired. After dinner Delia put on all her crooning records so that talk was unnecessary. Mrs. Brandon sat with her embroidery, but her fingers were idle and she looked more often than usual at her graceful hands and Miss Brandon's diamond ring. A gentle melancholy filled her as she thought of Aunt Sissie's legacy to Captain Arbuthnot, probably if one went by dates and ages the grandson of the woman who had for a season enchanted Captain Brandon. As Francis had said, it was the end of an old song. Captain Brandon and his lovely ladies were long forgotten; only in Miss Brandon's memory they had lived. Now she was dead and her memory too would soon be faint. Mrs. Brandon suddenly realized how great a compliment Aunt Sissie had paid her when she put Captain Brandon's gift on her finger. What she did not realize was that her indomitable, pagan old aunt had seen and respected in her, for all the silliness that she so trenchantly criticized, an integrity of spirit not so far from her own. The end of an old song.

When good nights had been said Mrs. Brandon remembered something she had forgotten, a phenomenon which was frequent in her life. She went to Miss Morris's room and tapped at the door. Miss Morris in her dressing-gown, her hair in two plaits, opened to her.

'I'm so sorry,' said Mrs. Brandon, 'I quite forgot to ask you about church to-morrow. Would you like to go to Little Misfit or Nutfield? I just wanted to know so that I could send word to Curwen.'

'I'd like so much to come to church with you if I may,' said Miss Morris.

XIII

MISS MORRIS'S LEGACY

SUNDAY passed over quietly. Francis and Delia were spending the day with friends, Mrs. Brandon and Miss Morris went to the eleven o'clock service, during which Mrs. Brandon did some very useful thinking about clothes for Miss Morris's possible spring wedding, Mr. Miller tried hard to keep his mind on his work, and Miss Morris betrayed no thoughts of any kind. The Grants were also there, in the vicarage pew, and when Mr. Grant saw every eye in the church turned upon his mother and her jangling accoutrements, he wished as usual that he were dead, for he was too good a son to wish that fate to his mother. The only thing that sustained him was the thought of the literary composition upon which he had already embarked. As soon as he and Mr. Miller had finished their horrid cold supper he had made an excuse of some work to do, and shut himself up with Jehan le Capet. During the evening he mapped out a rough draft of the novel suggested by Mrs. Morland and had written a chapter of very realistic description of Jehan le Capet's first mistress, the wife of the proprietor of a rather low eating house in the Quartier Latin called Le Chat Savant. In his enthusiasm he had almost identified himself with his hero and had emerged at about two o'clock in the morning from his work, dazed, exhausted, and with very cold feet, as the poet had often emerged from the side door of the Chat Savant. There was however this difference, that the proprietor's wife always sent her poet away with a little parcel of food in his pocket, whereas Mr. Grant having finished on the previous night a tin of biscuits that he kept in his room, and being afraid to go downstairs in case Cook or Hettie should hear him, had to go hungry to bed.

Outwardly all the congregation looked much as usual and no one, hearing Sir Edmund read the lessons in his usual orderly-room manner, taking all the difficult names in an unhesitating and often incorrect stride, would have guessed that he was reflecting upon his responsibility for preventing his Vicar and his old friend Mrs. Brandon from making fools of themselves.

After the service there was the usual talk outside the church door as the congregation dispersed. When the Vicar came out he approached the little group where Mrs. Brandon was standing with Sir Edmund and the Grants. He looked anxious, a fact which did not escape the keen eye of his churchwarden.

'Morning, Miller,' said Sir Edmund. 'That was a queer first lesson. Something to be said for having the Bible in Latin, eh? You look a bit queer too. Had a bad night?'

Mr. Miller said he hadn't slept very well.

'It was the Fête,' said Mrs. Brandon sympathetically.

'Got the accounts wrong again?' asked Sir Edmund.

Mr. Miller said he hadn't been through them yet.

'No, no, of course not. Sunday,' said Sir Edmund. 'Thirteenth after Trinity and all that. Never mind. They'll keep and I daresay you'll get them just as wrong to-morrow. Remember the year you were seventeen and threepence out of pocket. Well, be sure to let me know if there's any deficit. Mustn't muzzle the ox, you know, eh?'

Mr. Miller smiled feebly. Not that he in the least resented Sir Edmund's remark about the ox, or the implication that he lined his own pockets out of the takings of the Fête, for he knew his churchwarden's kindness of heart, but there were reasons why he could not bear to think of any deficit being made up by him. One does not like to take too much charity from a man whom one really likes very much and is trying not to dislike.

'Mr. Miller,' said Mrs. Grant, 'will you mind very much if I take my Boy back to lunch at the Cow? I feel I must see all I can of him before I go.'

Mr. Miller, who had counted upon Mr. Grant to do justice to the Vicarage roast beef and knew Cook would be annoyed if he said he really couldn't face a heavy lunch, said indeed, indeed she must have Hilary. Mr. Grant, who had only come to church out of kindness to his host, and was straining to get back to his novel, looked at his mother in black despair.

'We shall have a little festa,' said Mrs. Grant gaily. 'I have told Mrs. Spindler exactly how macaroni should be prepared, and we will imagine we are in Calabria.'

Mr. Grant looked as if this exercise of the imagination would afford him no pleasure at all, but said nothing.

'Mrs. Brandon,' said Mr. Miller, 'would I find you in sometime to-morrow afternoon? I very much want to speak to you, alone.'

Although he had said these words in a low voice, they had not escaped Sir Edmund's attention.

'Of course,' said Mrs. Brandon. 'Do come to tea and I'll tell Rose I am not at home, only I'm afraid we can't have tea in the garden in that case, because it is really quite impossible to say one is not at home when there one is in full view under the chestnut. I do hope it isn't the accounts, because I can't do them at all.'

Mr. Miller assured her that it was not the accounts, but only a small private matter. Sir Edmund, who deliberately overheard this, was more than ever perturbed and resolved to think the matter over seriously.

Mr. Miller went back to the Vicarage, told Hettie that Mr. Grant would not be in to lunch and sat down alone to a round of beef, which was what Cook and Hettie liked on Sundays. For a moment he thought of putting the helping he had cut for himself under Hettie's eye into an envelope and burying it, but he knew he would not be clever enough to conceal the crime and in any case would be acting a lie. So he chewed his way industriously through red meat, grey potatoes, damp cabbage, and stony apple-pie. With the uninteresting cheese courage was given him to tell Hettie he had had enough and didn't want any coffee as he had to go to Grumper's End. He found a faint satisfaction in sitting in Mrs. Thatcher's kitchen, giving her the latest news of Jimmy (who was going on well) and promising to take her to see him at the hospital next week. The cottage appeared to him in an even more deplorable condition than usual. Edna and Doris were washing their hair over the dirty sink, dirty dishes lay about, the younger That-

chers were playing on the dirty floor with their illegitimate young
nephew and niece, a few clothes, washed out in a slovenly way by
Edna and Doris, lay about the room because no one could be bothered
to hang them out in the sunshine. In the corner Thatcher, unshaven,
was enjoying his after-dinner pipe and reading in his Sunday paper
about the forthcoming autumn football pools. Everything smelt of
frostiness and stale food. Looking round upon the young Thatchers, all
of whom seemed to thrive upon their parents' slatternly methods, the
Vicar blamed himself severely for want of tolerance and wondered how
he would manage on thirty-five shillings a week.

Just as he was sitting down to his horrid cold Sunday supper his
pupil came in.

'I'm awfully sorry I'm late, sir,' said Mr. Grant.

'Come in, come in,' said the Vicar. 'I'm afraid it's only cold beef and
pickles. Hettie said they were too busy clearing up after the Fête to do
baked potatoes to-night. I am so sorry.'

'That's all right, sir,' said Mr. Grant. 'I'm off farinaceous food altogether since lunch. Mother had a most unholy row with Mrs. Spindler
about macaroni. She wanted to show her how to cook it and Mrs.
Spindler, who I must say is usually awfully nice, was a bit off colour
after the Fête and there were a lot of extra Sunday dinners for motorists
and things and she seems to have gone off the deep end altogether. Oh,
that's heaps, sir, thanks,' said Mr. Grant, hastily withdrawing his plate
upon which the Vicar had been heaping slices of beef while Mr. Grant
talked. 'We did get the macaroni, but it was not a success, and then it
was ground rice shape and I felt I must do something not to hurt Mrs.
Spindler's feelings, so I had two helpings. Oh Lord! Sorry, sir.'

'I am indeed sorry,' said the Vicar. 'I've never known Mrs. Spindler
be rude to a visitor before.'

'Well, you haven't known my mother before sir,' said Mr. Grant.
'But one good thing is that mother says she must go back to Italy. She
has lots of rows with the hotel people there, but somehow rows are
different in Italy and people always seem a bit cheered up by them, if
you know what I mean. How's Donne, sir?'

'I have been correcting the galley proofs,' said the Vicar, flushing
with mild pleasure at his pupil's interest. 'I must say the work has been
very well done, and I find very few mistakes. The only thing that
worries me now is the question of a dedication.'

'Who were you thinking of dedicating it to?' asked Mr. Grant, feeling
very respectful towards a person who had real proofs to correct.

'I had thought — —' said the Vicar, and then broke off.

'What about your old college, sir?' asked Mr. Grant. 'I should think
they'd be jolly pleased.'

'How nice of you,' said the Vicar. 'If it were a work on a classical
subject I should not hesitate to make a suggestion. But Donne —. I fear

the Master would think such a dedication frivolous. How is your own work?'

'I'm afraid I've been a bit slack lately,' said Mr. Grant, guiltily conscious of books unread and essays unfinished. 'I'll put in some solid work to-night and really get down to it next week.'

'I meant your own work,' said the Vicar.

'My own work?' said Mr. Grant, going bright pink.

'I suppose it's a novel,' said the Vicar.

'Yes sir. But how on earth did you know?'

'The usual sign,' said the Vicar mildly. 'I've had a good many pupils, you know. When they come down to meals looking drunk and sometimes very cross and nearly always peculiar in manner, it always means a novel. Besides, I wrote one once myself.'

'Did you really, sir?' asked Mr. Grant, suddenly seeing his tutor in a new and respectful light. 'Could I read it?'

'I'm afraid not,' said the Vicar, secretly flattered at this interest. 'I tore it up soon after I had finished it. But I remember exactly how I felt when I was writing it and how drunk – if we may use the expression – literary composition made me. I am afraid I wasn't always an easy companion during that period.'

'What was it about, sir?' asked Mr. Grant.

'Oh, nothing,' said the Vicar vaguely. 'Quite an ordinary story about two young people who thought they cared for each other and were separated by circumstances. One is told,' he added, more to himself than to his pupil, 'that first novels are nearly always autobiographical.'

He fell into a kind of muse, forgetful of his pupil's presence. Mr. Grant felt respectfully uncomfortable and being still young enough to believe that his own affairs must interest all his friends he rather shyly asked the Vicar if he would like to hear about what he was doing.

'What you are doing?' said the Vicar, bringing himself back to life with an effort that his young friend did not notice. 'Indeed, indeed, my dear Hilary, I should be delighted. Don't think I wish to press your confidence in any way, but it would really interest me immensely. Let us go into the garden. It feels so hot and heavy indoors.'

'I was doing a kind of monograph on that French poet, Jehan le Capet that I told you about,' said Mr. Grant, as they installed themselves on the seat by the heliotrope border, 'but I was talking about it to Mrs. Morland at the picnic and she was awfully helpful about publishers and things and then I met her again at the Fête and she said why not make a novel out of it?'

'Why not?' said Mr. Miller.

'So,' continued Mr. Grant, enchanted by this encouragement, 'I thought I'd have a stab at it. Mrs. Morland's awfully nice and she's a real author. I mean people ask for her books in libraries. And she's the

sort of person you can really talk to about anything. I mean things
you couldn't talk to other people about.'

'Yes, I should think Mrs. Morland is extraordinarily broad-minded
about things she really knows nothing about,' said the Vicar, a remark
whose unexpected profundity rather staggered Mr. Grant. 'And now
tell me how you propose to treat your novel.'

Encouraged by the growing darkness which enabled one to say words
like 'mistress' in front of one's tutor without feeling uncomfortable, Mr.
Grant embarked upon his subject, and having once begun saw no
reason to stop. The Vicar found his pleasant eager young voice no
hindrance to his own thoughts and they sat, each full of his own dreams,
till the late full moon had risen above the trees.

*

On Monday morning Francis, coming down just before half-past eight
to have his breakfast and go off to his work, was very much surprised to
find his dear mother already downstairs and walking about the room.
To see her so early and to see her restless were phenomena which, taken
together, could not fail to strike an intelligent observer.

'Good Lord!' said Francis, 'it's Monday.'

'The post is usually a bit late on Mondays,' said Mrs. Brandon,
looking out of the window.

'I say,' said Delia, as she came in, 'has the post come?'

'Not yet,' said her mother. 'He never does on Monday because of
helping his cousin at the dairy.'

'I do hope Miss Morris will get down before he comes,' said Delia.
'I want to see if she'll throw a fit or something when the news comes.
Do you suppose it will come this morning, Mother?'

'Mr. Merton said so,' said Mrs. Brandon, 'and he ought to know
because he's a lawyer.'

'People do sometimes die of shock when they get very good news,'
said Delia hopefully, but at the moment Miss Morris came in, looking
as neat and collected as ever, and this interesting conversation had to
stop.

Miss Morris ate her breakfast with good appetite, wondering a little
why Francis and Delia were talking in such a disjointed way.

'You don't often come down to breakfast, do you, Mrs. Brandon?'
she asked.

'Sometimes, but not very often, at least I hardly ever do, but just now
and then, or really hardly ever, unless you count the days one has to
get up early, like going abroad,' said Mrs. Brandon with the air of one
giving a thoroughly lucid explanation.

Francis and Delia began to laugh. Francis choked and Delia hit him
on the back and they would probably both have had hysterics had not
Rose come in with the letters. One might have heard a pin drop, as

Francis dramatically said to Mr. Grant later in the day, while Miss Morris looked over her little pile of letters.

'They all look like business,' she said. 'I shan't spoil my breakfast with them.'

If maddened frustration could kill, Francis and Delia would certainly have killed her on the spot. Even Mrs. Brandon thought vaguely that Miss Morris was perhaps a little inconsiderate but a fat envelope bulging with patterns of material for new curtains held her attention for the moment. Francis got up and went to the sideboard to find a little something to round off his breakfast. After cutting himself two slices of ham he returned to his place, and said to Miss Morris, as carelessly as possible,

'Why not look at them now, Miss Morris? It's unlucky to leave letters unopened at breakfast.'

He looked across at his sister to demand her sympathetic applause for this brillant piece of diplomacy, but Delia did not respond. To her brother's alarm she was sitting with a flushed face and her mouth open, and staring fixedly at nothing.

'Hi, Delia, what's up?' Francis asked. 'Has something stuck in your gullet? Wait a minute and I'll come and hit your back.'

To this kind suggestion Delia's only answer was the words, 'Two hundred pounds!'

'Pounds of what?' said Francis. 'Pull yourself together, my girl.'

'Aunt Sissie! Two hundred pounds!' Delia gasped. 'It says so in a letter. Mother, is it real, do you think?'

She pushed a letter across the table to her mother who read it with provoking coolness and said she thought it was quite real.

'Well!' said Francis, who had got up again and was reading the letter over his mother's shoulder, 'who would have thought Aunt Sissie had it in her. Now we can get those records, Delia.'

'I'll tell you what,' said Delia, 'I'll give you half.'

'No, you jolly well won't,' said Francis. 'Oh Good Lord! hang on a moment. I've got a hunch.'

He dashed back to his place, tore open his letters, held up one of them and said triumphantly,

'There! Two hundred pounds for me too. Well, well, well. Good old Aunt Sissie. Let's go to Monte Carlo and stake it all and double it and take away the number we first thought of. I'll give you half, Delia, to make up for the half you're giving me. I say, Mother, what about you?'

'Aunt Sissie gave me my ring,' said Mrs. Brandon, looking with complacency at her graceful hand which bore only her wedding ring and Captain Brandon's diamond. 'I am so glad she remembered you both, and two hundred pounds is such a nice sum, because you feel it isn't worth investing.'

Miss Morris then said, with every evidence of sincerity, how glad she was of this good fortune and quite agreed — she who had counted less than half that sum as riches for a year — that the great thing about two hundred pounds was that one could spend it; that it became indeed a kind of solemn duty to spend it. By the time she had finished saying this her young friends could have shaken her till every tooth in her head rattled, but the conventions forbid one to press one's guests, who may have very good reasons for their conduct, to open their letters in one's presence.

'Well, I must be off,' said Francis. 'If I get the sack for being late two hundred pounds won't support me till I get the Old Age Pension. How soon do we get the money, Mother?'

'I haven't the faintest idea, darling,' said Mrs. Brandon. 'Ask Mr. Merton.'

'When is he coming?' asked Francis.

Mrs. Brandon said she didn't know, but Mr. Merton had said he would telephone. Her son Francis looked at her and grinned at his sister.

'What you mean, darling, is that you asked him to ring you up,' said Francis. 'Well, I must be off.'

He made a last face at Delia, indicative of hatred for people who would not read their letters, and went away to his car. Delia, after gazing with silent animosity upon the unconscious Miss Morris, went into the garden. Mrs. Brandon, giving the whole matter up as a bad job, went off to see Cook in her sitting-room leaving Miss Morris looking at the advertisement pages of *The Times*. Cook was in a good mood and Mrs. Brandon was soon able to apply herself to her correspondence. She was in the middle of writing an account of the Fête to her old governess, who lived in Cheltenham, when Miss Morris came in and asked if she could spare a moment.

'Of course,' said Mrs. Brandon, laying down her pen with a gentle feeling of excitement. 'Can I do anything?'

'I don't quite understand this letter,' said Miss Morris, apparently as composed as ever.

Mrs. Brandon asked if she might see it. Miss Morris handed a letter to her and Mrs. Brandon noticed that her hand was shaking.

'Sit down and let me look at it,' said Mrs. Brandon, who knew perfectly well what the contents were, but wanted to give Miss Morris time. 'It seems quite clear to me. Aunt Sissie has left you ten thousand pounds, and I must say it does her the greatest credit, or did, or is it does?'

'But it's not fair,' said Miss Morris with unusual vehemence. 'Francis and Delia have two hundred pounds each and you have nothing, and I have all this money.'

'No, please don't look at it like that,' said Mrs. Brandon. 'As a matter of fact it is a very good thing for the children not to have any more, because they will both be really very comfortably off, and as for me I shouldn't know what to do with it, and besides, I have my diamond. Please, please do believe me that it is the nicest and best thing Aunt Sissie could have done, and let me say for us all how very pleased we are.'

With which words Mrs. Brandon got up and kissed Miss Morris warmly.

'I can't believe it. You are too generous,' said Miss Morris, in a voice which threatened tears.

'Drink this at once,' said Mrs. Brandon, unscrewing the top of the little flask of brandy that she kept in the top drawer of her bureau in case, and thrusting it into Miss Morris's hand. Miss Morris, hypnotized by her hostess's firm attitude, tilted the flask, drank more of the contents than she expected and coughed so violently that emotion was for the time being dispelled.

'I'm not really a bit generous,' said Mrs. Brandon, voicing as usual the first muddled thoughts that came into her head, 'because I didn't make the will, but I'm sure if Aunt Sissie had asked me I'd have said twenty thousand.'

'I can't take it,' said Miss Morris.

'You could subscribe to ever so many charities,' said Mrs. Brandon, 'and do good secretly, but I *do* hope you'll spend some on clothes and let me help you, because I know that's what Aunt Sissie would have liked.'

'Miss Brandon would have liked you to have pretty clothes. She wouldn't have approved of them for me,' said Miss Morris with ruthless realism. 'But if I could help anyone who is in need — — '

She paused and looked with a rapt expression into the distance.

'Of course you could,' said Mrs. Brandon, seizing her opportunity. 'Pomfret Madrigal is simply full of people in need and then there is our division of Barsetshire, and the whole county, and Zenana missions, whatever they are, and heaps of charities. Mr. Miller is coming to see me after tea and I could ask him about deserving cases in the village to start with if you like.'

'That would be true kindness,' said Miss Morris, 'and so like you. I think, if you don't mind, I had better go upstairs to my room and be quiet for a little. If only my dear father could see — — '

She broke off, too moved for further speech.

'He can see *everything*,' said Mrs. Brandon firmly, for though she had no particular conviction herself that the Rev. and late Justin Morris, who seemed to have been as selfish as they make them, was looking down from his particular brand of heaven upon his daughter with a benevolent and approving eye, yet she felt that any idea to that effect in Miss Morris's mind was eminently suitable for a clergyman's daughter and should be encouraged.

Miss Morris threw a grateful glance towards her hostess and escaped, to thank Heaven with grateful tears in her bedroom for making it possible for her to help the poor, and more especially the poor who were in Mr. Miller's flock.

Mrs. Brandon, left alone, amused herself by trying to calculate upon the blotting paper how much a year Miss Morris would have, but as she didn't know how much per cent one was likely to get and had a vague though mistaken idea that Compound Interest, which she could never do at school, somehow came into it with some letters of the alphabet, not to speak of blotting paper being a very unfavourable medium for arithmetical computation, she had not got very far when Delia came into the room, carrying a vase of flowers.

'I say, Mother,' she said, 'does Miss Morris know yet? I saw her going upstairs when I was bringing the flowers in, but I didn't like to ask, so I did the dining-room vases and this one for her room, but I didn't like to take it upstairs till I knew everything was all right.'

'Yes, she opened her letters just after you had gone out,' said Mrs. Brandon, 'but I wouldn't go up just yet. She is probably crying. Poor thing, how glad I am for her.'

'So'm I,' said Delia. 'I say, Mother, what about Hilary? Do you suppose he comes in on this? If not Francis and I must do something about it. He was just as much Aunt Sissie's cousin or whatever it is as we are.'

*

The object of Delia's interest had meant to get up at cockcrow to strike while the iron was hot, or in other words to continue his novel while the inspiration was upon him, but so soundly did he sleep that it was not till Hettie had knocked twice that he realized the precious early morning hours had flown. Having realized it he at once went to sleep again and did not wake till half-past nine. Full of shame he rushed through his bath and dressing and came downstairs three steps at a time only to find the dining-room empty. Hettie, coming in to ask rather grudgingly if he would like some fresh tea, said Mr. Miller had been sent for to Starveacres Hatches and didn't know when he would be back. Mr. Grant looked miserably at the tepid, black infusion in the tea-pot and said it would do nicely, and Hettie retired. He poured himself out a cup, drank shudderingly of it, looked with distaste at a cold poached egg, and decided on milk and bread and butter. Over this blameless meal he began to read his letters, and by this time it will surprise no one to learn that the second letter he opened was from Miss Brandon's solicitors, announcing a bequest of two hundred pounds.

His first thought was of pure joy at having two hundred pounds of his own, for though his father had arranged an income for him, it was not to be his own till he was twenty-five, until which time he had to live on the allowance his mother gave him, an allowance which, though not ungenerous, did not allow for much saving. Two hundred pounds would be a godsend. One could buy books, go to Iceland, have really good seats at the Opera and in short indulge one's fancy. His second thought was one of apprehension. Had his mother also received a legacy, and if not would she resent his having one. Her annoyance, if she had to be annoyed, would not last, but while it did last she was capable of flying into one of the scenes which, while part of calm every-day life to her beloved Calabrians, had the effect of volcanoes and geysers on the colder-blooded English and would put him to shame for ever in Pomfret Madrigal. With some annoyance he decided he had better neglect his classics and his novel and go down to the Cow before his mother went out. But on the way he passed the lane leading to Stories and could not resist the temptation of going up the drive to see if anyone was about. Catching sight of Delia through the morning room window, he came in and found her with her mother.

'Good morning, Hilary,' said Mrs. Brandon. 'Have you come to congratulate Miss Morris?'

'Because you can't just now,' Delia remarked antiphonally, 'because she's having a good howl in her room. Good old Miss Morris.'

'I'd rather forgotten about that,' said Mr. Grant, feeling brutal, 'but I'm awfully glad. She deserves it if anyone does. I really came to tell you something.'

'But what is *marvellous*,' said Delia, taking no notice of him, 'is that Aunt Sissie has left me two hundred pounds for myself. Good old Aunt Sissie. I say, Hilary, have you got anything? If not I'll give you half of mine.'

Mr. Grant suddenly felt so selfish that he could have sunk through the floor. All he had thought of was how to spend his own money, and now Delia, who must have as many secret wishes as he had, was offering him half her inheritance from sheer kindness. He tried to say something but stammered so badly that he had to stop. Mrs. Brandon, feeling that the young people must really deal with their affairs themselves, resumed her letter writing with some ostentation.

'All right, Hilary, no need to gobble,' said Delia kindly. 'Just as you like, only I'd awfully like to give you something. It might help your book along a bit.'

'You do have the most marvellous ideas,' said Mr. Grant, at last recovering partial control of his speech.

Delia looked pleased.

'You will have it, won't you?' she asked anxiously.

'It's absolutely *decent* of you,' said Mr. Grant vehemently, 'but as a matter of fact Aunt Sissie left me two hundred pounds too. I do hope you won't mind.'

'Delia darling,' said Mrs. Brandon, 'do take Hilary into the garden.

I must finish writing to poor old Miss Heaton about the Fête and I have just written hundred pounds instead of roundabout.'

Accordingly the young people went into the garden, where Mr. Grant, now himself again, told Delia all about Mrs. Morland's suggestion. Delia showed as much interest and excitement about the proposed novel as any author could wish, and it was she who made the brilliant suggestion that in the extremely remote case of the publishing trade being blind and misguided enough not to accept the novel, Hilary should use some of his legacy in paying for a part of the expenses of publication, thus conferring a lasting benefit on the reading public. So pleasantly did the morning pass that it was too late for Hilary to go to the Cow, and he had to hurry back to the Vicarage where lunch was at one.

'I really can't say thank you enough,' he said to Delia as he left. 'You simply are the only person I can really talk to about my book. You really understand.'

Pleased with her cousin's praise, Delia went back to the house and let Nurse try on a camisole without a single murmur, which made Nurse look at her a little suspiciously.

XIV

MRS. BRANDON AT HOME

MR. MILLER arrived punctually for his assignation with Mrs. Brandon, who had given orders that she would see no one till the Vicar had gone.

'Now, tell me all about everything,' said Mrs. Brandon, in her most comfortable voice.

'I really hardly know how to begin what I want to say to you, Mrs. Brandon, without a breach of confidence,' said Mr. Miller.

'Tell me exactly what it is then,' said Mrs. Brandon.

'You see, it concerns not only myself, but Mrs. Grant,' said the Vicar.

'Mrs. Grant?' said Mrs. Brandon, taken quite aback, and wondering whether Mrs. Grant had come to tell Mr. Miller that the Mafia were on her track, or alternatively whether he was going to propose to his pupil's mother. Neither alternative seemed probable.

'You see she came to the Vicarage on Saturday evening, after she had been at Stories, and told me something which perhaps I oughtn't to know, but which has caused me very grave concern.'

Mrs. Brandon simply couldn't think of anything at Stories which,

repeated by Mrs. Grant, could cause Mr. Miller any concern, and
looked at him in perplexity.

'My only excuse,' said Mr. Miller, 'is that I didn't realize what she
was talking about till it was too late.'

'And I shan't either,' said Mrs. Brandon, stung by his floundering to
what was for her an unusually sharp retort. 'What on earth did she say?'

'She said, but doubtless I understood her wrongly, that Miss Brandon
had left Miss Morris a sum of money in her will,' said Mr. Miller,
looking appealingly at Mrs. Brandon as if she might be able to reassure
him.

'That is quite true,' said Mrs. Brandon. 'Ten thousand pounds. I
don't know how much a year that comes out to, because Delia interrupted me when I was doing the sum, but it was very nice of Aunt Sissie.'

Mr. Miller said nothing. Mrs. Brandon, realizing that as usual she
would have to help him to express himself, took up her embroidery in a
soothing way and asked if he wanted to see Miss Morris who was
upstairs.

'No,' said Mr. Miller, jibbing violently. 'At least nothing would give
me more pleasure, but I feel it would be better not to. I had hoped so
much—she was so kind about the notices for the Fête—she helped in
the tea-tent—you saw how she dealt with Jimmy Thatcher. And then
she came to church with you yesterday. Perhaps I oughtn't to have
noticed that, but I couldn't help seeing her in your pew. But of course
this inheritance, about which no one can be more unfeignedly glad and
thankful than I, puts her in a position where it is impossible for me to
speak to her on a matter that is very near to my heart.'

Mrs. Brandon looked with great compassion on Mr. Miller, whose
halting words were obviously being forced from him with considerable
anguish, while he industriously picked to pieces a rose, fallen from a
vase.

'Miss Morris is very anxious to use some of this legacy in helping the
poor,' said Mrs. Brandon. 'She asked me particularly about the poor in
your parish, and I promised her I would find out. Perhaps if you made
a list of people who needed help you could talk it over with her, though
really we aren't a needy parish at all and no one is in the least grateful.'

'I could do that,' said Mr. Miller, carefully picking up the rose
petals and putting them on an ash tray. 'It is just like her to think of
such a use for the money. As a matter of fact a little judicious help would
be welcome at Grumper's End. Poor Mrs. Thatcher does nothing but
cry about Jimmy, who is in no danger at all, and Doris and Edna only
think of clothes and lipstick and the kitchen is worse than I've ever seen
it, with the sink full of dirty dishes and all the children on the floor.'

'That sounds just the thing for Miss Morris,' said Mrs. Brandon.
'I'm sure she'll adore it.'

Mr. Miller tried to explain that while on the one hand he did not for a moment mean that Miss Morris herself should go to Grumper's End, yet on the other hand the presence of anyone so helpful and kind would be of the utmost benefit to the Thatcher family, but he entangled himself so hopelessly in what he was saying that Mrs. Brandon cut him short by saying that she would tell Miss Morris about the Thatchers at once.

'I know she isn't doing anything to-morrow,' she said, 'so I'll tell her she might as well go down there about half-past eleven. No; Mrs. Thatcher will be getting the children's dinner then. Say about half-past three, and then she can be back here for tea. It was so nice of you to come.'

This was so unmistakably a congé, though said in the kindest way, that Mr. Miller rose. Mrs. Brandon laid down her embroidery and accompanied him to the front door, where he turned and took both her hands in his. He was standing on a lower step and their eyes were on a level.

'Thank you and God bless you,' he said. 'I can't see my path clearly, but you have been kind beyond measure to me and I shall never forget it.'

'How very nice of you,' said Mrs. Brandon, leaving her hands in his and vaguely noticing that someone was at the bottom of the steps. 'And don't forget; to-morrow at half-past three.'

'Bless you again, with all my thanks and devotion,' said Mr. Miller. He did not kiss her hands, for this might have savoured of idolatry, but he pressed them respectfully and went down the steps, nearly cannoning into Sir Edmund, who acknowledged his greeting with a kind of grunt.

'Came to see you about an investment, Lavinia,' said Sir Edmund, 'but now I'm here there's another matter I might as well speak about. Where's Delia? Don't want her and Francis coming in all the time.'

'Delia is out somewhere and Francis won't be back till dinner-time,' said Mrs. Brandon, 'so we are quite safe. Do come in.'

She led the way to the drawing-room and re-established herself with her embroidery. Sir Edmund let himself down into the armchair in which his vicar had been sitting and lit a cigarette. His feelings were at the moment in such a seething condition that he could hardly trust himself to speak. For some time he had had his suspicions of Mr. Miller, and the scene he had just witnessed had fully confirmed them. With his own eyes he had seen Mrs. Brandon and Mr. Miller standing on the front door steps holding hands like lovers; with his own ears he had heard Mr. Miller express undying devotion and Mrs. Brandon making an assignation. Neither of the guilty couple had even had the grace to look ashamed. If one looked at the matter calmly, as he erroneously imagined himself to have done since Saturday, there was no reason why a wealthy, charming widow, with a grown-up son and daughter, should not marry to please herself; and though Miller was poor, his character was excellent, his learning uncontested, and his family quite as good as Mrs. Brandon's. But it didn't seem right to Sir Edmund, and the more he thought of it the less he liked it. After a week-end of the honest but muddled mental process which Sir Edmund took for thinking, he had brought himself to the conclusion that Lavinia was on the verge of making a fool of herself and it must be stopped. After what he had just seen the folly was but too evident, and as for the manner of stopping it, Sir Edmund saw but one course open to him.

'Bit lonely here sometimes, eh, Lavinia?' he said, breaking the peaceful silence.

Mrs. Brandon said she never felt lonely. Francis was always back to dinner, and Delia was usually at home, and what with people coming to the house and one thing and another, she never seemed to have enough time.

'Can't keep Francis and Delia for ever,' said Sir Edmund. 'Leave the nest and all that sort of thing, you know.'

'Yes, I hope so,' said Mrs. Brandon. 'I think it is dreadful when children stay at home for ever. I have sometimes thought that Francis was attracted by the Archdeacon's daughter at Plumstead, such a nice girl, and the Dean's daughters are delightful too. Delia is a bit young, but I'm sure she'll be delighted to get married presently, and I shall let her have my second-best pearls and my grandmother's lace veil. And then I shall have the grandchildren here and Nurse will be quite happy for once.'

'That's not the point, Lavinia,' said Sir Edmund, who had waited with ill-concealed irritation for the end of her remarks. 'Point is, you're getting on. We're all getting on. Need to settle down a bit for our old age, eh?'

Mrs. Brandon said yes, she supposed so, and had Sir Edmund heard that Miss Brandon had left the children two hundred pounds each.

'Good God! what's happened to the property then?' asked Sir Edmund.

'Mr. Merton did explain, but I wasn't listening very much,' said Mrs. Brandon, matching a wool with her head on one side. 'It is all to be a home for somebody, a kind of charity. It seems a very good idea, because what with the damp and the distance from the main road, no one could live there.'

'Suppose Amelia knew her own mind,' said Sir Edmund doubtfully. 'More than most women do. Well, I'm glad you won't be at the Abbey. Can keep my eye on you better on this side of the county. Wish I could keep it on you a bit more. See what I mean, eh?'

'I'm afraid my business is rather a trouble for you sometimes,' said Mrs. Brandon plaintively, 'but I couldn't possibly do it myself.'

'Of course you can't. That's why I want to be in a position where I can look after you. If I were here, or you were over at my place, I could keep an eye on things properly. What about it, Lavinia. You know me pretty well and I know you pretty well. You've not much sense, but you're a good woman. Your Miss Morris could come as secretary to us both. Clever woman that.'

Mrs. Brandon, who was used to being scolded by Sir Edmund, and had not been listening much to what he was saying, came to life at the last words.

'Oh, but Miss Morris won't need to be a secretary now,' she said. 'Didn't you know? Aunt Sissie left her ten thousand pounds. How much would that be a year?'

'Don't be a fool, Lavinia,' said Sir Edmund, exasperated. 'How can I tell how she's going to invest it? If she's the woman I think, she'll leave it where Amelia had it. Good business woman, Amelia.'

'And what is annoying,' continued Mrs. Brandon, wrinkling her forehead over her wools, 'is that Mr. Miller is really very devoted to her, but he has that noble kind of feeling that I really call rather silly that he oughtn't to say so now.'

Sir Edmund stared at his hostess, his face and neck going such a deep purple that she was almost perturbed. Luckily Rose came in with brandy and soda, and as Sir Edmund gulped down a very stiff drink, his face assumed its ordinary brick-red appearance again.

'He came to me about it this afternoon,' Mrs. Brandon went on. 'Miss Morris wants to do something for the poor here, so I said to Mr. Miller, Why not give Miss Morris a list of people that really need help, and he said the Thatchers at once, so I said I'd tell Miss Morris to go down and have a look at them to-morrow at half-past three.'

Her mysterious mischief face was bent over her work and Sir Edmund was able to look at her at his ease. Seldom had he more admired his trying and charming friend. She might have no sense, but she had lightened his heart of an immense load. If marrying her had been the only way of saving her from marrying the Vicar, he had been prepared to do his duty, but not only had she apparently no thoughts of marrying Mr. Miller, but was actively engaged in scheming for him to marry Miss Morris. Sir Edmund heaved such a sigh of relief that Mrs. Brandon looked up in alarm.

'Most sensible thing you could do, Lavinia,' he said approvingly. 'More sense than I gave you credit for. Must be getting along now. I'll come in again about that investment some other time.'

Such was his pleasure at his escape that as he said good-bye to Mrs. Brandon he put an arm round her and kissed the side of her head. She accepted the attention in the spirit in which it was offered, laughed, and promised to let him know how things went.

When Francis came back a little later, he found his mother snipping off dead roses in a very elegant way in front of the house.

'Hullo, darling,' he said. 'I saw Merton in Barchester to-day, and he wants to know if you would give him a glass of sherry to-morrow.'

'Of course I will,' said Mrs. Brandon. 'Shall I ring him up?'

'No need,' said Francis sternly. 'I have saved your fair name by telling him to come unless he hears to the contrary. Anything happened to-day? I see in your face that it did.'

'Miss Morris was terribly pleased about the money and is going to do good to the poor,' said Mrs. Brandon. 'And Mr. Miller came to see me and then Sir Edmund came. And it has only just occurred to me, Francis, that he was trying to propose to me for a moment, but he got over it, I am glad to say, almost before he had spoken.'

'Really, Mother, you shouldn't say things like that,' said Francis. 'Come in. It's time to dress.'

*

On the following afternoon Miss Morris set out for Grumper's End on foot, refusing Mrs. Brandon's offer of the car. In her hand she carried her large, sensible bag containing her overall. Mr. Thatcher was out at work, but as school had not yet begun all the young Thatchers were making holiday in the narrow lane, or on the kitchen floor. Edna and Doris were absent-mindedly poking bits of tinned salmon into their unhallowed offsprings' mouths, and three hens and a very large half-caste dog were walking aimlessly in and out of the kitchen. As Miss Morris came down the lane, a couple of young Thatchers rushed into the cottage to tell their mother that Jimmy's Lady was coming, a piece of news that caused Mrs. Thatcher to dust a chair with an old stocking and begin to cry again.

Miss Morris appeared at the door and asked if she might come in. As Mrs. Thatcher could only sniff and gulp, and Edna and Doris burst into loud, primitive giggles, Miss Morris accepted this welcome, and sitting down on the chair that Mrs. Thatcher pushed at her, said it was a nice day and how was Jimmy. Mrs. Thatcher appeared to be incapable of speech. Doris nudged her sister Edna and smacked her child, and said Mr. Miller was coming to take mother to the hospital in his car.

'Well, if Mr. Miller is coming, we ought to get the kitchen a little tidier,' said Miss Morris.

Fascinated by this eccentric statement, Mrs. Thatcher stopped crying. Edna and Doris stopped giggling, and the children all crowded round to look at Jimmy's Lady. Miss Morris opened her bag, took out her overall, put it on, and assumed command. In answer to her questions Doris said there was a bit of soap somewhere, and Edna volunteered that the scrubbing brush was somewhere in the yard and she said the towel was somewhere. Miss Morris looked round, and recognizing Teddy, who had been in the sack race, gave him some money and told him to run up to the shop as fast as he could and bring back yellow soap, washing soda, a dish mop, a wire saucepan cleaner, a small bottle of Jeyes' Fluid, and three cloths for drying up. She then filled both the kettles. Doris, entering into the spirit of these preparations, carried them to the kitchen range, while Edna drove Ernie Thatcher out to bring in some more sticks, and chased all the other children into the garden, where they clustered round the door in horrified interest, gazing at Jimmy's Lady and their illegitimate young nephew and niece, who were tied to their chairs.

Just as the kettles were coming to the boil, Teddy came back with his shoppings and the change.

'Now, Edna and Doris, if you'll give me a hand we'll get the sink tidied up,' said Miss Morris, 'and then we can clean the children.'

Recognizing an irresistible natural force, Edna and Doris, again giggling irrepressibly, so exerted themselves that the unpleasant pile of dishes, plates, cutlery and saucepans was soon washed and neatly stacked, and the sink scoured with soda and disinfectant and clean enough to wash in. In a fury of zeal Doris dragged all her young brothers and sisters into the kitchen and washed their hands and faces, while Edna, disinterring from a loathsome heap of rubbish in a cupboard a broom with half a handle, swept everything that was on the kitchen floor out into the yard.

'That's very nice,' said Miss Morris approvingly. 'Now we'll just wash out these cloths and Teddy can hang them on the fence to dry. Suppose you and Doris tidy youselves a little, Edna. Have you a comb?'

Doris said she hadn't seen it not since Friday, when Edna was combing Micky. On inquiring which of the children Micky was, Miss Morris was informed that it was the large half-caste dog. Without showing any signs of emotion, that admirable woman took a small comb out of her bag and gave it to the girls, saying that they could keep it and she would send them some shampoo powder. While they wrestled with their tangled golden curls in front of a small chipped mirror, Miss Morris wiped the kitchen table, put a bowl of water on it, and applied herself to cleaning the children of shame, who were too young to mind.

While she was thus engaged, Mr. Miller, who had left the car at the corner because it was difficult to turn in front of the cottage, knocked at the open door and walked into the kitchen. Coming from the brilliant sunshine outside he was at first unable to see who was in the dark little kitchen, but a sense more intimate, more nostalgic than sight, suddenly seized upon his heart, making it stand still. For a moment he was a young man again on a hot summer morning, and Ella Morris in her check apron was scrubbing out the vicarage dustbin with Jeyes' Fluid before it was used for rubbish at the Church Lads' Brigade tea. Then, as his eyes became accustomed to the gloom, he saw Miss Morris, in an overall, seated at Mrs. Thatcher's kitchen table, washing the faces and hands of Purse (Percy) and Glad (Gladys) Thatcher; so he said good afternoon.

'How do you do,' said Miss Morris. She finished drying Glad's face, emptied the bowl, and shook hands with Mr. Miller. Mrs. Thatcher began to cry again.

'That's enough,' said Miss Morris with kind authority. 'One of you get your mother's hat. We mustn't keep Mr. Miller waiting.'

Doris took Mrs. Thatcher's hat from a peg behind the door, rammed it onto her mother's unresisting head, and jerked her onto her feet, telling her not to keep Mr. Miller waiting.

'Here's your purse, Mother,' said Edna. 'You don't want to keep Mr. Miller waiting.'

Mrs. Thatcher, sobbing loudly, was propelled by her family towards the Vicar's car.

'Could I give you a life, Miss Morris?' said the Vicar.

Miss Morris, who was folding her overall and putting it in her bag, thanked Mr. Miller and said she would enjoy the walk back to Stories.

'Of course,' said Mr. Miller doubtfully, 'I would not wish in any way to interfere, but if you could possibly see your way, without undue fatigue, to coming at least as far as the Vicarage, where I have to pick up the afternoon's post, I should be so very grateful. Mrs. Thatcher is certain to cry all the way to Barchester and probably all the way back, and as I have to drive the car I am really very much at a loss.'

'If I can be of any real help I will come with pleasure,' said Miss Morris, and got into the back seat with Mrs. Thatcher. Amid shrill cries from the Thatcher family the car moved off.

'I hope you made a good profit at the Fête, Mr. Miller,' said Miss Morris. 'Now, Mrs. Thatcher, you've had a nice cry and it's done you good and we all know you are very brave. Now you must be brave just once more for Jimmy. If he sees mother come into the ward, crying, it will quite upset him.'

'Jimmy was always easy upset, just like me,' said Mrs. Thatcher with some pride.

'Yes, we did very well, Miss Morris,' said the Vicar, speaking backwards, 'but a most unfortunate thing has occurred. Try as I will, I cannot get the accounts to balance, and the dreadful thing is that I seem to be seventeen and sixpence in pocket, quite apart from the profit.'

'Then the accounts must be wrong,' said Miss Morris with calm finality. 'There, Mrs. Thatcher, that's better. Now you mustn't cry any more, or we'll have to ask Mr. Miller to lend you a clean handkerchief.'

'Oh, Miss!' said Mrs. Thatcher, agreeably shocked and horrified, but much calmer.

By this time they had arrived at the Vicarage, where Mr. Miller and Miss Morris got out.

'Thank you very much for coming so far,' said the Vicar. 'I will just see if there are any letters for me and then I will take Mrs. Thatcher on to Barchester.'

'I don't know,' said Miss Morris, with what was for her unusual diffidence on her own subject, 'if I could help you with the accounts at all. I am pretty good at them, and there is no hurry for me to get back.'

'Would you really,' said Mr. Miller. 'Indeed, indeed I should be so grateful for your assistance. Everying is on my desk. If you would just allow me to show you my difficulties. And Hettie would bring you some tea.'

He led the way to his study, where a heap of bills, scrawled memoranda, receipts and odd documents lay in disorder on the writing-table. Miss Morris's eyes lighted at the sight and she took off her hat.

'Let me just get my spectacles,' she said, opening her bag. The overall in which she had been cleaning Mrs. Thatcher's kitchen was hiding everything else, so she took it out and laid it on the table. A strong smell of disinfectant filled the air.

'That is Jeyes' Fluid,' said Mr. Miller, his words spoken in a dead, level tone, forced almost with pain from him.

'You noticed it?' asked Miss Morris, feeling as if her own voice were coming from an immense distance.

'From the moment I came into Mrs. Thatcher's kitchen and saw you ministering to that poor family,' said Mr. Miller. 'Did you think I had ever forgotten?'

'I know that I hadn't,' said Miss Morris. 'It was the last day of happiness that I remember.'

'You were cleaning the vicarage dustbin in your apron,' said Mr. Miller, 'and your hair was blown across your face.'

'Do you remember that?' said Miss Morris. 'You put it back for me, because my hands were dirty. I suppose when things are far away there is nothing wrong in remembering them.'

She began to get her spectacles out, but found it difficult.

'Miss Morris,' said Mr. Miller, speaking with what was clearly almost agony, 'I had a deep respect for your father and I have never ceased to regret the pain that I gave him, the disappointment of which I was the cause. For that I offer you my humble apology. But I cannot change my convictions, even if I lose everything on earth that I hold most dear; even if I have to suffer the almost unbearable pain of wounding what on earth I most reverence.'

Miss Morris's spectacle case fell from her hands onto the table. She wondered vaguely why it was so dark and why Mr. Miller's voice came to her across infinite space. There was silence.

'I fear I have been discourteous,' said Mr. Miller. 'You will, I trust, forgive me. I must take that poor woman to Barchester.'

He turned to go, but Miss Morris's voice made him turn to her again, though he did not look at her.

'I loved and respected my dear father more than anything in the world,' said Miss Morris, in her usual clear, controlled voice, 'but I cannot help seeing that he was sometimes wrong. He was unjust to you. So was I. Forgive his daughter.'

Mr. Miller took a step towards Miss Morris. Her hair, as a rule so neat, was a little disordered by her work at Grumper's End and the drive back to the Vicarage.

'Your hair has blown across your face,' he said, touching it very gently. 'May I put it back?'

Then, because he and Miss Morris were so unused to outward forms of tenderness, they made no further sign.

'It has been a very long time,' said Miss Morris.

'Is that your only reproach?' said Mr. Miller. 'I don't know how to bear that.'

'I have never reproached you. I only loved you,' said Miss Morris. 'I will soon get these papers tidy. Mrs. Thatcher will be getting anxious.'

'How selfish happiness makes one,' said the Vicar. 'I will go at once. It doesn't take long.'

'Then I may still be here when you come back,' said Miss Morris.

'God bless you, very dear,' said Mr. Miller and went out. In a moment Miss Morris heard the car start. She put on her spectacles, sat down, and was at once absorbed in the papers on the desk.

*

The hot, golden afternoon passed agreeably for Mrs. Brandon. Having got Miss Morris safely away she lay down on the sofa in her room and went comfortably to sleep. At five o'clock she had tea with Delia, with a subcurrent of mild excitement at the thought of Noel Merton's visit. Hardly had they finished tea when a car drove up to the door and to their annoyance Mrs. Grant got out, followed by her son.

'What on earth does Mrs. Grant want to come in a car for?' said Delia, looking out of the window. 'It's Wheeler's big car from the garage and a lot of luggage. I hope she isn't taking Hilary away; it would be too sickening.'

But before she could indulge in any more theories, Mrs. Grant was upon them, wearing in addition to her usual homespun suit and necklaces, a kind of brigand's cape of coarse blue cloth.

'Addio!' she exclaimed, halting so suddenly and dramatically that her son nearly banged into her from behind.

'But why?' said Mrs. Brandon. 'You aren't going, are you?'

'I will sit down for five minutes,' said Mrs. Grant. 'I am a gipsy. I come and go as fate wills. I am very glad to have seen my Boy in surroundings which he finds congenial, but for me this life is not possible. I bear no grudge against Amelia Brandon, and there is now nothing to keep me in England. Mrs. Spindler, in spite of what Victoria Norton may say, does not wish to learn how to cook macaroni, and I refuse to eat her chops and puddings. I am going up to London at once and shall spend a day at my club, the Hypatia in Gower Street, and probably go to Italy on the following day. I believe there is a pilgrimage going to Rome and by joining it I could go more cheaply. It is quite a mistake to believe that Calabria is hot at this time of year. I am like the lizards, those graceful little creatures. I can spend all day with my brother the sun and feel refreshed. My Boy will join me there.'

'Oh, I say, Mother,' said Mr. Grant, 'I really can't. I've got heaps of work to do and I've got to read seriously all this autumn.'

'We will forget the fogs of London,' said Mrs. Grant, waving them joyously away. 'Hilary needs the sun.'

'I'm awfully sorry, Mother, but I simply won't,' said Mr. Grant with such determination that Delia stared at him in surprise. Much as she liked her cousin, it had never before occurred to her that he could assert himself against his mother, and she was at no pains to conceal her admiration.

'Then that is settled,' said Mrs. Grant, rising with a majestic sweep of her cloak and a jingling of all her necklaces. 'I never fight against destiny. Woman must yield to man. Good-bye, Mrs. Brandon. Good-bye, little Delia.'

Mrs. Brandon, guiltily conscious of not having done much for Mrs. Grant during her stay at Pomfret Madrigal, threw a passionate regret into her voice, to which Mrs. Grant responded with equal fervour, pressing Mrs. Brandon to visit her in Calabria at any time.

'I'd simply adore to,' said Mrs. Brandon, 'but somehow I never seem to get abroad. I did go to Cannes once with my husband, but he died there, so I came back.'

'Cannes — Frinton,' said Mrs. Grant musingly. 'The interweavings of destiny are strange. I shall miss my train. No, Hilary, don't come with me. Your gipsy mother needs no speeding on her way.'

With great agility she swept herself and her cloak into Wheeler's car, crying 'Avanti', which Bert from the garage, who was driving, rightly conjectured to mean Barchester Central Station, for such was the destination that Mr. Wheeler his employer had mentioned to him when giving him his instructions. The car disappeared down the drive.

'Come in the kitchen garden for a bit,' said Delia to her cousin. 'We might get some plums if Turpin isn't looking. I say, Hilary, you were marvellous with your mother.'

'I felt rather a beast,' said Mr. Grant, 'but after all I've got to work.

I mean I'm not going to starve, even without that beastly Abbey which thank goodness I haven't got, but one feels a frightful rotter doing nothing at my age, and mother doesn't understand that.'

'Besides, there's your novel,' said Delia.

'If ever my novel comes to anything, it will be all your doing,' said Mr. Grant, finely ignoring the patient listening of Mrs. Brandon, Mrs. Morland and Mr. Miller. 'If it weren't for you, I couldn't do it.'

'But it was Mrs. Morland's idea,' said Delia, anxious to be quite fair before she could accept this praise.

'Yes, she did suggest it,' said Mr. Grant, 'but you have been splendid about the whole thing from the beginning. I really feel there is no one I can talk to about myself and my work as well as I can to you. I awfully want to do something, Delia, and I wonder if you'd mind.'

'I'm sure I wouldn't,' said Delia. 'Hullo, Turpin wants to talk to me. What is it, Turpin?'

'I say, he looks dangerous,' said Mr. Grant, for Turpin was advancing towards them from the far end of the grass walk which, with its herbaceous borders, divided the kitchen garden in two, looking like a paralytic old countryman on the stage, shouting angrily, and brandishing a fork.

'Come and look, Miss Delia,' said Turpin, trembling with rage, 'come and look!'

He led the way towards the rich bed of manure where sprawled his beloved vegetable marrows. With a threatening gesture he jabbed his fork into the ground, stooped, and with infinite reverence turned the fattest marrow gently on one side. On its under surface, in mis-shapen letters, was too plainly visible the word HILARY.

'That's my name!' said Mr. Grant.

'Maybe it is, maybe it isn't,' said Turpin. 'What I want to know is who done it. I've laid awake thinking of that marrow, and now Sir Edmund's man'll have the laugh over me at the Flower Show. I'd have the laugh over the one that done it if I knowed who it was.'

'Well, I'm awfully sorry, Turpin, but I did it,' said Delia.

'You cut this young gentleman's name on my marrow, miss?' said Turpin. 'Of all the — —'

But instead of finishing whatever dire thing it was he was going to say, Turpin began to chuckle in such a coughing and rumbling way that Delia and her cousin were alarmed.

'Do you think he'll burst?' Mr. Grant whispered nervously to Delia.

But Turpin, his good temper miraculously recovered, was already moving away towards the tool-shed with his fork, chuckling to himself as he went, 'cut a young gentleman's name on my marrow, cut a young gentleman's name on my marrow,' until he was out of sight.

'That was the day we picked the gooseberries,' said Delia, not so much giving an explanation as a statement. 'I always frightfully wanted

to carve something on that marrow, and I thought it would be nice for
you to have your name on a prize marrow.

Mr. Grant was silent.

'Would you rather not?' said Delia.

'No, I like it immensely,' said Mr. Grant. 'I was never allowed to
carve my name on anything at home, not even on a pumpkin that we
had in a little glasshouse, so I know exactly how you felt. I was only
wondering if what I wanted to tell you would be a good sort of thanking
you.'

'What was it?' said Delia. 'I'm sure it would.'

'I thought I might dedicate Jehan le Capet to you,' said Mr. Grant,
trying to sound like a person who is in the habit of dedicating novels
every day.

'Oh!' said Delia. 'But I thought you were going to dedicate him to
mother.'

'That was when he was just a critical study,' said Mr. Grant. 'But a
novel is different, and I don't think your mother would understand
about le Capet's sex life, not really. So I thought I'd dedicate him to
you.'

'What would you say?' asked Delia eagerly.

'I might just say, "To Delia".'

'How marvellous,' said Delia.

'Or, "To Delia Who Helped". Or I did think of "For Delia", but I
think "For" is a little affected.'

'It would be rather nice to have something about the marrow,' said
Delia wistfully. 'I mean, the book and the marrow do make a good sort
of exchange, don't they?'

' "By just exchange one for the other given",' said Mr. Grant
musingly. 'You do hold mine dear, and yours, considering its size, I
simply cannot miss; but that's affected too. I'll tell you what. I'll put
simply, "To Delia Who Understood".'

'Oh!!' Delia said again. 'Oh, Hilary, do you think you could possibly
make it "Understands"?'

In her earnestness she stopped short and laid her hand on her cousin's
arm.

'Of course I could,' he said, looking down with some pride at the
intellect which, so he felt, he was calling into being. 'And what's more,
I will.'

For gratitude Delia rubbed her head violently against his shoulder.
Then they pursued their way towards the house and were soon laughing
about nothing again in the sunshine.

*

In the drawing-room all was a cool, delicious, scented repose. Mrs.
Brandon, reclining elegantly on the sofa, flowers massed on a table

behind her, flowers on a table by her side, was pensively doing nothing at all. On her face was an expression of amused and slightly guilty anticipation which her son Francis would have recognized at once.

Shortly after six o'clock she heard a car come up the drive, and a moment later Rose announced Mr. Merton. Mrs. Brandon, who was discovered working at her tapestry, looked up with a face of pleased surprise.

'How nice of you to come on this hot day,' she said to Mr. Merton, holding out her hand with appealing lassitude.

Mr. Merton held it for a second longer than was necesssary and restored it to her with great care.

'Nothing would have kept me from coming,' he said, in his deep agreeable voice. 'The only thing that might have detained me was Lydia, who is so unacquainted with man that her tameness is occasionally quite shocking to me, but luckily she had got Tony Morland for the day and they have gone up the river.'

'She is such a nice girl,' said Mrs. Brandon.

'I do love the entire lack of interest with which you made that remark,' said Mr. Merton.

Mrs. Brandon made no reply, but raised her eyes slowly from her work and looked at her guest with an air of complete candour.

'I can't tell you,' said Mr. Merton, who was already enjoying himself immensely, 'how much I hoped I might find you alone.'

'I thought we could talk so much more comfortably,' said Mrs. Brandon, again darting at her guest a soft glance, to which he delightedly attached its exact value.

After a little more desultory fencing, conducted with great skill on both sides, Mrs. Brandon asked after Miss Brandon's maid.

'She has gone to a married sister at Swanage, so my father's clerk tells me,' said Mr. Merton. 'She had fifty pounds a year left her by Miss Brandon, and all the contents of the sitting-room including the photographs. Also the gorillas.'

Mrs. Brandon was silent for a moment, thinking of Sparks in a room at Swanage, furnished from the Abbey, full of the Brandon family photographs, guarded by the gorillas, and hardly knew whether to laugh or cry.

'You feel things more deeply than other people,' said Mr. Merton.

'I know I do,' sighed Mrs. Brandon. 'It's so stupid.'

'Not stupid at all. You can't help being sensitive,' said Mr. Merton. 'Tell me – and then we will forget all these painful subjects – how is Miss Morris?'

'I don't exactly know,' said Mrs. Brandon, suddenly becoming quite natural, 'but I hope very much she is engaged by now. Our Vicar, a delightful person, is a very old friend of hers, and I think used to admire her. He is very unworldly and when he heard of her legacy he wanted to withdraw, but it would be so foolish of him to spoil her chance of happiness because she has a little money, so I arranged for them to meet this afternoon, and as that was at half-past three and it is half-past six now, I really feel that something may have happened.'

'How like you,' said Mr. Merton.

'One is so very grateful for any chance of making people happy,' said Mrs. Brandon. 'One hasn't always been very happy oneself, so one does want it desperately for others.'

'I don't like to think that you have been unhappy,' said Mr. Merton, throwing exactly the right shade of chivalrous admiration into his tone and look. So much indeed did he throw that his guardian angel, who was on the roof talking to Mrs. Brandon's guardian angel, came hurriedly down through the ceiling to see if he was safe.

'I wouldn't trouble if I were you,' said Mrs. Brandon's angel, following him. 'Mine can look after herself perfectly and I should say yours could too.'

'I daresay he can, but it's my duty to listen to everything,' said Mr. Merton's angel firmly. 'Go back again, there's an angel, and I'll join you in a minute.'

'You'll find me somewhere upstairs,' said Mrs. Brandon's angel and sped on strong wings into the cloudless blue sky.

Mrs. Brandon laid down her work and looked at her hands.

'I was married very young,' she said simply, 'and knew very little. It's a stupid story; but there are things one doesn't forget.'

'I wish,' said Mr. Merton, 'I could help you to forget them.'

'You do,' murmured Mrs. Brandon, but couldn't help giving Mr. Merton a conspirator's glance as she spoke.

'How charming of you to say so,' said Mr. Merton. 'And how I hope that you will look on me as a real friend, as one who would do a great deal to make things easier for you.'

At this point Mr. Merton's guardian angel nearly fell down off the ceiling in his anxiety to miss nothing.

'A friend,' said Mrs. Brandon in a low thrilling voice. 'A friend. I feel about that word as Shelley felt about love. "One word is too often profaned—"'

'I know, I know,' said Mr. Merton, in tones that matched her own. 'But you must also remember that one feeling is too falsely disclaimed for me, if I may be allowed to alter the poet's choice of pronoun, to disclaim it.'

He looked deeply into Mrs. Brandon's eyes and she looked deeply into his. What they saw there amused them so much that they began to laugh.

Mr. Merton's guardian angel, puzzled but on the whole satisfied, spread his wings and soon his path was vague in distant spheres.

BEFORE LUNCH

BEFORE LUNCH

BEFORE LUNCH

I

MR. MIDDLETON IS ALARMED

THE owner of Laverings looked out of his bedroom window on a dewy June morning. Not the large window that commanded a gently sloping view to the south of his garden, his meadows and a wooded plain with hills beyond, but the side window to the east that overlooked the little lane. In his hand he held a letter, with whose contents he angrily refreshed his mind from time to time. Neither the mild June air, nor the beneficent warmth of the sun, could counteract the evil impression that the morning post had made. Everything conspired against him, down to the fact that the White House, whose garden marched with his own, was undoubtedly empty, so that there was no valid excuse for not letting it to people that he didn't particularly want as tenants. Not that he disliked his widowed sister, Mrs. Stonor, but her two grown-up stepchildren were an almost unknown quantity and might come bursting into his privacy with the ease of neighbours who are remote connections by marriage and annoy him very much. All he knew about the young Stonors was that the son was delicate and the daughter, as he shudderingly remembered her, not delicate at all, and at the moment both states of health seemed to him equally repulsive.

Giving his camel's hair dressing gown a petulant twitch he walked back to the table where his breakfast tray and his letters had been put. The cup of coffee that he had poured out ten minutes ago was now tepid with a crinkling skin on its surface. It was more than flesh and blood could stand. He strode to the door, opened it and bellowed his wife's name into the passage. No one answered. He banged the door to, spooned the horrid skin clumsily into the saucer, drank the tepid coffee to which nauseating fragments of milky blanket still clung, and looked at the rest of his post. Business letters from the office, contractor's estimates. He slammed them angrily down again and returned to the east window, chewing the cud of his resentment against his sister, who by her inconsiderate wish to spend the summer near him had entirely and eternally wrecked his peace of mind.

Presently a creaking sound became audible, then the clop of a horse's hoofs at a slow walk, then a gentle clatter of harness and trappings, the

encouraging voice of a carter. Round the corner of the lane came a
bright blue farm cart with red wheels, drawn by a benevolent monster
with long hairy trousers and a shining coat. The cart was laden with
early hay, and one axle was in sore need of greasing. Perched sideways
behind the monster's hind quarters was a middle-aged man, giving
monosyllabic instructions to the horse, who took no notice at all knowing by long practice exactly what his driver was going to say. On the
side of the cart was painted in slanting white lettering,

J. MIDDLETON ESQ.
LAVERINGS FARM

At the sight of this equipage the watcher from the window felt an
exquisite sense of peace and well-being steal over him. There are various degrees of fame. Some would give their name to a rose, some to a
mountain, some to a sauce or a pudding, but John Middleton's secret
ambition, ever since boyhood, had been to have a farm cart of his own
with his name painted on it. He became vaguely conscious that earth
held nothing more satisfying than to look out of one's window on a
summer morning, warmed by coffee, glowing with anticipation of a
visit from one's only sister and her stepchildren, and see a blue farm
cart with red wheels, drawn by an imperturbable carthorse, driven by
Tom Pucken, containing fragrant hay, emblazoned with one's own
name.

'Morning, Pucken,' Mr. Middleton shouted from the window.

Tom Pucken looked up, showing a handsome, crafty, weather-lined
face, touched his disgraceful almost brimless hat, shouted some pre-
Conquest instructions to his horse, and was carried away towards the
gate that led to the farm. Mr. Middleton, refreshed by this encounter,
took off his camel's hair dressing gown, finished dressing, and went in
search of his wife. But did not, as one might have expected, go out of
his bedroom and down the staircase.

In his earnest desire to make life really comfortable for himself he
had arranged his house in an unusual way. For at least four hundred
years there had been a farm at Laverings and for most of that time it
had been in the possession of the same family, passing sometimes to a
son, sometimes to a daughter and the husband, so that however often
the name may have changed, the blood was the same. Even so the farm-
house itself had been altered, pulled down in parts and rebuilt, added
to, occasionally burnt, but had kept its own spirit and the name of its
original builder. When the last owner, having ruined himself by building the White House and trying to be gentry instead of sticking to the
farm, decided to sell the place and go to join a cousin with a motor
works in Canada, most of the land had been bought by neighbouring
farmers, but the house, with a few acres round it, remained derelict.

John Middleton, a rising architect, happened to pass Laverings on a

walking tour, recognized it at once as his house, but could not afford to
buy it. He had a simple confidence that he would always in the end get
what he wanted, a confidence which so far had never been disappointed,
though a generous habit of mind and an aged mother to support made it
very difficult for him to save money. For ten years Laverings remained
empty and desolate. At the end of this time a very unpleasant gentleman called Sir Ogilvy Hibberd suddenly made an offer for it. The
county, who disliked and resented Sir Ogilvy because he was a Liberal
and not quite the sort we want (though admitting that there had been
some perfectly presentable Liberals only one didn't really know them),
suddenly resolved itself into a kind of informal Committee of Hatred,
with Lord Bond of Staple Park near Skeynes, well known for having
voted against Clause Three of the Root Vegetables Bill, in the chair.
Lord Bond, who had more money than he knew what to do with, was
pushed by his masterful wife into buying Laverings, together with the
White House and four large fields, while Sir Ogilvy Hibberd bought
'The Cedars', Muswell Hill, which had come into the market on the
death of Mrs. C. Augustus Fortescue, (Fifi), only child and heiress of
Bunyan, First Baron Alberfylde.

Lord Bond had felt for some time that there ought to be a sound man
at Laverings. What Lord Bond meant by a sound man no one quite
knew, nor, apart from a strong feeling against anyone from Cambridge,
did he, but a chance meeting with Mr. Middleton settled his mind for
him. Mr. Middleton talked to Lord Bond for an hour and a quarter
without stopping and Lord Bond invited Mr. Middleton to stay with
him at Staple Park. On Sunday afternoon he walked his guest over to
Laverings to see the repairs he was doing on the house. By Sunday night
Lord Bond, a little dazed, had offered Mr. Middleton a long lease of the
house at an absurdly low figure and promised to make all the alterations
that his new tenant wanted. Mr. Middleton at once decided to have the
east end of the house entirely to himself, using the original kitchen as a
library with the old back stairs communicating directly with a bedroom,
bathroom and dressing-room, which he also used as a work-room, on
the floor above. His mother, who was unwillingly installed in the
country, preferred a hipbath in her bedroom and soon languished and
died. Her son mourned her sincerely with the largest wreath of expensive flowers that Skeynes had ever seen, which was described in the
local paper as a floral tribute, and then forgot about her, except when
sentiment got the better of him.

For ten more years Mr. Middleton lived alone at Laverings in great
happiness, going to town from Tuesday to Friday every week, working
with concentrated violence on Monday and Saturday morning and
talking to weekend guests from Saturday afternoon till late on Sunday
night or well into the small hours of Monday morning. During this
time he set up as a very mild amateur gentleman farmer and had lately

added to the little herd of cows he already possessed the blue farm cart with red wheels whose acquaintance we have just made.

When Mr. Middleton met his future wife she was an orphan and over thirty and Mr. Middleton was nearly fifty, so it seemed a suitable marriage enough and they had a large wedding in London with a reception at the Bonds' town mansion in Grosvenor Place and the bride said Thank Goodness now she need never see any of her family again. So she never did, for they lived in quite another county and hunted. Mr. and Mrs. Middleton had no children, but as Catherine Middleton truly said, once one had got over the mortification it was really a very pleasant life.

*

So Mr. Middleton went out by the door that led to his little back stair and descended to the library, a large, low, sunny room, with a French window onto the garden, lined with books, furnished with one very comfortable chair, a few less comfortable ones, three large tables heaped with books and papers, and a piano which no one ever played. He looked at the table where material for an article for the Journal of the Royal Institute of British Architects was accumulating, put his morning's post on another table and again bellowed aloud for his wife. This time his appeal met with more success, for Mrs. Middleton, who had been doing a little gardening, heard his call and came across the lawn. Her husband went out onto the flagged terrace to meet her and affectionately kissed the top of her head. Not that Catherine Middleton was a small woman, but Mr. Middleton's impressive bulk, topped by a slightly bald leonine head, was apt to make everyone else look frail and insignificant.

'How are you this morning, darling?' said Mrs. Middleton. 'You look very nice and peculiar.'

'I fail to see anything peculiar about myself,' said Mr. Middleton.

'That is because you can't see yourself, Jack,' said his wife. 'You really look very nice and I like you just as you are.'

Mrs. Middleton did not exaggerate in calling her husband's appearance peculiar, for ever since he had bought the farm cart, he had thrown himself vehemently into the part of gentleman farmer and, after a severe struggle with his tailor, ordered his clothes accordingly. This morning he was dressed in a blue shirt, a kind of shooting jacket in large checks with pockets capacious enough for a poacher, orange tawny plus fours, canvas gaiters and heavy nailed shoes. It is true that no gentleman farmer off or even on the stage ever wore so preposterous an outfit or wore it so unconsciously, but to go about looking like an eccentric gave Mr. Middleton such unalloyed pleasure that his wife had not the heart to point out to him the marks his nailed shoes made on the parquet floor of the library.

'I am glad you can tolerate me as I am,' said Mr. Middleton, still suspicious, 'for at my age it is very improbable that I shall change. Had I been a younger man when you married me, Catherine, a man more suited to you in age, you might have re-moulded my life, shaped me again to your liking. But you took pity on an ageing wreck, your young life twined itself round the rugged roots of a storm-shattered tree, and I cannot alter my way of living, I cannot change my spots.'

'I do love the way you say everyting twice over,' said Mrs. Middleton, 'and I would hate you to change your spots. What were you calling me for?'

Mr. Middleton's impressive face dissolved in a flash and became as formless as water.

'I called you because I needed you,' he said, suddenly becoming a heartbroken child. 'I called you once and you did not come.'

'And then you called me again and I did,' said his wife, whose adoration of her husband was unshadowed by any illusions about him. 'Can I do anything?'

'It is my sister Lilian,' said Mr. Middleton, recovering himself under his wife's bracing want of sympathy. 'I had a letter from her this morning. It is here, in my pocket. No, it is not. You see, Catherine, my memory is not what it was. It is on the library table.'

He turned and went indoors followed by Mrs. Middleton.

'Sit down, Catherine,' said Mr. Middleton, seating himself in the one comfortable chair, 'and I will read Lilian's letter aloud.'

When he had done so his wife asked him to give her the letter as it was much easier to understand things if one read them oneself. Rather offended he handed over the letter with a pained and studied courtesy which Catherine ignored.

'That sounds very nice,' she said as she gave it back to him. 'The White House is quite ready and aired. It only needs the beds making up and it will be great fun to have Lilian and the children, and as she says she will bring her own maid there will be no difficulty at all.'

'Children!' said Mr. Middleton.

'Well, Denis is twenty-five and Daphne is four years younger, and I could be their mother at a pinch. And at another pinch you could just be their grandfather, I suppose. I mean if you had had a son when you were sixteen and he had had a son when he was sixteen, that's thirty-two and you are sixty-two, so Denis could be thirty, which leaves him several years to the good.'

'Why Lilian had to marry a retired Colonel who did nothing but die and leave her with two grown-up stepchildren, I don't know,' said Mr. Middleton, determined to have a grievance.

'I daresay she didn't either,' said Mrs. Middleton placidly. 'One usually doesn't. Falling in love makes one do very peculiar things. Look at us. There couldn't be two people less suited, but we simply had to get married. I do love you, Jack.'

Mr. Middleton looked at his wife and his face which had been wearing an uneasy irritated expression melted to pure tenderness, a look that always pierced his wife's heart, though she did not think it good for him to know this, so she asked when Mrs. Stonor wanted to come. Her husband said next week and this was one of his working days and she must know that if he could not break the back of the day's work before lunch he might as well retire and leave his practice to a younger man. So she laid her hand on his shoulder and went across the garden to the White House.

*

Lord Bond when he bought the property had so altered and improved the White House that it made a very pleasant residence, forming part of the Laverings estate. Up till the beginning of the year it had been let to the widow of a retired General, and when she died Mr. Middleton decided to keep it as an overflow lodging for his weekend parties or to lend or let it to friends. Sarah Pucken, the carter's wife, was willing to oblige when the house was full and could usually produce a daughter for emergencies. Mrs. Pucken had been a kitchenmaid at Staple Park before she married and knew her place to quite an alarming extent. It still pained her to feel that her husband was one of the lower class, but she fed him very well and allowed him half a crown a week out of his wages for himself. Her three elder daughters were all in service in good houses. Two were still at home and showed rebellious symptoms of wishing to go into Woolworth's, but their masterful mother had already found a place as kitchenmaid with Mrs. Palmer at Worsted for Ireen whom no one but Mrs. Middleton called Irene, and had her eye on a sixth housemaid's place for Lou. This youngest scion of the Puckens had been christened Lucasta after Lady Bond, who had with overpowering condescension personally stood godmother to her ex-kitchenmaid's child, but it was well understood by the village that the name Lucasta was no more to be used than the best parlour.

Mrs. Middleton went down the flagged path, through the gate, across the lane and in at the White House gate. With the key that she had brought with her she unlocked the front door. To her surprise she heard voices at the back of the house and going to the kitchen found Mrs. Pucken and Lou having what Mrs. Pucken called a good clean. Everything in the kitchen was wet. The kitchen table was lying on its side while Lou scrubbed the bottoms of its legs and her mother scrubbed out the drawer. Mrs. Middleton stopped short on the step that led down to the kitchen and was one of the architect's mistakes, and surveying the damp scene with interest, said Good morning to Mrs. Pucken.

'I dessay you was quite surprised to see me and Lou, madam,' said

Mrs. Pucken in the voice of a conjuror who has produced a rabbit from a top hat. 'I was just passing the remark to Lou that Mrs. Middleton would be quite surprised to see me and her, didn't I, Lou?'

'Mum said you would be quite surprised seeing her and me,' said Lou, whom no efforts of her mother's could bring to say Madam, although she had no wish to be impolite.

'Well, I am surprised,' said Mrs. Middleton, feeling that by making this confession she might escape a repetition of the statement. 'And,' she continued hurriedly, 'I was just coming to ask you to give the house a good dusting as soon as you had time, because Mr. Middleton's sister, Mrs. Stonor, is coming down next week with her stepson and stepdaughter.'

'There now, Lou, what did I tell you?' said Mrs. Pucken. 'When Miss Phipps at the Post Office told me there was a letter from Mrs. Stonor gone up to Laverings I said to Pucken, Depend on it, Pucken, I said, we shall be having Mrs. Stonor down on us before we can turn round. So I hurried up with Pucken's breakfast and brought Lou along with me to give the kitchen a good clean out. When did you expect Mrs. Stonor and the young lady and gentleman, madam?'

Mrs. Middleton had long ago accepted Miss Phipps's inquisitions into the mail bag and was indeed inclined to admire her unerring memory for every correspondent's handwriting. Miss Phipps took the broadest view of His Majesty's Post Office regulations and would always keep letters back at the shop instead of sending them up to Laverings if Mr. Middleton telephoned that he was going up to town by the early train and would call in for his. More than once had she allowed him to hunt through the bag for his own letters, open them and alter a word or a figure, and if Laverings wanted to ring up any neighbour she always knew if the person wanted was at home, calling on a neighbour, or shopping at Winter Overcotes where the chemist would take a message. As she had never put her power and knowledge to any but kindly uses no complaint had ever been made and the Inspector, though he vaguely suspected something, could not put his finger on it.

Mrs. Middleton said she expected the Stonors on Saturday week.

'There,' said Mrs. Pucken, sitting back on her heels, 'it's a good thing I've got the kitchen clean. Monday me and Lou can do out the drawing-room and Tuesday the dining-room and Wednesday the best bedroom and Thursday — —'

'But you did them out only last week, after Mr. Cameron had been here,' said Mrs. Middleton, who had housed her husband's partner and another member of the firm at the White House for a weekend.

'I like that Mr. Cameron,' said Mrs. Pucken reflectively, 'and Lou wished she had his photo, didn't you, Lou?'

Lou giggled and set the table on its legs again.

'But I couldn't let Mrs. Stonor come in here not without I give the rooms a proper cleaning, madam,' said Mrs. Pucken. suddenly becoming businesslike. 'Come along, Lou. There's some nice suds in the pail and you can wash the scullery floor. I remember Miss Stonor as well as if it was yesterday, the time she came down to Laverings and the Jersey was ill. Miss Stonor was up with her all night and Pucken said she had a heap of sense, madam, not like some young ladies. Mr. Middleton quite took on about that Jersey, didn't he madam, Lily Langtry, that was her name.'

Casting her mind back to the last visit the young Stonors had paid them three or four years earlier, Mrs. Middleton thought that 'put out' but imperfectly represented her husband's state of mind at the time. His anxiety for his best cow to whom he believed himself to be fondly attached, though he never knew her from her fellows, was combined with intense distaste for the medical details that his sister's stepdaughter poured out at every meal during her attendance on the invalid.

'And young Mr. Stonor, he was took dreadful,' Mrs Pucken continued, enjoying her own reminiscences. 'The doctor came twice a day for a week and he looked like a corpse. I do hope he's better now, madam.'

Yes, reflected Mrs. Middleton, that part of the young Stonor's visit had not been a success either. It was not poor Denis's fault that he had been delicate and still got bronchitis when other people were having sunstroke, nor was it his stepmother's fault that she had been in America at the time and could not come and nurse him herself. But Mr. Middleton, while generously supplying money for nurses and doctors, had deeply resented the presence of an invalid in his comfortable house. He had a kind of primitive animal hatred of any kind of illness, except his own occasional colds which were in a way sacred and drove every other subject out of the conversation. Even his wife's rare ailments drove him almost to frenzy with fear and dislike and it was tacitly understood that no servant must be seen if she was coughing or looked pale. The result of Denis's unlucky illness had been that Mr. Middleton nearly quarrelled with his sister on her return from America and had refused to ask the Stonors to the house again. Mrs. Stonor, who really loved her brother, had concocted with her sister-in-law this plan for taking the White House, hoping that at a safe distance he and her step-children would get on. If only Denis would keep well and Daphne would be a little less healthy Mrs. Middleton thought it might do, and she looked forward to the Stonors as next door neighbours.

'Yes, he is better, Mrs. Pucken,' she said, 'and working very hard. You know he writes music.'

'Yes indeed, madam,' said Mrs. Pucken pityingly, for as she afterwards said to Lou no one didn't *write* music. Play the piano, or the ocarina, or turn the radio on, yes: but write, no. Then she disappeared into the scullery with the nice suds and Mrs. Middleton went upstairs. The bedrooms looked spotless in spite of Mrs. Pucken's threats of cleaning. Mrs. Middleton automatically straightened one or two pictures which Mrs. Pucken would certainly put askew again as she dusted them and looked out of the window. Through a little silver birch, across the cheerful flower borders and the grass, she saw Laverings comfortably mellow red in the sunlight and could almost see, through the open library window, her husband wrestling with his article for the Journal of the R.I.B.A. Her heart suddenly swelled with affection for her large, overpowering autocrat, who bullied his clients so unmercifully and needed her own strength for his own weakness. How weak he was very few people besides his wife knew. Mrs. Middleton thought of them. Lilian Stonor had never admitted it, but Mrs. Middleton had once or twice caught a fleeting glance that told her how exactly Jack was estimated by his sister. Mrs. Pucken, of all people, knew it and stood in no fear of the roaring domestic tyrant at all. As for Alister Cameron, the junior partner of the firm, she never quite knew what he knew. For ten years he had worked assiduously and untiringly with Mr. Middleton, shouldering all the drudgery of the office and never putting himself forward. Beyond the fact that he was absolutely trustworthy, read the classics for his own pleasure, reviewed books on them with cold fury, and had rooms in the Temple, no one knew much about him. That he loved and admired Mr. Middleton, she knew. How much his love was the protective pity that she herself often felt she did not quite want to guess. That her husband was a brilliant architect, a most unusual organizer and had an astounding gift for seizing the moment and making money for his firm she was well aware, but she feared that one serious check in his hitherto unchecked career might find him out. She had once hinted at something of the kind to Mr. Cameron. He had listened attentively and then said that success could make people very vulnerable. 'But,' he added, 'he will always recover himself because whatever events may do, you won't let him down; nor, though that is a minor consideration, shall I.' Mrs. Middleton had been much comforted by this remark and she and Mr. Cameron had become in a gentlemanly and unemotional way very fast friends. It was one of her treats when she went to town to have lunch in Mr. Cameron's rooms and exchange some ordinary remarks and share some unembarrassed silences before going on to a theatre, or a shop, or a hairdresser. And for her Mr. Cameron would occasionally drop his pose of detached tolerance and say exactly what he thought about women undergraduates or the Master of Lazarus's views on Plotinus, using his guest as an audience as freely as if he were Mr. Middleton himself.

She had sometimes in the earlier days of their acquaintance indulged in sentimental and romantic speculation about his past, imagining him like George Warrington, a blighting marriage or a dead romance in his background. But this pleasing illusion was dispelled one day when they were talking about husbands and wives (with special reference to Lord and Lady Bond) and Mr. Cameron had said he had never yet seen anyone he wanted to marry and hoped he never would, having had his blood curdled by two aunts and a governess in early life.

After that Mrs. Middleton had with feminine perversity felt obliged to gather the nicest girls in the neighbourhood to Laverings for his benefit, but though he was only about her own age they had all treated him as an uncle at sight and flung their arms round his neck with a freedom that certainly did not betoken any serious feelings.

In the distance Mrs. Middleton could hear the stable clock chiming eleven from Staple Park and roused herself. There was shopping to be done in the village, the report of the District Nursing Association of which she was secretary to be finished, and a dozen small household odds and ends awaiting her. Alister Cameron was coming down on Saturday week, the Stonors would be arriving on the same day and perhaps he and Daphne – and then she laughed at herself for trying once more to melt Alister's flinty heart and went off to the garage to get her car.

II

GUESTS AT THE WHITE HOUSE

ON the Saturday morning of the following week Mr. Cameron left the office with his weekend suitcase and made his way by underground to Waterloo. The one through train to Skeynes (for by all others you have to change at Winter Overcotes) was on the point of starting. The guard, who knew Mr. Cameron, held a door open and called to him to jump in, which he did just as the train began to pull out. The exertion of jumping in and the slight jolt as the train began to move caused him to stumble against some legs and he apologized.

'It's all right,' said the owner of the legs, a girl who was doing a crossword.

Mr. Cameron put his suitcase on the rack, looked to see whether it was a smoking-carriage, and saw with slight regret that it wasn't. The 11.47 was always rather full on Saturdays and the only vacant place was next to the girl over whose legs he had stumbled. So he sat down in it and being rather tired after some late nights and heavy days went to sleep, or at any rate passed into a state of suspended animation which lasted till the train got to Winter Overcotes. Here some rather primitive shunting which was being done by a white horse harnessed to some goods trucks made such a noise that he woke up and found most of the passengers had got out. A young man and woman were in the two far corners reading and the girl next to him was still doing her crossword. As he had very good long sight he could not help seeing that she had made very little progress since Waterloo and the words she had tentatively filled in were in several cases incorrect. At the moment she was struggling with 7 down, the clue to which was 'Tomorrow to . . . woods and pastures new (Milton), 5'. With fascination he watched his neighbour think, frown, lick her pencil and finally write the word *Green* in block letters. He could hardly control himself.

'I say, Denis,' said the girl. 'This seems all wrong. If I put Green for 7 down it makes sense all right but the letters don't seem to fit. I mean I'd got Socrates for 5 across, because it says "This call for help contains a large parcel," which was pretty good work, but now it will have to be Socratee. Do you think they spelt it Socratee sometimes? I mean in the accusative or something?'

The young man, evidently Denis, said he simply couldn't think.

'Oh, but then it wouldn't be S.O.S. for the call for help but S.O.E.' said the girl. 'I expect the man that wrote it did it all wrong. Someone told me that they stick next day's crossword up in the office, I mean the squares of it, and anyone who comes along can put in a word, so someone who didn't know much about Greek plays put it in wrong.'

'Sophocles you mean,' said Denis.

'That wouldn't do,' said the girl after a moment's hard thinking, 'unless you spelt it like sofa; because it's only eight letters.'

Mr. Cameron could bear it no longer.

'Excuse me,' he said, 'but I couldn't help seeing over your shoulder. It ought to be fresh.'

'What ought?' said the girl, evidently willing to receive any new idea but quite at sea as to his meaning.

'Green of course,' said the woman, who had come close to the girl and was looking at the clues.

'Oh, you mean it ought to be *fresh*,' said the girl, licking her pencil again and blacking in the word Fresh. 'Well, thy ought to explain properly and anyway they've got two letters the same. If I were the editor I'd see they did the crossword properly. Green woods is just as good as fresh woods.'

'It's really Milton's fault,' said Mr. Cameron apologetically.

'Oh, I did see it said Milton,' said the girl, 'but I didn't quite get the idea. Thanks awfully. Could you do any more of it?'

Crosswords were like drink to Mr. Cameron, who willingly took the job and finished it before the train had reached Skeynes, in spite of the Worsted tunnel where the railway company, in accordance with a tradition dating from the days of oil lamps, refused to put on any lights and the carriage windows were obscured with a sulphurous deposit that did not melt away till the train was halfway down the valley on the other side.

'Well, thanks awfully,' said the girl as the train slowed down for Skeynes. 'We're getting out here. Lilian, here we are.'

The woman shut her book and put it into a small suitcase. As she stood up, Mr. Cameron saw her face properly for the first time and recognized it. He got out of the carriage with his suitcase and called a porter, whom he delivered over to his fellow travellers.

'Oh, thank you so much,' said the woman, and then she looked questioningly at him.

'Yes, we have met,' said Mr. Cameron. 'It was stupid of me not to recognize you at once. My name is Cameron. I'm your brother's partner.'

'Of course,' said Mrs. Stonor. 'I met you once at Laverings. These are my stepchildren, Denis and Daphne. Denis has just had influenza. Are you going to stay with Jack? I have taken the White House for the summer. I asked Catherine to send a taxi to meet us, so perhaps we could give you a lift.'

As she was speaking they walked up the platform towards the exit, through which from the booking office surged the form of Mr. Middleton, intent upon meeting his sister and her party. He was in his country squire's dress, carrying the very large stick with which it was his habit to incommode himself on his walks. As he caught sight of his sister he raised the stick in greeting.

'Lilian!' he exclaimed, trying to throw into the name a wealth of meaning intended to disguise the fact that he didn't know what to say.

'That is very nice of you to come and meet us, Jack,' said Mrs. Stonor, 'and if you would put your stick out of Daphne's eye I could kiss you. Mr. Cameron, would you mind helping me with the luggage. I can't remember if I had twelve things in the van or thirteen, and the children are always ashamed of me in public.'

She drifted away followed by Mr. Cameron.

'That's all right,' said Daphne, as she got in under her step-uncle's guard and banged her face against his cheek.

'Wait a moment,' said Mr. Middleton, slightly annoyed. 'I will give the stick to Flora. She loves to carry it for me. Flora! Flora! Where are you?'

A stout brown spaniel who had been sending a crate of hens into hysterics by sniffing at the wooden bars, looked with kindly contempt at Mr. Middleton, wagged her tail and sat down. Daphne laughed a hearty laugh and said Flora was too fat to move.

'She is not fat,' said Mr. Middleton indignantly. 'She is twelve years old and needs her food. Flora! Come and take stick. Take stick for master.'

Flora slapped the platform with her tail and smiled tolerantly.

'Dog won't bite pig, pig won't get over the stile,' murmured Denis. 'How do you do, sir.'

Mr. Middleton looked coldly at his step-nephew, but could not ignore Denis's outstretched hand and had to shake it. Mrs. Stonor with Mr. Cameron in attendance was still fussing over her trunks outside the luggage van and Mr. Middleton had leisure to inspect the young Stonors whom he had not seen for two or three years. They were much as he remembered them and his memories were unsympathetic. Daphne was certainly a very handsome girl but had what appeared to him a terrifying air of good-humour and determination. Besides, she had called Flora fat. As for Denis, he was even taller and thinner than in Mr. Middleton's recollection. Huddled in a long coat on a balmy June day, his large dark eyes ringed with the marks of suffering, he reminded his step-uncle too much of an organ grinder's monkey. When Flora waddled up and inspected the newcomer's legs and Denis, stooping, took off his glove and patted her, his long bony hand seemed to Mr. Middleton to increase the resemblance, and he felt the vague unreasonable distaste that always overcame him at the sight of illness. To make up for this uncharitable feeling he informed Denis that Flora liked him.

'I wish I could think so,' said Denis, slowly straightening himself and putting his glove on again. 'I am afraid she knows I don't like her. Dogs always come to me because they know I see through them and they enjoy it. They are such masochists. I am always polite to them, but I wouldn't care if I never saw another one again. What a charming station you have, sir.'

Mr. Middleton became a prey to mingled emotions. To his mind, quick to grasp essentials, it was clear that Lilian's stepson was going to be a perpetual annoyance to him. He didn't like young men who wore gloves in the country and camel hair coats; people who didn't like Flora he could not away with. That a good many of his friends had no particular affection for her he was not aware, but so long as they veiled their true sentiments under a decent veil of hypocrisy he was willing to take a surface value. Young Stonor's analysis of his Flora's reactions he found almost indecent. Nor did he at all like the easy way in which the boy had dismissed Flora and condescended about the station. He looked angrily round. Charming appeared to him the last word one would choose for Skeynes station. It represented what might be called Mid-Victorian functional railway architecture, as far removed from the Gothic romanticism of Shrewsbury on the one hand as it was from the modern station with circular booking office, elliptical signal boxes and stepped-back waiting-rooms on the other. There was a decent squat row of grey brick offices with wooden floors which were watered from time to time during the hot weather to lay the dust that they engendered; the booking office and entrance hall still contained one of those advertisements, now much valued by connoisseurs, of a storage and removal firm whose vans had the peculiar property of exhibiting one side and one end simultaneously; the stationmaster had a little office chokingly heated by a stove with a red-hot chimney and furnished with yellowing crackling documents impaled on spikes; there was a waiting-room containing a bench, a table, an empty carafe of incredible thickness and weight, two chairs and a rusty grate full of smouldering slack; the porters had a room called Lamps which was always locked; and at the end of the down platform was a tank on four legs from which local engines still obtained their water supply through a leathern hose pipe. There were a few little flower beds, edged with whitewashed stones and containing varieties of flowers from penny packets of mixed seeds. On the wooden fence that separated the platform from the station yard was another prize for the amateur of railway art, enamelled on tin, a fine original example of the distich about the Pickwick, Owl and Waverley pens. The platform was sheltered by a corrugated iron roof with a wooden frill along its front and all the paint was an uncompromising chocolate colour.

From the foregoing description it will be easy to see how to Mr. Middleton and most of the inhabitants Skeynes was simply a station, while to Denis and some of his generation it was a period piece to be treated with protective reverence. When Denis, having done his duty by Flora and his step-uncle, strolled up to a chocolate machine and actually obtained a small slab of very nasty pink chocolate cream, he felt that a summer at Skeynes would not be unbearable.

By this time the luggage had all been put on a trolley and was on its way by the side gate into the station yard, where the Laverings car was in waiting.

'Oh dear,' said Mrs. Stonor, giving way to despair. 'Your car can never take all our luggage, Jack. Is there a station taxi, or could the station-master ring up something? We seem to have a frightful amount, but really for three months one does want everything one has in the English climate. I did think of not bringing my tweeds, but one never knows and it is such a nuisance if you haven't got your things when you want them. I always say if you *are* taking any luggage you might as well take what you need.'

'It's only thirteen things,' said Daphne, 'besides the things we had in the carriage with us. The car could easily come back for the rest. I say, Uncle Jack, you've still got that nice chauffeur you had last time I was here. Hullo, Pollett, how are you? You could easily get our things up to the White House, couldn't you?'

Pollett touched his cap to Daphne and without making any verbal reply, for he was a man of few words, favoured her with an expressive glance in the direction of his employer.

'Oh, I suppose Uncle Jack's one of those people that don't like luggage on their seats,' said Daphne, accepting this curious attitude towards the leatherwork of an expensive car as one of the inexplicable facts of life.

'Perhaps some of it could go up on the porter's trolley,' said Mrs. Stonor, talking aloud to herself and anyone who was unable to avoid hearing her. 'It's only a mile to the White House and not very much uphill and if I said which things we don't need so much as the others, it would do quite well if we didn't get them till after tea, or even by dinner-time.'

'I'd love to go up on this,' said Denis, who was sitting on a suitcase on the trolley with his long legs dangling over the side. 'Yes, Lilian, I know I should get axle grease on my trousers, but it is too late; I got it as soon as I came near the thing. It exudes death-rays of grease, yards away. I'll have to take them into Winter Overcotes and get them cleaned. I can't think why we haven't a car of our own. No, darling, I beg your pardon,' he exclaimed, getting off the trolley and putting his arm round his stepmother. 'I know it's because I'm such a damned expense with my foul diseases.'

Mrs. Stonor gave him a glance in which some anxiety mingled with a good deal of affection, pressed his arm, released herself and went over to her brother who was now talking to Mr. Cameron. But hardly had she begun to expound her plans for the luggage when a trampling, creaking noise came round the bend of the road, resolving itself as it approached into the blue farm waggon with red wheels, drawn by the shining monster with hairy trousers. Mr. Pucken, who was as usual seated sidways just behind the horse, addressed a few words to his charge who pulled up and stood quietly waiting for the next job.

'There, my dear Lilian, is the answer to your questions,' said Mr. Middleton. 'Tom Pucken will take your luggage up in the cart and I will take you all in the car, for it is already past lunch-time.'

'Never mind lunch,' cried Mrs. Stonor. 'We lunch at any time. I must look at your cart.'

Mr. Middleton, who lunched at half-past one and was already annoyed at being late, herded his sister towards the car. Pollett opened the door and Flora, bursting through among everyone's feet, hurled herself into the car and sat panting on the seat.

'Here, come out of that,' said Daphne, hauling Flora's unwilling dead weight out by a handful of her back. 'She needs training, Uncle Jack.'

'She doesn't,' said her owner indignantly, answering Daphne back as if they were children of the same age. 'Come to master, Flora, and sit on master's knees.'

But Flora, recognizing in Daphne a natural dog-ruler, was crouching slavishly at her feet with worship in her eyes and turned a deliberately deaf and disobedient ear to her master's invitation.

'Get in, Lilian,' said Daphne. 'I say, Uncle Jack, that's the best cart I've ever seen. I always wanted to know someone who had their name on a cart. "J. Middleton Esquire, Laverings Farm." It looks simply marvellous. Could I go up in it, with the luggage? Come along, Denis.'

Denis made a step towards his sister, but was stopped by Mrs. Stonor, who begged him to be sensible and come in the car. Denis, who was already feeling the effects of the heat and the wait in the station yard, was secretly glad of an excuse not to accompany his sister and obediently got into the car, looking extremely green in the face.

'I shall go in front with Pollett,' said Mr. Middleton hastily, not so much from unselfishness as from a wish not to be in the back of the car if young Stonor was going to faint or die in it. 'Come up, Flora. Come up with master.'

Flora bundled herself into the back of the car, and busied herself in guarding Denis's feet from possible enemies. Mrs. Stonor lingered for a moment to collect Daphne, but her stepdaughter was standing in the farm cart like Boadicea while Mr. Pucken put the luggage on board.

'I say, Mr. Cameron, it is Mr. Cameron, isn't it, your name I mean,' Daphne shouted, 'come up in the cart.'

Mr. Cameron looked from Miss Stonor to Mrs. Stonor in some perplexity.

'Yes, do,' said Mrs. Stonor in answer to his look. 'My brother will go mad if we wait any longer and I must get Denis back as quickly as possible. Please don't let Daphne drive the cart or ride the horse or go the long way round, and could you make sure that there are *three* blue suitcases, because if one is missing it is sure to be the one that is wanted, and could you see that the brown hat box is the right way up because I think some of Denis's medicine is in it and one of the corks isn't a very good fit and if the cork comes out — —'

But Mr. Middleton, angrily saying a quarter to two already, snapped his watch to in a terrifying manner and told Pollett to start, so Mr. Cameron never knew what would happen if the cork came out of the medicine bottle and found himself deserted in the station yard with the masterful Miss Stonor. How he was to stop her driving the cart or riding the horse or going the long way round he couldn't conceive, and could only hope that his interference would not be needed. So he went over to the cart and told Daphne that her stepmother wanted to know if there were three blue suitcases.

'I expect so,' said Daphne indifferently. 'Come up and we'll get going. You'll get a lot of hay on your clothes because Pucken was carting hay this morning, but he gave it a good sweep out he says.'

Mr. Cameron in a cowardly way gave up the question of the blue suitcases, and climbed into the cart where he sat on a holdall, feeling that Miss Stonor could deal with the situation far better than he could. Mr. Pucken was settling himself in his usual place on the shaft, when Daphne called down to him that she wanted to drive and would he chuck the reins up.

'All right, miss,' said Mr. Pucken, 'but mind you don't pull on them or he'll pull up. Just let them lay on his back, miss. He knows the way home.'

Daphne caught the reins and flapped them on the monster's back. Mr. Pucken rammed the remains of his tobacco further into his pipe, lit it and prepared to tolerate the gentry enjoying themselves. Daphne, taking his advice, perched herself on the front of the cart and let the reins lie slack, while Mr. Cameron wondered what subjects, if any, would interest her. Suddenly he remembered Mrs. Stonor's second request. Looking round he saw two brown hat boxes. They were shaped like drums and to the lay mind there appeared to be no reason why one way up should be more the right way up than another.

'Oh, Miss Stonor,' he said, 'Mrs. Stonor said there was some of your brother's medicine in one of the hat boxes and she wanted to be sure if the bottle was properly corked. Do you know which it would be?'

Daphne, who had been holding the reins with the air of one guiding the whirlwind and directing the storm, pulled them violently. The monster stopped. Daphne quickly opened one of the hat boxes, rummaged among a confused heap of scarves, woollies, gloves, silk underclothes, powder puffs, anything in fact but the hats for which the box was intended, and at last produced a small pink bundle with a brown stain on it. This she unwrapped and held up a bottle.

'What a mercy Lilian told you,' she said. 'Denis hadn't room for his medicine, so he gave it to Lilian and she hadn't room, so I said I'd put it in my hat box and I wrapped it up in my vest, but the cork must have worked a bit loose. Anyway there's hardly any of it spilt, but it's made a mess of my vest.'

She drove the cork firmly home, wrapped the bottle up again, thrust it into the pocket of the loose coat she was wearing and flapped the reins. The cart was once more put into action and the monster breasted the hill up to Skeynes village. Mr. Cameron then became aware that Miss Stonor was looking at him with what he felt, though he could not account for it, to be disfavour.

'I suppose,' she said suddenly and rather defiantly, 'you don't think there's anything wrong with Denis.'

'Wrong?' said Mr. Cameron, playing for time. 'Oh no, nothing wrong I'm sure.'

'Well, you must have noticed,' said Daphne severely, 'about his medicine. You've just seen it.'

'Yes, I did see it,' Mr. Cameron admitted, 'but lots of people have medicine. I have some awful stuff that I take myself sometimes.'

'Well, Denis is *really* not well, or he wouldn't be having medicine at all,' said Daphne. 'He's always been like that and it's a frightful shame. There's nothing really wrong with him, he just can't help it. Sometimes people think he looks like that out of swank, but he loathes it and he can't bear people to talk about it. So don't tell him he looks rotten or anything like that because he can't bear it.'

She ended her explanation with a flushed face and a break in her voice which Mr. Cameron found touching though a little unnecessary. She must be very fond of her brother to take him so seriously. He certainly looked pale and weedy, but by no means in mortal danger. However to be polite he said he was very sorry and he had noticed that Mr. Stonor seemed to feel the heat.

'Mr. Stonor?' said Daphne. 'Oh, Denis, you mean. Of course he did. That's why Lilian wanted to get him to the White House as soon as she could. She's an angel. Not a bit like a step. I really think she married father so that she could look after Denis and take me about a bit, at least I can't see any other reason. Father found us rather a bore, because he was a Colonel and he wanted army children and I was a girl and Denis was never well, so that was a wash-out. Mother died ages ago in India. Lilian was really our friend first. We warned her what it would be like marrying father, but she seemed to like it all right.'

In face of these interesting family details Mr. Cameron felt rather at a loss but luckily the monster turned into the little lane that led to Laverings and the White House, and all the suitcases lurched across the cart. Mr. Pucken, knowing that the horse would with Casabianca-like devotion go straight to his stable whatever Miss Daphne tried to do, slipped down from the shaft and went to its head, where he explained to it that a short halt would be necessary to unload the luggage, after which it would get its dinner. On hearing this the monster stood still, with one hoof delicately poised on the tip of its shoe like a ballerina.

Mrs. Stonor's maid, who had come the day before by motor coach, hurried down the garden path followed by Mrs. Pucken. By the greatest piece of good fortune Palfrey, which was the name of the maid, had taken a violent fancy for Mrs. Pucken and Mrs. Pucken for her. Owing to Mrs. Pucken's favourable introductions Palfrey was already on the best of terms with the village tradesmen and Miss Phipps at the shop, and Mrs. Pucken had spent the morning at Laverings drinking tea and doing a quantity of quite unnecessary cleaning, for the house was already spotless from her ministrations. Lou, to her eternal disgust, had been banished to the scullery to peel potatoes and shell a few peas for lunch, while her mother and Palfrey, whom Lou was instructed to call Miss Palfrey on pain of death, discussed the major mysteries of life, saying what a shame it was Mr. and Mrs. Middleton hadn't any children, though Mrs. Pucken gave it as her opinion that Mr. Middleton was nothing but a big child himself and Mrs. Middleton had her hands full.

'Your lady hasn't any children not of her own, has she?' said Mrs. Pucken.

'Oh no,' said Palfrey pityingly, 'being as Colonel Stonor was a widower when she married him.'

She looked Mrs. Pucken firmly in the face, as if challenging her to dispute this curious physiological phenomenon and such was her personality that Mrs. Pucken very slavishly nodded her head in a knowing way.

'The Colonel was very particular,' said Palfrey putting all the cushions askew on the sofa and chairs as she spoke. 'Very particular indeed. I was cook there for two years before he died and I never cooked for a gentleman that was more particular. Now madam and Mr. Denis and Miss Daphne they don't hardly seem to notice what they eat, though I will say for Miss Daphne she'a a hearty eater. But what Mr. Denis eats wouldn't feed a cat, Mrs. Pucken. A bit here and a bit there and as like as not leave it on his plate after all. That's why we've come down here, Mrs. Pucken, to see if the country does him good. Always playing the piano and going to the concert, in London. I wonder madam can stand it, I really do sometimes.'

At this point Mrs. Pucken said she heard the car so she and Palfrey went to see if there was any luggage, after which Palfrey ran upstairs to clean herself and Mrs. Pucken received Mrs. Stonor and Denis, who said how do you do to her very charmingly and sat down abruptly on a chair in the hall.

'Would you like some sherry, Denis?' said Mrs. Stonor anxiously. 'Jack said he had sent us some, and if Mrs. Pucken knows where it is and there is a corkscrew in the kitchen anywhere we could have some at once. I did put a corkscrew in my big trunk, the one that has your music in it, but it hasn't come yet, so that's not much use.'

Mrs. Pucken said the sherry was in the larder and there was a cork-screw on the dresser and the sherry glasses were in the pantry and she could get a bottle and have the cork out in a minute and did Mr. Denis like the dry or the sweet as Mr. Middleton had sent over both. Lord Bond, she said, liked the dry best and she had noticed that gentlemen usually did, but it wasn't a mite more trouble to open the sweet if Mr. Denis liked it. And as a preparation for the festival she called to Lou at the top of her powerful maternal voice. Denis controlled himself with an effort, hoping that neither the effort nor his attempt to conceal it would be visible to his stepmother and said he really didn't want any sherry and would rather wait for lunch. Mrs. Stonor who was acutely sensitive both to his fatigue and to his self-control saw nothing for it in the face of Mrs. Pucken's determined kindness but to accompany her to the larder and there hold her in talk about sherry and corkscrews till lunch was ready, leaving Denis to recover himself as best he could. If only the cart and the luggage with the hat box and the medicine would come soon.

Very luckily Lou had so far exceeded her instructions as to put the potatoes on, a phrase which should need no explanation, while Palfrey was cleaning herself. Her mind, if she can be said to have had any, was running on a bottle of bright red liquid nail polish which she had brought against her mother's orders and hidden in her other pair of shoes, so she naturally forgot to put enough water in the saucepan and just as Mrs. Pucken and Mrs. Stonor came into the kitchen Palfrey, summoned by a smell of burning, came clattering down the little staircase that led from the top landing to the kitchen and opened the door at its foot with a dramatic flourish. The storm burst over Lou's head, thunder and lightning from Mrs. Pucken and Palfrey, and Mrs. Pucken, sending her home to put her father's dinner in the oven, quickly washed a few of the smaller new potatoes and put them on so that they might be ready for the travellers as soon as possible.

By this time the sherry was forgotten and then the cart was heard and the staff rushed out to help with the luggage.

'Good-bye,' said Daphne to Mr. Cameron. 'I hope you enjoyed yourself. And don't forget what I said about Denis.'

'I enjoyed myself very much,' said Mr. Cameron truthfully, 'and I'll remember. I hope I shall see you again while I'm here.'

Then he went off to the right to Laverings, while Daphne went through the gate on the left to the White House. Here her stepmother met her, carrying an empty glass.

'Did you find the medicine?' Mrs. Stonor asked anxiously. 'I told Mr. Cameron to ask you about it, because I wasn't sure if the cork was in properly.'

Daphne pulled the vest out of her pocket and produced the bottle. 'Here you are,' she said. 'It's made my vest in a bit of a mess, but there's heaps left.'

'Thank goodness,' said Mrs. Stonor. 'Will you take it to Denis, or shall I?'

'You take it,' said Daphne. 'I want to say good-bye to Pucken, but I wanted to give you the medicine first. Poor old Lilian.'

Mrs. Stonor poured out Denis's medicine and took it into the drawing-room where he was standing at the piano, tapping a note here and there with one finger.

'To your great pleasure, Lilian darling, I will at once tell you,' he said in the rather high voice which she knew so well as a danger signal of nerves, 'that this little upright is quite impossible, so you will not be tormented with my playing at all. And a good thing too, I daresay,' he added, shutting the lid with great care. 'I always said I ought to compose without a piano and here is my chance. Oh, darling, you haven't got some medicine for me?'

'Daphne has just brought it,' said Mrs. Stonor, handing him the glass. 'It was in her hat box and if I had had any sense I would have told Pollett to put the hat box in the car, but I didn't think of it. I only thought of telling Mr. Cameron to tell Daphne to see if the cork had come out, and she wrapped the bottle up in her vest and it was rather stained.'

'I don't know what I'd do without you and Daphne,' said Denis, making a face. 'This is quite the most disgusting medicine I've had yet. What a useless encumbrance I am.'

His stepmother looked at him with mild reproach and took the empty glass.

'Quite right, darling,' said Denis, laughing in spite of himself. 'Too much self-pity. But don't you ever wish you had let that odious, unhealthy schoolboy die a natural death? You wouldn't have noticed if I'd died then, but now it is quite habit with you to take care of me and I think you would miss it. Do you know, Lilian, you've been standing between me and Kensal Green for nearly ten years?'

'Well, someone had to look after you,' said his stepmother apologetically. 'You looked such a wretched atomy, all eyes and bones.'

'And someone had to look after Daphne, who was a quite dreadful giggling schoolgirl then,' said Denis.

'And there was your father who wasn't bony or giggling,' said Mrs. Stonor almost sharply.

'Forgive me,' said Denis. And then Palfrey disdainfully banged a little gong which stood in the hall and they went in to lunch where the new potatoes were much admired and Denis actually ate two.

After lunch Denis was ordered to lie on a long chair on the little stone terrace in the corner of the L-shaped house and get as much sun as possible, and he was tired enough to obey with very little fuss. The sun was very hot. A lawnmower at Laverings made a pleasant distant drone and scent from the sweetbriar hedge drifted in the air. Denis felt that he might be quiet at the White House, he might find a little of the inward peace which he so desperately wanted. Whenever, in his experience, his mind settled to some kind of equilibrium, his body would give it a twist or a jerk. How often Lilian had saved him only he knew. She had never pretended to understand his mind, perhaps never thought it worth while to try, but her kindness, her patience, her affection had been as constant as day and night. What she didn't understand she accepted, and so naturally that one had gradually come to think of oneself as an ordinary person that happened not to be very well, instead of imagining, as that bony schoolboy had done, that one was marked out as different from other people and being savagely proud of it. His gratitude to her was so much part of him now that he sometimes forgot it. He suddenly thought of the words he and his stepmother had exchanged before lunch. As usual he had said something stupid, almost cruel, rousing even her tolerance to a protest. He and Daphne had never cared much for their father. Or perhaps, if one delved deeply enough for truth, always an unpleasant work, he had not got on with his father, and Daphne, who could get on very well with everybody, had with her younger sister's loyalty come over to his side and lost touch with her father. Between them they had decided that Lilian Middleton had married Colonel Stonor so that she could be a good stepmother to two motherless children. But as he got older Denis had realized, with some shame, that Lilian had probably married his father because she was deeply fond of him and had taken on the care of two children not so much younger than herself, not because she thought they were misunderstood or unkindly treated, but because anything that belonged to her husband was dear to her. Denis was thankful to remember how Lilian had so tamed him that he began to have good manners to his father, which were accepted with surprise and silent gratitude, and from his real effort to please had come at last an understanding not deep, but good enough to make life easier for them both. Daphne, pleased to do whatever her brother did, allowed herself to be affectionate to her father and improved vastly under Lilian's hand. If Lilian had burst out before lunch about her husband, even as little as she did, it meant that her feelings were deeply touched. Denis flushed hotly as he remembered with what fatuousness he had said, or almost said, that she had married his father for his sake, and as an afterthought, for Daphne's sake. How could he have been such an oaf. He prided himself on a certain sensibility, but there was nothing to be proud of in taking for granted that a woman had not loved very deeply the man she married: gross insensitiveness, was the best name he could give to it. That Lilian never suspected an unkindness and never bore rancour made it all the worse. Denis began to feel his heart beating too fast and an answering pulse in his head which would probably mean what were known as 'one of poor Denis's heads', as all this rushed over him. Five years ago he would have made a scene with his stepmother, accused himself, implored forgiveness, left her with a headache as bad as his own, but this at least he had learned, to keep his remorse to himself. So he lighted a cigarette and tried to think of his music, and gradually, though his head was no better, he was drowsy enough to hover not unpleasantly between waking and what was less sleep than a kind of blissful half-consciousness.

*

But meanwhile who can describe the rage of Mr. Middleton. Not only was he late for lunch himself, but when he got back, at two o'clock, he had to wait yet another fifteen minutes for Mr. Cameron. In vain did his wife offer him sherry or a cocktail. He was exhausted, a thing of no account, a mere purveyor of motors and general transport for sisters and nephews and nieces, and the whole world would have been taken into his confidence had it been there. As it was, he had to content himself with his wife and the parlourmaid for audience.

'No, no, Catherine, you well know that sherry is poison to me at this hour,' he exclaimed. 'And as for cocktails, this is no weather for them. There is only one thing that I could drink — —'

'Well if we have got it you shall have it,' said Mrs. Middleton.

'—and that,' said Mr. Middleton, 'is beer.'

'Shall I bring some beer then, madam?' said Ethel, the parlourmaid, who had brought in the sherry.

'When I say beer, none of you know what I mean,' said Mr. Middleton.

'Yes please, Ethel, off the ice,' said Mrs. Middleton.

'None of you are old enough,' said Mr. Middleton, addressing his wife and the departing figure of Ethel and suddenly becoming a pathetic nonagenarian, 'to know what beer was. Ah! the beer we used to drink before the war, long long before the war. It had savour, it had body, it was meat and drink to the thirsty body and the thirsty soul. Had Dr. Johnson drunk the beer we used to drink he would have amended his dictum to Beer for Heroes. You do not know what it was to come in after a long day's tramp, hot, sweating, tired as only the walker can be with a divine fatigue, stupefied with the strong air of the hills, the scent of gorse and heather, the salt tang of the sea, the sweet resinous smell of pinewoods above the fiords, the chill wind from the great glaciers, the glare from the sand dunes of the desert,' said Mr. Middleton, who seemed to have done his walking in a very composite kind of country, 'and grasping a tankard to feel the cool nectar slip down one's throat, grateful to the palate, to the throat, to the whole body. To relax the body in utter contentment and then to talk. Ah! how we talked in those days. Have I ever told you, Catherine, of my great, my epic walk with Potter and Bagshaw, both now with the great majority, men of infinite learning and humour, ascetics like myself, caring for little but the things of the mind and the use of a well-tempered body.'

'Yes, darling,' said Mrs. Middleton.

'I may have, I may have,' said Mr. Middleton, 'I know I repeat myself, for I get old, I have no longer the brain of the youth who could never be tired or worsted in argument, but bear with me, Catherine, while I repeat for myself, for my own enduring pleasure, the story of our walk up Kirkstone, over Fairfield, across to the long backbone of Helvellyn,' said Mr. Middleton, drinking at one long draught the glass of iced beer that Ethel handed him, '—again, Ethel; that was good, you have iced it to a nicety—down across the end of Thirlmere, up and over by Armboth, among the mosses to Watendlath, then unspoilt by the hand or pen of man, down into Borrowdale, up the Stye Head Pass, across Green Gable where we saw the rainbow of Valhalla spanning the valley at our feet, down again to Buttermere—thank you, Ethel, thank you. This beer is the best I have ever tasted. Where do we get it? I must have a cask to hold my high revels.'

'It's not in casks, sir, it's bottled, from the Fleece down in the village,' said Ethel. 'Light Lager.'

'Catherine, we must always have this beer,' said Mr. Middleton. 'I know beer. Few men know it as I do and this is *beer*.'

'It's what we always have, sir,' said Ethel.

'It may be, it may be,' said Mr. Middleton rather crossly. 'No thanks, no more. It is not so good now as it was before.'

With which Shakespearian echo he reassumed his fit of gloom.

But almost at once Ethel announced Mr. Cameron and they were able to go straight in to lunch. The meal was so good that conversation fell to a pleasantly low level and when they had finished their coffee Mr. Middleton carried Mr. Cameron off to the library to talk business.

'I shall go over before tea and see if I can do anything for Lilian,' said Mrs. Middleton. 'She looked so worried about Denis. That poor boy.'

'I hope he isn't going to be ill again,' said Mr. Middleton. 'Ask them all over after dinner to-night, Catherine. After all Lilian is my sister. I may be busy, I may have to work, but she will be welcome, and so,' he added battling with his lower self, 'will her stepchildren. Do not forget, my dear Catherine, to order more of that excellent beer.'

'I did, yesterday,' said Mrs. Middleton. 'The Fleece like sending on Saturdays, so I usually order on Fridays. What time do you want to dine, Jack?'

After a great deal of talk it was decided that after so late a lunch it would be agreeable to have dinner at a quarter past eight, and the two men went off to the study while Mrs. Middleton prepared to visit her sister-in-law, for it was already almost four o'clock.

III

GUESTS AT LAVERINGS

It was one of Mrs. Middleton's special gifts that her servants stayed with her. In most households a sudden demand for lunch at a quarter past two and dinner at a quarter past eight would have been met with sulks and followed by notice. But though Mr. Middleton was entirely inconsiderate of his staff, or perhaps because he was so whole-heartedly inconsiderate, they all felt a protective adoration for him and never left except to marry. The more people came for the weekend, the more unexpected guests turned up for lunch, tea and dinner, the more the Laverings kitchen rose to the occasion. It was not the good wages, nor the large Christmas tips, not the lure of seeing and hearing famous people, for the Middleton's circle though very well known had not the names that adorn the cheaper Sunday papers. There was in it some of that rather sentimental British feeling for children, drunken men, very small things and dogs; not that Mr. Middleton exactly surprised in himself, in Count Smorltork's words, all or any of these elements, unless it was his occasionally childish attitude. A great deal of the kitchen contentment must have been due to Mrs. Middleton, who had the excellent housekeeping tradition of her family, infinite patience in listening to stories of misfortune, and never lost her head or her temper, unless deliberately. A story was current in the kitchen that she had once thrown some Benger's Food, feeding cup and all, out of Mr. Middleton's bedroom window because it was not properly made. The Benger's Food was by now in a fair way to becoming a leg of mutton, or a turkey with trimmings, and added greatly to her reputation in the village. Even Lady Bond, who kept her servants by the reign of terror which the better class of that race still admires as being a proof of good blood, had to admit that Mrs. Middleton was a past mistress in the art of keeping a staff.

Therefore, when Mrs. Middleton wanted dinner at a quarter past eight, she merely gave the order to Ethel and was able to go over to the White House without any foreboding or sinking of the spirit.

She crossed the lane and went into the Stonors' garden. Everything was very quiet. Mrs. Pucken had gone home, Palfrey was reading about the Home Life of the Royal Family in the kitchen, on the other side of the house. The only person to be seen was Denis, lying on a chair in the sun, his hat tilted over his eyes, so whether he was dead or asleep she could not tell. As a matter of fact he was neither, but still in that state of blissful half-consciousness that only the right time and place can bring. The slight noise of Mrs. Middleton's approach broke this calm. He looked up and saw what for the moment he took to be a stranger, for he had not seen Mrs. Middleton since he had been ill at Laverings some years ago. He looked at a woman no longer young, with a face that proclaimed good breeding, rather tired eyes and a mouth that told him nothing till it broke to a smile and he suddenly knew who she was and incidentally where he was, for his waking had left him for a moment confused. He sat up.

'Don't get up, Denis,' said Mrs. Middleton. 'I'm so glad to see you again.'

Denis, fearing that he was being treated as an invalid uncoiled himself as quickly as possible and shook hands. Mrs. Middleton was a tall woman, but she had to look up to see Denis's face. In it she saw more than she liked of the invalid whom she had helped to nurse, so she at once said that he was looking much better.

'Oh, I'm quite all right, thank you,' said Denis. 'I expect you want to see Lilian, don't you. She was going to unpack, but it's nearly tea-time. Will you come in?'

'I can't tell you,' said Denis as they went into the house, 'how sorry I was that we made Mr. Middleton late for lunch. It all seemed to be rather a muddle with our luggage and Flora and Mr. Cameron, and darling Lilian did so much explaining. I'll go and find her and Daphne.'

'Wait a moment,' said Mrs. Middleton sitting down. 'I want to know about you. Are you really better? And how much do you feel like doing? Jack wants you all to come over to-night after dinner, but if it would tire you, please tell me. We have so many people at Laverings and I want you to feel free to come in when you like and stay away when you like. We have rather a good piano if that would amuse you.'

'That's a hideous temptation,' said Denis. 'I was congratulating myself on the badness of this little piano, because I ought to work at composing without a piano, which this odious little affair would give me every encouragement to do. And now you mention a good piano and all my good resolves go flying away.'

Mrs. Middleton suggested that he should give way to his evil impulses in the middle of the week when her husband was in town and so avoid disturbing him. In a few minutes Denis was telling her his plans for some ballet music that he had almost been commissioned to write. Palfrey, bringing in the tea things, was asked to let Mrs. Stonor know that Mrs. Middleton had come and in a very short time Lilian came downstairs and kissed her sister-in-law with great affection.

'You look very well, Lilian,' said Mrs. Middleton. 'And ridiculously young to have such grown-up children.'

'It isn't as if they were really mine of course,' said Lilian seriously. 'I could nearly be their mother, but not quite.'

'All this talk about mothers is sheer vanity and one of Lilian's favourite ways of showing off,' said her undutiful stepson. 'She likes people to think I am really her son so that they will say how surprising and they never would have thought it possible.'

Mrs. Middleton laughed, but secretly she thought, with compassion, that though Lilian might look younger than her years, poor Denis looked far older than his. Then she asked about Daphne.

'Daphne was in a very good job with a doctor,' said Mrs. Stonor. 'She did secretary work for him and then he most selfishly died, so she wants another job, but I rather hope she won't find one just yet. It would be so nice to have her down here for the summer. She gave the greatest satisfaction to Dr. Browning and has a gift for adding up figures that I simply can't understand, besides knowing people when she sees them again. Oh, Daphne, here is Aunt Catherine.'

Daphne embraced Mrs. Middleton, enquired warmly after Lily Langtry and was delighted to hear that her ex-patient, now a thriving grandmother, was well and had beaten Lord Bond's Staple Selina in the milk competition, though coming second to Mr. Palmer's Phaedra.

'What a funny name for a cow,' said Mrs. Stonor.

'Mr. Palmer called her after some amateur theatricals they had,' said Mrs. Middleton, which explanation satisfied everyone. 'Jack wants to know if you will all come over after dinner. We shall be alone except for Alister Cameron whom you know.'

'Oh how lovely,' said Daphne, 'and we'll play Corinthian bagatelle. Or did Uncle Jack break it to pieces? He said he would when Denis was ill, the night you and I, Aunt Catherine, do you remember, and that nurse that was always taking offence made such a noise.'

'Yes, Uncle Jack broke it to pieces himself. And then he repented, because the British Legion would have liked it, so he bought them a new one, much better than ours.'

'But it was yours, wasn't it, Aunt Catherine?' said Denis.

'Yes, I suppose so,' said Mrs. Middleton. 'Lilian, all this "aunt"-ing. Need your family be so polite? They call you Lilian, so I really think they might call me Catherine.'

'I'd love to,' said Daphne. 'I always do except when I'm talking to you. It's an awfully nice name somehow.'

Denis said nothing. Catherine was a comfortable kind of name, but he didn't feel he particularly wanted to use it. One could always manage by saying 'you' to people. The Aunt Catherine who had been so kind to him, whom he had expected to see when his stepmother brought him to Skeynes, had mysteriously vanished. Her place had been taken by a stranger, charming enough, but someone he must get to know all over again. When he woke and found her looking at him his first feeling had been a faint resentment that he had been taken unawares. He so wished never to be treated as an invalid and she had stolen upon him, found him having what Nannie used to call a nice lay down, taken him altogether at a disadvantage. Then looking at her as his consciousness emerged from the confusion of a light sleep, he saw her eyes, and it had become, though he only realized it now, extremely important that they should look less tired.

Mrs. Stonor went back to Laverings with her sister-in-law to look at the improvements in the garden and the young Stonors were left alone. They went out onto the terrace and strolled into the little wilderness where a stream had been coaxed into miniature pools and waterfalls and planted with delicate clumps of flowers and shrubs.

'I call it very clever of Catherine to make all this,' said Daphne. 'She did a lot of it when you were ill at Laverings. I wish I were about six inches high.'

Denis thought six inches would be too small. One wouldn't be able to cross such a roaring torrent, he said, if one were that size. He thought about a foot high, tall enough to enjoy the scenery without being frightened of it. Daphne pointed out a very good place for fording the river if there were a few stepping stones and for the next hour they worked industriously at making travel easier for people one foot high and laughed so much that they didn't hear Mrs. Stonor coming towards them. So she stopped to look at them, full of gratitude that Denis looked so happy, hoping that it was a good omen for a successful summer. The one grief of her happy married life had been that she could not remove her husband's anxiety about the boy whom he loved and couldn't understand. If Colonel Stonor had lived she believed the understanding would have grown as Denis's health improved, and already there had been a hopeful basis of more toleration from the father, more patience from the son. Since she had been a widow she had devoted herself more than ever to her step-children, with a vague feeling that if Daphne had a happy time and the right clothes, and Denis was nursed and persuaded into better health, her husband would be pleased. It had meant a good deal of economy for they were not well off, but her own wants were few and she was not easily tired. She was one of the rare people in whom perfect health goes with real compassion for the weak and to Denis she had given from her strength with both hands.

Denis, perhaps unconsciously conscious of her presence, looked up and saw her. His tired lined face melted into the smile that always touched his stepmother to the quick, in which she saw all the affection and gratitude that the greediest woman could want; and she was not greedy. She came nearer, admired the stepping-stones and suggested one or two small improvements suitable for people a foot high.

'Oh, a dreadful thing,' she said suddenly, putting the last stone to a flight of steps by which travellers would get to the top of the beetling river bank, 'Lord and Lady Bond are coming in after dinner at Laverings. I did hope we would be alone, but they are agitated about something somebody wants to build somewhere and they said they must come and talk to Uncle Jack about it. If you feel too tired, Denis, Daphne and I will go and I will say you are going to bed, which will be nearly true because you will be going to bed sometime in any case.'

'I remember Lady Bond,' said Daphne. 'She came to lunch the day the Jersey calved and she knows a lot about cows, but I had been reading the Stock Breeders' Gazette when I was sitting up with Pucken the night before waiting for the calf and I caught her out once. She is one of those people that ought to have been a Colonel's wife in India if you see what I mean.'

'I'm glad she isn't,' said Denis. 'I'd love to see you arguing with her about cows and I certainly shan't go to bed. I shall read up Cow in the Encyclopaedia and confound her with my knowledge. Also I shall play the Ranz des Vaches to her on the Laverings piano.'

Daphne said she betted he didn't know what the Ranz des Vaches was.

'Of course I do,' said Denis. 'It is the tune that Swiss waiters all over the world get homesick when they hear.'

'When they hear it, you mean,' said Daphne. 'You can't say It's the tune when they hear.'

'Well, It's the tune when they hear it wouldn't make much sense either,' said Denis. 'You don't know English Usage, my girl.'

*

The party at Laverings were having coffee in the library when the Stonors came across from the White House. Mrs. Middleton told Ethel to bring three more cups and some fresh coffee, Mrs. Stonor protested that they had had coffee at home and didn't want any more, and after the senseless hubbub demanded by the conventions, got her own way. Mr. Middleton, who had made up his mind that Denis would arrive fainting, in a shabby velvet coat (for such was his rapidly conceived idea of an invalid who was a musician), was agreeably surprised to see his guest in a very ordinary smoking jacket, clean and tidy, his hair (which Mr. Middleton for no particular reason expected to have grown several inches since their brief meeting that morning) neatly cut. The boy was certainly no beauty, if not downright ugly, but he looked healthy enough in the waning summer light. And now that there was no danger to his own sensibilities, Mr. Middleton was ready enough to be sympathetic. So he asked Denis to sit by him, offered him a cigar which Denis refused and enquired how he liked the White House, and what he proposed to do during the summer. Denis said he liked the White House very much and hoped to write some music for a ballet.

'Lilian,' said Mr. Middleton to his sister, who was talking to her hostess and did not in the least wish to be disturbed, 'this boy of yours tells me he is going to write music for a ballet. That is excellent, excellent. The ballet is one of the best exercises for the young musician, for it gives him the rigid framework which is so necessary; the trellis on which the vine can put forth its luxuriant growth. The same applies to all forms of art. The picture must have a limit, hence the arbitrary shape, square, oblong, the lunette, the tondo. Sculpture too has its boundaries; the triangular pediment, the square lines of the tomb, even the actual shape of the mass of marble from which the skilled artist will release the imprisoned group or figure. Similarly with music it has been found necessary to impose upon it the form of the symphony, the sonata, to prune what is excessive that the plant may grow with more vigour. Alister!' he called to Mr. Cameron who was happily talking to Daphne about a river in Scotland where he had once fished, 'one moment. Would you or would you not agree with me when I say that of all the arts literature, at any rate in England, is that which stands least in need of bounds. That the strength of that glory of our country is such that it can climb and wander at its own will, careless of forms, or creating its own form as it goes.'

Having thus forcibly attracted the attention of his whole audience Mr. Middleton, without waiting for the reply which Mr. Cameron knew him far too well to waste his time in making, was enjoying himself immensely, when Ethel, seizing a moment between two sentences, announced Lord and Lady Bond.

As her ladyship bore down upon the company Denis at once recognized what his sister had meant when she said that Lady Bond ought to be a Colonel's wife in India. It was quite obvious that she would arrange the life of any of her friends or acquaintances without the faintest regard for their feelings, bully all the tenants for their good, be on every committee, and in short be a despotic benefactress to the whole country. Her husband, a little roundfaced man with a white moustache, followed her closely.

'How are you, Bond,' said Mr. Middleton. 'This is my sister's stepson, Denis Stonor. He is composing a ballet.'

'Are you a Russian then?' said Lord Bond. 'No, no, stupid of me, Middleton couldn't have a Russian sister.'

'I'm quite English all over,' said Denis, 'and it's an English ballet I'm trying to do the music for.'

'English ballet, eh?' said Lord Bond. 'Now that's most interesting. I thought it was Russian ballet. I know my wife took me to something Russian last summer. Not much in my line, but there was a nice bit of music by that fellow that wrote the symphony—what is its name, the one my wife's musical friends are always talking about, the Seventh. You know I always think it's a funny thing writing a symphony and calling it the seventh. I knew a man, before your time he was, Abel Fosgrave, he had a very good taste in wine and called his first daughter Septima.'

Denis said gravely that there must be something in the number seven. Lord Bond said he was probably right and the name of the fellow that wrote the symphony was Beethoven, but it didn't sound Russian, which seemed to depress him so much that Denis kindly offered to play him some of his own ballet on the piano. But before Lord Bond could answer, Lady Bond, having said what she considered fit to Mrs. Stonor and Daphne, demanded the attention of the whole room.

'Something has happened of so serious a nature that I felt I must see you at once, otherwise Bond and I would not have interrupted your family party,' said her ladyship, whose habit of speaking of her husband by his name without a prefix was the admiration of all who heard her.

'You know,' said Lady Bond, graciously including all her audience whether interested or not, 'Pooker's Piece.'

Most of them didn't, but they were too cowardly to say so except Mr. Cameron, who simply said No.

'No, you wouldn't know it,' said Lord Bond kindly. 'It is on the edge of my property, just above High Ramstead.'

'Just where we march with Mr. Palmer,' said her ladyship in a feudal way, 'on the other side of the Woolram, above the hatches.'

'Oh, you mean Overfolds,' said Mr. Middleton.

'No, no, Mr. Middleton,' said Lady Bond. 'Overfolds is the name of that triangle where Mr. Palmer's larches come down the hill. Pooker's Piece is the part at the bottom, by the little lane that runs up past old

Margett's cottage to Upper Worsted. Any of the old people would tell
you its name.'

'I thought — —' Mrs. Middleton began.

'Yes, Mrs. Middleton?' said Lord Bond kindly.

'Oh, nothing,' said Mrs. Middleton weakly, remembering that envious shepherds to whom she had talked gave that particular field a
grosser name, though Lady Bond did Pooker's Piece call it.

'Well, that is the bit of land I mean,' said Lady Bond firmly. 'And
what do you think we have heard?'

'Pooker's Piece,' said Mr. Middleton. 'The survival of these pre-
Norman names, even so near London, is excessively interesting. Pooker,
Pook, or Puck — —'

'Pooker wasn't pre-Norman,' said Lord Bond, 'I found out all about
him a few years ago. You know the living of Skeynes Agnes is in my gift.
I had to go through the records of the church there and it appears that
the Reverend Horatio Pooker was vicar from 1820 to 1843. He bought
that field from sheer spite, because my great-grandfather and Palmer's
great-great-uncle both wanted it, and left it to the Charity Commissioners.'

'And that,' said Lady Bond, determined not to be forestalled in her
news, 'is where the trouble comes. You remember Sir Ogilvy Hibberd?'

Everyone said Yes: some because they did, the others because they
felt it would save trouble.

'Well, he has bought Pooker's Piece,' said Lady Bond, 'and wants to
put a teashop and garage there. As soon as I heard of it I said to Alured
that we must see you as soon as possible.'

It was a tribute to the importance of the occasion that Lady Bond
should have used her husband's Christian name, which was only
wrenched from her by severe emotion. There was a brief silence of con-
sternation, broken by Daphne who asked who Sir Whateverhisnamewas
was.

'A Lloyd George Knight,' said Lord Bond, 'something in shipping, I
believe, from Goole. I have had to meet him once or twice on committees but my wife does not know him.'

'How did you hear about it?' asked Mrs. Middleton.

Lady Bond opened her mouth to speak, but Mr. Middleton, who had
hitherto been silent, suddenly uttered the words, 'This touches me very
nearly.'

Daphne said Why, but catching an appealing look from her stepmother, said no more.

'Pooker's Piece,' said Mr. Middleton in an enormous voice, contemplating an unseen audience in a building about twice the size of the
Albert Hall. 'If I had been asked to name one place in which the spirit
of England breathes, in which oak, ash and thorn still shelter who knows
what woodland divinities under a rustic guise, untouched since the days

of the Heptarchy, I should have named Pooker's Piece. Many is the tramp I have taken over wood and common in this countryside, with Flora enjoying every moment of it as much as I do, with that wonderful dog's instinct for what is best — not only best because Master likes it, but best in itself. Many, I say, is the tramp we two friends have taken together, but none have been so wholly blessed to us as our walks over Pooker's Piece.'

Having thus delivered himself he snapped his fingers affectionately towards Flora, who opened one eye from the rug where she was sleeping, looked at her master with complete lack of recognition or interest and went to sleep again.

'And now, Bond,' said Mr. Middleton, 'I would like to pick your brains. My man Pucken says that the little pond down beyond his cottage goes dry regularly, every seven years, whether the season is wet or dry, and is therefore poisonous to cows. I think it is an excuse to save himself trouble when the cows are in that field and he doesn't want to bring them up to the higher pond, but you know the country better than I do. Have you ever heard about it?'

Lord Bond knew Mr. Middleton well enough to be quite sure that picking his brains was only his way of saying that he meant to talk about his own views on folk-lore for at least fifteen minutes, but he was none the less flattered, having a touching belief in professional men, especially in one of his own finding. But Lady Bond put an end to his hopes by asking again in a commanding way what was to be done about it and answering her own question by saying that they had better call a meeting in the Village Hall, or better still have a drawing-room meeting first to decide who was to be asked to the general meeting.

'I don't think your room is large enough, Mrs. Middleton,' said Lady Bond, 'so it had better be at Staple Park.'

If Mrs. Middleton felt annoyed at this cavalier treatment of her house she gave no sign of it.

'You must all come, of course,' said Lady Bond graciously. 'You of course, Mr. Cameron.'

Mr. Cameron said with great presence of mind that his work made any day except Sunday impossible.

'—and Mrs. Stonor and her young people,' her ladyship continued, Juggernauting over Mr. Cameron as if he were not there.

Daphne, who had been bursting to speak ever since her stepmother checked her, saw an opening and said Denis loathed that sort of thing but she would come and help with pleasure. She was, she added, pretty good at meetings and could typewrite the notices if Lady Bond liked.

'Oh, do you typewrite?' said Lady Bond. 'That is delightful. You must come over to lunch and we will make out a list of useful people to invite.'

Daphne at once took possession of Lady Bond and so absorbed did her ladyship become in her plan of campaign that the rest of the company, to their great relief, were able to talk among themselves. Mr. Middleton and his sister sat together on the sofa while Mr. Cameron and Mrs. Middleton talked comfortably about nothing in particular. Denis, rather bored, was wondering if he could slip out and go home to bed, when Lord Bond, almost apologetically, reminded him of his offer to play some ballet music.

'I do so like a good tune,' he said, 'and I never feel the wireless is the same as a piano. I used to play a little piece by Chopin myself once. It was quite short. I wonder if you know the one I mean. It had three of those things like noughts and crosses at the beginning, and three-quarters written on the lines. Of course I only played it by ear. De-*doo*-de-doo-doo-doo, it goes, and then the same thing over again only the notes are a little bit different. De-*doo*-de-doo-doo-doo. And then the same thing again, only with just a little change, De-*doo*-de-doo-doo-doo —you don't know it?'

Denis recognized the little piece with no difficulty as the little Prelude in three-four time which everyone has played badly at one time or another. He obligingly sat down and played it with the soft pedal so that the conversation of his elders should not be disturbed.

'Thank you very much,' said Lord Bond when Denis had finished. 'I do like a good tune so much. My wife and my son like this highbrow stuff, but I do like something with a tune in it and not too long. You were going to play me one of your own tunes.'

Lady Bond from the other end of the room said, 'So amusing to hear some Chopin. Do go on, Mr. Stonor. I can't tell you, Miss Stonor, what a handicap I find it with my secretary away, and her mother's illness will be a very long one, I fear.'

Mr. Middleton sang a few bars of the Chopin in a rather tuneless falsetto and said Denis should study Bach.

Mrs. Middleton looked across with great gratitude at anyone who could amuse Lord Bond, and Denis, interpreting her look, sent her one of the smiles that so changed his ugly face. If pleasing Lord Bond would please Catherine, it should be done, though he very much doubted if his ballet music would give Lord Bond any real pleasure, when suddenly, with what he afterwards considered to the be direct guiding of Providence, a thought came to him.

'I'm afraid my stuff doesn't go very well on the piano, sir,' he said to Lord Bond. 'You see it's written for orchestra, and piano isn't quite the same. But I was wondering if you like Gilbert and Sullivan.'

Lord Bond's face, which was usually quite devoid of any expression but earnest dullness, suddenly lighted up.

'If you really could play some, not too loud,' he said, looking nervously at his wife, 'I would enjoy it so very much. My dear mother took me to *Pinafore* when I was seven, it was the first play I had ever been to and I shall never forget the impression it made on me. My wife doesn't much care for that sort of thing, but if you really could play some of the songs, I should enjoy it immensely. I suppose you don't know the words, do you?'

'Not very well,' said Denis, amused, 'but perhaps you would help, sir.'

Without waiting for an answer he began to play the Judge's song from *Trial by Jury*, very softly, while Lord Bond, transfigured, half sang, half spoke the words in a hoarse whisper. At the end of the last verse he shook Denis warmly by the hand.

'We'll have some more another time,' he said in a low voice. 'Come up to Staple Park one day when my wife is in town, mustn't disturb her you know, and we'll have what I call a real concert together. We've a grand piano in the drawing-room and I'll make them find the key, they lost it at Christmas when the piano tuner came, and we'll enjoy ourselves. And I've some really good port; you look as if a glass or two would do you good.'

He went over to his wife, leaving Denis to reflect upon the probable condition of a piano whose key appeared to be permanently lost and the best way of avoiding port which upset him at once. But he liked Lord Bond and was very willing to amuse him.

'Come and talk to us, Denis,' said Mrs. Middleton. 'We'll go outside, it's so hot indoors.'

Denis and Mr. Cameron walked out with her onto the stone flags and sat down on a bench. The late summer twilight still lingered in the north, behind the house, while before them the landscape was fading into darkness.

'You and Daphne are going to be the greatest success,' said Mrs. Middleton. 'If you can amuse Lord Bond and she can hold her own against Lady Bond, Skeynes will be more peaceful than it has been since I came here.'

'She is a good woman,' said Mr. Cameron, 'but stupid, stupid. I don't know anyone that so exhausts the air from any room where she is. Half an hour of Lady Bond makes you look more tired, Catherine, than three nights in a train. And I know what I am talking about. Mr. and Mrs. Middleton and I,' he explained to Denis, 'all went on the Orient Express one summer because Mr. Middleton wanted to meet someone who knew more about Balkan architecture than anyone else. You looked like the inside of a mushroom, Catherine, when we got to Prasvoda. But Lady Bond can produce exactly the same effect on you in three minutes. I dislike her.'

'Was the interview a success?' said Denis, who felt he ought to slur over Mr. Cameron's very unchivalrous comparison of his hostess to the inside of a mushroom, and rather resented it.

'A great success,' said Mr. Cameron. 'The man — he was an ex-prime minister whose name I could not pronounce at the time and have never remembered since – could not talk a word of English and only a few words of French. Mr. Middleton's French is, to be candid, entirely inadequate to any situation. It was the height of summer when Prasvoda is quite empty and there was no interpreter to be found. So Mr. Middleton talked to the ex-premier for three days and three nights without stopping, not even pausing to suck an orange, about the influence of Graeco-Roman civilization in Prasvoda with divagations on the Greek element in Shelley, Keats and Goethe.'

'And then?' said Denis, suddenly very tired, but amused by the story.

'We came home,' said Mr. Cameron, 'and Mr. Middleton wrote a most remarkable article on the architecture of the Orthodox Entente, Prasvoda and all those little states, between 1900 and 1936.'

'But did he need to go there to write it?' asked Denis. 'I mean if he couldn't understand what they said and they couldn't understand what he said – –'

He paused.

'How Mr. Middleton comes to know anything is an eternal mystery,' said Mr. Cameron. 'He has never been able to communicate with any foreigner unless he can speak English, and as far as I can gather from various interviews at which I have assisted none of the people whose brains he says he picks have ever got a word in edgeways. He has an extraordinary power of absorbing not only atmosphere but facts. And he never forgets anything.'

'No, I suppose not,' said Mrs. Middleton quietly.

Denis, sensitive to voices, couldn't quite make out if her words were a statement, or a question to herself. But any further reflections on this subject were cut short by his host calling Mrs. Middleton's name. One did not keep Mr. Middleton waiting, so much Denis had already discovered, and all three rose and went in.

'Catherine, I needed you, and you were not there,' said Mr. Middleton pathetically.

'I was just outside the window and I heard you at once and here I am,' said Mrs. Middleton. 'What is it, Jack?'

She laid her hand on her husband's shoulder and he looked up very affectionately.

'I need your advice, Catherine, as always. Lady Bond thinks that perhaps for a preliminary meeting Staple Park would be too large.'

He looked round him wildly, like a child who only knows half its lesson.

'What about the White House?' said Mrs. Stonor. 'I don't think the drawing-room would hold more than five people at a pinch, what with the way it goes round the corner, but we could pull the piano out into the hall, only then I suppose people could hardly get in.'

Lady Bond said with a smile of gracious impatience that she feared it would be hardly what they needed and looked at Mr. Middleton, who appeared to have forgotten his cue.

'We were wondering,' said Lady Bond, 'if it would in any way upset Mrs. Middleton's arrangements – but you can put it better than I can, Mr. Middleton.'

Mr. Middleton groaned.

'We could easily have it here, Lady Bond,' said Mrs. Middleton, adding with faint malice, 'If we have it in the middle of the week when Jack is in town, it will put no one out.'

Lady Bond protested against her host's absence and said it must certainly be on a Saturday when all the weekend residents would be obtainable. 'But not that young couple over at Beliers,' she said. 'They are Communists and the woman wears shorts and the young man has a beard.'

As no one had ever heard of the young couple at Beliers Mrs. Middleton was able to promise that they should not be asked.

'Then I think to-day week, no I am busy that day, to-day fortnight will suit us all,' said Lady Bond. 'Miss Stonor, if you will come up to the Park on Monday we could arrange about invitations and you could begin typing the notices. And perhaps you would look at the accounts for me as Miss Edwards is away and I would give you lunch of course.'

'Thanks awfully,' said Daphne. 'Dr. Browning paid me three guineas a week for doing his secretary stuff, but this won't be a regular job, so shall we say half a crown an hour and then I can come as much or as little as you like. I worked four hours a day for five days for Dr. Browning, so this would work out a little cheaper, but it's the country and nothing important, so I think that's quite fair. Then when your secretary comes back she won't be able to have the Union down on you for using blackleg labour. It'll be great fun.'

Several of the party saw in Lady Bond's eye how little she had intended to pay Daphne anything at all and felt that Providence was for once taking an intelligent part in affairs at Skeynes. Daphne's remark about the unimportance of the job also gave great pleasure, for though everyone now hated Sir Ogilvy Hibberd and wished him to be baulked at every point, he was a distant foe, and to see Lady Bond bearded in Mr. Middleton's den was a triumph that could be rolled on the tongue and thoroughly enjoyed on the spot. But her ladyship, who prided herself on doing things in a handsome way said that the arrangement would suit her very well, and catching up Lord Bond in the whiff and wind of her departure, took her leave.

'I always expect,' said Mr. Cameron, 'that Lady Bond will pick her husband up under one arm and carry him out of the room.'

'Oh, she's all right,' said Daphne tolerantly. 'You only want to get her where you want her. Most people are like that.'

'Want, up to the present, has been my master, and certainly Lord Bond's master,' said Mr. Cameron, and then Mrs. Stonor, who had for some time been worried about Denis, said they must go home.

'Yes, my dear Lilian, you must be tired,' said Mr. Middleton looking with benevolent solicitude at his sister. 'You have done much to-day. Much,' he added, so that no one should get a word in while he took breath. 'But here you will I hope find complete repose. I like to think that at Laverings and equally at the White House, the influence of many hundreds of years of settled occupation, of peaceful tilling of the soil, of the rearing of cattle, a contribution to the well-being of the country to which I am far from indifferent, having taken an infinite amount of trouble to obtain the best Jersey cows and feed and shelter them on the more modern and scientific lines, all these forces, I say, must work together to create an atmosphere in which the tension of latter day life is relaxed, is dissipated. Laverings — —'

'Pucken says Lily is going to calve again in August,' said Daphne, her handsome face alight with anticipation.

'Laverings,' Mr. Middleton continued, raising his voice several tones against this distasteful interruption, 'Laverings was already in existence, though not in its present form, before the Conquest. Wait,' he said as no one was doing anything else, though much against most of their wills, 'I should like to read you an extract from the Domesday Book in which Gorwulf-Steadings, the site of the present Laverings Farm, and the name yet survives in Guestings, one of Lord Pomfret's places in this neighbourhood, is mentioned in some detail.'

'I think I had better take the children home now, Jack,' said Mrs. Stonor getting up. 'Let's have the Domesday thing to-morrow. I am really rather tired after to-day. I don't know why, for after all the railway journey is quite short, and I had finished practically all the packing the night before and Palfrey and Mrs. Pucken had got everything in perfect order here and I had a most restful sleep this afternoon, but somehow one does get fatigued by any kind of move, so we will say good night.'

'Bear with me one moment, Lilian,' said Mr. Middleton with a patient yet gay smile. 'When my hand is on the plough I do not like to look back. Cameron, you will find the volume of which I was speaking in the third shelf from the top of the shelves to the right of the fire. I know every book as if it were my child.'

Mr. Cameron, who had at once got up and gone to look, said it was not there.

'You mistake, unless I am gravely in error,' said Mr. Middleton, rising in affronted majesty.

But even as he embarked upon his search for the book his wife said good night to the Stonors with a gentle finality that left them no choice but thankfully to slip away by the open French window.

'I have it, I have it,' cried Mr. Middleton, turning from the book-case. 'Lilian! Where is Lilian?'

'She has gone home,' said Mr. Cameron, who was standing at the window looking after the departing guests.

'I regret it,' said Mr. Middleton gravely. 'And the more so as I have just remembered that I have that book upstairs in my room. Shall I go and get it, tired as I am? I will, I will, and I will read you the passage in question.'

He made as if to go up by his little staircase, but with such a bowed gait and almost shuffling step, as of a man grown old in the service of his country and now unjustly thrown aside, that his wife went upstairs, found the book and brought it to him before he had finished his noble and vacillating journey from the bookcase to the door.

'There you are, Jack,' said Mrs. Middleton. 'And now I am going to bed. Good night, Alister.'

'Bear with me for one moment, Catherine,' said the persecuted veteran. 'I must read the account of Laverings to you and Cameron. I had promised myself the pleasure of reading it aloud, and though Lilian and her young had left us, a promise is a promise. I feel I shall not sleep if a promise is not fufilled.'

Mrs. Middleton sat down and smiled at him.

He read aloud for some ten minutes an account, extraordinarily dull to anyone who was not interested, of the manor of Gorwulf-Steadings and its appurtenances, while his wife sat apparently thinking of nothing and his partner smoked a pipe. On coming to the end of the extract he shut the book with some violence, and looked round.

'Bed, bed!' he cried. 'It is far too late for us, Cameron. We have to work to-morrow and I shall take you over to Pooker's Piece, where we shall talk to old Margett, who is wise with the wisdom of his ancestors. He knows me well and will talk to me when he would be silent with another man. And you, my Catherine, should have been in bed an hour ago.'

So saying he went upstairs.

'Good night, Catherine' said Mr. Cameron. 'You look tired.'

'You said Jack never forgot anything,' said Mrs. Middleton rather vaguely.

'You mean the whereabouts of that book,' said Mr. Cameron.

'Yes, I suppose I do,' said Mrs. Middleton with what might have been a sigh but was probably, Mr. Cameron thought, a yawn, and she went away, asking her guest to shut the French window before he went to bed. Before he shut it he took a turn on the flagged path outside and saw one light still shining through the trees at the White House. He thought it might be that amusing girl, Daphne Stonor, whose routing of Lady Bond filled him with awed admiration. As a matter of fact it was the light from Denis's room, who was too tired to go to sleep. He was

thinking about the evening at Laverings and how he had let himself in
for playing Lord Bond's locked piano and having to refuse his excellent
port. Mr. Cameron's story of his chief's visit to Prasvoda had been very
amusing. Then he remembered how Mr. Cameron had said that Mr.
Middleton never forgot anything. Mrs. Middleton's non-committal
answer came back to his mind. She had not seemed quite sure if Uncle
Jack remembered everything and Denis felt a dawning certainty that
the one thing Uncle Jack regularly and unconsciously forgot was his
wife. This thought appeared to him so worthy of attention that he
turned out his light, the better to consider it. From Laverings Mr.
Cameron saw the light go out, shut the window and went up to bed.

IV

STAPLE PARK

MRS. Middleton and Mr. Cameron were alone on Sunday morning,
for Mr. Middleton preferred as usual to breakfast in his own room. Sun
poured into the dining-room and Mr. Cameron imprisoned two wasps
in a glass jam-pot which, as he said, was all very well, but he wished he
had taken a second helping before they found their way in.

'I suppose you aren't going to church, Alister,' said Mrs. Middleton.
'Oh look, one of your wasps is getting out at the spoon hole.'

'You ought to have spoons with fatter handles,' said Mr. Cameron.
He took a small piece of the soft inside of his toast, moulded it in his
fingers and stopped up the hole. The wasp, who had twice got his head
and shoulders out, fell down again discouraged and lay kicking among
the raspberry seeds. 'No, Catherine, I am not going to church. I should
like to come and sing out of the same hymn book as you, but my employer will probably want to talk with me this morning, or rather to use
me as a talking horse, if the expression may be allowed. And apart from
the great pleasure of sharing a hymn book with you, I find the so-called
music extremely trying. Why are all hymns and psalms so high that one
can't get there? And if one sings, as I do, an octave lower, one's voice
makes no noise at all.'

'Perhaps it is all for the best,' said Mrs. Middleton. 'I always pretend
that the print is too small for me to see the words and don't sing at all
and try to look as if I were meditating. I don't suppose it really counts,
but one must go or there would be no one in the Laverings pew and the
Rector would be unhappy. Alister, would you very kindly go over to the

White House and see if any of them would care to come with me. It is so nice if one can make a good show for the Rector and even three in a pew, if one spaces them out, are a help. Church is at eleven.'

'Then I'd better go now,' said Mr. Cameron, looking at the clock. 'It's after ten. Shall I let my wasp out? He might bite Ethel.'

'Don't bother,' said his hostess. 'Ethel likes dealing with insects. She has never forgotten or forgiven an earwig that got away from her last summer by what she considered unfair means. She was just going to stamp on it when Flora ate it, so she is getting her own back on wasps this year.'

'That decides me,' said Mr. Cameron. 'I always was one for cruelty to animals, but unfairness I cannot abide. If Ethel wants to kill earwigs, well and good; but to punish a wasp for the crime of another is beyond the limits.'

He took his bread stopper out of the jam-pot. The wasp elbowed its way out indignantly and Ethel, who had come in a moment too soon, gave Mr. Cameron a glance of cold disapproval.

'I will go over to the White House now,' he said. 'What a delightful sister-in-law you have, Catherine. Why haven't I seen more of her? I never met anyone whose rather irrelevant flow of conversation covered such real heart.'

'It was clever of you to see that,' said Mrs. Middleton. 'Most people don't get beyond the talk. I think she was so unhappy when her husband died that she took to talking as a kind of defence. Not but what talking runs in the family. How Jack and Lilian ever manage to tell each other anything, I don't know, as neither of them ever listens.'

'Yes, but you know what my employer is,' said Mr. Cameron. 'He talks to you all the time, but six weeks afterwards you find he knows exactly what it was that his flow of words wouldn't let you say to him.'

'Yes, I know,' said Mrs. Middleton. 'It may be the same with Lilian, though I don't know her well enough to be sure. She certainly understands Denis and Daphne, if anyone can ever be said to understand anyone.'

'I like Daphne,' said Mr. Cameron. 'I wish we could have a secretary like her in the office. The young lady we have now is a refined product of the London School of Economics. I wouldn't mind her trying to run her pink politics down my throat, for that is a malady most incident to youth, though I never see why being a Communist should make one abhor washing and have bad manners, but she thinks she knows how to run the office so much better than I do that it leads to unpleasantness.'

'Daphne does want a job,' said Mrs. Middleton, 'but perhaps Jack's office — —'

'Yes, you are right,' said Mr. Cameron. 'My employer has always been against nepotism and though one's sister's stepdaughter is hardly a relation, I don't think it would do. And here am I standing talking with the best of them, while the fate of the Laverings pew hangs in the balance.'

He went across to the White House, found the Stonors still at breakfast and was hospitably pressed to join them.

'Well, I wouldn't say no to toast and honey,' said Mr. Cameron, 'because a wasp got into the jam-pot and I couldn't have a second helping. But what I really came for, Mrs. Stonor, was to say from Catherine that she wants volunteers for church.'

There was an immediate and gratifying response to this appeal. Mrs. Stonor said she always went to church in the country, though never in town, because church never seemed quite church in London, if Mr. Cameron saw what she meant, and they had services at such extraordinary times at Westminster Abbey. Daphne said she wanted to see what Lady Bond's Sunday hat was like and if the village idiot was still quite well, while Denis said that he would go anywhere if there was a chance of hearing Jerusalem the Golden, which he liked better than any tune in the world, especially where it went up so high that one had to squeak or stop singing altogether. This led to a very interesting discussion between him and Mr. Cameron on Russian basses which so prolonged itself that Mrs. Stonor and Daphne went over to Laverings to collect Mrs. Middleton, leaving the men to follow them.

As Mr. Cameron and Denis, still deep in argument, were about to separate in front of Laverings, the one to be talked at by his employer, the other to go across the field to the church, Mr. Middleton appeared at the garden door with a furrowed brow. It was, he said, after a perfunctory greeting to his visitors, one of the great griefs of a life now nearing its close that every Sunday brought with it duties that made it impossible for him to go to church. This very morning he had intended to accompany his wife and his sister and refresh himself in that spring of living waters the English Liturgy. But, he continued, after a rapid sketch of the development of the Book of Common Prayer, a cursory survey of the Salisbury Rule and a bird's eye view of the Reformation and its effect on the English language, his wish was not to be fulfilled. There was work waiting for him, Work, he added.

'Will you want me?' said Mr. Cameron, who had a sudden wish, that he didn't trouble to analyse, to go to church himself.

All his life, Mr. Middleton said reverently, he had played a Lone Hand. Others had wives, children, devoted friends, but he had borne the heat and burden of the day alone. Alone.

Denis thought secretly that though Mr. Middleton might not have had wives, he had a wife, but didn't like to say so. Mr. Cameron, who through long practice knew exactly the value to attach to his partner's words, said very well, he would go to church and strode off.

'Didn't he want you?' asked Denis as soon as they were out of earshot.

'Not a bit,' said Mr. Cameron. 'What he wanted was to smoke a very large cigar and go down and talk to Pucken about the cows and the hay. Which is much better for him than sitting indoors talking to me about Bitruvius. Come on, that's the last bell.'

They got into church just ahead of the Rector and went into the Laverings pew, which was right up in front with an excellent view of the Bonds' pew in the chancel. Lady Bond's hat was all that Daphne had hoped. A massive erection of brown velvet crowned with the produce of field, flood and grove, it was perched high on its wearer's head with fine disregard of fashion. Lady Bond, whose mother was Scotch, had been brought up in the best tradition of Edinburgh hats, a tradition which dies hard and still dazzles the rash beholder's eye at afternoon concerts in the Usher Hall, and always got her hats from the same shop in Prince's Street. Mrs. Middleton maintained that she had identified on Lady Bond's Coronation year hat a lobster, two hares' claws, a pineapple, a large bunch of parma violets and a fox's mask and though no one believed her, everyone admitted that she had the root of the matter in her. With Lady Bond were her husband, a female friend, and a young man, unknown to the Stonors. Mr. Cameron had the pleasure of sharing a hymn book with Mrs. Middleton, but as it was one of those hymn books with double columns and *Brilliant* type, and both worshippers were long sighted, neither was able to join in the singing, though in any case they would not have done so. To Denis's great satisfaction Jerusalem the Golden was the second hymn, and he exercised himself very happily in singing in various octaves as the tune soared or sank. Mr. Cameron greatly admired the way in which Daphne, who had a pleasant voice and no diffidence, forged gallantly through everything, when everyone but the choir (four rebellious little boys and two farmer's daughters) had failed.

'I say,' said Daphne accusingly to Mr. Cameron as they came out of church. 'Why didn't you sing?'

Mr. Cameron answered that no one could sing if they couldn't see the words.

'Well,' said Daphne, 'why didn't you put your spectacles on? People *ought* to sing. That's what one goes to church for.'

Mr. Cameron felt unequal to this religious argument and contented himself with saying that if his spectacles were double million gas microscopes of extra power he might be able to read double-columned *Brilliant*. Daphne looked at him tolerantly, said that was out of Scott or someone wasn't it, and let the subject drop. Mr. Cameron felt that he was somehow hopelessly in the wrong: first as a shirker, then as a highbrow and pretentious quoter, and though reason told him that Daphne's opinion was of little value, he had an inexplicable desire to make a better impression on her.

As the Laverings party and the Staple Park party coalesced in the churchyard, some introducing took place.

'I want you,' said Lady Bond to Mrs. Middleton, 'to know my friend, Miss Starter. It is so annoying. Miss Starter is on a diet and has to have a special bread called Kornog, which is practically starch-free. She brought part of a loaf with her — —'

'It was what I hadn't finished from the loaf I got on Thursday,' said Miss Starter, a thin middle-aged lady in black, with a faint air of royalty about her and a high black net collar. 'I usually get one on Monday and one on Thursday, which last me for a week, as I only have two slices, or at the most three, for my breakfast, very crisply toasted.'

' — and,' continued Lady Bond, looking with some pride at her exhibit, 'Miss Starter unfortunately did not bring an extra loaf, thinking she could get one here, but we find that they do not keep it at Skeynes. My cook has telephoned to Higgins with whom we usually deal and to Foxham, the other baker, but they say there is no demand for Kornog.'

'Have you tried Mopsall at Winter Overcotes?' said Mrs. Middleton. 'When Jack was on a diet two years ago we used to get a special bread from him. It wasn't Kornog, but I'm sure he would get it. I think ours was called Pepso.'

'Pepso is only starch-reduced,' said Miss Starter earnestly. 'Sir Barclay did think of it for me, but he came to the conclusion that Kornog was more what I needed.'

'Miss Starter has been attended by Sir Barclay Milvin for some time,' said Lady Bond. 'He specializes in diets, as you doubtless know. I shall certainly try Winter Overcotes. And I do hope you will come up to tea this afternoon and bring your sister-in-law and her young people. I have my son at home for a few weeks before he goes back to New York. he is doing very well there. C.W.' she called to the young man who had been hanging back during the discussion of starch-free bread, 'come and meet Mrs. Stonor, and Miss Stonor and Mr. Stonor.'

This formal introduction so paralysed all concerned that they shook hands in silence, and in silence followed Lady Bond to the lychgate, till Daphne said to Lady Bond's son,

'I say, what's your name? Your mother said C.W., but that's only initials. Haven't you got a real name?'

'Yes,' said Lady Bond's son simply, 'but I'm rather ashamed of it. My people have always called me C.W., and somehow it stuck. I think they must have been a bit ashamed of it themselves.'

'What is it then?' asked Daphne.

'Well,' said Lady Bond's son rather nervously, 'you know my father is called Alured and there's a sort of superstition that he is a bit Anglo-Saxon or something of the sort, some kind of descendant of King Alfred, only there's a gap of about eight hundred years unaccounted for, so one can't be sure. But anyway Mother thought they ought to keep up the spirit of the thing so they called me Cedric Weyland.'

'Good Lord,' said Denis sympathetically. 'I thought my name was bad enough – it's Denis – but yours must be a perfect curse.'

'There's only one thing to be thankful for,' said young Mr. Bond, 'and that is that schools aren't what they were. In my father's time a boy with a name like that would have been persecuted till he hanged himself or was taken away and sent to an agricultural college, but no one minded it a bit at Hocker's. They thought it was pretty foul of my people and I was always called C.W. And of course at Eton nothing matters.'

'Were you at Hocker's?' said Denis, interested. 'I was there for two years till I got sent abroad for a bit. Do you remember Miss Hocker's parrot?'

The two young men fell headlong into prep school reminiscences and would gladly have gone on till lunch-time, but Lady Bond after condescending to the Rector's wife had rescued Lord Bond from the senior churchwarden and called to her son to get into the car.

'We're all coming up to tea,' said Daphne, 'so you and Denis can have a good talk then. Would you like us to call you Cedric or C.W.?'

'Whichever you like,' said young Mr. Bond, getting in beside the chauffeur. 'No one I like ever called me Cedric, only governesses and awful things like that.'

'All right, we'll take the hoodoo off and say Cedric,' said Daphne. 'If I'm coming to do secretary stuff for your mother I'll have to call you something.'

Young Mr. Bond seemed to be taken aback by this news, but the car rolled away before he could make enquiries.

*

'C.W. is such a nice boy,' said Mrs. Middleton as they walked homewards. 'His parents have been a sore trial to him at times, but he bears with them wonderfully. He is in some business firm with a branch in New York. Of course, when Lord Bond dies he will have to live in England and look after the estate and all Lord Bond's interests. Denis, would you care to come over to Laverings before tea and try our piano? Jack and Alister are going for a walk after lunch, so you wouldn't be bothered.'

Denis thought that most people would have said You won't be a bother, and gratefully accepted.

*

Sunday lunch at Laverings was always the same; what Mrs. Middleton called the sacred Sunday joint, followed by a pie of whatever fruit was in season, which happened to-day to be cherries. She herself would like to have ordered milder and cooler food for a hot June day, but any attempt to change the ritual made the iron eat so deeply and loudly into her husband's soul, that she had quite resigned herself. What with beef and cherry pie and beer, Mr. Cameron would gladly have stretched himself on one of the long chairs outside the house and gone to sleep till it was time to go to Staple Park, but his senior partner was inexorable, so Mr. Cameron made up his mind that he would at least walk him off his legs in revenge.

'Don't forget, Jack,' said Mrs. Middleton as the two men were starting, 'that we are all having tea with the Bonds about five.'

Mr. Middleton groaned.

'I had it in my mind,' he said, 'to take Cameron first to Pooker's Piece, where we shall talk as man to man with old Margett, talk racy of the soil, and then to tramp, burning the long miles beneath our feet, over to Worsted, by the ruins of Beliers Abbey, to Skeynes Agnes and so home, talking as we go.'

'That is about fifteen miles,' said Mr. Cameron grimly.

'If you did the walking, Jack could do the talking,' Mrs. Middleton murmured. 'If I leave it to you will you get him to Staple Park by 5 o'clock?'

Mr. Cameron said he would. Mr. Middleton called loudly for Flora who was sleeping off her dinner in the sun. She got up and sauntered towards her master, but suddenly realizing that she was pampering him sat down with her back to him and thought of other things.

'If you don't want to come, don't,' said Mr. Cameron.

Flora at once got up and approached him, her liquid eyes fixed adoringly on his face.

'Here, Flora,' said Mr. Middleton, 'carry Master's stick. Many is the mile that she has carried my stick or my newspaper, rejoicing in her dear doggy mind that she can be of help to Master. Here Flora!'

Flora, who understood and resented this statement, took the proffered stick and trotted into the library, where she laid it on the floor by her master's desk and returned for applause.

'No, no, Flora. Master's stick for walkies,' said Mr. Middleton. 'Fetch stick for walkies.'

But as Flora, who had no intention of encumbering her walk with a large stick, remained deliberately stupid and oafish, Mr. Middleton had to go and fetch his stick and announced himself ready for the walk. Flora, who liked long walks, decided that her master had been sufficiently put in his place, pushed her nose against his hand and led the way to the garden gate.

Mrs. Middleton went into the library and cleared some books and papers from the piano in case Denis wanted to open it. Then she picked up a book and lay down on the large sofa. The summer peace of Laverings reigned undisturbed. Mrs. Middleton opened her book, but her thoughts immediately slid away to the White House. She had a great fondness and a deep admiration for her sister-in-law, although circumstances had never allowed them to become very intimate. Colonel

Stonor had not been an easy man to live with and Mrs. Middleton knew that only a woman so entirely selfless as Lilian could have dealt with her difficult situation as she had done. From an embittered and disappointed father and two rebellious children, one of them a perpetual anxiety in his health, she had somehow in the few years that Colonel Stonor had lived made a united if not always an harmonious family. With Daphne and Denis she had never attempted to exercise any authority, but both children had felt that it would be a shame to be unkind to so confiding a creature. Owing to her unceasing kindness and her apprehensive nature, Denis had called her the pleasing anxious being, adding not unkindly that the only forgetfulness she wasn't a prey to was a dumb one, for her vague talk ran on, just as did her brother's more reasoned flow of speech. Everyone felt when Colonel Stonor died that Providence had arranged quite nicely, for Daphne would surely marry and Denis could live with his stepmother and be cared for. Daphne had not yet married and the three of them lived happily together. That she should marry again herself had not entered Mrs. Stonor's head and it is improbable that Denis or Daphne had thought of it either, for though she was so little older than Denis, one's father's wife wasn't a person that one connected with marriage, except of course to one's father, a subject from which one mentally shied, feeling that 'that sort of thing' wasn't at all in keeping with a person so obviously destined to look after one as Lilian.

Lilian Stonor was of firmer character than her brother, and this Mrs. Middleton quite realized, having found that behind her vague loquacity there were reserves and reticences that no one could approach. She had no intention of trying to penetrate these defences herself, in fact liking her sister-in-law all the better for them. What Lilian thought of her she could not guess, but she hoped that the summer would bring a closer relationship, involving no sentiment, founded on respect and liking; for Mrs. Middleton was often alone, or lonely, she wasn't sure which word to use. Her masterful husband leaned so heavily on her for strength that though she grudged nothing she felt from time to time a weariness of the spirit. It might be more blessed to give than to receive, but there had been times when she would have given a year's life to be the receiver and not the giver. Her longing to step aside for a moment, to lean on a shoulder, to give gratitude as freely as she gave help was very great, so she had taught herself that one can't have things both ways and mocked herself for sentimental weakness. Good friends she had, but none to whom she spoke much of herself, except in a gentle sardonic way that made them find her good if baffling company. Alister Cameron was probably the nearest to a confidant that she had ever known, but even so their bond was largely their common wish to defend her husband who must be allowed to show his façade of strength to the world, unhindered by his own weakness.

So hot it was, and so confusing are one's thoughts of oneself, thoughts that are apt to tend to self-pity unless one laughs in their face, that Mrs. Middleton went to sleep, or something so near sleep that Denis, coming in by the garden door, thought he had better not play the piano and sat down patiently to wait. Though he was very quiet and didn't even light a cigarette, the consciousness of a presence in the room troubled her light oblivion and she sat up suddenly, shedding book, spectacles, spectacle case, bag and one shoe.

'Oh thank you so much,' she said, as Denis collected her property and restored it to her. 'I am so sorry. Why didn't you amuse yourself with the piano?'

'Well, I did think of it,' said Denis, 'but thought I it would be too affected.'

'Affected?' said his hostess. 'But you were coming over specially to play.'

'I know,' said Denis, 'but I mean you were asleep and besides being rude to wake you up, it would have been rather too much theatre to awaken sleeping heroine with soft music, don't you think?'

'Perhaps,' said Mrs. Middleton absently, suddenly recognizing in her guest a spirit almost as self-mocking as her own. 'Yes. I expect you were right,' she added with more vigour. 'But do play now. I can write some letters and not disturb you in the least.'

Denis begged her not to as he wouldn't be disturbed whatever she did and then felt this was rather a proud, conceited way of putting it and began to stammer so much that Mrs. Middleton quickly asked him about his ballet music. He looked at her from his dark sunken eyes with a moment's suspicion that he was being offered a toy or a sweet to keep him quiet, but reassured by the entire truthfulness in her face he did tell her about his ballet music, with such growing interest in himself that it was suddenly half-past four, and his stepmother and Daphne were on the terrace.

'Good heavens! Lady Bond! 'cried Mrs. Middleton. 'I'll be ready in a moment. Come in, Lilian, and be cool. Denis was telling me about his ballet.'

'Did you play that bit to Catherine that I never can remember?' said Mrs. Stonor. 'The bit I like?'

Denis, who appeared to recognize this particular bit with no difficulty from her description, said he had only told her about it.

'Denis!' said his sister reproachfully. 'Telling's no use at all. Why on earth didn't you play?'

'It was a matter of the finer feelings,' said Denis pretentiously. 'Come and play the Merry Peasant.'

Daphne, all willingness, sat down at the piano with her brother and they performed a version of that beginner's bane arranged by Denis for four hands as vulgarly as possible, which always made them have the giggles, and the giggles they were still having when Mrs. Middleton came down and carried them all off in the car to Staple Park.

Staple Park, the seat of Lord and Lady Bond, had been built by Lord Bond's great-great-grandfather Jedediah Bond, a Yorkshire manufacturer of woollen goods who had come south to spend part of his vast fortune and found a family. He had acquired fame in his own part of the world by paying his operatives less and working them longer than anyone in the South Riding and had with his own hands shot three ringleaders in a gang of machine breakers dead, and dragging two others into his counting-house by their collars had fought them both till they lay bruised and bleeding on the floor. He had then jumped down fifteen feet into the yard, picked up a child of one of the strikers, its arm and leg broken in the tumult after the shooting, galloped with it ten miles to the nearest surgeon and paid for the treatment that led to its subsequent complete cure. A few years after the Repeal of the Orders in Council he was able to retire to the South, and built a mansion upon an approved slope overlooking an ornamental water, a Palladian bridge that led from and to nowhere in particular and a wall the whole way round the estate. It was before him that the regrettable gap of eight hundred years in the Bond's Anglo-Saxon pedigree appeared, and though he called his eldest son Ivanhoe, no researches were able to supply with even a reasonable degree of probability the thirty generations or so that were missing. Ivanhoe Bond had gone into Parliament for one of Lord Pomfret's rotten boroughs; his son Athelstane Bond had entered the House after an expensive but on the whole honourable election and pushed his way resolutely to the front on philanthropy, and his son Ethelwulf had carefully married money and received a peerage in 1907. Alured the second and present Lord Bond was as good a man of business as his great-great-grandfather Jedediah, and fully as philanthropic as his grandfather Athelstane; but besides being almost more dull than any peer has a right to be, he had an extremely kind heart and looked after his tenants with an amount of real kindness that would have shocked his grandfather, who calculated his love of his fellow men on a basis of two and a half per cent. He had married Lucasta, half-sister of the present Lord Stoke, with whom he had a more or less friendly rivalry in pedigree cows. When he succeeded to the title his wife who never forgot that she had been an Honourable in her own right, became the great lady of the district to that extent that she had made a good many enemies; but the various charities and deserving causes of the county knew very well that provided she was allowed to be Lady Bountiful her cheque book and her really invaluable services as chairman were always at their disposal.

Their only son, whom we have already met, was a faint, a very faint disappointment to them, for though his career had been steady and he was a dutiful son, he saw amusement in things that his parents did not

find at all funny and had shown no wish to marry. A few years earlier
he had greatly admired a niece of Mr. Palmer, the most important
neighbouring landowner, but his parents had so fostered and encouraged the attachment that it had died almost as quickly as, under the
influence of amateur theatricals, it had arisen. For a family, which with
the slight gap before mentioned, ran back to Alfred to have no grandson was a disgrace that Lady Bond did not wish to contemplate, and
the disgrace was if possible made more acute by the fact that when her
half-brother Lord Stoke died, her son, unless Lord Stoke had absent-
mindedly married his cook, would also come into Rising Castle, though
not into the title which would become extinct.

Thr Laverings car, driving up the mile and a half of scented lime avenue, turned round with a swish of gravel in the large sweep and drew
up before the majestic flight of stone steps on which so many guests at
dinners and balls had got wet until Lord Bond's father had built a little
side entrance with a covered way for rainy weather. The immense
pillars of the portico were golden in the afternoon light and to pass into
the cool black and white marble front hall was to be dazzled by darkness. Tea was being served in the long inner hall. This uncomfortable
room was the core on the four sides of which the gigantic suite of drawing-room, dining-room, saloons, octagon rooms, garden rooms, were
built, and owing to its position was lighted from a lantern in the roof,
except for such light as came through the great glass doors of the marble
hall. On its gloomy walls, covered with a deep red paper of everlasting
quality, the founder of the family had hung an enormous number of bad
but highly varnished copies of second-rate Old Masters. The floor was
encumbered by tables with gilt lions' claws and inlaid marble tops,
cassoni, copies of Canova and Gibson, screens of stamped leather, and
two enormous globes, one terrestrial and one celestial.

The butler steered the Laverings party through the half-light to
where Lady Bond in a useful coat and skirt and wearing a useful felt
hat was installed on a sofa that had belonged to Pauline Borghese, pouring out tea. Miss Starter was the only other guest present. The company
were accommodated with chairs of various degrees of discomfort and a
couple of Chinese stools which the Prince Regent had given to young
Ivanhoe Bond in very inadequate repayment for certain money lost at
cards. Denis and Daphne politely sat on the stools, which were so low
that they felt like children looking over the edge of the nursery table.

'Spencer. Get some cushions for Miss Stonor and Mr. Stonor,' said
Lady Bond.

The butler brought two massive cushions of faded red velvet trimmed
with tarnished gold insinuated them onto the stools and departed. Denis
and Daphne sat down again and found themselves so high above the
table that the rest of the company looked like dwarfs. Brother and sister
began to laugh.

'Those cushions,' said Lady Bond, 'were brought from Brussels by my husband's great-grandfather. They always used to be on the sofa in the little yellow satin room, but I had them brought into the hall last year.'

This interesting piece of history was of a nature to kill conversation and everyone sat dumb, Lady Bond apparently not minding in the least, till Miss Starter said that there was a shop in Brussels where she had once got some very good charcoal biscuits.

'I love charcoal biscuits,' said Daphne. 'When we had them for a dog of ours I always ate half the tin. I suppose one gets black all over inside if one eats enough.'

'Oh, *no*,' said Miss Starter, shocked, but on being pressed by Daphne for her reasons could not give any.

'I expect your young people would like to see the house, Mrs. Stonor,' said Lady Bond. 'When Bond and C.W. come in I will get C.W. to show them the rooms. He and Bond have been looking at the heifers. We expect to do well with our cows at the Skeynes Show. How are yours doing, Mrs. Middleton?'

'I believe they are all quite well,' said Mrs. Middleton. 'Jack talks to Pucken about them every day, not that he really knows anything about them.'

'Lily Langtry will be calving about then; it's an awful shame,' said Daphne. 'She'd have loved to go to the Show, Pucken says. Is Mr. Palmer sending his Phaedra up, Lady Bond?'

'She is calving too,' said her ladyship, with some satisfaction. 'But my brother, Stoke, will probably have a walkover. No one has a cow-man to touch his. Lord Pomfret would give anything to get him.'

So happily did this conversation go on that Miss Starter was able to annex Mrs. Stonor and tell her all about the use of bran as a corrective. Miss Starter, who was really an Honourable, was the daughter of that Victorian statesman, litterateur and bearded impostor Lord Mickleham, whose photograph by Mrs. Cameron, draped in a rug and wearing a kind of beefeater's hat, is familiar to all students of the Mid-Victorian period. Lord Mickleham was the author of *Cimabue: a Poetical Drama in Prologue, Five Acts and Epilogue*, which was once performed by Irving and never again. As he had married three times his descendants consisted largely of nephews and nieces who were older than their uncles and aunts, thus causing much social perplexity, but the Honourable Juliana Starter, the youngest of his eighteen children, had the whole family at her finger tips and was always ready to explain it to anyone who wanted to know.

'It was when I was In Waiting to Princess Louisa Christina,' she said, 'that Dr. Williams, a very delightful man and quite in advance of his times, recommended bran to Her Highness.'

'We used to have bran pies when we were small at Christmas,' said Mrs. Stonor.

'Dr. Williams certainly did not recommend it to Her Highness as a pie,' said Miss Starter, doubtfully.

'In a wash tub with red baize round it,' said Mrs. Stonor, her eyes shining wistfully at the thought, 'and we always made a frightful mess.'

Mrs. Middleton, who had been listening, thought it time to interfere before Miss Starter went mad under her eyes, so she asked if Princess Louisa Christina was not a daughter of Old Prince Louis of Cobalt. This at once led the talk onto the Royal Family and its relations, a practically unlimited sphere for people who know their Debrett well to triumph quietly over their friends and even Miss Starter's well-bred, plaintive voice was raised a little.

'Well, I feel quite certain somehow that Princess Louisa of Cobalt was a Hatz-Reinigen,' said Mrs. Stonor. 'I can't think why I feel it, but I feel as if I had heard it or read it somewhere in the way one does you know.'

'I don't quite think so,' said Miss Starter. 'Princess Louisa's sister married one of them, but the Princess — dear me, I should know her name as well as my own. Here comes Lord Bond, we will ask him. Lord Bond,' she said as the owner of Staple Park and his son came to the tea-table, 'we were discussing the mother of Princess Louisa Christina. Do you remember — — ?'

'Princess Louisa Christina?' said Lord Bond. 'Her mother used to drive a brougham and pair. Married old Cobalt. Her marriage was annulled. Shocking business; shocking. Where's Middleton, Mrs. Middleton?'

Mrs. Middleton said he was out walking with Mr. Cameron and might be back at any moment.

'When you have drunk your tea, Alured,' said Lady Bond, 'will you take Mrs. Stonor's young people through the principal rooms. I feel sure they would be interested.'

Lord Bond obediently gulped his tea and stood up.

'I'll come with you,' said young Mr. Bond, who could not abide Miss Starter, and avoiding his mother's eye he joined Denis and Daphne for the tour of the house.

Lord Bond had a real passion for his ancestral seat and if he had not been so well off would have been quite happy to show people round it at sixpence a head every day. Unfortunately for him the house was only shown to visitors when he and Lady Bond were away. He had once made an excuse and hurried back to Staple Park from Aix-les-Bains, hoping to enjoy the pleasure of the sightseers, but his butler had been so unkind and cutting that he had not even dared to ask if he might spend the night in his own house and had to go over to his brother-in-law Lord Stoke, who was not only an archaeologist but very deaf and incredibly boring. So he gladly seized the opportunity that his wife gave him of showing the house to his visitors and led the way through the marble hall to the dining-room.

'That's the marble hall,' he said as they walked across it. 'Black and white marble. We had a very good central heating system put in a few years ago and that's where one of the mantelpieces was cracked when the men were in the house. Here is the dining-room. We don't use it much unless we are a large party. You can't see it very well with all the shutters closed.'

'I'll open them, father,' said young Mr. Bond.

'No need, no need,' said Lord Bond. 'Plastered ceiling and all that, you know. It's very much admired. Portraits of my family and their wives. All want cleaning I think, but my wife likes them as they are. I was talking to a man at the club last time I was in town, forgotten his name. He said he cleaned his with slices of raw potato, but old Carruthers who was there said he did his with soap and water. Now we come into the south octagon room.'

The south octagon room, lined with locked bookcases with gilded grills across their front, was admired but Lord Bond left them little time to express their admiration, hurrying them on through a door masked with sham books. Daphne lingered.

'I do like those doors with books on them,' she said. 'If I had a house I'd have one and choose the names of the books.'

'I always thought I'd like to do that,' said young Mr. Bond, lingering with her. 'My great-something-or-other that built this place hadn't much imagination. He just thought of one book for every shelf and said Vol. I, Vol. 2 and so on.'

'I see,' said Daphne, examining a shelf which contained twenty-four volumes of an imaginary work entitled *Historical Survey of Taste*. 'If I had a door like this I'd have a lot of names of real books like *History of England* or *Life of Gladstone* and then when people tried to get them out to read they couldn't.'

'I don't suppose anyone would want to get out a *Life of Gladstone*,' said young Mr. Bond doubtfully. 'One would have to have an awfully dull set of friends to want books like that.'

'But don't you?' said Daphne. 'I mean judging by Miss Tartar I should say you did.'

'Miss Starter,' young Mr. Bond corrected her.

'Well, I said Miss Tartar,' said Daphne. 'Oh, Miss Starter. I see. Well, she's dull enough.'

'I can tell you I'll be glad to get back to New York,' said young Mr. Bond fervently. 'I love this place and my people are jolly decent, but the kind of guests they have. . . . Let's go round the rooms the other way.'

Accordingly they went back to the dining-room where young Mr. Bond opened some of the shutters and let in the afternoon sunlight so that Daphne could admire the ceiling, exquisitely plastered in low relief with sheaves of corn, wreaths of vine leaves and tendril and bunches of grapes, painted in what were called Pompeian colours.

'I don't know why father was in such a hurry,' said young Mr. Bond as he closed the shutters again. 'Come across the hall and I'll show you the yellow satin room and the musical boxes that my great-grandmother collected.'

'And tell me about your cows,' said Daphne.

If she and her companions had stayed with Lord Bond they would have discovered the reason for his hurry. His lordship paused inside the room they now entered and said reverently to Denis, 'Look!'

Denis looked. In front of him was one of the most nobly proportioned long drawing-rooms he had ever seen, lighted by six long windows almost the height of the room. The ceiling and the walls were decorated with exquisite carvings, painted white and gold, and the fireplace was a masterpiece in pale golden marble. A few English landscapes of the early nineteenth century hung on the white walls. The furniture, serene, fitting, unobtrusive, must have been there since the house was built. Denis almost gasped with pleasure at its quiet mellow beauty.

'I thought you'd like it,' said Lord Bond. 'My old great-great-grandfather and his son spent a lot on the furniture. It's been in Country Life. But there's something I really wanted you to see. Look there!'

Taking Denis by the arm he pivoted him round so that he looked into the corner of the room to which his back had hitherto been turned. In it stood the largest, most hideous, most elephant-legged grand piano that Edwardian money could buy. Over its bloated form a piece of Turkish embroidery, glistening with little bits of looking-glass was carelessly draped. On it stood two large bronzes of matronly nymphs in the respectful embraces of decent satyrs, a huge green glass vase of coloured pampas grass on an oxidised silver stand representing the Three Graces in Art Nouveau style, three elephants' tusks, at least a dozen signed photographs of royalty in massive chased silver frames and a richly bound volume of the songs of Alicia Adelaide Needham.

'I knew you'd like that,' said Lord Bond, as his visitor stood spellbound. 'My old pater gave it to my dear old mater the year he got his peerage. The most expensive English piano on the market. And we've always kept it exactly as it was when she used it. The pater bought those bronzes at the Paris Exhibition in 1900. The mater was very fond of flowers. I remember those grasses when I was a boy, and the mater used to sing to me before I was taken to bed.'

Denis, gazing awestruck on the late Lady Bond's memorial, wondered how on earth her ladyship had managed to use a piano which could only be opened with the aid of two or three strong men, for each of the bronzes must have weighed half a hundredweight, and came to the conclusion that she preferred to make her effects in a small way.

'She had a way of playing all her own,' said Lord Bond, almost echoing Denis's thoughts. 'She always put the soft pedal down and played the notes one after the other.'

'Arpeggios?' Denis suggested, fascinated by the vision.

'That's it,' said Lord Bond. 'She said it put more expression into the music. Now, I wonder where the key has got to? The butler used to have it in his pantry, but when the piano tuner came on his yearly visit the Christmas before last Spencer was away for two nights owing to the death of his wife who lived in Wolverhampton and the key could not be found. So I put it in the drawer of the writing table and when I went to look the other day it wasn't there. But we'll find it, we'll find it, before you come and play to me.'

'I hope so,' said Denis.

'Of course we will,' said Lord Bond. 'Where have your sister and C.W. gone? Is your sister musical?'

'She's got a nice voice, sir,' said Denis.

'We'll have a concert, all to ourselves, some day,' said Lord Bond. 'My wife isn't musical, she's artistic. Well, now I expect you'd like to see the rest of the rooms. We'll find your sister and my boy somewhere about.'

So saying he led Denis through the farther door of the drawing-room.

*

Meanwhile in the hall Lady Bond, free from her family and the young Stonors, had outlined to Mrs. Middleton her scheme for the drawing-room meeting at Laverings. As far as Mrs. Middleton could make out it was to be Lady Bond's party, chosen by her, at her own time, but Laverings was to supply the tea.

Mrs. Middleton had often wondered if it was worth while standing up to Lady Bond, but every time she had come to the conclusion that it wasn't. It was in her nature to give way, to be silent, and she followed her nature, not without inner mocking at herself. If her husband wanted Lady Bond to use their drawing-room, it would be less trouble to arrange for a few chairs and some cakes than to argue the point. Sometimes she wondered if there was in her anything strong enough to stand up to facts that she didn't like, but to demand one's own way always seemed an unnecessary and almost ridiculous glorification of self, so she let things slide, contenting herself with keeping her house perfectly appointed, cultivating a few friends and being a loving companion and supporter of her husband's quick moods of overbearing wilfulness or despairing abasement.

Miss Starter said she wished the dear princess were still alive, as she would gladly have taken the chair.

'Of course you must come to the meeting if you are still with us,' said Lady Bond. 'I think your husband must take the chair, Mrs. Middleton; unless of course my brother — —'

She paused. Mrs. Middleton, reflecting that either suggestion would annoy her husband so it didn't much matter, said nothing.

'Then that is settled,' said Lady Bond rising. 'Your men are very late, Mrs. Middleton. Let us go and see what my husband and the young people are up to.'

As they went into the marble hall they met Mr. Middleton and Mr. Cameron.

'We have been waiting for you,' said Lady Bond with grim graciousness. 'I will have some fresh tea made, or would you prefer a drink?'

Mr. Cameron at once said a drink, so Lady Bond told the butler to bring drinks into the yellow satin room, and swept the whole party onwards. By this time Lord Bond and Denis had been round the whole suite of rooms and rejoined Daphne and young Mr. Bond who had been amusing themselves by listening to the musical boxes that Athelstane Bond's wife had collected and talking about cows, so her ladyship had no idea of the length of time that her son and Miss Stonor had been alone together.

'It was a marvellous walk, a marvellous walk,' said Mr. Middleton, who felt that it was quite long enough since proper attention had been paid to him. 'Flora — where is Flora by the way?'

'I told the butler to shut her out,' said Mr. Cameron. 'She had been twice through the duck pond in the village and the water is low.'

'So be it,' said Mr. Middleton. 'Bond, this was a walk that you would have loved. The whole soul of England was abroad on the hills to-day.'

'Crowded, eh?' said Lord Bond. 'That's the worst of all these cheap excursions by rail and coach on Sundays. Spoils all the walks. Why didn't you go over by Pooker's Piece? No one goes that way.'

'We did,' said Mr. Cameron.

'Well, I'm surprised that you found it crowded,' said Lord Bond.

'And what a talk we had with old Margett,' said Mr. Middleton, ignoring the misunderstanding.

'I expect he did all the talking,' said young Mr. Bond. 'He's as deaf as a post now, but he does love the sound of his own voice. It was very kind of you, sir. The old fellow doesn't often get an audience.'

'I didn't hear Margett say much,' said Mr. Cameron to a private audience of Mrs. Middleton and the Stonors. 'He did say Good afternoon when we found him and I think he said Good evening when we left him. Middleton was in great form.'

Mrs. Middleton looked at him half in amusement, half imploringly, while her nephew and niece burst into delighted laughter.

'It is quite extraordinary how much Jack can talk,' said Mrs. Stonor. 'It was just the same when we were small. I sometimes think it is because he hasn't quite grown up.'

'Darling, I do love you when you are mystic,' said Denis. 'I am sure you are right, but do tell me what you mean.'

'Well,' said Mrs. Stonor, frowning in painful chase of a thought, 'you know the way children do all their thinking aloud because they are too silly to think to themselves and how dull it is. Jack still does his thinking aloud, though of course it isn't dull, and it must run in the family because I do too, and I know I say a good many silly things, but it seems to me the only way to get at what one really wants to say. I'm doing it now.'

She looked round for her audience's opinion.

'I think your criticism is extraordinarily good, but you aren't quite fair to yourself,' said Mr. Cameron seriously. 'I don't suppose you ever are.'

'That's clever too,' said Denis. 'She isn't.'

Lady Bond's voice now dominated the party, asking how far the walkers had been.

'We left Laverings at three o'clock,' said Mr. Middleton. 'No; no sherry I beg. A whisky and soda if I may. It is now nearly six. Say four good miles an hour, for Cameron and I are stout walkers, that would be ten miles, eleven miles or so. But it did not feel like half so much.'

'It often doesn't if you don't notice it,' said Lord Bond. 'I remember once walking round the park here, nearly five miles that is if you keep to the wall, with Carruthers when he was Under Secretary for India, and when we got back we only had just time to get dressed for dinner. Extraordinary how time flies.'

'And I'm afraid we must be going,' said Mrs. Middleton.

Good-byes were said and Lady Bond reminded Daphne that she was to enter upon her secretarial duties to-morrow.

'That's right. Half a crown an hour,' said Daphne. 'Thanks awfully. I'll love it.'

Lord Bond courteously came to the door to see his guests off, the Middletons and Mrs. Stonor in the car, Mr. Cameron and the young Stonors walking. When he turned back into the marble hall he found his butler looking at him with an air of disapproving though long-suffering ennui that Lord Bond could hardly bear. Every memory of old wrongs sprang to his mind. The time he had come home from Aix-les-Bains and been practically driven out of his home. The key of the piano. His old wounds burned and bled anew.

'Spencer,' he said in an off-hand way, 'I can't find the key of the drawing-room piano. I left it in the writing table drawer.'

'I found it in the eskritaw drawer, my lord, when I was Giving a Look Round,' said the butler, fixing his employer with a basilisk eye, 'so I took it into My Pantry where it belongs.'

'Well, put it back in the escritoire drawer,' said Lord Bond, finding himself much to his annoyance using his butler's nomenclature. 'I might want it at any time.'

'Yes, my lord,' said Spencer. 'I was merely thinking, my lord, that when the piano tuner came it would be advisable to have the key where I could Put My Hand On It.'

'Never mind that,' said Lord Bond, too cowardly to remind his butler of the Christmas when the piano tuner had come and the key could not be found.

The butler bowed acquiescence and went away in the opposite direction from his pantry, thus leaving his employer in a state of pleasing uncertainty as to whether he meant to obey orders or not.

*

The walking party were going back to Laverings by the foot path. It led them by fields of springing wheat, through pasture land, followed the course of disused lanes where the hedges were pink with dogrose and yellow flags grew in the ditches. The heat was intense and no breath of air stirred.

'How far did you really walk, Mr. Cameron?' said Denis. 'Was it ten miles?'

'When your uncle said that we left Laverings at three and got to Staple Park before six, he was speaking the truth,' said Mr. Cameron. 'But he didn't say that we got to Pooker's Piece at half-past three and that he talked to old Margett—notice that I don't say with old Margett—till half-past four, or that we stopped at the Beliers Arms at a quarter to five for a soft drink, where Mr. Middleton harangued the soft drinking public on the iniquity of building on Pooker's Piece. I should say four miles at the very outside.'

'Uncle Jack is a bit of a windbag,' said Daphne. 'I sometimes can't think how Catherine sticks it.'

'She is very fond of him you know,' said Mr. Cameron.

'Of course she is,' said Daphne. 'I mean when people are married to each other they have to be, unless they are getting divorced or something. Oh, let's hurry up. I can hear the six-twenty hooting before the viaduct and we'll be in time to see it go over. I love that.'

She quickened her pace, followed by her companions, and in a very short time they had reached the top of a hill where some cows were grazing. In front of them lay the valley of the river Woolram, spanned at this point by a handsome viaduct, the work of Brunel. Even as they looked a toy train came puffing out of Mr. Palmer's woods on the left, puffed across the viaduct and ran into the cutting on Lord Bond's property on the right. Daphne drew a deep sigh of pleasure.

'I adore looking at that train,' she said. 'Come on.'

'I'm coming,' said Denis, who had been leaning against a tree, surveying the panorama.

Daphne looked at him with a peculiar expression that Mr. Cameron did not understand. They continued their walk at a slower pace and Mr. Cameron thought that Daphne was not in her usual spirits. In fact she almost snapped at him once or twice and so much did this prey on his spirits that he dressed for dinner in a very low frame of mind and did not trouble to set Mr. Middleton right when he boasted again of the long tramp they had taken that afternoon. Later in the evening Mrs. Middleton said she must take a scarf that her sister-in-law had left in the car over to the White House, so Mr. Cameron said he would come with her. They found Mrs. Stonor and Daphne playing six pack bezique.

'How nice of you, Catherine,' said Mrs. Stonor as soon as she saw the scarf. 'I knew my scarf must be somewhere, because I had it when I started and when I got back it wasn't there. Poor Denis was so tired that I sent him to bed and made him have his dinner there. Luckily it is Palfrey's Sunday out, so I was able to take his dinner up without offending her. Do come up and see him, Catherine. He can never sleep when he is overtired and company is a good distraction. Mr. Cameron, do you play bezique? If you do you could finish the game with Daphne. I never like to leave a game unfinished. Not because of superstition, because I really don't think there is any special superstition about it, but it seems so untidy and one always hopes one might have won.'

Mr. Cameron sat down at the card table, when Daphne startled him by picking up all her cards and banging them down on the table in a heap, saying defiantly that she was a beast. On being questioned she said that anyone who wasn't a beast and also a born fool would have seen that to make Denis hurry up the hill in the heat was an idiotic thing to do and she wished she were dead. Mr. Cameron, trying to comfort her, said it was just as much his fault, but Daphne, scorning such an easy sop to conscience, said rubbish.

'You didn't know,' she went on, banging violently at each eye with her handkerchief rolled into a tight ball, and then glaring at Mr. Cameron. 'It wasn't your fault a bit. Denis always gets knocked out with the heat and I was an idiot to make him hurry. Now he'll be on Lilian's hands for a couple of days, while I do Lady Bond's silly invitations. I wish I was dead and everyone was dead.'

'Not everyone,' said Mr. Cameron, as he sorted the cards and put them neatly into their box.

'Well, pretty well everyone,' said Daphne with less heat.

'I'll tell you what,' said Mr. Cameron. 'If Mrs. Stonor sees you have been crying it will be very upsetting for her on the top of Denis being unwell.'

Daphne said she knew that, and anyway she hadn't been crying.

'So,' said Mr. Cameron, ignoring this untruthful remark, 'we had better fake the score for the game we didn't finish and put a good appearance on things. Who would have won, do you think?'

Daphne looked at him with admiration.

'You do have good ideas,' she said, 'and I was a beast not to think of it. Lilian was seven hundred and fifty ahead of me, so let's say she won.'

'Wouldn't she feel more comfortable if you won?' asked Mr. Cameron.

'Yes, she would be more comfortable, but she'd be a bit suspicious, because I never do win. Give me the markers and I'll fix it.'

In this agreeable task of forgery Daphne forgot that she was a beast and confided in Mr. Cameron that she liked doing secretary work, but would much rather live in the country and have a cottage and keep pigs, but she couldn't possibly do that because if she and Denis and Lilian all lived together it was fairly easy, but none of them could really afford to live alone. She then enquired where Mr. Cameron lived and on hearing that it was the Temple said it must be awful to live there, which depressed Mr. Cameron a good deal.

'Of course,' said he, after a short silence during which he had been following his own train of thought, 'your uncle manages to have his home in the country and do his work in London. It might be possible.'

'But Uncle Jack's *quite* different,' said Daphne. 'I mean he earns pots of money and Catherine is rather rich herself. We'll have to stick to London.'

'I wasn't thinking so much of you,' said Mr. Cameron thoughtfully.

'Who of then?' said Daphne. 'We weren't talking about anyone else.'

Mr. Cameron suddenly realized that he couldn't easily explain that he was thinking how to organize his own life so that anyone who happened to be married to him could live in the country while he went up to town every day, but luckily Mrs. Middleton and Mrs. Stonor came downstairs. Mrs. Stonor was much happier about Denis and said he was all the better for Catherine's visit.

'He really is getting stronger,' she said as she accompanied her guests to the gate. 'Dr. Hammond always said he would outgrow his delicacy and I believe he will. If only he could get away on his own. I do wish he could get a job and Daphne would marry someone very very nice, and then I should feel comfortable.'

'And what about you?' said Mrs. Middleton very affectionately. 'Wouldn't you be lonely?'

'Oh, I'd be all right,' said Mrs. Stonor vaguely. 'I might have a very small flat somewhere and take up my painting again. I don't seem to have had time to do any for years. Thank you so much for bringing the scarf, Catherine. I simply knew it must be somewhere, because of having started with it and then not having it when I got back. Good night, Mr. Cameron. Do come again whenever you are down here. Denis likes you so much. I must see if Palfrey remembered to take the back door key, otherwise I'll have to sit up for her, but I don't suppose she'll be late.'

Mrs. Middleton and Mr. Cameron walked for a few moments in the garden before they went in.

'That was a tremendous compliment that Lilian paid you,' said Mrs. Middleton. 'She makes Denis a kind of touchstone for her friends; not a bad one.'

'He is a very nice boy,' said Mr. Cameron, 'but I thought he was too much wrapped up in himself and his music to notice people.'

'I think he sees an enormous amount without looking,' said Mrs. Middleton. 'Some kind of sixth sense. At any rate you have a passport to Lilian's heart now. Let's go in and talk to Jack. By the way did you and he really go ten miles on this boiling day?'

'Not more than four at the outside,' said Mr. Cameron. 'But I didn't think it worth mentioning at the Bonds'.'

By now they had reached the library door and the light shone on Mrs. Middleton's face as she threw him a look of grateful understanding, and they went in.

V

DAPHNE GOES TO WORK

On Monday morning Mr. Cameron went back to town without seeing any of the Stonors. Denis had quite recovered from the effects of the heat and began work again on the score of his ballet, while Daphne pumped up her bicycles tyres and rode over to Staple Park. Leaving her bicycle at the foot of the stone steps she rang the bell.

'I say,' she said when a footman appeared, 'do you think I could leave my bicycle there, or will someone pinch it?'

The footman thought he had better ask Mr. Spencer and shortly returned with that official who looked at her bicycle as if it were a new and loathsome species of beetle and told the footman to wheel it into the bottle room. The footman went down the steps and Daphne followed the butler across the marble hall.

'What's the bottle room?' she asked.

'The room where the empties is kept, miss,' said Spencer. 'Being on the ground level, Charles can wheel your bike in there with no exertion and will bring it round for you when required. Miss Stonor, my lady,' he said, opening a door in the dark centre hall.

Lady Bond's sitting-room was a pleasant room at a corner of the house, furnished with bright uninteresting chintzes. Her ladyship in another useful coat and skirt was walking up and down smoking.

'Good morning, Miss Stonor,' she said. 'Would you like a glass of milk before starting work, or some biscuits?'

Daphne thanked her and said she never ate anything in the morning.

'Quite right,' said Lady Bond approvingly. 'But Miss Starter has such a habit of glasses of milk at odd hours that one gets into the way of expecting it. You will be glad to hear that the man at Winter Overcotes whom Mrs. Middleton recommended can supply Kornog. I think it is all rubbish myself, but Miss Starter has a very delicate digestion and having no other occupation since Princess Louisa Christina died she thinks a great deal about it. Now, if you will sit at that table I will dictate a list of the names for the drawing-room meeting and a circular letter to accompany each invitation.'

This she did in a certain masterful way that Daphne could not but admire. When she had finished she said she had to go and see the head gardener and would be back in an hour. Miss Stonor would find paper, carbons and everything necessary in the table where the typewriter was. Daphne took the cover off the machine and made a face at it as she recognized a very old out-of-date model, but she had to make the best of it, so she sat down and began her work. After some time the door opened. Daphne who was wrestling rather angrily with the typewriter didn't look up.

'Mother,' said a voice, adding 'Oh, it's you.'

Daphne looked up and saw young Mr. Bond.

'Hullo,' he said, 'are you secretarying?'

'As far as this machine will let me,' said Daphne. 'I'm going to tell your mother she ought to have a new one.'

'I'd like to see my stenographer's face in the New York office if anyone gave her a machine like that,' said young Mr. Bond examining the gigantic and cumbersome superstructure with awe. 'Are you staying to lunch?'

Daphne said she was.

'All right,' said young Mr. Bond, 'I was going to cut lunch to avoid the Starter, but now I shan't.'

'O.K.' said Daphne. 'Oh, damn this machine.'

'When you see me at lunch, please give a start of surprise,' said young Mr. Bond and left the room.

When Lady Bond got back Daphne handed her a pile of envelopes correctly addressed, each containing a letter explaining the object of the drawing-room meeting and an invitation card. Lady Bond approved and Daphne asked where she would find the stamps.

'Oh, Spencer stamps all the letters,' said Lady Bond. 'And now I want to discuss with you a letter to the local newspaper and one to our M.P.'

Daphne opened her shorthand book and laid it on the table.

'Before I start taking down the letters, I'd better tell you that this machine is hopeless,' she said kindly. 'I don't suppose you use it yourself so you couldn't know. It must be a pre-war model and it can't have been cleaned since it left the works.'

'Is it really as bad as that?' asked Lady Bond, examining the typewriter, about which she obviously knew nothing. 'I can't think why Miss Knowles, my secretary, never mentioned it.'

'I expect she hadn't the nerve,' said Daphne. 'But I'm sure she'd be awfully grateful and work twice as fast if you got her a new one.'

'Well, I'll ask my son about it,' said Lady Bond. 'He knows all about offices. You were right to mention it.'

The rest of the morning passed quickly and Daphne found she enjoyed working with Lady Bond, who wasted no time and knew exactly what she wanted to say. When they went in to lunch Miss Starter, who was measuring her medicine at the sideboard, told Daphne how delighted she was to find that Kornog bread was procurable.

'Of course,' she said, as she took her place at the table, 'I could have written to London for it, but it all takes time and I certainly could not have got a loaf before Wednesday, whereas now, thanks to your prompt action, Lucasta, I shall have it this afternoon. Will you thank your aunt very much, Miss Stonor, for her kind help.'

'Well, she's really not an aunt at all,' said Daphne. 'She only married my stepmother's brother. But I'm awfully fond of her.'

Although Daphne did not really much care whether young Mr. Bond came in to lunch or not, she felt he needn't have made such a parade of secrecy over something that he was going to forget at once. The dining-room door opened and she looked up, but it was Spencer, who bending over Miss Starter's chair said confidentially,

'I thought you would be glad to know, miss, that your diteetic loaf is come. I have given instructions for your usual slice, lightly toasted, to be brought to you immediately'.

He had hardly finished speaking when a footman came in with a small silver toast rack containing a slice of Kornog, lightly toasted and cut into four small triangles. This he placed beside Miss Starter.

'Thank you so much,' said Miss Starter. 'Oh, but Spencer, they have cut off the crusts again. I did ask for the crusts to be left on, as my doctor says half the good lies in the crusts.'

Spencer said deferentially that he would Let Them Know about it, but with a wealth of implication that froze Daphne's blood. He then signed to the footman to remove the toast rack, but just as that underling was carrying it away young Mr. Bond came in by the service door and nearly cannoned into him.

'What have you, Charles?' he said. 'Toast? I adore toast. You didn't think to see me, Miss Starter,' he continued, dangling the toast rack from one finger. 'I found I wasn't out to lunch after all, so I came back through the kitchen, and Mrs. Alcock said there was cold salmon so here I am. How do you do, Miss Stonor. Have some toast.'

'Don't eat that, C.W.,' said Miss Starter imploringly.

'Why not?' asked young Mr. Bond, putting about four ounces of butter on one of the small triangles and munching it. 'No, Spencer, no macaroni, it's too hot. Just the salmon and rather a lot of it, especially if there's one of those bits that have what one might call a little salmon fat between the flesh and the skin. Is it poisoned, Miss Starter?'

'The crusts have been cut off,' said Miss Starter.

'I'm all in favour of that,' said young Mr. Bond, carrying another butter-laden triangle to his mouth. 'I always give my crusts to the dogs since I got too old to hide them under the rim of the nursery tea-tray.'

'But practically the whole dietetic value lies in the crusts,' the guest persisted. 'Besides, toast and salmon entirely neutralize each other. That is why I am not having any. Just the salad.'

'It seems awful waste to have salmon if one doesn't eat it,' said Daphne, in whose life Scotch salmon did not occur very frequently.

'Well, I can neutralize anything,' said young Mr. Bond with fine want of logic. 'Cider please, Charles.'

'That is really enough, C.W.,' said his mother. 'And I want your advice. Miss Stonor says the typewriter is not in very good condition.'

'I've always wondered how poor old Knowles stood it,' said young Mr. Bond, taking an enormous helping of Charlotte Russe and emptying the cream jug over it. 'All right, mother, this isn't greedy; it's only taking what you ladies have left. That typewriter must have been left over from the year grandfather got his peerage. I believe he bought one to answer the congratulations.'

'Then I had better order a new one,' said her ladyship, 'and I shall scold Miss Knowles for not having mentioned it before.'

'I don't suppose she dared,' said young Mr. Bond. 'I'll choose you one and have it sent down. Which machine do you use, Miss Stonor?'

Daphne said she liked a Revotina, but Lady Bond ought to choose. Miss Starter said that the princess's secretary always used a Gladinon, so young Mr. Bond said he would have a Revotina sent down as soon as possible if his mother approved.

When they had had their coffee Daphne asked Lady Bond if the same time to-morrow would do, and said good-bye. Young Mr. Bond opened the dining-room door for her and managed to shut himself outside.

'Shall I run you home?' he asked.

Daphne said her bicycle was in the bottle room.

'The devil it is,' said young Mr. Bond. 'Do you mean to say you ride one of those things.'

Daphne said she was poor but honest, and why not, so they went across the marble hall, through a door, along a stone passage with several corners, down a flight of stone stairs, past what looked to Daphne like several hundred bells all hanging curled up and ready to spring with their names written above them on a board, and so past the boot room to the bottle room.

'By Jove, we do have a lot of empties,' said young Mr. Bond. 'I wonder who gets the twopences on them.'

'Your butler I should think,' said Daphne. 'And I bet he does pretty well over the stamps too. Your mother says he stamps all the letters.'

'I always wondered how my letters got stamped,' said young Mr. Bond reflectively. 'I must ask my lordly father to let me see Spencer's book. I have an idea that there is some dirty business on foot. One gets suspicious in New York. I say, may I try to ride your bike? I haven't been on one since I was ten.'

Daphne gave permission, and to the uncontrollable joy of three under-gardeners and a couple of under-housemaids who had no business on that side of the house at all, the heir to the estate was seen wavering down the drive till he fell off into the rhododendrons. So enchanted was he with this new toy that he insisted on accompanying Daphne home, sometimes riding the bicycle till he fell off, sometimes running behind her while she rode, and sometimes wheeling it while they both walked. By the end of the journey he had so much improved his style that he said he would get a bicycle for himself and they would go for picnics.

'You'd better hire one,' said Daphne. 'It's no good your buying one if you won't be staying here. When did you say you went back to New York?'

'Not till September. I'm doing a job of work for them over here,' said young Mr. Bond, 'but I don't always need to be in town all the week. Could I have a drink of water or something? It's a thirsty sport.'

'You'd better stay to tea,' said Daphne. So young Mr. Bond did stay to tea, and found Mrs. Stonor so easy to talk to that he told her a great many quite uninteresting things about himself and enjoyed himself vastly.

'I'm sorry I forgot the start of surprise at lunch,' said Daphne when he at last tore himself away. 'And I forgot to call you Cedric too. I somehow wasn't sure if your mother would approve.'

'Probably not, but she will,' said young Mr. Bond. 'Call me anything you like so long as it isn't Seedric as matron at my prep school used to say. Was Miss Plimsoll there in your time, Denis?'

'Yes, indeed. It was in my second term that her lower teeth fell out of the bathroom window,' said Denis, 'and a boy called Pringle thought they were a gift from heaven and kept them in his best knickers pocket for two days, till Miss Plimsoll found them herself when she was getting out clothes ready for chapel on Sunday.'

'All right, I'll say Cedric,' said Daphne. 'And it's awfully nice having you here. What with you and Catherine and all the cows, it's going to be a lovely summer. And Mr. Cameron at weekends. I like him almost better than anyone I've ever met, don't you?'

Upon this artless declaration young Mr. Bond walked all the way home in deep gloom and nearly didn't send for the typewriter after all. But reflecting that if he didn't Daphne might give up coming to Staple

Park altogether, he wrote to the Army and Navy Stores that very night.

*

The next two weeks passed uneventfully. Lady Bond found Daphne extremely helpful with the accounts and on several occasions kept her on till tea-time. Daphne enjoyed seeing into the works of a big house and garden and made one or two suggestions to Lady Bond which her ladyship passed to her husband, who said Miss Stonor had a head on her shoulders. Young Mr. Bond had to be in town daily, but managed to see a good deal of the Stonor family in his spare time. He and Denis laughed together over their reminiscences of Hocker's, and Mrs. Stonor listened kindly to all he had to say about himself.

When Mr. Middleton was in town in the middle of the week, some-times spending a night or two at his club, Mrs. Middleton took to dropping in very frequently at the White House to gossip with her sister-in-law, whom she got to like more and more. On the first occasion of her husband's absence she sent word to Denis that the piano would be at liberty and he came over at tea-time.

'I didn't come sooner,' he said, 'because I thought you might be resting.'

Mrs. Middleton, who had indeed been resting but would not at all have minded the piano, was touched by this consideration and told Denis that he must use the piano whenever he liked so long as Uncle Jack wasn't at home. So he gradually lost his shyness and came over every afternoon while his difficult step-relative was away. Mrs. Middleton went in and out, sometimes gardening within earshot of the music, sometimes writing letters in her sitting-room next door, sometimes sitting with a book, or only musing while Denis played and frowned and put down hieroglyphics on scored paper and complained that her good piano was ruining him as a composer. By the end of the second week he had so far conquered his diffidence as to play Mrs. Middleton most of the music that he was composing for a ballet. When he had finished playing Mrs. Middleton said nothing. At last she said, 'It sounds very grown-up to me.'

'I am grown-up, you see,' said Denis. 'I rather think it's my misfortune.'

'Very few of one's friends are,' said Mrs. Middleton. 'I'm not; and I think that's my misfortune. So how discontented we all are,' she added laughing.

Denis looked at her with one of his quick searching looks.

'I knew that the first time I saw you,' he said. 'Not when I was here before, when I was ill, but as soon as I saw you the first day we were here.'

Ethel now brought tea in and while they partook of it Mrs. Middleton asked Denis when the ballet was likely to be produced.

'That's the trouble,' he said, with a quick darkening of his eyes. 'The artist is there for the decor — no one you've heard of but very clever; the choreographer is there and understands every note I write; I have nearly done my music and it is right for dancing; that's what makes it sound grown-up probably. But as usual the people who would like to put it on haven't any money to back it. Meanwhile it's fun, and if I go on feeling as well as I do here I'll be able to get a cinema organ job. I wouldn't mind going up and down on a golden lift five or six times a day with bears' grease on my hair and bowing in a pale and interesting way to the audiences. Uncle Jack can build me a super cinema, and Lilian shall be receptionist because she loves fussing over people, and Daphne shall be secretary. A family affair.'

'Do I come into the family?' asked Mrs. Middleton.

'Of course. You'll be here, ready to comfort Uncle Jack when he says he is certain he forgot to allow for the weight of the audience on the dress circle. And Daphne and Lilian and I will come down to you all rich and jaded on Saturday night late, in a car full of champagne bottles, and go back after Sunday lunch for the five o'clock session.'

'That sounds very nice,' said Mrs. Middleton. 'And talking of nothing in particular, do you all realize that this Saturday is the drawing-room meeting here about Pooker's Piece?'

'We do, indeed we do,' said Denis. 'It has cast a blight over our lives for days. Daphne seems to have done nicely with the invitations, and half the county is coming. I hope Uncle Jack will come up to the scratch. Can I bring over some chairs from the White House? There is one my bedroom that squeaks and one in Daphne's room that has one leg shorter than the others.'

Mrs. Middleton said she would love to give the one with the squeaky leg to Lord Stoke, who was deaf, and then Ethel came in to announce that Mrs. Pucken wished to speak with Mrs. Middleton and was waiting in the kitchen to that end. She was told to bring her in and shortly conducted Mrs. Pucken into the drawing-room.

'Good-afternoon, Mrs. Pucken,' said Mrs. Middleton. 'Do sit down.'

Mrs. Pucken, feeling the immense moral superiority to be gained from standing, said she would prefer to stay where she was and would like to speak to Mrs. Middleton.

'Is it about Lou?' said Mrs. Middleton.

Mrs. Pucken said Lou was a handful of trouble and then looked so ominous that Denis offered to go.

'Don't disturb yourself, sir,' said Mrs. Pucken. 'Lou's a troublesome girl, but it's not what you call trouble this time. Not like my eldest niece. That girl's got herself into trouble again, madam, that is to say she doesn't know if it's trouble yet, so we hope for the best and expect the worst. But Lou is a good girl, at least as far as that goes.'

She paused for effect and Denis nervously began to put his music together.

'I'm sure I don't want to disturb you and the young gentleman, madam,' said Mrs. Pucken looking severely at Denis who stopped arranging his music and sat down again. 'It's this meeting, madam, about Pooker's Piece. Seems Pucken's old grandfather used to live up there in Margett's cottage as is now, and Pucken always talked a lot about the Piece. He has a kind of fancy his people used to live there in the old days and it used to be called Pucken's Piece. A lot of ideas he gets into his head,' said Mrs. Pucken, to whom the word ideas meant rubbish, 'but he gets talking about it of an evening sometimes. I don't pay no attention to Pucken, but Lou she's a regular dad's girl and listening to Pucken keeps her out of harm's way, for they do say it's at the pictures that most of the harm gets done.'

She looked at Denis, who felt that she suspected him of practising debauchery in the sixpenny seats at the Winter Overcotes Odeon and wished he could get under the piano.

'Well, Mrs. Pucken,' said Mrs. Middleton.

'It's this way, madam,' said Mrs. Pucken. 'Miss Daphne's been talking about this meeting Lady Bond's having about Pooker's Piece and nothing will content my young lady but can she come and hear the speeches. Rubbish, my girl, was what I said when she began about it, don't you get getting ideas into your head, but she goes on about it enough to drive you wild, so at last I said, "Look here my girl, I've had enough of this. I'll speak to Mrs. Middleton about it and see what she says. But don't think you can scamp your work." '

'Well,' said Mrs. Middleton, 'I really don't see why Lou shouldn't come. I'm afraid she'll find it rather dull.'

'She's quite a one for an outing,' said Mrs. Pucken. 'And I'll see she cleans herself proper before she comes. It's very good of you I'm sure, madam. Perhaps I'd better come along of Lou myself to keep an eye on her and I could give Ethel and the others a hand with the washing up afterwards.'

'Yes of course, do come with Lou,' said Mrs. Middleton, feeling that things were gradually getting out of control.

'Thank you very much, madam, I'm sure. And Miss Palfrey is taking quite an interest in the meeting too.'

'Miss Palfrey?'

'Lord, I didn't know Palfrey was a fan of Lady Bond's,' said Denis.

'Mrs. Stonor's maid, madam,' Mrs. Pucken explained. 'Her father was a naval captain in an oil tanker.'

'You'd better ask Mrs. Stonor then,' said Mrs. Middleton firmly. 'If she can spare her maid of course you can bring her. Good afternoon, Mrs. Pucken.'

Mrs. Pucken, who always knew when the gentry had had enough of her, withdrew and Mrs. Middleton and her guest fell into helpless laughter. Why the staff of the White House should want to attend a drawing-room meeting on preserving the amenities of rural England was beyond their comprehension. Denis said they could now give Mrs. Pucken the squeaking chair with a clear conscience and let Lou, who was skinny, have the chair with one short leg. Then he gathered up his music and said good-bye.

'Come again next week for music, Denis,' said Mrs. Middleton.

'It's a funny thing, but I still don't say Catherine to you,' said Denis irrelevantly. ' "You" is the nearest I can get.'

'It's not very near,' said Mrs. Middleton, truthfully.

'Well, I wish your eyes didn't look tired,' said Denis, and went back to the White House. His stepmother and Daphne were in the garden by the little stream and he told them how Mrs. Pucken and Palfrey wanted to come to the meeting. They were amused, but quite as much at a loss as he was. After dinner they all sat outside again. From the kitchen came a ceaseless babbling of voices, mixed with the clash of silver and china in the sink. Denis said there seemed to be a good deal of company to-night.

'Only Mrs. Pucken and Lou,' said Mrs. Stonor. 'Mrs. Pucken is always in the kitchen lately. I only pay her for the mornings, but she comes up nearly every night with Lou. She and Palfrey are great friends and it means I never have to think of what to do with remains of pudding or cold potatoes. What they talk about all the time I can't think.'

The subjects of the foregoing remarks were finishing the after-dinner wash-up. Lou had just been scolded by her mother for leaving the knives in the sink while she dried the china.

'How many times have I told you that's not the way to do the knives,' said Mrs. Pucken to her daughter. 'Take all them knives out of the sink and put them in that white jug. Now you can put some hot suds in the jug but don't let it come up to the handles. Rot the handles right off the blades, my girl, that's what you'll do, leaving them in the sink like that. Why the cook I was second kitchenmaid under when I first went out, she'd have thrown the rolling pin at me likely as not if she'd seen me done a thing like that. And no giving back sauce neither,' said Mrs. Pucken accusingly to Lou, who had not yet opened her mouth.

'My father used to take the slipper to we girls if we didn't have everything the way he liked it,' boasted Palfrey. 'I'm glad of it now though. Same as Lou will be glad you spoke to her about those knives. Don't forget what your mother says, Lou. And you do the fish knives and forks the same way, and the little tea knives if they have nice handles, and the carvers. Now you can pour away those suds out of the jug and fill it up with hot water and then take the knives out and dry them.'

Lou emptied the suds out of the jug, letting one knife escape with a clatter into the sink, thus causing Palfrey to draw in her breath with a hissing sound. She then put the jug under the tap and refilled it with hot water. As she withdrew it she hit the jug against the tap. A crash was heard and a three cornered piece of china fell into the sink.

'All right, my girl, you don't go to the meeting to-morrow,' said Mrs. Pucken in gloomy triumph. 'Here, give me the cloth. Miss Palfrey and me'll finish the drying. You're just like your dad, all thumbs. Put the cloth on for supper and don't forget the cruet.'

While Lou, sniffing loudly, laid the table, the two elder ladies rapidly finished the wash-up and the dry-up. Mrs. Pucken said she would just wash the cloths through and hang them up, as Miss Palfrey wouldn't be boiling till Monday, if Miss Palfrey would put out the things. By the time she had done this Palfrey had set the cold lamb, the cold potatoes, a bottle of Piccalilli, the remains of a trifle and a large piece of cheese on the table and they sat down.

'That's enough, Lou,' said Mrs. Pucken sharply to her daughter who was sniffing, 'and there's others besides you wants the cruet. Pass it to Miss Palfrey. I shan't be coming up to-morrow night, Miss Palfrey. I'll stop on at Laverings and give the girls there a hand. There'll be a big wash-up after the meeting and tea, and four for dinner with Mr. Cameron coming.'

Here Lou stopped sniffing and gave a yelp.

'Whatever *is* the matter,' said her exasperated mother.

Lou was heard to mumble that she wanted to go to the meeting.

'All right, go to the meeting, only stop that noise. Nobody said you wasn't going,' said Mrs. Pucken, who like a true mother had forgotten her threat as soon as she had uttered it. 'You'll be able to have a good look at Lady Bond, Miss Palfrey, and young Mr. Bond too, I expect.'

'We've seen plenty of young Mr. Bond round our place,' said Palfrey. 'Always coming to tea he is. I must say though,' she added, wishing to give credit where credit was due, 'that it's a treat to see him eat. I don't suppose he's Spoken yet.'

'Get on with your supper, Lou, listening like that to what Miss Palfrey says,' said Mrs. Pucken to her daughter whose eyes, ears and mouth were wide open.

'Do you mean Mr. Bond will Ask Miss Daphne?' Lou breathed in a hoarse romantic whisper.

'If you was to get on with your supper, Lou, the way your mother tells you, you wouldn't need to be asking all them questions,' said Palfrey, with fine kitchen logic. 'It's my belief, Mrs. Pucken, it's as good as Settled. But she's quite right not to be too easy with him. Does them good to wait. I've been walking out nine years now with my friend.'

'Quite right too,' said Mrs. Pucken. 'The worst day's work I ever did was giving up a good place at Staple Park to marry Pucken when we'd only been going together three years and I hadn't even met his mother. A fine old lady she was. She had seven sons and she made them all give her their wages every Friday night. Of course when I took Pucken I took care of his money, so the old lady went off it was a fair treat they say and that's how I never met her after all. Well, we must be going, Miss

Palfrey. I'll be in to-morrow early, so don't bother about the rest of the wash-up to-night. Has Miss Daphne got Mr. Bond's photo in her room?'

'I couldn't say, I'm sure,' said Palfrey, suddenly becoming a faithful retainer. 'Not on the mantelpiece where the other photos are.'

'But she's got a snap of Mr. Cameron,' said Lou, her virgin heart impelled by Aphrodite to express her passion. 'I sor it on the table the day I was doing the room out with you, Mum.'

Upon this shameless statement both ladies fell on Lou with accusations of prying and Nosey-Parkering and prognostications of a bad end, so that she went home bellowing loudly, but not on the whole unhappy, for had she not borne witness for her chosen hero just like Glamora Tudor in *The Flames of Desire* when she told wicked Lord Mauleverer that it was really the Duke she loved.

As for Daphne, she had taken the snapshot of Mr. Cameron in the garden at Laverings the previous weekend and liked to see her own handiwork. She still thought him one of the nicest people she had ever met, but was also much attached to young Mr. Bond, and really thought very little about either.

VI

PRELUDE TO A MEETING

On Saturday morning a kind of ferment was going on in all the houses which we already know and in various others with which the reader of this work may already be familiar. At Worsted for example Mr. and Mrs. Palmer at the Manor House were having one of those differences of opinion which sometimes made breakfast a little alarming to visitors. Mrs. Palmer, although professionally a rival of Lord Bond and Mr. Middleton where cows were concerned, felt that public spirit about the amenities of Pooker's Piece should rise above any private feelings. His wife, who was of sterner stuff, regarded any meeting held by the instigation of Lady Bond as anathema, for she had never forgotten the day on which the Bonds' cowman had allowed a bull to get mildly out of control and been indirectly the cause of a slight accident to her youngest niece.

'Yes, yes, Louise,' said her husband, 'that's all very well, but it wasn't Lady Bond's fault that the bull got loose. And the meeting isn't at Staple Park, it's at Laverings. Nice woman, Mrs. Middleton. We ought to go, my dear. Can't let this fellow build on Pooker's Piece.'

Mrs. Palmer said Lucasta Bond was capable of anything, and how Mrs. Middleton could submit to having Lucasta's meeting in the Laverings drawing-room she didn't know. Her husband wisely retreated behind the Stock Breeders' Gazette and when Mrs. Palmer had said a little more of what she felt towards Lady Bond she suddenly remembered that she had heard that Mrs. Middleton's sister-in-law's step-daughter, who was doing secretarial work for Lady Bond while Miss Knowles was away, was a nice girl and good-looking, and might be available as fresh theatrical talent; for Mrs. Palmer's production of Greek plays and Shakespeare in a converted barn was one of the celebrated features of Worsted, and *Twelfth Night* was already in rehearsal. So she said presently that she supposed they would have to go and she would order the car for three o'clock and had promised to take the Tebbens. Mr. Palmer replied that Lord Stoke had bought a bull from Mrs. Leslie at Rushwater and so the discussion closed.

At about the same moment Mr. Leslie who hated the telephone and Lord Stoke who was very deaf, were deliberately misunderstanding each other on the telephone about the delivery of the bull. After some very unhelpful conversation Mr. Leslie tried to convey to Lord Stoke that he meant to go to the meeting at Laverings that afternoon and would discuss the matter with him there if he were going. As Lord Stoke was reminded by the word Laverings that he had quite forgotten that he had been asked to take the chair or propose a chairman, he wasn't sure which, and took full advantage of his deafness not to hear any of Mr. Leslie's attempts to speak, Mr. Leslie banged down the receiver, though not before he had expressed his views on other people's want of sense, leaving his lordship placidly repeating himself to a dead wire, all to the infinite pleasure of the telephone exchange. And it was owing to the deep interest taken by the young lady operator that Mrs. Tebben at Lamb's Piece was unable to get unto the Worsted shop and order some tinned apricots for a cold supper when she got back from the meeting.

'It is too provoking, my dear,' she cried gaily to her husband who had heard her trying to telephone and hoped it wasn't anything he need pay attention to. 'The exchange won't answer at all. I wanted to get some of those Empire apricots, cheaper than Californian and quite as good, for our little meal to-night. Well, cheese is always our great stand-by and the piece we have left needs finishing. You are coming to the meeting about Pooker's Piece, dear, aren't you? Louise Palmer said they would drive us.'

Mr. Tebbens, who wanted with all his soul to stay at home and write an article for the Journal of Icelandic Studies on Bishop Ogmund, said he didn't think he need go. His wife replied, yet more gaily, that needs must when the devil drives and Louise was coming for them soon after three or else a little before and she must go and cut a cabbage.

'Think!' she added dramatically. 'Our own cabbage! I shall tell Mrs.

Phipps to shred it very fine with just a taste of onion and we shall have an excellent salad from our own garden, except for the onion which I must confess is the last of that string of them I bought from the man who was all looped with them and went bad so soon.'

Her husband, vaguely wondering who the devil in this particular case was, and why a man looped with onions had gone bad, turned eagerly to his work again and was re-absorbed into sixteenth-century Iceland.

At Pomfret Towers old Lord Pomfret was in the estate room looking at the Ordnance map with his agent, Roddy Wicklow.

'Can't think why the Government allows people like Hibberd,' said his lordship angrily. 'Had him once on a committee. Feller was wearing a Guards' tie. Extraordinary the way these new men don't know anything. Pooker's Piece. Nice little bit of meadow-land and Palmer planted a nice screen of larches on the north side,' said his lordship who knew every inch of the country. 'Like the feller's infernal impudence to want to build on it. I suppose I'll have to go over to the meeting. Laverings: that's down the narrow lane half a mile outside Skeynes, isn't it. I remember that lane. Nearly killed there when I was a young man. Driving a dog cart and we met a waggon full of hay. I was a silly young fool then and tried to pass it. We went right into the ditch and broke one wheel and the mare couldn't be used again for a month. Well, I'll go, but I know the car will stick in that lane.'

'I couldn't go for you, could I?' said Roddy Wicklow, who was not only devoted to his employer, but a kind of connection, as his sister had married Lord Pomfret's cousin and heir.

'No, no, you've got to see Sir Edmund Pridham and the Council Clerk about those County Council Cottages,' said Lord Pomfret. 'No good my going, I'd only lose my temper. Confounded counterjumper that clerk is. I'll go to Laverings. Daresay I'll lose my temper there too, but that won't matter. Heard from your sister to-day?'

'Yes sir. They seem to be having a splendid time at Cap Martin and little Giles is getting brown all over.'

'That's right,' said his lordship approvingly. 'I'll be glad to see them back though. House seems a bit empty without the little chap.'

And Lord Pomfret fell into a muse as he thought of the six months old baby who was later to bear the title of his only son, killed so long ago.

*

At Staple Park Lady Bond was being driven almost to frenzy by Miss Starter's anxiety about the tea at Laverings.

'If,' said Miss Starter plaintively as they sat down to lunch, 'I could be sure that Mrs. Middleton had *real* China tea, I should feel more at ease, but so many of one's friends have what they call China tea and certainly isn't, for half an hour after drinking it I always have a peculiar feeling. Now real China tea, like yours Lucasta, leaves me feeling absolutely free from any feeling at all. I suppose I shall just have to do without my tea altogether.'

Lady Bond always invited Miss Starter to Staple Park for a long visit in the summer because she was an old friend of the Bond family and bore genteel poverty in London lodgings very courageously. But every three or four days her guest so exacerbated even her not very sensitive nature that she heartily wished she had not been so kind. Since the Kornog bread had been got from Winter Overcotes Miss Starter had been unusually placid, but for the last twenty-four hours she had talked of China tea till her hostess could have bitten her with pleasure.

'Well, Juliana,' she said, 'we will take some of my tea with us and I'll ask Mrs. Middleton if she will have a pot made specially for you.'

'Oh dear me, no,' said Miss Starter. 'I should feel so nervous and uncomfortable that I am sure all my feelings would come on, worse than ever. You know worry is really at the basis of everything; it can poison the most healthy person. I say to myself every night, "Do not worry. Do not worry. Do not worry."'

'That's all wrong, Miss Starter,' said young Mr. Bond, who had been hoping for some time that his mother's guest would choke on a fishbone and die. 'What you ought to say is "I am not worrying." Keeps the old Ego in much better order.'

'Oh, is that what you do?' said Miss Starter.

'Well, not exactly. The fact is I simply don't worry at all. It saves me a lot of trouble. More of those nice little new potatoes, Spencer. They look a bit young to have been killed, but they taste uncommonly good.'

Miss Starter said earnestly that they were poison, which caused young Mr. Bond to put six into his mouth at once, give a single chew and swallow them. Lord Bond, who came in just then from seeing about a drain down in the seven acre field, said talking of poison they had found a vixen dead down near the stream undoubtedly poisoned, and the question was who had done it.

'Miss Starter says it is potatoes,' said young Mr. Bond.

'Potatoes?' said Lord Bond. 'Never knew a fox eat potatoes.'

'Perhaps vixens do,' said young Mr. Bond. 'Ladies in an interesting condition have queer fancies — at least that's what one reads,' he added hastily, meeting his mother's eye. And then without giving either of the ladies time to interfere he plunged into a discussion of the possible vixen poisoner with his father, leaving Miss Starter so discomposed that she quite forgot about her tea.

'We are leaving at a quarter past three,' said Lady Bond as she rose from the lunch table. 'Juliana, you will rest of course. Alured, who is to take the chair? My brother or Mr. Middleton?'

'Well, my dear — —' his lordship began.

'So it had better be Mr. Middleton, as it is his house,' said Lady

Bond. 'Will you catch Stoke as soon as he comes and make him understand that he is to propose Mr. Middleton.'

'Stoke is getting very deaf,' said Lord Bond plaintively.

'I said Make him understand,' said Lady Bond. 'You can drive us, C.W., as I have ordered the small car. Ferguson is having the weekend off as I shall be taking him to town next week.'

Her ladyship swept Miss Starter out of the room in front of her, leaving her husband and son together.

'I didn't know your mother was going away next week,' said Lord Bond. 'I wonder who will drive me if she takes Ferguson. Young Phipps is the only man I'd trust and he won't be back from his holiday. I suppose you wouldn't, C.W.?'

'I'm awfully sorry, father, I really would if I could,' said young Mr. Bond quite seriously, 'but I have to be at the office all next week. Can't you hire someone?'

'I suppose I'll have to,' said Lord Bond with a sigh. 'But I'll tell you what,' he added, cheering up. 'I'll get that nice young Denis Stonor to come and play Gilbert and Sullivan to me. His sister sings and we'll have a nice little concert together. I do hope Spencer will let me have the piano key by then. I don't like to ask him every time and I can't quite burgle his pantry while he's out. Well, well.'

He looked longingly at his son, half hoping that he would offer to knock Spencer out in fair fight and bear away the piano key as the spoils of victory. But young Mr. Bond had not heard the end of his father's remarks for it had suddenly come over him how pleasant it would be to hear a little music, and how easily he could run down for an evening in his car now that the evenings were so long.

*

At Laverings Mr. Middleton had retired to his dressing-room for the morning to do some work, while the library was made ready for the meeting. As this plan had been arranged the day before it did not come as a surprise to anyone except Mr. Middleton himself, who came downstairs at intervals to tell his wife, Alister Cameron, the three Stonors, and any of the servants who were helping, what it meant to him to be an exile from his own room.

'A precious morning and a precious afternoon wasted, lost!' he exclaimed, suddenly appearing at the door of his private staircase. 'The whole world is basking in sunshine and I alone am condemned to toil.'

'Why not go down to the field and have a talk with Pucken,' said his wife. 'It certainly does seem a pity to be indoors on such a lovely day.'

'How can I talk to Pucken when I have work to do? And without the kindly shelter of my own room, I feel outcast, unwanted. Better perhaps had I stayed in London for the weekend.'

'If you really did work in here there would be some sense in what you say,' said Mrs. Stonor, who was putting paper and pencils on a table at the far end of the room. 'But after all, Jack, you keep all your plans and things upstairs, which is a delightful room, and I haven't seen you working here, I mean only writing letters or doing nothing, though sometimes when one is doing nothing one is really thinking very hard. When Denis is composing he often looks as if he were quite mad or thinking about nothing at all.'

'I do,' said Denis. 'I sometimes see myself in a glass and say "Good God". But I don't see what that has to do with Uncle Jack working upstairs, darling.'

'Good morning, Uncle Jack,' said Daphne coming in with a jug of water and two glasses on a tray. 'How lucky you are, doing nothing on such a divine day. We are all sweltering to death. I say, could I have those two chairs you aren't using in your work-room? I didn't like to take them without asking you, but I saw them when I looked in, when I went up to Catherine's room to see if she had some blue sewing silk she promised she'd lend me. Your room looked so lovely and cool, and I read a bit of an awfully good book you left on the table where your plans are.'

'I am always needing nice books for my library list,' said Mrs. Stonor. 'What was it called, Daphne?'

'Something about Blood,' said Daphne. 'And there is an awfully good bit about where the detective gets on the track of an Argentine white slaver and the wardrobe suddenly turns round on a hinge and there he sees a girl's body hanging up by the heels and she had nothing on and has been dead for *days*. Oh, "All Blood Calling", that's the name.'

Mrs. Stonor said it sounded a very nice book and she would put it on her list. Denis said if he were a white slaver he would make a better job than that and he would never have the same respect for Argentines again.

'And could I take those two chairs, Uncle Jack?' said Daphne.

'Certainly not,' said Mr. Middleton. 'I want them. I need them. I require them, to put things on. And what is that jug of water for?'

'For the chairman,' said Daphne. 'At least one glass is for him and the other for anyone else, and the jug is so that they can give themselves some water.'

'And who is the chairman?' asked Mr. Middleton, rather glad of a diversion from the subject of his leisure reading.

'Didn't Lady Bond tell you?' said his wife.

'No one in this house tells the master of it what is happening,' said Mr. Middleton with tragic dignity. 'I know nothing. I cannot work. I cannot go out and enjoy the beneficent sunshine.'

'But Jack,' said his sister, 'why not? If you must work you can't go out, and if you go out you can't work, but you can't have it both ways.'

To have it both ways was exactly what Mr. Middleton wanted and usually got. Crushing a desire to strangle his sister he said coldly that he had better put on a hat, for this was hardly a day to walk in the direct rays of the sun, and see Pucken about that manure.

'Then can I have those two chairs if you don't want them, Uncle Jack,' said Daphne.

'NO!' said Mr. Middleton. 'Catherine, I appeal to you. Is this my house or is it not?'

'Yes, darling, it is,' said Mrs. Middleton. 'At least as long as we pay the rent. And if you could possibly spare time to speak to Pucken about that manure I shall be so glad, because we really need it for the marrows. I know how busy you are, but it won't take long. I saw Pucken go down the field just now.'

Mr. Middleton stood for a moment irresolute. That he wanted to walk about in the sunshine and gossip with Pucken he well knew, and knew that his wife knew it, but to admit that he didn't feel like work, especially after Daphne's very trying and tactless description of the thriller he had been reading was a mortification to his spirit. A way out must be found which would not impair his dignity.

'I yield, I yield,' he said, making his way among the chairs to the French window. 'I sigh as a worker, but I obey as a husband.'

Pleased with this neat parody, he repeated it, adding with sudden anxiety,

'And no one is to have those chairs, Catherine. That is quite understood.'

'Quite, darling,' said his wife.

She stood for a moment at the window, watching him go down towards the field, and then returned to the work of preparing the library for the meeting. There was really very little to be done now except to wait for half-past three. The chairman's table was neatly laid out with water jug, glasses, paper, pens, ink, blotting paper and pencils. Chairs were arranged without too much formality. In her sitting-room teathings were laid out for the twenty or thirty guests that might come.

'That is always what happens,' she said. 'One gets everything ready much too early and then feels flat. It's only a quarter past twelve. I'll tell Ethel to bring some drinks into the garden. Would you ring, Alister.'

Mr. Cameron rang, the order was given and the whole party wandered across the lawn to where a willow drooped in a most becoming manner above a stone-rimmed pond in which goldfish swam among green weeds. Here in the shade chairs and a garden seat were set and Ethel came wheeling a double-decked trolley towards them, laden with drinks.

'Beer, and lemonade, and cider, and ice,' said Denis gloating. 'No sherry, thank goodness, Catherine. How clever of you not to have sherry on a hot day. It makes one come all-overish. May I pour out?'

He helped everyone and sat down with a glass of cider on the edge of the pond, near his hostess. Mr. Cameron joined Mrs. Stonor on the wooden seat, for he always enjoyed her company. Whether it was the country air, or the pleasure of the Middletons' company, or a lessened anxiety about her stepson, or all three, she looked much younger than when she arrived at Skeynes. Mr. Cameron felt it to be quite ridiculous that she should be Mr. Middleton's sister. True she was a very much younger sister, and Catherine had told him that she was about her own age, but Mrs. Stonor, to his mind, looked younger than Catherine. Partly perhaps because she was very fair, partly because her greenish eyes danced so agreeably while she spoke, partly because she had, as she herself had said, a child's way of doing her thinking aloud. With Catherine one never knew what her thought was till it suddenly dashed out at one, and if one didn't understand it she never troubled to explain. Take it or leave it. And she couldn't let life slip easily over as Lilian, in spite of all her difficulties, had done.

'What are you thinking about?' said Mrs. Stonor.

'I was thinking, Lilian,' said Mr. Cameron, and then stopped, confused.

'Yes, Alister?' said Mrs. Stonor.

'I don't know what I was thinking of,' said Mr. Cameron. 'I do apologize. I always think of you as Lilian.'

'Well, it seems to me quite reasonable,' said Mrs. Stonor. 'You are almost one of the family, in fact in a way you are more in the family than I am because you see a lot of Jack and Catherine and I see so little. I've got to know Jack better as a brother in the last few weeks than ever in my life before. And as for Catherine she is a great deal too good for him, or for anyone else for that matter, but luckily neither of them know it. So I really don't see why you shouldn't call me Lilian. The children always speak of you as Alister behind your back, but of course that means nothing in their generation. Ours is still a little more backward about Christian names.'

'That is very nice of you,' said Mr. Cameron gratefully.

As usual Mrs. Stonor's talk had ramified into a confusing number of by-paths, each of which he would have liked to explore with her but hardly knew where to begin or how to find time enough. What she said about her brother and his wife appeared to him to be so bristling with home thrusts that he could have reflected upon it for a very long time. And what she said about the children, about Denis and Daphne, was double edged, though he hardly thought she meant it to be so. It was quite true that Daphne and he were of different generations, but really not a whole generation apart, only each fresh crop of young trod so quickly on the footsteps of the last that one felt like a great-grandfather at forty-eight. And probably Daphne felt a grandmother compared with all the young creatures between seventeen and the early twenties.

Age, it seemed to him, mattered far less than it used to. Meanwhile it was very pleasant to see Lilian looking better and younger day by day.

'And now, what was it you were thinking?' said Mrs. Stonor again.

'I was really thinking how much better you looked since you came here,' said Mr. Cameron.

'It's because I feel better,' said Mrs. Stonor, accepting with great calm a compliment that most women would apply entirely to their faces. 'The children are so happy here. Daphne is always well, thank goodness, and Denis is so very much better, and when he is better I feel so relieved that I feel much better too, and feeling better usually makes one look better. Did Daphne show you the snapshot she took of you last week? It came out very well. She has it in her room — —'

Mr. Cameron's heart rose in his bosom.

' — with all her other snapshots. She takes a lot.'

Mr. Cameron's heart swooped down to the very depths of his inside and then came to equilibrium again. After all it was something to be even one among many snapshots. Mrs. Stonor went on talking of her step-children with a fondness and admiration that Mr. Cameron found not only suitable, with special regard to Daphne, but wholly delightful in a stepmother. Denis looked up from trying to tease goldfish and gave his stepmother one of his quick looks.

'Are you talking about me, darling?' he enquired. 'If so I will tell you that I am very well as this leaves me at present, and I do like you so much, and if only someone would leave me a thousand pounds, or even five hundred, to get my ballet put on I would be quite well and happy for the rest of my life. Catherine, I am tickling for goldfish. Wouldn't it be dreadful if I caught one? It might die on me before I could put it back in the water. Would you mind?'

'Not so long as I didn't actually see it die,' said Mrs. Middleton.

'I love your truthfulness,' said Denis laughing. 'I won't pursue my tickling. Daphne, I'll have sixpence with you on the Great Goldfish Derby. I am backing that far one with a silver fin.'

Daphne objected, on the grounds that all goldfish were exactly like each other and anyway they never raced, only swam about. Denis said they would each put a crumb on the water then, and whichever gold-fish got it first would win sixpence for the owner, and there was absolutely no difficulty in telling them apart if you took pains. But as there were no crumbs about the idea had to be abandoned. Denis, who said he felt an overmastering passion to bet on something, offered to go up to the house and find a crumb, when Mr. Middleton and Pucken approached.

'You look hot, darling,' said Mrs. Middleton. 'Come and sit down and have a drink.'

Mr. Middleton accepted the glass of beer which Denis got up and fetched for him, but remained standing.

'What about Pucken?' Denis said softly, bending over Mrs. Middleton as he passed behind her chair.

'Beer? No, please not. He has as much as is good for him when the Fleece opens.'

'Right,' said Denis, sitting down on the edge of the pond again, feeling a little confused, perhaps from bending so low to whisper to someone in a deckchair.

'What about the manure, Pucken?' said Mrs. Middleton.

'Well, mum, it's this way,' said Pucken.

'Denis darling, are you sure the stone isn't cold?' said Mrs. Stonor. 'You have been there a long time.'

'It may have been cold in the beginning, though I didn't notice it, but it certainly isn't now,' said Denis. 'The sun was shining violently upon it while I got Uncle Jack's beer.'

'Well, do be careful,' said his stepmother.

'Bless your innocent heart,' said Denis, blowing her a kiss.

'Can't you get it?' said Mrs. Middleton as Pucken remained tongue-tied.

'Well mum, it isn't exactly that,' said Pucken.

After a great deal of questioning it appeared that the Fleece was responsible for the whole affair. Pucken had the promise of a load of manure, not none, he said, of your mucky pig manure, but a good clean load from Lord Bond's farm stables, as sweet manure as a man could wish to see. But words having passed between him and Lord Bond's second gardener, who was down at the Fleece, that gardener had said he was danged if Pucken should have so much as a wheelbarrow of manure off the place, and so the matter had remained. He could, he said, get a load off Farmer Brown, but where was the use? There was nothing in the county to touch his lordship's manure and set his heart on it he had for the marrows.

After hearing this Mrs. Middleton said she supposed she had better speak to Lord Bond about it.

'Or will you Jack?' she asked her husband. 'You will be seeing him at the meeting to-day, you know.'

But Mr. Middleton showed such signs of becoming a complete nervous and physical wreck if he had to take the responsibility that his wife said she would do it herself. Pucken was told to be more careful at the Fleece and went happily away talking to himself about the excellent qualities of the Staple Park manure. After this the party broke up for lunch.

*

The first arrival was Lord Stoke who enjoyed any kind of meeting so much that he always came a quarter of an hour too soon, to get his bearings he said, though neither he nor anyone else knew exactly what he meant. As his car drew up at the garden gate Pucken, who was hanging about to watch the arrivals, touched his cap. Lord Stoke, who knew every face connected with cows in the whole county and had twice seen Pucken at the Skeynes Agricultural Show, touched his hat in return.

'You're Mr. Middleton's man, aren't you?' said his lordship. 'Pucken, that's the name isn't it?'

Pucken, much gratified, scratched the back of his neck and grinned.

Lord Stoke enquired what cows Mr. Middleton was sending to the Show, expressed great interest, not unmingled with relief, at the news that the Jersey was in calf again and so, gossiping with Pucken, moved slowly down the lane towards the field where the cow sheds were. As Pucken was too shy to answer except in monosyllables, his lordship's deafness did not prevent conversation and time passed very happily.

After Lord Stoke came the Palmers, carrying with them Mr. and Mrs. Tebben. Mr. Tebben torn unwillingly from Bishop Ogmund was heartily wishing that Sir Ogilvy Hibberd, the source of all these woes, were spread-eagled. Mr. Middleton who had come out on hearing the sound of cars to catch Lord Stoke was greeted by Mrs. Palmer.

'I don't think you know my friends Mr. and Mrs. Tebben,' she said. 'Their daughter married my nephew Laurence Deane. And I've brought Ed Pollett over. Come here, Ed.'

A man, stiff with consciousness of his Sunday suit, who was sitting beside the Palmer's chauffeur, dismounted and came awkwardly towards her.

'I thought you wouldn't mind,' Mrs. Palmer went on, 'his coming with us. He's having his holiday.'

'Certainly not,' said Mr. Middleton, courteous but perplexed. The name Pollett seemed familiar to him, but the bearer of it he could not place. He had heard that Mrs. Palmer had strange theatrical guests. . . .

'Brother of your chauffeur,' said Mrs. Palmer, her quick eye at once detecting her host's dilemma. 'You must have heard of Ed. He is the under porter at Worsted Station and has a perfect genius for cars, but a little bit wanting.'

In giving this character of Ed, Mrs. Palmer took no pains to moderate her voice, but Ed bore no grudge, appearing indeed to take some pride in this publicity.

'Well, he'd better go and find Pollett, he's somewhere about,' said Mr. Middleton. 'You didn't pass Stoke's car on the way, did you? I want to speak to him.'

Ed gave Mr. Middleton a respectful nudge and pointed towards a car a little further down the lane, saying 'That's her.'

'Who?' said Mr. Middleton, for no female was visible.

'He means Lord Stoke's car, sir, don't you, Ed,' said the Palmer's chauffeur coming to the rescue. 'Ed can pick out any car, sir, once he's seen it, can't you Ed?'

'That's her, O.K.,' said Ed.

'Well, I must have missed Stoke somehow. I expect we'll find him in the house,' said Mr. Middleton. 'Come in.'

Mr. Tebben had brightened perceptibly at the name of Lord Stoke, for a labourer while digging a drain on his lordship's estate in a field called Bloody Meadow had lately turned up some bones, which might as well have been those of a Viking as anyone else. It was more or less authentically proved that a battle had been fought in the vicinity of Rising Castle between a local ruler and a Danish force stiffened with a roving contingent of Norsemen, and Mr. Tebben had a secret hope that the bones might prove to be those of a hero called Thorstein Longtooth who was mentioned in a Norse ballad over which Mr. Tebben and the President of the Snorri Society had quarrelled violently through the medium of the Journal of Icelandic Studies. If he could get from Lord Stoke a description of the bones, or better still permission to see them, his afternoon would not have been wasted, so he followed his host with a somewhat lighter heart.

Mrs. Tebben paused to cry aloud in ecstasy over the beauty of some delphiniums, but was hustled along by Mrs. Palmer who wished to get front row seats as her husband was a little deaf.

'All the same, Louise,' said Mrs. Tebben. 'I do think my plan of getting a few packets of seed from Woolworth's, quite at random, simply by the delightful coloured pictures on the outside, and sowing them here and there in our little garden in a spirit of adventure has often been most successful and seldom more so than this year. You haven't seen that little corner down by the ash-pit lately. I have put nasturtiums there and it is going to be quite a splash of colour.'

Mrs. Palmer took no notice of her friend and bore the whole party into the house where Mrs. Middleton was receiving her guests, most of whom knew each other, though not always on speaking terms, so very little introducing was needed. Mrs. Palmer was moving towards the front row, but Mrs. Tebben lingered to exclaim gustily over the beauty of the view from the library window and so lingering found herself face to face with the Bonds. Mrs. Tebben did not in the least mind Lady Bond's title, wealth, position or domineering ways, but on one subject she would brook no rivalry. She and Lady Bond each had an only son and each knew that her own son was quite perfect, though without prejudice to a good deal of fault-finding in the home. Neither lady appeared to have any idea that her husband was in any way responsible for the qualities of her child, each gathering all credit to herself. The race on the whole had been even. Young Mr. Bond had a very good job and would eventually inherit a title, while Richard Tebben was doing very well in an engineering firm and had excellent prospects. There was however one triumph which Mrs. Tebben could not forget and had no intention of letting Lady Bond forget. A few years earlier, before the two young men went out into the world, Richard Tebben at the annual cricket match between Skeynes and Worsted had caught young Mr. Bond out with a spectacular catch never to be forgotten at the Fleece in Skeynes or the Woopack in Worsted. The result had been a violent friendship lasting for one day, since when the young men had never met, young Mr. Bond going to New York and Richard Tebben on a three years' job to South America. But neither of the mothers had forgotten the event. At the sight of Mrs. Tebben Lady Bond automatically became more the county magnate than ever, while Mrs. Tebben could not help conveying by her air that she had taken a first at Oxford and had a son who caught other people's sons out.

'How are you?' said Mrs. Tebben to Lady Bond. 'And how is C.W.? Still playing cricket?'

Young Mr. Bond, who thought this question was addressed to himself, was about to say that he looked forward to the match against Worsted and was sorry Richard couldn't be there, when his mother, morally elbowing him out of the way, said he was quite out of practice as he only played polo in America. She then wished she hadn't said it.

Mrs. Tebben, horrified by the inverted snobbism that at once overcame her against her will said polo was alas! too expensive a game for Richard, but he had had a perfectly wonderful time during the opera season at Buenos Aires, having heard Strilla and Taglino every time they sang.

Lady Bond, who was usually rather proud than otherwise of being entirely unmusical, felt that this boast was aimed at her and in a voice that she didn't quite recognize as her own said That was very nice. Luckily Lord Bond and Mr. Palmer now began to discuss the Skeynes Agricultural Show in a way that relegated women, even Lady Bond, to their proper place, and no blood was shed.

By this time the room was nearly full and it was twenty-five minutes to four. Lord Stoke had not yet arrived, nor had Lord Pomfret, and Lady Bond was beginning to chafe and told Mrs. Middleton so.

'I know Stoke had started,' she said, 'because Spencer rang up to enquire just before we left home. I do hope he hasn't had an accident. He is so deaf now.'

'But he doesn't drive himself, does he?' asked Mrs. Middleton.

'Stoke? He never tried,' said Lady Bond. 'He is a perfect fool about machinery. But it is worrying. Mr. Middleton,' she called as her host came in. 'Stoke hasn't come, has he?'

'He has come all right,' said Mr. Middleton, 'but I can't find him. His car is in the lane, but I can't see him anywhere about.'

'Then he is down in the field talking to your cowman,' said Lady Bond, who knew her brother's peculiarities. 'C.W., you had better go and look.'

'Certainly,' said young Mr. Bond. 'Which field would he be down, sir?'

Daphne said she would show him and they went off together, to the simultaneous annoyance of Lady Bond and Mr. Cameron, who were both even more annoyed when Lord Stoke came in by the French window.

'Oh, there you are, Stoke,' said Mr. Middleton. 'It is time we began.'

'I've been having a most interesting talk with your cowman,' said Lord Stoke. 'I remember his father quite well. He fell into a ditch coming back from the Southbridge Cattle Show one year and a waggon of hay overturned just at the same spot. When they got the waggon right next day and reloaded the hay, of course Pucken was dead. Suffocated. Don't suppose he suffered, though. He must have been quite drunk when he fell in. At least they had refused to serve him with any more beer at the Stoke Arms and you know what Glazebury was, old Glazebury I mean; he'd go just as far as the law would let him and if he refused to serve a customer it meant that customer was pretty tight already.'

'Well, we ought to move a chairman,' said Mr. Middleton. 'You are going to do it, I believe.'

'Eh?' said Lord Stoke.

'We ought to be getting down to business,' said Mr. Middleton, not quite patiently and rather loudly.

'Business, eh? Quite right. Who is that woman sitting in the back row, Middleton? I ought to know her face,' said Lord Stoke, who had been surveying the audience with much interest.

'That's Mrs. Pucken,' said Mr. Middleton unwillingly.

'Of course, of course,' said his lordship. 'Sarah Margett she was. Her brother keeps the shop at Worsted. Used to be Lucasta's kitchenmaid. I must have a word with her. Well, Sarah, how are you?'

Mrs. Pucken got up and shook Lord Stoke's proffered hand and said she was nicely.

'And how are the new lowers?' said his lordship.

Mrs. Pucken smiled broadly with a slightly seasick motion of her lower teeth and said there wasn't really nothing she couldn't eat now.

'Lou here wants a set like mine, my lord,' she said. 'Her teeth are something awful. But I say Just you wait a bit, my girl, we can't have everything we want not all at once, didn't I, Lou?'

But Lou, a step further than her mother from familiar terms with the aristocracy, went bright scarlet and although she opened and shut her mouth several times was bereft of the power of speech.

'That's right,' said Lord Stoke approvingly, for he was used to finding his friends inaudible and took it for granted that Lou had spoken. 'Always do what your mother tells you. Called after Lady Bond, isn't she?'

Mrs. Pucken replied that in a manner of speaking she was, implying that she fully realized Lady Bond's condescension in lending her name. Lord Stoke would have lingered indefinitely, asking after the various

members of Mrs. Pucken's family, but Mr. Middleton, made quite
desperate, seized his distinguished guest by the arm and propelled him
to the other end of the room. Lord Stoke, seeing an armchair, and being
used to taking the chair on every possible occasion, sat down in it and
Mr. Middleton, who had rather meant to conduct the meeting himself,
was forced to take the inferior seat at his lordship's side. Denis caught
Mrs. Middleton's eye and received from her a look expressing amusement combined with despair.

Lord Stoke lost no time in telling his audience that they had been
convened to discuss a public meeting to be held about the proposed
building of a garage on Pooker's Piece. As everyone had already been
informed of this by the leaflet of invitation, and in many cases by word
of mouth, the news created very little sensation. He then by easy stages
passed to the suitability of Pooker's Piece for grazing land, his own
opinion of pure-bred Jerseys as against a mixed strain of milker and a
pressing reminder to his hearers of the importance of the Skeynes
Agricultural Show. At this point Lady Bond, who had been listening to
her brother's words with growing disfavour, wrote on a visiting card the
words 'Let Mr. Middleton speak' and handed it up to the chairman's
table.

'What's that?' said Lord Stoke. 'Middleton speak? Of course Lucasta,
of course. I am just coming to that. Well, Middleton, what have you to
say, eh?'

Seizing this favourable moment Mr. Middleton rose to his feet and
launched into a spirited defence of the amenities of Pooker's Piece, with
special and lengthy reference to the pleasure it had so often given him
to ramble over it with Flora, who barked at her own name and had to be
suppressed by Mr. Cameron, glad of an excuse to vent an unaccount-
able irritation of feeling upon a dumb beast. Mr. Middleton's rolling
periods gave his audience time to think in some cases about nothing, in
others about their own affairs. Flora at intervals gave an hysterical
whimper, till Lou, sitting just behind Mr. Cameron and at the end of a
row, was moved to an heroic impulse.

'Shall I take her away, sir?' she said hoarsely. 'She knows me.'

Flora, on hearing this, made a wild struggle as of a beast starved and
tortured to escape to freedom, for with the profound instinct of her kind
she associated Lou with bits of food surreptitiously bestowed whenever
she went into the Pucken's cottage or the kitchen of the White House.

Mr. Cameron thankfully allowed Lou to pick Flora up bodily and
take her out by the service door and relapsed into gloomy meditation
till he saw Mrs. Stonor looking anxiously and sympathetically at him.
Somehow this sight cheered him a good deal and he began to wonder
what everyone else had already been wondering for some time, whether
Mr. Middleton would ever stop. This question was suddenly settled by
Lord Stoke, who looked at his watch, and uttered an exclamation.

'Good heavens, Middleton, it's half-past four,' he said. 'Sorry I must be off. Sub-Committee of the County Council at Southbridge at five. Most interesting meeting. Does a lot of good getting people together.'

He then descended among the crowd and began saying good-bye to his hostess. Everyone got up or shuffled their chairs, eager for Mrs. Middleton's good tea. Mr. Tebben, driven to desperation by a wasted afternoon in which nothing whatever had been accomplished except the ruin of his working day, got between Lord Stoke and the door.

'Excuse me one moment, Lord Stoke,' he said.

'Yes?' said Lord Stoke stopping courteously.

'It's about that find of bones,' said Mr. Tebben.

'Eh?' said Lord Stoke.

'Bones!' said Mr. Tebben at the top of his voice. 'Viking's bones! My name is Tebben.'

'Tebben?' said his lordship. 'Good Lord! Tebben! Snorri Society. I read your paper on the Laxdaela Saga in their transactions. Most interesting. I'd like you to come over and see those bones. At least what there is of them. Most of them were broken and a lot crumbled away, but we've got the rest up at the Castle for the moment.'

'And do you think they are definitely of that period?' said Mr. Tebben.

'Couldn't say,' replied Lord Stoke. 'Bones aren't much in my line. Might be a man's, might be a dog's as far as I'm concerned. But come over to-morrow and have a look. I'll send the car for you. Or come to lunch. That's it, lunch, one-thirty, and we'll have a good look at the excavation. Is this your wife?' he added as Mrs. Tebben who had a passion for Getting to the Bottom of Things came up to see what it was all about. 'Will you introduce me?'

Mr. Tebben introduced Lord Stoke to Mrs. Tebben, adding quickly that he was going to lunch at Rising Castle on the next day.

Mrs. Tebben, who held that an invitation to a husband should include a wife, was about to be disappointed when a thought struck her.

'That will be splendid, my dear,' she said. 'I had meant to have a little bit of neck of lamb for lunch to-morrow and open a tinned tongue for to-night. But if you are going to Lord Stoke we will keep the roast till Monday and I shall have a picnic on some Heinz beans by myself for Sunday lunch. Or, I wonder, would the lamb keep till Monday in this weather? Perhaps it might be wiser to have it to-night. It is such a small piece that there will be time for Mrs. Phipps to put it in the oven for our supper when we get home, and I shall have time to hurry down the garden and get some peas.'

She paused, her hat a little on the back of her head with enthusiasm.

'Well, that's splendid,' said Lord Stoke, who had but imperfectly understood Mrs. Tebben, but gathered that her inclinations were friendly. 'Now I must really be getting along. My car will fetch you at one o'clock to-morrow, Tebben. Lamb's Piece at Worsted, isn't it? I used to know old Margerison who owned it. Married his housekeeper —high time too.'

But just as he was going his eye was caught by Ethel, important and flustered, speaking to her mistress. His lordship who had a violent curiosity about everyone with whom he came in contact, paused to listen.

'Show him in, of course, Ethel,' said Mrs. Middleton. 'Jack, Lord Pomfret is here.'

'Then we'll get something done,' said Lady Bond, whose disapproval of her brother and her host had been increasing rapidly. 'Don't let the people have tea yet, Mr. Middleton. One moment,' she added to the room in general in her committee voice.

The rush towards the tea was stemmed and Lord Pomfret came in.

'I am so glad you could come,' said Mrs. Middleton, 'but I'm afraid the meeting is almost over. Would you care to say anything?'

'Depends on what's been said,' said Lord Pomfret looking suspiciously around.

'Absolutely nothing at all,' said Lady Bond. 'I understood that this meeting was called to arrange for a public meeting about Sir Ogilvy Hibberd's plan for building on Pooker's Piece, but nothing has been settled at all.'

'Not much good my coming then,' said Lord Pomfret. 'However as I'm here can I have a cup of tea, Mrs. Middleton?'

'Of course,' said Mrs. Middleton. 'Willl you come into the dining-room?'

'Crowd there,' said Lord Pomfret. 'I'd rather have a cup here with you.'

Mrs. Middleton, who liked Lord Pomfret but did not intend to be bullied, said she must look after her guests and would send some tea to him and come back herself before long. She then introduced her sister-in-law to Lord Pomfret and went away.

VII

EPILOGUE TO A MEETING

In the dining-room the fun, as Mrs. Tebben said, was fast and furious. Most of the other guests were gorging on Mrs. Middleton's excellent cakes, telling each other that they were on a diet but when you were out to tea it didn't count. Denis and Mr. Cameron were being very obliging with strawberries and ices. Mr. Cameron had always found that hard work was a good way of taking one's mind off things, and to fill people's plates seemed better than to wonder where Daphne and young Bond were; so he industriously did both.

As a matter of fact Daphne and young Mr. Bond, having conducted the most perfunctory of searches for Lord Stoke, had gone down to the cowshed and had a delightful conversation with Pucken, who obliged them with his valueless views on the Milk Marketing Board. They then discussed the cows, the probable date of Lily Langtry's expected calf and the chances of the various exhibitors at the Skeynes Agricultural Show, after which young Mr. Bond gave Pucken a cigarette and followed Daphne to the strawberry beds. Here they performed a difficult but humane deed by rescuing a thrush who had entangled himself in the net and deeply resented their kind interference.

'By Jove, he has bitten me to the bone,' said young Mr. Bond as the thrush gave one last vindictive dig at his hand and fled shrieking to the wood.

'That always happens if you help people,' said Daphne. 'I expect you'll see that thrush walking up and down outside your window tomorrow with a placard saying "Mr. Bond Unfair to Thrushes".'

'If he does I'll jolly well drive my car up and down outside his wood with a placard to say "Thrush Ungrateful to Mr. Bond".'

'Well, that's about all,' said Daphne straightening herself. 'I don't think there's a single one we haven't eaten. It won't matter because I know Catherine has got all she wants for to-night. I suppose we'd better go back to the meeting.'

'Need we?' said Mr. Bond.

'Well, not for pleasure,' said Daphne, 'but Catherine might want me to help and I'd hate to let her down.'

Young Mr. Bond, who really had a sense of duty, at once recognized the justice of Daphne's remarks and admired her for them, so they went back to Laverings, entering the library by the French window just as Mr. Cameron was bringing a tray of strawberries and cream for Lady Bond, Mrs. Palmer and their parties.

'Hullo, Alister,' said Daphne. 'I'd adore some of those.'

Mr. Cameron smiled at her and brought his tray.

'I should have thought you'd had enough,' said young Mr. Bond. 'Guzzling away under the strawberry net.'

'Well, they do make me come out all over spots sometimes,' said Daphne candidly. 'Thanks awfully, Alister, but I'd better not.'

Mr. Cameron took his tray away and saw that Lady Bond, Mrs. Palmer and Mrs. Tebben were properly looked after. Lord Pomfret, Lord Bond, Mr. Palmer and Lord Stoke, who had now decided that it was too late for the Sub-Committee, were deep in professional talk about cows, and Mr. Middleton for once in life found so little attention paid to his remarks that he was glad to give Mr. Tebben his views on the Icelandic sagas. Lady Bond, still annoyed by the very inconclusive character of the meeting and what she inwardly called the maunderings of her brother and Mr. Middleton, was in her most aggressive humour and had already had one or two sharp passages with Mrs. Palmer. Mrs. Middleton, who had come back as she promised, found that Lord Pomfret was immersed in cow talk so she tried to pour oil on the rising billows of their politeness, though without much success.

'What play are you giving this year, Mrs. Palmer?' she asked.

Mrs. Palmer said they were having a complete change from Greek plays and doing *Twelfth Night* in modern dress.

'We are still short of principals,' she said. 'I suppose Mrs. Stonor, your daughter wouldn't help us by doing Olivia?'

'Well,' said Mrs. Stonor, who had been listening with some amusement to the bickerings between the other ladies, 'she is really my stepdaughter, but I don't see why she shouldn't be able to act. I'll ask her. Daphne!'

'It is quite in the nature of an experiment,' said Mrs. Palmer. 'Everyone is as far as possible to be his or her natural self. My butler, for instance, is doing Malvolio and the doctor's twin girls are doing Viola and Sebastian, and the Rector's parlourmaid will be Maria.'

'It seems a pity, Louise, that Ed Pollett couldn't do the fool,' said Mrs. Tebben. 'Of course he can't ever remember his lines and has no voice, but I daresay someone else could sing his part off.'

'Ed isn't a *fool*, Winifred,' said Mrs. Palmer sharply. 'He's only wanting. Miss Stonor, would you care to do Olivia for us?'

'Not if it's Shakespeare, thank you,' said Daphne retreating. 'We did a lot of him at school.'

'It is in modern dress,' Mrs. Palmer urged.

'But that wouldn't feel like Shakespeare,' said Daphne, basely changing her tactics. 'I mean you can generally get away with it with robes and things, but I'd feel an awful fool in my ordinary clothes.'

'Well, think it over,' said Mrs. Palmer graciously. 'We have a most enthusiastic audience. Our high water mark was the production of *Hippolytus* a few years ago.'

'That was the year Richard made his wonderful catch,' said Mrs. Tebben, beaming at the thought.

Lady Bond who did not like this allusion to her son's defeat said nothing in a very marked manner, but young Mr. Bond with perfect honesty said what fun it was and what a splendid tea the two elevens had had afterwards.

'That was the year Mrs. Palmer's niece, Betty, did Phaedra so well,' Mrs. Tebben continued. 'Didn't you think her splendid, Mr. Bond?'

Young Mr. Bond, with less enthusiasm, said she was awfully good.

'We all thought they would be engaged,' said Mrs. Tebben aside to Mrs. Stonor and Daphne. 'I have never seen anyone so struck as Mr. Bond was. Betty is such a nice girl. She has just taken a first in Greats at Oxford.'

Daphne's face expressed her opinion of nice girls that took first in Greats so clearly that Mrs. Palmer began to bristle for her niece.

'She tells me she saw quite a lot of you, C.W., while you were in America,' said Mrs. Palmer, glad to show Lady Bond that a Palmer niece was properly valued by the heir of Staple Park. 'I believe she is going back to Bryn Mawr to do a post-graduate course, so doubtless you will see her when you go back to New York. It will be nice for her to have you there.'

Young Mr. Bond, acutely sensible of Daphne's disapproval, said it would.

'I didn't know you were such a friend of Miss Deane's, C.W.,' said his mother.

Young Mr. Bond began to flounder so miserably that Mrs. Middleton quickly asked Lady Bond why Miss Starter had not come to the meeting.

'Oh, Juliana had one of her bad days,' said Lady Bond. 'She has headaches that are quite unlike anyone else's, so she is staying in bed with the blinds down and will just have a little toasted Kornog bread for tea and perhaps come down to dinner. C.W., I think we ought to be going. Tell your father I am ready.'

At the same moment Lord Pomfret, saying that the Bishop was dining at Pomfret Towers and he must get back, broke up the cow conference. A welter of good-byes ensued.

'Good-bye, Mrs. Middleton,' said Lord Pomfret. 'I never had my cup of tea with you. You must let me come over again one day. I don't get about as much as I did since my wife died. She liked you. You look tired. Don't overdo it.'

Mrs. Middleton said it was only the heat and she was afraid that they had rather wasted Lord Pomfret's time.

'Not a bit,' said the earl. 'I've learnt what I wanted to know. Drawing-room meetings are no good. I'll have to think about that feller Hibberd. My wife liked Pooker's Piece. We used to ride there when we were first married. Can't have a garage on it.'

He took his leave, as did Lord Stoke and the Palmers, accompanied by Mr. and Mrs. Tebben, which last named lady expressed the greatest appreciation of her afternoon's treat.

'I do hope you will be able to come to tea with me one day,' she said to Mrs. Middleton. 'Your tea was delicious, but we have a way of doing cake that I am sure you would like to know. When I have a cake that has got really stale and I don't want to make a trifle with it, I cut it into slices and toast them and spread a little butter on them and pile them up in a dish and leave it in the oven for a few moments. You have no idea how good it is. I had a cake last week that had somehow got into a corner and been overlooked and when I had just cut off the little mildewed bit and toasted and buttered it, we all enjoyed it so much.'

Mrs. Middleton thanked Mrs. Tebben warmly. The rest of the guests were going and after some more handshaking and thanks for the tea she found herself left with her family and the Bonds.

'Cows!' exclaimed Mr. Middleton. 'The whole subject of cows is one on which, I say it without pride, I am competent to speak, but I must confess that for the moment I am tongue-tied. In the face of Lord Pomfret and Stoke and Palmer I must perforce be silent. How they talked, Catherine; how they talked. Never have I been so borne down, so overwhelmed by sheer force of words, a veritable Niagara of talk. Bond, you will bear me out in what I say.'

'I'll never do anything against Stoke as long as he has that cowman,' said Lord Bond mournfully. 'But he won't leave. I know for a fact that Pomfret would give him twice what he's getting now. But I still don't agree with Stoke about those Friesians. Mark my words. . . .'

While Lord Bond said what he felt about Friesians and Mr. Middleton explained at great length how impossible it was for him to speak, Mrs. Middleton, on the sofa which had been put at right angles to the chairman's table, her back to the window, wondered what use anything was. The great drawing-room meeting had taken place, nothing useful had been said or settled; the one success of the afternoon had been the tea, and if people wanted tea she would far rather give it to them in a friendly way, a few at a time, than have the whole house upset. Denis sat down beside her, a glass in each hand.

'One is sherry, one is brandy and a little soda,' he remarked. 'Which are you going to have?'

'Thank you so much, but I really don't think I want either,' she said kindly.

'I know you don't,' said Denis. 'Which are you going to have?'

'The brandy please,' said Mrs. Middleton meekly. 'Not because it brings back the colour to my pale cheeks as in novels, but because I like it better.'

Denis gave her a curiously ferocious glance and went away to look after the rest of the party. Lord Bond, on the pretext of mixing his whisky and soda himself, accompanied Denis to the table where the drinks stood.

'About that concert,' he said. 'My wife's going to town next week and Juliana is going to visit her widowed sister at Tunbridge Wells. Suppose you and your sister come up one evening to dinner and I'll get the piano opened.'

'I'd love to, sir,' said Denis. 'I'll ask Daphne.'

He fetched his sister, who was loud in her approval of the scheme.

'But you needn't mention it to my wife,' said Lord Bond anxiously.

'Are you concealing something from mother?' said young Mr. Bond, who had naturally gravitated to Daphne.

His father explained the plan.

'Jolly good idea,' said young Mr. Bond. 'Make it Wednesday and I'll run down for dinner.'

'That's right. We'll be four then,' said Lord Bond, feeling like Guy Fawkes.

Daphne, without looking at young Mr. Bond, said would Lord Bond think it awfully rude if she asked if Mr. Cameron could come. He was staying at Laverings for some time and was most awfully nice and she knew he liked Gilbert and Sullivan.

Lord Bond, who delighted in hospitality, said of course Cameron must come and wouldn't Mrs. Stonor come too. In view of Lady Bond's well-known gift of spotting at once what was going on the invitations had to be given with great care and secrecy, but both were gladly accepted.

'There, that's splendid,' said Lord Bond to the conspirators. 'Now we shall be six. Oh, one thing though. My wife is taking the Rolls to town and I haven't got anyone to drive the other car. Young Phipps is the only one I'd trust and he is away on his holiday. Tell you what. I'll get the car from the Fleece to bring you over and take you back. Would that be all right?'

'I could fetch them all on my way down from London, father,' said young Mr. Bond, 'and take them back.'

Daphne said he might have an accident or a puncture on the way down and then where would they all be.

'Quite right, Miss Stonor,' said his lordship. 'Much better to have the car from the Fleece. Do you remember, C.W., the time you were to fetch Juliana from Tunbridge Wells and forgot all about her? Wouldn't do to forget Miss Stonor. Where were you that day, C.W.?'

Young Mr. Bond, suddenly feeling a profound dislike for his father, said rather sulkily Which day.

'The day you forgot Juliana,' said Lord Bond. 'I know. You were driving Mrs. Palmer's niece to Oxford. Betty; that's the name. Betty Deane. Handsome girl that. You'd like her, Miss Stonor.'

Daphne said she was so glad she had never been at Oxford, because all the girls she had known who went there were perfectly ghastly. Lady Bond then summoned her husband and son and everyone walked to the garden gate with them. By their car Ferguson, the Bonds' chauffeur, and Pollett, the Middletons' chauffeur, were deep in discussion, with Ed Pollett standing by.

'Excuse me, my lady,' said Ferguson, who like most of the Staple Park employees looked to his mistress for orders, 'but if his lordship was wanting anyone to drive the car while I am away, Mr. Pollett's brother is quite as you might say a wizard with cars. Of course I wouldn't have suggested it, my lady, but Mr. Spencer, who was in the dining-room at the time, happened to pass the remark that his lordship said he didn't know who to have seeing that young Phipps was away.'

Lord Bond said almost pettishly that he wished Spencer wouldn't gossip in the servants' hall, but his wife who never let anything pass without investigation asked who Mr. Pollett was and, hence, who his brother.

If Ferguson had been among his equals he would have said that Mr. Pollett drove Middleton's car, but in deference to his employer's class prejudice he said that Mr. Pollett was Mr. Middleton's chauffeur.

'Can I speak to your man?' said Lady Bond to Mr. Middleton, thus grossly offending Ferguson's class consciousness. Then without waiting for Mr. Middleton's assent he set up a Board of Inquisition on Pollett, harrying and browbeating him in a way to which his free mechanic's spirit was quite unaccustomed. Pollett's ancestors had lived at Worsted ever since there was a Pollett in England; respect for the gentry had been bred in the family since the days of Gorwulf who lived at Gorwulf-steadings and had a Pollett as serf; and all Pollett's education, his training in motor works, his experience with armoured cars in Mesopotamia during the war, fell from him like dust before the broom under Lady Bond's eye.

'Well, Mr. Middleton,' she said after a few moments' talk, 'your man's brother appears to be distinctly wanting, but I gather that he has a licence and understands cars, and your man says he is absolutely trustworthy, so I daresay he will do for a few days. Will that suit you, Alured?'

Lord Bond would, on the whole, have preferred not to be driven by what he not unnaturally took to be the village idiot, but if his wife said it was to be he supposed he had better agree. Besides he liked Ed Pollett's face and thought he might get some amusing local gossip out of him. So he agreed.

'Then I'd better have a word with him now,' said Lady Bond. 'Ed!'

Ed, roughly awakened from the pleasant day-dream about nothing at all which was his normal state, came nervously forward.

'Do you understand, Ed?' said her ladyship in a clear voice. 'You are to come up to Staple Park on Monday and your brother will show you the car you are to drive, and you will drive his lordship till the end of the week.'

Ed looked at his brother for confirmation.

'Say Yes to her ladyship,' his brother prompted.

'That's O.K., miss,' said Ed.

'It's a little Denham,' said Lady Bond, quite unperturbed by her temporary chauffeur's mode of address. 'Do you know them?'

Ed smiled blissfully.

'Of course Ed knows them,' said young Mr. Bond who had been wondering where he and Ed had met. 'Do you remember the play at Mrs. Palmer's two or three years ago, Ed, and how Mr. Richard Tebben's car got stuck and you put her right? She was a Denham, wasn't she?'

'That's right, sir,' said Ed, smiling more benignantly than before.

'He'll be all right for you, father,' said young Mr. Bond, with the happy assurance of the young that their elders are so dull as to be immune from accident. 'You'll drive my father nicely, won't you, Ed?'

'That's O.K., sir,' said Ed, and then said something to his brother that the audience couldn't catch.

'Excuse me, my lady,' said Pollett, 'but Ed wants to know if he can have a uniform, because he's only got the one good suit and he wouldn't like to spoil it and he doesn't think Mr. Patten, the station master at Worsted, would like him to wear his railway uniform. I could lend him my old one.'

This matter being satisfactorily arranged Lady Bond was just going to get into her car when a thought struck her.

'Oh, Mr. Middleton,' she said, 'we have arranged nothing about the public meeting after all. I really don't know what my brother was thinking of.'

'Of cows,' said Mrs. Middleton. 'They all do at this time of year. Would it be better to put the meeting off till after the Skeynes Agricultural Show?'

'Perhaps you are right,' said Lady Bond. 'Daphne, if you will come up to the Park on Monday I will give you a list of people and we will settle a date and then you could get on with the typing while I am away.'

Daphne was quite ready to do this at half a crown an hour and at last the Bonds went away. Ed went to get his tea at his brother's cottage before catching the 7.33 from Skeynes to Worsted, a journey which he intended to perform either in the cab of the engine driver, Sid Pollett, his first cousin, or in the van of the guard, Mr. Patten, his aunt's husband.

Laverings and the White House all sat in chairs on the terrace and drank what they fancied.

'I can't think,' said Mrs. Stonor, 'why people ever have meetings. It really seems to be the one way of not getting anything done. I think it would be so much easier if someone would simply write to Sir Ogilvy Hibberd and explain. He would be much more likely to take notice of a person than a meeting. Jack, why don't you write?'

'I write, Lilian?' exclaimed Mr. Middleton. 'No, no.'

'But why not?' asked his sister.

'My dear Lilian!' said Mr. Middleton, ever active in avoiding things he didn't want to do. 'My dear Lilian,' he added, hoping to find something to say. 'My dear Lilian, the thing is impossible. My name may carry some little weight. I have tramped the country about Pooker's Piece year in year out, under blazing June suns, under the bitter blasts of winter, under the slanting showers of April — — '

'And do not forget the golden shower of autumn leaves,' murmured Denis, catching Mrs. Middleton's eye, who wanted to laugh and frown at once and compromised by a glance of reproving sympathy.

' — till every flower, every hedgerow, every blade of grass is as familiar to me as the palm of my hand — — '

Mrs. Stonor said she wondered why the palms of people's hands should be familiar to them. She for one, she said, never looked at hers, because it always seemed to be the back of one's hands that one saw, or one's finger nails if they suddenly happened to be dirty when one thought they were clean, which was always happening in London. It was really, she thought, because London water was so hard, certainly much harder than it used to be when she was a girl and it was an extraordinary thing that the water seemed to be getting harder all over England; and it was all very well to say Collect the rainwater in a butt, but when you lived in London it was quite impossible to have a butt in a flat, because first it wouldn't go in at the front door and then there would be nowhere to put it unless one could have it on the roof and padlock it so that other people couldn't use it and in any case London rain was so dirty, as anyone who left her window open when it was raining and saw the white curtains afterwards would agree, that it would really hardly be worth while unless one had a filter. Her hair-dresser, she added, had a water softener machine which was very nice.

' — but,' continued Mr. Middleton, who had been champing while his sister unburdened herself, 'though I am, as it were, one with this countryside, bone of its bone, soil of its soil, there are others who have a yet greater and long claim on it, affection towards it, and to them I must yield pride of place. Besides I don't know the man.'

'But that doesn't matter, does it?' said Daphne. 'I mean if you begin Dear Sir it's all right. People get heaps of letters from people they don't know. Lady Bond gets about six or seven every day asking her to be a patroness for a ball, or sell tickets for something.'

'Of Lady Bond's post bag I know nothing,' cried Mr. Middleton, goaded beyond endurance, 'but the cases are entirely dissimilar, entirely. I do not wish to ask Sir Ogilvy to patronize anything, to take tickets for anything. I do not wish to have anything to do with him at all. I do not know him, I repeat. In fact nobody knows him.'

'But they must, Uncle Jack,' said Daphne, severely practical. 'You can't be a person that nobody knows them, unless it was a kind of mystery film.'

Mr. Cameron laughed, so Daphne laughed too, though she didn't quite know why. Then Mrs. Stonor took her family back to dinner, with a promise to return later in the evening.

'How did you and Mrs. Pucken enjoy the meeting?' said Mrs. Stonor
to Palfrey while she was carving a chicken and Palfrey was handing
breadsauce, gravy, peas and new potatoes.

'It was very nice, thank you madam, I'm sure,' said Palfrey with such
a wealth of sinister meaning that Denis and Daphne got the giggles.

'Couldn't you hear?' said Mrs. Stonor. 'Lord Stoke wasn't very
distinct.'

'It wasn't that, madam,' said Palfrey in a manner carefully calculated to stimulate curiosity.

'Well, I hope you got a nice tea afterwards,' said Mrs. Stonor, dis-
missing the whole affair in what Palfrey considered an unfair and
unsympathetic way.

'Well, I always said no one could make breadsauce like you, Palfrey,'
said Denis, helping himself to far more than his share. 'What was wrong?'

'It was Lou, Mr. Denis,' said Palfrey.

'What happened?' asked Denis. 'Was she sick after tea?'

'Yes, Mr. Denis. She is very given to be bilious. I was just the same
when I was her age, the least thing, like a pork chop, or prawns and
cocoa upset me. But it wasn't so much that. Mrs. Pucken was quite
shocked, and it's not to be surprised at.'

'Well, what was it?' said Denis, 'or forever after hold your peace,
because I shan't ask you again. I got quite a bit of work done yesterday,
Lilian, and I want to try it on Catherine's piano.'

'I'm sure I would be the last to say anything,' Palfrey began.

'So you are,' said Denis, 'but do go on.'

'Well, madam,' said Palfrey, retransferring her patronage to her
mistress, 'Mrs. Middleton's dog, that Flora, was making quite a nuisance of himself while Mr. Middleton was speaking.'

'It's not him, it's her,' said Daphne. 'She's a bitch, Palfrey.'

'Whining and making a nuisance of himself he was,' said Palfrey,
who had a rooted conviction, born of her extreme delicacy, that all
dogs were he and all cats, or pussies, she: as indeed they too often are.
'Sitting by Mr. Cameron's chair he was, so that everyone where we was
sitting passed the remark what a nuisance he was. And then what must
my lady, do but take the dog as bold as brass and away she takes him
to the stable and shuts him in and then comes back to eat her tea.'

'But I think it was very kind of Lou to take Flora away,' said Mrs.
Stonor. 'She was making a horrid noise.'

'It wasn't that, madam. It was Putting Herself Forward, just to show
off to Mr. Cameron. She won't hear the last of it from her mother. Well
Lou, I said to her, I'm really ashamed of you I am. Of you and for you,
I said. If Mr. Cameron was Marleen or Donald Duck you couldn't act
more silly, I said.'

'Well, that was quite dreadful,' said Mrs. Stonor sympathetically.
'What is Lou doing now?'

'Mrs. Pucken gave her a dose of salts and sent her home, madam,' said Palfrey. 'She was crying so much she dropped one of the dessert plates and broke it. That makes only four we've got now, madam.'

Feeling that this parting line could not be improved she made her exit to the kitchen, leaving her audience stunned.

'Poor Lou,' sighed Mrs. Stonor. 'And of course it would be one of the good dessert plates. I had better put the rest away. And yet perhaps I hadn't, because it is silly not to use things just because some of them are broken.'

'Wear them and tear them, good body, good body,' said Denis sympathetically. 'Or why not have them gummed onto plush frames and hang them on the wall? Or have numbers painted round them and stick some hands through the middle and you'll have four tasty clocks.'

'Don't go on like a Women's Institute, Denis,' said his stepmother severely. 'I shall simply take no notice of those plates and go on using them exactly as if nothing had happened.'

'That's right, darling,' said Denis. 'Never let dumb objects get the upper hand. But I think Alister ought to be warned about Lou, or he will find she has stolen his shoes to have the pleasure of cleaning them. Why Lou has to pick on a middle-aged man for the first object of her young passion I can't think. I suppose it is fate. I've never loved anyone so much as I loved Mrs. Miller, the drill sergeant's wife at school and heaven knows she had four married daughters.'

'When you call Alister middle-aged, you simply don't know what you are talking about,' said Mrs. Stonor, suddenly roused. 'And everyone falls in love at one time or another with someone who is much older than they are. I think you are very unkind to laugh at Lou. I might as well laugh — —'

She paused, and Daphne who had been thinking along her own lines, paying as usual very little attention to her stepmother, said she liked Alister awfully and people were much more interesting when they were a bit older and she was awfully glad he was going to be at Laverings for some of his holiday and could they have coffee outside because it was so hot.

So they had coffee outside with the last sunlight on delphiniums and roses, almost too good to be true. Mrs. Stonor was pleased to learn through Daphne that Mr. Cameron would be at Laverings for part of the summer. She liked him very much and didn't mind how much he talked to her about himself and about Daphne. Her only anxiety was on his account, an apprehension that he might be caring for Daphne a little more than would be good for his peace of mind. What Daphne herself felt she could not guess. Her stepdaughter's frank avowal of a preference for older people might be personal, might be general. She had noticed for some time past that Daphne was more than ready to express a flattering desire for Mr. Cameron's company, but all these young

Dianas hunted the prey of the moment with wholehearted gusto, leaving no room for sentiment. It had also crossed her mind that Daphne liked young Mr. Bond, but young Mr. Bond's pitch had been queered that afternoon by Mrs. Tebben's indiscreet remarks about Betty Deane. It was possible that Daphne was punishing poor Mr. Bond for an earlier flame by throwing herself with even less than her usual hail-fellow-well-met lack of reticence into Mr. Cameron's arms; tropically so, of course, for Daphne was all against what she called sloppiness. It looked to Mrs. Stonor uncommonly as if young Mr. Bond were going to be hurt by her unrestrained Daphne, and though she had no fear that he would die of it, she hated to see anyone suffer. This thought led her to wonder with her ever anxious stepmother's mind if Daphne were going to let herself be unhappy about young Mr. Bond, and from this it was but a step to wondering how much Mr. Cameron might be hurt if Daphne used him as a whip for young Mr. Bond. Altogether there was too much chance of people being hurt and the sunshine took on a livid hue and the roses became dun. If Mr. Cameron were going to suffer she would not at all enjoy standing by and seeing it. Not at all.

Then her mind wandered to Denis. She was glad she hadn't finished what she had begun in a spirit of resentment to say. It was not fair for Denis, who found so much pleasure in Mrs. Middleton's society, to laugh at poor Lou whose affections were set on an equally unattainable object. Mrs. Stonor was extremely fond of her sister-in-law, but had no guess as to what was in her mind. So kind was Catherine Middleton to everyone that her kindness to Denis was nothing to notice, but if Denis were going to be a little too grateful for the kindness, it might hit him as hard as a real passion. He would not die of his emotions any more than young Mr. Bond would. Mrs. Stonor had not nursed him through a difficult youth without knowing that his music was on the whole his life and would always be so, but she suddenly felt a little pang of jealousy in case anyone should by a kind look innocently undo some of the good work that she had patiently been building up for years, set her nervous Denis back a step on the road to health that was so necessary if he was to use his music seriously. For the moment everything looked twisted. Everyone she cared for was in danger. Not ferocious danger, but danger of a little pain, a little disillusionment, a little spiritual hardening. It had looked as if it would be a perfect summer, but that was ridiculous to expect. Probably she was worrying and exaggerating quite morbidly. Quite unnecessarily. Better to think of something real, like the dessert plate, a definite annoyance.

'It is all too difficult,' she said half aloud.

'What is, darling?' said Denis. 'Lou and the dessert plate?'

'Yes,' said Mrs. Stonor, looking affectionately at her stepson's mocking affectionate eyes. 'Lou and the dessert plate and life. I suppose we had better go over to Laverings now. Are you going to bring your music, Denis?'

'No, darling. Being a genius it is all in my head,' said Denis modestly. 'I did finish writing it down this afternoon in case I died and then a great work would be lost to the world, but as far as playing it on Catherine's piano goes I need nothing but my musical brain and my long, agile, yet powerful fingers.'

They found the Middletons and Mr. Cameron in the library because of mosquitoes, so Denis had to keep his music to himself while Mr. Middleton discussed, if a monologue may be termed a discussion, the events of the afternoon.

'He has never stopped since the beginning of dinner,' said Mr. Cameron to Mrs. Stonor, surveying his senior partner with exasperated pride. 'It is true that he has managed to include the Conquest of Peru, the Thermae of Diocletian, the philosophy of Confucius, the Repeal of the Corn Laws and the Counter-Reformation in his survey of this afternoon, but the principle is the same.'

'It is quite extraordinary how many things Jack manages to talk about,' said Mrs. Stonor. 'He has always been exactly the same since I first remember him when he was a big schoolboy and I was a very little girl. I can't think how he thinks of so many things to say. I mean I could think of a fair number of things to say about things like sewing, or nursing, or books I'd been reading, or cooking, or places I'd been to, but I wouldn't ever get so far as thinking them worth saying. Of course I daresay they wouldn't be. My mother used to scold me a little because when she took me abroad I wouldn't speak French, which I really knew fairly well, though I never can think why when people say abroad they mean France as a rule, and yet most other places are much abroader than France, but people who have been to Russia and Turkey and Iceland never say they have been abroad, and I used to try to explain to her that it wasn't that I was too shy to talk French, but I never had very much to say in English, so there didn't seem to be any more to say in French. I wonder how Catherine bears it. I suppose it wouldn't do any good if she didn't. No one has ever stopped Jack talking. And then of course she is very, very fond of him and that makes one so happy that one minds nothing,' said Mrs. Stonor a little wistfully as she thought of her difficult moody husband and how their great affection had made a working partnership which was becoming easier and more peaceful every year, when he had to die.

'Yes, Catherine is very fond of him, bless her,' said Mr. Cameron. 'And I think she could bear anything quite happily for someone she loved; certainly not show it if she were hurt in any way. She has unusual self-control.'

That word Hurt again, thought Mrs. Stonor a little angrily. Too many feelings about as usual.

'And Jack is extremely fond of her,' said Mrs. Stonor almost defiantly.

'Yes, he is,' said Mr. Cameron. 'He sometimes dissembles his love

almost to the point of kicking her downstairs, but he is entirely dependent on her affection.'

'Nobody is entirely dependent on affection,' said Mrs. Stonor, half to
herself. 'You only think you are. My husband and I were just as fond
of each other as Jack and Catherine, but he is dead and here am I still
alive. And if he were suddenly alive again there would be one heavenly
moment, and then so embarrassing. Not so bad as the Monkey's Paw
of course, but bristling with difficulties.'

'You are marvellous,' said Mr. Cameron, almost laughing. 'I never
knew anyone who put things as you do.'

'I don't put them at all,' said Mrs. Stonor in serious surprise. 'I was
only telling the truth.'

But at that moment her brother, anxious for the whole company to
benefit by what he was saying, broke across their conversation.

'You my dear Lilian, you Cameron,' he said, 'will bear me out when
I say that the whole of the unfortunate debâcle of this afternoon is due
to one man, and that man — —'

He paused dramatically. His wife and Mr. Cameron who were
accustomed to these rhetorical pauses which he merely introduced in
order to have the pleasure of filling them up himself, said nothing. His
sister, who had seen so much less of him in late years, was rash enough
to say Lord Bond.

'No, no, Lilian, *not* Bond,' said Mr. Middleton. 'Bond, a well-meaning
ass, would have done his best. He was, I understand, prepared to
explain to Stoke, whose deafness make him really unfit to transact any
sort of business now, that he was to propose me as chairman. But if
Stoke, knowing that his presence at the meeting is essential, chooses
rather to go and inspect my cows with my cowman than to do his duty
as a citizen, what is to be expected. It was useless for Bond to try to tell
Stoke what was expected of him. He came in late, would listen to no
explanation, took the chair himself and talked about cows. I may say
without undue pride that I know as much about cows as most men,
but a drawing-room meeting convened for the purpose of defending a
piece of our national heritage against an invader is not a fit moment to
discuss Jerseys and Friesians. I wash my hands of the whole thing.'

'Well, Uncle Jack,' said Daphne, anxious for fair play. 'You did
mostly talk about Flora when you made your speech, you know.'

Mr. Middleton was about to quell his niece by marriage with his
thunder when a thought struck him.

'Where is Flora?' he asked. 'My doggie has not come to see her
master to-night. Was she at dinner, Catherine?'

Mrs. Middleton said she thought not and appealed to Mr. Cameron
who said he didn't remember seeing her. Mr. Middleton's agitation
became very marked. Mrs. Middleton rang the bell. Denis and Daphne,
rather bored, went over to the bagatelle board. Ethel came in.

'Do you know where Flora is, Ethel?' asked Mrs. Middleton.

Ethel said she was sure she couldn't say and Cook had said she hadn't come for her supper. She then waited in a baleful and unhelpful way, hoping for tragedy.

'My doggie,' said Mr. Middleton, agitated. 'She will not sleep unless she has her good-night talk to master. Perhaps she has gone to my bedroom to look for me.'

He looked round helplessly.

'She's not upstairs, sir,' said Ethel, rejoicing in the bad news, 'because Alice looked for her when she went up to tidy the rooms. Cook said You might as well look for Flora, Alice, while you are up there, so she looked, but there wasn't a sign nowhere. Cook thinks she's gone hunting.'

'She would never go alone,' said her indignant master, 'never. She always waits till master has hat on head and stick in hand before she will cross the threshold.'

'She brought in a partridge last Tuesday, sir,' said Ethel, 'but Cook said not to mention it in case you was upset, so she gave it to Pollett.'

'Thank you, Ethel,' said Mrs. Middleton, 'that will do. I expect she will come back soon.'

'A light must be kept burning,' said Mr. Middleton.

'Really, Jack,' said Mrs. Stonor, 'it isn't as if Flora was your erring daughter that had run away, and a candle in the window to guide her home.'

'Of course we can leave the electric light on, darling,' said Mrs. Middleton, 'but the question is which. As all the doors and the ground floor windows are shut, she couldn't get in and I am afraid she would howl.'

'Then,' said Mr. Middleton nobly, 'I should hear her.'

'And so would everyone else in the house,' said Mrs. Middleton, 'except the maids who never hear anything and wouldn't get up if they did. We might go down to the wood and call her.'

'No. I will not go down to the wood. She will expect to find master at home,' said Mr. Middleton. 'But I will sit on the terrace and call her from time to time. She may hear me and come.'

Accordingly he went out onto the terrace and established himself in a garden chair. Mrs. Stonor accompanied him.

'I say, Uncle Jack,' Daphne suddenly shouted from the bagatelle board. 'I say. I have only just thought of it. Flora is in the stable. Lou locked her up when she was interrupting your speech and then Mrs. Pucken gave her a dose of salts and sent her home, so I expect she forgot.'

It naturally took some time for the united forces of the company to explain to Mr. Middleton that it was Lou, not Flora, who had had the dose of salts, and why Lou, who was not on the Laverings establishment, happened to be in the drawing-room that afternoon, but when he did understand his indignation knew no bounds.

'Flora was being a devilish nuisance to put it mildly,' said Mr. Cameron, 'and deserves all she got. I'd leave her there all night.'

Before Mr. Middleton could marshal his indignation in suitable words, Daphne said she would go and fetch Flora and invited Mr. Cameron to go with her. Followed by Mr. Middleton's voice beseeching them quite unnecessarily to be kind to Flora, they vanished into the dusk towards the stable where the monster cart horse lived, laughing as they went. Mrs. Stonor felt again the little stir of uneasiness that had assailed her earlier in the evening, but put it away and drifted back into talk about old days with her brother.

'I suppose,' said Denis rather diffidently to Mrs. Middleton, 'this wouldn't be a possible moment for me to play a few notes on your piano, would it?'

Mrs. Middleton, seeing her husband and sister-in-law comfortably gossiping farther along the terrace said she would love him to play.

'I'll keep the soft pedal down all the time,' said Denis. 'It's just a movement of my new ballet. I've got it all down on paper and I want to have a little debauch and play it on the piano. I'll swear not to tell you when the oboe comes in, or how nice the 'cellos sound just here. May I put one or two books on my chair? I like it a little higher.'

Without waiting for permission he took a couple of large volumes that were on a table by the piano.

'Duets,' he said, looking at one.

'Yes. I used to amuse myself with them,' said Mrs. Middleton.

'I didn't know you played,' said Denis.

'I don't,' said Mrs. Middleton, 'I did before I was married and when I lived in London, but one can't play duets alone somehow. I ought to have a little piano in my sitting-room, but even so it would make rather a noise.'

Denis at once realized that Mr. Middleton would find music disturbing and wondered what the point was of having a grand piano in the library if no one could use it. But he did not say this. He said what an amusing collection of duets she had and how he adored all that modern French stuff.

'We might try some of them one day when Uncle Jack is away,' he said, sitting down to the piano. 'Or would it bore you?'

Mrs. Middleton said it would be great fun, only she must have the bass and the pedals, so that she could cover up all her mistakes.

'That will be perfect,' said Denis, beginning to play with the soft pedal down as he had promised, 'and I will do the counting. Do you like One and, two and, or Wuh-un, too-oo? Some people are proud about counting, but I think it's half the fun of duets. Now,' he went on, half speaking, half following the melody, 'this is where all the lovers have

had a picnic in a grove, all very Watteau, and they all go off two and
two and there is one unfortunate gentleman left who has no one to
make love to, all in lovely blues he is to be if only I can keep the
designer and the producer off putting him into white tights, and he has
a sad little pas seul to himself to express the pangs of having no one to
love, all graceful and melancholy. And this is where the critics will say
"Mr. Stonor should guard against the primrose path of a too facile gift
for melody." Facile! Catherine, I would sooner invent six hundred
pages of stark atonality than one real tune. I nearly killed myself over
this facile little melody.'

'Keep the pedal down,' murmured Mrs. Middleton.

'I will keep it down if it is with my last drop of blood, not that that
would be much use,' said Denis, 'although a pint of pure water does
weigh a pound and a quarter. And what is more I will stop playing at
once if it is likely to inconvenience anyone,' he added, with a quick
glance unlike the leisurely mode of his speech.

'It is no inconvenience,' said Mrs. Middleton and resigned herself to
the facile melody if Denis liked to call it that. A long tiring day. Denis,
looking once more at her, decided that she ought to be allowed to rest,
and he amused himself on the piano, always keeping the soft pedal
down, till the sound of voices and an odious sound of barking shattered
his music.

'That,' said Mr. Middleton loudly from the terrace, 'is Flora.'

No one contradicted him.

'I shall call her,' said Mr. Middleton. 'Flora!'

' "Tell me, shepherds, have you seen," ' Denis remarked as he shut
the piano and put the duets back on the table.

The whole party now met on the terrace.

'And what did my doggie think, shut up alone, no master to love
her?' cried Mr. Middleton. 'How her faithful heart was tried!'

'She was having a marvellous time, Uncle Jack,' said Daphne. 'There
are a lot of rats in the stable and she had a splendid fight. When Alister
and I got there, there was such a row we couldn't hear ourselves speak.'

'I didn't know spaniels had it in them,' said Mr. Cameron, 'but all
the blood of the Macdonalds must be in Flora. The way she got that rat
down was a pleasure, a grisly one I admit, to the connoisseur.'

'So I gave her some coffee sugar that I'd taken with me,' said the
practical Daphne, 'and she buried the rat and then we took her for a
walk and I got my shoes absolutely sopping. There's a lot of dew about.
I *have* enjoyed myself. I say, Uncle Jack, could Denis and I play our
duet? I feel I ought to celebrate the death of the rat. I know you aren't
musical, but it wouldn't take long and it doesn't make much noise, not
really much.'

Flushed with excitement she dragged Denis back into the library and
opened the piano.

'Catherine!' said Mr. Middleton, 'I appeal to you. That I loathe and abhor this modern cacophony that goes by the name of music is true enough, but of the classics there is no more ardent worshipper than I. Bach, wise, serene, human in the deepest sense; Beethoven, a troubled mortal like ourselves, foretelling in his later works all the struggle, the turmoil of the world we live in to-day, a true prophet crying in the wilderness — —'

Mrs. Stonor said one must always remember that he was deaf.

'—Mozart, that prince among his peers,' Mr. Middleton continued, raising his voice, 'who filled his brief life with pure bright sound. One cannot but love him. There is a little melody of his from a violin-sonata that I whistle to Flora. She loves it,' he said looking round for possible disagreement. 'That universal language is music even to her doggie ears. Flora!'

'I think she has run away again,' said Mr. Cameron.

'You and Daphne had better go and find her then,' said Mrs. Stonor, 'or Jack will talk all night. Daphne!'

'Hullo!' shouted Daphne from the library where she and Denis were fighting for the pedals.

'Flora is lost again,' said Mrs. Stonor. 'Hadn't you and Alister better find her?'

'I expect she's gone to unbury the rat,' yelled Daphne. 'Come on now, Denis. Ready?'

The cheerful sound of a duet to celebrate the death of a rat filled the evening air. Mr. Middleton winced in a noticeable way, but owing to the gathering darkness no one saw him. Mr. Cameron began to talk about Daphne to Mrs. Stonor. Mrs. Middleton wandered down the path to look at the white Canterbury bells which were her pride at the moment. In her white dress she was almost indistinguishable among them now. Luckily the duet was short and before Mr. Middleton could arrange suitable periods in which to express his disapproval the performers had finished and come out again.

'There is Flora,' said Daphne, as a brown form came lightly trotting over the lawn. 'What did I say?'

Flora, a look of conscious pride on her face, came up to her master and deposited at his feet with tender care the mangled and mould-covered corpse of her rat.

'Oh Diamond, Diamond, what hast thou done?' said Mr. Middleton, shrinking from the offering.

'I say, Uncle Jack, you oughtn't to talk to her as if she was Cain,' said Daphne indignantly. 'She has killed a jolly good rat and I expect Pucken will be as pleased as anything. I'll ask him to bury it properly so that she can't dig it up again.'

'Flora! Good dog!' said Mr. Middleton, feeling that this was the attitude required of him.

But Flora, having paid this formal tribute to her master, turned her back to him and attached herself to Denis with loving and unwelcome gambols.

'Well, good night, Uncle Jack,' said Denis, feeling that the end of the evening had not been a success.

'Yes, you go to bed, Denis,' said Mrs. Stonor, who was a little anxious about the night dew for her stepson since Daphne had so vividly described its effects. 'I'll come along with Daphne in a few moments.'

Denis walked down the path towards the gate. On the way he stopped by the Canterbury bells.

'Good night and thank you so much,' he said to his hostess.

'And thank you for the music,' said Mrs. Middleton. 'We will try the duets when Jack is in town.'

'White flowers, and you all in white,' said Denis. 'Could you keep Flora? She has taken an embarrassing affection for me.'

Mrs. Middleton stooped and held Flora by her collar till she heard the latch of the garden gate click behind Denis. Then she went back to the house, asked Mr. Cameron to take the rat in the library tongs and put it in the dust bin, and applied herself to soothing her husband. Flora, pleased with a well-spent day, was obliging enough to go to sleep at Mr. Middleton's feet, so the evening ended more harmoniously than might have been expected. Mr. Cameron walked back to the White House with Mrs. Stonor and Daphne and it was not till well after midnight that Mrs. Middleton heard him come back. She guessed that he had been talking to Mrs. Stonor about Daphne and about himself, and it is probable that her guess was not far out. As she went to sleep she wondered how soon Mr. Cameron would find himself impelled to talk to her about Daphne. Friends come and go. Alister might be a friend that was soon to go a little from her. Would any newer friend come a little nearer?

VIII

HUNTING THE FOLK-SONG

ALTHOUGH Lord Bond fully realized that his wife was a woman of inflexible determination who could carry out her intentions at whatever cost to others, it was not until he had seen her set off for London in the large car that he breathed freely. But not for long, for a difficult task lay before him.

He had been so well brought up, first by an autocratic mother and then by an autocratic wife, not to speak of a black period during which he had been brought up by both ladies, who sometimes used him as a pawn against each other and at other times joined forces to crush him, that he had a feeling of guilt on those very rare occasions when he set out to enjoy himself in his own way. When he met Denis Stonor and was deluded by his kindness into thinking that he had discovered a fellow-enthusiast for Gilbert and Sullivan, he had invited Denis to dinner and music without thinking of the consequences. When he came to think of them he was uneasy, but kept his uneasiness to himself. Then the slight intoxication of being in league with a fellow man against the regiment of Lady Bond had encouraged him to the further excess of inviting Daphne, Mr. Cameron and Mrs. Stonor. And as his son was coming they would now be a party of six, but of this he had not breathed a word to his wife. The only drawback to this secrecy was that he knew Lady Bond had gone to London leaving word that his lordship would be alone that evening, and he would have to face Spencer with the news that there would be a small party. Desperate ills need desperate remedies, so Lord Bond went into the library and rang the bell. Spencer appeared, with the faint and provoking air of relaxation which Lady Bond's absence always produced in the household and which was bitterly if dumbly resented by the master of Staple Park.

'Yes, my lord,' said Spencer.

'Oh, did her ladyship mention that we should be six to-night?' said Lord Bond, plunging into the subject.

'No, my lord,' said Spencer.

'Yes, six,' said Lord Bond, temporizing.

'And that, my lord, would be . . .?' said Spencer with irritating deference.

Lord Bond wanted to say Five friends of mine and it doesn't matter to you who they are and give me the key of piano at once and take a month's notice and I hate you.

'Mrs. and Miss Stonor and Mr. Stonor and Mr. Cameron,' he said in an unnatural voice.

'That would be four, my lord; five together with your lordship,' said Spencer. 'Shall I tell Mrs. Alcock five?'

'No, I said six; didn't you hear me?' said Lord Bond, beginning to revolt. 'Mr. Bond is coming down.'

'Very good, my lord. Anything else, my lord?' said Spencer with weary tolerance.

'Yes. That champagne in the fourth bin,' said Lord Bond, 'and the 1875 brandy. And the key of the piano.'

Spencer bowed and went away. Neither side had won; or more correctly both sides had lost. Spencer had been ordered to produce wine and brandy which he considered suitable for better dinner parties and knew that he could not disobey. Lord Bond had demanded the key of his own piano, but Spencer would not give it up till the last moment and even then Lord Bond feared that he might be reduced to the ignominious position of having to beg for it again in front of his guests. On the whole, Spencer's game. The only person who was pleased was Mrs. Alcock who was always on the verge of giving notice because her employers did not entertain on a scale suited to her ambitions. Six was hardly a party, but it would at least give her an excuse to harry the scullerymaid and the two kitchenmaids.

At eleven o'clock the small car came to the front door to take Lord Bond over to Southbridge on business. Something unfamiliar struck him, which on investigation turned out to be a strange face in the chauffeur's seat.

'Who is that driving?' he asked Spencer, forgetting for the moment the blood feud between them.

Spencer, who never forgot what was due to himself, said coldly that he understood that Pollett's brother was taking Ferguson's place while Ferguson was in town with her ladyship and he supposed that was the young man. He accompanied these words with a look of such thinly veiled contempt that Lord Bond, feeling for Ed Pollett a sympathy which Ed, blissful in his brother's old uniform, did not in the least require, seated himself in front beside his temporary chauffeur. Spencer, who knew to a nicety how employers should behave, nearly gave notice on the spot, but remembering that the piano key was still in his keeping, decided to rest on his laurels and reserve the question of notice till a more pressing occasion. He stood on the steps till the car disappeared and then returned to the establishment which he felt was, with the trifling exception of that second window in his pantry, almost all that a butler could wish, especially when his employers were not contaminating it with their presence.

*

At Laverings Mr. Middleton had decided to take a week at home, partly to recover from the meeting on Saturday, partly because things at the office were slack enough at the moment to justify the absence of the two senior partners, and if it came to that he and Mr. Cameron could discuss the preliminaries of the new buildings for the College of Epistemological Ideology which a gentleman, described by the Press as a super-steel magnate, had just forced upon the unwilling University of Oxbridge, just as well in the country as in town. So Mrs. Middleton and Denis had not yet played their duets.

On the day of Lord Bond's dinner party Mr. Cameron, wandering as he so often did into the garden of the White House, found Mrs. Stonor peacefully getting the peas for lunch, and accompanied her on the other side of the peasticks, talking through the prosaic but exquisite trellis of leaves and tendrils.

'Daphne isn't helping you with the peas, is she?'

Mrs. Stonor, after looking carefully round, said she wasn't. In fact, she added, Daphne had gone into Winter Overcotes in the bus with Denis to see if they could get a copy of the *Gondoliers*, as Denis had felt it in his bones that Lord Bond would want him to play 'Dance a Cachuca' and wasn't quite sure if he remembered it, while Daphne had equally felt it in her bones that Lord Bond would require 'Poor Wandering One' and wanted to get a copy of the *Pirates*.

Mr. Cameron said how very kind Daphne was, adding that he had never heard her sing and how much he looked forward to the evening.

'She doesn't really sing,' said Mrs. Stonor. 'She knows all the words and the music of lots of songs, but it isn't a voice. She and Denis just have fun together.'

Mr. Cameron was faintly shocked by this criticism. However doubtless Mrs. Stonor wasn't really musical and didn't know. Mrs. Stonor, sorry for his obvious disappointment at not finding Daphne said they would probably be back on the twelve o'clock bus and wouldn't he stay till half-past twelve on the chance, and if he would excuse her while she took the peas in they could sit in the garden. So she took the peas in to Palfrey, and came back to Mr. Cameron.

The next hour was not an easy one for Mrs. Stonor. Her guest, while trying to conduct polite conversation on ordinary topics, was so obviously pulled back to the subject of Daphne again and again as if he were a tethered golf ball on an elastic cord, that she felt a great deal of pity for him. Even when she led the conversation to the work that he and Mr. Middleton were engaged upon at the moment, he could only bring a limited amount of his attention to bear, and Mrs. Stonor well knew that if a man is incapable of being a bore on his own subject, it must mean that his feelings are very deeply occupied. Her compassion led her to relate a number of very dull stories of Daphne's school career of her subsequent training at a Secretarial College and of the various positions she had held, winding up with the Dr. Browning whose death had thrown her temporarily out of employment.

'I suppose one oughtn't to call him selfish,' said Mrs. Stonor, 'because death seems to be something beyond one's control, but it really was annoying, just as Daphne had settled down to the work. One really would think doctors could do something about it, but I daresay they get so used to the idea of people dying that they don't really notice it in themselves.'

Mr. Cameron, paying but scant attention to this interesting theory, said he wondered if Mrs. Stonor would let him ask her something, but perhaps there was hardly time now.

Mrs. Stonor looked at him. What she had half feared must be only too true. She liked Alister Cameron very, very much. He was now going to hurt himself a good deal, and hers would be the unpleasant role of seeing him suffer and not being able to help him; for sympathy is often difficult to offer and difficult to accept and even so does not get to the root of the matter. That foolish child Daphne had called him middle-aged, which just showed how silly the young were, for Alister Cameron was what Mrs. Stonor regarded as a very reasonable kind of age and was moreover, she felt, the sort of person one could depend on, the sort of person it would be a very blessed relief and relaxation to depend on.

'I don't think,' said Mr. Cameron, who had expended some ingenuity in preparing this approach to his subject,' that you have ever seen my rooms in the Middle Temple.'

'No, I don't think I have,' said Mrs. Stonor. 'In fact,' she added in a burst of candour, 'I am sure I haven't, because I have never been in them.'

'I have a particularly delightful view,' said Mr. Cameron. 'Very green and peaceful.'

'That must be enchanting,' said Mrs. Stonor. 'It is extraordinary what lovely views there are in London. Absolutely as quiet and green as the country. At least not at all really, because there is always the noise and the smuts, but one would hardly notice the difference except for the way you can't hear yourself speak and the smuts come off on your clothes. When I was little we lived in Cadogan Square and I used to get absolutely filthy in summer, playing in a corner of the Square under some laurels.'

'Perhaps,' said Mr. Cameron with a visible effort, 'you would come to lunch or tea with me one day.'

Mrs. Stonor said she would love to.

'And bring anyone you like, of course,' said Mr. Cameron.

'Well, I don't think that would matter,' said Mrs. Stonor, 'because the Temple isn't like Albany.'

'Do you have that feeling about Albany?' said Mr. Cameron, more human than he had been that morning. 'How splendid.'

'I am absolutely convinced,' said Mrs. Stonor, 'that a Guardsman is lurking in every set of chambers in Albany to Ruin people's reputation.'

'Instead of which it is women now, and young men with beards,' said Mr. Cameron morosely. 'If you wanted to have your reputation ruined there is really nowhere to go nowadays. I'm afraid we can't even make a pretence of it in the Temple, but I do hope you'll come all the same. And of course,' he added, with a return to his former nervous manner, 'do bring someone with you if you'd care to.'

'I'm sure Daphne would love to come,' said Mrs. Stonor, sorrier than ever for Mr. Cameron's difficulties.

'Oh, Daphne. Yes, that would be very nice,' said Mr. Cameron, with an airy manner which he flattered himself entirely disguised his feelings. He then fell so uncomfortably silent that his hostess was paralysed and hunted wildly for some remark to break the embarrassment.

'It's funny,' she said desperately, 'how well we have got to know you this summer, Alister, without really knowing anything about you.'

She then wished she had not said it, for it sounded exactly as if she were a real mother asking her daughter's suitor what his intentions and position were. But Mr. Cameron appeared to be rather glad than otherwise of the opportunity.

'There's practically nothing to know,' he said. 'My parents died when I was at school and left me pretty well off, and when I left Oxford I went into an architect's office and then I came in as partner to Middleton and the firm is doing very well.'

'I *am* sorry about your parents,' said Mrs. Stonor, with such genuine sympathy that Mr. Cameron was moved to tell her a great deal more about himself. In the course of this narration it was discovered that he was almost exactly two years older than Mrs. Stonor, that his father had been in Colonel Stonor's regiment and that his old nurse came from the same village as Palfrey. By this time it was one o'clock and Mrs. Stonor said the children were probably having lunch at Woolworth's and would come out by the half-past one bus, so Mr. Cameron said good-bye and went back to Laverings. Half-way down the garden he remembered that what he really went to the White House for was to ask Mrs. Stonor whether she thought he would have any chance if he urged his suit upon Daphne, but he had so much enjoyed himself that the moment never seemed to arise. He wished she had not spoken of Daphne and Denis as the children. The word child seemed to open a wider gulf than he liked between him and Daphne. On the other hand it had put him and Mrs. Stonor into a pleasant conspiracy together against the disturbing element of youth. Daphne was horribly disturbing, no doubt of it. So very friendly, so very remote; so sympathetic, so unconcerned. A riddle well worth solving, but it was sometimes dangerous to read a riddle aright.

*

After lunch Mr. Middleton went up to his room to do some concentrated work, leaving his wife and his partner in the library. Mrs. Middleton described rather amusingly how she had wrestled with a Woman's Institute Committee meeting in Skeynes and then asked Mr. Cameron how he had spent his morning. He said he had been over at the White House.

'I though Daphne might be there,' he said, 'but she and Denis had gone to Winter Overcotes, and I stayed and talked to Lilian. I hope she and Daphne will come and lunch in my rooms in the autumn. You must come too, Catherine, and make a fourth.'

'Too many women,' said Mrs. Middleton. 'One too many certainly; possibly two too many.'

'What do you mean?' asked Mr. Cameron.

'I don't exactly know,' said Mrs. Middleton. 'Do you know yourself, Alister?'

'I still don't understand,' said Mr. Cameron. 'You wouldn't be one too many ever, Catherine.'

'Not as a general rule,' said Mrs. Middleton, 'but on occasion, yes. And on such an occasion I am rather wondering who else would be a little superfluous.'

'Dear Catherine,' said Mr. Cameron, 'how straight you look at things. I don't know what I'd do without you. Of course you know what I feel about Daphne.'

'Yes,' said Mrs. Middleton, 'and I am not going to talk about it. I'll give you my blessing, or I'll bind up your wounds, but not now. Not till one or the other is needed. Was Lilian nice?'

Mr. Cameron said she couldn't have been nicer. One of the most sympathetic women he had ever met. They had had, he said, a perfectly delightful conversation.

'About what?' said Mrs. Middleton.

Mr. Cameron said she had asked him a good deal about himself. Then, with a little hesitation, he said did Mrs. Middleton think that was a good sign.

'It depends,' said Mrs. Middleton. 'It is certainly a sign that Lilian is a very intelligent person, but I have known that for a long time. Very intelligent.'

'Oh!' said Mr. Cameron.

'As you ought to know if you have any intelligence yourself, Alister,' said Mrs. Middleton in a detached way. 'But I rather think you haven't just now. You will never find out what Daphne thinks by talking to her stepmother.'

'You couldn't − −?' Mr. Cameron began.

'Certainly not,' said Mrs. Middleton. 'I believe in non-intervention. If Daphne is your fate, Alister, speak to her yourself.'

Mr. Cameron pointed out to his hostess that he had already waited all morning in vain to try to see Daphne and then by degrees began to talk about Daphne and himself, gradually widening his treatment of the subject to include himself and Daphne and at length treating it on so ample a scale that Daphne vanished and he only spoke about himself. Mrs. Middleton listened kindly and sometimes let her thoughts wander. By the time tea came Mr. Cameron, who as a rule spoke so little, had talked himself nearly dry, but after a refreshing cup he showed every symptom of running on, when luckily Mr. Middleton summoned him to his work-room to discuss the central heating system for the Epistemological Ideological College. Mrs. Middleton, feeling the need of a change, went for a walk by herself down the fields to the coppice and thought with her accustomed tolerance of several things. Alister was certainly to go a little further from her, taking all he could before he went, all the attentive listening, the cool advice which she never gave unless asked, never spared if it was really wanted. And Denis was coming to play duets with her one day, when Jack was in London and would not be disturbed by the piano.

*

At a quarter to eight Lord Bond's little car, with Ed Pollett at the wheel, came to collect the Stonors and Mr. Cameron. Denis, who had heard that Ed knew one of the local folk songs hitherto unedited, went in front to explore this unworked mine. Ed, with the true countryman's caution, heightened in his case by his slightly defective mentality, would not commit himself, on the grounds that 'she', by which he meant the song, belonged to old Margett at Pooker's Piece. Denis, enchanted by this survival of the singer's property in a song, asked Ed if he thought old Margett would sing it, but was dashed by hearing that Margett, apparently a Puritan in his mode of thought, considered it unsuitable for the lay ear.

'Now if you was old Mr. Patten up at Skeynes Agnes,' said Ed, 'old Mr. Margett he'd sing her for you.'

On further enquiry Denis learned that old Margett and old Patten each had a song which he guarded jealously but would sing for the other, honour among bards being a marked quality. Ed, being a nephew of Mr. Patten the station master at Worsted, grandson of old Mr. Patten, and well known to be wanting, had from time to time been admitted to these bardic feasts and with an intellect unspoilt by school-ing, to which he had been practically immune, had retained the songs in his mind.

'You'd had ought to be there last Christmas,' said Ed, 'when old Mr. Margett sang her and old Mr. Patten he played the mouth organ. That was a fair treat.'

Denis, with the cunning of the collector on the warpath, asked Ed if he liked mouth organs.

Ed expressed the greatest admiration for that instrument and said he had a lovely one but it fell on the line and was flattened by the 6.47 down. His mother, he said regretfully, to whom he gave all his wages, wouldn't allow him two shillings to buy another and them sixpenny ones didn't seem to sing like. Enflamed by this poetic flight Ed, to Denis's great terror, took both hands off the wheel and went through the actions of playing a first class mouth organ.

'That's how she goes,' said Ed, carelessly taking the wheel again.

'I'll tell you what, Ed,' said Denis. 'I've got a mouth organ at home. She cost me five shillings and sings like a crooner. If you sing me old Mr. Patten's song, you can have her.'

On hearing this Ed would undoubtedly have upset the car into the ditch in his rapture, but for the opportune arrival of the Winter Over-cotes motor bus which debouched upon the road they were following.

As the driver, who also gave out tickets and knowing all his passengers was agreeable about giving credit to ladies who had left their purses at home or spent all their money at Woolworth's, was a second cousin of Ed's, Ed felt obliged by family pride to play a kind of cup and ball with the bus, finally outdistancing it by the narrowest of margins and turning triumphantly into Staple Park. Denis, who had been almost rigid with fright, realized that Ed's skill in driving was something out of the common and was quite ready to laugh at his own fears by the time they arrived.

'Now this is what I call really pleasant,' said Lord Bond as he greeted his guests. 'You will all have some sherry, won't you. Dinner nearly ready, Spencer?'

'Mr. Bond is not yet here, my lord,' said Spencer reproachfully. 'I was given to understand, my lord, that he would be here for dinner.'

'Well, if he isn't, we won't wait,' said Lord Bond pettishly.

Spencer managed to express without speaking that he could easily reduce Lord Bond to a charred cinder by a glance and only refrained from doing so out of consideration for the guests assembled. He then left the room and shortly reappeared to announce in a voice of Christian resignation that dinner was served.

'I must apologize for that boy of mine,' said Lord Bond as they took their seats. 'He was to be next to you, Miss Stonor, between you and your brother.'

Daphne said it didn't matter a bit and very likely he had forgotten. Shen then devoted herself to talking to Denis and Mr. Cameron, while Lord Bond and Mrs. Stonor laid the foundations of a sympathetic friendship, each talking on the subject uppermost in his or her mind, but listening with great courtesy to what the other had to say and never interrupting.

'I hope you are liking our part of the world, Mrs. Stonor,' said Lord Bond, speaking not so much as royalty, as representing the landowners of the county.

'I simply love it,' said Mrs. Stonor. 'And do you know, talking of the country, my maid Palfrey whom you wouldn't know, though she did come to the meeting and enjoyed your speech so much, comes from the same village as Mr. Cameron's nurse. Isn't it extraordinary?'

'Cameron's nurse, eh?' said Lord Bond, looking at Mr. Cameron rather nervously.

'His nurse when he was a baby,' said Mrs. Stonor. 'He doesn't have one now, though I believe he has quite a nice housekeeper, but of course it's not the same. Foxling-in-Henfold.'

'Eh,' said Lord Bond.

'The village,' Mrs. Stonor explained.

'Oh, Foxling; of course, of course. Used to go there when I was a boy. The Rector was a friend of my father's. He used to shoot jackdaws in the church tower and used incense. Now I'll tell you a remarkable thing. There was a farmer at Foxling who had a good Jersey, splendid milker. He tried crossing the strain with a West-Midland Shorthorn. What do you think happened? The calf, nice little heifer she was with a crumpled horn, won every prize she could at the Barchester Agricultural next year, but she never did any good after that. I told the farmer so, Hopgood his name was, I told him the heifer hadn't got the stamina. And I told Stoke so. That heifer won't have any stamina, I said. Extraordinary how often I've been right in things like that.'

'One often is,' said Mrs. Stonor. 'And what is even more extraordinary his father was in my husband's regiment.'

By the time Lord Bond had elucidated the fact that it was Mr. Cameron's father, not the father of Farmer Hopgood or the Rector of Foxling that was in question, Spencer was pouring champagne with a scorn that no one noticed.

'I hope my chauffeur brought you here comfortably,' said kind Lord Bond, turning to Daphne on his left. 'He is only temporary, but Mr. Middleton's chauffeur, whose brother he is, highly recommends him.'

'He's a jolly good driver,' said Daphne. 'I thought he'd hit the motor bus but he didn't.'

'He is going to sing me one of old Margett's songs,' said Denis, 'Do you know them, sir?'

'Yes, yes,' said Lord Bond. 'We'll have a talk about them after dinner.'

And with what Denis thought a curious want of interest in one so devoted to his neighbourhood, Lord Bond changed the subject and then Mr. Bond came in, full of apologies, having been detained he said in town. He slipped into his seat between Daphne and Denis, apologised again to everyone for not having changed, and applied himself to catching up on the two previous courses, which he quickly did, talking to Daphne at the same time. But Daphne, not as a rule a stickler for etiquette, seeing her stepmother and Mr. Cameron in talk, found that duty compelled her to turn to the deserted Lord Bond and discuss cows with great animation, having had a talk with Pucken to that very end during the afternoon. Young Mr. Bond was not altogether happy. He had been looking forward to this evening with almost excitement. To snatch an evening with Daphne without his mother's rather cramping presence had seemed to him a delightful adventure. He found Daphne one of the nicest girls he had ever known, perhaps the very nicest, and had no reason to think she felt otherwise than kindly disposed towards him. Now all was changed. Daphne was distinctly avoiding his conversation. Not so had the nymphs of New York treated the heir to an English title; not so did the nymphs of the London season treat a good dancer with a good car. Was it for this that he cut a very dull dinner and even duller dance and had motored forty miles on a lovely summer evening? He turned to Denis and gave him an account of a new ballet company he had lately seen, which turned out to be the company who might do Denis's ballet. What with the champagne and a very good ice pudding and the subsequent strawberries the two young men were quite happy when Lord Bond called down the table.

'I heard some news to-day that will interest you, C.W.,' he said. 'Palmer told me. He was on the bench with me at Southbridge. It's about his niece Betty, your great friend. Nice girl. She's just back from America — —'

Whether this was the end of the sentence no one ever knew, for Mrs. Stonor suddenly remembered that she could not remember whether or not she had remembered to tell Palfrey to remember to tell Mrs. Pucken to catch the butcher's boy at the end of the lane about the cutlets, and as they had all finished dinner Lord Bond asked Mrs. Stonor if she and Daphne would care to have coffee in the library where the men would shortly join them. Owing to the position of the dining-room door Daphne was able to turn a scornful shoulder on young Mr. Bond as she got up, at the same time issuing a pressing invitation to Mr. Cameron not to be long.

The two ladies were not long alone, but long enough for Mrs. Stonor to wonder uncomfortably whether Daphne was behaving badly by accident, which was not at all like her, or on purpose, which was not like her either. What the ins and outs were, Mrs. Stonor was not quite sure, but that Lord Bond's reference to Mr. Palmer's niece had annoyed Daphne was to her almost maternal eye only too clear. If pique with young Mr. Bond was going to make Daphne, no good hand at dissembling her feelings, show an even more open interest in Alister Cameron, she was afraid of the consequences. It seemed to her that in this unnecessary game of hurting people, not only were Alister and Daphne to be involved, but also C.W., whose only fault was that he had a great many female friends and perhaps a tactless father. If Daphne, so tolerant, so easy-going, had to be rude because Lord Bond said he had news of Mr. Palmer's niece, it was all a pretty kettle of fish. She looked at her stepdaughter, but that young lady, whom she had never tried to control except by kindness, was scowling so truculently at herself in a mirror that Mrs. Stonor dropped any idea she had of trying to make her reasonable.

'Well now,' said Lord Bond, as the gentlemen came in from the dining-room where, owing to the blessed absence of the ladies, they had all got on very well, 'what about our little concert? Let's go into the next room.'

He led the way to the drawing-room at whose grace and beauty in the level sunset light Denis marvelled anew.

'You see I've had the bronzes moved,' Lord Bond said proudly as he went up to the piano. 'Oh dear! Spencer has forgotten the key. Stonor, would you mind ringing. Or no, I'll ring myself.'

With a feeling that he could not assert himself too strongly Lord Bond went over to the fireplace and pulled one of the bell ropes that were part of the original decoration. While the vibration travelled over several hundred yards of bell wire to ring one of the seventy-two bells in the basement and summon a footman to tell Spencer that it was the drawing-room, Lord Bond fussed uneasily over his guests, pressing various chairs, ottomans and sofas upon their notice.

'Did you ring, my lord?' asked Spencer, standing majestically in the doorway.

'The piano key,' snapped his lordship. 'I told you this morning I wanted it.'

'I am sorry, my lord,' said Spencer, which convinced nobody and was not meant to. 'I did not understand that it was for this evening that your lordship was requiring it. It is in its usual place of safety in My Pantry. Shall I get it, my lord?'

Lord Bond angrily assented and Spencer presently came back with the key. Walking, as Denis subsequently averred, straight through his employer, he unlocked the piano, raised the lid from the keyboard and made as though to retire.

'You can leave the key,' said Lord Bond, staking all on one throw.

'I understood that the key was to be in My Charge, my lord,' said Spencer.

The whole room was mute in admiration of the battle now joined.

'Hi!' said Daphne. 'You'd better let me have the key, Spencer. I'll want to lock up when we've finished.'

It was part of Spencer's code that though employers could hardly be in the right, it was almost impossible for guests to be in the wrong. He therefore handed the key to Daphne, for whom he had acquired an unwilling admiration, and withdrew.

'Good *girl*!' said Lord Bond, patting Daphne on the arm. 'Now Stonor, we are all ready. I am really looking forward to this little treat. What shall we have first?'

'Anything you like, sir,' said Denis.

'Let's have a good chorus to start with then,' said his lordship, pulling a chair close up to the piano the better to enjoy himself. 'There's a very nice tune in the *Gondoliers*. Something about a fandango – you'll know what I mean.'

Denis, exchanging a satisfied glance with Daphne, began to play. Lord Bond, his eyes closed in ecstasy, conducted with a paper knife, tapped the measure with his feet on the floor, and sang all the words he could remember in a tuneless baritone, assisted by Daphne who had a pleasant voice and no illusions about it and sang soprano, alto, tenor or bass or all four with equal abandon. The years fell from Lord Bond as he demanded tune after tune and when Daphne sang 'Poor Wondering One' tears stood in his eyes. Apart from an occasional brief pause while

Lord Bond spoke of the glories of the Savoy in his young days, the concert went on without interruption till nearly eleven, when Lord Bond suddenly remembered that he had been neglecting Mrs. Stonor for more than an hour and a half.

'Bless my soul!' he exclaimed as looked at his watch. 'What will your stepmother think of me. I don't know when I've enjoyed an evening so much. Made me feel quite young again. You must come again, Denis, and you too, Miss Stonor.'

'I wish you'd say Daphne,' said that young lady. 'I never know who people mean when they say Miss Stonor.'

'Daphne is a very pretty name and couldn't suit you better,' said Lord Bond. 'Now I must really go and talk to Mrs. Stonor. Nicest evening I've had for a long time.'

'I suppose I'd better lock the piano again,' said Daphne. 'Suppose I put the key in the drawer of that writing table, Lord Bond. Isn't that where it ought to be?'

'It really ought,' said Lord Bond, 'but Spencer won't leave it there.'

'All right,' said Daphne. 'I'll lock the drawer. You keep the key of the drawer and then you can get the piano key whenever you like. Tell Spencer I've got it if he gets fresh.'

With profound admiration for Daphne's courage and strategy Lord Bond pocketed the key of the bureau and went over to Mrs. Stonor, with many apologies.

'But I liked the music,' said Mrs. Stonor. 'It always seems so peculiar to have musical children, though of course people don't call Gilbert and Sullivan music nowadays, because I'm not in the least musical myself, but of course being only my step-children does make a difference. And I had a talk with your son, Lord Bond. How nice he is. He told me a lot about himself.'

Lord Bond, gratified, said that C.W. was a good boy, and observed with pleasure that his son was approaching Daphne, doubtless to compliment her on her performance. He then fell into chat with Mrs. Stonor.

Young Mr. Bond, accompanied by Mr. Cameron, came up to Denis and Daphne.

'I say Daphne, I did like your singing,' said young Mr. Bond. 'I don't like Gilbert and Sullivan as a rule, but you make it sound quite different.'

Daphne said in an unpleasant voice that she adored Gilbert and Sullivan more than anything in the world and if she made it sound different she must have been singing very badly. She then begged Mr. Cameron to tell her all about the pictures in the room, because he was an architect and they always knew.

Mr. Cameron felt far from comfortable at being asked to do cicerone in front of the on of the house and was just beginning to say that pictures weren't exactly his line and here was Mr. Bond who would know all about them, when Daphne, taking his arm in a flattering way, walked him off with determination to the other end of the room where a large painting of the Campagna, entirely in tones of brown varnish and attributed on no particular grounds to Wilson, claimed her attention.

Young Mr. Bond looked so stunned that Denis felt very sorry for him. What exactly was happening he did not yet know, but Daphne had been surprisingly rude to one of her hosts, with no visible grounds, and Denis felt he ought to make up for it. So he offered young Mr. Bond a cigarette.

'It's a bit stuffy in here,' said young Mr. Bond. 'Suppose we go outside.'

Accordingly the two young men slipped out of the drawing-room and went into the garden. In the deepening light of late evening Ed could be seen, his head in the bonnet of the car.

'Hullo, Ed, anything wrong?' asked young Mr. Bond.

Ed said he was only waiting to take Them, by which and a jerk of his thumb he indicated Lord Bond's guests, back to Laverings, and the engine was running that sweet it was a treat to look at her.

'What about that song of old Margett's, Ed,' said Denis, sitting on a stone balustrade. 'Do you know anything of old Margett, Cedric? He seems to have a song that is his peculiar property and I rather wanted to find if it is worth collecting. Ed says he knows it and I want him to sing it.'

Young Mr. Bond said that Margett had a wonderful memory for old country songs, mostly quite unprintable, but he thought they had all been collected by a society with a gramophone and put into a collection with slightly chastened words.

'Old Mr. Margett he didn't sing her to no gramophone,' said Ed firmly.

'Then it's probably even less printable than the rest and that's saying a good deal,' said young Mr. Bond. 'I heard some of them at the Fleece and I can assure you that I didn't know which way to look, though it's just possible that old Margett exaggerated a bit that evening because the curate was there exuding fellowship. Let's have it, Ed.'

Ed grinned sheepishly.

'Come on, Ed,' said Denis. 'Remember you get my mouth organ if you sing me that song. What's it called?'

'Old Mr. Margett, he calls her "The Old Man's Darling",' said Ed.

'Good God!' said Denis. 'We have probably struck the juiciest folk song on the market. Fire away, Ed.'

Ed twisted his body about and said his mother didn't like him singing it.

'I expect you are right then,' said young Mr. Bond to Denis. 'Mrs. Pollett isn't at all particular. That's why Ed is a bit queer. They say it was one of Lord Pomfret's under keepers who had to be discharged for selling pheasants, but no one ever knew. If she objects to the song I'd very much like to hear it. Come on, Ed.'

After a little more persuasion Ed with an expressionless face suddenly uplifted a tuneful tenor into the following refrain, in rollicking waltz time.

> 'She was a dear little pussycat, pussycat,
> 　Soft little velvet paws.
> But now all my money is gone, little kittycat
> Shows me that kitties have claws.'

On hearing this interesting fragment Ed's auditors were struck dumb and then laughed so much that they couldn't stop. Young Mr. Bond was the first to recover himself.

'Good eighteen-ninety vintage, I should say,' he remarked to Denis.

'I would even put it a little earlier,' said Denis as seriously as he could. 'It has to me the definite ring of the Lion Comique, which would place it a little further back.'

'Don't you like her?' said Ed, puzzled.

'We like her very, very much,' said Denis.

'Thanks, Ed,' said young Mr. Bond. 'She's a winner.'

'When I had my mouth organ,' said Ed mournfully, 'I did used to play a bit of a worlse like at the end.'

'Well, if you are driving us back I'll give you the mouth organ to-night,' said Denis, 'and you can play waltzes all over the place.'

Ed grinned seraphically and returned to his loving inspection of the car. The two young men went back towards the house.

'I don't know what has come over Daphne,' said Denis. 'But one often feels a bit queer and excited after doing music.'

'I expect I was butting in at the wrong moment,' said young Mr. Bond. 'I ought to be getting back to town. Look here, Denis, will you tell father I had to hurry, and say good night to Mrs. Stonor for me. I'll be down again sometime soon.'

So saying he got into his car and drove away.

Denis went back to the drawing-room and gave the messages. Lord Bond and Mrs. Stonor were sorry not to have said good-bye and continued their conversation which was about Miss Starter's family and very dull. Denis thought that Daphne must be tired by all her singing, for the life had suddenly gone out of her and she returned very stupid answers to Mr. Cameron's remarks. Very soon Mrs. Stonor said they must go. Lord Bond saw them to the car, repeating that he hadn't had such a nice concert for years.

'You must come again, you and your sister, Denis,' he said as they came down the steps. 'I do like to hear a girl sing without any fuss. When that niece of Palmer's comes down to Worsted we must have her over. You'd like her, Daphne. You'd get on very well.'

As they drove away Daphne surprised her family and Mr. Cameron by bursting into loud unrefined sobs and saying she hated Staple Park and never wanted to go there again. Her stepmother who had been anxiously observing her all the evening and had heard her being rude to young Mr. Bond about Gilbert and Sullivan, saw that the trouble she anticipated was coming upon them. What to do about it she couldn't yet say, so she applied herself to comforting Daphne, ably seconded by Denis who was also beginning to guess the reason of his sister's peculiar behaviour. She had behaved very badly to Cedric, but she was his own Daphne and he was going to take her side whatever she did.

As for Mr. Cameron he was disappointed that the evening, so pleasantly begun, was for no visible reason ending in disaster. Daphne's tears moved him deeply, yet he felt at the same time that her abandon was perhaps excessive and admired her stepmother's calm handling of the situation. At the gate of the White House he took leave of the Stonors.

'I do hope Daphne will be all right to-morrow,' he said to Mrs. Stonor. 'I expect so much music was too much for her. She is rather sensitive.'

'I shall put her to bed at once and she will be quite all right to-morrow,' said Mrs. Stonor.

'One couldn't help being all right with you,' said Mr. Cameron and went into the Laverings gate. As he undressed he suddenly thought that Mrs. Stonor had looked tired. However he had settled it in his mind that it was Daphne who was sensitive, so he dismissed the thought, which then kept him company until he went to sleep.

Denis found the mouth organ and gave it to Ed with a parting injunction not to play any waltzes till he was safely in the garage. Ed smiled mysteriously, mumbled a few words of heartfelt thanks and drove the car back to Staple Park, hardly using his right hand at all.

IX

MR. CAMERON IS WARNED

NEXT day Daphne had quite recovered and no allusion was made to her outburst. Mr. Cameron went to Oxbridge about the new college and was to be away for ten days or so. Lady Bond came back at the end of the week and as she was not particularly interested in her husband's doings she did not enquire closely how he had spent his time, and the dinner party remained a secret from her. Not that Lord Bond would have denied it, but in his opinion when Lucasta was quiet it was as well to let sleeping dogs lie. Then Miss Starter came back for the rest of her visit with a new diet which she had collected at Tunbridge Wells and there was the usual excitement about the Skeynes Agricultural Show on Bank Holiday, for which Lord Bond was entering some livestock, and Lady Bond was full of fresh plans about a public meeting to save Pooker's Piece, and the wheels of life went on.

Denis went up to town several times about his ballet. His stepmother thought London in the heat a bad plan, but as he came back none the worse and indeed in very good spirits except for the permanent difficulty of getting any backers for the company, she stopped worrying.

Daphne was over at Staple Park every day, so Mrs. Stonor spent a good deal of time with her sister-in-law.

The friendship, the growing intimacy between Mrs. Middleton and Mrs. Stonor was of a very gentlemanly kind. Each had an immense respect for the other, unexpressed; each deliberately refrained from looking closely into the life of the other. Mrs. Middleton's silences, Mrs. Stonor's vague talk, were in their essence the same, a screen for personal feelings, a shrinking from any betrayal of deep emotion. Mr. Middleton, with one of his occasional alarming flashes of insight, said he did not know which was the more significant in moment of stress, Catherine's agony of silence or Lilian's agony of speech.

Mrs. Middleton, who rarely made intimate friends, was finding in Mrs. Stonor what she had always hoped to find, an intimacy untouched by sentiment. She knew that whatever she did she would find Lilian exactly the same, anxious and changing on the surface, absolutely dependable in herself. Apart from their affection from different angles for Mr. Middleton, neither woman with many illusions about her husband or brother, each ready to protect him, they had a further bond in their affection, again of quite different degrees, for Alister Cameron and Denis. But each of them saw something the other couldn't or wouldn't see and each had a hidden anxiety for her friend.

If Mrs. Middleton had been asked by the right person what she felt about Alister Cameron she would probably have said without any particular emphasis that she was devoted to him, or that she loved him, which would have been true enough. His association with her husband, their constant meetings, a silence of nature that agreed with hers, a tacit understanding that Mr. Middleton must have life made smooth for him, had created a very strong bond. She and Alister were perfectly at their ease with one another, often met, often corresponded, trusted each other and would have felt very deeply any crack in their friendship. She had grown so used to his companionship, together or apart, that it would be impossible for her not to feel an emptiness when another door opened and he went forward witout her. She had long ago made up her mind to have no sentimentalizing when that moment came, but now the moment seemed to be near she found it difficult to be entirely

happy. That Alister should care for Daphne did not pain her at all;
that was natural, perhaps inevitable. But if Alister were going to break
his late flowering affection against Daphne's young indifference, that
would be hard to watch. And she wondered, never even putting her
wonder consciously into words, whether Alister were not overlooking
his true happiness in his pursuit. But of this she could not speak to
Lilian, nor indeed to anyone else. To Denis, who was so genuinely
devoted to his stepmother, she might have spoken, but the oftener Denis
came to Laverings the less there was to say. Denis would play to her and
there had been long peaceful silences; at least she supposed he had
found them peaceful, for if he wasn't playing he would sit quietly in the
sun, looking better every day. She found them peaceful, as she thought,
but there was a disconcerting quality in them as well. Sometimes she
raised her eyes from a book or some work and looked at Denis; sometimes as she read and sewed she was conscious that he had looked at her.
But the occasions when their eyes met were rare. A sudden, answering
look, gone before she was fully aware of it.

Mrs. Stonor's anxiety about Alister and Daphne had not lessened
since the evening at Staple Park. Of young Mr. Bond there had been no
sign. Daphne had shown an irritability most unlike her usual self, but
was always at her nicest with Alister. Mrs. Stonor had asked him over a
good deal, hoping he would cheer Daphne up, but now he was away
and she was wondering whether she had done a foolish thing. It was so
clear to her that he came to the White House only to talk about Daphne,
and she saw no solution to the problems involved. If Alister were really
in love with Daphne she would not in any way discourage him, but it
all looked out of drawing to her. Daphne's feeling for young Mr. Bond
and his for her was an unknown quantity, liable to make an explosion
at any moment. She had tried to discuss it with Denis, but he had
shrugged his thin shoulders and said one couldn't interfere and been
more than usually affectionate to her. Her vague apprehension of some
hurt to come to Denis remained. She made no pretence of understanding him and had never invited a confidence, but her sensitive
affection for her stepson who was in a way a creation of her own making,
of her own saving, made her too aware of undercurrents in his mind. As
far as she knew his heart had never been seriously touched. He had
laughed at himself with her over various passing fancies, had always
protested that she was the only woman he could bear to live with. But
she had observed that Catherine was a person about whom he had not
laughed, and she would like to have known whether this meant that he
didn't think about her much, or thought about her a little too deeply.
Her one secret comfort was that whether Denis was affected by Catherine or not, he never wavered in his devotion and kindness to herself;
and she hoped that as she had never failed him in the past when he was
a delicate, hideous fledgling, she would never fail him in the future.

Mrs. Middleton and Mrs. Stonor were doing a little quite preposterous gardening at Laverings, where the gardener took a tolerant view of employers and let them cut off dead roses or pick freely among his sweet peas.

'How is Lady Bond getting on with her meeting about Pooker's Piece?' Mrs. Middleton asked.

'Daphne has typed a lot of letters about it,' said Mrs. Stonor, 'but she can't fill in the date till after the Skeynes Agricultural Show. Why, I do not understand, but the Agricultural appears to wreck the county for so long before and after it takes place that nothing can be decided. I am just going to put these dead roses on the rubbish heap. Shall I take yours?'

'Don't bother,' said Mrs. Middleton. 'Put them on the border and Pucken can clear them away when he comes. I do hate green fly when it gets squashed on one's hand. Jack asks about the meeting at least once a day. He has worked himself up to feeling that he ought to write a personal letter to Sir Ogilvy Hibberd and I expect he will do it. His letters are apt to be intemperate.'

'I should think Sir Ogilvy would be intemperate too,' said Mrs. Stonor. 'I daresay they will both boil over into *The Times*. They'll print anything and Pooker's Piece would make a good Silly Season heading. Denis went to play to Lord Bond last night when Lady Bond was at the Women's Institute Meeting at Winter Overcotes and he says there is no talk of Mr. Bond coming down till the Agricultural. He has to make a speech then. Oh, dear!'

'Is Daphne still cross?' said Mrs. Middleton, who knew quite well what her sister-in-law's exclamation meant.

'Suppressed crossness,' said Mrs. Stonor. 'It's good of her to suppress it, but I sometimes think it would be less trying if she didn't. She and Denis went to lunch at Skeynes Agnes, but they'll be back to tea.'

'Alister will be down this afternoon,' said Mrs. Middleton. 'He got back from Oxbridge yesterday and wants to have a few days with Jack.'

'Oh, dear!' said Mrs. Stonor again.

'I know,' said Mrs. Middleton. 'But I don't see what we can do about it. Come and have some tea. I believe Lady Bond is coming over, but that can't be helped either.'

Mr. Middleton joined them for tea, full of the letter he proposed to write to Sir Ogilvy Hibberd.

'There is much to be said,' he began, 'for the personal approach.'

'I am sure there is, Jack,' said his sister without malice.

'Much to be said,' Mr. Middleton repeated, glaring suspiciously at his sister. 'I have weighed every pro and con in my own mind. Whether, I have said to myself, would it be better to hold this public meeting which owing to Stoke's very selfish behaviour here seems to be fated never to come to birth, and in any case I very much doubt whether

Hibberd, a hard-headed business man, hard-headed in every sense of the word, would be in any way influenced by an appeal of that kind, or, taking up the cudgels myself and laying aside all personal pride – and I am a proud man, Catherine, you know it; you too know it, Lilian – to put clearly and dispassionately before Hibberd what the wanton vandalism that he proposes to inflict on this precious corner of England would mean to Me. I have thought long and painfully on the subject and come to the conclusion that there is no more to be said. Do you agree?'

'I am sure there is no more to be said, darling,' said Mrs. Middleton, 'and if there were you would certainly say it. And as Lady Bond is coming to tea you had better discuss it with her, for Lilian tells me that Daphne says notices for the meeting are all typed and only waiting to go out till the Agricultural is over.'

As his wife spoke Mr. Middleton's face assumed an expression of horror which she rightly interpreted as a wish that her ladyship were not coming.

'It's no good, Jack,' she said. 'You told me that you had asked her to tea yourself when you met her in town last week.'

'You will make her my excuses,' said Mr. Middleton piteously, rising as he spoke. 'Tie up the knocker, say I'm sick, I'm dead.'

'That would be quite impossible,' said Mrs. Stonor, turning with some severity upon her brother, 'because well you know that there isn't one.'

'And well you know, too,' said Mrs. Middleton, 'that Lady Bond never comes by the front door in summer. She always comes round by the garden to show that she knew you before I did.'

'And here,' said Mrs. Stonor antiphonally, 'she is.'

Mr. Middleton, groaning more audibly than the rules of hospitality admit, sank back into his chair as Lady Bond appeared at the library window.

'Here is Lady Bond, darling,' said his wife, looking at him with mocking affection.

Mr. Middleton got up again.

'Don't move, don't move,' said Lady Bond. 'Here I am you see, Mr. Middleton. And I am so glad to find you, Mrs. Middleton, and Mrs. Stonor too. I have brought – now where are they, oh, here they are, they were merely admiring your border – Miss Starter, who I am glad to say is finishing her summer holiday with us, and Mrs. Palmer's niece, Betty Deane, of whom you have heard me speak.'

Miss Starter came in followed by a tall, handsome young woman with dark hair, heavy eyebrows, a well-shaped nose and mouth and a general air of overpowering statuesqueness.

'Betty is staying with her aunt Mrs. Palmer, for a few days,' said Lady Bond, 'and they came over to lunch. Mrs. Palmer had to go on to Southbridge, so I thought you wouldn't mind if I brought Betty to tea. I shall drop her at Worsted on my way home.'

Having made this very frank and handsome apologia for her guest she seated herself by Mr. Middleton and began to tell him about the public meeting.

'We cannot fix the date till after the Agricultural, as everyone is so busy at that time,' she said. 'But possibly about the tenth. Most of the people who matter will be down here then and we shall avoid the twelfth.'

'What twelfth?' asked Mr. Middleton, no sportsman in spite of his feudal status.

'The moors,' said Lady Bond, leaving Mr. Middleton to brood, perplexed, upon a procession of swarthy Africans who were somehow to be avoided. 'Juliana, have you told Mrs. Middleton about the new bread that Dr. Picton recommended to you at Tunbridge Wells? It is quite a new discovery. Not only is it almost starch free, but you can eat any quantity of it without any effect whatever, good or bad. What did you say its name was, Juliana?'

'That is exactly what I can't remember,' said Miss Starter, lamenting. 'When Dr. Picton told me about it I said, "Now do write it down, Dr. Picton, for everything you tell me goes in at one ear and out at the other," so he wrote it down on a piece of paper. I am sure I put it into my bag, but I cannot find it anywhere.'

'That is a Dememorizing Fixation,' said Betty Deane, who had not hitherto spoken, being, as she said, entirely opposed to people speaking unless they had something of value to say. 'You ought to go to Prack at Cincinnati and be analysed. He is *the* man on all Memory Fixations. I went to some of his lectures when I was over there. I couldn't understand much because he is a Mixo-Lydian refugee, but his book is very good. You ought to read it.'

Miss Starter said that she felt herself that quite enough was done for refugees and there was a woman psychopath in Surbiton who had done wonders for a friend of hers.

Betty Deane favoured her with a baleful stare and was silent, obviously finding Miss Starter of no value at all.

'I think,' said Miss Starter, who as an ex-lady-in-waiting on minor royalty was immune to snubs,' that although many people get great help from such healers, it is better — I speak for myself of course — to trust to the Church. The Bishop of Barchester wrote an article in the *Evening Headline* on the subject of faith which would I am sure interest you, Miss Deane.'

Betty said that religion was all very well for people who believed in that sort of thing, but she herself had been an agnostic since she was sixteen and could not take any interest in creeds which simply atrophied the intellect.

'Isn't it interesting,' said Miss Starter mildly, 'to find that young people are still agnostics. I thought that had quite gone out. My grandfather was an agnostic, he was a great friend of Huxley and in many ways one of the most deeply religious men I have every known. I must lend you a little book of his, Miss Deane, *Essays in Anglican Agnosticism*, you would like it. We were all brought up as agnostics and of course one's early training counts for so much, but I remember my father, a great friend of Bishop Colenso, saying, "Without the Church of England where would we agnostics stand?" And it has always seemed so true to me. This new bread of Dr. Picton's is called Ita-lot, pronounced Eat-a-lot, and I get it by post twice a week from Bishop's Stortford which is the only place where it is made. You should try some, Mrs. Middleton.'

Betty Deane, her guns spiked, publicly convicted of a Mid and Late Victorian creed, was darkly silent, meditating on Milton's Satan, a character for whom she had an intellectual affinity, or so she felt, waiting for an opportunity to crush someone.

'I have given much thought to the matter,' said Mr. Middleton to Lady Bond, 'much thought. I am not a man to take lightly any step in which my own name, my position such as it is, are involved but when I see a duty plainly before me, that duty becomes to me a sacred — what at the risk of tautology I find myself unable to call anything but a sacred — duty.'

'You will come to the meeting then,' said Lady Bond.

'No, no, dear lady, you misapprehend,' said Mr. Middleton. 'Without undue pride I may say that my name carries a little weight. I shall write to Sir Ogilvy Myself.'

'Well I wouldn't if I were you,' said Lady Bond, entirely unimpressed. 'No good writing to a man like that. He can always be ruder than you can. I think we'll have the meeting on the ninth rather than the tenth. The tenth might clash with the Barchester Infirmary Fête. Ah, here is Daphne. That is very nice. I want her and Betty to meet. Betty has some very interesting news for us.'

As when two bulls of milk-white fleece, ranging the slopes of Illyrian Timavus, espy afar off the heifer, grazing, ah! beneath the ilex whose cold shadow the careful farmer will avoid to seek as roof for the golden swarm lest haply the stored sweetness of the honey turn to maleficent vinegar baneful as the Centaur's blood on the fatal shirt doomed to lead the club-bearer to the gloomy realms of Dis, anon they paw the ground with equal foot, this flashing forth fire from his eyes as the careful husbandman strikes the spark from tinder that will burn the dried stalks of beans to a rich ash meet for increasing tenfold the produce of his paternal fields (twenty lines of description of various forms of artificial fertiliser are here omitted), that, similar in shape and form to this, shaking wide his flowing locks and with the ivory spears of his forehead turning the turf till sods fly fast as the scudding sails upon the Adriatic what time Boreas plunging from where Taygete the Pleiad westers to the

Median Hydaspes, causes fishes to be caught up from the waters, where they, ah! now in vain, guard their thousand young destined now to perish waiting a father's care, whirling them aloft on his wings till they, bereft of Neptune's element, lie gasping on the shore where to-morrow maidens, washing linen in the sea foam, may haply weep for silver scales stained with blood purple at the Tyrian's dye, gained by him in no not remote seas from the shelly flocks of Proteus —

To be short, taking young Mr. Bond as the heifer, so did Daphne and Betty take a violent dislike to each other at sight, having determined to do so long before they met. Daphne had heard quite enough, she felt, of how good-looking and nice Betty Deane was from Lord Bond, while Betty did not wish to hear any more thank you about Daphne Stonor who was such a help to Lady Bond and so much liked by everyone. Their antipathy sent out such waves of dislike that everyone except Lady Bond became acutely conscious of it and talked in an unnatural way.

'Did you have a nice time in America?' asked Mrs. Stonor.

'It is difficult to say yes or no when America, or rather the United States, is such a large place,' said Betty, 'but I enjoyed what I did see very much. I had an extremely interesting time in New York and made lots of friends. I hope to go back again and do a course at Bryn Mawr. Cedric Bond goes back in the autumn and I might go with him. You ought to go,' she added looking at Daphne.

Daphne said she was sure she would loathe New York.

'You can't say till you've been there,' said Betty. 'No one can understand it till they have.'

Mrs. Stonor, distracted, said she had once been to New York, the year Denis was so ill at Laverings, and thought the flower shops were so nice. She remembered, she said, what particularly beautiful gladiolus there were in the shops that winter.

'Oh, do you say gladiolus,' said Miss Starter. 'I always say gladiolus.'

A short and ill-informed discussion on the subject was terminated by Betty who said coldly, that as both were incorrect it was of little importance. The i and o of gladiolus were both short she said, and an equal stress should be laid on each syllable, as far as possible approximating to the form gladyolus.

'Well, Betty must know. She got a first at Oxford,' said Lady Bond.

'When do you expect your son down again, Lady Bond?' asked Mrs. Middleton, seeing Daphne about to express her opinion of the female members of that University.

'We don't quite know,' said Lady Bond. 'He is very busy at the office at the moment. For the Agricultural in any case. Betty dined with him last night. She had something very special to say to him which we shall all know before long,' said Lady Bond with a stately archness that froze her hearers.

She then collected Miss Starter and Betty and went away. Daphne said in an uncertain voice she wanted to write some letters and would go home. Her departure was watched with sympathetic anxiety by her stepmother and Mrs. Middleton. It had not escaped the notice of either of these ladies that Betty Deane was wearing on the fourth finger of her left hand a very expensive-looking sapphire ring, and they could not imagine that Daphne had not observed it. It was no use going after Daphne in her present condition, so Mrs. Stonor sat unhappily with the Middletons, comforted alternately by her brother's entire want of perception and Mrs. Middleton's unspoken sympathy. Mr. Cameron arrived a little later.

'Ha, Cameron!' said Mr. Middleton, who was longing to finish a thriller that he had left upstairs. 'We will have a talk indeed about all you have done. We will tire the sun with talking, though Summer Time makes the feat more of a test for us than for our old Samian friend. But for the moment, for the moment, Cameron, I must leave you with Catherine and Lilian. You will not be in bad hands. Later, washed and refreshed, we will meet again.'

Upon which he went quickly out of his private door and upstairs.

The two ladies did their best with Mr. Cameron, but he was not very attentive and looked often towards the garden. Finally he interrupted Mrs. Stonor to ask if Daphne was coming over or if he would find her at home.

'I really don't know,' said Mrs. Stonor. 'She was here, but then she went away. She isn't very well. At least she is very well indeed but rather upset — I don't mean upset so much as harassed, really about nothing at all and I must say she didn't behave at all well, did she, Catherine?'

'Lady Bond brought Mrs. Palmer's niece Betty Deane to tea,' said Mrs. Middleton, 'and the two girls didn't get on well. I think Daphne was a little rude and went away to get over it. I must say Betty is very trying.'

'I'll go and find her,' said Mr. Cameron. 'I brought a new kind of film for her camera that she said she wanted to try.'

'You have been warned,' said Mrs. Middleton, a little sadly, but Mr. Cameron did not hear, or did not notice, and went over to the White House. The ladies said nothing and returned to their gardening, snipping off dead, dying, or even slightly faded heads with savage intensity, Mrs. Stonor even going so far as to walk deliberately on a couple of small snails, a thing she would in calmer moments have shrunk from.

*

Poor Daphne went back to the White House with a swelling heart. Betty's words, the ring on Betty's finger, had told her only too clearly what had happened. It wasn't that she loved Cedric in the least, in fact she looked upon him with indifference if not with hatred, but hypocrisy and deceit were what she could not bear, and of all the horrid, stuck-up, affected girls she had ever met, Betty Deane was the one. Betty would make a very good wife for such a stupid creature as Cedric and she hoped they would both be very unhappy, or be drowned on the way to America, or gored by bulls; and the more she thought of these delightful consummations the happier and more exulting she felt, till at last her happiness took the form of a prickling behind the nose, a gulping in the throat, a wish to tell everyone, especially the Honourable C. W. Bond and Miss Betty Deane, exactly what she thought of them, and such an uprising of hysterica passio that all she could do was to rush, blinded by tears, past the back door where Lou was sitting on a kitchen chair shelling peas into a colander, and bury herself in the darkest recesses of the garden. So it was that when Mr. Cameron came to the front door and asked Palfrey if Miss Daphne was in, he was told that she had gone over to Mrs. Middleton's, but Mr. Denis was at home. Denis was writing out a score.

'Hullo, Alister,' he said, 'I say, I simply hate to behave as if it mattered, but if I don't get this bit written down I'll forget where the bassoon comes in. I shan't be a minute.'

He plunged furiously into his notes again and Mr. Cameron, not at all offended but slightly dashed, wandered out again, not even daring, such was his layman's respect for the musician's frenzy, to ask if he knew where Daphne was. Without thinking much where he was going he walked past the back door and seeing Lou shelling peas he said Good evening. Lou, whose young movie-struck mind viewed the world as little but a setting for love and who would willingly have laid her heart in a puddle that Mr. Cameron might walk dry-shod, was suddenly visited by one of the most noble and entrancing thoughts ever vouchsafed to mortal. She had seen Miss Daphne go down the garden in tears. Now came Mr. Cameron, looking anxious and moody. The inference was clear. They had had a lovers' quarrel and had Broken Apart, Miss Daphne to cry herself into her grave, Mr. Cameron (probably) to go with set face and reckless courage where the danger was hottest. Lou knew well, too well, that Mr. Cameron could never be her Ideel Lover except in day-dreams, but here was an opportunity to display a nobility which even Greta or Norma could hardly hope to emulate. All in a flash she saw the lovers reunited by her help. Together they would visit the little grave marked by naught but a fresher turf where daisies sprang, together their tears would mingle as they thought of Little Lou who had given her life for their happiness. Tears of melancholy bliss welled to Lou's eyes as she carefully put down the colander of peas, for even romance paled for a moment when she thought of her mother's wrath if they were spilt, and followed her secret heart.

'Please, Mr. Cameron,' she said.

'What's the matter, Lou,' said Mr. Cameron. 'You've got a nasty cold, haven't you.'

At these words Lou nearly died of maudlin bliss, but true to her ideal she sniffed and said,

'It's Miss Daphne. She went down the garden. She was crying. She's in the pea-sticks, Mr. Cameron.'

'WHAT?' said Mr. Cameron. And without a word of thanks, he hastened towards the pea-sticks, leaving Lou literally gasping with excitement and romance. There, sure enough, was Daphne, standing between two rows of peas, shelling the youngest pea-pods and eating their crisp contents in a melancholy way, pausing every now and then to blow her nose violently.

'Daphne!' said Mr. Cameron. 'Darling, what is it?'

Daphne looked up. There was Alister looking as kind and nice as he always did, and the thought of a kind shoulder to cry on was too much for her. With a gulp she hurled herself against him and abandoned herself to the full luxury of grief, repeating amid her sobs how glad she was he had come. Mr. Cameron, hardly able to believe his luck, patted her shoulders, kissed the top of her head, said everything was all right and gradually managed to restore her to sanity.

'I *am* so glad you have come back,' said Daphne. 'Everyone was *ghastly* and I thought I'd die. Oh, Alister, I *am* so pleased to see you. How did you know I was here?'

'Lou saw you go down the garden,' said Mr. Cameron. 'Daphne, are you sure I'm not too old?'

'For what?' said Daphne.

'Well, I am a good deal older than you are,' said Mr. Cameron, 'but it's better than being a good deal younger. After all Jack Middleton is much older than Catherine and they are very happy.'

It then occurred to Daphne for the first time, like a thunderbolt, that she was now engaged to Mr. Cameron. Being of a practical turn of mind she thought she had better get it clear.

'You mean,' she said, looking at him steadily, 'that if we get married you will be older than I am.'

'Just about that,' said Mr. Cameron.

At the bottom of her heart Daphne knew that though Alister was quite the nicest person in the world, she didn't in the least want to marry him. But everyone else was ghastly and it would be too difficult to explain now that crying on a person's shoulder wasn't at all the same as being engaged, still less married, so like a soldier's daughter she determined to make the best of a forlorn hope.

'Well, I daresay by the time I'm about forty you won't seem so much older,' she said cheerfully. 'One gets used to people. Oh Alister, shall we have to tell everyone?'

'I should like to sow the fact in mustard and cress all over the garden

like the gentleman in the song,' said Mr. Cameron, 'but we'll do just
as you like. Would you rather only tell your people and not have it in
The Times just yet?'

'*The Times!*' said Daphne. 'Oh no. It would look as if we were really
going to get married.'

'But we are,' said Mr. Cameron.

'I know,' said Daphne. 'But people get broken off too. Oh, not *The
Times*, Alister. I'd feel safer if we didn't.'

Mr. Cameron naturally found her folly the most delightful thing that
he had ever seen and they walked back to the house, eating a handful of
young peas with which Daphne had thoughtfully provided herself. At
the back door Lou, who had finished the peas, was peeling far more
potatoes than were wanted, hoping to see the result of her noble action
before her mother called her. Her expression of open-mouthed rapture
was such that the lovers stopped.

'It's all right, Lou,' said Mr. Cameron kindly. 'I found Miss Daphne.'

'They say finding's keeping,' said Lou, moved by her romantic spirit
to literary flights which she had never suspected in herself.

'So it is,' said Mr. Cameron. 'Only don't tell your mother, or Palfrey,
or anyone else, because it's a secret for the present.'

'Won't you have no ring, Miss Daphne?' said Lou, who had somehow hoped that a ruby the size of a pigeon's egg would materialize on
Daphne's finger.

'Oh, Alister, I needn't have a ring, need I?' said Daphne, to whom
the word ring brought back such searing memories of Betty Deane's
sapphire that she nearly went back to the pea-sticks.

'Of course not,' said Mr. Cameron. 'But I would like to give you one.
Perhaps a little later, when it is in *The Times*.'

But at the word *Times* Daphne's face began to crumple so suspiciously
that he quickly said they must go and tell Lilian and Denis, and leaving
Lou with their secret they went into the house, where Denis was still
furiously scribbling spidery hieroglyphics on a huge sheet of scored paper.

'Hullo, Alister,' he said, 'back again? Give him a cigarette, Daphne.
I must get this thing off my chest,' and he applied himself again to his
music.

'I'm not staying,' said Mr. Cameron, emboldened by love, 'I only
want to tell you that Daphne and I are engaged.'

Denis blinked himself into the daylight from the inner world where
he had been furiously living and looked startled.

'Everyone was ghastly,' said Daphne, 'and I went into the pea-sticks
to cry, but we aren't going to tell anyone yet except you and Lilian and
Uncle Jack and Catherine. Oh, and we told Lou, but she promised not
to tell.'

'Well,' said Denis, getting up and giving his sister a hug, 'that's very
nice indeed. I really couldn't think of anyone nicer for Daphne to

marry. I can't say that I feel like a brother to you, Alister, because never having had one I don't know the feeling, but I am delighted. I shall give you a breakfast service and a very large Persian cat. Have a drink, Alister.'

Mr. Cameron accepted some sherry and Denis toasted the bridal pair and expressed again and again his pleasure in the engagement, but it was rather uphill work. Something seemed wrong to him. Daphne looked happy, Alister looked happy, but he missed the rapture which in his mind should go with an engagement and then blamed himself for being so particular.

'I shall have to go now,' said Mr. Cameron. 'Will you be all right, darling?'

'Quite all right,' said Daphne. 'And, Alister, if you see Lilian at Laverings you'd better tell her and Catherine. I don't suppose Uncle Jack would notice if you told him or not.'

Mr. Cameron laughed, put his arm round Daphne's shoulders for a moment and went away. Denis arranged his music paper and his rough drafts with meticulous care.

'You don't mind, do you?' said Daphne suddenly.

'Of course I don't mind, you goose,' said Denis, his conscience pricking him for the want of enthusiasm he had shown. 'Alister is a very good chap indeed, who would do anyone credit as a brother-in-law. And what's more, though I don't suppose it has occurred to you, he is what is known as quite a good match. You will be able to live in luxury, darling, which is more than any of the Stonors have ever done yet.'

'Denis,' said Daphne, and then stopped.

'Out with it,' said Denis. 'Do you want me to forbid the banns? I've always dearly longed to see it happen and I can imagine no greater pleasure than to get up in church and say "I do", and be invited to the vestry to explain while all the audience die of curiosity.'

Denis had rambled on simply to fill in time, because his sister had an inscrutable expression to which even he, who knew her so well and so fondly, had no clue.

'It all sounds very nice,' she said dolefully, 'but oh! Denis, I'd much rather stay with you and Lilian.'

Upon which she went upstairs and could shortly be heard having a bath.

Denis tried to tell himself that girls often had a moment's revulsion or fright at having committed themselves, but he was uneasy. If it were in his destiny, which he felt it never would be, to love and be loved, he could imagine a way of love quite different from what he had just seen. Probably Alister and Daphne's matter of fact behaviour was the best and safest for life as it was now, but he had thought of half-lights, undertones, reticences, a hand that trembled when it brushed against his, silences that hung like perfume about him, quick answering glances.

'Romantic fool,' he said aloud to himself. And as there was no chance of getting at the bath till Daphne had finished, he applied himself once more to his ballet and was presently immersed in the music of his mind.

*

Mr. Cameron found Mrs. Middleton and Mrs. Stonor still hard at work in the rose garden and stood about in so marked a way that they were in no doubt as to what had happened.

'Did you find Daphne?' asked Mrs. Stonor, who had never yet been afraid to face a situation.

'We found each other,' said Mr. Cameron in a terse voice.

Again both ladies knew quite well what he meant, but with a touch of vindictiveness towards the male sex in general each determined that he should jolly well explain himself and not leave them to take the trouble of extracting his meaning for him. So they remained silent, snipping off roses.

'Lilian,' said Mr. Cameron, 'could I say something to you?'

'Certainly,' said Mrs. Stonor in a cheerful voice.

'I do hope you won't mind,' said Mr. Cameron, 'but Daphne and I are engaged. I thought I'd better tell you.'

Mrs. Stonor put down the basket of dead roses and came round the flower bed to him.

'I am perfectly delighted, Alister,' she said, 'and I am sure her father would have been pleased. And I hope you will accept me as a very affectionate stepmother.'

As she said this she took both his hands.

'And I am enchanted too,' said Mrs. Middleton. 'I hope you will be as happy as Jack and I are and have dozens of children.'

'It is all rather private for the present,' said Mr. Cameron uneasily. 'Daphne didn't like the idea of *The Times*.'

Mrs. Middleton said she quite understood the feeling and when they had told her husband they would not let anyone else know. Mr. Cameron, feeling vaguely that he ought to shelter Mrs. Stonor, offered to see her home, but she preferred to go alone. When she got back to the White House she found Denis still at his work.

'Well, darling, I see you have heard the news,' said Denis. 'I do like Alister and I do love Daphne, but — oh, I don't know. Am I a beast not to feel very happy?'

'If you are a beast, I am a beastess,' said Mrs. Stonor. 'I'd like nothing more in the world than for Daphne to be happy — and Alister to be happy — but — oh, I don't know either.'

She and Denis sat and looked at each other with concern, each longing to persuade the other that everything was all right, but quite unable to work up any conviction about it.

'I'm being very silly,' said Mrs. Stonor firmly.

'You are not, darling,' said Denis. 'Well, we will give Daphne a slap-up wedding and live on bread and cheese for a year and settle down together to a bachelor life. No one will ever want to be engaged to me, and just as well, and I shall be the prop of your declining years. In youth you sheltered me and I'll protect you now.'

'I wish you could, Denis,' said his stepmother.

'So do I,' said Denis ruefully. 'Never mind, you shall protect me, which will really give you much more satisfaction, being a motherly sort of woman. There is the water running off and I'll rush and have my bath if you don't mind.'

Dinner passed off peacefully. Daphne appeared to be quite herself again and though she went to bed early it was not to toss on a wakeful couch but to sleep off in a very natural way the effect of so much excitement.

*

Dinner at Laverings fell alive into the hands of Mr. Middleton, who read aloud to himself from rough drafts visible to his inner eye, the various letters he had thought of sending or not sending to Sir Ogilvy Hibberd, calling occasionally upon his wife or his partner for their comments, to which he paid no attention at all. Under cover of this his hearers were able to think their own thoughts which were not altogether comfortable ones. Mrs. Middleton had the doubtful pleasure of seeing some of her gloomier prognostications verified with every probability of the rest coming true; for anything less like her idea of a blissfully engaged lover there could not be. Mr. Cameron, after an instant of pure happiness when Daphne had cried in his arms, had experienced a peculiar sinking of the stomach which reason told him was excess of bliss but instinct defined as a mixture of terror at what he had done and irrevocable regret for something, not very clear to his mind, that he had not done.

'So,' said Mr. Middleton when the dessert was on the table,' I shall send the letter, but not till after the Agricultural.'

'Why put it off?' said his wife.

'My dear,' said Mr. Middleton, 'when you live at Rome, do as the Romans do. At this time of year every event in our Country Calendar is calculated from before or after the Agricultural. Probably a survival from the old Hiring Fair at Beliers which used to take place at about this time, but was unfortunately allowed to fall into disuse, together with the Abbey of Beliers, after the Reformation. As a loyal inhabitant of this part of the world it pleases me to conform.'

'Then your letter to Sir Ogilvy and Lady Bond's notices of the public meeting will go out at about the same time,' said Mrs. Middleton.

'Precisely,' said Mr. Middleton. 'The one will add weight to the other.'

'You don't think they'll interfere with one another, do you?' said his wife.

Mr. Middleton, who had just had that thought, said with great dignity that there were certain subjects on which women were hardly qualified to judge, and became remote.

'And now that that is settled,' said Mrs. Middleton, 'I am going to tell you something. Alister and Daphne are engaged.'

'Blind that I am!' cried Mr. Middleton, striking his forehead with his clenched fist, though cautiously. 'An exquisite story has been playing itself out before my very eyes and I have seen naught. You must forgive me, Cameron. My perceptions are usually far more acute, but I have been an old, a weary man, I have had much on my shoulders.'

He paused and became Atlas, the world's weight upon his neck.

'As a matter of fact we were all surprised,' said Mrs. Middleton.

'Yet I knew, I knew,' said Mr. Middleton, brushing this tactless remark aside, 'that something was astir, something burgeoning, the eternal miracle of high summer reflected in the mirror of human hearts. This news has made me very, very happy. The friend with whom I have worked, with whom I have always had such cordial relations, has plighted his troth to my sister's stepdaughter, whom I love as if she were my own, my own daughter I mean not my stepdaughter, and under this very roof.'

'It was at the White House,' said Mr. Cameron, 'and as a matter of fact not under a roof at all, because Daphne was in the pea-sticks.'

'No matter, no matter,' said Mr. Middleton. 'And you love her, Cameron, and she returns your love. Forever will you love and she be fair. Make much, Cameron, of these golden hours.'

He mused, a little obtrusively, for a moment, while his wife and his partner exchanged an amused glance of embarrassment.

'Time like an ever rolling stream,' said Mr. Middleton, by way of a suitable quotation for a newly engaged couple. 'And that reminds me, Cameron, we shall have to reconsider the whole question of the water supply for that College. There has been a question of contamination in the reservoir and I must find out exactly what is happening.'

Mr. Cameron said he knew a man on the Town Council at Oxbridge whose father had been a scout at his old College and thought something might be done through him. Then the talk became so happily and enthusiastically technical that Mrs. Middleton left the men and thought she would go over to the White House, feeling vaguely that her sister-in-law might need her. Laverings dined much later and sat much longer over its dinner than the White House, so it was now after ten o'clock. When she got to her own garden gate she found Denis in the lane.

'Lilian and Daphne have gone to bed,' he said, 'and if I could stop working, I'd go too. I suppose you know about Alister and Daphne.'

'Yes,' said Mrs. Middleton.

'I wish,' said Denis, leaning his elbows on the top of the gate, 'that I had a nice contented easy-going disposition. But I haven't. And Daphne was really all I've got except darling Lilian, and now I have lost her. Oh, I don't mean because she's engaged, but I suddenly have no clue to her and I don't like it at all.'

'Yes, I suppose she and Lilian are all you have,' said Mrs. Middleton quietly and then was silent. The silence became so deep that it menaced like a betrayal. 'I wish,' she said, forcing herself to speak, 'that there were more rapture about it. But I suppose I am romantic.'

'Oh, yes,' said Denis. 'You are romantic.'

He took his elbows off the gate and melted away into the dark shadow of the lane. Mrs. Middleton did not move for some time. Then she went back to the house where she found her husband and Mr. Cameron still deep in technicalities, so she said good night.

'You are tired,' said Mr. Middleton accusingly.

'I don't think so,' said Mrs. Middleton, suddenly conscious, as if his words had released a spell, of boundless fatigue.

'I know you so well, Catherine,' said Mr. Middleton, 'and every shadow on your face. Don't get tired.'

Mrs. Middleton lingered, her hand on her husband's shoulder.

'No, Jack, I won't get tired,' she said. 'Good night, Alister.'

X

THE AGRICULTURAL AT SKEYNES

By a miracle of self-restraint on the part of everyone concerned, helped by Mr. Cameron's return to London and his work, Daphne's engagement remained a secret for the next fortnight. There was a kind of agreement that it should be announced in *The Times* after the Skeynes Agricultural Show, that Grand Climacteric of the rural year. Mr. Cameron came down twice to spend the day at the White House and on each of these occasions Daphne was urgently wanted at Staple Park. She explained to her stepmother that if she made excuses to Lady Bond and her ladyship happened to discover, as she certainly would, that the excuses coincided with Mr. Cameron's visits, the county would know the news within twenty-four hours. So Mr. Cameron talked to Mrs. Stonor, who listened and listened, doing very fine sewing which needed a great deal of attention.

Mrs. Middleton and Mrs. Stonor were a great deal together, gardening, working, talking on some subjects, silent on others. Mrs. Middleton, kneeling among damp rock plants, a smear of mud across her face from pushing her hair back with a dirty gardening glove, did once go so far as to say that life was very tiring, and Mrs. Stonor, picking up from the flagged path a large basket of very earthy weeds which she had just upset, added as a kind of rider that she hoped transmigration wasn't true, because one life was quite enough. Otherwise, being philosophers in their own way, they left philosophy alone.

As invariably happened the weather got worse and worse as the Agricultural drew nearer, till on the weekend of the Bank Holiday a kind of equinoctial gale arose, accompanied by driving rain and a falling barometer. A chimney pot crashed onto the terrace at Laverings, hurting no one; the smoke poured downwards from the White House kitchen chimney, smothering the kitchen in fine soot and forcing its way out through hitherto unsuspected crevices into Palfrey's bedroom. Over at Skeynes the big marquee was nearly blown over in the night and Pucken said with gloomy relish that if Lily didn't calve on Monday night he was a Dutchman. What with the engagement and the weather and the prospect of a wet Bank Holiday and Lord and Lady Bond's dreadfully dull dinner party which they gave every year after the show, partly to do their duty by the county, partly to show that Bank Holidays made no difference to their well-organized staff, everyone was cross. Denis, obsessed with musical composition and the improbability of ever getting his ballet produced, was almost snappish with his stepmother, who in her turn rather crossly told Mr. Cameron, at Laverings for the weekend but spending most of his time at the White House, that he and Daphne must really make up their minds about announcing the engagement and thinking of the wedding, while Mr. Cameron sat with Mrs. Stonor and Mrs. Middleton alternately, in a state of gloom very unlike him. Daphne had a cold and when having tea at Laverings on Sunday blew her nose so often that Mr. Middleton became almost demented with fear of infection and drenched his handkerchief with eucalyptus. Mrs. Middleton was very quiet and did her best to smooth matters, for there seemed to her little else to do.

On Monday morning the weather was worse than ever and the kitchen chimney more disordered. Lou, whose nerves had been much affected by her oath of secrecy, sulked when Palfrey told her to wash the kitchen dresser and mind she got all the soot off, and answered back. Her mother for once took her side and rounded on Palfrey, saying that it was a shame to put upon the girl and what was the use of washing the dresser with the soot coming down like that. Palfrey said there were some that were glad of *any* excuse not to do their work; Mrs. Pucken retorted that Lou was only coming to oblige, being as she wasn't getting any wages; Palfrey sniffed, all three ladies cried and the bacon was burnt.

Daphne's cold was better, but her stepmother made her stay in bed till lunch, as a preparation for Lady Bond's dinner party, and when Mr. Cameron came over after breakfast Mrs. Stonor was so short with him that he went back to Laverings and shut himself up with the plans of the new water system.

After lunch a treacherous gleam of sun appeared and everyone said in a hollow way that it would be quite nice for the Agricultural after all. With umbrellas and mackintoshes and in some cases galoshes the inhabitants of Laverings and the White House made their way up the sloppy lane to Skeynes. Only Mr. Middleton remained at home, alleging an anxiety about Lily and her calf that deceived nobody.

The Agricultural was an event eagerly looked forward to by a large part of the county. All those landowners, great or small, who were interested in cattle, pigs, sheep, dead bunches of the greatest variety of wild flowers collected by school-children, and whatever else is shown at an Agricultural Show which is also a Flower Show and a Fun Fair, found it an invaluable opportunity for seeing the friends and enemies that they had been seeing on and off all the year round. Perhaps the best known and most important figure was Lord Stoke, wearing a kind of truncated grey top hat, copied from the hat his father always wore, tweed jacket and leather leggings, and followed in a feudal way by his cowman Mallow, cousin of Mr. Mallow the station master at High Rising. Mallow, as befits the best cowman in the county, was dressed in his hideous Sunday best, but not even the thought of what Mrs. Mallow would say when he got home with his boots and the bottoms of his trousers smeared with the sticky clay of the field where the Agricultural was always held prevented him from enjoying every moment of the afternoon to the full. The only competitor he had feared was Mr. Middleton's Lily Langtry, and in her absence the Rising Castle entries had had little or no opposition to face. Rosettes of the first class decorated every one of his entries, while Lord Pomfret, Lord Bond, and Mr. Palmer had to be content with second and third class or even Highly Commended.

Lord Pomfret usually attended the Skeynes show in person to encourage local industry, but his agent Mr. Wicklow had telephoned that morning to say that his lordship had to be in Barchester to fight the County Council who were trying to build ten cottages in a lane that had been impassable when the floods were out every year since the oldest inhabitant could remember. But Lord Bond and Mr. Palmer had been there ever since nine o'clock and after lunch were joined by their wives. Mrs. Palmer, who was wont to boast with considerable truth that she didn't care what she looked like, was squelching about in gum boots, despising Lady Bond who, in very neat woollen stockings and heavy brogues, felt an equal contempt for her friend's footgear.

Lady Bond had determined to use the day, with its chances of meeting most of the neighbouring landowners, to prepare the ground for her campaign against Sir Ogilvy Hibberd. The invitations for the Public Meeting were now all ready to be sent out and Lady Bond had planned to enlist everyone's sympathy at the Show, give them Monday night to think it over, and post the invitations on the Tuesday afternoon, so that they would be found on every breakfast table on Wednesday and clinch the matter. Seeing Mrs. Stonor and Denis at the entrance to the grounds, she bore down on them, demanding Daphne, whom she wished to accompany her on her crusade and make mental notes of likely converts. Mrs. Stonor, looking rather draggled in a shapeless old tweed coat and an old tweed hat which was the most suitable toilette she could think of for a wet afternoon among animals, said she was keeping Daphne in bed with a cold.

'That is very annoying,' said Lady Bond. 'I wanted her to go round with me. I hope she is coming to our party to-night.'

'Yes, that's exactly why,' said Mrs. Stonor. 'I thought if I kept her in bed till tea-time she would be able to come to your dinner, because it isn't an infectious cold, or I would have rung you up at once to say so, but she sneezed twice and I never think sneezing colds matter, it is the ones that begin with a sore throat that are infectious and she has no throat, absolutely no throat at all. But what with the wet walk here and standing about in all this mud among bulls I felt she would be far better in bed.'

'Open air is much the best thing for colds,' said Lady Bond eyeing Mrs. Stonor's coat with disfavour, and forgetting, as she was apt to do, that a well-cut tweed suit, an expensive felt hat and a Burberry are not within everyone's reach.

'But not for Daphne's,' said Denis agreeably. 'Hers are quite different from anyone else's, or anyone's else, if one can speak of an else. She will be quite well to-night.'

'Well, I shall look froward to seeing you all,' said Lady Bond with vice-regal graciousness and passed on, thinking as she went that Denis, bareheaded and wearing a mackintosh which had obviously spent much of its life on the floor of a car, near an oil can, was even more unsuited to an Agricultural Show than his stepmother.

'Why did we come here, darling?' said Denis to Mrs. Stonor.

'I can't think,' said she, 'except that everyone seemed to think we were. I suppose one would call it mass hysteria. Besides we ought to see Lord Bond's cows as we are dining with them to-night. It would only be polite.'

'If it is to please Lord Bond, I will take you to see the cows at once,' said Denis, 'though at dining with them I draw the line. I do like his lordship. His misfortunes do but mellow his character.'

'Misfortunes?' said Mrs. Stonor, startled.

'I mean Lady Bond,' said Denis. 'If I had a wife like that I'd take it out on everyone younger and poorer than myself. Few deeds in my ill-spent life had given me greater pleasure than playing bits from *Pinafore* to Lord Bond of an evening, bless his heart.'

'Well, I hope you will have a *very* nice wife,' said Mrs. Stonor, seizing on what struck her as the most important feature of his remark.

'Don't hope too much, darling,' said Denis. 'One can't have everything and I am very happy as I am.'

He led his stepmother away in the direction of the cows. Each wondered a little what the other was thinking, but for all their intimate affection neither of them would trespass on the other's reserves, now or ever.

Lady Bond had a very shrewd guess as to where her next objective, her brother Lord Stoke, was to be found, and wasting no time on any hens, ducks, wild flowers, or vegetables from the allotments, she went straight to the pens where Barsetshire's squarest, most bristly pigs were enshrined. Here, as she expected, she found Lord Stoke gloating over a hideous matron, gently scratching her scaly back with his stick. His herdsman, Mallow, who thought but poorly of animals with less than four stomachs, was standing by registering contempt for employers.

'I want you, Tom,' said Lady Bond, laying her hand on her brother's arm.

'Eh!' said Lord Stoke, asserting his deafness in a defensive way. 'Now look at her, Lucasta. There's a sow! Pomfret's showing her. When I look at her I wonder how I ever came to go in for cows. Isn't she a beauty?'

The beauty, who was the shape of a giant petrol tin with a snout at one end and a twirly tail at the other, looked with hatred at Lord Stoke out of her small, vicious eyes, and turned herself a little to indicate a spot at which more scratching would be acceptable.

'She got a man down the other day and nearly did for him,' said Lord Stoke, as proudly as if the sow were his own. 'Nasty thing a pig's bite. I'd sooner be bitten by a mad dog than by most pigs I know. Remember that old fellow that used to work about the place when the governor was alive? Old Ted they called him. He used to go wherever the bees were swarming because he said bee stings were good for rheumatics. Nasty thing happened to him with a pig when he was a lad. I don't quite remember the rights of it, but he wore one of the pig's teeth on his watch chain on Sundays. I think they got the tooth out of his arm. Ought to write all these things down, you know. Make a book about them like that book of Pomfret's that everyone talked about. Come over now, old lady,' said his lordship, prodding affectionately at the sow's portentous flank.

'I've been looking for you, Tom,' said Lady Bond in a louder voice. 'You are coming over for dinner, aren't you?'

'Dinner, eh?' said Lord Stoke. 'Bless my soul, yes, Lucasta. Always dine with you after the Skeynes Agricultural. Anything wrong?'

'No, nothing's wrong,' said Lady Bond. 'But I want you to beat up everyone for the meeting about Pooker's Piece.'

'Pooker's Piece?' said Lord Stoke. 'Now, it's a curious thing about that field, Lucasta, but you cannot get good butter from any cow that grazes in it. No one can account for it, but there it is. I let old Margett who was farming it in nineteen-two have one of my best Jerseys there for a week, and the butter wasn't fit to eat. Old Mrs. Margett, Margett's mother, said her grandmother told her a highwayman was buried there, but that wouldn't account for the taste of the butter. No, there's more in it than meets the eye.'

'Well, you don't want Sir Ogilvy Hibberd to build on it, do you?' said Lady Bond, who had barely been able to control her impatience during her brother's recital.

'Build on it, eh? Certainly not,' said Lord Stoke. 'Wonderful thing, Lucasta, not a bit of a pig goes to waste. Hams, pork pies, roast loin, hand of pork, pig's face, Bath chaps, pettitoes, sausages, bacon, black puddings, pigskin, leather; and that's only a beginning. I never heard,' said Lord Stoke, giving the sow a final prod behind her ear, 'of anyone eating their eyes, but I daresay old Margett did. He once ate three live frogs for a wager. You wouldn't find a man to do that now. It's all the Education Act.'

Lady Bond, far from being depressed by this evidence of modern decadence, once more shouted commands at her brother not to forget the meeting, and as an afterthought asked him how his cows had done.

'Four firsts and the silver cup, my lady,' said Mallow, breaking silence for the first time. 'Good thing Mr. Middleton's Lily wasn't showing this year, my lady, or we might have got a second. If Lily knew what she was missing, my lady, she'd be in a rare way.'

Lord Bond who had just come up asked if there was any news of Mr. Middleton's cow, and was informed by Lord Stoke's cowman that Mr. Middleton's cowman expected to be up all night, not being one to take any chances. Mr. and Mrs. Palmer now added themselves to the party. Mr. Palmer's cows had only got seconds, but his butter and cheese had secured several firsts, popularly attributed to his dairymaid having stirred the milk with a twig from Hangman's Oak, a large, blasted tree near the common, known historically to have been so called because a certain Lucius Handiman, Gent., had in 1672 planted a number of acorns brought back by him from Virginia, of which this was the only survivor, but naturally connected in the popular mind with gibbets and a mild form of magic.

'Afternoon, Bond,' said Mr. Palmer, whose success in butter and cheese had made him well-disposed towards all the world, 'I see your bull-calf has done well. But what about that duty on mangolds, eh? I always said that third clause of the Root Vegetables Bill would mean trouble. Said so to Louise, three years ago, wasn't it?' he said, appealing to his wife. 'The year Leslie's bull got loose in our lane. I said to Louise, I see Bond has been voting against the third clause of the Root Vegetables Bill and that will mean trouble. Now they're going to take that duty off Brazilian mangolds and where shall we be then? No, no; bad business, bad business.'

Lord Bond said that clause was still in Committee.

'We all know what *that* means,' said Mr. Palmer. 'Lot of old women —no offence, Bond—that don't know a swede from a turnip.'

Lord Stoke said that his governor had always stood for a sliding scale duty on mangolds, and began to scratch the back of a small black pig in the next sty.

'Now that we are all here,' said Lady Bond, whose determination to stick to her point was one of her most annoying and sterling qualities, 'what about the Pooker's Piece meeting? I have all the invitations ready to send out for the ninth, and I think if we all made an effort to-day to interest the farmers and the local people we could work up a very good feeling. Mrs. Middleton,' she called, as that lady together with Mr. Cameron came up, 'I am sure you will help us to beat up supporters for the Pooker's Piece meeting on the ninth. We count on your husband of course.'

'Well, you know what Jack is like,' said Mrs. Middleton, acting on her usual instinct to protect her husband. 'If he can come he will simply love to come, but he might be away.'

'I shall count on you in any case,' said Lady Bond, 'and on Mr. Cameron, I hope.'

'Did you say the ninth, Lucasta?' said Lord Stoke, suddenly taking an interest. 'Can't have it on the ninth.'

Lady Bond asked why not.

'Now, wait a moment, Lucasta,' said Lord Stoke. 'Never flog your horses. There's something against the ninth, can't tell you what. If I had my old notebook here I'd tell you. I find it a great help,' said Lord Stoke, deserting the black pig and leaning his back against its pen as he addressed his circle of auditors, now swelled by several pig fanciers, 'to jot down everything of importance in a note-book. Addresses and dates and things of that sort. I usually carry it in my breast pocket, but I suppose I forgot it to-day. Funny thing,' said Lord Stoke, taking handfuls of small portable property out of various pockets, looking at them and putting them back again, 'I seem to have everything else here. Must have left my notebook in my other tweed jacket. Always have two tweed jackets going at once, Palmer. Then if one wants mending or a button sewing on, I have the other to slip on. My governor taught me that. "If you are ordering one suit, Tom my boy," he used to say, "always order two." You wouldn't remember that, Lucasta. You were in the nursery.'

As Lord Stokes's autobiography showed no signs of coming to an end, Lady Bond used a sister's privilege and cut across what he was saying to make another appeal for the public meeting on the ninth.

'The ninth,' said Mr. Palmer. 'Louise, there is Mrs. Tebben. You must tell her, Lady Bond. She will be a most enthusiastic helper.'

Mrs. Tebben, who had come by the day excursion from Worsted to Skeynes and was very hot from walking up the hill in her mackintosh, greeted everyone and said it reminded her of some pastoral scene near Vergil's Mantua.

'Banbury?' said Lord Stoke. 'Beastly bit of country. I bought a cow there once. Only time I've been really disappointed, except that time in 'thirty-seven when Pomfret got a mare from me ten pounds too cheap, and of course that time when — —'

Lady Bond, who was by now almost pawing the ground with impatience, said she hoped Mrs. Tebben would tell everyone in Worsted about the public meeting on the ninth about Pooker's Piece. Mrs. Tebben, her face shining with damp heat and enthusiasm, said she would tell *everyone*, though she believed it was the Buffaloes' Outing. And did Lady Bond, she said, know the excellent plan for reserving seats which she herself always practised.

'We get so many cards of invitation for societies and private views and meetings,' said Mrs. Tebben, 'and I keep them all, in a drawer. Then if I need a card for anything I take one of them and use the blank side of it. I have quite a collection, and if they would be of any use to you I would willingly send you some, either by post or by the train to Skeynes. They will always take small parcels and any of your people that were down at the station could pick them up. I usually make a large cross on the printed side in red or blue chalk to show that the invitation has nothing to do with the meeting in question, and then on the blank side you could write the numbers of the seats. I have had a great success with this plan at scout concerts.'

Lady Bond thanked Mrs. Tebben very much but said she would not trouble her as she did not intend to reserve seats.

'Nonsense, Lucasta,' said Lord Stoke, suddenly hearing very well. 'Must reserve seats. How do you suppose people will hear if they come late and have to sit at the back of the hall?'

The number and complication of the issues raised by this question appalled everyone except Mrs. Tebben who said, Then they could just write Reserved on some of the biggest cards, for instance the cards of which she and her husband had not been able to make use for the Royal Academy Soiree, the Conversazione of the Royal Society and an invitation to a reception at the Liverpool Guildhall, though why they had been invited to that she had never been able to make out.

'And now,' she added, 'I shall visit the exhibits and then I must get the 4.10 back, as our good Mrs. Phipps is out to-night and I must be the cook. Just an omelette, made in a delightfully economical way with hardly any butter and a little chopped parsley out of the garden, and the cold semolina pudding cut into slices in a glass dish with some of my home-made rhubarb jam. I can't tell you how much my husband enjoyed his visit to your excavations, Lord Stoke. He hasn't been able to talk about anything else since.'

'Not able to talk, eh?' said Lord Stoke. 'What's wrong? Talked all right the day he lunched with me. Tonsils, I expect. You ought to take him to Slattery. He's the man for tonsils. Has 'em out as soon as look at you.'

But Mrs. Tebben was so occupied with good-byes to everyone that she did not hear him.

'I shall take off my mackintosh and carry it,' she said brightly. 'Now that the rain has stopped I find it hardly necessary. Good-bye, good-bye. I shall not forget the cards, Lady Bond.'

She went briskly off towards the big tent and the Palmers followed her. Mrs. Middleton asked whether Miss Starter was at the Show. Lady Bond explained, rather proudly, that her guest could not go near cows without getting hay fever, so she was spending the afternoon resting in preparation for the dinner party that night.

'C.W. ought to be here,' said her ladyship. 'He was going to drive over from Rushwater House where he spent the weekend with the Leslies and said he would come to the Show before he went home. He felt, rightly, that he ought to show that he takes an interest. Oh, Mrs. Stonor, there you are again. You haven't seen C.W. anywhere, have you?'

'Yes,' said Mrs. Stonor. 'Denis and I saw him in the cow enclosure. He said he was going to look for you.'

And even as she spoke young Mr. Bond came up. He had already learnt from Denis that Daphne was not at the Show and did not quite know if he was sorry or glad. He had spent so much time trying not to think about her that he had thought of very little else, and while one half of him wished to show proper pride, aversion and scorn, the other half wanted nothing better than to cast itself at her feet and offer her its heart and hand. And if anyone disbelieves the strength of young Mr. Bond's attachment, we can only say that even the thought of what his mother might say did not weigh with him in the slightest degree. He congratulated his father and his uncle on their various successes and enquired from Mrs. Middleton about the cow Lily's health.

'Pucken says he is going to sit up all night with her,' said Mrs. Middleton. 'I don't think there is any real need to, but he enjoys it. He takes a lot of old sacks and a can of tea and some bread and fat bacon down to the cowshed and gets away from Mrs. Pucken. If it weren't for your dinner party I expect Daphne would be there too,'

'I could easily run her over if she is really keen,' said young Mr. Bond eagerly, but Mrs. Middleton made a non-committal reply.

The sky, which had been lowering hideously for the last half-hour, now made up its mind to spoil the rest of the Agricultural Show as thoroughly as possible. Heavy drops came spattering across the ground on a chill gust. Mrs. Tebben put on her mackintosh again, saying gaily that she must foot it swiftly to the station. The Palmers said Rubbish, they would take her home in the car, which they very kindly did, while Mrs. Tebben discussed with herself at great length whether the railway company would refund anything on the return half of a day excursion ticket, price one and sevenpence halfpenny. It was not till Mr. Palmer had pointed out that the day return cost exactly as much as an ordinary single that she was at all appeased, but the subject rankled and she was able to continue it, as what she called a purely academic discussion, with her husband over the economical omelette and the cold semolina pudding.

Young Mr. Bond offered to drive Mrs. Stonor home, hoping to see Daphne, but Mrs. Stonor said she was so wet she would rather walk. The Bonds were just moving to their car when Lord Stoke, who despised all forms of weather and intended to finish doing the Show thoroughly, called them back.

'What is it, Tom?' said Lady Bond. 'Be quick, because Ferguson doesn't like to be kept waiting when it's raining.'

'Remember I said something about the ninth?' said Lord Stoke, turning his coat collar up. 'It came to me just now what it was. I knew there was something wrong with that day.'

'Well, you must come, Tom, whatever it is,' said his sister.

'You remember old Uncle Fred?' said Lord Stoke. 'No, you wouldn't; before your time. He died when I was a youngster. The governor was very fond of him and Uncle Fred left him those Chinese Chippendale cabinets. The money all went to his children — illegitimate of course, but blood's thicker than water. I saw the boy not long ago. When I say boy, he's about my age and doing very well on the Stock Exchange. Don't know what happened to the girl, married a feller in India, I think. Well, as I was saying,' he continued, suddenly becoming aware of his sister's expression, who looked as if she would like to run him through with her shooting stick, 'Uncle Henry never liked the number nine. His unlucky number. No accounting for these things. I knew I'd remember what it was.'

His lordship then went off to look at a ploughing contest.

The walk back to Laverings was far from pleasant. The lane was shoe-deep in slippery clay, the wind lashed hair and hat furiously and penetrated with icy breath Mrs. Stonor's shabby old tweed coat. Mr. Cameron, who was walking beside her, had one of his shoes sucked off in a particularly sticky rut and swore violently under his breath as he tried to get it on again. As they turned the last corner a blast met them that nearly took Mrs. Stonor off her feet and she was thankful to clutch Mr. Cameron's coat sleeve to steady herself, so he quite naturally went into the White House with her.

'Oh my goodness!' said Mrs. Stonor, taking off her hat and coat and kicking her shoes into a corner. 'You'd better stay to tea, Alister, and I'll have your shoes dried. I'll just go and see if Daphne is coming down. Denis must have gone back with Catherine.'

She ran upstairs and came back with a pair of Denis's shoes for Mr. Cameron and the news that Daphne would be down in about half an hour. Palfrey brought in the tea and took away the wet shoes.

'Alister,' said Mrs. Stonor, so suddenly that he nearly jumped. But having let loose this word, she appeared unable to go on.

'Yes?' said Mr. Cameron, eating a cake that he didn't want.

'Alister,' said Mrs. Stonor again. 'It is dreadful to talk like a parent, but after all there is no one else to do it and though Denis is really the head of the family he is even less her parent than I am.'

'It is certainly very difficult to think of you as a parent,' said Mr. Cameron. 'You don't look fit to be responsible for Denis and Daphne.'

'I really do my best,' said Mrs. Stonor apologetically.

'Good God, I don't mean that,' said Mr. Cameron. 'I mean — I really don't know what I mean. I'd better go back to Laverings.'

'But I must say it before you go,' said Mrs. Stonor. 'Your engagement with Daphne. It was to be put in *The Times* after the Agricultural.'

'What does Daphne say?' asked the fervent lover.

'She won't talk about it at all,' said Mrs. Stonor mournfully. 'She always says wait a few days. I did mention it to her just now and she said to ask you. And will you *please* tell me what to do.'

Mr. Cameron looked at her with despair. Mrs. Stonor suddenly felt her heart wrung with anguish for all the muddle, and because in spite of all her vagueness she had a very clear mind about people she loved, she saw that her concern was far more for Alister Cameron's happiness than for the happiness of her much loved Daphne. Then she was so ashamed of this revelation that she sat quite silent, in a violent storm of confusion. Mr. Cameron, looking at her, allowed himself to know what he had known ever since the day among the pea-sticks, and wondered exactly how deeply Lilian Stonor would despise him if she knew. As soon as Daphne would make up her mind he would put the engagement in *The Times* and pray that Lilian would never know the disloyalty of his heart. That Daphne might ever suspect it did not occur to him at all.

'I suppose,' said Mrs. Stonor at last, in a conversational voice, 'people occasionally make mistakes.'

'Yes,' said Mr. Cameron. 'And then they have to back up their mistakes like gentlemen, or as near gentlemen as possible. Would you mind if I went now, Lilian?'

'No,' said Mrs. Stonor, not looking at him.

So he went into the hall and suddenly finding that he had Denis's shoes on, went to the kitchen to ask for his own. Lou was alone, keeping guard for Palfrey who had gone off to the Show as soon as she had brought tea in.

'Are my shoes here, Lou?' said Mr. Cameron. 'And why aren't you at the Show?'

'I'm going to-night, Mr. Cameron,' said Lou, reverently fetching his shoes from the kitchen fender. 'It's lovely at night with the lights and the boys throwing crackers. Excuse me asking, Mr. Cameron, but aren't you going to say nothing? I mean about you and Miss Daphne? I never said a word, the way you told me.'

'Quite soon, Lou, I expect,' said Mr. Cameron, tying his damp shoes. 'You've been a good girl.'

'Miss Palfrey and Mother and me always thought it was to be young Mr. Bond,' said Lou, emboldened by her hero's praise and the delightful intimacy of a tête-à-tête in the kitchen. 'Miss Daphne seemed quite taken by him. She had his photo under her pillow, because I found it one day when I was helping Mother make the beds, but I hid it away ever so quick, so Mother shouldn't see, in Miss Daphne's handkerchief drawer. I hope I did right,' she added anxiously, seeing a peculiar expression on Mr. Cameron's face.

'Quite right, Lou,' said Mr. Cameron.

'You hadn't ought to sit in those wet shoes, Mr. Cameron,' said Lou as her guest rose to depart.

'I shan't,' said he. 'I shall go for a long walk.'

When Lou went into the drawing-room a few minutes later in answer to the bell, Mrs. Stonor asked her to bring fresh tea for Miss Daphne who was coming down. Lou who cried loudly and freely herself on the slightest provocation, knew at once that Mrs. Stonor had been crying. As Lou could see no reason for the gentry to cry except Lovers' Quarrels, she was much exercised. For Miss Daphne to cry would have been reasonable, but why Mrs. Stonor?

'Has Mr. Cameron gone?' said Mrs. Stonor.

'Yes, Mrs. Stonor, he came into the kitchen to get his shoes and said he was going for a nice long walk. He *is* a nice gentleman, Mrs. Stonor, and said it didn't matter a bit when I told him about Miss Daphne's photo.'

'What photograph?' said Mrs. Stonor, not much interested in the girl's chatter.

'Mr. Bond's photo that Miss Daphne put under her pillow,' said Lou, half frightened, half full of a delightful sense of power and the unchaining of unknown forces. 'Mother didn't see it, Mrs. Stonor. I slipped it into Miss Daphne's handkerchief drawer as quick as anything.'

'All right, Lou, that will do,' said Mrs. Stonor, much to her informant's disappointment. 'And bring the fresh tea the moment Miss Daphne comes down.'

When Daphne did come down she looked so wretched that her stepmother had not the heart to say anything about the engagement, and very soon went upstairs herself to lie down before dinner, for her head and her heart were both aching so much that she didn't know which she disliked more.

*

While Mrs. Stonor and Mr. Cameron turned into the little gate of the White House, it was but natural that Denis, who has been walking with Mrs. Middleton, should accompany her into Laverings. Ethel, who was just bringing in tea said that Mr. Middleton had taken Flora and gone for a tramp over Worsted way.

'He will do it on wet days,' sighed Mrs. Middleton, 'and Flora is one mass of mud. However it doesn't seem to do him any harm. You had better have tea with me, Denis, and we will look at those duets. Jack won't be back till six at least if he has gone to Worsted.'

As they drank their tea before the fire that Ethel had thoughtfully lighted, rain and wind beating on the windows outside, Mrs. Middleton asked Denis how his ballet was. He was not much inclined to speak of it at first. The excitement of the mood had passed and he was in the Slough of Despond that so often follows some prolonged mental exertion. He saw all its faults and more clearly still he saw the extreme improbability of its ever being performed. But the temptation to unburden himself was too great, and gradually he found himself talking about his hopes and plans just as he so often did.

'And now I have tired you,' he added, in a fine glow of self-accusation. 'You shouldn't let me.'

'How can I help it?' said Mrs. Middleton.

'Do I know what you mean by that?' asked Denis after a silence.

Mrs. Middleton said she wished he would tell her again exactly how much money would be needed to get the ballet company going. Denis mentioned the sum that would put the company on its feet. Ethel came in and cleared tea away. While she was in the room Mrs. Middleton and Denis talked about the Agricultural. When she had gone there seemed to be no need to talk and a silence fell that was full of disquietude. Mrs. Middleton tried to speak, but as no sound came from her she gave it up and reflected, with the nightmare clarity that is given by an anaesthetic, that not to speak was the very best way of laying up irremediable trouble for two people, and possibly for a third for whom her long affection and devotion were very deep. It did not help her at all when Denis said in a carefully ordinary voice 'If you look so tired I don't know how to bear it.' But seeing that she must help him even if she couldn't help herself, she wrenched her mind back savagely from its far wanderings, got up, and said she would look out those duets. The music was piled on the piano. She began to turn it over. Denis threw his cigarette into the fire and came to her side.

'I think,' said Mrs. Middleton, 'not duets, Denis. Duets are a perpetual battle for the loud pedal. Music for two pianos is much more fun. If we had two pianos in the library — —'

Then because Denis's hand touched hers she was speechless and powerless.

'I think you are quite right about duets,' said Denis, speaking to the top of her head. 'You always are right. Also kind. Also too tired. I am going home to see how Daphne is. I am only talking because it is extremely important that someone should talk at this moment. When I first saw you again at Laverings I wanted more than anything in the world to make you look less tired. I still want that, but I have made no kind of success of it. Indeed a failure. I shall see you at Lady Bond's horrible dinner to-night.'

Then Mrs. Middleton was left alone. So she put away the music and wrote some dull letters and before long Mr. Middleton came back.

'A giant refreshed, Catherine,' he called to her as he came in. 'I have walked in good English rain and mud since three o'clock. So has Flora. She delights in everything that her master loves. Now to prepare for Bond's dinner party. I feel that I shall be in vein to-night. Did you enjoy the Agricultural, my dear?'

Mrs. Middleton said it had been very nice and they went upstairs to dress. While they were waiting for the car Mr. Middleton looked anxiously at his wife.

'There is a cloud,' he said. 'Can you tell me?'

'It is just a small, secret grief,' said Mrs. Middleton, faintly amused that she was capable of so accurately analysing her own feelings.

'Keep it then, my dear,' said her husband with all his kindness. 'I wouldn't interfere with your secret griefs. But let me know when I am needed.'

XI

MR. CAMERON ESCAPES

THE dinner table at Staple Park was round on ordinary occasions, and by the addition of various leaves it could seat as many as twenty-four. Tonight there were to be eighteen, so it was not developed to its greatest extent, but even so it looked highly impressive and Spencer felt that it was on the whole worthy of him. Lord Pomfret was always invited to the Agricultural dinner and always declined. The other local landowners present were Lord Stoke, Mr. and Mrs. Palmer with their niece Betty Deane, the Middletons and Mr. and Mrs. John Leslie, a very nice, rather dull couple who came as representatives of Mr. Leslie and

Lady Emily Leslie at Rushwater. These, with Miss Starter, Mr. Cameron, the Stonors and the Dean of Barchester and Mrs. Crawley made up the party.

Poor Daphne found herself between Mr. Cameron and young Mr. Bond, and as Mr. Bond was getting on extremely well with Betty Deane on his other side, she wished more than ever that her cold had been bad enough to keep her in bed. On the same side of the table Mrs. Stonor in the intervals of talking to Mr. Leslie and renewing an old acquaintance with the Dean, was able to look across at Denis, between Mrs. Leslie and Mrs. Palmer, and wonder what exactly had happened that afternoon, for that something had happened she was perfectly sure.

'I hope, Mr. Dean,' said Lady Bond to her left-hand neighbour, 'that you and Mrs. Crawley will be able to come to a meeting in the village on the evening of the ninth about preserving Pooker's Piece. You will have an invitation by Wednesday morning.'

The Dean said that if there was an Evangelical humbug in England it was the Bishop of Barchester, who had arranged a meeting at the Palace for that evening. What the meeting was about he could not at the moment precisely remember, but if it was intended to further any of the Bishop's plans, he ought to be there to lead the opposition.

'You know it is Sir Ogilvy Hibberd who has bought Pooker's Piece,' said Lady Bond. 'He wants to build a road house.'

'Hibberd?' said the Dean. 'A pestilent fellow. One of those clerically-minded laymen that are such a thorn in our flesh. I had the pleasure of blackballing him for the Polyanthus. I'll come if I can, Lady Bond, and if not I'll send my secretary. He is young and vigorous to a degree that quite exhausts me and will lead any movement with the greatest of pleasure. In fact if you would switch him onto the Preservation of Pooker's Piece it would be a real godsend to me and perhaps he would allow me to answer some of my own letters.'

As the talk between Lady Bond and the Dean was long and animated, lasting well into the saddle of lamb and red currant jelly, Mrs. Stonor on the Dean's other side had to go on talking to Mr. Leslie, which was easy enough if one asked him about his two young children; and the next couple, Betty Deane and young Mr. Bond, were similarly thrown into each other's arms. As they had many American friends in common, and young Mr. Bond took no notice of Betty's peculiar manner, they got on very well and indeed made a good deal of noise, which was far from inspiriting to poor Daphne. And, as a stone thrown into water spreads a ripple over the pond, so did the ripple from the Dean and Lady Bond reach Daphne, forcing her to talk to her affianced on her other side. In justice to this unhappy pair it must be said that they did their best. Daphne told herself again and again that Alister was one of the nicest people she had ever met and asked him a great many questions about the College of Epistemological Ideology, but she couldn't

help hearing the gay and heartless chatter between young Mr. Bond
and Betty Deane, nor could she help turning her head from time to
time to lacerate her eyes with the sight of the huge sapphire on Betty's
left hand. Mr. Cameron told himself what a darling girl Daphne was,
and how well she looked even with the remains of a cold and how nice
it would be to have a wife who took an interest in damp courses and
reinforced concrete, but he thought a good deal about Lilian Stonor and
people making mistakes and honourably living up to them, and often
answered Daphne's questions rather at random, which made no difference, as she was not listening to the answers.

On Mr. Cameron's other side Mrs. Crawley was talking comfortably
to Lord Bond about the shocking state of the Deanery coal cellar, while
beyond them Mrs. Middleton fed Mr. Palmer with questions about his
dairy and how his nephew Laurence was getting on. She could not see
Denis, two couples away, and wished she could and was glad she
couldn't. As for Miss Starter and Lord Stoke they became almost in-
separable at once, for Lord Stoke's mother had once been proposed to
by Miss Starter's father, and after crying for twenty-four hours, for
Lord Mickleham was poor and a poet and quite ineligible in spite of
his title, had married old Lord Stoke, while Lord Mickleham had
immediately married the first of the three wives who had brought him
his eighteen children. Miss Starter, having lived with semi-royalty, was
extremely good at Debrett, a book of which Lord Stoke made an almost
religious study, and cousins and connections by marriage flew between
them like so many shuttlecocks, till Miss Starter quite forgot her diet
and took melted butter and a piece of ordinary toast, both of which
were well known to be death to her. Beyond them Mrs. Leslie talked
gently to Denis about her two young children, her sister-in-law Agnes
Graham and her six children, her brother-in-law David who always
had such an amusing time, her nephew Martin Leslie who was down
from Oxford now and working in his grandfather's estate office, and
how much she liked Littlehampton. Her mild babble gave Denis every
chance of wishing he could see Mrs. Middleton, two couples away, and
being glad that he couldn't. And Mrs. Palmer and Mr. Middleton were
doing their best to talk each other down on the subject of the Post
Impressionists, both having very decided views combined with a distinct
difficulty in remembering whether Manet and Gauguin were Monet
and Van Gogh or someone else.

Altogether Lady Bond was able to tell herself, as she always did, that
her party was being a complete success and even Spencer relaxed a
little as the roar of contented diners-out rose louder and louder. But the
happiest of parties must be broken up when the fatal moment comes for
the hostess to take a gracious leave of her first partner and set to her
second. Much as Lady Bond would have liked to go on talking to the
Dean, who was speaking evil of his Bishop in a way that was balm to

her staunch High Church spirit, she saw that the turning point had arrived, said the Dean must tell her more about the Palace later on, and seizing a lull in the discussion on Post Impressionism asked Mr. Middleton for news of Lily, thus releasing Mrs. Palmer to talk to Denis.

'What's the matter with your stepmother?' said Mrs. Palmer. 'She doesn't look well.'

Denis said she had been nursing Daphne, who had a cold.

'I suppose she wears herself out over you young people,' said Mrs. Palmer, and then softening to Denis, for she had no children and was very fond of her nephews and nieces and the young in general, she put him through a rigorous cross-examination about his own past life, health, work and prospects. Denis liked her blunt kindness and answered all her questions as well as he could.

'Of course a wife is what you need,' said Mrs. Palmer. 'Someone like Betty who would look after you. Pity you didn't meet her sooner. How well she looks to-night, and no wonder.'

Denis looked across at Betty, who certainly looked handsome and animated beyond her wont talking to young Mr. Bond, and shuddered at the thought of managing her.

'You young men will not wear enough clothes,' said Mrs. Palmer, noticing the shudder. 'This weather is very treacherous. I'll tell you what you ought to do.'

So she told him, and next to him Mrs. Leslie told Lord Stoke about her children, and her husband's relations, and Lord Stoke thought she was a nice sensible little woman and told her about the new kitchen range at Rising Castle.

Miss Starter, abandoning with regret her genealogical talk with Lord Stoke, turned to Mr. Palmer, and asked him, for she had acquired a royal memory for faces and names, whether she had not seen him and his wife at Homburg before the war. Mr. Palmer, who had never forgiven the Germans for making it impossible to take his usual cure for several years, said they were a bad lot and now he had quite stopped trying to see any good in them he felt much more comfortable. Miss Starter was able to tell several harrowing stories of insults accorded to her at minor German courts where she had been in attendance on H.H. Prince Louisa Christina, courts where, in spite of their intolerable stickling for rank and precedence, she, an English Honourable, had been treated as a commoner. Mr. Palmer put forward the comprehensive view that all foreign titles were rubbish and there was nothing abroad to touch an English Duke, to which Miss Starter agreed so heartily that she ate some ice pudding, a delicacy absolutely forbidden by her physician.

'You look a little tired,' said Lord Bond to Mrs. Middleton. 'It was very good of you to come to the Agricultural, but it's too much for you on a day like this. Sorry Middleton couldn't come.'

'He was rather busy with work,' said Mrs. Middleton, feeling that any kindness was more than she could bear.

'Nice of Mrs. Stonor to turn up too,' said Lord Bond, in great content with his party. 'She looks a bit run down. Nice girl that stepdaughter of hers. Plenty of character Miss Daphne has. Only person I ever knew that got the upper hand of my butler. I've had the piano key ever since she told him to give it back to me. And Denis is a nice boy too, a very nice boy. I'd as soon listen to him playing Gilbert and Sullivan as anything. What's he going to do with his music, eh? Not much money in music, I suppose.'

Mrs. Middleton said he had written the music for a ballet but it cost a lot to get that sort of thing produced, naming the sum that Denis had mentioned.

'Ballet, eh?' said Lord Bond, looking down from the head of the table at his young guest with increased respect. 'Pretty girls in tights and crinolines, eh? Is it pretty music? I did mean to ask him to play me some, but we always got back to Gilbert and Sullivan. He likes it as much as I do.'

Mrs. Middleton said it was very pretty music.

'I must have a talk with that young man,' said Lord Bond. 'Now you know what you need is a good holiday, Mrs. Middleton. Go off on a cruise or something.'

So he gave her a great deal of very kind and quite useless advice, and she wondered why to say a person's name was so difficult and was thankful that she had been able to speak of Denis as 'he' when Lord Bond was asking about him.

Mrs. Crawley and Mr. Cameron both knew Mr. Barton, the architect who was doing some repairs to Hiram's Hospital in Barchester, an old building in which the Crawleys were much interested, so they got on very well, and now Daphne found herself left with young Mr. Bond.

'I've been longing to talk to you ever since dinner began,' said young Mr. Bond.

Daphne wanted to say 'So have I,' but a stranger that had got inside her and was hurting her dreadfully said in a rather horrid voice that he had seemed very happy with Miss Deane.

'She's a splendid girl,' said young Mr. Bond enthusiastically. 'I wish you could know her better, but she's going to America so soon. You know we are going on the same boat. I wish you were coming too.'

The stranger said she knew she would simply loathe America.

'I say, Daphne,' said young Mr. Bond anxiously, 'I haven't done anything stupid, have I? I thought I might have annoyed you about something last time I was down here and you know I'd die sooner than be a nuisance. Can't you tell me what it is and I'll apologize like anything, even if I haven't done it.'

'It's nothing,' said Daphne, pushing the stranger aside. 'It's only — —'

But before she could finish, Betty Deane, deserting her other partner, Mr. Leslie, leant over to young Mr. Bond and said, 'I say C.W., did you know your father means to announce it when he gives his Agricultural Toasts? It's a bit shame-making, but I don't like to spoil his fun.'

'Good girl, Betty,' said young Mr. Bond, patting her on the arm. 'Please excuse me,' he continued to Daphne, 'I couldn't help it.'

'It doesn't matter a bit,' said the stranger with icy politeness. 'I never noticed you doing anything particular. I really wasn't thinking about it. I just thought you might like to know that I am engaged to Alister Cameron. It's a secret, at least it was, but we're going to have it in *The Times* at once, so I thought I'd tell you.'

Young Mr. Bond went perfectly white and said he congratulated her with all his heart and Cameron too.

'Thanks awfully,' said the stranger. 'I expect we'll be married almost at once, even before you are.'

'What on earth do you mean, Daphne?' said young Mr. Bond. 'You are mad, or I am. Why should I get married? You know perfectly well — —'

But here he was interrupted by a genteel banging of spoons of handles of dessert knives on the table. It was Lord Bond's very embarrassing annual custom to give a few healths at the dinner after the Skeynes Agricultural Show and make a little speech. Much as his wife detested this outburst she was for once powerless to check him. Luckily most of the guests were old friends who were used to their host's mild form of eccentricity, and Lady Bond had to conceal her disapproval as best she could, drawing but faint comfort from the knowledge that Spencer was the only person who fully shared her feelings. In fact every year Spencer determined to give notice after the dinner, but realizing what he owed to himself, he always thought better of it next day.

Holding a small piece of paper on which he had made some illegible notes, Lord Bond ran through practically the whole list of prizewinners and gave an historical survey of the Agricultural Show from its inception in 1890 to the present day, reminded his hearers after a little calculation that the fiftieth anniversary would shortly be upon them, regretted the absence of Lord Pomfret, applauded the presence of Lord Stoke, Mr. Palmer and Mr. Middleton, thought of making a joke about the Dean being a kind of shepherd himself but suddenly felt it might be in bad taste or at any rate more applicable to a Bishop than to a Dean, and so floundered happily through nearly twenty minutes of intolerably dull and sometimes, when he had to look very closely at his notes, almost inaudible oratory. Young Mr. Bond tried hard to get Daphne's attention, but with averted head she took an apparently absorbing interest in what his father was saying.

When he suddenly found himself at an end of what he had to say Lord Bond raised his glass.

'I will now give you our usual toast, the Skeynes Agricultural Show,' he said, 'but before we drink it I want to tell you all a delightful piece of news. Miss Betty Deane, our old friend Palmer's charming niece, has allowed me to congratulate her publicly on her engagement.'

He ceremoniously bowed to Betty and sat down.

'You didn't say who to, Lord Bond,' said Betty in her usual commanding tones.

'Bless my heart, no more I did,' said Lord Bond. 'What is his name, my dear? I know he's a friend of C.W.'s but for the life of me I can't remember it.'

'Woolcott Jefferson van Dryven, father,' said young Mr. Bond. 'One of the nicest fellows in New York.'

Betty's health was politely drunk by the company, who were only too thankful for a change from the Agricultural, and a buzz of congratulations surrounded her. With a smile of gracious exasperation Lady Bond rose and led her ladies from the room. As young Mr. Bond held back Daphne's chair for her to go out she looked at him with such a piteous plea for forgiveness in her eyes that he nearly kissed her on the spot, and if he refrained it was not so much from fear of what anyone, even his mother, would say, as the knowledge that a girl who has just told you she is engaged to another man is not the person you honourably ought to kiss.

Daphne toyed for a moment with the idea of suicide as the ladies made their progress to the long drawing-room, but it all seemed too difficult, so she did the next best thing, planted herself firmly by Betty Deane and said how awfully glad she was about the engagement.

'Thank you so much,' said Betty. 'It will be in *The Times* to-morrow, but Lord Bond wanted to tell people to-night and it is always a mistake to thwart people's impulses, even at his age. You never know what kind of complex you may be creating.'

Miss Starter, settling herself in an uncomfortable chair with her back extremely straight, added her congratulations to Daphne's and said she had known Mr. Van Dryven's father when he was American Minister at the Grand Ducal court of Schauer-Antlitz.

'He's dead,' said Betty. 'He got a lot of inhibitions in the diplomatic service and when he tried to get rid of them in America it was too much for him. Woolcott is quite different. He has had every inhibition psychoed and is perfectly free. You'd like him.'

'And what does he do?' enquired Miss Starter, with the gracious temporary interest of fallen royalty.

'He looks after his money, and does a spot of archaeology. He took a Classical Excavation Diploma at Pittsburgh. Of course it doesn't carry the same weight as a First in Greats,' said Betty, who never underestimated her own achievements, 'but it's pretty good to get that Diploma in three months.'

'His father was a really scholarly man,' said Miss Starter severely. 'And where will you be married?'

'Oh somewhere,' said Betty. 'Marriage is doomed as an institution of course, but one might as well please one's parents. St. Margaret's, I suppose.'

'It makes me feel quite young to hear you say that,' said Miss Starter. 'My dear father did not believe in marriage at all, which was quite advanced in those days. It is quite amusing to hear you young people still holding those views. He was married three times, first at St. George's, Hanover Square, then at St. Peter's, Eaton Square, and finally, to please my dear Mother, at St. Jude's in Collingham Road. I am sure you will be very happy. You must bring Mr. van Dryven to see me in Ebury Street, number two hundred and three, the top floor.'

This invitation was so clearly in the nature of a royal congé that Betty, who had meant to pulverize Miss Starter, found herself to her great surprise getting up and going away.

'Cutsam Porck van Dryven would certainly not have liked her as a daughter-in-law,' said Miss Starter, surveying Betty's departing form dispassionately. 'Now tell me about yourself. I have always been so grateful to your delightful aunt Mrs. Middleton for finding out about Kornog bread for me. Are you staying here long?'

'I don't know,' said Daphne, and then said desperately. 'You see I'm engaged too, to Alister Cameron, and we might get married quite soon. I don't want to leave the White House, but I suppose if one is going to be married one might as well get it over, don't you think?'

'Or break it off,' said Miss Starter, looking at nothing in particular.

'Oh, but one couldn't,' said Daphne, too surprised and too wretched to resent this advice. 'I mean if one is engaged to someone awfully nice and one is very fond of, even if one finds someone else one thought was engaged to someone else really isn't, one can't exactly back out.'

'I think I understand you,' said Miss Starter. 'I have eyes in my head and I have seen a good deal of life. You wouldn't do badly at Staple Park.'

Upon this paralysing remark she got up and joined the elder ladies, leaving Daphne a prey to conflicting emotions. She knew now so fatally what she wanted and what she didn't want that it was quite unbearable. Suicide being out of the question she felt that even at the cost of being rude she must get away and if possible get home. Her stepmother was now deeply engaged in talk with Mrs. Crawley and Daphne thought if she went round the other way, by the room with all the musical boxes in it she could find Spencer and ask him to tell Pollett that she wanted to go home at once and send a message to her stepmother that her cold was coming on again and apologize next day to Lady Bond. It was a very muddled, ill-conceived scheme, but all she could think of for the moment. It was dusk outside and only a few lights were turned on, so

Daphne was able to slip away unnoticed and make her way to the yellow satin room, from which she knew she could get hold of one of the footmen by the little stone passage that led to the servants' quarters. In the room was young Mr. Bond.

'Hullo,' said he. 'Father wants to show the Dean the Marie Antoinette box and I'm not sure which it is; the one with the bird that flaps and twitters when you press the spring. Do you know which case it's in?'

'I must go home,' said Daphne. 'I can't tell you why, but I must.'

'I'll drive you, if it's important,' said young Mr. Bond. 'Only please tell me first that I didn't hear you properly. You aren't really engaged to Cameron, are you?'

'Yes I am,' said Daphne, 'and it's too awful, because I do think he is the nicest person almost I ever met, but I thought you were engaged to Betty Deane and I hated her, and I thought if I got engaged to Alister it would stop me minding, but it made it much worse, and I do think he is so very nice, but then you weren't engaged to Betty and it was all too ghastly, and I wish I was dead. I think the Marie Antoinette box is in the table with the glass top and the red plush lining.'

'Oh damn the box and the table,' said young Mr. Bond. 'You aren't going to marry Cameron and you are going to marry me. Is that clear? Besides you haven't even got an engagement ring. It's all nonsense.'

'I didn't want a ring,' said Daphne. 'I thought it wouldn't seem like being really engaged so long as I didn't have a ring and didn't have it in *The Times*.'

'Then it isn't an engagement at all,' said young Mr. Bond.

And at that moment the door opened and Mr. Cameron, who had a passion for musical boxes and thought he might play with some quietly while the others discussed cows, came in and looked piercingly at the guilty couple.

'It isn't Cedric's fault, Alister, it truly isn't,' cried Daphne, with visions of a duel.

'What isn't?' said Mr. Cameron.

'I do really think you are the nicest person I have ever known, Alister,' said Daphne, 'and I am terribly fond of you, but it was so awful and I always thought Cedric was engaged to Betty.'

Mr. Cameron was not surprised. He understood Daphne's incoherent words quite well. Lou's indiscretion had only been the last eye-opener and he knew he had known from the beginning that the whole thing was a mistake. Not unnaturally he experienced for a moment a pang of intense mortification, but even as that subsided a hope rose to fill its place.

'If you would like our engagement to come to an end, Daphne,' he said, 'it can do so this very minute.'

'Alister, *darling*,' cried Daphne, flinging her arms round his neck and embracing him heartily.

'Are you sure you don't mind?' said young Mr. Bond.

'To be perfectly truthful, though I am very, very fond of Daphne, I was never so relieved in my life,' said Mr. Cameron.

Then he and young Mr. Bond shook hands and began to laugh so much that Daphne had to join them, though she didn't quite know what it was about, and as they were laughing Lord Bond came in.

'Well, amusing yourself, young people?' he said benignantly. 'Can't you find the Marie Antoinette box, C.W.? I do want Crawley to see it.'

'It's in the glass table, Lord Bond,' said Daphne, lifting the lid and taking out the little chased golden box with its royal monogram.

'Good girl. You know the place better than I do,' said Lord Bond.

'Oh, father,' said young Mr. Bond, 'Daphne and I are engaged if that's all right.'

'Bless my soul! And on the Agricultural night too,' said Lord Bond. 'Well, I couldn't have been more pleased if I'd got every first prize at the Show. She's a treasure, C.W. A girl that can get the better of Spencer will do anything. But what about your mother, my boy?'

'I think, Father,' said young Mr. Bond, 'that if I didn't tell her till to-morrow I'd feel stronger then. Could we have it for a secret to-night?'

Lord Bond kissed Daphne warmly and said they would say nothing till next day and he must get back to the dining-room or the Dean would be wondering where he was.

'And I'll get back too,' said Mr. Cameron. 'I suppose no one else is to know till to-morrow? What about Lilian?'

'Oh, I'll tell her, of course, and Denis when we get home,' said Daphne. 'And it will be lovely to tell Uncle Jack and Catherine to-morrow, and Palfrey and Mrs. Pucken. Oh — —' she added with a kind of shriek.

'What?' said young Mr. Bond.

'I've just remembered Pucken said Lily would probably have her calf to-night,' said Daphne. 'Oh Cedric, do you think anyone would notice very much if we drove back to see? I do *adore* new calves.'

'I should think they'd notice like anything,' said young Mr. Bond, 'but we may as well be hanged for a calf as a lamb. Come on. Cameron, you can make some excuses, can't you.'

He swept Daphne away, leaving Mr. Cameron with his shattered romance and much happier than he had been since the dreadful day among the pea-sticks. He went back to the dining-room and took a pleasant part in the conversation, though occasionally embarrassed by the looks of complicity that Lord Bond cast in his direction. When the men joined the ladies Mr. Cameron mentioned to Miss Starter, who would, he thought, spread the news as well as anyone else, that Daphne and young Mr. Bond had gone over to Laverings to enquire about a calf.

'A good thing too,' said Miss Starter, eyeing Mr. Cameron in a way that made him jump, so clearly did it tell him that she knew exactly what was going on.

But apparently no one else did, and on such an Agricultural evening it seemed perfectly natural that two of the party should drive five miles each way on a rainy night to make enquiries after a cow.

The Leslies, who were the first to leave, offered to drop Mrs. Stonor and Denis at the White House, an offer they gladly accepted, as the Middletons showed no sign of moving. Lord Bond, who had immensely enjoyed being host at so pleasant a gathering, came to see them off.

'One minute,' he said, detaining Denis. 'Can you come up and see me to-morrow morning? Come when your sister comes. We'll have a little talk about music. Don't forget.'

Denis, pleased to give pleasure, and feeling that anything would be better than being at home, where Lilian's keen sense would detect that he was troubled, said he would certainly come up, and so went off with his stepmother and the Leslies.

When the Laverings party got back Mr. Cameron, who had controlled himself heroically all the evening, said he would just see if Daphne had come home, and went across to the White House. Mrs. Stonor and Denis were in the drawing-room and almost at the same moment Daphne burst in, followed by young Mr. Bond.

'Lilian darling,' she shrieked, hugging her stepmother violently, 'it's a divine calf and I'm engaged to Cedric. Oh Denis,' she continued, hurling herself at her brother, 'isn't it heavenly. Pucken says it's the nicest little heifer calf he ever saw and he's going to call it Daphne if Uncle Jack doesn't mind.'

There was a perfect welter of joyful congratulations, much better ones, Mr. Cameron sardonically reflected, than his ill-starred news had produced.

'Well, I must get back,' said young Mr. Bond. 'I suppose you'll be coming up to-morrow, Daphne, as usual. I'll come and fetch you. You have kissed everyone except me to-night, Daphne. It's unreasonable.'

Daphne checked a gigantic yawn, kissed everyone with great impartiality, including her betrothed, and fled upstairs to bed.

'Do I have to ask any one's permission?' said young Mr. Bond.

'Technically, no,' said Denis, 'as Daphne is twenty-one and no one has ever attempted to control her. But Lilian and I, unofficially, are enchanted, and if she shows any signs of backing out, rely on us to bring her up to the scratch.'

Young Mr. Bond thanked them cordially and went away.

'Is it all right, Alister?' said Denis, looking over the stairs on his way up to bed.

'I've not felt so happy since I can't think when,' said Mr. Cameron.

'Good,' said Denis, disappearing.

'Good-night,' said Mr. Cameron to Mrs. Stonor.

'Is it really all right?' she asked.

'Really. And more than ever right if you will forgive me for anything and everything,' said Mr. Cameron.

'If you are really content, that is perfect,' said Mrs. Stonor, giving him her hand.

He went back to Laverings, and Mrs. Stonor remained quite still till she had heard both the garden gates click.

After midnight the wind fell, the clouds shredded and melted, the stars were seen again. In the hush after the storm, in the grey hours before the summer dawn, Mrs. Middleton was able to tell herself how glad she was that she had had no further opportunity of speech with Denis that evening. Denis waking again and again in panic from nightmare dreams was able to point out to himself, with all the coolness and detachment suitable to the hour, how it was really for the best that he had been unable to exchange so much as a look with Mrs. Middleton during the dinner party. Nothing could have been more calming and satisfactory for both of them.

XII

BEFORE LUNCH

On the following morning Lord and Lady Bond and Miss Starter were seated at breakfast. Sunshine flooded the room. Outside the gardeners were busily removing every twig and leaf brought down by the storm and raking over the gravel sweep. Young Mr. Bond was not there and his mother concluded that he was still asleep.

'I must tell you a very interesting thing, Lucasta,' said Miss Starter. 'Last night I actually took some melted butter and a piece of toast; not my own toast, but ordinary toast. I was so much interested in your brother's conversation that I quite forgot about myself for once. And the extraordinary thing is that I have felt no bad effects at all.'

'I always told you you imagined a lot of your complaints, Juliana,' said Lady Bond, who was rapidly going through her correspondence.

'You have such a wonderful constitution that you don't understand suffering as I do,' said Miss Starter, which was most provoking of her, for however well people may be themselves they like to think that they are more sensitive than their neighbours. 'And another really most extraordinary thing that has just, only just occurred to me is that I ate some ice pudding, which every doctor I have been to says is Poison for me.'

'Sounds like faith healing, or Christian Science or something of the sort,' said Lord Bond. 'Glad to hear it, Juliana. I hope we'll see you eating a leg of mutton before you leave.'

'I fear not,' said Miss Starter reprovingly. 'One can do much when mentally distracted – I do not mean deranged, merely entertained or amused – that one cannot do under ordinary conditions. The whole flow of bile is affected.'

'We must get Stoke over again then while you're here,' said Lord Bond. 'You ought to try a pinch of bicarbonate, Juliana. Never known it fail.'

'When I leave you on Thursday,' said Miss Starter, speaking very pointedly to her hostess, 'I shall go to my doctor at once and tell him what happened here. He will be immensely interested.'

'Spencer,' said Lady Bond, 'remind me that I shall have a number of letters for the afternoon post. It's important.'

'Very well, my lady,' said Spencer.

Presently Miss Starter went to her room to write letters, a Victorian accomplishment which she had never lost, driving the housemaids mad wherever she went, as they had to have her bedroom tidied and cleared far earlier than they thought suitable. Lord and Lady Bond discussed some plans and congratulated each other on the party. Lady Bond then expressed some dissatisfaction at her son's late hours.

'I think C.W. had breakfast more than an hour ago, my dear,' said Lord Bond. 'I saw him going off in his car while I was shaving.'

'He might have said good-bye,' said his unsuspicious mother.

'I don't think he has gone to London,' said Lord Bond. 'Only to Skeynes.'

'What would he want to go to Skeynes for?' said Lady Bond in an annihilating way, and gathering up her letters she went to her sitting-room, where, to her surprise and annoyance her husband followed her and began fidgeting with the books on a table till she could hardly bear it.

'Do you want anything, Alured?' she asked.

'No,' said Lord Bond. 'No,' he added thoughtfully, looking out of the window, 'no. Not exactly. There's C.W.'

'Then I suppose we shall know why he went to Skeynes,' said Lady Bond, seating herself at her desk and opening her engagement book. 'Could we dine with the Leslies at Rushwater on Friday week, Alured? Lady Emily sent a message over by John last night. Well, C.W., you were up very early. Good morning, Daphne. Did you bicycle?'

'Good morning, Mother,' said young Mr. Bond, kissing the side of his mother's forehead. 'I brought Daphne over, because we are engaged and I thought you'd like to know.'

Lady Bond behaved very well, merely asking her son to say again what he had just said.

'We got engaged last night,' said young Mr. Bond. 'You must have seen it coming, Mother. So I thought I'd better bring Daphne over this morning and I brought Denis too, Father, because he said you wanted to see him about something. He is in the drawing-room because you said something about music.'

'Quite right, my boy,' said Lord Bond. 'I'll go to him in a minute. Well, Daphne my dear, I'm just as pleased about it this morning as I was last night. And so will my wife be.'

'Do you mean to say you knew last night, Alured?' said Lady Bond.

'I couldn't help telling father,' said young Mr. Bond, now joyfully reckless of all consequences, 'because he saw us when he came to look for the Marie Antoinette musical box.'

'I don't understand this at all,' said Lady Bond.

'Well, I'm awfully sorry, but Cedric and I got engaged last night,' said Daphne.

In Lady Bond's rather slow-moving mind a struggle was going on between her natural tendency to disapprove of everything which she had not originated herself and a real wish to show pleasure in her son's choice, even if it were not quite her own. She also would much have liked to relieve her feelings by bullying her husband for his complicity. The result was that she remained completely silent and everyone felt uncomfortable, none more so than Lord Bond, when a distraction was mercifully offered by the sound, too rare alas, of horses' hoofs on the gravel.

'Good God,' said Lord Bond, who was still at the window. 'It's Pomfret and young Wicklow. Wonderful the way Pomfret goes on riding. Over eighty and I've hardly ever seen him in a car in his own part of the country. I wonder what he wants. If it's the Barsetshire Benevolent Association I suppose I'll have to be steward again, though fifty guineas is pretty stiff.'

Daphne and young Mr. Bond did not know whether to stay or to slink from the room, but before they could decide Lord Pomfret was announced and came in followed by his agent Roddy Wicklow, whose sister Sally had married Lord Pomfret's heir.

'It is very nice to see you so early, Lord Pomfret,' said Lady Bond getting up.

Lord Pomfret shook hands with Lord and Lady Bond and nodded to young Mr. Bond.

'You know Wicklow,' he said. 'Just got engaged to Barton's daughter Alice. Nice girl she is. Come on a lot lately.'

'Good luck, Wicklow,' said young Mr. Bond, seeing a good opportunity to consolidate his position. 'I've just got engaged too,' he added, taking Daphne's hand.

'That's right,' said Lord Pomfret. 'Young man like you, coming into a nice little place, can't get engaged too soon. Keep you steady. Congratulations, young lady. What's your name, eh?'

'Daphne Stonor,' said Daphne, a little overawed by Lord Pomfret'
impressive size, his bald head, his bushy eyebrows and his fierce little eyes
'Any relation of Stonor of the twenty-third?' said Lord Pomfret.

'He was my father,' said Daphne.

'My boy was in the twenty-third,' said Lord Pomfret, alluding to hi
only son Lord Mellings who had been killed as a young man in a
frontier skirmish. 'Good regiment. Glad to have met you, young lady
Now, Bond, I daresay you want to know why I've come. I was riding
round with Wicklow to look at that drain where the vixen got drowned
last February, and I thought I'd look in to say I've settled Hibberd for
good.'

'Do you mean he won't build on Pooker's Piece?' said Lord Bond.

'Wait a minute. Let me tell it my own way,' said Lord Pomfret
glaring at everyone. 'No, I won't sit down. Sit quite enough as it is. I
met Hibberd yesterday afternoon in Barchester at the County Club
Can't think how the feller got in, but they have anyone nowadays. So I
told him what I thought. Didn't mince matters. Said it would be
damned uncomfortable for him in the county if he went on like that
only I put it a bit more strongly.'

'Then what will he do with Pooker's Piece?' said Lady Bond.

'Won't do anything,' said Lord Pomfret with a bellicose chuckle. 'I
bought it. He said he'd take a hundred more for it than he gave. No
no, I said, that won't do. No profiteering. I'll give what you gave, or
you can take the consequences. I frightened him, I think,' said his
lordship meditatively.

'Well, that's very public-spirited of you, Pomfret,' said Lord Bond
'We are all extremely grateful. Have you decided what to do with it?
It's rather far from your property.'

'Now don't think you or Palmer are going to get it,' said Lord
Pomfret. 'Too old a bird to be caught by that sort of chaff. No, I'm going to make it over to the National Trust or one of these damned
meddling affairs, to be kept as it is, in memory of my wife. Children can
play there and that sort of thing. Edith would have liked it.'

There was a moment's silence, for everyone knew that Lord Pomfret
missed his countess more than he would allow. Then Lord and Lady
Bond congratulated and thanked him again warmly.

'I'm going on to tell Middleton.' said Lord Bond. 'Bit of a gas-bag
that feller, but I like his wife. Well, good-bye. Good-bye, young lady.
This place needs a few children about. Brighten things up.'

'Thanks awfully, Lord Pomfret,' said Daphne. 'I mean to have about
six.'

'Do you really think so many, Daphne?' said young Mr. Bond,
slightly alarmed by this access of maternity.

'Young lady's quite right,' barked Lord Pomfret, 'and don't you
meddle with her, young man. She knows her own business.'

Upon which he went away, followed by his silent and devoted agent and accompanied by Lord Bond.

During the interruption Lady Bond had managed to get her feelings under control and was quite ready to accept and embrace Daphne, but the thought of victory was still uppermost in her mind and she had to express it before yielding to the softer emotions.

'Lord Pomfret has done the county a great service,' she said impressively. 'It will be a great weight off everyone's mind.'

'Then now we needn't send the invitations to the Public Meeting,' said Daphne. 'I'll tear them up. Where are they, Lady Bond? I thought I left them on your desk, to go this afternoon.'

'Are you sure you didn't put them in a drawer?' said Lady Bond.

'Quite. They couldn't have got posted, could they?'

'I gave Spencer special orders that they were to go by the afternoon post,' said Lady Bond.

'Then I bet he's sent them by the morning post,' said Daphne. 'Shall I ring?'

Without waiting for an answer she rang with a violence that set every bell in the basement jarring and made the third footman rush to Spencer's pantry without putting his coat on to say that her ladyship's sitting-room was ringing like mad. Spencer crushed his underling and proceeded at his own pace to Lady Bond's room.

'I say, Spencer,' said Daphne, 'did you post those letters?'

'What letters, miss?' said Spencer.

'I particularly said I wanted my letters to go by the afternoon post,' said Lady Bond, 'and I can't find them anywhere.'

'I understood your ladyship to say that the letters was to go particularly by the afternoon post,' said Spencer, 'and as one of the men was going down to Skeynes on his bike I thought I would take advantage of the event to give him the letters. They will catch the twelve o'clock post, my lady, and be delivered earlier than by the afternoon post.'

'It is most vexatious,' said Lady Bond.

'Yes, my lady,' said Spencer. 'Was that all, my lady?'

'No, it wasn't,' said Daphne, roused to indignation on her future mother-in-law's behalf. 'It was frightfully interfering of you, Spencer, when Lady Bond said the afternoon post, and it's going to make a frightful muddle and be a great nuisance to everyone and all your fault. What is the good of people telling you things if you don't listen. Don't do it again.'

Of course under any other circumstance Spencer woul have given notice on the spot, but Something, as he reverently said when describing the scene to Mrs. Alcock the housekeeper later on, told him that something was up between Miss Stonor and Mr. Bond and under these peculiar circumstances he felt he had better leave things be.

To everyone's intense surprise he said,

'I'm very sorry, my lady, very sorry indeed, miss. It shall not occur again,' and left the room.

Lady Bond gazed at Daphne with an admiration past words.

'I'll tell you what,' said Daphne. 'There's still time to get the letters back. It's only eleven, and we'll all look awful fools if they are posted now that Lord Pomfret has settled it all.'

'But, my dear, we can't,' said Lady Bond piteously. 'They are in the post now.'

'Miss Phipps will get them out if I ask her,' said Daphne negligently. 'Look here, Cedric, you run me down at once and we'll rescue them before the twelve o'clock collection. Would you like to come?' she added kindly to Lady Bond. 'I'm afraid you'll have to hurry.'

Luckily Lady Bond kept a felt hat and some gloves in the hall against sudden incursions into the garden and in two minutes young Mr. Bond was driving much too fast down the drive, with Daphne and Lady Bond in the back seat.

'Don't go right up to the Post Office,' said Daphne, poking her affianced in the back. 'Miss Phipps mightn't like it if it was you. I'll go in.'

So young Mr. Bond drew up in front of the Fleece and Daphne went over to the Post Office. Opening the door of the little cottage, she walked into the office and said good morning.

'Good morning, miss,' said Miss Phipps. 'I'm sorry I haven't got those peppermint bull's eyes in yet, but I'm expecting them at every minute.'

'That's all right,' said Daphne. 'I'll come in again. Oh, and that idiot from Staple Park posted a whole lot of letters I'd written for Lady Bond by mistake. Be an angel and let me have them out or I'll get into frightful trouble. They're all typewritten, with the crown thing on the flap, so they'll be quite easy to find.'

'Well, miss, I really oughtn't,' said Miss Phipps.

'Of course you oughtn't,' said Daphne. 'But you'll save me a frightful blowing up from Lady Bond if you do. Let's have a look.'

Very obligingly Miss Phipps emptied the contents of the mail bag onto the counter. Daphne sorted out the invitations with no difficulty.

'Thanks awfully, Miss Phipps,' she said. 'You're an angel. And if you hear something about me in a day or two, don't be surprised. I'll come in for the peppermints later.'

She ran back to the car with her treasure. Miss Phipps, also guided by a Something. followed her to the door and looked out. What she saw evidently satisfied her, for she remarked aloud to herself, 'And a very nice young ladyship too,' and went back to her Post Office, where she served her next customers with such scorn, born of a secret knowledge which she had no intention of using except to mystify and tantalize her clients, that several of them said she was on her high horse again.

'Here you are, Lady Bond,' said Daphne, putting the pile of letters on the back seat and getting in beside young Mr. Bond.

'I can't thank you enough, my dear,' said Lady Bond. 'Kiss me.'

Daphne turned round in the seat and leaning into the back of the car gave Lady Bond a very hearty hug.

'I'm afraid,' she said, 'I had to make you out a bit of a Tartar to Miss Phipps. I hope you don't mind.'

'I dare say I deserved it,' said Lady Bond magnanimously. 'And now, my dear, I think we will go on to the White House. I would like to tell your stepmother how delighted Lord Bond and I are, and we can discuss the date for the wedding. I suppose you and C.W. will want to get married before he goes back to New York.'

As the millennium appeared to have arrived Daphne and young Mr. Bond accepted the miracle gratefully and the car's head was turned towards the Laverings Lane.

*

Mr. and Mrs. Middleton and Mr. Cameron had also breakfasted very comfortably in the sunny dining-room. Mr. Cameron had decided to tell his host and hostess about his lucky release when breakfast was over, but he could not conceal a happiness which came as a relief to Mrs. Middleton after all the gloom of the last fortnight, though she could not quite account for it. When breakfast was over they went out onto the terrace, where the form of Pucken, who had been hanging about to catch them, presently became manifest.

'Well, Pucken, did you get that manure?' said Mr. Middleton.

Pucken said he thought he'd got her all right and a lovely load she was, and then stood twirling his hat in his hands. Mrs. Middleton, understanding that he had something else to say, asked after Lily. With a broad grin Pucken said she had a fine little heifer calf.

'And I never knew!' cried Mr. Middleton. 'This event upon which all my thoughts, my hopes have been centred, has come and gone, and this is the first I hear of it.'

'Well, darling, if it only happened last night you could hardly have heard sooner,' said his wife. 'Besides you do remember, don't you, that Daphne and Mr. Bond left the party early last night to see how Lily was, so you must have known that something was happening, and really you are practically the first person to know.'

'Practically!' said Mr. Middleton bitterly. 'However, we must now find a name for this newcomer. Have you any suggestion, Cameron?'

'Beyond Epistemological Ideology, none,' said Mr. Cameron, rather bored with cows and wanting to get on to his own news.

'Miss Daphne she wants to call her Miss Daphne' said Pucken, 'but I said to my old woman this morning, Miss Daphne is a pretty name for a heifer, but Mrs. Bond would be better. My old woman she told me to hold my tongue, but I've eyes in my head as well as another I said to her, and you mark my word, I said — —'

'That will do, Pucken,' said Mrs. Middleton. 'Daphne will be a very nice name for the calf and now you might stake those dahlias.'

Pucken went off, chuckling at his own wit and Mrs. Middleton looked at Mr. Cameron.

'It happened last night,' he said guiltily, 'but when I got back from the White House you had gone to bed. I was going to tell you now, when Pucken came pushing in. I think Daphne and Bond will be very happy and to be perfectly frank I'm very happy myself. Daphne couldn't have been nicer about it nor could Bond and we are all safely out of a foolish mistake, which was really a great deal my fault.'

Mrs. Middleton expressed her pleasure with a warmth that Mr. Cameron again mentally compared with her lukewarm congratulations over his engagement. Mr. Cameron, who had seen young Mr. Bond driving off with Daphne and Denis a little earlier, said he thought he would go for a walk, and sauntered elaborately down the garden and into the field.

'I am very glad that engagement is over,' said Mr. Middleton. 'Daphne was much too young. Someone like Lilian would be much more suitable for Cameron.'

'I think so too,' said Mrs. Middleton.

The morning passed on. Mr. Cameron did not come back from his walk and Mr. Middleton read the Journal of the R.I.B.A. in the sun. Mrs. Middleton drove down to the village to get some more stuff to spray the green fly and then cut roses for the house, talking to him as she came in and out of the library window. A little after half-past eleven the sound of hoofs made them both look up and in the lane they saw Lord Pomfret and his agent.

'This is very nice to see you,' said Mrs. Middleton over the gate. 'Will you come in?'

'No thanks,' said Lord Pomfret. 'Got to get back. Morning Middleton. I just stopped to tell you that you needn't worry about Pooker's Piece. I'm buying it from Hibberd. Thought you'd like to know. That's the end of him. No more meetings. Well, I must be moving.'

Touching his hat he rode off, followed by the silent and devoted Roddy Wicklow.

'What a relief,' said Mrs. Middleton. 'It was all such a muddle, and I'm sure Sir Ogilvy would have won. Now you can walk over Pooker's Piece quite happily for the rest of your life.'

'I know one person who will rejoice even as I do,' said Mr. Middleton.

'Lots, I should think,' said his wife, 'but who specially?'

Mr. Middleton pointed to Flora, who was lying half asleep on the hot flags. A fly passed too near her and she twitched angrily.

'My doggie knows, even in her sleep,' said Mr. Middleton, making a statement for which there was not the slightest foundation. 'She knows that Pooker's Piece is free for her to run in with Master, that Sir Ogilvy has retreated, leaving us our unsullied English countryside, that — —'

His voice suddenly died away. The look of panic that Mrs. Middleton knew so well suddenly invaded his face and dissolved its apparently firm lines as if a sponge had been passed over it.

'What is it, Jack?' she said.

'Fool that I am,' said Mr. Middleton, hitting himself not too hard, 'fool, fool.'

'Yes, darling, but how?' said Mrs. Middleton.

'I wrote to Hibberd last night,' he groaned. 'With all the force that is in me, all the passionate love of England which is the one thing that my worst enemy cannot deny, I wrote to him. I made it clear that I would be grievously offended by what he proposed to do, that it would be a blow aimed against ME. I humbled myself, Catherine; proud though I am I abased myself to that man, and now Pomfret has in his usual high-handed way taken the very ground from under my feet. I shall be a laughing-stock.'

'When was it posted?' Mrs. Middleton asked.

'What do I know of posts?' Mr. Middleton groaned. 'I wrote it last night when you, Catherine, were I hope asleep. I left it on the hall table with the other letters, including one, as I remember, to the Army and Navy Stores about Pollett's uniform.'

'Then the postman would have fetched them when he brought the morning post,' said Mrs. Middleton, 'and they would go by the twelve o'clock delivery. I think we can save it. It's lucky I didn't put the car away.'

Before her husband could ask her more than twice where she was going, she had driven off towards Skeynes, leaving him with a bitter sense of desolation which he expressed in vehement language to the uninterested Flora. As Mrs. Middleton stopped outside the Post Office the church clock struck eleven which meant twelve, owing to Summer Time. An attempt had been made a good many years previously to alter the clock, but its works so deeply resented being put on an hour in spring and even more being put on eleven hours in autumn (for it put to back an hour was found to be a mechanical impossibility) that it had been found better to leave it to itself. Mrs. Middleton clicked the latch of the Post Office door and went in.

'Good morning, Miss Phipps,' she said. 'Mr. Middleton has posted a letter he didn't mean to post, as usual. Do you think I could get it back?'

'There now, if you aren't in luck, Mrs. Middleton,' said Miss Phipps. 'I ought by rights to have had the bag ready, but I was doing a bit of ironing, so I told the postman to call back in ten minutes. It was an organdie blouse for my niece to wear to go to the cinema at Winter Overcotes with her young man and she wanted to get the ten-past-twelve bus, and I'd just got the iron nice and hot, so I said "You'll burn it if you do it, Gladys," for she never thinks what she's doing. "Let auntie do it," I said, so I've just finished it as you come in. Here's the bag.'

For the second time that day Miss Phipps generously poured out the letters on the counter. Mrs. Middleton saw her husband's letter to Sir Ogilvy Hibberd, took it and thanked Miss Phipps.

'I hear we may expect some joyful news about Miss Daphne before long,' said Miss Phipps, suddenly becoming extremely genteel.

'Well, I don't know anything official,' said Mrs. Middleton and escaped before Miss Phipps could begin asking questions. She did wonder a little how Miss Phipps came to suspect what was, as far as she knew, only known to the immediate family and Pucken, but the subject did not hold her mind long. No subject could hold her mind very long from its anxious avoidance of one thought. She remembered a message for the President of the Women's Institute, an excellent creature who lived three miles out of Skeynes, and with a faint and affectionate vindictiveness towards her husband for giving so much trouble she decided to go round that way before lunch.

*

Mr. Cameron, having walked down to the field in a way that certainly did not deceive Mrs. Middleton, took the footpath that led back to the garden of the White House, passed the pea-sticks without a tremor, and came to the little stream, where Mrs. Stonor was grubbing about with rock plants. She looked up anxiously when she saw him, half afraid that he might have been exaggerating his relief the night before and be now contemplating suicide. But he asked after Daphne in such a cheerful voice that she felt her fears to be groundless.

'Daphne is very well,' she said. 'All the excitement seems to have cured her cold and Cedric took her and Denis to Staple Park about half an hour ago. I must tell you, Alister, because it is rather funny and I hope you won't think it brutal, how she celebrated her engagement to Cedric, which was by throwing all her photographs of her men friends, which is a dreadful expression but what else can one say, into the waste paper basket. I thought it rather heartless, but after all what *can* one do with photographs and snapshots that do clutter up the house so? I found her waste paper basket in the kitchen, so I just looked to see what it all was and that snapshot she had of you wasn't there, so I expect it is the only one she kept, which is in a way rather touching.'

Mr. Cameron thought he had never heard anyone talk such delicious nonsense and said he had come to say he was going back to town that afternoon and wasn't likely to be down again for the present, as they were going to be very busy at the office and he would probably be spending his weekends at Oxbridge. On hearing this Mrs. Stonor poked a small plant very viciously into a hole and forced the earth down round its roots till it nearly screamed. Mr. Cameron, rather frightened by her determination and her silence, went on talking about the office and the new college and various plans in a very blithering kind of way, not quite knowing what he was saying.

'Do you *ever* talk about anything but yourself?' said Mrs. Stonor in a pause, pulling up one or two small weeds as she spoke. 'You and Jack are just the same. I wonder how Catherine and I can stand it.'

'I am sorry,' said Mr. Cameron, abashed.

'Of course Catherine is very fond of Jack,' said Mrs. Stonor, 'which makes a difference.'

'Well, I am very fond of you, if that makes any difference,' said Mr. Cameron. 'I know I've no right to say so after the way I've behaved, but as I am going away to-day it doesn't much matter, and I am going to say it. I am very fond of you. In fact I love you quite dreadfully. I won't say it again, but I must say it this once, I absolutely adore you and if I thought there were the faintest hope of your considering marrying me I'd ask you at once, but as there isn't, will you forgive me and let me go on being a friend. Only I shan't be able to help loving you. Damn it all, Lilian, everything I say sounds quite idiotic and like people in books, but I do mean it and you can't help my wanting to give you everything I have to give even if you don't want to take it. Good-bye.'

He put out his hand. Mrs. Stonor looked up from where she was kneeling on the edge of the little stream.

'I was thinking of Denis,' she said, ignoring Mr. Cameron's farewell gesture.

Mr. Cameron felt so strongly that stepsons were not suitable subjects for the thoughts of people to whom one was offering one's whole heart, that he could have killed Mrs. Stonor on the spot, loving her as he did.

'You see,' said Mrs. Stonor, looking up very seriously at her admirer, 'I have really brought Denis up by hand, as you might say, and I do feel responsible for him. He gets on very well with me and it would be quite dreadful for him if suddenly he had no home. He is so much better this summer that it is really very encouraging, but I couldn't bear him to feel that he was being turned out, and you know what lodgings are. Of course he might be lucky and some landladies are very kind, but one never knows. If we could perhaps wait for a little. I don't mean to be grasping, and of course one can't have one's cake and eat it, but do you think that would be possible?'

'You mean,' said Mr. Cameron, thinking very hard over his beloved's rather jumbled speech, 'that if it weren't for Denis you wouldn't mind marrying me.'

Mrs. Stonor looked up with swimming eyes.

'*Don't*,' said Mr. Cameron.

'Very well,' said Mrs. Stonor and did her best not to.

'Denis could quite well live with us,' said Mr. Cameron, 'and I'd like it. I like Denis very much indeed.'

'It wouldn't do,' said Mrs. Stonor decidedly. 'It is silly enough for me to be his stepmother considering how old he is, but you would be a step-stepfather, if there is such a thing, and I don't think it would work. Besides, he is apt to play the piano a good deal.'

'Look here. Will you marry me?' said Mr. Cameron.

'Of course,' said Mrs. Stonor patiently. 'That's what I've been saying for ages, but you don't seem to understand. Only I must think of Denis.'

'There is Denis,' said Mr. Cameron, looking up the little garden as he heard the gate click. 'Now we'll settle this thing at once. I won't be thrown into the waste paper basket twice in one day. Denis!' he called.

*

When Lord Bond had seen Lord Pomfret off, he went to the drawing-room, where Denis was waiting his pleasure. But instead of asking him, as he had expected, to play him something from the *Mikado*, Lord Bond had enlarged upon the pleasure he felt in having Daphne for a daughter-in-law, till Denis glowed with pleasure at hearing his dear Daphne so well appreciated.

'And now there's one more thing,' said Lord Bond, walking up and down. 'You've given me a lot of pleasure, Denis. You've played me all the old tunes I like, and I know you young people like something more up to date. Now, about this ballet of yours. From what I hear what is wanted is a backer.'

'Yes, sir,' said Denis.

'Well, I believe in you, and I am willing to put up something,' said Lord Bond, naming a sum that Denis had come to look upon as impossible. 'Mind you, it's business. I shan't expect to see any of it back, but there have got to be accounts. If I lose money I like to know exactly how. And if your ballet pays, then I shall get some interest. Now don't thank me, because I like to do it.'

'I hardly know how to thank you, sir,' said Denis. 'How did you guess what we wanted?'

To Denis's incredulous joy Lord Bond said that a little bird had told him how much money was needed. He longed for Lilian to be there and share his pleasure in actually hearing those words said.

'You'd better go to town as soon as possible,' said Lord Bond, 'and see my lawyer. I'll write to him about it to-day.'

'There's only one thing,' said Denis, 'my stepmother. You see the ballet people are in Manchester now and it would mean living up there for a time. Lilian will be losing Daphne and I don't quite like to think of her alone. I have always looked after her since my father died – at least we have looked after each other.'

Lord Bond very kindly said that Denis was quite right to think of his stepmother, but she was a sensible kind of a woman and would see that a young man couldn't always live at home. Denis finally said that he would consult her and at any rate go up to town and see Lord Bond's lawyer at once. He tried again to express his thanks, but was silenced by his kindly host, who ordered the little car to take him home. The drive to Laverings was not long enough to give Denis much time for consideration. The anxious avoidance of one thought was always uppermost in his mind. To go to London, then to Manchester would perhaps be flight, but it would be quite worth while being a coward oneself if it would make life easier for anyone else. Then he thought he was perhaps being a little conceited to imagine that his presence or absence might affect anyone. But his heart told him quite fatally that there was no conceit about it; merely a statement of fact and a fact that needed facing.

He thanked Lord Bond's chauffeur and went in at the garden gate. Mr. Cameron's call reached him and he went down to the little stream. If he had been feeling less peculiar himself he would have noticed that his stepmother and Mr. Cameron were looking a little peculiar themselves, but between excitement and the foreboding of grief his usual sensitiveness to atmospheres was rather dulled.

Mrs. Stonor in whom no amount of emotion could dull her perception of what was happening to one of her nurslings asked Denis if anything had happened. He said it had, but he hardly knew where to begin.

'I really don't know where to begin either,' said Mrs. Stonor.

Mr. Cameron began to behave like a man, but was at once squashed by Mrs. Stonor who begged with the utmost firmness to be allowed to explain things in her own way. On hearing this Mr. Cameron sat down on a dry stone and lit a cigarette, ready to bear with the utmost possible patience his beloved's serpentine methods.

'Of course Daphne getting married will mean that you and I will only be two instead of three,' said Mrs. Stonor to Denis. 'Of course if you ever *wanted* to be a bachelor, I mean technically a bachelor, at least you know what I mean, and live in lodgings where I am *sure* the landlady would neglect you, you mustn't worry about me, because I can always manage very well. Only you must consider that our two incomes separately aren't as much as they are together, not on my account, I mean, but you would be surprised how expensive househeeping is when you are on your own, so please do consider very carefully, because I'd love to have you live with me always but not if you felt you couldn't bear someone else in the house.'

Mr. Cameron knew that he would burst soon, but managed to control himself.

'Darling, said Denis, pulling up a few long grasses and plaiting them together, 'heaven knows I don't want to leave you, because nothing can be nicer and more spoiling than being with you, but after all I have to do something some day. You know I'm much better what with all this hot weather and the fresh milk and that damned cock that wakes me at three every morning, and I really ought to be up and doing. Only I'd much rather do nothing for the rest of my life than desert you: it sounds rather gigolo but you know what I mean. If you happened to get a bit sick of me I could manage quite well on my own; but as long a you like to have a man about the house, count on me.'

'I really think, Denis, you ought to know — —' Mr. Cameron began.

'No, Alister,' said Mrs. Stonor. 'Denis is my stepson, not yours. Well, darling,' she went on, 'nothing on earth could induce me to get sick of you and I do like a man about the house, so let's just leave things as they are for the present, shall we?'

'But Lilian — —' Mr. Cameron protested.

'Very well,' said Denis, trying hard not to feel a dull disappointment, 'if you really like having me and I am any kind of help, we'll leave things as they are, just as you say.'

'Then we'd better go in. It will be lunch-time soon,' said Mrs. Stonor, annoyed with herself for feeling so unhappy. 'Will you stop to lunch, Alister?'

Mr. Cameron wanted to say No and walk off into the infinite, but he couldn't. So he said Yes and followed Lilian and Denis to the house. And no sooner had they reached it than Lady Bond and young Mr. Bond and Daphne came in, all of them radiant, Lady Bond's majestic felt hat for once a little crooked after Daphne's daughterly hug.

'I can only hope, Mrs. Stonor,' said Lady Bond, advancing upon her hostess, 'that you are as pleased as I am. C.W. couldn't have chosen better and I hope you will let them be married before he goes back to New York.'

'And we are going on the *Normandie*, first class!' said Daphne. 'And I could get a lot of clothes in New York. Oh, Lilian darling, do say yes.'

'It wouldn't do any good if I said no,' said Mrs. Stonor to Lady Bond, 'so certainly I say yes. And thank you so much for being pleased. And Lord Bond has always been so very kind to Denis. It couldn't be nicer.'

'So Denis has told you, has he?' said Lady Bond. 'My husband mentioned it to me last night and I quite agreed with him that it would be an excellent thing. Denis has given my husband a great deal of pleasure this summer, when I'm sure he would really much rather have been playing jazz. Bond told me what a delightful evening you had when I was away.'

After this kind of Speech Denis did not like to protest against Lady Bond's conception of his character as a jazz fiend.

'Told me what?' said Mrs. Stonor.

'I hadn't mentioned it, darling, because of not wishing to seem un-grateful if you needed me,' said Denis, 'but Lord Bond did most nobly offer this morning to put up the money for the ballet, and that would mean living in Manchester for a bit. But if you'd rather not I can quite well, without being a bit noble about it, go on as I am.'

'But I'd like you to go more than anything in the word,' said Mrs. Stonor, in a voice that carried no reservations at all. 'It's the best news I could possibly have. We'll have a talk about it. How very, very kind of your husband, Lady Bond.'

Lady Bond said graciously that they looked upon Denis as one of the family now and she must be getting back to lunch.

'Thanks most awfully, Mrs. Stonor,' said young Mr. Bond. 'It's rip-ping of you. And could Daphne come back to lunch?'

'Of course,' said Mrs. Stonor, mildly surprised that anyone should ask her permission. 'I suppose I ought to kiss you, Cedric, but it seems so unusual.'

'That's all right,' said young Mr. Bond and taking her hand he kissed it quite naturally, a gesture that left Daphne speechless with admiration.

'Well, mother-in-law,' said young Mr. Bond very impertinently to his mother, 'come along.'

But as they went into the hall such a dreadful noise of unrestrained crying from the kitchen smote upon their ears that Mrs. Stonor, with an apology, went to the kitchen door, followed by Lady Bond who had a lively curiosity about domestic affairs. An informal court of justice was being held by Mrs. Pucken and Palfrey, with Lou, her face swollen with tears, in the dock.

'What *is* the matter?' said Mrs. Stonor.

Palfrey said she shouldn't wish to say.

'Well, Sarah, what is it?' said Lady Bond to her ex-kitchenmaid.

Mrs. Pucken, at once recognizing and reacting to the voice of authority, said it was quite shocking the way girls carried on nowadays. As good as stealing, she called it, and her own daughter, called after her ladyship and all.

'Ah yes, that is Lou, isn't it,' said Lady Bond. 'What has she been doing?'

'I didn't steal it,' blubbered Lou. 'Miss Daphne threw it in the waste paper basket and I didn't think there was no harm in taking it.'

'Taking what?' said Lady Bond.

'Mr. Cameron's photo that Miss Daphne threw in the waste paper basket, my lady,' said Mrs. Pucken. 'When a young lady gets engaged she does quite the right thing to throw away the photos of the other gentlemen. And what does my lady do,' she continued, pointing at her unhappy daughter, 'but pick Mr. Cameron's photo out and had it down the front of her dress of all places. Nice goings on. And it fell out of her when she was washing the scullery floor and that's what all the noise is

about, because I threw it on the kitchen fire. I'm reely very sorry, Mrs.
Stonor, all this disturbance with Miss Daphne just engaged and the
joint in the oven. Lou can't come up here no more, not if she can't
behave.'

'And how did you know about Miss Daphne?' said Mrs. Stonor.

'Pucken he was up with Lily last night,' said Mrs. Pucken, 'and Mr.
Bond and Miss Daphne they came to see the calf and Pucken said anyone with half an eye in his head could see what was up. I gave Pucken
a piece of my mind, talking like that, but I'm sure I wish them joy.'

'A big girl like Lou ought to be in proper service,' said Lady Bond. 'I
shall need a vegetable maid next month. Tell Lou to wash her face and
go up and see Mrs. Alcock this afternoon, Sarah. And tell Pucken not to
talk so much.'

Lady Bond retreated feudally from the kitchen, leaving Lou to receive
all the good advice and terrifying prognostications that her mother and
Palfrey could give. She did not stop crying, it is true, but her tears and
yells gradually passed from sheer despair to an expression of pleasurable
anticipation about Staple Park where she would no longer be under her
mother's domination. Young Mr. Bond drove his mother and Daphne
off to Staple Park, so that they wouldn't be late for lunch.

'I didn't know you were Clark Gable,' said Denis, who together with
the rest of the party had been a fascinated spectator of the scene in the
kitchen, to Mr. Cameron.

'Poor Lou!' said Mrs. Stonor.

Something in her voice made her stepson look at her piercingly.

'I'm so pleased about the ballet,' said Mrs. Stonor. 'And I'm sure it
will be the greatest success and I'll come to your first night. And if you
are really going to Manchester it will be in a way most convenient,
because it sounds rather stupid that Alister was engaged to Daphne and
of course I was really delighted about it if I thought either of them
would have been happy, which they obviously wouldn't, so probably
things are much better as they are and you will always, always come to
us when you are in London, won't you, darling.'

'I suppose — —' said Denis hesitatingly.

'Yes,' said Mr. Cameron. 'Lilian, I *will* speak. Your stepmother,
Denis, has forgiven me for being the most blithering ass that ever was.
I can't explain to you how the muddle happened, but thank God it was
cleared up. We shall be married, though not in such a violent hurry as
Daphne, and if you don't object to a kind of step-father-in-law, I'll be
very, very glad.'

'And if you felt like giving me away, it would be quite perfect,' said
Mrs. Stonor, 'unless of course Jack wanted to. He might take offence.'

Denis, feeling that nothing was left remarkable beneath the visiting
moon, kissed his stepmother most affectionately and said he would do
anything she liked and it couldn't be nicer.

'I daresay I'll look on you as Mr. Murdstone at first,' he said to Mr. Cameron, 'but it will pass.'

'And now Alister can stay to lunch,' said Mrs. Stonor.

Mr. Cameron said he had better go and tell Mrs. Middleton that he wouldn't be back.

'I'll tell her,' said Denis. 'If you are going up this afternoon, Alister, will you take me with you? I've got to go and see Lord Bond's lawyer.'

'Certainly,' said Mr. Cameron. 'Only I've got to start directly after lunch. Two o'clock too early?'

'Perfect,' said Denis. 'I might have lunch at Laverings to make up for your having lunch here. I'll just put some things in my suitcase and go over and tell Catherine.'

He went upstairs and packed his clothes for a few nights in town. Laverings lunched later than the White House, so there would be time to go over. What with Daphne and Cedric and Lilian and Alister, not to speak of Lou's contribution, he felt a little dizzy. His own safe world had suddenly cracked under his feet. A new world was before him, thanks largely to Lord Bond, a world unknown, unsafe, difficult, but the world where he ought to be if there was anything in his music. In his musician's self he had the terrifying confidence of the artist; as for his private self he thought it would often be very homesick and lonely. And all that remained to be done now was to make his loneliness more desolate, lest a natural longing to comfort and be comforted should bring bitterness in the end to a heart that he hardly knew. He went out into the hot sunshine. In the lane he saw Mrs. Middleton, who had just put the car into the garage. She had a letter in her hand.

'I've been rescuing a letter from the Post Office,' she said, falling into step with Denis and walking slowly down the lane. 'One of the letters Jack repents when he has written them. I don't know what we would do without Miss Phipps.'

'Alister asked me to say he wouldn't be back for lunch, if you will excuse him,' said Denis. 'He is going to marry Lilian. It is all rather complicated, but she will explain it to you. It seems very satisfactory to me.'

'I'm so glad,' said Mrs. Middleton. 'I've thought so for a long time.'

'I'm going up with him directly after lunch,' said Denis. 'Lord Bond has been extraordinarily generous. He is putting up money for my ballet. How he knew how much we need I don't quite know. Did you tell him?'

'Not exactly. I mentioned it,' said Mrs. Middleton.

'You would,' said Denis. 'Thank you. I am going to see his lawyer and then go to Manchester where the ballet company is working just now.'

'And then back here? said Mrs. Middleton.

'I think not at present,' said Denis. 'It seems better not to.'

Mrs. Middleton stopped, determined, whatever darkness and roaring of a thousand waters overwhelmed her, however the ground seemed to rock under her feet, that she would not take Denis's arm or ask him for help.

'Is that — —' she began, and couldn't go on.

'Is that — —' she said again, with extreme care but no more words would come from her.

Denis wondered to what point self-control could be borne, and what defence there was against the terrifying weight of silence.

'Is that,' she said for the third time, speaking as if each word had to be brought with pain from some infinitely remote darkness, 'for you or for me?'

'For us both, I think,' said Denis, and began to walk back towards Laverings. Mrs. Middleton walked beside him, but her steps so lagged that he was afraid.

'I am pretending to Lilian' he said when they reached the gate, 'that I am having lunch with you. As a matter of fact I shall go for a walk and come back when Alister is starting. I don't know what I'll do without you.'

'You will do quite well; oh, very well,' she said, opening the garden gate.

'And you, which is all I care about?' said Denis.

'Oh, I shall do well; quite, quite well,' she said searching for each word in that darkness where she was helplessly bound.

'Good-bye,' said Denis and took her hand.

She held his hand closely to her in both of hers for a moment, then turned and walked away down the flagged path without a backward glance. Denis watched her till she went in by the library window. Then he shut the gate and went down the lane into the fields. In three quarters of an hour he could start with Alister.

*

In the library Mrs. Middleton found her husband, his face still ravaged, what hair he had in wild disorder.

'Here is your letter, Jack,' she said, handing it to him.

'Thank God, thank God,' said Mr. Middleton, tearing it open and reading it. 'I regret in a way that Hibberd could not have seen it. It is well expressed, Catherine, well expressed. When something has to be said, Catherine, I can always say it. Facts marshal themselves, my pen becomes a trumpet. You may remember the letter I wrote to Tolford-Spender about the restoration, rather the wanton desecration of the church at Monk's Porton; that was a letter. He was forced to admit himself in the wrong all along the line and that little gem of pure East Anglian Transitional was saved. And now Pooker's Piece is saved,' said

Mr. Middleton triumphantly, as though his intercepted letter to Sir Ogilvy Hibberd had been the means of its salvation.

Mrs. Middleton was still standing, for she felt that if she sat down she would never get up again. She made no answer.

'You are tired, my dear,' said her husband with real concern. 'You went to the Post Office in the fierce noontide heat and by your own methods, whether legal or illegal I shall not enquire, rescued my letter and saved me from eternal shame and opprobrium. You must lie down this afternoon.'

He put his arm kindly round her. Mrs. Middleton rested her head on his shoulder, thankful for support and affection.

'I don't know what I would do without you, Catherine,' said he earnestly.

'Nor do I, darling,' said Mrs. Middleton.

Ethel then announced lunch, with deep disapproval of the intimate attitude of her employers, so they went into the dining-room.

'We are alone?' said Mr. Middleton. 'I thought Cameron was with us till the afternoon.'

'I quite forgot to tell you,' said Mrs. Middleton, 'that in the middle of everything else he and Lilian have decided to be married, so he is having lunch at the White House.'

'An excellent thing, an excellent thing,' said Mr. Middleton. 'Will I have to give her away?' he added with sudden terror.

'Not if you don't like, Jack,' said his wife. 'Denis could always do it. Lord Bond has been most generous and put up some money for Denis's ballet scheme, so he is going to Manchester.'

One might as well say his name. People said if you had been thrown from a horse it was best to ride again at once, to show your nerve had not gone. She had said his name twice.

'Good God!' said Mr. Middleton. 'A day of wonders. Daphne and young Bond, Hibberd, Pomfret, the calf, the manure, Denis, Lilian and Cameron, your brilliant *coup* with the letter. I stand amazed. That so many things should have happened at once. And all before lunch.'

And Alister has gone, Mrs. Middleton thought, and Lilian will go. Then shutting her mind resolutely against the deeper pain, which she knew would pass with time, though it was at the moment almost unbearable, she said,

'Yes. It is extraordinary how many things can happen before lunch.'

CHEERFULNESS BREAKS IN

CHEERFULNESS BREAKS IN

I

HASTE TO THE WEDDING

To all those who had admired and disliked the lovely Rose Birkett it appeared (with the greatest respect for the Royal Navy) quite inevitable that she should marry a naval man. As the elder daughter of the Headmaster of Southbridge School she had every opportunity for trying the effect of her charms on as many as three hundred and twenty-seven members of the opposite sex, ranging from the newest comer in the junior school to Mr. Walker who dealt out the very highest mathematics to a privileged and harassed few and was popularly supposed to be coeval with the late Queen Victoria, but except for one or two junior masters to whom she simply couldn't help getting engaged, a term which appeared to her parents to mean absolutely nothing except that she would always neglect the man of her choice for any later arrival, the whole school united in a total disregard of 'that Rose', as they called her on the infrequent occasions when they bothered to think about her. Young gentlemen up to eighteen, or at a pinch, and if one can't pass one's School Certificate and is really good at cricket, nineteen, rightly regard their Headmaster's daughter as beyond the pale, while the senior masters had little but dislike for the exquisite nitwit who played havoc with their juniors' hearts and work. Everard Carter, Housemaster of the largest House, had particular cause to feel annoyance with Rose, as she had three years ago so devastated his second-in-command, Philip Winter, that he could willingly have shaken her till her lovely head fell off her perfect shoulders.

Since the fateful summer when Rose had first got engaged and then got unengaged, to use her own description, to Philip Winter, she had plighted her troth to at least six admirers and with equal fervour unplighted it. Her parents, who had not the faintest control over their wayward child, began to fear that she would live with them for ever, when Lieutenant John Fairweather, R.N., who had made her the object of his attentions for several years whenever he was on leave, came into a very nice fortune and was appointed Naval Attaché to the South American capital of Las Palombas. Immediately on the receipt of these pieces of news he proposed to Rose, was at once accepted, for such was her artless custom when wooed, and told her parents he was very sorry but he must marry her at once.

Mr. and Mrs. Birkett, who had known Lieutenant Fairweather ever since he and his brother were in the junior school, made a faint protest for form's sake and then arranged with joy to have the wedding in the school chapel two days after school broke up for the summer holidays, a date which only gave Mrs. Birkett a fortnight to get her daughter's trousseau and send out invitations. In this her husband would, she well knew, be little or no help, partly because he wouldn't in any case, partly because end of term occupied his every moment, but in the joy of getting rid of her daughter she would willingly have undertaken a far more onerous task. It was difficult to believe that in two weeks Rose would be safely married and no longer drive everyone mad by coming down late, combing her hair and making up her face all over the house, bringing young men in for drinks at all hours and being very rude to her parents, or having equally exhausting fits of remorse accompanied by loud crying and yelling, but if any effort of hers could help towards this long-desired end, Mrs. Birkett was ready to make it. In all her preparations she was loyally seconded by her younger daughter, Geraldine, who while not envying her elder sister her beauty or her admirers (for she was an intellectual), very much looked forward to having the old nursery, which Rose had in vain attempted to rechristen a sitting-room, for her sole use and to receiving there such old girls of the Barchester High School as she happened to favour.

Under normal conditions it would have been perfectly easy to Rose to get unengaged within a fortnight and even get engaged to someone else, but two things contributed to make her love burn with a steadfast glow. The first was that her mother firmly took her up to town for such an orgy of dress-buying that even Rose's delicate frame, proof against a twenty-four hour day of cinemas, driving in fast cars, dancing at night-clubs and listening to the wireless at full blast while she talked to all her friends, was slightly affected; the second that she had nearly learnt to play the ocarina and did not wish to lose any moment in which she might be perfecting herself on that uninteresting instrument.

There had been moments when Mr. and Mrs. Birkett had suffered from compunction, wondering whether they had done right in delivering an Old Boy into the hands of their lovely Rose, and Mr. Birkett had gone so far as deciding to enlighten his old pupil as to the character of his daughter. For this sacrificial act he had chosen a Sunday evening after dinner. Lieutenant Fairweather had been spending the week-end at the school and had filled his future parents-in-law with admiration by telling Rose that if she couldn't be down and dressed by ten o'clock on Sunday morning he wasn't going to wait for her, as he had promised to meet Everard Carter on the Southbridge Golf Links at half-past. Rose, sauntering down at five minutes to ten, her golden locks tied up in a scarlet fish-net, her exquisite figure draped in a yellow short-sleeved shirt and grey flannel slacks, her feet with their gleaming red toe-nails thrust into blue beach shoes with soles two inches thick, carrying her ocarina under one arm and a large, dirty, white vanity bag under the other, found her betrothed sitting on the front doorstep of the Headmaster's house in the sun.

'You can't come like that, my girl,' said Lieutenant Fairweather, looking with affectionate disgust at his Rose.

'Don't be so dispiriting, darling,' said Rose.

'Four minutes and a half to put on some decent clothes,' said the Lieutenant, turning his back on his beloved, going down the steps to his car and looking with great interest at the bonnet. He then took a neatly folded piece of wash-leather out of a pocket in the car and began to polish some chromium work. When he had finished he folded the wash-leather neatly up again, put it away and got into the driving seat. As he did so Rose in a becoming light woollen coat and skirt (for the day, though near the end of July, was not very hot), her hair confined by a neat bandeau, her beautiful legs and feet in silk stockings and brogues, ran down the steps and round the car and took her place beside him, remarking as she did so that he was foully dispiriting.

'Not half so dispiriting as that pumpkin of yours, my girl,' said the gallant Lieutenant, and taking the ocarina from Rose he stretched out his long arm and put it in one of the stone flower-pots at the bottom of the steps.

Rose said that was *too* dispiriting and foul.

'That's all right,' said Lieutenant Fairweather, starting his high-powered sports car with a jump and roar that would have shaken the teeth out of anyone less toughly made and insensitive than the exquisite Rose. 'It'll do nicely in the flower-pot. Grow into an ocarina tree. Isn't there a book called that by some fellow?'

Rose said it sounded a pretty dispiriting sort of book and she daresaid it was one of those foul books Mummy got from the library.

'Fellow called something or other,' said the Lieutenant, swinging the car out of the school gates into the main road on one wheel while he lighted a cigarette. 'Morn, or Morm, or something. The Torpedo Lieutenant of the *Anteater* lent it me and I lost it.'

The rest of this intellectual conversation was lost in the joys of over-taking every car on the road and the happy pair were not seen again till dinner-time. Sunday dinner, for the loathsome meal called Sunday supper Mrs. Birkett had always managed to avoid, was the usual mixture of family, three masters, and a couple of rather spotty senior boys, upon all of whom Rose lavished her charms with great impartiality and but little success, for the masters talked shop with the Headmaster as a relaxation from talking shop with him all the week, and the boys regarded her much as Hop o' My Thumb regarded the Ogre's daughter, finding her sister Geraldine a much better sort of fellow. Lieutenant Fairweather talked very happily with Mrs. Birkett about old days in the junior school and his elder brother in the Barsetshire Regiment, and when Rose sauntered out of the room no one missed her in the least.

When the guests had gone Mr. Birkett looked at his wife and in an offhand way invited Lieutenant Fairweather to come into his study and smoke a pipe. As the Headmaster and most of his guests had been smoking pipes ever since supper the invitation might have struck an unprejudiced observer as quite unnecessary, but the Lieutenant, who took everything as he found it unless he wanted to alter it, at once got up.

'Good night,' said Mrs. Birkett, 'I suppose I ought to call you John, but I always think of you as Fairweather Junior.'

'Well, I always think of you as Old Ma Birky,' said the Lieutenant. 'Jove, those were the days, Mrs. Birky. Do you remember the boxing competition when I was in the Lower Fourth?'

'Of course I do,' said Mrs. Birkett. 'You and Swift-Hetherington were in the under four stone class.'

'And Mrs. Watson went out of the hall till the fighting was over because she was afraid young Watson might bleed,' said Lieutenant Fairweather. 'He was a glutton for a fight.'

'Now Bill is waiting for you,' said Mrs. Birkett, always a good Headmaster's wife.

Lieutenant Fairweather knocked his pipe out against the revolting tiles of the drawing-room fireplace, put in at vast expense by the Governing Body under the influence of one of their members who had been to the Paris Exhibition of 1900, and followed his old Headmaster to the study. The long summer evening was drawing to its close and from the study window lights could be seen in the various Houses across the school quad. Mr. Birkett turned on the light at his writing-table.

'Sit down, Fairweather,' he said.

'Makes me feel quite young again,' said the Lieutenant, taking a chair within the little pool of light. 'Those were the days, sir. One used to get the wind up like anything when you sent for us. I remember you giving me six of the best for cheeking Mr. Ferris in the Upper Dor., when I was in the Lower School.'

'Did I?' said Mr. Birkett, feeling more and more how awkward it was to have to warn an Old Boy against Rose, especially an Old Boy whom he had beaten for cheeking that dreadful Ferris who had since become one of H.M. Inspectors of Secondary Schools and the right place for him too.

'I don't suppose you'd remember, sir,' said the Lieutenant, warming to his memories. 'Rose was yelling like anything that day because Mrs. Birky wouldn't let her bang her toy drum in the hall.'

'Yes; Rose,' said the Headmaster absently. 'Yes. Fairweather, I feel I ought to speak to you seriously about Rose.'

He paused. Much as he disliked his exquisite daughter he must be loyal to her and between this feeling and his deep loyalty to all Old Boys he must decide.

'Sounds a bit like the Chaplain's jaws before we were confirmed, sir,' said Lieutenant Fairweather cheerfully. 'Of course we knew all about facts of life but we used to give him his head.'

He laughed cheerfully.

'It's not that,' said Mr. Birkett in great discomfort. 'Rose is a very good girl, but I don't think you quite understand what you're undertaking. I'm afraid my wife and I have spoilt her rather.'

'Take it from me, sir, you have,' said the Lieutenant. 'But this is where the Navy puts its foot down. Do you mind if I smoke, sir?'

He filled his pipe again and began lighting it. From the far corner of the room where by now it was quite dark came a low sound as of a melancholy and not very musical owl hooting in syncopated time.

'Hi! Rose!' said Lieutenant Fairweather, quite unperturbed. 'Come out of that.'

At his loving words Rose with her ocarina came slowly and gracefully towards the table, remarking that it was quite dispiriting if one couldn't practise because people would talk so much, and she had nearly got "Hebe's got the jeebies but they're not so bad as Phoebe's" right.

'Right, my girl? You wouldn't get it right if you tried for a fortnight,' said the Lieutenant. 'And listen; that things of yours is not coming on my honeymoon.'

'Don't be so foul, John,' said Rose. 'Daddy, I think it's too dispiriting to be told one's spoilt.'

Mr. Birkett, though he knew that he was in the right and his lovely daughter an intruder, an eavesdropper and a nuisance, felt more embarrassed than ever and was quite delighted when his younger daughter Geraldine came into the room with an avenging expression and went up to Rose.

'You've taken my stockings again,' said she.

'I couldn't find mine, and anyway they're a foul pair,' said Rose languidly.

'They aren't,' said Geraldine coldly. 'They are my good new pair that Mrs. Morland sent me for my birthday. Rose, you *are* a mean beast. You always take my things and you know I wanted specially to keep this pair for your wedding.'

Rose played a few uninterested notes on her ocarina. Mr. Birkett's heart sank. This was a judgment on him for trying to warn Fairweather against Rose. Now he had seen Rose in this very unfavourable light he would break off the engagement and Rose would go on living at home, probably for ever. At this thought the Headmaster almost groaned aloud.

'Come, come, my girl, that's not cricket,' said Lieutenant Fairweather getting up. 'Give Geraldine her stockings. No, not now,' he added, as

Rose began pulling up her skirt and showing apparently yards of a very elegant silk-clad leg. 'Go along now, and give them to Geraldine when you get upstairs.'

Rose dropped her skirt again and went towards the door.

'And don't forget to say good night,' said the ardent lover. 'Your father first, my girl.'

To her own great surprise Rose kissed her father good night, an attention to which he was little accustomed, and then put her face up for her betrothed to salute her, which he did with great affection, at the same time taking the ocarina from her, saying that she would keep everyone awake all night.

'Darling John, I *do* love you,' said Rose, clinging heavily about his neck.

'Of course you do,' said Lieutenant Fairweather, 'you're not a bad sort when one comes to know you, Rose. Good night, Gerry. Let me know if Rose tries to put it over you about those stockings.'

Geraldine, who as a rule resented any shortening of her name, kissed her future brother-in-law with almost as much affection as Rose had done and the two girls went off together, perfectly reconciled.

'You know I'm awfully fond of Rose,' said Lieutenant Fairweather, sitting down again, 'and you needn't be anxious about her, sir.'

'No, I don't think I am,' said the Headmaster.

'Nor about me, sir, if it comes to that,' said the Lieutenant, looking his future father-in-law straight in the face with an immovable countenance.

Mr. Birkett came as near blushing as a middle-aged Headmaster can do and was silent for a moment.

'It's a queer world, Fairweather,' he said at length. 'We can't tell what's going to happen and none of us feels very safe. My wife and I rely on you implicitly.'

Lieutenant Fairweather again looked steadily at the Headmaster with his sailor's concentrated gaze.

'I think I get you, sir,' he said. 'If there is any trouble about and I have to join my ship instead of going to South America, I shall get a special licence and marry Rose out of hand. I've known her ever since she was a little girl, and I know she's been engaged to lots of fellows, but this time she's for it, so don't worry, sir.'

Mr. Birkett's first impulse on hearing that he need not fear that his lovely daughter would be left on his hands was to say, 'Thank God,' but as headmasters have to keep up a pretence of being slightly more than human he merely said that he hoped things wouldn't be as bad as that and inquired after the Lieutenant's elder brother, Captain Geoffrey Fairweather, who was at the moment doing a staff course at Camberley and was going to be best man.

*

The last few weeks of the term sped away, the prizegiving and breaking-up took place, boys were whisked away to Devonshire, or the South of France, or walking tours in Scandinavia, or Public Schools camps at the South Pole, while masters prepared to pretend they were ordinary people for six or seven weeks. The matrons of the various Houses had left everything sheeted and tidied and gone to join their married sisters at Bournemouth or Scarborough, and an unwonted hush lay on the school quad, only broken by the occasional roar of a car as the guests who were coming for the night before the wedding arrived.

Everard Carter, the senior Housemaster, and his wife were among the few members of the staff who were still in residence. Mrs. Carter's brother, Robert Keith, had married Lieutenant Fairweather's elder sister Edith, which made Mrs. Carter almost a relation, and under the Carters' roof Lieutenant Fairweather was to spend his last bachelor night. There had been talk of dining in town that evening, but London is not at its best at the end of July, most of Lieutenant Fairweather's friends were away and his brother reported that Camberley seemed a bit sticky about giving leave, so the idea was abandoned. Rose had then suggested that they should all go to a cinema at Barchester, but this her mother vetoed, with firm support from the bridegroom, who told his Rose it was simply not done and she would see quite enough of him when they were married. Rose had shed a few very becoming tears and then forgot all about it in the excitement of unpacking a large china pig with pink roses on its back, the gift of the matron of Mr. Carter's House.

The party at the Carters' was not large. Everard Carter was tired at the end of term, Lieutenant Fairweather was quite happy to smoke with his host and talk with his hostess, and there were only three other guests at dinner. One was the Senior Classical master, Philip Winter, who had been engaged to Rose for a few months of the hot summer three years before, an engagement which he had bitterly repented and from which he had only been saved by the fit of temper in which Rose had thrown him over, since which time he had almost loved her for not marrying him.

The two ladies, if one may use the expression, were Geraldine Birkett and Lydia Keith, Mrs. Carter's younger sister, who had been at the Barchester High School together and were to be bridesmaids next day.

Miss Lydia Keith at about twenty-one had toned down a little from her schoolgirl days, though not so much as her mother might have wished. Her family had thought that when she left school she might wish to train for some sort of work in which swashbuckling is a desirable quality, though they could hardly think of any form of employment, short of Parliament, that would give Lydia's powers sufficient scope. But to everyone's surprise she had preferred to stay at home, where she wrested the housekeeping reins from her mother and ran the house with a ferocious yet tolerant competency that made her mother prophesy dolefully that Lydia would never get married, though on what grounds she based this opinion, or indeed any other, no one quite knew. To all such young men as were prepared to accept her as an equal Lydia extended a crushing handshake and the privilege of listening to her views on all subjects. As for any more tender form of feeling no one had ever dared to approach the subject with her and Lydia's general idea of matrimony appeared to be that it was an amiable eccentricity suitable for parents in general who were of course born too long ago to have any sense, her sister Kate, and really silly people like Rose Birkett. In these matters her sentiments were echoed by Geraldine Birkett who had been her admiring follower ever since she used to do Lydia's maths. at school and Lydia did Geraldine's Latin. In fact, except that Lydia was tall, dark-haired and good-looking while Geraldine could only be described as a girl with a rather clever face, they were twin souls and had often toyed with the idea of breeding Cocker spaniels together. But Mr. Birkett wouldn't hear of it and as Lydia's mother had developed a heart Lydia couldn't be spared. Most of Lydia's contemporaries would have regarded an invalid mother as an additional and cogent reason for leaving home and breeding dogs, but Lydia, in spite of her swashbuckling, had too good a heart and, though she would have died sooner than admit it, too firm a sense of duty to desert her mother and led on the whole a very contented life.

'Who are the other bridesmaids?' asked Philip Winter, who had not taken much interest in the wedding.

'Delia Brandon,' said Lydia, 'you know, the one that her mother's Mrs. Brandon at Pomfret Madrigal and one of the Dean of Barchester's girls that is called Octavia.'

'And how,' said Geraldine, who had a passion, her only trait in common with her sister Rose, for American gangster films.

'How?' asked Philip, amused.

Before Geraldine could reply Lydia, fully armed, leapt lightly to the breach, as she nearly always did when it was an affair of answering a question, whether addressed to her or to someone else, preferably someone else.

'Anyway,' she said scornfully, 'if I had a lot of daughters I wouldn't call one of them Octavia, even if she *was* the eighth. It seems invidious, if you know what I mean,' she added, glaring belligerently at the company.

Her sister Kate Carter who was so good and sweet-tempered that one would hesitate to apply the word dull to her if there were any more suitable description said that after all it showed she *was* the eighth.

'As a matter of fact she isn't,' said Geraldine, seizing her chance where mathematics were in question, 'because two of them were boys and one died quite young, really before he was born I think.'

Kate quietly and anxiously changed the subject by saying that the delphiniums in the School Chapel looked quite lovely and a blue wedding would be so nice and bridesmaids always looked nice in blue. But her sister Lydia, who despised such palterings with stern facts, said even if the brother hadn't really been born someone must have known about him or they wouldn't have known, and it might have seemed unkind to give him a miss when they were counting up the family.

'And anyway,' she continued, slightly raising her powerful voice, 'being called Octavia doesn't really show. I mean Octavian, the one who was Augustus you know, Philip,' she said to the Senior Classical master, 'there's nothing to say that he was the eighth, whether anyone was born or not. At least if there is I haven't read it and it's not in Shakespeare,' she added with the air of one making a handsome concession.

Kate with an effort wrenched the talk round to the wedding guests and the preparations for refreshments afterwards, which quite distracted Lydia and Geraldine from the problem of the Dean's daughters, and the talk became more general.

Lieutenant Fairweather, who had said nothing because his pipe was drawing well and he did not know the Dean or any of his daughters, asked Mr. Carter about various Old Boys and school notorieties.

'Did you know Harwood was dead?' said Everard Carter.

'No, sir. By Jove!' said Lieutenant Fairweather, rather weakening his interjection by adding, 'Who was he?'

'Of course I forgot, you wouldn't know him. He only took the Senior boys,' said Everard.

'He was the cricket coach,' said Kate, coming to the Lieutenant's rescue.

'By Jove, yes,' said Lieutenant Fairweather. 'He had that ripping cottage in Wiple Terrace. Who lives there now?'

'People called Warbury,' said Kate. 'He is something in the films, I think, and she is an artist; at least she paints. And they have a son who I am sure is very nice.'

'Out with it, Kate,' said Philip Winter. 'Your understatements are worth their weight in gold.'

'Well, I dare say he is quite nice,' said Kate, defending herself and modifying her statement simultaneously. 'Often it is only shyness that makes people seem conceited.'

'Then he must be uncommon shy,' said Philip dryly. 'And if shyness makes him so confoundedly rude and patronizing in the Red Lion bar, I wish he would get over it.'

Kate then invited anyone who liked to come and see Bobbie Carter aged nearly one in bed. Lydia and Geraldine accepted the invitation and the men were left alone.

'You were engaged to Rose, weren't you?' said Lieutenant Fairweather to the Senior Classical master.

'Yes,' said Philip, rather wondering if the bridegroom proposed to fight a duel, or keelhaul him. 'But it was some years ago—not for long.'

'Don't apologize,' said the Lieutenant. 'That girl has a genius for thinking she is in love. I thought she might get tied up before I could cut in. One doesn't get much chance with a sailor's life, you know. But that's the end of it. I hope she didn't give you much trouble.'

Philip politely said none at all. Everard Carter said that his wife was not the only person with a genius for understatement and that Rose had nearly wrecked the peace of his House during her brief engagement to Philip.

'She only needs handling,' said Lieutenant Fairweather. 'I've got her pretty well where I want her and she knows it, and it's the best day's work I ever did in my life. The Dagoes will go quite mad about her, bless her heart.'

Everard asked when he was leaving for South America.

'Day after the wedding,' said the Lieutenant. 'I had a sort of idea I might be recalled to my ship, but it doesn't look like a scrap now. I shan't be sorry to get a couple of years ashore. What are you and Mr. Winter doing, sir?'

Philip said he was going into camp with the Territorials after the wedding and then to Constantinople to do some work, unless of course there were a scrap and then he supposed Senior Classics would know him no longer.

'I thought you were a Communist, sir,' said the Lieutenant. 'Do you remember that time my brother and I came over to see Rose when her people took Northbridge Rectory, and you told us all about Communism? Geoff and I thought it was jolly interesting to meet a chap that knew such a lot, but it didn't worry us. One has enough to do in the Navy without worrying.'

'I think you were right,' said Philip, colouring a little. 'I wasn't busy enough then. I dare say I'm still a Communist if it comes to arguing, but for all practical purposes I have quite enough to do being a schoolmaster.'

'And if it came to a scrap, sir?' said Lieutenant Fairweather.

'Then I suppose I'd have enough to do being a Territorial,' said Philip, after a moment's thought.

'Excuse me, sir, I didn't mean to barge in,' said Lieutenant Fairweather, 'but when one isn't a brainy chap it bucks one up a lot to find that the brainy chaps see it the same way the rest of us do.'

At this ingenuous compliment Philip Winter coloured even more deeply to the roots of his flaming hair, feeling that to be called sir and deferred to by a naval officer, even if he was really only Fairweather Junior in disguise, made him almost older than he could bear. Everard, who was a good deal older and had even been called 'sir' by the brilliant young Attorney-General of a short-lived Administration, took it all more calmly and said he expected to do nothing but go on school-mastering.

'If anything did happen,' he said, carefully choosing a form of word that would not be likely to let any Higher Powers know what he was talking about (for to such superstitions even a Housemaster may be prone) 'we have our work more than cut out for us, because we are going to take in the Hosiers' Boys Foundation School.'

Lieutenant Fairweather sat up.

'The Hosiers' Boys, sir. But aren't those the chaps who had a week's camp down by the river the summer I left school. I mean they were very decent chaps — —'

There was a silence, so charged with agreement that Philip almost expected an immediate vengeance for snobbish feelings to fall on them all three. Then Kate came back with the girls and a very interesting conversation took place about the horribleness of the physical exercises mistress at Barchester High School. When we say conversation it is of course to be understood that Lydia did most of the talking, backed by Geraldine, while the others listened, amused, and Lieutenant Fair-weather smoked and thought of an improvement in the fourth hole at Southbridge golf course, after which Geraldine went home and they all went to bed.

II

THE BRIDESMAIDS' TALE

IF IT was inevitable that Rose Birkett should marry a naval man, it was equally inevitable that the day of her wedding should be the most perfect day of unclouded sun tempered by a breeze not powerful enough to disarrange her hair or her veil. Mrs. Birkett, going into her elder daughter's bedroom at half-past nine o'clock, found her in bed with two large, loose-jointed, depraved-looking dolls and a rather dirty plush giant panda, the wireless turned on at its loudest to an enchanting programme from Radio Luxembourg sponsored by the makers of a famous corn cure, eating an enormous breakfast off a tray balanced on her knees and blowing melancholy blasts on her ocarina between mouthfuls.

'Hullo, Mummy,' said Rose, 'they're doing *Lips of Desire* at the Barchester Odeon, you know, the film about the Brownings, the ones that were poets, and Glamora Tudor is Mrs. Browning and to-day's the last performance. It's too dispiriting for words.'

Mrs. Birkett, wondering in an exhausted way if Rose would rather go to the cinema than be married, turned the wireless down, for the noise made it very difficult to converse.

'*Don't*, Mummy,' shrieked Rose, spilling a good deal of tepid coffee into her bed as she reached towards the wireless and turned it on again. 'I'd nearly got "Hebe's got the jeebies" right on Radio Luxembourg. Mummy, the first house is at twelve o'clock. Couldn't I and John go? We'd easily get back in time for the wedding.'

Mrs. Birkett, praying to keep her temper for the few hours during which Rose was yet under her wing, said, Certainly not.

'If I rang up Noel Merton, he's staying at the Deanery, could I go with him then?' said Rose.

Mrs. Birkett said with some severity that Rose did not seem to understand that a wedding was a wedding and that until she was married she was not going to leave the house. Rose clasped the giant panda and her lovely eyes filled with tears.

There was a knock at the door and Mr. Birkett came in.

'Good morning, Rose,' he said. 'Everything all right? I was just looking for you, Amy.'

'Oh, Daddy,' said Rose, gulping. 'It's too foully dispiriting. It's the last performance of *Lips of Desire* and Mummy won't let me go.'

'Now, be sensible, there's a good girl,' said Mr. Birkett giving his daughter's shoulder a nervous but well-meant pat. 'Amy, the Dean has just rung up to say his car is out of order, and his secretary is going to drive him over.'

'Then if I went to *Lips of Desire* at the 12 o'clock session the Dean could drive me back,' said Rose, throwing the panda on the floor, jumping out of bed and slipping on a flowered dressing-gown in which she looked like Botticelli's Flora, except that intelligent mischief was an expression entirely beyond her powers. 'Oh, Mummy! Oh, Daddy! Could I?'

Mrs. Birkett snapped at Mr. Birkett for bringing such a foolish message. If the Dean were coming in any case, she said, it was quite immaterial how, and she only hoped all the buttons would fly off his gaiters, and Rose had better go and have her bath and see about finishing her packing. Rose picked up the panda again and clutching it to her bosom began to cry. Mr. Birkett, considerably alarmed by the storm he had innocently helped to raise, was trying to get away unseen when Geraldine came in, followed by Lydia Keith.

'I thought you and daddy wouldn't have much grip to-day,' said Geraldine, speaking with the kind firmness of a District Visitor to the Deserving Poor, 'so I brought Lydia along to help. The man from Barchester about the extra glasses and things is here, Mummy, and there's a man called a name I couldn't hear like Gristle it sounded that wants you on a trunk call, Daddy.'

The distracted parents, only too glad of the excuse, left the room.

'Who can Gristle be?' said Mrs. Birkett to her husband, who replied that he hadn't the faintest idea.

Rose, left alone with her unsympathetic bridesmaids, at once became her normal self and taking a box of chocolate creams out of her stocking drawer shared the contents with Geraldine and Lydia. Geraldine, as a sister and an intellectual, objected to the number of chocolates Rose had bitten into to see if they were soft, but Lydia, who liked hard ones, said it would save her biting them herself, and Rose and Geraldine could have all the soft ones. The head housemaid, sent by Mrs. Birkett to assist with the packing, was dismissed by Lydia who having seen an elder sister into matrimony was an authority on trousseaux. What with packing, trying some of Rose's face creams, listening to the wireless, playing swing records on the gramophone, discussing the probable cast for a film about Building the Pyramids in which Rose hoped that the Marx Brothers would be Totems or whatever it was (which Geraldine was able to explain by saying Rose meant hieroglyphics and even then it wasn't sense), getting Rose by degrees bathed, partly dressed and made-up, the morning passed as swiftly as lightning. At half-past twelve Mrs. Birkett, feeling that she would rather not see Rose again for the present, sent up cold lunch on a tray and all three young ladies made a hearty meal. Over the depraved dolls and the plush panda there was a slight difference of opinion, Geraldine maintaining that they ought to be sent to the Barchester Hospital, Lydia that they would be invaluable for her mother's Jumble Sale, and Rose, who after all was their mistress, declaring that nothing would part her from them and anyway the panda zipped up the back and made a splendid bag for her ocarina.

Then Mrs. Birkett, bearing her courage in both hands, came in with the head housemaid and Rose was dressed in her bridal robes. The head housemaid said Miss Rose looked just like her name and everyone saw what she meant. To Mrs. Birkett's intense relief, not only had Rose entirely forgotten and forgiven the scene she had made earlier in the morning, but so far did her forgiveness extend that she actually kissed her mother and said it was rotten not seeing *Lips of Desire* but perhaps they'd have it at Las Palombas and she supposed there would be an Odeon or whatever people called it out there.

Geraldine and Lydia, who had brought her bridesmaid's dress over from the Carters' house in a suitcase for the occasion, suddenly thought they had better get dressed too and at a quarter to two they escorted Rose to the drawing-room where the other bridesmaids, Delia Brandon and Octavia Crawley, were waiting.

'Hullo, Rose,' said Delia Brandon, 'you do look gorgeous. I wish I could have a wedding dress like that.'

Rose said she thought white satin was a bit dispiriting, but Mummy would have it.

'And anyway,' she said with great simplicity, 'if there was a war or anything and John got killed or something, I could have it dyed black.'

Octavia Crawley, who did not look her best in blue, or indeed in any other colour, nice girl though she was, said if there was a war or anything she would drive an ambulance and then she needn't go to dinner parties in the Close, but she knew there would be no such luck.

Rose said it would be just like her luck to be at Las Palombas if there was a war and too foully dispiriting.

'If there did happen to be a war, not that there will,' said Delia Brandon, 'I shall go to Barchester General Hospital as a V.A.D. I've done all my exams. In the War they had some perfectly *ghastly* face wounds there,' said Delia, her kind heart aglow with hopeful excitement. 'I'd like to see Sir Abel Fillgrave operate more than anything in the world.'

Rose thought it sounded a bit dispiriting.

*

When Mrs. Birkett got downstairs from Rose's room, she found Mr. Tozer, the representative of Messrs. Scatcherd and Tozer, Caterers, of Barchester (described by Geraldine as the man about the extra glasses and things) waiting for her in the dining-room. Already trestle tables had been set up and spread with what in fiction used to be known as fair white cloths, though rather badly ironed by the Barchester Sanitary Laundry. Two skilled underlings disguised as waiters were setting out glasses, cups, saucers and plates, and erecting the giant urns or samovars from which Messrs. Scatcherd and Tozer dispensed tea and coffee. A large cylindrical object in a corner promised ices, and the sandwiches and cakes were stacked in cardboard boxes. In the middle of the largest table graceful folds of butter muslin kept the wedding cake from contamination.

Mrs. Birkett took this all in with the well-trained eye of a headmaster's wife, used to entertaining on a large scale. Everything appeared to be in order. Messrs. Scatcherd's representatives had often worked for her before and knew what was required, but there was a feeling of silent enmity about that froze Mrs. Birkett to the marrow.

'Mr. Birkett said you wanted to speak to me, Mr. Tozer,' said Mrs. Birkett. 'Is everything all right?'

Mr. Tozer coughed behind his hand and said it was always a pleasure to do the arrangements at Southbridge School. Always a pleasure, he added.

'I haven't much time,' said Mrs. Birkett.

'It is like this, madam,' said Mr. Tozer, who really despised anyone not in orders and had particularly strong feelings about lay headmasters, though he spoke of Mrs. Birkett as a lady that understood how things should be done, 'there is a slight hiatus about tumblers. Your order was for three hundred guests. We had fully assumed that we could meet any calls upon us, but owing to the militia camp at Plumstead having co-opted us to assist with their catering, we are short on the small tumblers.'

'I suppose you can make up with large wine-glasses,' said Mrs. Birkett. 'They would do quite well for lemonade.'

'That is precisely what I was going to suggest, madam,' said Mr. Tozer. 'We have plenty of large wine-glasses; not the champagne size, for they would be required for champagne, but the largest size of non-champagne if I make myself clear. Though of course lemonade should *never* be drunk except from small tumblers,' said Mr. Tozer with a slight shudder.

'Well, the wine-glasses will do nicely,' said Mrs. Birkett.

'We shall be lucky if we have them this time next year with the Hun creating the way he is,' said Mr. Tozer whose military vocabulary belonged to the years 1914–18 during which he had been a mess waiter on Salisbury Plain. 'Some say it will all blow over, madam, but I say to talk like that is tempting Providence. Expect the worst and then it can't get you down is what I say.'

As Mr. Tozer was well known for never leaving off talking, Mrs. Birkett was accustomed to drift away from him, leaving him to finish his periods to the circumambient air, but the feeling of silent enmity that had approached her at her first entrance was now just behind her right shoulder and turning slightly she saw her butler, Simnet, holding the champagne-nippers in his hand in a very threatening way.

'What is it, Simnet?' said Mrs. Birkett.

'I was merely waiting, madam, till Mr. Tozer had finished,' said Simnet with icy politeness, 'to inquire who is to open the champagne.'

Mr. Tozer, speaking to an unseen audience, said that when he arranged the reception at the Palace for the colonial bishops, he had personally opened every bottle himself and His Lordship had said everything couldn't have gone off better.

Simnet, by saying nothing, managed to convey that he had planted, pruned and watered the vines, picked the grapes, personally trodden them in the wine press, bottled and labelled every pint of the wine, superintended its shipping to England, retailed it to Mr. Birkett and (which was indeed true) fetched it up from the cellar that morning with his own hands.

To the outer world he merely remarked in a distant way that he understood His Lordship to have allowed one bottle to every ten guests, but perhaps that was as well, being as some of them were black.

Mr. Tozer, whose feelings about people in orders included a conviction that a coloured bishop was a contradiction in terms, found his position considerably weakened. To say that a tenth of a bottle was enough for a dusky prelate would have been a betrayal of the whole

Established Church; to say it was not enough would have reflected upon the Bishop of Barchester's celebrated want of hospitality. So he said nothing and the battle hung suspended in a chill silence.

But Mrs. Birkett, who though she never tried to organize the school had to order practically everything else for her husband, and was used to composing quarrels between matrons, head housemaids, parlour-maids and cooks, was, except where her daughter Rose was concerned, a woman of practical decision.

'If you are announcing the guests, you can't open the champagne, Simnet,' she said. 'Mr. Tozer will be good enough to open it and I dare say he has brought his own champagne nippers.'

Only the genius of a born organizer could have prompted Mrs. Birkett to say this. Some sixth sense told her that the champagne nippers were to Simnet a mysterious badge of authority which he would sooner die, or at any rate be very disagreeable about, than give up.

Mr. Tozer without a word produced two pairs of champagne nippers from behind the wedding cake. Simnet said that he had put four dozen bottles on the table near the service door and if Mr. Tozer would give him the word, he had several dozen more on ice in his pantry.

As more than half an hour had been wasted Mrs. Birkett after an anxious look at her watch went to dress. She and Mr. Birkett were to have a sandwich lunch in his study and she hoped to get a few moments' peace with him and ask who Mr. Gristle was, but so late was he that the Dean of Barchester and his secretary arrived on his heels and Simnet severely removed the rest of the sandwiches as partaking of blasphemy.

The Dean took Mrs. Birkett's hand.

'As it is neither morning nor afternoon, I must say good-day,' he announced. 'And a good day in every sense of the word it is. Ha, Birkett,' he said to the Headmaster.

'Ha, Crawley,' said Mr. Birkett, who had been at Oxford with the Dean, though Dr. Crawley, being in his earlier years a young and penniless clergyman, had naturally married much sooner than Mr. Birkett and had a much larger family.

'You know my secretary, Thomas Needham,' said the Dean, present-ing a young clergyman with a pink cheerful face. 'He has driven me over like Jehu.'

'We only touched sixty once, sir,' said Mr. Needham deprecatingly.

'And so Rose is going to be married,' said the Dean. 'Ah.'

As the whole of Barchester had known this for some weeks and the Dean was about to perform the ceremony, assisted by the School Chaplain, Mr. Smith, there seemed to be no real answer. Mrs. Birkett told Simnet, who was tidying away the last remains of lunch, to tell Mr. Smith that the Dean was here.

Young Mr. Needham, who had been looking round the walls, sudden-ly exclaimed, 'By Jove, there's my uncle!'

'Where?' said the Dean.

Mr. Needham pointed to a photograph of fifteen boys in jerseys, shorts and football boots with a blurred background of school buildings.

'Your uncle?' said Mr. Birkett. 'I thought I knew every name, but I don't remember a Needham.'

'My mother's brother, sir,' said Mr. Needham, 'Oldmeadow is the name. That's him with his legs crossed, in the middle. Good old Uncle Tom.'

'Tom Oldmeadow?' said Mr. Birkett. 'Of course I remember Tom. He was Captain of Games in his last year. You remember Oldmeadow, Amy?'

'Of course I do,' said Mrs. Birkett. 'He had measles twice running in one term. Where is he now?'

'I think he's in Switzerland,' said Mr. Needham, 'mountaineering, but he's in the Reserve of Officers, so he might have to come back any time if there's a row. It makes me a bit sick that I didn't go into the Army now, but I might get out as a stretcher-bearer with luck.'

He then went bright red with confusion and looked at his employer to see if he had given offence. The Dean said it was laid upon us to love our enemies but one might be allowed to distinguish between enemies and devils, and then in his turn wondered if he had gone too far. But the School Chaplain cut short the conversation by coming in with a cordial greeting and the remark that the nuptial hour drew on apace and would the Dean like to be preparing himself. The Dean looked at his secretary, who said the doings, he begged his pardon, the robes, were in the suitcase outside and should he bring them in. Mrs. Birkett, feeling that she might be consumed with fire if she profaned these mysteries, said she would go and see about Rose. The School Chaplain said this parting was well made and he would himself conduct the Dean to the School Chapel and see that Mr. Needham was suitably placed among the congregation.

'You know, Smith, that Oldmeadow is Needham's uncle,' said Mr. Birkett as he too left the room.

The Chaplain, who had played for Cambridge as a young man, was so enchanted to find that the Dean's secretary was a relation of the best football player the School had ever produced that he took Mr. Needham under his wing, extracted from him that he had played for a well-known club and discussed with such ardour the chances of the Universities for the autumn that the Dean was metaphorically and almost literally elbowed into a corner and had to get on with his robing as best he could.

As it was now time for the ceremony the School Chaplain led the way by the private passage from the Headmaster's study to the little vestry or anteroom of the Chapel.

*

At Mr. Carter's House, Everard, Kate and Philip Winter marvelled as they watched Lieutenant Fairweather eat through fish, eggs and bacon, cold ham, scones, toast, butter and marmalade, and drink two large cups of coffee, that love could have so little effect on the human appetite. Lydia, who it is true was not going to be married, ate neck to neck with him over the whole course till they got into the straight when with no visible effort she came in first by a large piece of toast thickly spread with butter and potted ham.

'It's a pity,' she said reflectively, 'that bridesmaids don't still go on the honeymoon like Miss Squeers with Mr. and Mrs. Browdie. I'd love to come to Las Palombas.'

'Come and visit us,' said Lieutenant Fairweather, 'and stay as long as you like.'

'I do wish I could,' said Lydia, 'but Mother has a heart and I rather look after things for her, and Father seems to need me a bit. I know it sounds awfully priggish,' she added apologetically.

Kate looked at her younger sister with admiring affection. Everard and Philip felt, as they often did, what an extraordinarily good fellow Lydia was.

'Well, we shall be there for two years,' said Lieutenant Fairweather, 'unless there's a scrap and they want me back, so come along any time.'

'Thanks most awfully,' said Lydia. 'Old Bunce, you know, at the Northbridge Ferry, says he knows there's going to be a war this autumn because he knows the signs, but he won't say what the signs are and anyway no one believes him.'

Philip said from his brief experience of Old Bunce, the summer he stayed at Northbridge with the Birketts, the signs must be several extra pints of old and bitter at the Ferryman's Arms. Lydia went over to the Headmaster's House with her suitcase and peace reigned until eleven o'clock when Captain Geoffrey Fairweather of the Barsetshire Regiment arrived in a roaring little car to be best man to his brother. The two brothers and the two schoolmasters sat in the garden and kept an eye on Master Bobbie Carter who was imprisoned in a kind of square sheepfold on the lawn and surprised himself very much by standing up and falling down from time to time. The conversation was chiefly about the Fairweathers' days in the junior school, and a great deal of news was exchanged about Old Boys and the fate of various masters.

'I don't know if you remember Johnson,' said Everard. 'He did quite well at Oxford in Modern Greats, though it is a falling-between-two-stools school that I personally deplore, and is coming here next term as a master in the Junior School for a bit, unless — —'

He stopped, sacrificing the end of his sentence to a craven wish to propitiate any deity that might be about.

'Johnson was a bit junior to me,' said Lieutenant Fairweather. 'He had a bottle of hair fixative in the Junior School and we all used it. Hard luck.'

What Everard and Philip felt about the hard luck, to give it no harder name, that might tear all their ex-pupils (for they could not help looking at the situation from their own schoolmastering point of view and especially from the point of view of their own school) from their various avocations and pitchfork them into the paths of glory which may lead but to the grave, was so mixed that neither of them could quite have put it into words. When you have done your best for your pupils, you hope to have fitted them in some measure for the conduct of life, but you always envisaged a life that is to go on, not a life that is very possibly to take its place in a living rampart and so be given up. You sicken at the thought of the waste, yet you cannot call it waste. You are thankful for those who can remain undisturbed, yet you cannot altogether be glad for them. There seems to be no end to the warring loyalties in your mind, except the certainty that the end is appointed.

'Yes, it's jolly hard luck on those youngsters,' said Captain Fairweather from his twenty-five years and the immense tolerant kindness of the real professional for the amateurs. 'Still, even if there is a scrap I dare say it'll be over before most of them get out. You can't make an army in three weeks.'

'I must say I'll be sick if there is a show and I'm at Las Palombas,' said Lieutenant Fairweather. 'You blighters have all the luck, Geoff. What do they say at your shop?'

Captain Fairweather said the Lord alone knew, but apart from a certain stickiness about leave the Brass Hats hadn't given tongue, and as far as he was concerned his leave was due in the middle of August and he was going to Scotland to have a shot at a grouse. He then applied himself to the entertainment of Master Bobbie Carter whose language he at once understood and they enjoyed themselves very much together till Nurse came out and said Baby must thank the soldier for playing with him so nicely and come along and have his din-din.

'I suppose I am a soldier,' said Captain Fairweather, straightening himself and looking vengefully after Nurse, 'but she needn't rub it in. That chap of yours is very intelligent, sir,' he said to Everard. 'He got the hang of my moustache almost at once. By Jove, I thought he'd have it out by the roots.'

If a Housemaster can simper, Everard almost simpered.

'He *is* a bit intelligent,' he admitted. 'You should see him in his bath. If he wants his celluloid fish and Nurse gives him his duck, he begins to howl at once.'

Captain Fairweather said it was certainly *jolly* good to know a fish from a duck at that age and he'd like to see him in his bath if there was time before he went back to Sparrowhill Camp. Lieutenant Fairweather

expressed sincere regrets that the fact of getting married and starting on
his honeymoon would deprive him of this treat and said that talking of
getting married he supposed he had better put his uniform on before
lunch. So they all went in.

III

GO, LOVELY ROSE

THE School Chapel really looked very nice, just as Kate had said it
would, though nothing could disguise its complete hideousness. It had
been built about seventy years previously by the same architect who
had built Lord Pomfret's seat, Pomfret Towers, and though the architect, hampered by the restrictions of space, had not been able to carry
out his Neo-Gothic wishes to full effect, he had managed to combine
inconvenience and darkness in a manner hitherto unparalleled in any
of his work. The Chapel was a very long, narrow, lofty building, richly
panelled in pitch-pine. The windows which were placed near the roof
were of most elaborate tracery, filled with lozenges of green and purple
glass. The pews, also of pitch-pine, had specially constructed seats, not
only very narrow, but with a slight forward tilt that obliged the worshipper to brace himself against the encaustic tiled floor with both feet.
The stalls at the east end were so profusely ornamented with carving
that they constituted a kind of Little Ease for the senior boys and masters
who occupied them, and were furnished with seats which folded back
on a hinge at such an angle that at least two boys were able to say that
their seats had fallen down with a bang of themselves at every service.
The Great East Window, presented by former pupils in memory of the
Rev. J. J. Damper, Headmaster from 1850 to 1868, when he retired to
an honorary canonry of Barchester which he held in a state of mild
imbecility for the next ten years, was one of the finest examples of the
Munich school of stained glass in the country, sustaining very favourably a comparison with the glass in St. Mungo's, Glasgow. It cast
indeed, as the School Chaplain had more than once said, a dim religious
light, so that the electric fittings (installed in 1902, as a memorial to
Old Boys killed in the Boer War, in the finest *art nouveau* style) had to be
used all through the year. As for the organ (now electrically controlled),
the lectern, given in memory of an unpopular master who was killed
in the Alps because he would not take his guide's advice but had a rich
mother (who also put up a less expensive memorial to the guide in his
village church), the tiles on each side of the altar (copied from those

used in the kitchen at Pomfret Towers), they are described (with five stars) in all guide books to Barsetshire, so we will say no more.

Short of burning it all to the ground, there was not much to be done, but Mrs. Birkett had put lilies and delphiniums all over the choir and up the altar steps and, greatly daring, ordered quantities of blue carpet to cover the aisle and the handsome Kidderminster rug that lay in front of the altar and vied in richness of colour with the East window.

Soon after lunch the guests began to arrive. Mr. and Mrs. Birkett naturally had an enormous number of friends and acquaintances, nearly all of whom had sent a present to Rose because they were fond of her parents, and so had to be asked. A certain number were already abroad, or dispersed in far parts of England and Scotland, but even so there were enough acceptances to make Mrs. Birkett a little anxious about accommodation in the Chapel. However, the more people are jammed together at any social function, the more they will enjoy it, so from her place of vantage in the choir stalls she was able to survey the audience without too much discomposure.

It is well known that proper weddings in a church, as distinguished from hole and corner affairs for conscience' or convenience' sake in what even quite well-educated people will call registry offices, are conducted entirely for the benefit of the bride's mother and the bridesmaids. The bride, beyond a general feeling that it will be marvellous to be married, has usually been reduced by dressmakers, presents, nervous and unintelligible advice from her very ignorant mother, visits to her lover's great-aunts, and doubts about the setting of her hair, to a state of drugged imbecility in which she would as easily be led to suttee (or sati, if you prefer it, both being probably incorrect) as to the altar; while the bridegroom is merely an adjunct or bleating victim. As for the bridegroom's family and friends, everyone knows that they are only there by courtesy, being as naught, and relegated to the right or decani side of the church which for some ecclesiastical reason is the less honourable. And what is more, it is rare for the bridegroom's friends to turn up in such force as the bride's, so that the ushers are fain to hustle poor relations of the bride's, old governesses, nannies, and obvious members of the domestic staff into the bridegroom's side to fill up the pews, while the bridegroom and his best man have to hang about in new boots with no particular *locus standi* as it were.

But on the left or cantoirs side, how different is the scene. All the bride's friends have come to talk to each other, all her parents' friends have turned up, majestic, distinguished, and except for an aunt or two, well dressed. Everyone says, 'Where is the bride's mother? Oh, there she is. Doesn't she look well in that blue (or purple, or flowered silk or whatever it may be). Dear Elsie, she looks as happy as if she were going to be married herself. I suppose those are his people up in front. I don't think I've met them. Taunton, isn't it, or somewhere in Yorkshire.

Look, there is Cynthia. Come into our pew, my dear, there's heaps of room and I have something I want to tell you.'

So on this occasion did the Birketts' party and Rose's large body of bosom friends surge into the church and storm the pews. So did Mrs. Birkett look quite delightful in a shade of cyclamen that she had not been quite sure about and dispense welcoming smiles to anyone who caught her eye and co-opt into her pew her old friend Mrs. Morland, the well-known novelist, whose youngest boy Tony had been through Southbridge School from the bottom of the Junior School to the top of the Senior School and had just left in a cloud of glory with a Former-ship (corrupted from Formaship and pronounced Formayship), because scholars were supposed to apply for free tuition *in forma pauperis* at Paul's College, Oxford. Mrs. Morland's hat was too apt to lose its moorings on her head, her abundant brown hair was too apt to escape and rain hairpins on the floor, but no one could call her undistinguished, and Mrs. Birkett was very fond of her.

As for the bridegroom's parents they were both dead, which simpli-fied everything very much, and Philip Winter, who was doing duty as usher for Lieutenant Fairweather, saw to it that the front pews were filled with the best specimens of the bridegroom's friends, including some very pretty young wives of Old Southbridgeians who had been at school with the Fairweathers, and the Dean's secretary who was well known as a football player by all the younger men and so gave lustre to the scene.

The organ pealed forth, though never except in fiction does it do this, rather blaring and bursting, or in more refined cases quavering. In every heart began to spring that exquisite hope, seldom if ever realized, that the bride will have had a fit, or eloped with someone else.

Meanwhile Mr. Birkett was approaching the drawing-room, more nervous than he had ever been since he had to explain to the Dean of his College why he had frightened the wife of the President of St. Barabbas next door by stumbling against her camp bed in the garden at three o'clock on a June morning, an action formally deprecated but privately condoned by the Dean, who did not hold with married Presidents, or indeed anyone else, and most especially not with people who slept out of doors in the summer, as he himself had slept with all his windows shut for nearly seventy years, and who also defended the members of his own College against all comers, whatever the offence, and that with such venom and gusto that only the President of St. Barabbas's fear of his wife had driven him to make the complaint. Mr. Birkett had been dismissed with an injunction not to be a young fool and the information that in his, the Dean's, young days when under-graduates *were* undergraduates, the way back into College via St. Barabbas was condemned as milk-soppery and child's play by all self-respecting men, who took the higher road by the crocketted gable end of Colney House, then but lately built for non-denominational non-collegiate students. At the present moment Mr. Birkett felt that he would rather face the Dean, or even the President of St. Barabbas's wife, than the ordeal of escorting Rose to the Chapel, but it had to be done, so he pulled himself together and went into the drawing-room, where Octavia Crawley and Delia Brandon were practising Court curtsies, much despised by Lydia and Geraldine, while Rose made up her face.

'It's time, Rose,' said Mr. Birkett, finding an odd difficulty in speaking.

'Oh, Daddy, need I?' said Rose, with rather impeded articulation as she applied a lipstick to her beautiful mouth.

'Now come along, Rose,' said Mr. Birkett helplessly. But he might have appealed in vain had not Lydia Keith taken Rose's bag and lipstick away from her and put her bouquet into her hand. Rose was so surprised that she allowed her father to tuck her arm into his and lead her through the private passage to the anteroom, from which one door led to the choir, the other to the west end of the Chapel. Lydia and Geraldine arranged themselves behind the bride, Delia Brandon and Octavia Crawley followed, and the bridal procession began to move up the aisle towards the Dean. There was an audible gasp from the audience as Rose appeared on her father's arm and they all turned their heads to look. Never had her exquisite figure shown to more advantage than on what Everard Carter's House Matron described in a letter to her married sister as the Day of Days, and if her lovely face appeared to be vacant of all expression her friends were used to it. Lydia, who with Geraldine's passive acquiescence had constituted herself chief bridesmaid, was pleased by the admiration around her, and collecting Rose's bouquet prepared to stand by. To her old friend Noel Merton, who had driven Mrs. Crawley and a selection of the Deanery girls over from Barchester in his car, she had something of the air of a very competent second, bouquet in hand instead of a sponge, ready to give first aid between the rounds.

And indeed it looked at one moment as if her services would be required, for Rose, suddenly recognizing her bridegroom, was about to say, 'Hullo, darling, isn't this marvellous.' Her lips had actually parted to say the words; her father's frown was unnoticed, and Noel Merton told Mrs. Crawley afterwards that he was certain Lydia would have garrotted Rose. But Lieutenant Fairweather, who had no illusions at all about his lovely bride, saw with his sailor's eye what was in the wind and stepping forward one pace gave his Rose a warning look that for once silenced her completely. Mr. Birkett stood back, weak with relief; the Dean and Mr. Smith did their duty; Captain Fairweather produced the ring at exactly the right moment; and with a feeling of loss and an even deeper feeling of thankfulness Mr. and Mrs. Birkett saw their daughter and her husband kneeling together, Rose's dress perfectly arranged, Lieutenant Fairweather, as seen in perspective, appearing to consist chiefly of the soles of his boots. For the brief moment of silent prayer Mrs. Birkett wondered if she had been a bad mother, and decided with her usual admirable common sense that she had made the best of a difficult job. Her mother's heart was divided, one half feeling a so natural pang at the sight of her lovely daughter setting out into a new life in a distant country, far from her parents' care, the other and by far the larger half feeling a gratitude amounting to idolatry for the son-in-law who was going to relieve her of a child that had done her best for the last five or six years to drive her parents mad.

Relations and old friends began to move towards the vestry. Lydia marshalled the bridesmaids and herded them along, stopping for a moment to exchange greetings with Noel Merton.

'Hullo, Noel,' she said, 'hullo, Mrs. Crawley, come along and sign the register.'

Noel Merton said he would gladly accompany Mrs. Crawley, but didn't think he would sign as he hardly knew the Birketts.

'Rot,' said Lydia. 'You were at Northbridge with us in the summer Rose got unengaged to Philip and threw his ring into the pond. You can't call that not knowing her. Come on.'

As there was no point in resisting, Noel followed with Mrs. Crawley as Lydia swept them into her wake.

In the vestry the register was lying ready. The Dean himself conducted the bride to the table and showed her where to sign.

'Your full name,' he said, 'Rose Felicity Birkett.'

'Not Birkett,' said Rose, 'Fairweather.'

'For this last time,' said the School Chaplain kindly, 'you sign in your maiden name.'

'But I can't,' said Rose, looking round for sympathy. 'I mean I've just got married, haven't I, and it works the minute you're married. I mean if anyone talked to me that I didn't know them, they'd say Mrs. Fairweather.'

The Dean and Mr. Smith, who had never been up against this particular difficulty before, looked at each other with what in anyone but a professed Christian would have been despair, when Lieutenant Fairweather, who had waited out of respect for superior officers, saw that the moment had come for the secular arm to assert itself.

'Don't argue, my girl,' he said. 'You know nothing about it. Write Rose Felicity Birkett or you won't be married at all.'

Rose threw an adoring look at her husband, and murmuring that it was foully dispiriting and on one's wedding day too, did as she was told and immediately recovered her spirits. The other requisite signatures were quickly affixed and a general orgy of kissing took place.

'I'm glad it wasn't me,' said Lydia to her friend Noel Merton, giving him a violent hit on the arm. Noel, who in spite of being a very distinguished barrister and about fifteen years older than Lydia was always treated by her as an equal and enjoyed it, inquired whether it was the bridegroom or the ceremony that she objected to.

'Oh, John's all right,' said Lydia negligently, 'I mean all this marrying business. Do you remember, Noel, a very good conversation we had about getting married the first time you stayed with us or the second and you said you didn't think you'd get married and I said I probably would if it was only not to be like the Pettinger.'

'Look out, she's just behind me,' said Noel, casting a warning glance in the direction of the Headmistress of the Barchester High School, who was exercising the fascination of a snake over a small bird upon the Dean's secretary, Mr. Needham.

'Well, I've changed my mind,' said Lydia, taking no notice of Noel's warning, 'and I think I'll not get married. Supposing one had a daughter like Rose.'

'I can promise you that you won't,' said Noel. 'And if you do think of marrying anyone, be sure to tell me, and I'll see if he's nice enough for you and have proper settlements.'

Lydia said of course she would, only if Noel wanted to marry anyone he had better not tell her till afterwards, as she was sure it would be someone ghastly that she'd absolutely loathe. This compact having been made, it was time to reform the bridal procession. The organ suddenly trumpeted like an elephant and Rose on the arm of Lieutenant Fairweather, followed by her bridesmaids, passed down the aisle, between their admiring friends, out at the little door and so by the private passage back to the drawing-room where the reception was to take place.

'Here you are,' said Lydia firmly, as she handed Rose her bag. 'You can stick on some more powder and lipstick if you like, but I think you've quite enough, don't you, John?'

'Don't be so dispiriting,' said Rose, 'and this lipstick doesn't come off anyway.'

'I should think not,' said her husband. 'I wouldn't let you put it on if it did. That's enough, Lydia. Take it away.'

'Darling John,' said Rose, relinquishing the bag to Lydia.

And now Simnet in all his glory began to announce the guests. Rose kissed everyone with fervour and said it was too marvellous of them to have given her such a marvellous present, while Lieutenant Fairweather shook everyone's hand in a very painful way and smiled, for there seemed to him no particular reason to say anything. Considering that it was the end of July Mrs. Birkett had collected a very good bag. Lord Pomfret, who had been for many years a Governor of the School, was unfortunately abroad, but had sent a silver rose bowl chased, as

Philip Winter had said, within an inch of its life. Lord Stoke too was absent, enjoying himself very much at an Agricultural Congress in Denmark, and was represented by a messotint (framed). But there were several parents with titles, and some Old Boys who were distinguished in various walks of life, among them a young Cabinet Minister, two actors, a film star who had endeared himself to the public by always acting with his wife, whoever she might happen at the moment to be, an Admiral, and an Indian prince who had been in the School Eleven. Add to these a good sprinkling of dignitaries from Barchester Close, quantities of subalterns and young naval officers on the Fairweather side and enough pretty girls to go round, and it will be seen that Mrs. Birkett had cause for satisfaction. For half an hour she did her duty in receiving guests as they flowed steadily through the room, and then she felt free to do what she really wanted, which was to talk to as many of the Old Boys as possible. There was not a boy who had been in the Junior School when she and her husband were there, but liked and admired Ma Birky, and before long she had twenty or thirty young men about her, competing for her attention, so that Rose's friends had to content themselves with the older, more distinguished, and to their minds much duller men.

It was a long time since Mrs. Birkett had had so many of her chickens under her wing at once and questions and answers flew between them, with much laughter. All the naval men and the subalterns were eager to tell her what they planned to do on their next leave, and all said much the same thing. So long, Mrs. Birkett gathered, as there wasn't a scrap, or a blow-up, they proposed to climb, fish, tramp, bathe, shoot for every moment of daylight. If there was any sort of trouble, they said, it would be jolly hard luck on the fellows who were in India, or on the China station, or attached to Embassies, but of course nothing was likely to happen, because we had had quite enough trouble over Munich to last us for a long time and anyway Old Moore said it was going to be all right. Mrs. Birkett was sensible of a chill that she didn't stop to analyse, told herself not to be silly, and felt that a world with so many very nice healthy young men in it couldn't be so very wrong.

Mr. Birkett had also neglected his guests for various old Oxford friends, mostly in public life. As they too talked of their summer plans one or two said that it looked like trouble with the railway men again and how annoying it would be to be held up at Dover on one's way back from the Continent if there were a strike.

'Strikes are a nuisance,' said the President of St. Barabbas, 'but nothing to the nuisance we shall have if there did happen to be any trouble. The Government want to take over part of the College for the Divorce Court. We should have to send half our men to St. Jude's and it will upset the work greatly, besides making us a laughing stock. And Judges expect much more comfort than we can give. They expect bathrooms!' said the President with the just indignation of one who had lived on a flat tin bath ever since he first came up to Oxford.

'The only man who is going to enjoy it is Crawford at Lazarous,' said Mr. Fanshawe, the Dean of Paul's.

'He was my predecessor here,' said Mr. Birkett.

'I hate a crank,' said Mr. Fanshawe dispassionately, 'and Crawford cranks about Russia till most of us are thoroughly ashamed of him. He's got a queer lot at Lazarus now, all doing Modern Greats and thinking they understand politics. He has managed to get the promise of the Institute of Ideological Interference being billeted on Lazarus, if there is any question of its leaving London. They are going to bring a lot of typists, and his men will have to go to St. Swithin's. Do them good,' said Mr. Fanshawe with gloomy pleasure. 'St. Swithin's are the hardest drinking college in Oxford just now and they'll lead Crawford's flock astray all right. I don't think any of this is likely to happen, but I must say I rather hope there will be some evacuating from London, just to serve Crawford right. Never ought to have got the Mastership. Ha!'

'You should hear my butler, Simnet, on Crawford,' said Mr. Birkett. 'He was a Scout at Lazarus but resigned because he didn't hold with the Master's political and social views.'

As he spoke Simnet suddenly materialized at his side and murmured, 'Mrs. Birkett says The Cake, sir.'

'You were on No. 7 staircase at Lazarus, weren't you?' said Mr. Fanshawe, whose knowledge and memory of Oxford characters were unique. 'I'll have a word with you later.'

The guests were then swept into the dining-room where Lieutenant Fairweather and Rose were standing by the cake. Mr. Tozer was plying champagne nippers with demoniac fury, his satellites, reinforced by the Headmaster's staff and some of the servants from the Houses, were already speeding about the room with trays of glasses. Simnet corralling by the power of his eye the most distinguished of the guests, served them himself. A photographer from the *Barchester Chronicle* suddenly elbowed his way to the front. Lieutenant Fairweather drew his sword, and offered the hilt to Rose. The flashlight went off. Rose, her hand guided by her husband, gave a loud shriek and cut into the cake. The photographer disappeared. Mr. Tozer then fell upon the cake with a kind of caterer's hacksaw and dismembered it with the rapidity of lightning. Healths were drunk, Simnet produced unending supplies of champagne for Mr. Tozer, and Mrs. Birkett suddenly wished it were all over.

'How are you bearing up, Amy?' said Mrs. Morland at her elbow.

Mrs. Birkett said as well as could be expected, and she must get Rose away to change soon.

A young man in rather disreputable clothes approached Mrs. Birkett with a glass of champagne.

'You ought to drink this,' he said gravely, offering it to Mrs. Birkett. 'It will do you good.'

'Tony!' Mrs. Birkett exclaimed, suddenly recognizing Mrs. Morland's youngest son.

'I thought you weren't coming,' said his mother.

'I wasn't,' said Tony, 'because I was mending my bike, but as I got it mended I thought I'd come, but the pedal came off at the level crossing so I left it at a shop to be mended.'

'Let me know if you'd like me to fetch you and the bicycle from anywhere on my way back, darling,' said Mrs. Morland.

'It would be too complicated,' said Tony. 'If I had a car of my own, Mamma, it would save you a lot of trouble.'

'And give me a lot of trouble,' said Mrs. Morland with some spirit. 'Well, good-bye, darling. It was so nice to see you.'

Tony, divining that his mother might kiss him, sketched a salute to the two ladies and with gentle determination forced his way to the thickest of the crush where Lieutenant and Mrs. Fairweather and the bridesmaids were to be found.

'Many happy returns of the day,' he said politely to Rose. 'Hullo, John. Hullo, Geoff. Hullo, Geraldine. Hullo, Lydia.'

'Come and stay with us when you're out of camp,' Lydia yelled above the tumult.

'Can't,' said Tony. 'My mamma will take me abroad.'

'There'll be a railway strike and you'll never get home,' shouted Lydia. 'I heard someone say so.'

'It all comes of listening to the wireless,' said Tony. 'You ought to learn to think for yourself.' And before Lydia could counter this accusation he had slipped away.

Mrs. Birkett now approached her married daughter and said it was time to change. Rose, who was vastly enjoying a flirtation with all her husband's and her brother-in-law's friends, said in rather a whining voice Need she really?

'Indeed you need, my girl,' said her husband, looking at his wristwatch. 'Half an hour. At half-past four, you'll find me clean and sober at the front door, so get up steam.'

'All right, angel,' said Rose and followed her mother from the room.

Lieutenant Fairweather, accompanied by a large body of select friends, went to Mr. Birkett's dressing-room to change his uniform and the crowd began to disperse. Mr. Birkett, who was acting host while his wife was with Rose, stood and shook hands with his guests. He was tired and felt as if he were somehow apart from the scene, and as if for a hundred years people had shaken his hand and said they would be seeing him when term began again unless anything happened, though of course it wouldn't.

Presently only the near friends of the two families and some uninteresting relations were left and then Lieutenant Fairweather came down with his bodyguard. Captain Fairweather put the bridegroom's suitcase into his car, which was already loaded with Rose's luggage. Simnet brought more champagne into the hall where the remains of the party were now waiting for the bride. The school clock chimed two quarters. Lieutenant Fairweather went to the bottom of the stairs and shouted 'Rose!'

Even as he spoke his wife came downstairs in a ravishing silk coat and skirt, clasping the two depraved dolls in one arm and the plush panda in the other.

'Here, Geraldine,' said Lieutenant Fairweather, 'take those dolls.'

'Oh, John — —' Rose began.

'And give me that other thing,' said her bridegroom, laying hands on the panda.

'John, *don't* be so dispiriting,' said Rose.

'What on earth have you got inside him?' asked Lieutenant Fairweather, and without waiting for an answer he unzipped the panda's back and the ocarina fell out.

'You might take that coco-nut thing away,' said Lieutenant Fairweather to Simnet, who was in deep converse with Mr. Fanshawe. Simnet was so surprised that he stooped and picked it up.

'Catch!' continued the Lieutenant, tossing the panda to Lydia. 'And now say good-bye, Rose.'

He then embraced his mother-in-law very kindly, kissed all the bridesmaids and shook hands with his father-in-law.

'Don't you worry,' he said. 'I'm going to look after Rose with all my might and all my heart. Thank you all. Bless you all. Come along, Rose.'

Rose hugged her parents tempestuously, and kissed everyone in a careless way. Mrs. Birkett, who could hardly bear it now that the moment of parting had come, saw that Rose's lovely eyes were brimming.

'John!' she said, laying her hand on her son-in-law's arm and looking towards Rose.

'It's absolutely all right,' he said very kindly. 'Anything wrong, Rose?'

'No,' said Rose, bursting into tears. 'It's only because of leaving mummy and daddy, but I do love you better than anything in the WORLD, darling.'

In proof of which she flung herself sobbing into her husband's arms.

'That's absolutely all right,' said he, patting her back. 'And now we'd better go.'

He took Rose's arm. Her tears ceased as if by magic, leaving her face unravaged. On the bottom step he suddenly turned and ran back to her mother.

'Mummy, *did* they put my little blue suitcase with my bathing things in the car,' she asked earnestly, 'because we're going to bathe to-morrow if there's time.'

Geraldine said it was all right. Rose ran down the steps again and got into the car. With a frightful noise it leapt forward and the married couple whirled away down the drive. The younger guests who had been making up parties for cinemas or dancing went off, taking Delia Brandon and Octavia Crawley with them. Mr. Fanshawe said he had much enjoyed his talk with Simnet and had got the low-down on Crawford, and would now walk to Southbridge station and take the next train that came, which he found more restful than being driven by his wife.

'Come and sit down, Amy,' said Mrs. Morland, who was staying to dinner. 'You look tired.'

'I am,' said Mrs. Birkett. 'Oh, must you go, Dr. Crawley? It *has* been so good of you to come. I think Rose will be very happy.'

'I couldn't help hearing her last words to you,' said the Dean. 'They reminded me so curiously of a story my grandfather used to tell about the late Lady Hartletop. It was when she married Lord Dumbello, before he succeeded to the Marquisate. They are a kind of connection or ours, you know. My Aunt Grace married Major Grantly who was Lady Hartletop's brother.'

'But it was a moiré antique she wanted, wasn't it,' said Mrs. Morland, 'not a bathing dress.'

The Dean laughed and said good-bye.

*

Dinner was very quiet. As Geraldine had gone back with Lydia to dine at the Carters', taking with her Captain Fairweather who wanted to see Bobbie Carter in his bath before going back to camp, only the Birketts and Mrs. Morland were there to eat the crumbs of the wedding feast. Mr. Tozer had cleared away with his usual thoroughness and the dining-room was quite habitable again. Simnet with great tact had put away the unopened champagne, feeling that it would remind his employers too vividly of their loss and had, without waiting for orders, brought up a very good claret under whose soothing influence everyone relaxed. Mrs. Morland spoke of her plans for going to France with Tony unless anything happened.

'Everyone has said that to-day,' said Mrs. Birkett wearily. 'Oh, Henry, who was Gristle that rang you up this morning? I've been meaning to ask you all day.'

'Gristle?' said the Headmaster. 'Not Gristle; Bissell. He is the Headmaster of the Hosiers' Boys Foundation School. If there is any evacuating of the London schools,' he continued, addressing himself to Mrs. Morland, 'we are taking them in, damn them. I'm sorry; the day has been trying. But it will be a difficult job with the best will in the world.

If anything did happen, not that I think it will, but one must be prepared, a good many of our younger masters will have to go automatically. So will my secretary.'

Mrs. Morland did not stay late. Before she went she said to Mrs. Birkett:

'I was wanting to ask you, Amy. If there is any trouble, which I shall *not* encourage by talking about it, my publisher Adrian Coates and his wife, George Knox's daughter, you know, rather want to take my house. I don't suppose there'll be any air raids, but if there were Adrian wants Sybil and the three children to be in the country. Tony will be at Oxford, so I wondered if it would be any use to you if I came to you for a bit, as a secretary, or a P.G., or anything you like. But only if you'd like it. Think about it.'

'I shan't think at all,' said Mrs. Birkett, 'I'd love to have you. You can P.G. if you'd feel happier and have Rose's room to write in. Bill, wouldn't it be nice if Laura came to us in the autumn if things get difficult?'

'Very nice indeed,' said Mr. Birkett warmly. 'And there isn't another parent, past, present, or future, that I'd say that to. Do come, Laura.'

Mrs. Morland stared into vacancy and took a deep breath.

'I am *not* superstitious,' she said firmly, 'and though I don't believe in encouraging things by talking about them, it is silly not to face facts. If there is a war, I will come to you. There!'

'I always said you saw things clearly,' said Mrs. Birkett. 'You can tell the truth better than anyone I know. If there is a war, come to us.'

'And now let it do its worst,' said Mrs. Morland heroically but irrelevantly, and so took herself away.

'I still don't think it can happen,' said Mrs. Birkett to her husband, 'but I'm glad Rose will be safely away.'

'I don't believe it either,' said Mr. Birkett, 'for to admit it would be to admit the possibility of the Hosiers' Boys coming here, which will undoubtedly be worse than death. I think John will look after her.'

IV

THE STORM BEGINS TO LOWER

On a September afternoon about six weeks later than the interesting events just described Mrs. Morland drove up to the Headmaster's House at Southbridge and rang the front door bell. Simnet, who was prepared for her arrival, opened the door and himself removed her suitcases from the car and took them up to what, to Geraldine's secret resentment, was still called Miss Rose's room. Mrs. Morland went straight to Mrs. Birkett's sitting-room where she found her friend writing letters.

'Well, here I am,' said Mrs. Morland dramatically.

Mrs. Birkett embraced her friend and rang for tea.

'Tell me about everything,' said Mrs. Morland.

'There's not much to tell,' said Mrs. Birkett. 'The Hosiers' Boys Foundation School has decided to extend its holidays, so they don't come here till the 25th. All the masters who were Territorials won't be coming back of course, including Philip Winter whom we shall miss very much. Bill and Everard Carter go mad together for hours every evening, trying to work out a time-table that will satisfy Mr. Gristle, though I suppose I must remember to call him Bissell.'

Mrs. Morland, who knew that the present disturbed state of things made people rather unlike themselves, looked piercingly at her friend to see if she were going mad.

'Gristle?' she said.

'That was what Geraldine said his name was when he rang up on Rose's wedding day,' said Mrs. Birkett, 'and the name somehow stuck.'

'There is a carpet-sweeper called Bissell,' said Mrs. Morland thoughtfully, 'and one forgets to empty the rubbish out of it and then it puts dirt on the carpet instead of taking it off. But I suppose everyone has electric ones now.'

'He may or may not be a carpet-sweeper,' said Mrs. Birkett, 'but he is the Headmaster of the Hosiers' Boys Foundation School and very, very well meaning. He is coming here for the night to talk to Bill, so you'll see him at dinner. I have asked the Carters, so we shall be six.'

'Where is Geraldine then?' said Mrs. Morland.

Mrs. Birkett sighed.

'She did First Aid last spring,' she said, 'and is working with Delia Brandon at the Barchester Infirmary. When I say work, they sit there all the time with nothing to do, because all the patients were turned out last week which was *most* depressing for all their families that thought they had got rid of them. And none of the doctors are allowed to take any private cases, so it is very dull for everybody. Better, I suppose, than having hundreds of wounded soldiers, yet in a way if one didn't know any of the soldiers one would be glad to think of the nurses and doctors being employed.'

Mrs. Morland felt this question too difficult for her and asked after Rose. Mrs. Birkett said proudly that she had written by every mail and was loving Las Palombas and very happy, and offered to show Mrs. Morland some of her letters. Mrs. Morland with great kindness accepted the offer, but her kindness was not unduly tried for Rose's large scrawling hand though it covered a great deal of paper, had nothing particular to impart except that Las Palombas was marvellous which she spelt with one 'l', and the language a bit dispiriting and mummy and daddy must come out and see her as soon as they could and she supposed the war must be a bit dispiriting and sent tons and tons of love. Mrs. Morland said how nice the letters were and they gossiped about the wedding and so time passed and it was time to dress for dinner.

When Mrs. Morland got down to the drawing-room she found Mr. Birkett talking to a stranger whom she rightly guessed to be Mr. Gristle or more correctly Bissell. The Headmaster of the Hosiers' Boys Foundation School, erroneously described by its well-wishers as one of our Lesser Public Schools, was a lean middle-sized man of about thirty-five. He wore a neat blue suit and looked as if he wasn't sure if he ought to attack his hosts, or be on the defensive.

Mr. Birkett introduced Mrs. Morland and Mr. Bissell, who shook hands and said he was pleased to meet her, and was sorry the wife wasn't with him as she was a great reader. Mrs. Morland, who in spite of some fifteen years of ceaseless and successful novel writing had no opinion of her own works at all, thanked Mr. Bissell warmly for his kind words and asked which of her books Mrs. Bissell liked best.

'Not but what they are all the same,' she added, 'because my publisher says that pays better and I have to go on earning money for the present, because although the three elder boys have been supporting themselves for some time except of course for Christmas and birthday presents which I always make as large as I can, I still have my youngest boy at Paul's and you know what Oxford is.'

Mr. Bissell said not being a Capittleist he didn't.

'But aren't there heaps of scholarships and things?' said Mrs. Morland. 'I thought everyone had a Field-Marshal's bâton in his knapsack now, only that isn't exactly what I mean.'

Mr. Bissell said Conscription was one of Capittleism's most unscrupulous methods of attack on its enemies, so that Mrs. Morland who could not bear unpleasantness was very thankful when Mrs. Birkett came in, closely followed by the Carters and sherry was handed, which Mr. Bissell refused. Mr. Birkett, making a shrewd guess that Mr. Bissell was refusing owing to a social code which forbids one to show enthusiasm, or indeed gratitude, for what is offered, pressed his fellow Headmaster to try the sherry, to which Mr. Bissell answered that he didn't mind if he did take a glass, remarking as he tossed it off that Mrs. Bissell had a lady's taste in wines and liked hers sweet and he must say he could not altogether deprecate her taste.

Before Mr. Birkett whose dry sherry was rather well known could recover his balance, the door opened and his daughter Geraldine in her Red Cross uniform walked in and peeling off her gloves flicked them together in a very professional way.

'Geraldine darling, I didn't know you were coming home,' said her mother. 'This is Mr. Bissell, the Headmaster of the Hosiers' Boys Foundation School.'

'How do you do,' said Geraldine. 'Sorry, Mummy, if it's a dinner party, but they've actually got a patient at the hospital, a flying man from Sparrowhill with jaundice, so Matron said some of us could have the week-end off, otherwise there'd be too many trying to nurse him.'

Mrs. Birkett inquired if her daughter wanted a bath before dinner in which case she was sure Mr. Bissell would excuse them if they waited ten minutes. Mr. Bissell said, Pleased, he was sure, though no pleasure appeared to be in him, but Geraldine, again flicking her gloves in a swaggering way said she wouldn't bother to change and anyway Mr. Bissell wasn't changed either, so she would keep him company. Mr. Bissell would dearly have liked to explain that he had a dinner jacket suit and tails, both of which he was quite used to wearing in their proper place, with a rider on the Capittleist habit of changing for what he had learnt not to call tea but did not think it reasonable to call dinner, seeing that one dinner at midday should be enough for any man, but Simnet coming in with an air of triumph announced Captain Winter, and Philip appeared in uniform.

For a few moments there was such a joyful crossfire of questions and answers that Mr. Bissell was quite forgotten. Philip explained that he had got an unexpected week-end's leave and decided to run down to the School. He begged Kate to forgive him for not letting her know, but the telephone lines had been crowded out and a telegram would have arrived no sooner than he did.

'It doesn't matter in the least,' said Kate, her soft eyes shining at the prospect of overhauling Philip's uniform, and indeed every stitch on him during the week-end. 'Your room is always ready for you and Bobbie *will* be so pleased to see you. He stood up to-day and pulled the table-cloth so hard that two cups and saucers fell off and were broken,' said Kate proudly.

'He knew quite well what he had done,' added Everard with equal pride.

Everyone, except Mr. Bissell, knew that Master Carter could not possibly be pleased to see Philip, even if he was one of his godfathers, and would be far more likely to yell at the sight of a complete stranger in unknown clothes, but they were so fond of Everard and Kate that they allowed the subject to drop. Simnet announced dinner, Mrs. Birkett said she hoped cook would have found something for them all to eat, and they went into the dining-room.

'I must tell you,' said Kate, who was next to Mr. Bissell and in her kindness was afraid he might feel out of it, 'that Bobbie is our little boy. He is just one and called after my brother Robert, at least his full name is Robert Philip, after Mr. Winter, whom I really ought to call Captain

Winter now, but it all seems so unreal. How many children have you, Mr. Bissell?'

Mr. Bissell, thawed by Kate's obvious sincerity and interest, said it was a great grief to Mrs. Bissell and he that they had no chicks. Kate saw in Geraldine's eye a professional nursing wish to ask him why, and knowing that no sentiment of what was suitable would keep her from her purpose, plunged into an interesting account of Bobbie's first birthday and how he had been sick with excitement at the sight of his birthday cake, a plain sponge cake with one candle on it, but had subsequently recovered. During her soothing monologue Mr. Bissell began to feel at home and although he could not reconcile dinner jackets with his principles he enjoyed the good food and wine without knowing it and softened towards the representatives of Capittleism and an effete educational system more than he would have thought possible.

It was not till Mrs. Morland unfortunately spoke of a book she had been reading about the Russian ballet that Mrs. Birkett had any cause for anxiety about her dinner party. Even as Philip Winter a few years ago had bristled at the name of Russia, so did Mr. Bissell now look defiantly about him, anxiously watching for his chance to become a martyr. Nor did he have long to wait, for Philip put forward the opinion that it was just as well we hadn't had a trade pact with the Russians, as they would have turned round and bitten us. This was not to be borne.

'Have you ever been to Russia?' said Mr. Bissell, not quite sure if he ought to say Captain, but deciding against it as of a militarist tendency.

'No,' said Philip, and he and Everard began to laugh.

Mrs. Birkett asked what the joke was.

'It was when I was staying with you that summer at Northbridge,' Philip answered her, 'and the Oxbridge Press accepted my little book on Horace. I was going to Russia, but Everard said if the proofs were sent to me there they might be confiscated, so I went to Hungary with him and Noel Merton instead.'

'You missed a most valuable opportunity,' said Mr. Bissell. 'It is practically unknown for letters to go astray in Russia.'

Philip, baulking the main issue in a very cowardly way, said he hadn't got the proofs till November, so it wouldn't really have mattered.

'Mark me,' said Mr. Bissell.

Everyone looked at him with interest.

'Mark me,' he said, 'Russia is a Power to be reckoned with. Look what she has done for civilization.'

A confused hubbub rose about him in which the words Tchekov, Ballet, Rimsky, Diaghilev, Tschaikovsky, Flying over the Pole were heard. Mr. Bissell, who meant something quite different, found it impossible to make himself heard.

'It is more like Flying over the Poles now,' said Mrs. Morland in her tragedy voice. 'I never quite know how large Poland really is, because it seems to get bigger or smaller in history till one is quite giddy, but to have Russians there must be quite dreadful. Cossacks, only I don't think they fly, and why the French are always allies of Poland I cannot think.'

Mr. Bissell seizing upon a second's silence said no one could begin to understand the World Problems of to-day who did not reckon with Stalin.

'That's what you used to say, Philip,' said Geraldine accusingly.

Philip said he used to say Lenin, but the principle was the same, only he found himself too busy ever to think of either of them when he was in camp.

'Anyway,' said Mrs. Morland, pushing her hair back, 'they got it all from us.'

'Got what, Laura?' said Mr. Birkett.

'You know perfectly well that you know what I am talking about and that I can never explain what I mean,' said Mrs. Morland severely. 'The Italians getting sympathy from us for the Risorgimento and look at them now, all Fascist and Abyssinian. And reading books in the British Museum, which is *free*, for weeks and months at our expense like Karl Marx. And the Russian ballet at Covent Garden charging the most frightful prices for everything, that *we* have to pay, though I must say it's worth it, because when one goes to an English ballet one has to say how wonderful it is considering what a short time it has been going on.'

Mr. Bissell felt himself reeling. Capable of close, sustained argument, with facts of all kinds at his finger tips, he was as baffled by Mrs. Morland's mental flights as one of his own junior boys would have been by the differential calculus. How the Franco-Polish friendship, the Risorgimento, Karl Marx, and English ballet had sprung from Stalin he could not conceive. Either he was mad, or Mrs. Morland was mad, and a Public School Headmaster with his Senior Housemaster and his Senior Classical Master, now a Captain in the Army, not to speak of wives and daughters, were taking her irrelevant and illogical ramblings seriously, and therefore must be mad too. Exactly how much he longed for the bracing atmosphere of a debate at the Isle of Dogs Left Wing Athenaeum no one but himself knew, but Mr. Birkett, Everard and Philip had a fairly good guess, and much as the Birketts loved Mrs. Morland even they found her swallow flights of thought a little confusing at times. Mrs. Birkett looked at her husband and rose with her ladies. As they left the room Geraldine who had been silent, or as she preferred to imagine thinking things out, stopped near Mr. Bissell.

'If you want to nationalize the hospitals I'm your man,' she said, rather threateningly. 'Of course the Government ought to pay for them and not us. We pay a jolly sight too much for things like hospitals and education that no one really wants. I've thought it all out and I'll tell you what you ought to do — — '

But Philip, who saw Mr. Bissell going mad before his eyes and was on very old-friendly terms with Geraldine, pushed her kindly out of the room and shut the door.

'Have some port, Bissell,' said Mr. Birkett. 'No? I'm afraid Geraldine is a little overpowering. She can't think of more than one thing at a time and just now it is hospitals. She is entirely uneducated and you must forgive her. She was never good at anything but mathematics. I got Carter here to-night so that we could have a good talk about the fitting in of our timetables and I am glad Winter has turned up, as he will be a great help. If you really don't want any port, suppose we all adjourn to my study. And then to-morrow we'll go over the school and I will show you exactly what we propose to do and you will doubtless have some suggestions to make.'

Accordingly the four men went to the study where Simnet brought them coffee. Philip spoke of his month in camp and his chances of staying in England and being sent abroad, and posted himself up in school matters. While the three Southbridge masters talked Mr. Bissell reflected upon the extraordinary people among whom this war was going to force him to live. As far as he could see, though they were all very kind and obliging, not one of them had any clear idea about anything. Mr. Birkett and Mr. Carter, whom he must remember to call Birkett and Carter, were what was called educated men who had been to Oxford (though here he was wrong, for Everard was a Cambridge man) and Captain Winter, whom it would perhaps be all right to call Winter, had learnt Classics, a degree that one knew to be really difficult, though pure waste of time and getting you nowhere. Yet these men could sit and listen to conversation that the Isle of Dogs would not for a moment tolerate. When he and Mrs. Bissell went to tea with Mr. and Mrs. Lefroy of the Technical School, and Mr. Jobson from the Chemical Works and Mrs. Jobson, and Mr. Pecker from the Free Library and his unmarried daughter who taught music and folk dancing at the L.C.C. evening classes were there, then there *was* conversation. Mrs. Bissell, Mrs. Lefroy, Mrs. Jobson and Miss Pecker were in a woman's proper place. At tea the talk would be general; Mr. Jobson would tell Mrs. Bissell about the indigo trade, Mr. Lefroy would tell Mrs. Jobson about the new wood-carving class and what Miss Makins of the art weaving class had said, Mr. Pecker would give Mrs. Lefroy information about the Borough Council's stinginess in the matter of gum for the labels, while he himself would explain to Miss Pecker the latest developments in his feud with the officials responsible for University grants, after which the men would retire to Mr. Lefroy's den, so-called apparently because it was the back room in the basement and had bars at the window, though to keep burglars out rather than

Mr. Lefroy and his friends in, and discuss the coming Social Revolution and Russia's part in it, with well chosen reasoning (mostly chosen from sixpenny books of a Red and tendentious nature) and almost complete unanimity of view. After this they would go early on account of Monday morning, spiritually much refreshed.

How Mrs. Morland, who wrote books that Mr. Pecker often handed out at the Free Library and therefore must be intellectual, could be allowed to talk as she did, with no visible chain of thought and a total want of depth and earnestness, he could not imagine. And Miss Birkett, though she might be good at mathematics, seemed to have no knowledge of economics whatever. Mrs. Birkett and Mrs. Carter were certainly nice, but in any revolution they would obviously be the first to go. Still, he had made up his mind when this war began in which Russia, betrayed by England, had so far forgotten herself as to make a pact with the Ryke, that though he could not conscientiously approve of anything here or elsewhere, his duty to his profession was to meet everything as coolly as he could, carry out orders, look after his boys and masters, keep Mrs. Bissell's spirits up and never grumble at anything. So he put the disquieting behaviour of his hostess and her friends away in his mind for future reflection and prepared himself for discussion.

*

Mr. Birkett and Everard, when the subject of sending London schools to the country had first been raised, had secretly hoped to get one of the London public schools, but pressure had been put on them to take in the Hosiers' Boys Foundation School, and thinking with their guest that their obvious duty was to do what came to their hand, had during the preceding spring a good deal of correspondence with Mr. Bissel, so that they knew pretty well the numbers and requirements of the school, luckily not a very large one. As a larger number of boys were leaving than usual they were able to clear one of the boarding-houses for a number of the Hosiers' Boys. The rest were to be put in a large empty house owned by the Governors which had been fitted up as a boarding-house, largely by Kate's energy and common sense in all domestic matters. The Hosiers' Boys would have their classes partly in the School itself, partly in some wooden huts that Mr. Birkett's foresight had collected before the rush began. It might be possible to pool some of the junior classes, but the whole arrangement still needed a good deal of consideration. However two hours' solid work did a great deal and then Mr. Birkett said they would all go to bed.

'By the way, Bissell,' he said as they went into the hall, 'what about you and your wife? Will you live with your staff in the boarding-house? We haven't considered that.'

'I hadn't thought of it either,' said Mr. Bissell. 'Mrs. Bissell would be quite agreeable I'm sure. She isn't one for thinking of herself. Of course she isn't used to sharing, but we talked it over, her and I, and I'm sure she feels like I do.'

Mr. Bissell looked so tired as he made this noble but not very helpful statement that Everard felt sorry for him. To have to move a hundred boys or so into new surroundings, to make yourself responsible for them as boarders when most of them were day boys, to have to share school accommodation with unknown and possibly hostile strangers, to leave your own home, it was all quite difficult enough, without having to eat and live with your staff and forty boys. On an impulse he said:

'I don't know how the idea would suit you, Bissell, but if you and your wife cared to come to us for a bit and see how you like it, we would be delighted. Ask her and let me know.'

Mr. Bissell said he daresaid Mrs. Bissell wouldn't mind, and Everard understood him. Simnet came forward with the news that Mrs. Carter had gone home some time ago, so Everard and Philip said good night and walked across the School Quad, in silence. Kate was still up when they came in and while they had drinks she asked how everything had gone. Everard said very well, and next morning they were to go over the boarding-house reserved for the Hosiers' Boys and settle about some of the classrooms.

'I asked Bissell and his wife to come to us for a bit, Kate,' said Everard. 'It doesn't seem quite fair for them to have to live with their masters and boys. They couldn't even have a sitting-room of their own. Is that all right?'

'Quite right,' said Kate, her eyes assuming the far-away expression which always meant very sensible thoughts about practical things and which Everard still thought the most enchanting sight in the world. For had not she looked with just such eyes at a loose button on his waistcoat when he had first met her. 'Quite right. If I give them the spare room I could turn the dressing-room into a sitting-room and let them use the other bathroom. The only thing is that Philip would have to share the bathroom with them when he comes back on leave, or else use the prefects' bathroom. Would you mind, Philip?'

Philip said of course he wouldn't and Everard and Kate were angels and personally he would far rather be in a draught-ridden hut on Sparrowhill than shut up with Mr. Bissell and the unknown Mrs. Bissell.

'Well it won't be for ever,' said the practical Kate, 'and I was so sorry for Mr. Bissell when he said they hadn't got any children. Would you like to see Bobbie asleep before you go to bed, Philip?'

*

Mr. Birkett and Mr. Bissell looked into the drawing-room to say good night. Much to Mr. Bissell's relief Geraldine had gone to bed and as the two other ladies were very sleepy good nights were said at once.

'Did you have a good evening?' said Mrs. Birkett when she and her husband were alone together.

'Quite good. We got a lot of work done and can finish the practical details to-morrow. Laura was very Lauraish to-night.'

'She was tired,' said Mrs. Birkett. 'She didn't enjoy having to rush home from France with Tony when things began to look bad, and the elder boys will probably be in the army, except John who is the sailor, and she doesn't know if anyone will be buying books now. I'm very glad we've got her here.'

'Bissell doesn't realize the intelligence of what he must look on as uneducated women,' said Mr. Birkett, 'and I thought he would go mad at the dinner table. I suppose Geraldine simply must bore people about the hospital. Well, thank goodness Rose is out of it.'

So they went to bed. And Mr. Bissell in the second-best spare room wondered at the peculiar surroundings in which his lot had been cast and saw but little hope for the future if the so-called educated classes were so hopelessly ignorant and shallow. Birkett, it is true, would be a good man to work with and Mrs. Carter was very sympathetic, and after all the boys were the chief thing to be considered. So, with less distrust than he had felt on his arrival and great thankfulness that Miss Birkett would mostly be at the Hospital, he too went to sleep.

V

A ROOM WITH A PICTURE

NEXT day, much to Mr. Bissell's relief, he had breakfast alone with his host, after which they walked across the School Quad to the Carters' house. Here they collected Everard and Philip and with them made an extensive tour of the proposed new quarters of the Hosiers' Boys. By midday everything was settled and Mr. Bissell was able to feel that his school would not be badly housed.

'By the way,' said Everard, 'have you thought about coming to us with Mrs. Bissell? No hurry, but my wife would like to know in time to get things ready for you.'

Mr. Bissell had forgotten all about it. But even as he heard Everard speaking he realized that to share a house with other people, however sympathetic their wives, was the one thing he and his wife could not do. Their house they would leave dust-sheeted and empty, their books and furniture and picture (a coloured reproduction of the Van Gogh sunflowers) they would abandon, but if they were to keep their balance in this new and peculiar world where no one knew what dialectic meant, they must somehow be alone in their spare time. The thought of evenings spent with the Carters was more than he could face. Even at the risk of giving offence he must strike out for freedom. In halting words he began to explain that to stay at the Carters' house would give very great pleasure to Mrs. Bissell, and he, but his misery was so apparent that Philip Winter on an impulse came to his rescue.

'Before Mr. Bissell decides,' said Philip to Everard, 'what about taking him to see that cottage in Wiple Terrace? I know it's empty because Jessie's brother delivers the milk there and he says it is to be let furnished. Jessie is the head housemaid at Carter's,' he added to Mr. Bissell, 'and her brother does the milk round for Abner Brown who grazes one of the school fields and carts coal.'

Everard's relief at this suggestion was not less than Mr. Bissell's. He liked Mr. Bissell and felt that they could pull together, but the thought of housing indefinitely a fellow worker who regarded the School as a product of Capittleism was not bliss, the more so as he knew his own code would not let him point out to Mr. Bissell that the Hosiers' Boys was supported by one of the richest of the City Companies on money obtained partly from their appropriation of several very wealthy abbeys under Henry VIII, partly from the investment of funds obtained by rather piratical trading with the East in the seventeenth century, and that its original purpose was to educate the sons of Hosiers and enable them to enter the church through one of the Universities. So he said that he thought it a good idea, but Mr. Bissell must feel perfectly free to come to them or not.

'My wife will be delighted if you do come,' he said truthfully, knowing that his Kate enjoyed any guests, even Mr. Holinshed, a parent who had disgraced his family by suddenly taking orders at an unusually advanced age and having family prayers, which he insisted on conducting wherever he stayed, regardless of the embarrassment he caused his hosts before their servants, 'but of course if you and Mrs. Bissell prefer to be on your own we shall quite understand.'

He then wondered if he would ever dare to call Mrs. Bissell 'your wife' to Mr. Bissell; put away from him as harsh the thought that 'the wife' might be tolerated, vaguely wondered again if that lady's Christian name would ever be made known to him and thought probably not. Philip said he would take Mr. Bissell down to the village and he could have a look at the cottage, and they might drop in at the Red Lion and talk to Mr. Brown, Abner Brown's uncle, who was a useful man to know. Mr. Bissell unexpectedly said he could do with a pint and the doctor had put Mrs. Bissell on stout last winter which had done her a lot of good; so they went off across the playing-fields, by the footbridge over the river, across the allotments, and so by the lane that led into the backyard of the Red Lion.

During the eighteenth and early nineteenth century the Red Lion had been, as its capacious stables showed, a coaching inn on a fairly large scale, and its handsome red brick front on Southbridge High Street was to be seen in more than one engraving, copies of which can still be picked up in antiquarian shops in Barchester. Now its stables were used as garages except for one wing where a young woman kept a few hunters and hacks on hire, and through the great archway under one side of the hotel came nothing more exciting than a flock of sheep or a drove of cows once a month on market day. Philip led Mr. Bissell into the public bar.

'There is a Saloon, why so called I can't imagine,' he said, 'but it despises one and the drinks cost more. Besides here we get Eileen. Look at her.'

The most dazzling blonde Mr. Bissell had ever seen, dressed in skin-tight black, was behind the bar, passing the time of day with two commercial travellers and a farmer. Catching sight of Philip she bent her swan-like bust forward over the counter and asked if he would have the usual. Philip said yes and would Mr. Bissell like the same, namely Old and Mild.

'I'll have Old and Bitter if it's all the same to you,' said Mr. Bissell to the vision, only just stopping himself saying 'Miss.'

The vision drew two pints and as a mark of special favour did not put them on the counter, but saying to the commercial travellers and the farmer, 'Well, ta-ta boys, I must be looking after my guests,' brought them herself on a tin tray to Philip's table.

'Thanks, Eileen,' said Philip paying. 'This gentleman is the Headmaster of a school in London and he is coming down here with all his boys.'

'Well, I'm sure!' said Eileen. 'More of them evacuees, poor things, and really, Mr. Winter, what they have on their heads or in their heads as you might say makes you want to give Hitler a kick in the pants as the saying is. Three my married sister has, and the number of those nasty creatures they brought with them, well as I said to her, Gladys, I said, if there's a word I do not like it is lousy, but I wouldn't be doing those poor kids justice if I didn't say it. So she does them three times a week and I give her a hand and a nicer set of kids I must say you couldn't find. Greta, Gary and Gable their names are, not triplets as you might think, but hardly ten months between them and their mother, she's at the Vicarage, expecting again, poor thing, but always look on the sunny side I said to her and now your husband's at sea brighter days may be in store.'

Philip saw that Mr. Bissell would shortly burst at Eileen's misconception of his young charges and hastened to inform her that Mr. Bissell's boys were not evacuees, but a school like Southbridge, only in London. The look of relief on Mr. Bissell's face on hearing this noble lie was so great that Philip could almost see the Recording Angel drop his expunging tear upon it.

'Come along then, Bissell,' he said, 'and we'll find Mr. Brown. Where is he, Eileen?'

Eileen said he was out in front talking to the beer, so the two school-masters went out into the High Street, and there was Mr. Brown talking to the driver of a fine dray full of casks and bottles, the property of Messrs. Pilward and Sons Entire.

'Morning, gents,' said Mr. Brown. 'Beer's up a penny.'

'That's bad,' said Philip. 'This gentleman is looking for a small cottage, Mr. Brown. Do you know if Maria Cottage is still to let?'

Mr. Brown said that rightly speaking it was and the key was at Adelina Cottage and he knew Miss Hampton was in because Bill had just taken the usual over, six gin, two French, two Italian, two whisky and a half-dozen syphons that was, as regular as clockwork once a week, besides what Miss Hampton bought extra and what she drank when she came in, and he'd been in the street himself ever since and would have seen Miss Hampton go out.

'Thank you,' said Philip. 'This is Mr. Bissell. He is the Headmaster of a London school and they are all coming down to us in case of air raids.'

'I was at a London school myself,' said Mr. Brown, looking at Mr. Bissell with interest. 'My Grandfather, Grandfather Smith that was, had a tied house in Camden Town and when my mother, his daughter that was, married my father and came down here to manage because Grandfather Brown was beginning to fail, she used to send me up to keep him company for a bit when I was a nipper. And I went to the Old Sewerworks Road Board School. Elementary they call them now,' he added explanatorily to Mr. Bissell, 'but boys are boys call them what you like. Hope we'll see more of you, sir.'

As this was clearly in the nature of a royal congé Philip moved on with Mr. Bissell, hoping that his colleague would not have resented the comparison of the Hosiers' Boys with a London Board School in the eighties. Could he have seen into Mr. Bissell's mind he would have found no resentment, only an intense bewilderment at a world where every value seemed to be wrong and an increasing wish to find a roof under which he and his wife could be safe from the turmoil and misunderstanding of this new life.

'Just across the road,' said Philip encouragingly.

Mr. Bissell looked and saw a little Terrace of four two-storied cottages in mellow red brick, with a wide strip of grass lying between them and the road. They were surmounted by a stucco pediment on which the words 'Wiple Terrace 1820' were visible. Mr. Wiple, whose monument is to be seen in Southbridge Church, though rather the worse for wear and in parts illegible owing to the lettering being painted and not incised, was a small master builder of the village who had erected the terrace as a monument to his four daughters, Maria, Adelina, Louisa and Editha, calling each cottage after one of them. The property now belonged to Paul's College, who also owned the Vicarage and the living, but was always run in a very friendly way, the tenant of longest standing have a shadowy claim to pre-eminence. It was on this account that Miss Hampton, a spinster lady residing at Adelina Cottage with her friend Miss Bent, was in possession of the key of Maria Cottage which the Vicar's aunt, who had gone to join her husband at Gibraltar, wished to let furnished. Of the other two cottages, Louisa Cottage, residence of the late cricket coach at Southbridge School, was tenanted by the Warburys of whom mention has already been made, and Editha Cottage by the Vicar's other aunt who was a widow and would have Nottingham lace curtains, but otherwise will not, I think, come into this story at all. Each cottage had a very narrow flower bed at the foot of its wall, divided from the footpath by low white posts with chains. Maria Cottage had a red door, Adelina a green, Louisa a yellow and Editha, owing to the insistence of the Vicar's other aunt, imitation oak grained with so many twiddles and such a liberal coat of varnish that all highbrow tourists stopped to exclaim at it and the Nottingham lace curtains as Perfect Period.

'That's the empty one,' said Philip pointing out Maria. 'We'll go and ask Miss Hampton for the key.'

Mr. Bissell said it was quite Old-World.

At Adelina Cottage Philip rang the bell. The door was opened by a rather handsome woman with short, neatly curled grey hair, not young, in an extremely well-cut black coat and skirt, a gentlemanly white silk shirt with collar and tie, and neat legs in silk stockings and brogues, holding a cigarette in a very long black holder.

'Come in and have a drink,' said Miss Hampton.

'Certainly,' said Philip. 'This is Mr. Bissell, the Headmaster of the Hosiers' Boys Foundation School, who is bringing his staff and boys down here and wants to find a cottage. Brown says you have Maria's key.'

'French or Italian?' said Miss Hampton, who had already three-quarters filled four very large cocktail glasses, or indeed goblets, with gin. 'Bent has just taken Smigly-Rydz out, so I might as well mix hers too. She won't be a moment.'

'Is Smigly-Rydz a new dog?' said Philip. 'It was Benes last winter.'

'Gallant little Czecho-Slovakia!' said Miss Hampton in a perfunctory way. 'But it's gallant little Poland now, so we've changed Schuschnigg's name; Benes's I mean, but one gets a bit mixed, everyone being gallant.'

'And wasn't he Zog at Easter?' said Philip.

'So he was. Gallant little Albania,' said Miss Hampton. 'We bought him after Selassie died. We buried Selassie in the garden. Put it down,

Philip, and you too, Mr. Bissell. That's the name, isn't it? I never forget names. So you keep a boy's school; and in London; interesting; much vice?'

Mr. Bissell spilt a good deal of his cocktail and remained tongue-bound.

'Come, come,' said Miss Hampton filling his glass up to the brim again. 'We're all men here and I'm doing a novel on a boy's school, so I might as well know something about it. I'm thinking of calling it "Temptation at St. Anthony's"; good name, don't you think?'

'Excellent,' said Philip.

Mr. Bissell was pretty strong on psychology and had for years been accustomed to explain certain facts to his pupils, drawing his examples from botany, then from nature study, and later from outspoken serious talks, from which most of his boys had emerged with a very low opinion of their Headmaster's intellect, who could think them such chumps as he evidently did. He had also had many an interesting and intellectual exchange of views with other authorities at conferences, but his soul was extremely innocent and when he thought of exposing Mrs. Bissell to such a woman as Miss Hampton he heartily wished the war had never been invented. But he lacked the social courage to flee, and the strong cocktail was reacting unfavourably on his legs, so he looked at her, fascinated, and said nothing.

'Well, here's fun,' said Miss Hampton, taking a deep drink of what Mrs. Bissell saw with terror to be her second cocktail. 'I study vice. Interesting. It's a thing you schoolmasters ought to know about. Prove all things, you know, and stick to what's good. Here comes Bent. She'll tell you about vice.'

The door of the little sitting-room burst open and a black dog came in dragging Miss Bent after him. The dog, presumably Smigly-Rydz-Zog-Benes-Schuschnigg, was one of those very stout little dogs with a black shaggy coat, short in the leg, with a head as large as an elephant's and mournful eyes. Miss Bent, whom he had just taken round the village, was a rather flabby edition of Miss Hampton. Her coat and skirt of an indefinite tartan had obviously been made locally, her figure bulged in a very uncontrolled way, her short hair of a mousy colour looked as if she trimmed it with her nail-scissors, her stockings were cotton and rather wrinkled, her shoes could only be called serviceable, and she wore several necklaces.

'Come along, Bent,' said Miss Hampton, handing the fourth cocktail to her friend. 'Put it down. Here's Mr. Winter come for Maria's key. Mr. Bissell has a boy's school and I'm going to pick his brains for my new novel.'

'Hampton sold one hundred and fifty thousand of her last novel in America,' said Miss Bent, looking very hard at Mr. Bissell. 'That was one that was the Banned Book of the Month here. But of course one can't hope for that luck again. After all, other people must have their turn. I have a friend on the Banned Book Society Council and he says Esmé Bellenden's *Men of Harlech* will probably be the next choice. Have you read it?'

Mr. Bissell, helpless with confusion and cocktails, said he hadn't, and was Esmé Bellenden a man or a woman.

'I couldn't possibly say,' said Miss Bent, 'and what is more I don't suppose anyone could.'

Miss Hampton who had been staring at Philip for some time said, 'Do my eyes deceive me, or are you in khaki?'

'Indeed I am,' said Philip, 'and only on twenty-four hours' leave, so if we can have Maria's key we will look at her now. I have to get back to camp and Mr. Bissell to London, and incidentally we both have to get back for lunch.'

'Will you fight?' said Miss Bent in a deep voice.

'I haven't the faintest idea,' said Philip. 'It all depends where they send me. Probably I'll get stuck on Ilkley Moor, with or without a hat, till the war is over, doing gunnery courses.'

'It is only a mockery to fight now,' said Miss Bent, giving herself another cocktail. 'You should have fought Italy, four years ago.'

Philip, who was used to Miss Bent's ferocity, only smiled, but Mr. Bissell, in whose pacifist soul gin and French were doing their appointed work, took the wind out of Miss Bent's sails by saying:

'If we had fought Franco three years ago, all this wouldn't have happened.'

'That,' said Miss Bent, 'is where you are entirely wrong. Civil war is quite, quite different. Besides Franco is a Churchman, or what corresponds to a Churchman in Spain, though under the Bishop of Rome who has *no* jurisdiction in England, so we should try to understand him. Have you ever been in Spain?'

Mr. Bissell had to admit that he hadn't.

'No more have I,' said Miss Bent, 'so it is absolutely no good arguing with you. We'll go and look at Maria.'

Accordingly she took a large key off the mantelpiece, but Miss Hampton said before they went they must just look over Adelina, so the whole party inspected the rest of the cottage, which consisted of a kitchen behind the sitting-room, a narrow breakneck staircase, a bedroom overlooking the street almost entirely filled by a very large square flat divan which made Mr. Bissell back out of the room in terror, a little bedroom behind called the guest room, and a tiled bathroom, all spotlessly clean.

'Mrs. Dingle comes three times a week to clean,' said Miss Hampton. 'You can have her the three other days. She's a treasure. You can trust her with any amount of drink.'

'She is Eileen's sister and a very nice woman,' said Philip.

Then they all went next door and Miss Bent put the key in the lock and opened Maria. The moment Mr. Bissell saw Maria he knew that in spite of the terrifying (and yet rather attractive) proximity of Miss Hampton and Miss Bent, this was where he and Mrs. Bissell could be happy. If the Vicar's aunt had been his own aunt and a nice aunt at that, she could not have made a house more after his heart's desire. He could almost have fancied himself back at 27 Condiment Road, E48, except that no trams clanged down the road and there was a long garden instead of a little back yard. In the hall was the fumed oak umbrella stand with hooks above it. The sitting-room, carpeted up to the walls, had a sofa (or couch as Mr. Bissell preferred to call it) and two arm-chairs that made both ingress and egress impossible, the dining-room-kitchen had the same red-tiled linoleum as his own. Upstairs the bathroom he was pleased to see had a geyser of the same type as that at No. 27, so he knew it would not blow him up, or if it did, exactly when and how. The guest room had two narrow divan beds and a fumed oak chest-of-drawers. In the front bedroom, also carpeted up to the walls, were twin beds (not divan) and a fixed basin, a luxury he had always secretly coveted, and facing him, above the fireplace, was a coloured reproduction of the Van Gogh sunflowers. There was no doubt that the house must be his if he could afford it. So kind was Fate that Mr. Hammer, the estate agent, had just not gone out for his dinner, the rent was most reasonable, and within twenty minutes everything was settled, with the enthusiastic assistance of the ladies from Adelina Cottage.

Miss Hampton and Miss Bent were delighted with their new neighbour, the one hoping to pick his brains, the other to improve his political outlook, and offered to negotiate with Mrs. Dingle, to which end they kept Maria's key.

'Good-bye,' said Miss Hampton, as they all left the agent's office. 'Bring your wife in for a drink any time. She doesn't wear trousers, does she?'

'Trousers?' said Mr. Bissell, who could hardly believe his ears.

'That's all right,' said Miss Hampton. 'Can't abide those women who go about in slacks trying to look like men.'

'I suppose you mean Mrs. and Miss Phelps,' said Philip.

'I do,' said Miss Hampton, 'and how Admiral Phelps can stand it I don't know. Women don't need trousers to drive motor ambulances, and the Southbridge ambulance is only the baker's van, 1936 Ford. Drove an ambulance all over the North of France myself in the War and never once thought of trousers. Good-bye. I must take Bent home. We'll hardly have time for a drink before lunch.'

So saying she took a firm grasp of Smigly-Rydz's lead and walked away with Miss Bent. Philip, seeing the grocer's motor van passing, hailed it, asked if it was going up to the school, and within three

minutes had landed himself and Mr. Bissell at Mr. Birkett's back
door.

'We had given you up, Mr. Bissell,' said Mrs. Birkett placidly, 'but
luckily it's a Monday-ish sort of lunch. You'll stay, Philip, won't you?'

'Many thanks,' said Philip, 'but I must get back to the Carters, so
I'll say good-bye. Good-bye, Bissell, and good luck with Maria Cottage.'

Mr. Birkett took him to the front door.

'You'll be seeing me here on and off when I get leave,' said Philip.
'My love to Geraldine, though I know it's wasted. If I turned up as a
casualty with one leg and half my head blown away she would take far
more interest.'

'Do you remember Featherstonhaugh?' said Mr. Birkett irrelevantly.

'The Captain of Rowing in '37?' said Philip. 'He went into the
Nigerian Police, didn't he?'

'Yes. And he was coming home on leave and was in the *Lancashire*
when she was torpedoed. He wasn't among the rescued. That's the
beginning, Philip. Good-bye.'

Mr. Birkett went back to lunch and Philip ran across to the Carters,
who had also given him up for lost and welcomed him with rejoicing.
Everard's joy that Mr. Bissell was not to live with him was unfeigned,
and though Kate visibly regretted the housewifely turmoil that their
coming would have meant, she was so fond of her husband that she
bore it very well. The talk all through lunch was of school shop, in
which the two men were still deeply engaged when the front door bell
rang.

'That must be young Holinshed,' said Everard.

'I remember giving young Holinshed C minus in his General
Knowledge paper three years ago,' said Philip, 'and never did boy
more deserve it. What does he want?'

'I don't know,' said Everard. 'He wrote to ask if he could come and
see me as he was in trouble, which might mean anything. He's pretty
sure of a mathematical scholarship in December if he sticks to it, and
he may be worrying. If you aren't in a hurry, Philip, come and see him.'

The two masters left the dining-room and went to Everard's study
where young Holinshed was waiting. He shook hands with his housemaster and seeing a stranger in khaki said, 'How do you do, sir.'

'I'll give you C minus again, Holinshed, if you cut me,' said Philip.

'Good lord, it's Mr. Winter,' said young Holinshed. 'I *am* sorry, sir.
I didn't know you were in the army.'

'Captain Winter, to be accurate,' said Everard. 'Anything wrong,
Holinshed?'

Young Holinshed went bright red and looked so wretched that
Everard and Philip wondered again which of the usual scrapes a boy
of seventeen had got into and how long it would take to explain to him
that whatever he had done did not mean death and damnation.

'Would you rather talk to me alone?' said Everard, and Philip made as if to get up and go.

'It's nothing of that sort, sir,' said Holinshed desperately. 'It's this war, sir. I simply *can't* get into it.'

At this unexpected confession the two masters' surprise and relief were so great that they could almost have laughed.

'Tell us about it,' said Everard, 'and I dare say Captain Winter can help a bit. Have you had any lunch?'

Young Holinshed admitted that he hadn't. Everard, leaving him with Philip, found Kate and put the situation before her. Kate was enchanted to do a little fussing about food, and in an incredibly short time a tray of lunch was brought into the study. Holinshed was told to get on with his lunch and talk at the same time if he could, as Mr. Winter had to get back to Sparrowhill.

'It's like this, sir,' said Holinshed, pitching into his food with an appetite undimmed by mental agony and addressing himself to Everard. 'I didn't tell you I tried to get into the Navy in Munich week last year and I was awfully sick that they wouldn't have me, but they made it pretty clear that no outsiders were wanted. Of course I was only a kid then.'

'Sixteen,' said Everard to Philip, aside.

'Well, when they started the same racket over again, I felt I must do something or burst. And I've tried *everything*, sir, and no one will look at me. I've got terrific biceps,' said Holinshed doubling his arm, 'and I won the Half-mile in the sports and I've got my Certificate A in the O.T.C., but I might as well be a humpback for all the notice they take. All I get is "Go away and play," or "Wait till you're wanted." I simply *can't* go on being at school, sir. I tried to tell my pater about it, but he said something about my duty to stay on at school, and if anyone says duty to me again I'll go mad. Both the Fairweathers are serving, and you are in the Army, Mr. Winter, and heaps of fellows I know are doing something and if I can't join in I'll go mad, sir, I really will. Couldn't you or Mr. Winter do something for me? I could easily say I was older than I am. I wouldn't mind being a private a bit.'

As he finished his apologia Holinshed looked so wretched that Philip's mind suddenly went back to the summer when a boy called Hacker, now at Lazarus, and a certainty for the Craven and the Hertford, had offered him his much-loved chameleon as thanks for coaching before a scholarship exam. Before Philip kindly refused it he had seen in Hacker's face what he now saw in Holinshed's, and if he had had a Fairy God-mother's wand he would have given Holinshed a Colonel's commission in the Guards at once, sooner than see his misery. But that couldn't be, and now that his official connection with the School was so slight, per-haps not to be renewed for a long time, perhaps never again, Everard must handle the job. And he had to admit that Everard did it well, for after an hour's talk, during which young Holinshed had been allowed to interrupt, storm, rage and rebel as much as he liked, he gradually began to see a faint glimmering of reason on the following points:

(*a*) that the Navy had no use for untrained amateurs;

(*b*) that he was only seventeen;

(*c*) that the Army didn't at present want anyone till he was twenty;

(*d*) that if he got his scholarship in December, finished his school year, went on to the University and started his engineering course, or even, if circumstances were favourable, finished it, he would be every day and in every way better fitted to kill a great many enemies than he was at present.

'Thanks most awfully, sir,' said Holinshed. 'It's most awfully good of you to have bothered and I know I've been rather an ass. The only thing is, do you think there'll still be a war by then?'

Everard said he would do his very best to see that a bit was kept back for him and he had better come and see Mrs. Carter and have some tea. Kate was delighted to see a boy in the holidays as the house seemed so empty when they were all away, and young Holinshed, undeterred by a large lunch at two-thirty, ate an enormous tea at four o'clock and much fortified physically and mentally went off again.

'We'll have more trouble of that sort,' said Everard. 'About twenty of the senior boarders here and in the other Houses went quite mad last year in Munich week. Some of them went mad at home, which was very trying for their parents, and some came and did their going mad here, which was fairly trying for me. However they all turned up on the first day of term and we heard no more about it.'

Mr. Bissell was then announced. He had come to say good-bye to Mrs. Carter and thank her for her kind offer of hospitality. Kind Kate assured him that if by any chance Maria Cottage didn't suit him, or was uncomfortable for the first few days, he and his wife must use the House for meals, baths, or anything they liked. Mr. Bissell, while not quite liking the use of the word 'bath' as applied to Mrs. Bissell, was none the less grateful.

'If you're going to the station, I'll run you into Barchester in my car,' said Philip. 'It will save you a change, and it's a pretty drive.'

Mr. Bissell said he didn't mind. This being rightly interpreted as an expression of great gratitude by the company, good-byes were said, and Mr. Bissell and Philip went to the front door, accompanied by Everard.

'It's been a pleasure to meet you, Carter,' said Mr. Bissell, remembering his manners. 'I'm sure we shall pull together. The world has deteri'ated of late, and it's up to we schoolmasters to make it a better place for the boys.'

Everard's eye met Philip's with extreme gravity as he said good-bye. With a sudden inspiration he told Mr. Bissell that he reciprocated his sentiments and then went indoors.

'I am so sorry,' said Kate when he came back, 'that the poor Bissells have no children. I wonder why?'

'I didn't ask, darling,' said Everard, 'but I'm sure you'll have it out of Mrs. Bissell an hour after you have made her acquaintance.'

VI

THE WORKING PARTY

In due course the Hosiers' Boys Foundation School came down to Southbridge, partly in motor coaches, partly in its parents' cars. Masters and boys were duly installed in their new quarters and got into their routine pretty quickly. By great good luck very few of the masters were married and those that had wives were able to find lodgings for them in the village, or in Barchester. Mr. and Mrs. Bissell took up their residence in Maria Cottage, with the enthusiastic help of Miss Hampton and Miss Bent. Miss Bent it was who showed them the crack in the scullery sink, but it was Miss Hampton who bearded the agent in his office and got it repaired at once, quite out of its turn. Mrs. Birkett helped her husband and the staff with her usual quiet efficiency and in a very short time the two schools had arrived at a working arrangement about the hours for games, the use of the masters' common room and other vital interests. The masters on both sides were on the whole heroic in concealing their feelings about the things they disliked in each other and it was only when goaded beyond bearing by Mr. Hopkins, the science master of the Hosiers' Boys who loudly proclaimed himself a Conscientious Objector although he was forty-five and limped, that Everard said to Mr. Birkett he had never quite known what common room meant before.

Everything being in tolerably good order, Mrs. Birkett and Mrs. Morland decided to go over one afternoon to Northbridge and call on the Keiths. They had heard, through Kate, that Mrs. Keith was not quite so well, and felt sorry for Lydia whose ardent spirit would, they knew, have liked to fling itself into uniform or some kind of war job.

Nothing could have been more lovely and more peaceful than the drive to Northbridge, in those early autumn days. The road skirted the river for a few miles, water meadows on one side and the downs on the other. On their lower slopes the stubble was pale gold, while from their grassy heights came the melancholy yet pleasing dissonance of sheep bells. Then, avoiding Barchester and a great loop of the river, the road mounted the downs, ran for a mile between wide stretches of thyme-grown turf where juniper bushes deployed their crooked armies of fantastic men and animals, with an infinitely wide, hazy distance encircling the world, and dropped again to the river. The short lime avenue that led to Northbridge Manor was beginning to turn yellow, and Michaelmas daisies shone in every amethystine colour below it. It seemed quite useless to speak of this peaceful beauty, which needs must make one think of other autumn fields where the earth was red, the trees broken, the harvest ravaged, so neither lady said anything about it.

Mrs. Morland, who was driving her own car, had to park it at some distance from the house, as the little circular sweep before the front door was already occupied by half a dozen cars.

'Oh, dear,' said Mrs. Birkett, 'it must be the Sewing Party to-day. I had forgotten that Mrs. Keith has it on Tuesdays. Well, it can't be helped. We'll go straight in.'

As is so often the pleasant custom in the country the outer door of the house was kept open through the warmer months, and all friends were accustomed to turn the handle of the inner glass door and walk straight in. A wide passage ran through the house from front to back, and glass doors open at the farther end showed a vista of a wide gravel walk between grass plots and a magnificent cedar, while on one side creepers were reddening on a brick wall. A sound of confused gabbling on the left showed that the Sewing Party was in full progress. Mrs. Birkett opened the drawing-room door and went in, followed by Mrs. Morland. A dozen ladies or thereabouts were sitting among billows of rather unpleasant-looking flannelette and art woollens, with Mrs. Keith in nominal command, but Mrs. Birkett was uncomfortably struck by the change in her friend since they had last met before Rose's wedding. There was no doubt that Mrs. Keith was far from well and Mrs. Birkett didn't like it.

'I'm afraid we've come on the wrong day,' she said, 'but it is the first free afternoon I've had since term began. You know Laura Morland. She is staying with me for the present.'

Mrs. Keith said she remembered Mrs. Morland's nice boy that she had brought to tea once so well and how was he.

'He is very well, thank you,' said Mrs. Morland, who had also noted Mrs. Keith's altered appearance and was impelled by nervous sympathy to talk far more than was necessary. 'At least I suppose he is, but he is staying with hunting friends and doesn't write. Of course the hunting season has been over for some time, but they may be cubbing, though whether they cub as early as this, I don't know. It is extraordinary how little one knows about hunting when one doesn't have hunting friends or take much interest in it and has never ridden.'

She looked rather wildly round her for corroboration.

'Can you sew?' said Lydia, suddenly surging up from a group of workers and speaking in a threatening way to Mrs. Morland, while she carelessly snapped a large pair of scissors.

Mrs. Morland said she could.

'Here's a pyjama leg, then,' said Lydia. 'I'm not much good at sewing myself, but I can cut out, which is more than most people have the sense to do,' she added with a withering glance at the workers. 'And if you want a needle and cotton, or pins, or anything, you'll find one in the basket on the table, unless Mrs. Warbury has taken them all.'

With which words of help Lydia returned to her cutting out.

Mrs. Morland, after greeting several ladies who were known to her made her way to the basket on the table. The basket was quite full of an empty needle-book, a large pincushion with no pins in it, and two or three dozen reels of cotton of different colours, all with long ends trailing from them and all of these trails hopelessly entangled. There were also half a dozen thimbles, some made for giants with large hands, others for undersized dwarfs. Mrs. Morland, always diffident, stood hovering over the basket, the pyjama leg dangling from her hand.

'Mrs. Morland, isn't it,' said a lady who was sitting in a very comfortable arm-chair sewing, though owing to the size and fatness of the arms of her chair she was pinioned as it were and could only sew by holding her work high in the air.

Mrs. Morland said it was.

'I am Gloria Warbury,' said the lady, a dark, ravaged, intense creature. 'You wouldn't remember me.'

'No, I wouldn't quite,' said Mrs. Morland, always truthful, 'Was it somewhere we met?'

Mrs. Warbury laughed in a profound way.

'Do you remember,' she said, 'a cocktail party at Johns and Fairfield?'

Mrs. Morland cast her mind back to several cocktail parties at the house of the well-known publishers with whom, despite their blandishments and her refusal to listen to them, she had always been on excellent terms, and asked if Mrs. Warbury meant the one where everyone was so drunk.

'You were talking,' said Mrs. Warbury, ignoring this question, 'to a man.'

She said the word man in such a way that all conversation ceased and every worker looked up from her sewing.

'I expect I was,' said Mrs. Morland, 'unless it happened to be a woman. Were you there?'

She put this question with such anxious if idiotic interest that Mrs. Warbury, while finding her almost half-witted, could not suspect any malice.

'Yes, I was there, with my husband,' she said. 'I expect you know him. We live in Wiple Terrace.'

Mrs. Morland said she didn't *quite* know Wiple Terrace and was it S.W.7.

'No, no,' said Mrs. Warbury, laughing even more profoundly, 'in Southbridge. Oscar is in Dante-Technifilms. They have moved down here from London. I knew I had seen you somewhere. My boy Fritz is down here too. He is on the production side of course. You must come in and have a drink and bring your husband.'

'Well, I can't exactly *bring* him,' said Mrs. Morland with the air of one making a concession, 'because he is dead, and I am not living in my own house at present, but if I could find any pins or a needle I could start on this leg. Lydia thought you might have some.'

Mrs. Warbury, saying with her contralto laugh that she had a fatal attraction for pins, rummaged about in her chair and produced a small pincushion quite well stocked which she handed to Mrs. Morland, who thanked her, sat down as far away as possible, and began industriously to pin the seam of the leg together.

'Here's a needle,' said Lydia, who managed to keep a firm eye on all the party. 'You'll need one. And Miss Hampton will give you some of her cotton. This is Mrs. Morland, Miss Hampton.'

The rest of the party, mostly nice local people who might just as well have been anyone else, were again silent. Every one of them had read at least one of Mrs. Morland's and one of Miss Hampton's books, in most cases one that was in a sixpenny edition, and they all hoped to hear a clash of intellects and really literary conversation.

'Glad to meet you,' said Miss Hampton. 'Been wanting to meet you for some time. You and I do the same sort of job, so I gather from Mrs. Birkett.'

'Well, I've never been a Banned Book of the Month, I'm afraid,' said Mrs. Morland, 'and I never could be. My publisher wouldn't like it, and I'm afraid I'm not up to it.'

'Bah!' said Miss Hampton vigorously. 'Banned Books! Why do you think I write them?'

Mrs. Morland said she had always wondered.

'Four nephews to support,' said Miss Hampton. 'And you have four sons, Mrs. Birkett tells me. They take a bit of supporting. They are all off my hands now, two in the Army, one in the Navy and one in the Consular Service, but it took a bit of doing.'

Upon this the two celebrated authoresses fell into a heart-to-heart conversation about boys which lasted without a break till Miss Hampton wanted a pair of scissors. Although Mrs. Keith provided several pairs for the working party they always became absorbed during the afternoon, and by tea-time there was usually a single pair which was passed from hand to hand like the eye of the Graiae. On the present occasion the scissors were run to earth in the folds of the hostess's work, which was not considered quite fair, and Miss Hampton continued the story of her fourth nephew, the one in the Consular Service in Spain, while Mrs. Morland, an excellent listener in spite of her own sons and their doings, sewed industriously away, running and felling.

'I say,' said Lydia, coming round on a tour of inspection, 'you must be ready for that other pyjama leg. Here it is.'

Mrs. Morland took it and compared it in a puzzled way with the leg on which she had been working.

'You've sewed your leg up all the way round, Mrs. Morland,' said Lydia pityingly. 'Give it to Miss Hampton and come and talk to Mother.'

Mrs. Morland obediently went across to her hostess and listened with real kindness and interest to what she had to say about her married son Robert and his three children, her daughter Kate Carter and her younger son Colin. As Mrs. Morland saw the Carters nearly every day she was able to give Mrs. Keith the latest news of Master Bobbie Carter. That phenomenal child had just cut another tooth and his grandmother enjoyed herself very much telling Mrs. Morland the approximate dates of every tooth of all her children and her other grandchildren. While this entrancing conversation was going on, tea had been brought in on a trolley by Palmer the parlourmaid whose expression clearly showed what she thought of sewing parties in her drawing-room. Mrs. Keith called Palmer to her side.

'Oh, Palmer,' she said, 'Mr. Keith tells me that there was a bright light in one of the maids' windows when he came in last night from the garage. I don't know whose it was, but you must be careful, or we shall have the police down on us.'

Palmer stiffened all over.

'I'm sure it wasn't me, madam,' she said, with a good servant's immediate reaction to any criticism of the staff, namely to take the criticism as directed especially and venomously to herself and angrily rebut it. 'And it couldn't have been Cook nor the girls, madam, as they was in bed quite early and Cook passed the remark to me, only this morning while we were drinking a cup of tea, that Mr. Keith was very late home last night and banged the garridge door so loud she thought it was the air raids.'

Having thus established the good servant's second reaction, namely the solidarity, surpassing that of any trade union, which makes her shelter any other member of the staff with lies, if necessary, of the most unblushing incredibility, Palmer became even more rigid and stood over her mistress in a very unpleasant way. Mrs. Keith suddenly looked very grey and tired.

Lydia, who appeared to be like Niobe all ears (as Mrs. Morland subsequently said when relating the incident to Mrs. Birkett who had been at the other end of the room talking to the Vicar's wife and had not heard this encounter, or, said Mrs. Morland, was it Argus she meant) suddenly materialized at her mother's elbow.

'It doesn't matter whose window it was, it mustn't happen again,' said Lydia, still brandishing her cutting-out scissors as a kind of wand of office. 'I did all the black-out myself and I know it's all right, so if anyone shows a light, it's their own fault.'

'Well, I'm sure Miss Lydia,' said Palmer, retiring to her third line of whining self-justification, 'no one could be more careful than I am. When I go to bed I turn on the light and first thing I do is to go straight to the window and draw the curtains the way you said, and there's not a chink of light showing, because I asked Cook to oblige me by going out and having a look and she said if there had been a corpse in the room it couldn't have been darker.'

Lydia, entirely unmoved by Cook's remarkable appreciation of a good black-out, said she had told Palmer that the black-out must be done every night before lighting-up time and if it wasn't she would put blue bulbs into the maids' bedrooms.

Palmer, with a face that forboded at least twenty-four hours' sulks, said the girls had quite enough to do as it was and their bedrooms were all at the back of the house, so no one could see. With which piece of reasoning she scornfully collected the tea-things and took the trolley away.

'I don't know why it is,' said Mrs. Morland, 'that so many people think air raids can only come in at the front windows. One ought to be just as careful at the back, and after all a lot of people's houses point the wrong way. I mean if the back of your house is east you ought to be particularly careful because one never knows.'

The Vicar's wife said the danger of unscreened lights was that they could be seen by enemy aircraft above, a statement so eminently reasonable as to paralyse all further conversation on the subject.

'I wanted to ask you about our next week's work, Mrs. Keith,' she said. 'The billeting officer tells me that the evacuees have all got night-gowns now, but a lot of them will be needing frocks and knickers. I thought we might be getting on with some, if Lydia has a pattern.'

'We've got plenty of green stuff and of blue too,' said Mrs. Keith. 'Lydia, where are those two frocks we made?'

Lydia went over to some neatly stocked shelves and produced two frocks, one the colour of dead spinach, the other a dull peacock blue, saying they were a bit Liberty but Mrs. Foster, the head of the Personal Service parties, had sent the material over from Pomfret Towers so they might as well use it.

The Vicar's wife examined and approved the frocks which she found very satisfactory except that the necks, she said, wanted arting up a bit, as the frocks were so very plain in cut. To this end she advised a little embroidery, something like a few flowers or leaves done in floss silk. She had at home, she said, some transfers that she could iron off on to the necks of the frocks when Lydia had cut them out. To this Mrs. Keith and Lydia agreed and the party began to break up.

'Stay a minute,' said Mrs. Keith to Mrs. Birkett and Mrs. Morland. 'I haven't seen you at all.'

Miss Hampton shook hands warmly with Mrs. Morland and pressed her to visit Adelina Cottage. Any one of her nephews, or all of them, might turn up at any moment on leave, she said, but there was always a spot of drink somewhere. Mrs. Warbury, coming up to Mrs. Keith, said she felt too frightfully *de trop*, but her husband was coming to fetch her on his way back from the Studios, so might she wait. Mrs. Keith looked very faint and said of course and would Lydia ring for some sherry. Lydia did as she was asked and then accompanied Miss Hampton to the front door. Mrs. Birkett, who knew her well, saw that she was boiling up with rage against Mrs. Warbury who would undoubtedly tire and exhaust her mother, but was controlling her feelings in a way that she would have been incapable of six months earlier. Palmer with deep displeasure brought in the sherry which Mrs. Warbury quaffed, for no other word can express her sweeping manner of handling a glass, with abandon.

'And now I want to know all about your wonderful boy, Mrs. Keith,' she said.

'He is very well. He has cut a new tooth,' said Mrs. Keith.

'A wisdom tooth, I suppose,' said Mrs. Warbury, 'at his age.'

'If you mean his father, he cut all his wisdom teeth years ago,' said Mrs. Keith, 'and then had to have them all out, so wasteful, but Nature doesn't seem to have got used to teeth yet. You would think that after so many thousand or is it million years of evolution she would know that we don't need wisdom teeth, but nothing seems to teach her.'

'But I didn't know he was married,' said Mrs. Warbury. 'Such a *nice* boy.'

It had become evident to Mrs. Birkett that her hostess and Mrs. Warbury were at cross purposes, so she intervened.

'I think, Helen,' she said to Mrs. Keith, 'that Mrs. Warbury is talking about Colin.'

'I really forget if he cut his wisdom teeth or not,' said Mrs. Keith in a very tired voice.

'It is Mrs. Keith's little grandson who has cut a tooth,' said Mrs. Birkett to Mrs. Warbury. 'Her daughter's little boy. Colin is somewhere in England with his gunners.'

'What a pity — that *nice* boy,' said Mrs. Warbury.

'I don't think it a pity at all,' said Mrs. Keith, almost sharply. 'He has been in the Territorials for a long time and I must say he looks wonderfully well, better than he has for months, for the life in London didn't really suit him. And there are a lot of other lawyers in his regiment, so they get on very well.'

'But the WASTE,' said Mrs. Warbury.

No one answered.

'You must be thankful that your boy isn't old enough to be conscripted, Mrs. Morland,' said Mrs. Warbury, with a hiss on the 's' of conscripted that caused her hearers to shudder.

Mrs. Morland, who was very truthful, said she supposed she was, and paused.

Mrs. Warbury, helping herself to another glass of sherry said if only all young men refused to fight and we gave back all our colonies to their rightful owners, the world would be a different place. With this sentiment all her hearers agreed, though not quite in the sense she intended. Mrs. Keith felt so unwell that she could not argue the point. Mrs. Birkett, who had no sons, kept silence, feeling that a woman with no sons to lose could not sit in judgment upon a woman who had a son, however disagreeable he might be. Mrs. Morland realized that the defence of anything that she and her friends cared about was in her hands. Heartily did she wish that Lydia were there to do reckless battle, but Lydia did not reappear. Mrs. Morland knew herself to be at her worst in a crisis. To be flustered, as she always was by people she didn't like, made her talk wildly and at far too great length, and she knew it. Looking madly about her she collected her wits for a reply. It was true that of her four sons the eldest was on an exploration expedition in Central South America and was in any case well over the present military age, the second was with his regiment in Burma, and the third a professional sailor, while Tony, her youngest, was a good eighteen months under military age, but even because of that she felt that it would seem like boasting to speak of what they were doing, or not yet able to do.

'Well,' she said apologetically, 'I don't see how one can stop them. And of course if one is in the Navy there one is, and it's much the same with the Army, or exploring where you get no news for six months, and Tony really likes the O.T.C. At least he didn't much like it the first time, but after that he met a sergeant-major in the regular army who swore more dreadfully than anyone he had ever heard which made him feel a real interest. I'm sure your boy must feel the same.'

As she spoke she heard herself getting sillier and sillier, but was quite unable to do anything about it. Mrs. Birkett and Mrs. Keith exchanged glances of surreptitious amusement at their friend's flounderings.

'Luckily my boy Fritz is in a reserved occupation,' said Mrs. Warbury, making up her lips again after the sherry.

'Is he a dentist?' said Mrs. Morland in a final outburst of trying to be intelligent and do her best.

'Films,' said Mrs. Warbury in a voice that implied, 'my good woman.'

To this there was no answer. A glacial silence, to which Mrs. Warbury appeared quite insensible, descended upon the room, while the three other ladies cudgelled their brains in vain for anything to say. To their great relief and surprise Lydia then came back, bringing Miss Hampton with her.

'I say, Mrs. Warbury,' said Lydia in what her mother distinguished as a peculiar voice, 'your husband rang up to say he was stuck on a film or something, so Miss Hampton is going to take you back.'

'Must get back at once,' said Miss Hampton. 'Red Lion opens at six and it's that now. Can't keep Bent waiting.'

With which stalwart words she hustled Mrs. Warbury out of the room and into her car before that lady knew what was happening.

'Lydia!' said Mrs. Keith accusingly, but in a very affectionate way.

'Well, I had to do something, Mother,' said Lydia. 'I couldn't have that ghastly spy boring you to death till her awful husband came and wanted a drink. So I told Miss Hampton and we rang up the film studio and told Mr. Warbury that his wife had gone home.'

'But you'll be found out!' said Mrs. Morland dramatically. 'They will compare notes and discover that you told a lie!'

'I must say,' said the unregenerate Lydia, 'that it was rather fun telling that one. I didn't know I had it in me. Mother, do you think you ought to rest before dinner?'

But Mrs. Keith, who had recovered a little since her horrid visitor had left, said she thought not, but she would lie down on the sofa if no one minded. So she did, and Lydia produced a hot-water bottle almost at once and put a light shawl over her mother, while Mrs. Morland thought how nice Lydia was and Mrs. Birkett, who had known her intimately for several years, thought how admirably she was teaching herself to be kind and thoughtful in a gentle way; for of hearty indiscriminate good nature there had never been any lack.

The four ladies talked very peacefully for half an hour about families and friends. Mrs. Keith asked Mrs. Morland if she was writing a new book. At first Mrs. Morland drew in her horns and retreated into her shell, for as we well know she had no opinion of her own work at all. After much pressure, applied with genuine interest, she said she was trying to work on a new story, centring as usual round the dressmaking establishment of Madame Koska, but her great difficulty was to know what nationality to make her distressed heroine. The head villain, who had taken a job as commissionaire at Madame Koska's shop in Mayfair the better to spy upon the English aristocracy, was of course a member of the Gestapo, but the heroine, a countess of exquisite form, face and breeding, had to be a refugee and the trouble was, said Mrs. Morland, that refugees were as bad as chameleons and kept on being someone else. On being pressed for an explanation she said she had begun by having a Czecho-Slovakian, but had been obliged to change her for an Albanian and was at the moment turning her into a Pole, which, she added, was extremely difficult because their names were all alike except Paderewski and in any case she would probably be out of date before the book was published and one couldn't turn her into a Belgian, or a Swiss, or whatever the next refugees were going to be, when the proofs had been passed. And, she added, with deep meaning, and in a slow emphatic voice, she knew Whose fault it was.

'Whose fault, Mrs. Morland?' said Lydia eagerly.

'Do you know that pair of stockings with black marks on them that I sometimes wear?' said Mrs. Morland to Mrs. Birkett.

Mrs. Birkett said she was afraid she didn't.

'You must, Amy,' said Mrs. Morland, 'because you noticed them. All speckled down the front.'

'Do you mean those stockings you had on the evening the Crawleys came to dinner and I thought you must have put them on by mistake?' said Mrs. Birkett.

'And what evening was that?' said Mrs. Morland, so portentously that all her hearers and especially Lydia felt that they would burst with so much mystery.

Mrs. Birkett said with a tinge of impatience that it was the evening the Crawleys came.

'And the day the *Royal Oak* was sunk,' said Mrs. Morland.

She then looked round her as if confident that everyone must now understand everything. But Mrs. Keith, who was never very good at understanding things and had the dogged character of the rather stupid, said One thing at a time and what Lydia had asked was Whose fault it was, though what the fault was about she could not now remember.

'It all hangs together,' said Mrs. Morland, 'and I was just explaining to Lydia about my stockings. You see, Tony and I were in France when all this trouble began and most luckily I read in someone else's old *Times* that there was going to be a railway strike in England, so I said really if there were going to be a strike we had better be at home. So we came back in great discomfort and crossness and of course when we got back the strike was off. Then Tony and I went down to High Rising and did the black-out which was very difficult because my cook Stoker doesn't approve of it and then the last straw came.'

She stopped and looked vengefully into the distance.

'Yes, Laura,' said Mrs. Birkett encouragingly.

Mrs. Morland started, tucked a strand of hair behind one ear and began in a very noble narrative style.

'I had blacked out everything,' she said, 'except the kitchen and scullery, because Stoker said if Mr. Reid at the shop was the Air Raid Warden we were all right. It was a fine evening and I hadn't drawn the curtains yet and I waited to take a sixpenny bottle of ink and some manuscript from my bedroom where they really had no business down to the drawing-room. I began carrying them downstairs, but the landing was rather dark. I was just going to turn the light on when I suddenly remembered that the curtains weren't drawn. So I determined to go on, very carefully. But I stumbled a little, just where that bit of carpet is always getting loose at the corner and the ink bottle fell on to the floor, and the cork came out, and a shower of ink spurted over the floor and over my stockings.'

She paused and glared at her audience with the expression of the Delphic Sybil.

'I can forgive a great deal,' said Mrs. Morland. 'Air raids are air raids and there they are, and Stoker got the ink off the floor, but there is one thing I shall never forgive and that is that pair of stockings. It isn't as if I had a pair on with darns in the heels. They happened to be new, and that is what I cannot forgive. And when I think who it is that deliberately made me spill ink on my stockings and makes it impossible to know who will be a refugee at any given moment, you will understand my feelings.'

By this time Mrs. Morland had, by her remorseless logic, left all her friends in various degrees of bewilderment. Mrs. Keith had long ago given up any attempt to follow the argument and was thinking about the sheet that had come home from the laundry with a corner torn. Mrs. Birkett was thinking that they really must be going soon. But Lydia, scenting high romance, could hardly contain her interest.

'Do you mean, Mrs. Morland, that you are always going to wear those stockings when anything awful happens like London being blown up, or Peace?' she asked.

But her question was never answered. The drawing-room door was opened, a kind of vision of men in khaki struggling with Palmer was seen, and two uniformed figures appeared, one of whom came quickly forward.

'Colin!' Lydia shrieked at the top of her voice, and flung herself into the arms of her brother.

Colin gave her a hearty hug and putting her firmly aside went to his mother on the sofa. Mrs. Keith, suddenly looking much younger, sat up and greeted her son with joy. Mrs. Birkett was also delighted to see him, for he had been a junior master at Southbridge School for a term a few years ago. Mrs. Morland was added to the party and a happy confusion reigned.

Meanwhile the second arrival stood by the drawing-room door, smiling in an amused way at the family hubbub. Colin was explaining to his mother that he had wanted to arrive unannounced, but Palmer had not seen eye to eye with him, which accounted for the fracas at the drawing-room door.

'If I hadn't had Noel with me,' he said, 'I think she'd have won. Where is Noel? Has he gone to help Palmer in the pantry and soothe her ruffled spirits?'

'Indeed I haven't,' said Noel Merton indignantly, 'but I felt that the homeless wanderer should not intrude on the family circle in this moment of reunion. How are you, Mrs. Keith?'

He came over to the sofa and kissed Mrs. Keith's hand, a gesture which filled his friend Lydia with mingled admiration and contempt.

'Hullo, Noel,' she said. 'I know what's wrong with you. You're an

officer. Why didn't you tell me? I thought you were much too old to
be in the Army.'

'So I was,' said Noel Merton, 'but a friend of mine said that my
quick mind and trained intelligence, not to speak of my distinguished
bearing, would benefit any army. So he got me a second lieutenant's
uniform and here I am.'

Everyone knew that Noel was doing himself less than justice, but
judged it more tactful to let him tell his story in his own way. After a
few moments' talk Mrs. Birkett collected Mrs. Morland and took her
away. Mrs. Keith evidently wanted to have a motherly talk with Colin,
so Noel, disregarding Colin's piteous signs of distress, carried Lydia off
to the library.

'First of all,' said Lydia, stopping and looking at him with a housekeeper's eye, 'do you want to stay the night?'

Noel said he would like it of all things if not inconvenient.

'Don't be silly,' said Lydia severely. 'You know it'd always be convenient. I will just go and tell them about a room for you — you can
have Robert's that we keep for him — and dinner. I shan't be a
second.'

She strode resolutely towards the kitchen. Noel Merton, left alone,
stood by the fire in amused and faintly melancholy meditation. A few
years ago, when he first became acquainted with the Keith family, he
had mapped out his career very neatly for himself. He was doing very
well at the bar and intended to do better. He had a large circle of friends
among whom he was much in request for dinners, dances, week-ends,
shooting, yachting, and the hundred agreeable activities that life offers
to a rising young man with pleasant manners. Marriage, he had decided,
was not in his line, and he infinitely preferred to amuse himself with
charming married women who could keep the shuttle-cock of heartwhole flirtation briskly flying. There had been a moment when his
heart was gently attracted to Lydia's sister Kate, but the attraction had
been so slight that it died in the bud at the moment when he found that
Everard Carter was in love with her, and now, in spite of his admiration
for Kate's sterling qualities and sweet temper, he was very thankful that
he had stopped when he did, for to be bored was no part of his scheme.
At that time Lydia had been an extremely bouncing and irrepressible
schoolgirl, and why these two so very different creatures had become
great friends nobody could understand. Mrs. Keith, seeing her younger
daughter, still in her revolting school uniform, carry off the much-
sought-after barrister as captive of her bow and spear, had been considerably flustered and prophesied woe. But as she really minded
nothing very much except novelty, her apprehensions soon wore off,
the more so as her younger son Colin who was reading law in Noel
Merton's rooms liked him very much and often brought him down to
Northbridge Manor.

Here it had become Noel's custom to pass a good deal of his time with Lydia with whom he walked, played tennis, and had endless discussions about life and literature. Lydia, for whom life had very few fine shades and literature meant the books she happened to like, began to apprehend through Noel that there were other worlds where her violent and downright methods might not pass muster, where there were values of which she was ignorant. Like many wilful natures she could be very docile where she was conscious of meeting her match, and had a natural quickness of wit that told her what to copy. Noel had never deliberately tried to alter or improve his young friend, liking her very well indeed as she was, but from time to time he was amused and a little touched to see Lydia modifying her uncompromising manner of speech and judgment by something he had said, or repeating as an original and striking thought something he had told her.

As for being in uniform he was nearly as surprised as Lydia. Nothing had been further from his thoughts when he last stayed with the Keiths in August. Looking at his age and his entire want of military qualifications he saw nothing for it but to go on as he was and make the best of it. Various applications for employment in the fighting services had led nowhere and he was reduced to frank envy of Colin who, like Philip Winter a Territorial, had gone into camp about Bank Holiday and had remained in the Army ever since, enjoying himself on the whole and putting on a stone and three inches round the chest. Then suddenly a highly placed friend had sent for Noel and in a short mysterious interview had asked him if he would feel like doing some Intelligence Work. Noel said he would like it very much and within three days he found himself a Second Lieutenant. Upon this he ordered a very good British warm from his tailor and went off to a place whose name was never mentioned (though quantities of people knew where it was) to do a very severe intensive course with twenty or thirty other temporary subalterns many of whom turned out to be personal friends in various walks of life. From this course he had just emerged with a week's leave, and meeting Colin Keith in town, also on leave, had accepted his invitation to come down to Northbridge for a night.

Although Northbridge Manor was outwardly unchanged he was conscious of a difference. His welcome was as warm as ever, the garden lay steeped in sunset autumn peace, Lydia was arranging for his comfort but he was not altogether part of it. He had a journey before him, whither and for what purpose he did not yet know, whether to some place overseas or to an office in Whitehall or elsewhere, whether a voyage for the body or for the mind. But as soon as the traveller knows he must be gone, he has already left the place that has been his home, and though Noel was in his own country and among old friends, he felt that a thin sheet of glass was between him and them. There would be much in his new life that he could not share with them and a part of him

would from now onwards have reticences where he had been used to
speak very much at his ease. Then he told himself that he was being
fanciful, but he knew that he wasn't, and was very glad when Lydia
crashed back into the room.

'I *am* glad you and Colin have come,' said Lydia. 'Mother hasn't
been very well and it will cheer her up like anything. It seems frightfully
funny you being a Second Lieutenant and Colin a Captain though.'

Noel said he had every hope of turning into a Captain before long,
as he was going to meet all sorts of people who simply couldn't speak
to anything as low as a subaltern.

'Will you vanish into the unknown like Richard Hannay and then
turn up at Constantinople or somewhere?' said Lydia. 'I'll write to you
all the time. Where are you going?'

Noel explained that he didn't know and even if he did he wouldn't
be allowed to say, but if Lydia would write to his chambers her letters
would all be faithfully passed on.

Lydia was silent for a moment and then asked how he thought her
mother was looking.

'Not so well as I'd like,' said Noel without hesitation, knowing that
Lydia required facts.

'Nor as I'd like either,' said Lydia. 'Dr. Ford says she must be very
careful. We had a ghastly time with evacuee children for a month. Six
children and two teachers. I think they really made Mother so ill,
because they worried her so.'

'Poor Lydia,' said Noel.

'Poor Mother, you mean,' said Lydia. 'But a most fortunate thing
happened which was that all the children were so revolting, and the
teachers, who were called Miss Drake and Miss Potter but they called
each other Draky and Pots, did nothing but walk about the garden with
their arms round each other's waists, that Dr. Ford went and bullied
the Billeting Officer like anything and they were all moved to Southbridge. Oh Noel, I *am* pleased to see you.'

'So am I,' said Noel, 'as pleased as anything. And I hope you won't
get any more evacuees.'

Lydia said not, because her father had offered to take troops if
Barchester was too full and had said he would rather have a hundred
of the Barsetshire Light Infantry camping in the grounds, with the run
of the squash court, tennis court, and billiard room, than one child or
one teacher.

'It took three coats of whitewash and two coats of paint to make the
rooms where the children were not smell of child,' said Lydia, 'not to
speak of the teachers being so horrid to Palmer that she nearly gave
notice.'

'I expect Palmer was pretty horrid to them too,' said Noel.

'She was,' said Lydia, 'I am glad to say. But it made Mother have a bad heart attack, because Miss Drake and Miss Potter came and were very red in the drawing-room.'

'Red?' said Noel.

'Red, Communist, you know what I mean,' said Lydia. 'Being very rude and arguing about Russia. I was over at the Vicarage helping them to make marrow jam or it wouldn't ever have happened. Would you like a drink before dinner?'

Noel said it was his heart's desire. Lydia mixed cocktails very professionally and handed one to Noel.

'I believe I ought to say "All the best" or something in that line as I'm an officer,' said Noel, 'but it goes against the grain. Here is to your health.'

'And to yours,' said Lydia. But instead of drinking she paused and set her glass down again. 'Noel,' she said very earnestly, 'could you tell me something?'

'Short of betraying my country's secrets I'll tell you anything,' said Noel.

'Do you think Mother is going to die?' said Lydia.

Used as Noel was to his dear Lydia's straightforward ways, he was taken aback by her question. He had no particular experience of people with hearts, but seeing Mrs. Keith after an interval he had been struck and indeed horrified by the change in her appearance. His first thought was to tell a thumping lie and say he had never seen her look better; his second thought was that Lydia believed in him so much that he could not dare to wreck that belief by a lie which she would undoubtedly detect; and between the two he hesitated for a fraction of a second too long.

'Don't say anything,' said Lydia. 'Anyway it's a good thing I'm here to take care of her. And I've made her let me do the house accounts and Father lets me do the estate accounts and go round the place with him, and Robert tells me about the family finance, so I can be a bit of help. I did think it would be fun to go as a V.A.D. to the Barchester Hospital with Delia Brandon and Geraldine, but one can't expect to have fun all the time, can one? You'd better go and get washed for dinner now.'

Noel did as he was told, as indeed most people did when Lydia took their interests in hand. While he was washing his hands and hunting for the clean handkerchief which, together with his other scanty effects, Palmer had unpacked and hidden with as much virtuosity as if he had brought two cabin trunks, he reflected again upon Lydia. That Lydia, the domineering, the devil-may-care, the rebel from domesticity, should have turned into a housekeeper, a thoughtful guardian of her mother's frail health, a useful companion to her father, was a change for which, in spite of his fondness for her, he was not at all prepared. He could only suppose that seeing her again after an interval in which so much had happened had made him notice what had been slowly going on for some time. Although he could think of few things more revolting than to be a V.A.D. with that dull Geraldine Birkett at the Barchester Hospital, he quite realized that Lydia had made a considerable sacrifice in giving up her plans. The more he thought of her general conduct the more admirable it appeared to him. He stood in a trance, the damp towel in his hands, considering the change from the Lydia who had so ungracefully taken possession of him a few years ago to the Lydia who appeared to be thinking sensibly and affectionately of the needs of others; and not of new and romantic friends, but of her parents, a creature which few of his younger friends considered as human in any way. And yet the same violent, confiding Lydia. The gong sounded and he went downstairs.

Mr. Keith had got back by this time and was quietly delighted to see Colin and had a friendly greeting for Noel. He had meant to give up the solicitor's office in Barchester altogether that summer, leaving it in Robert's capable hands, and retire to the management of his little estate, but the turmoil of the world had made it impossible. Robert who had been taking on various important unpaid jobs in the town and the county found himself needed for many more, and could not give the necessary time to the office. One of the younger men had, like Colin, gone into camp with the Territorials in August and remained there, another had been called up for the Air Force, so Mr. Keith had gone back to his work and made himself useful in every department. At the same time his bailiff, a retired naval man, had vanished at the call of the Admiralty, and he found himself with more work than he ever thought at his age to be doing. When Lydia said she helped with the accounts she was understating. The bailiff had been a great friend of hers, and with him she had learnt in the last two years all that he could teach her about the farm and the men, so when he left she informed her father that she would look after everything, which with the help of the head cowman, to whom the bailiff had bequeathed her as a valuable legacy, she did. Mr. Keith was at first nervous about the experiment, but finding that Lydia was perfectly pleased to discuss things with him, he allowed her to go her own way, though whether he could have stopped her is another question.

To Noel's amusement the earlier part of dinner was devoted to a discussion of cows and winter kale, upon which subject Lydia imparted her views with great freedom. After that the conversation ran upon books, a concert or two that Lydia had heard in town, a little legal business on which Mr. Keith asked his younger son's views with pleasant pride, and the continued horribleness of Miss Pettinger, who was now housing the Hosiers' Girls Foundation School and being as overbearing to their very nice Headmistress as she could possibly be.

No one wanted to hear the nine o'clock news, for as Mrs. Keith truly said one could read all the disgusting things that had happened in *The Times* next day, and it was better to be depressed in the morning than at night.

'And,' she said, 'you *read* the paper, instead of hearing those ladylike young men talking from Bangor or wherever they are.'

Lydia said she expected if *The Times* could speak it would have a voice like that but luckily it couldn't.

Colin said he had taken to the *Daily Express* and found it wonderfully soothing because he now knew exactly what to think and needn't ever be broadminded again.

'Quite right too,' said Lydia. 'No one ought to be broadminded now. I'm not.'

No one contradicted her.

Mr. Keith said he could bear anything, even the Income Tax, if only *The Times* would stop fiddling about with the Crossword Puzzle and put it in its proper place, down in the right-hand corner of page three or possibly page five. And as for putting it in that small print, he would take in the *Daily Telegraph* if it went on. One must have something to cling to in this world of shifting values, he said, and the Crossword appeared to him to be essential. In this he was heartily supported by the company, with the exception of Mrs. Keith who had never yet succeeded in grasping the principle of the crossword.

At about ten o'clock Lydia said she was going to bed if no one minded, as she had to go round the farm next morning before she went to Barchester to a Red Cross meeting and then on to lunch with Mrs. Brandon at Pomfret Madrigal about a sewing party. Noel escorted her to the drawing-room door.

'I just wanted to ask you,' said Lydia, 'if you've got everything you want. I've got some spare tooth-brushes if you didn't bring one. I don't suppose I'll see you again if you are going up with Colin as I shall have my breakfast early.'

'I have got a toothbrush, though Palmer thinks poorly of it,' said Noel, 'and has hidden it behind my sponge instead of planting it bravely in the toothbrush vase, or whatever it is called. But thank you all the same. You are as good as Kate at making people comfortable.'

'I *couldn't* be,' said Lydia, genuinely surprised.

'Well, you are,' said Noel, but did not add and a great deal more amusing, because he knew that Lydia's loyalty to Kate would resent such a remark. 'And I'll come down to your early breakfast if you'll tell me when.'

'No, honestly don't,' said Lydia. 'I never know how early I'll be and you ought to sleep. Let us know next time you get leave.'

Noel promised that he would and furthermore pledged his word not to leave England without coming in person to say good-bye. Lydia hesitated and then said:

'Would you mind if I asked you one more thing, Noel?'

'Not a bit,' said Noel.

'When you said about sending letters to your chambers to be for-warded, you didn't mean because you thought I'd tell anyone where you were if it's a secret, or be a Traitor, did you?' said Lydia earnestly.

'If I am allowed to tell my address to one single person you shall be the one,' said Noel. 'Even my clerk doesn't know. He only sends them on to a mystic address at the War Office.'

Lydia wrung his hand violently and went upstairs.

'And Lydia,' Noel called after her, 'do give Mrs. Brandon messages from me. That woman is the joy of my heart.'

'All right,' shouted Lydia and continued her journey upstairs. In the intervals of having her bath and getting into bed she thought with some pride of the compliment Noel had paid her. That it was untrue she well knew, for no one could make a home as really comfortable as Kate did, and Lydia was only too conscious of how far she fell short of that ideal, but that Noel should even pretend that she was as good as Kate made her heart feel comfortably warm. The thought of a heart suddenly roused some slightly unpleasant echo. She got into bed and opened *Wuthering Heights* in which she was at present indulging, but the echo teased her so much that she shut her book and turned out the light.

To-morrow she must get round the farm by ten o'clock. She would take her car and go straight on to Barchester getting there before eleven and then take Pomfret Madrigal on the way home. The echo sounded again. A heart. The joy of a heart. She knew that Noel and Mrs. Brandon, who were both quite grown-up, talked in a way that she did not quite understand though she looked with tolerance upon their childishness. But suddenly because of a word Noel had said, a light word she knew, spoken with his customary exaggeration, she felt far more like a child herself than was pleasant. She liked Mrs. Brandon very much and admired her looks and ways without the slightest wish to imitate them, and to envy her had never for a moment crossed her mind. So she decided not to envy her. After all Noel had promised to tell her and her alone what his address was, if he was allowed to tell, and on this comforting thought she fell asleep.

VII

MRS. BRANDON AGAIN

LYDIA, after a good night's sleep, had her breakfast early, went round the farm, spoke severely about a cow and a hedge, and pursued her way to Barchester. The Red Cross meeting was at the Deanery, so she drove into the Close and parked her car. In the drawing-room she found Mrs. Crawley sorting a number of papers in a very efficient way.

'Good morning, Lydia,' said Mrs. Crawley. 'You are the first. Octavia is so sorry she won't see you. She is on night duty at present and has just come off and had her breakfast and gone to bed.'

'Can I go up and see her?' asked Lydia.

Mrs. Crawley rather unwillingly gave permission, and Lydia went upstairs. The Deanery, a fine early Georgian house, was as inconvenient as it was beautiful. The low rooms on the ground floor made excellent libraries and offices for the Dean's work, and the lofty white panelled rooms on the first floor with their tall sash windows overlooking the Close were perfect for entertaining, but after that the house split up into so many staircases and corridors and small bedrooms carved out of large bedrooms, and bathrooms carved out of nowhere, that many of the inferior clergy who hadn't a sense of direction and were afraid to ask the servants had wretched memories of a night under the Dean's hospitable roof, unable to find a bathroom and late for dinner. Until the middle of the nineteenth century the Deanery had been little changed. The Arabins it is true had put in a bathroom about the year 1876, but this was a massive affair in a heavy mahogany surround with a battery of taps called Sitz, Douche, Plunge and other ominous names, hitting the unwary visitor full in the tenderer parts of his (for no lady visitor ever used it) anatomy with jets of water sometimes scalding, sometimes ice cold. It was set up in a large dressing-room (for there were then no small ones) thus making it impossible to put a married couple into the West Room and wasting a very good brass double bedstead with a good feather mattress on single members of the Church of England, though not on professed celibates for such Dean Arabin did not tolerate, broad-minded as he was in other ways.

This state of things continued till the beginning of the twentieth century when a bachelor Dean, ex-Master of an Oxford college, angrily had the bath removed on the ground that a flat tin bath was good enough for him and hence for anyone else. After his death the new Dean, who had married a grand-daughter of old Mr. Frank Gresham, who used to be Member for East Barsetshire, with a fine fortune, had modernized the house as above described and after a running fight with the Ecclesiastical Commissioners, conducted with great spirit on both sides, had got his own way at his own expense, and so cut the bedrooms up that four bathrooms and a servants' bathroom had been extracted from the existing rooms.

The present Dean and Mrs. Crawley, who were comfortably off for their station, left things much as they were and loved the house so much, though it was expensive to keep up, that they never repined. Indeed they often had cause to bless their predecessor for making something of a rabbit warren, as otherwise their eight children would have had to sleep several in a bed. All these children were grown-up and most of them married, and Octavia, the only one left at home, was able to have the biggish room on the second floor looking into the garden and down the river for her own, with easy access to the third best bathroom.

Here Lydia found her fellow bridesmaid in dressing-gown and pyjamas, looking out of the window with a pair of opera glasses.

'Hullo,' said Lydia. 'Your mother said you were in bed.'

Octavia turned round and explained that she was looking across the river at the hospital.

'I should have thought you saw enough of it,' said Lydia. 'Have you any patients?'

'Three,' said Octavia proudly, 'and two of them are in my ward. They were on anti-aircraft and fell over a pig in the dark and one got a broken wrist and one had shock; shell-shock it would be if the pig had been a shell.'

Lydia said that was better than nothing, or even than one patient.

'Yes, but the snag is,' said Octavia, 'that Matron who is the limit, is putting one of my patients into D. Ward and Geraldine will get him. Sister is furious and so is Delia. I can't see the sense in a war if there aren't any casualties. I wish my people had let me drive an ambulance. Ambulances quite often run over people in the black-out.'

Lydia looked admiringly at her single-hearted friend, though she could not feel her enthusiasm, and asked what Octavia wanted to look through opera glasses for.

'Delia promised she'd wave a swab out of the window at eleven o'clock if Matron really takes our patient away,' she said, 'and I was waiting. Have a look. It's the fourth window from the left on the top floor.'

Lydia adjusted the glasses and looked earnestly at the hospital. The cathedral bell boomed eleven times.

'There's something waving,' she said, handing the glasses to Octavia, 'but it's bigger than a swab.'

'It's probably a draw-sheet then,' said Octavia without interest, and drawing the curtains she got into bed. 'I wish I could get a first-aid job in a munitions factory. People get blown up or caught in the machinery there.'

'Well I must go to the meeting,' said Lydia, and went down again.

In the drawing-room she found nine or ten ladies already seated in a kind of semi-circle in front of Mrs. Crawley's writing-table at which Mrs. Crawley, the convener of the meeting, was sitting. Among the audience Lydia recognized young Mrs. Roddy Wicklow whose husband was Mrs. Foster's brother, the Archdeacon's daughter from Plumstead, and some friends of her mother's of great worthiness and dullness. At the far end of the semi-circle were Mrs. Birkett and Mrs. Morland, and to them Lydia betook herself.

'Are we all here?' said Mrs. Crawley.

Everyone looked at everyone else.

'Well, I am not really here,' said Mrs. Morland, 'but as I am staying at Southbridge, Mrs. Birkett thought it would be all right.'

Mrs. Birkett explained that her friend Mrs. Morland was staying with her for the present and was helping her with the Red Cross in Southbridge, so she was sure Mrs. Morland would be a welcome addition to the committee.

Mrs. Roddy Wicklow turned her large dark timid eyes upon Mrs. Morland and asked in a whisper if it was THE Mrs. Morland.

One of the dull worthy ladies said with a laugh that none of them would dare to read Mrs. Morland's next book as she was sure Mrs. Morland would have a scene about a Red Corss committee. Mrs. Morland, who detested being recognized in her professional capacity more than anything, tried to smile. Another dull worthy lady said she had been asking for Mrs. Morland's new book at Gaiters' Library ever since the beginning of September but it was always out and she felt sure Mrs. Morland would be pleased to know how popular her books were. Mrs. Morland again tried to smile, though nothing is more annoying than to be told that people can't get your book because Messrs. Gaiters or P. B. Baker & Son, Ltd. will not buy a few more copies. The second dull lady, leaning across the Archdeacon's daughter, said to the first dull lady, Whom *do* you think she had seen in the Close as she came along but Canon Banister, at which the first dull lady laughed and the Archdeacon's daughter said Well now they would be hearing what really *did* happen at the funeral. All the Barchester ladies then talked at once till Mrs. Crawley, who had finished writing some notes, said that they were delighted to welcome Mrs. Morland and all remarks must be addressed to the Chair.

During the brief silence that followed, the minutes of the last meeting were taken as read.

'And now,' said Mrs. Crawley, 'I have to put before you a special appeal for books from the Barchester Hospital.'

A lady got up and said she was so very sorry she must be going, but she had a teacher billeted on her who had to have lunch at twleve and she must get home as she couldn't manage separate lunches. Another lady said she was afraid she must go too, as her three evacuees also had to have lunch at twelve to attend afternoon school and she didn't like to leave it to her one maid. Two more hostesses had to leave at the same time, one to take her evacuee boy to the doctor because she felt sure it was impetigo whatever anyone might say and *such* a nice bright little fellow, the other to receive an angry father and mother from Dalston who threatened to remove their girl because the mother was expecting to have another baby and wanted Janice to look after the house as she wouldn't leave her husband and *such* a nice bright little girl it seemed really a pity, but what can you do. The first dull lady said that time alone would show whether evacuation had been a wise move. The second dull lady said that whatever the wisdom of the scheme there would be no two opinions as to the importance of removing young children and more particularly expectant mothers from danger areas. It was well known, she said, that many people were now a mass of nerves because they had been born during the last war after the air raids had begun.

'I must say,' said Mrs. Morland, following as usual a personal line of thought, 'that I have a very poor opinion of prenatal influence. Two of my boys were born in London during the war and are not nervous in the least, though I was, at least of the noise our own anti-aircraft guns made in Hyde Park, far far more frightening than any bombs exploding though I never heard one. But, on the other hand,' she added impressively in her deepest voice, 'a friend of mine who was perfectly sane and so was her husband had a baby which was born in 1913 and turned out a hopeless idiot, and is still alive, but of course in a home, where it will probably live for ever at great expense like people that are left annuities.'

Mrs. Roddy Wicklow, who was very kind, said it seemed dreadful about idiots but what was one to do, and as it was now twelve o'clock the meeting broke up and Mrs. Crawley said she would see about the books herself.

'Do come and see us soon, Lydia,' said Mrs. Birkett as she and Mrs. Morland took their leave.

'I'd love to,' said Lydia, 'but I don't know how the petrol ration will work out. I've put in for extra on account of Red Cross and working parties, but I mayn't get it. Anyway Sanders, our chauffeur, has a huge secret hoard somewhere.'

As Lydia went through the hall Mr. Needham the Dean's secretary came out of the small study, so obviously waylaying her that she stopped.

'I'm awfully sorry, Miss Keith,' he said, 'I don't suppose you remember me at Miss Birkett's wedding, but Mrs. Crawley mentioned at breakfast that you were going on to Mrs. Brandon's, so I wondered if you would mind taking me, as the Dean has gone to Courcy Castle in the car and my motor bicycle is being repaired where I ran into the market cross at High Rising in the black-out. Mrs. Brandon, whom I don't know, has very kindly asked me to lunch to meet the Vicar, Mr. Miller, who is an old friend of my father's, and his wife, and I can get a train back but there isn't any train before lunch except the 11.12.'

Lydia said of course.

'You know Miss Pettinger, don't you, Miss Keith?' said Mr. Needham.

Lydia said if you called a person being one's headmistress knowing them, she supposed she did.

'She will ask me to come in to social evenings after dinner,' said Mr. Needham plaintively, 'to meet Miss Sparling, the Headmistress of the Hosiers' Girls Foundation School, who is an extraordinarily nice person, and then she is rude to her and I feel so uncomfortable. I suppose one oughtn't to say one's hostess is rude, but she really is.'

'She's always been like that,' said Lydia, 'and I expect if I kept a High School I would be too. But why do you go? Can't you say the Dean wants you?'

'I would, even if it wasn't true,' said Mr. Needham, 'but she finds out from Octavia, who seems to like her, what evenings the Dean is out.'

'Of course Octavia was potty about Miss Pettinger at school,' said Lydia scornfully, 'and I must say she isn't much better now, only it's the hospital.'

'I think the way Octavia has taken her war work is magnificent,' said Mr. Needham firmly. 'Sitting in the hospital day after day with nothing to do. I almost find myself praying for a few casualties for her on Sunday.'

Lydia felt privately that Mr. Needham was much nicer when he didn't have a clergy-voice and that anyone who thought Octavia magnificent was potty too, but where a few years ago she would have expounded those views with the utmost frankness, she now merely accelerated and took the hill at Little Misfit at quite an alarming pace.

Stories, Mrs. Brandon's charming Georgian house, was looking its best in the peaceful late September sunshine. When Lydia stopped the car there was no sound. At least no natural sound, for something like the voices of children came from the house, and as Mrs. Brandon's son and daughter were unmarried there seemed to be no particular reason for it. Lydia, who was at home with Stories, opened the front door and was going into the drawing-room when Rose the parlourmaid appeared and taking up a Catherine Barlass attitude before the door said Mrs. Brandon was in her sitting-room. The babble of children was quite clear behind the door. Lydia, followed by Mr. Needham, went into the sitting-room. Here Mrs. Brandon was established on a sofa with a great bag of embroidery silks beside her. At the sight of her visitors she took off her large spectacles and got up, dropping her work all over the floor.

'Lydia!' she said, folding her guest in a warm, scented, unemotional embrace, 'I am so glad to see you. And Mr. Needham? You were going to bring him with you. At least Mrs. Crawley rang up just now to say that you were.'

'He's on the floor,' said Lydia.

Mr. Needham, who had chivalrously been picking up the profusion of scissors, needlecases, thimbles and material that his hostess had let fall, got up and shook hands.

'It is such a pleasure to have any friend of Mr. Miller's here,' said Mrs. Brandon, gazing into Mr. Needham's eyes.

Mr. Needham said he didn't exactly know Mr. Miller because he had never seen him, but his father had known him at college and he hoped Mrs. Brandon didn't mind. It was quite evident to Lydia that Mrs. Brandon was having her usual unconscious but quite inevitable effect upon Mr. Needham and she wished Delia were there, so that she could share the pleasure.

Mrs. Brandon said vaguely that old friends were such a help and she didn't know what one would do without them. She then looked so piercingly at Mr. Needham's neck that he began to wonder if his collar was dirty.

'Of course,' she said. 'Mr. Miller said you had been ordained lately, and now I see what he meant. I thought he said *it* was ordained, and I didn't know what. Of course you are a kind of relation of his now.'

Mr. Needham, unable to remove his eyes from Mrs. Brandon, said not a relation. It was only, he said, that his father had been at Mr. Miller's college. He didn't mean, he added stutteringly, that Mr. Miller had a college, but that Mr. Miller had been at his father's old college. He then felt that he might have expressed it all better and became dumb.

'I only meant a spiritual relation,' said Mrs. Brandon, looking, so Mr. Needham thought, exactly like a Murillo Virgin, for that was where his tastes lay. 'But Mr. and Mrs. Miller will be here soon and will explain everything. You will like Mrs. Miller so much. She was companion to my husband's old aunt and has been a perfect blessing in the parish. And her father was a clergyman too, but an odious one. I suppose I oughtn't to say that to *you*,' she added, suddenly stricken by conscience, 'but he was extremely Low Church, so I daresay you won't mind.'

'Mrs. Brandon,' said Lydia, who felt that her hostess had had a long enough innings, 'who are the children? Are you having evacuees?'

'Not exactly,' said Mrs. Brandon. 'I mean they aren't dirty or difficult, so I suppose they really have no right to the name.'

By severe cross-questioning Lydia managed to get from Mrs. Brandon a fairly reliable account of her guests, but it will save everyone's time and temper to explain in an omniscient way what had really happened.

When the question of receiving children from danger zones was first discussed, Mrs. Miller, who had taken on the ungrateful job of Billeting Officer, had been inspired to put all the children — luckily not a very large number, for Pomfret Madrigal was a small village with a very small Church School — into cottagers' houses. Here the eight shillings

and sixpence a week provided for the evacuees by a grateful if bewildered country were extremely welcome and the London children,
apart from their natural nostalgia for playing in dirty streets till midnight and living on fish and chips, settled down almost at once into the
conditions of licence, dirt, overcrowding and margarine to which they
were accustomed. The special Paradise, much envied by such children
as were billeted elsewhere, was Grumper's End, the congested district
of Pomfret Madrigal, and in that Paradise the most longed-for house
was the Thatchers'. Here Mr. and Mrs. Thatcher, with eight children
of their own, found no difficulty in housing four more, and to their
hospitable kitchen, where cups of strong tea and bits of tinned salmon
were almost always to be had for the asking or the taking, most of
Pomfret Madrigal's twenty evacuated children gravitated. As they only
went to school in the morning, the afternoon being kept for the village
children, they had played, screamed, fought, made mud pies, or fallen
into a little pond covered with green slime for four blissful weeks and
all called Mr. and Mrs. Thatcher Daddy and Mummy. As for Percy
and Gladys Thatcher, the children of shame of the two eldest Thatcher
girls, they had never enjoyed themselves so much in their very young
lives. Pulled about in an old soap box on to which Ernie Thatcher their
young uncle by shame had fixed wheels, stuffed with the sweets which
all the evacuee children bought with postal orders sent every week by
their parents, carefully instructed in all the latest bad words fashionable
in the select locality round King's Cross Station from which St.
Gingolph's (C. of E.) School had been evacuated, they became so overbearing that Mr. Thatcher said more than once that he'd have to take
the stick to them, while Mrs. Thatcher, feeling that with so many
children about everything was all right, went out charing from morning
to night, so that what with the money she earned and the money that
Edna and Doris, the mothers of the children of shame, were earning as
daily helps at the Cow and Sickle, which was doing very well owing to
officers' wives who wanted to be within reach of Sparrowhill Camp, Mr.
Thatcher was able to lose more on the dogs than ever and was later to
lose in the Football Pools an amount of money that earned him the
deep respect of everyone in the Cow and Sickle Tap.

As for the really difficult children, Mr. and Mrs. Miller, who were as
good as gold, had taken them into the Vicarage and though Mrs. Miller
had not the faintest hope of reforming them (for she was a very sensible
and practical woman) she managed to keep her eye on them to that
extent that they found it less trouble on the whole to do what The Lady
said. All the jobs she found for them in house or garden were cunningly
chosen to include dirt or destruction in some shape, and after a Saturday
on which they had helped Cook (of whom they were in as much awe as
their natures permitted) to clean out the flues of the kitchen stove, had
helped the gardener to fetch a load of pig manure from a neighbouring

farm, and to empty the septic tank near his cottage, they all burst into tears at the sight of their parents who came down on Sunday for the day to see them, hit at their mothers, used language to their fathers which surpassed anything that St. Gingolph's had yet produced, and said they would never go home.

At the beginning of all this trouble Mrs. Brandon had opened her purse with her customary generosity and said she would do her very best with any children that Mrs. Miller liked to send. But Mrs. Miller, who was as we have said extremely sensible, saw on the faces of Rose the parlourmaid and Nurse, Mrs. Brandon's faithful and tyrannical ex-nannie, exactly what opposition such a plan would meet. So with great cunning she discovered a little private nursery school which was anxious to get its young pupils out of danger, and taking advantage of a Saturday morning, which was the moment when Mrs. Brandon with Nurse's help did the fresh flowers for the church, cornered them both up against the chancel rails and describing the school, said she was at her wits' end where to billet it. In Nurse's eye she at once saw, as she had hoped, the lust for power over babies, ever near the surface with all good nannies, quickly rise. With Nurse's zeal and Mrs. Brandon's kind toleration, all difficulties were smoothed away, and within a few days ten very young children with two teachers were installed. The Green Room and the Pink Room were turned into dormitories for the children. The teachers were perfectly nice about sleeping one in each dormitory, and were given the Green Dressing-room as a sitting-room for themselves, while the large drawing-room was turned into a school and play-room, with a dining-room curtained off at one end. Mrs. Brandon and Nurse vastly enjoyed the fuss of having the best drawing-room furniture and the carpets stacked away in the spare garage, and furnishing the dormitories and schoolroom. Mrs. Brandon went so far as to say to her son Francis that the teachers had restored her faith in human nature.

'That is impossible, darling,' said Francis, 'because in the first place you don't understand human nature in the least and in the second you can't restore what you never lost. All I say is, don't put a refugee into my bedroom when I am waving a sword on the field of glory, or I shan't be able to come back a handsome though multilated cripple to drag out my last days in my ancestral home.'

'You know well, Francis, that the Army won't have you till you are young enough to register,' said Mrs. Brandon.

'I know what you think you mean, darling,' said Francis, 'which comes to much the same thing. What you are trying to say is that I am an aged dodderer, well above military age; damn it,' he added.

Any display of temper by Francis was so unusual that his mother was almost perturbed.

'It isn't that I want to hide you when the recruiting officer comes,' said Mrs. Brandon, her eyes brimming with unexpected tears—as unexpected to her as they were to her son. 'But in a wicked kind of way I can't help being glad that you are still a little over age.'

'You aren't wicked, bless you,' said Francis, hugging his mother with one arm, for he had his attaché-case in the other and was just leaving for the office where he worked in Barchester.

'I couldn't be anything as definite as that, I suppose, said Mrs. Brandon, with one of her rare flashes of insight. 'And I wouldn't let a refugee have your room if he were *starving*.'

'You mustn't say things like that, Mamma,' said Francis, much shocked, 'though I must say I'd rather think of an enemy alien in my bed than some of those Mixo-Lydian refugees over at Southbridge. They show a degree of determined ingratitude and unpleasantness that confirms me in my never-wavering belief that Mixo-Lydia will once again be a free and revolting nation. Bless you, darling. I must fly.'

After this explanation, or digression, it will be easy to see how what Mrs. Brandon nearly always managed to stop herself calling My War Work, was little or no trouble. Nurse, after looking at the teachers with the eye and nostril of a suspicious rocking-horse, and holding aloof in awful politeness for two days, was entirely melted on the third by being begged by Miss Driver, the senior teacher, to come and look at Baby Collis who wasn't quite the thing. After this she took Miss Driver and Miss Fielding, the second in command, under her wing, superintended much of the children's toilet and meals, and became so absorbed in what she would to Delia's indignation call 'Our Babies' that she quite forgot to keep up her enmity with Rose, and even allowed the head housemaid to mend Celia's stockings.

Rose now announced Mr. and Mrs. Miller. As all their friends know, the Vicar of Pomfret Madrigal and his wife, then Miss Morris, had cared for each other when they were young, had been separated by the very intransigent attitude of Miss Morris's father, the Rev. Justin Morris, about young Mr. Miller's High Church tendencies, and had not met for many years. After being companion to several old ladies Miss Morris had gone to old Miss Brandon at Brandon Abbey, and on her employer's death had been manoeuvred by Mrs. Brandon into the Vicar's company. The middle-aged lovers had made up their minds almost at once and had been married under the eye of Mrs. Brandon who had personally superintended Miss Morris's wedding outfit (which was a very neatly-cut coat and skirt, a felt hat, crocodile shoes and bag) and insisted on paying for it herself with such real kindness that Miss Morris could not refuse. Mrs. Brandon had also wished to give her an unassuming fox fur, but here Miss Morris was adamant. Not only did the expense seem to her almost wicked, but she had convictions about wearing fur, feeling very strongly that all fur-bearing animals were skinned alive and left to perish in slow agony while their hapless children starved. In vain did Francis Brandon point out to her that no fur hunter would be so wasteful and that practically all silver foxes were now bred on a commercial scale and well-treated, nay pampered, till the day of their unexpected and painless death. Miss Morris remembered reading something somewhere about ospreys, and went pink whenever the word silver fox was mentioned. So the idea of a fur was abandoned, but Mrs. Brandon got even with the new Mrs. Miller by putting a modern stove and a separate furnace for the hot water into the Vicarage while the Millers were on their honeymoon, which was Oxford, and Stratford-on-Avon, where they saw *As You Like It*. When the Vicar and his wife got back, Mrs. Miller could only thank Mrs. Brandon with her usual composure but in a tremulous voice, while the Vicar said Indeed, indeed a hot bath every day would be a luxury he had never expected and how truly kind Mrs. Brandon was. He then wondered privately whether the Ecclesiastical Commissioners would mind and hoped they wouldn't.

'So you are my old friend Needham's son,' said the Vicar, very kindly, as he shook the young man by the hand.

Mr. Needham, eyeing anxiously the cassock which he knew his present employer would strongly disapprove, said Yes in a mumbling sort of way.

'My dear,' said the Vicar, turning to his wife, 'this is Needham's boy. My wife.'

His pride, even after more than a year of marriage, in those two words, was so great that Mrs. Brandon felt her soul swelling inside her, but wisely said nothing about it.

Mrs. Miller, who had heard a great deal about Mr. Needham since her husband had discovered that he was secretary to the Dean of Barchester, and was quite prepared to see a young man in a clerical collar, bore up very well and shaking hands said, also in a very pleasant way, that she had heard a great deal about him and was so glad to meet him. Everyone then fell silent, while Lydia looked at the two clergymen with dispassionate interest, rather hoping that they might argue about the Thirty-Nine Articles; for she had been giving her attention to that admirable composition of late and was burning to air her views, but didn't see how to begin. Mrs. Brandon went on with her embroidery placidly, for she was one of those lucky beings to whom silences are never awkward.

'Ha!' said Mr. Miller at length. 'Yes; Needham. He rowed seven in the Lazarus Boat. "Mangle" Needham, we used to call him, but I can't remember why.'

Mr. Needham felt himself going crimson from the feet upwards and was dumb.

'How *is* your father?' said Mrs. Miller, who as the daughter and wife of the clergy was well used to keeping a mild conversational ball rolling.

'Oh, *Father*. He's awfully well, thank you,' said Mr. Needham. 'And so's Mother and both my sisters, and Father said to give his love to Goggers Miller. At least that's what he said, sir, I hope you don't mind.'

He stopped, paralysed by his own fluency. Mrs. Miller was sorry for anyone who so recklessly spent the whole of his small change of conversation in one breath. Mrs. Brandon chose some blue silk and threaded her needle.

' "Goggers",' said Mr. Miller, laughing. 'Indeed, indeed it is many a day since anyone called me by that nickname. I must tell you, my dear,' he added, turning to his wife, to whom it was his habit, partly from shyness, partly from affection, to address most of his remarks, 'the story of that name. It was just after the Summer Term of 1911, or possibly 1912. Needham and I and a man called Holroyd-Skinner, he was killed, poor fellow, in the early days of the war and I see his mother from time to time, but owing to her health she lives on the Riviera so it is only on her, alas, too rare visits to England that we meet, rowed down from Oxford to Kingston, spending the night at riverside inns, and on the second day we were discussing St. Thomas Aquinas, and somehow that name stuck to me.'

It was just as well that Rose announced lunch at that moment, or Mr. Needham, who was not accustomed to Mr. Miller's manner of speech, might have gone mad. Mrs. Brandon got up, dropping all her embroidery again, which the gentlemen precipitated themselves to pick up.

'What are you working at now, Mrs. Brandon?' said Mr. Miller.

'Well, I can't really call it work,' said Mrs. Brandon as they went into the dining-room, 'but Nurse made a lot of aprons for our babies of coloured linen, green and blue and yellow and I thought it would look so pretty if I embroidered them, so I am embroidering them. Mr. Miller, you will sit by Lydia, won't you; and Mr. Needham, come between me and Mrs. Miller. I am so sorry we are five, which is an odd number, but after all there is the Pentateuch, or do I mean Pentagon, isn't there, Mr. Miller?'

With which sop to the Church she smiled dazzlingly at her Vicar.

The excellent food and the excellent light wine soon restored animation and Mr. Miller and Mr. Needham talked happily across the little round table about Oxford. Mr. Miller had not heard that brick boat houses were beginning to supplement and were eventually to replace the barges, and nearly burst with sorrow at the news. The number of ways of getting illegally into Lazarus College was discussed and the Vicar was much interested to hear of a seventh way, unknown in his time and only made possible by the instalment in the Master's Lodgings of a second bathroom, which provided a drainpipe of very solid construction, a boon to Alpinists. Mrs. Miller and Lydia, wisely ignoring their hostess, discussed the possibility of a working party once a week

for such Northbridge and Pomfret Madrigal men as were in the Royal
Navy or the Royal Merchant Service, but owing to petrol rationing
were not quite sure if it could be arranged. Mrs. Miller said she knew at
least five workers who bicycled and Lydia undertook to rally some from
Southbridge, and as Mrs. Brandon had offered her dining-room for the
working party, there would be the added attraction of a very good tea.
After that Mrs. Miller and Mrs. Brandon had a very interesting conversation about the Vicarage stove, during which Mrs. Brandon
showed great intelligence, while Lydia listened attentively, conceiving
kitchen stoves to be part of her self-appointed work.

Just as they were finishing lunch, Rose came in and said Could Sir
Edmund Pridham see Mrs. Brandon.

'Well, he could if he came in,' said Mrs. Brandon, who was always
pleased to see her old friend and trustee, now busier than ever, if that
were possible, over committees of all sorts and every job that called for
a great deal of work and no pay. 'Come in and have coffee, Sir Edmund.
Here are the Millers, and you know Lydia Keith. And this is Mr.
Needham who came over with Lydia.'

'Another of your young men, eh, Miss Lydia?' said Sir Edmund, who
stuck to this charming if demoded address for young unmarried ladies.

'Of course not, Sir Edmund,' said Mrs. Brandon severely. 'Mr.
Needham is a *clergyman*, as you would see if you looked at him.'

'Afternoon, Mr. Needham,' said Sir Edmund, sitting down heavily
between Mrs. Brandon and Mr. Miller. 'No; no coffee, Lavinia. Makes
me bilious after lunch. I won't say no to a glass of port. Nothing to be
ashamed of if you were. Parsons often carry off the prettiest girls, eh
Miller?' said Sir Edmund, poking his Vicar in the waistcoat, or about
where the waistcoat, under a cassock, would be.

Mr. Miller felt, as he often did, that if his valued and excellent
Churchwarden could not control himself, he would have to give notice.
But Sir Edmund's poke was, he knew, inteded to imply that he, Mr.
Miller, had carried off one of the prettiest girls, and as in his eyes his
middle-aged wife was still the girl whose wind-blown hair he had gently
put aside on the day of the Church Lads' Brigade tea, more than a
quarter of a century ago, he could not find it in his heart to chide Sir
Edmund, and certainly had not the courage to do so.

'He's the Dean's secretary, Sir Edmund,' said Lydia.

'Which bedroom have they given you?' asked Sir Edmund, turning
on Mr. Needham. 'That last Dean's secretary had a room I wouldn't
put a dog in.'

Mr. Needham said, rather stiffly, that he had a very comfortable
room on the second floor looking out over the Close.

'Busman's holiday, eh?' said Sir Edmund. 'Anyone heard the one
o'clock news?'

'Well, everyone here was here at one o'clock and we didn't have it on.

so I don't suppose they have,' said Mrs. Brandon, with an air of great lucidity.

'Upon my word, Lavinia, you get sillier every day,' said Sir Edmund. 'Well, I haven't heard it either. Was over at Little Misfit at the British Legion. So we needn't talk about it. I won't have the wireless in my house. Never had one in the last war and won't have one in this war. Read my *Times* in the morning and that's that. Tell you what's wrong with this war though,' he added, looking round in a challenging way, 'it's not like the last one. Barsetshire Yeomanry in camp ever since the trouble began. Last time we had 'em out in France in three days and cut to pieces, by Jove, in the Retreat.'

Everyone knew that Sir Edmund, after commanding the Barsetshire Yeomanry with distinction for two years and taking more than a father's interest in his men, had been invalided out of the Army with a permanently crippled leg, and they respected his annoyance.

'We had men like Kitchener then,' Sir Edmund continued, 'and Beatty and Joffre. Not got them now.'

'Well, you couldn't,' said Lydia. 'They're all dead.'

'Good thing if I was too,' said Sir Edmund. 'Useless old man. I'd have a smack at the Boche now if I could. So'd you, young man,' he added, suddenly rounding on Mr. Needham.

Mr. Needham thought wildly of looking at his own collar in an appealing way, to show Sir Edmund his position, but the physical difficulties were too great.

'My dear Sir Edmund,' the Vicar protested.

'Don't talk to me about his cloth,' said Sir Edmund angrily, although the Vicar hadn't. 'What's the Church Militant for, eh? Eh, young man?'

Mr. Needham was heard to mumble something about military chaplains and the Bishop.

'Bishop of Barchester's an old woman and we all know that,' said Sir Edmund. 'Never you mind him, young man.'

Mr. Miller felt that as an unworthy son of the Church he could not listen to such subversive remarks, so although he disliked the Bishop as much as he had ever disliked anyone, he thought he ought to change the subject and reminded Sir Edmund that the following Sunday was the Day of National Prayer and he supposed the British Legion in Pomfret Madrigal would attend in full force.

'Bad thing when it comes to having a Day of National Prayer,' said Sir Edmund gloomily. 'It's all this Government. Wouldn't have had one if Churchill had been Prime Minister. Or Lloyd George. Mind you I never liked the man, never trusted him, in fact I'd have had him shot, but I'm a fair-minded man and I say it shows things are in a bad way. It's no good. I'm an old man and I don't understand these new ways, I suppose, but it's all beyond me.'

The Vicar, who was really devoted to Sir Edmund and knew his ceaseless care for and interest in every corner of the parish and every family that lived there besides all the work he did in the country, felt deeply sorry for his old friend. That a good deal of his grumbling was habit he was fully aware, but he was equally aware that Sir Edmund was cruelly troubled by the changing times and could not understand that 1940 was not 1914.

'Indeed, indeed, the times are troubled, Sir Edmund,' he said, 'but we must remember that we are all in God's hands.'

'I know we are,' said Mrs. Brandon earnestly, laying her hand on the Vicar's sleeve, 'and that is just what is so perfectly *dreadful*.'

This appalling truth drove everyone into a frenzy of unnecessary conversation which lasted until Sir Edmund went. The party then broke up, the Millers going back to the Vicarage for a Mothers' Meeting and Lydia taking Mr. Needham back to Barchester. Just as she was leaving she remembered Noel Merton's message and being a thoroughly conscientious girl gave it to Mrs. Brandon.

'How nice of Mr. Merton,' said Mrs. Brandon. 'If he is in Intelligence perhaps he could find a job for Francis. And there is our cousin Hilary Grant, who is due to be called up about the same time and speaks Italian so well, which would be very useful if they wanted anyone who can speak Italian. Will you ask him, Lydia?'

Lydia promised she would, took Mr. Needham aboard and set off for Barchester. Mr. Needham spoke at some length of the charm and virtues of Mrs. Brandon who, he said, was more like his idea of a saint than anyone he had ever met. Lydia listened kindly. She had given Noel's message to Mrs. Brandon, and Mrs. Brandon had at once suggested that Noel should find jobs for her son and her cousin, and this, she didn't quite know why, had been very soothing. Her liking for Mrs. Brandon remained undimmed, but her opinion of Mr. Needham fell slightly.

'I say, Mr. Needham,' she remarked, as they entered the Close.

'I wish you wouldn't say Mr. Needham,' said that cleric. 'Everyone calls me Tommy.'

'All right, Tommy then if you like, only of course you must say Lydia,' said Miss Keith, 'I suppose Octavia will be getting up soon.'

Mr. Needham said he thought about 6 o'clock.

'Then you'll be able to see her when you've done your work or whatever it is you do for Dr. Crawley,' said Lydia, determined that her friend should not suffer from Mrs. Brandon's fatal charm.

Mr. Needham said he sometimes went for a walk with his employer's daughter before she had dinner and went off to her night shift. Lydia nodded approvingly, wrenched Mr. Needham's hand in a way that reminded him of the time his wrist was broken in a rugby match in Wales, and careered away towards Northbridge and her responsibilities.

VIII

THE BISSELLS AT HOME

IN spite of Sir Edmund's gloomy views the Day of National Prayer passed off without incident. At Southbridge School Mr. Smith the chaplain preached to a large congregation of his own boys and the Hosiers' Boys, doing his best to say in one and the same breath that they must go on with their work as if nothing had happened, prepare themselves earnestly for what was before them, remember that the youth of all countries held the future of the world in their hands, and certainly not forget that the youth of certain countries had been so mis-led by what it was now the fashion to call totalitarian methods, though he was himself old-fashioned enough to believe in the Powers of Dark-ness, that the world's future must never be allowed to rest in its hands. But as everyone was used to him, no one minded.

At the Headmaster's House Mrs. Morland, who when she concen-trated was far from unintelligent, especially about other people's affairs, did a good deal of secretarial work for Mr. Birkett, worked away in-dustriously at her new novel and made a good many friends in the School. To her great surprise, for she was an unassuming creature, she found that a number of the masters and the older boys were among her constant readers. This she attributed largely, and possibly with some justice, to the fact that several of her books were now in a well-known sixpenny series, but it all cheered her up. Her youngest son Tony appeared to be very happy at Oxford, her invaluable cook Stoker sent her good accounts of her house at High Rising where her publisher's wife and children were now staying, so apart from a general feeling that she was of no use at all, she was happy enough.

For some time she and Mrs. Birkett had been in consultation about calling on Mrs. Bissell. It was publicly known that Mr. Bissell had taken Maria Cottage and there installed his wife, but no one had seen her, and Mr. Bissell had not been communicative. More than once Mrs. Birkett had said to Mr. Bissell that she would like so much to call on his wife. To each suggestion Mr. Bissell had replied that Mrs. Bissell was settling the things in. What the things were Mrs. Birkett and Mrs. Morland could not exactly understand, for Maria was fully furnished and news had reached them via the carrier, who was also the coals, that the Bissells' luggage had consisted of three suit-cases. But they felt that something was wrong and wished they had a book of etiquette that would tell them about calling on the wives of headmasters of evacuated schools.

'In Simla,' said Mrs. Morland, who had never been there, or indeed in any part of India, but had read a great many novels about Anglo-Indian life, 'you have a letter-box, at least whatever you do have in

India, on the front gate and when new people come they put their
cards in your box.'

Mrs. Birkett wondered how they knew which boxes to put them in.

'I suppose an A.D.C. or someone tells them,' said Mrs. Morland.
'But Amy, though it seems snobbish to say so, perhaps Mrs. Bissell
doesn't have cards.'

Mrs. Birkett thought this quite probable, which led to a discussion as
to whether people who didn't have cards would think it an offensive
act of Capittleism if people who had cards left them on them. As their
premises were based on entire ignorance the argument was very inconclusive. The only people who were known to have made Mrs. Bissell's
acquaintance were Miss Hampton and Miss Bent, but as Mrs. Birkett
didn't know them very well this did not help matters. Philip Winter,
whose friendship with those ladies, begun in the Red Lion bar and
ripened at Adelina Cottage, would have been a link, was at a place
known officially as 'somewhere within fifty miles of Bath', but known in
the Masters' Common Room, the School Debating and Literary
Societies, the Red Lion, and practically the whole of Southbridge as
Tiptor Camp, Nr. Bumblecombe, Somerset, and could not help.

The solution to this social impasse was at last provided by Mr. Bissell
himself, who under cover of returning a book on the Antiquities of
Barchester that Mr. Birkett had lent him, told Mrs. Birkett that Mrs.
Bissell had got things a bit settled and would be very pleased if Mrs.
Birkett would come to tea with her. Mrs. Birkett, who knew that tea
and Tea were different things, warily inquired what time Mrs. Bissell
was expecting them and was told four o'clock which was a relief, for
though she would willingly have gone to Tea at six or even six-thirty,
and eaten heartily for the sake of the School, she knew that she could
not eat another hearty meal at eight o'clock; and that would fidget her
husband.

'And do you think,' said Mrs. Birkett, 'that Mrs. Bissell would allow
me to bring Mrs. Morland?'

Mr. Bissell said that Mrs. Bissell had hardly liked to ask Mrs. Morland but would be very pleased, and on this double-edged statement
took his leave.

Accordingly Mrs. Birkett and Mrs. Morland walked down to Southbridge and knocked at the door of Maria Cottage (for the Vicar's aunt
had a brass Lincoln Imp for a knocker and refused to have a bell). The
door was opened by a small, plumpish woman with very neat hair and
a singularly sweet and placid expression.

'I said to myself,' said Mrs. Bissell as she ushered her guests into the
drawing-room, 'as I saw you cross the green, "That must be Mrs.
Birkett and Mrs. Morland." This is a great pleasure and I'm sure I'd
have asked you before, but it does take time to settle things.'

Mrs. Birkett, who had known Maria Cottage when the Vicar's aunt lived there, looked round. Every piece of furniture that could be moved had been placed cornerways instead of square. A tea-table was standing askew in front of the fire with a lace cloth laid diamond-wise upon it and five plates each with a small folded napkin lace-edged. There were two plates of sandwiches reposing on lace doyleys and a large cake on a doyley with fringes. In the corner of the room a little girl was playing with some coloured blocks.

'Come and say how do you do, Edna,' said Mrs. Bissell.

'I?' said the little girl.

'Now we know we mustn't say "eh",' said Mrs. Bissell.

'Wot sy?' said the little girl.

'No, Edna, we don't say "What did you say",' said Mrs. Bissell. 'What is it we *do* say?'

'Pardon,' said the little girl, who looked remarkably like an idiot.

'That's right,' said Mrs. Bissell cheerfully. 'And now come and say How do you do.'

'I?' said the little girl.

'I think we'll leave her for the present,' said Mrs. Bissell composedly. 'She is a dear little thing, a niece of Mr. Bissell's niece by marriage, but both her her parents were mentally defective. She was to be evacuated with the M.D. school, but she is liable to fits. In fact it has been quite a business deciding if she ought to be at an M.D. or a P.D. school — mentally defective and physically defective I should explain perhaps — so I said I would take her. She is really improving I think since we came down here with this beautiful air and we are getting on quite nicely with our lessons. She goes to the village school and is quite good, and if she looks like having a fit the mistress just phones me up and I come and fetch her.'

While she was speaking Mrs. Bissell had poured out tea, handed sandwiches, cut the cake, all with a placid efficiency that deeply impressed her visitors. Conversation then flowed pleasantly and genteelly on the weather and the school. Mrs. Birkett said, with great truth, what a pleasure it had been to her husband to work with Mr. Bissell. As she afterwards confessed to Mrs. Morland, she had perhaps given this praise rather in the manner of a Lady Bountiful and was justly rewarded for her pride, for Mrs. Bissell appeared to take all the praise as a matter of course and with perfect simplicity let her understand that Mr. Bissell had been quite relieved to find vestiges of civilization in a public school.

'Of course,' said Mrs. Bissell, 'the day of the public school is over. After this war we shall have nothing but State-supported schools. The same with Oxford and Cambridge of course. There won't be any place for young men to waste their time and their parents' money and be turned out useless burdens on the country. Mr. Bissell has supported himself with scholarships and grants ever since he was fifteen.'

There was something about Mrs. Bissell that made it quite impossible to resent her calm statements. Even Mrs. Morland, who always meant to be modest about her children and always failed, didn't like to mention that her sailor son had supported himself from an even earlier age than Mr. Bissell, though, owing to being much younger, not for so long; or that her two eldest boys had not for some years had any money from her except the voluntary (she would have refrained from saying handsome) presents she gave them for Christmas and birthdays; or indeed that Tony had contributed largely to his education from the day he took a Scholarship to the Senior School up till the present moment. For she felt certain that Mrs. Bissell would regard all such self-help as proof of the advantages accruing to the sons of Capittleists; though why the fact of her husband having died many years ago leaving her to earn the money to clothe, feed and educate four boys should make her be a Capittleist she could not see, but an inner instinct told her that Mrs. Bissell would see it in that light.

A shadow passed the window.

'I dare say you wondered,' said Mrs. Bissell, 'who that extra plate was for. That's for Daddy. He always gets home for a cup of tea. Pardon me, but he likes me to let him in.'

Accordingly she went to the front door ad returned with Mr. Bissell. Mrs. Morland and Mrs. Birkett on comparing notes afterwards found they had both expected Mrs. Bissell to admit an aged and decrepit father also living in Maria Cottage, so Mr. Bissell's appearance was a relief.

'Good afternoon, ladies,' said Mr. Bissell, who on crossing the threshhold had shed the schoolmaster and become the domestic host. 'Has Mother been looking after you?'

'Is your mother here too, then?' said Mrs. Morland.

Mr. Bissell explained that though he and Mrs. Bissell had the misfortune to have no chicks, they had always used those sweet old names and little Edna thought they were her real mother and daddy. The guests felt that little Edna was incapable of such a flight of reasoning but said nothing.

'And how do you like our little home?' said Mr. Bissell to Mrs. Birkett, who was loud in her commendation of his charms and with great tact said she liked the way Mrs. Bissell had arranged the furniture.

'Of course it's only our peedatair,' said Mr. Bissell, 'but Mrs. Bissell has quite the art of making a home.'

Mrs. Morland, feeling that as a woman of letters something was expected of her, said Mrs. Bissell had given the cottage a really homey atmosphere and she hoped the *pied-a-terre* (which she tried not to pronounce in too affected a way) would be their home for a long time.

Mr. Bissell said that Mother was quite a country girl having lived at Sevenoaks so it was quite like old times for her to be in the country again and little Edna looked quite different.

'And it must be so nice for you to have the school and the masters here,' said Mrs. Morland, nobly sacrificing herself in the cause of making conversation.

Mrs. Bissell was very noticeably silent.

'Of course I wouldn't say this officially,' said Mr. Bissell, wiping his mouth on the lace-edged napkin and pushing his cup away, 'but as we are all among friends and not speaking ex-cathedral, I must in honesty confess that some of my colleagues, though a splendid, loyal, conscientious, hard-working set of men,' said Mr. Bissell, obviously crushing down his lower self, 'are not exactly what I would call quite.'

His guests may have imagined that the sentence was not finished, but it evidently was.

'I know what you mean,' said Mrs. Morland, nervously pushing a stray hairpin into her skull. 'They haven't got that kind of broadness.'

'There you have hit the nail on the head, Mrs. Morland,' said Mr. Bissell, shifting himself and his chair along the floor nearer to her. 'Mr. Hopkins for instance, a fine scientific man with a very good degree from Aberystwyth, and excellent at keeping discipline, isn't exactly the type the Hosiers' Boys want. "Russia was all very well, Hopkins," I said to him no later than last Tuesday, "when she *was* Russia, but when — and we will let alone," I said, "any question of whether we should or should not have made a Trade Pact with her, for that is foreign to the trend of the present discussion — when," I said, "Russia deliberately plays into the hands of the Ryke, all I say is she has let the N.U.T. down, and that will go very heavily against her. And don't answer me, Hopkins," I said, "for I know exactly what you are going to say, and you can say it at the N.U.T. Congress and see how *they* take it." '

'Is Mr. Hopkins a Trade Unionist then?' said Mrs. Morland.

'National Union of Teachers,' said Mrs. Birkett hastily, hoping to retrieve the honour of the bourgeoisie, though without much hope.

'Of *course*,' said Mrs. Morland untruthfully. 'But everything's initials now and it is so difficult to remember. And then we call Russia, at least some people do but I won't, U.S.S.R. and the French, who are supposed to be so very logical, call it U.R.S.S., which being our allies seems quite unreasonable. But nothing will stop me saying St. Petersburg,' she added defiantly and looked round for support.

Mr. Bissell had gone mad once already under Mrs. Morland's divagations and it was clear that he was rapidly going mad again. He cast a frenzied glance at his wife who was taking it all very well, realizing that people like Mrs. Morland who wrote books must obviously be quite uneducated and were probably doomed. But it was a relief to everyone when Miss Hampton and Miss Bent were suddenly dragged into the room by Smigly-Rydz.

'Knew I'd find you here,' said Miss Hampton to Mrs. Birkett. 'Elaine told me you were coming and I saw you go in. Bent and I are going to the Phelps's. You'd better come too. The Admiral shakes a good cocktail. Well, Elaine, how's little Edna?'

'I never told you,' said Mr. Bissell proudly to Mrs. Birkett, 'that Mother's name was Elaine. Her father was a great reader of Tennyson and knew the *Idles of the King* by heart.'

'It's a lovely name,' said Mrs. Birkett, 'and very suitable,' and then she hoped she had said the right thing.

'You're right there,' said Mr. Bissell, casting a look of adoration at his wife that quite melted Mrs. Birkett. 'She'd have had all the Sir Galahads after her in the Olden Times.'

Mrs. Morland, who complained afterwards that she always coloured too quickly from her surroundings, said she was sure Mrs. Bissell didn't need a Sir Galahad with Mr. Bissell there, and was thoroughly ashamed of herself. But Mr. Bissell's lean tired face shone with gratitude.

Mrs. Bissell said Edna was a good girl and getting on nicely at school.

'Why don't you teach her yourself?' said Miss Hampton.

'I'd love to,' said Mrs. Bissell, 'but though I am no longer a member I fear it would be disloyal to the N.U.T.'

'My wife was a teacher before I married her,' said Mr. Bissell proudly. 'She did Psychology and understands all the complexes. She and Miss Hampton took to each other like ducks to water and many an interesting chat have we had, Mrs. Bissell on the theoretical side, Miss Hampton on the practical. Mrs. Bissell was offered the post of head-mistress in a very good secondary school.'

'I thought married teachers weren't allowed,' said Miss Bent. 'It takes a single woman to explain life to girls. Married women are one-sided in their views.'

'I did think of keeping on my job,' said Mrs. Bissell, 'and I discussed it very carefully with Mr. Bissell, but the Income Tax stood in the way. I should have been taxed on his income as well as mine, which made it hardly worth while. It is really much more economical to live in sin if it can be done without attracting attention. We discussed that alterna-tive quite frankly and decided that it wouldn't suit us as we are both home birds. Come along now, Edna, it's time to go to bed.'

'I?' said Edna.

'Put the blocks away, dear,' said Mrs. Bissell. 'Another way is to live with a woman. It is far more economical for Miss Hampton and Miss Bent to live together as they do than if they were married. Now put the lid on nicely.'

'Wot sy?' said Edna.

'We say "pardon", not "what did you say",' said Mrs. Bissell. 'You must excuse her, she's a wee bit tired. I must say I cannot quite agree with you, Miss Bent. I admit that one learns much at Teachers' Training Colleges, but it is all bricks without straw. I would advocate married teachers in every case, with a suitable amount of leave on half-pay with every child. But the Income Tax laws would have to be revised first. Say good night, Edna.'

'I?' said Edna.

'She's tired, poor little thing,' said Mrs. Bissell and picking up her adopted child she held it tenderly in her arms, smiling at it. Mrs. Morland afterwards maintained that Edna had smiled back at her, but Mrs. Birkett, who was more prosaic, said the child had shown no change of expression at all. Mrs. Bissell went upstairs with Edna. Mrs. Birkett said they must go and thanked Mrs. Bissell warmly for a delightful tea-party.

'Now you have once found the way you must come again,' said Mr. Bissell, and escorted the ladies to the door, which was tight work with five people in a very narrow passage. Smigly-Rydz pulled Miss Bent violently out of the drawing-room and fawned heavily on Mr. Bissell.

'No biscuits today, old fellow,' said Mr. Bissell, patting the dog's enormous head.

'Mustn't spoil him,' said Miss Hampton, getting out of the front door. 'He expects biscuits every time he comes.'

'He has a hopeful disposition,' said Mr. Bissell, by now entirely at his ease. 'I think Panderer must have been his sponsor.'

With this classical allusion he shook hands warmly with all his guests and went back into the house to wash up the tea-things.

'What *good* people,' said Mrs. Morland earnestly, as soon as they were out of earshot. 'They make me feel ashamed. When I saw them so fond of each other and so good to that dreadful idiot child, I felt I ought to go to Poland, or become a munition worker, though I don't suppose I could do either.'

'Saints, both of them,' said Miss Hampton. 'Drive you mad to live with, but saints all the same. She got a good one in on you and me, eh, Bent?'

And Miss Hampton laughed loudly.

'I don't agree with her at all,' said Miss Bent. 'I am perfectly prepared to pay Income Tax for the sake of my principles. What is the good of all the women like Rory Freemantle who have worn themselves out to make the world a safe place for us if we are not allowed to shoulder our part of the burden. If I had to pay Income Tax on Hampton's income to-morrow I would be proud.'

'Nothing to prevent you sending conscience-money to the Chancellor of the Exchequer to-morrow,' said Miss Hampton, 'but you won't. Coming into the Phelps's, Mrs. Birkett?'s

At any other time Mrs. Birkett would have refused, but so weak did she feel after the unexpected developments of her tea-party that she said After all she did owe Mrs. Phelps a call and might as well pay it now. So as they were now opposite the Admiral's house, they rang the bell.

Rear-Admiral Phelps was a retired naval man who had chosen

Southbridge for his retirement, bringing with him his wife and a grown-up daughter. He was a small dry-faced man, quiet and meek in the home, quiet and industrious in all forms of Social Service. There was hardly a Committee, an Institute, a Good Work of any kind in South-bridge on which he was not an active worker, besides being Secretary of the British Legion, the Boys Scouts, and the District Nursing Associa-tion, and one of the churchwardens, keeping the Vicar rigorously in order. His wife, a great, bouncing, masterful woman, was so exactly what one kind of Admiral's wife is supposed to be that it was almost like a miracle. She also took an immense and overpowering interest in village life, treating everyone as if she were on the quarter-deck; the Vicar as ship's chaplain, his wife as non-existent, such gentry as there were in Southbridge, a very small village, as captains and commanders, the higher-class tradesmen like Mr. Brown of the Red Lion as lieuten-ants and midshipmen, the lower class as warrant officers, and everyone else as ratings. For some time she had been unable to fit Miss Hampton and Miss Bent into her scheme, but appeared finally to have placed them as a kind of marines of an amphibious nature, as indeed they were. The Birketts, who did not live in the village, had given her some difficulty, until she decided that Mr. Birkett being in charge of some four hundred men and boys might hold brevet rank as a captain, and to Mrs. Birkett as the captain's wife she extended her friendship.

Mrs. Phelps was one of those happy women for whom wars are made and ever since September the 3rd had not been seen in a skirt except at church. She had become head of the local A.R.P. almost before it was thought of, and managed to combine these duties with running the Red Cross in the village, besides laying down a number of hens, rabbits and goats to save tonnage.

Her daughter Margot, who was as bouncing and masterful as her mother, though not yet so fat, seconded her ably in all her doings, and knitted at incredible speed a vast number of comforts for the Royal Navy. Her ill-wishers said she knitted during the sermon, but this was not true, and choir practice is quite different.

Jutland Cottage, as the Admiral had re-christened The Hollies when he took it on his retirement, was not only a centre for every village activity, but a port of call for any naval officer who had ever served with or under the Admiral. There was indeed a legend among the younger men that Mrs. Phelps had accompanied the Admiral on some of his cruises, bringing with her a cow and some poultry for personal use, but this would hardly be possible in the twentieth century, so we need not believe it.

Only a few intimate friends knew that the Admiral was often in pain from a wound received at the battle from which his house took its name, and even fewer knew how badly off the Phelps's were and with what courage they faced not only the rest of their own lives, but their daughter's future, for Miss Phelps was nearly thirty and so used to being regarded as a brother by the navy that nothing else had ever come into her head.

The Admiral himself opened the door. His guests walked in and were immediately enveloped in heavy black folds of some material and, as the Admiral shut the door, in complete darkness.

'To the left,' said the Admiral in his quiet precise voice. 'This is my light-lock for the black-out. A good invention, don't you think. You come in: no light can get out of the house through the curtain: you shut the door: then you turn left and come through into the sitting-room.'

Guided more by the sound of his voice than by his directions, the ladies extricated themselves from the folds, turned to the left and passing under a curtain held aside for them by the Admiral, emerged into the little sitting-room which was also hall, dining-room, smoking-room, and often a bedroom for visiting officers. Here Mrs. Phelps in blue serge trousers of a very nautical cut, her abundant bosom but imperfectly restrained by a blue serge zip-up lumber jacket, and a spotted handkerchief round her reddish-grey hair, was entertaining two young men in naval uniform whom she introduced as Tubby and Bill, and the Vicar. She warmly welcomed the newcomers and addressing the Admiral as 'Irons' told him to mix the drinks.

Mrs. Birkett begged to present her friend Mrs. Morland.

'Now, wait a minute,' said Mrs. Phelps. 'There's a Lieutenant Morland in the *Flatiron*. She's on the China station now.'

Mrs. Morland said she expected that was her third son Dick, as he was in the *Flatiron* on the China station.

'Dick, that's it,' said Mrs. Phelps. 'My husband had a destroyer in the Iron class and we take a great interest in them. He was Commander of the *Scrapiron* and Captain of the *Andiron* and was with the *Gridiron* on her trials. All his friends call him "Irons". I saw your boy at Malta two years ago, just before the Admiral retired. Tubby, you knew Dick Morland, didn't you?'

Tubby, whose other name is unknown to history, said Rather, and with very little encouragement told Mrs. Morland all about himself. Mrs. Morland, who on seeing so many naval men had suddenly thought that the heroine of her present novel might be rescued from the fangs of the Gestapo agent by an officer on leave listened with great attention, for though she did not exactly know what she wanted to ask, she knew that the strangely working mind that writes books for one would choose and remember a few points that would be useful, so she smiled on Tubby and drank her cocktail and let it all gently soak in.

Miss Hampton and Miss Bent, to whom one cocktail was as naught, tossed theirs off, but refused any more.

'Now, you must have another,' said the Admiral. 'Drinks are the last economy we are going to make. Must give our friends a drink when they come aboard.'

But Miss Hampton refused for herself and her friend, saying she had promised Joe Brown to be in the bar of the Red Lion at opening time and must keep a steady head. Mrs. Birkett had a shrewd guess that both ladies had a steadier head than most men and were really considering the Admiral's purse, and liked them none the less for it.

'These boys were torpedoed a month ago,' said Mrs. Phelps, 'and they are joining their ship to-morrow.'

Tubby tore himself from his conversation with Mrs. Morland to say it had been bad luck to be so long ashore and Bill broke a cheerful silence for the first time to say he wished he hadn't lost his ocarina with his kit, because he had never had a better one. Mrs. Birkett was just going to speak when Miss Phelps, dressed like her mother, but very muddy about the legs of her trousers, came in from the back of the house and said it had taken her half an hour to catch the goats and they weren't milked yet.

'And what's more,' she said, 'that Mrs. Warbury and her husband came by in their great whacking car and stopped and looked over the hedge and never even offered to help and then they had the cheek to say they were coming round to have a drink. Give me a strong one, Tubby, before they get at the bottle.'

'We can't refuse them drinks,' said Mrs. Phelps, to whom the laws of hospitality were sacred, 'but I'm sure they are spies. Mrs. Warbury has a refugee maid.'

'So have I,' said Miss Hampton. 'Loathe Mrs. Warbury like the devil, but must be fair.'

'Is that your Czecho-Slovakian?' said the Vicar, who had been talking quietly to Mrs. Birkett about the Restoration Fund.

'It was,' said Miss Hampton. 'But she would tell me how much better everything was in Czechoslovakia than in England, and I couldn't stand it. Got her a very good job in Barchester. No, it's a Pole now. Must support the Empire.'

'Oh, well, a Pole,' said Mrs. Phelps. 'After all that doesn't count. But Mrs. Warbury has an Austrian refugee and we all know what that means.'

Several people said Vienna was such an enchanting place before the last war, and how gay and courageous the Viennese were.

'Mrs. Warbury's maid *may* be gay and courageous,' said Mrs. Phelps, 'but I think she looks very suspicious, and I have told the Admiral repeatedly that he ought to do something about it. And the Warburys only changed their name from Warburg in the last war. The Admiral ought to get them interned. Especially their boy.'

Miss Hampton said he was a nasty piece of work and far too often in the Red Lion bar.

'Always there when Bent and I go in,' she said, 'cadging drinks and listening to what people say. To be quite fair, I don't know what he could find out there except the price of potatoes and what fat stock fetched last market day, but he isn't up to any good. When our men begin coming home on leave I shall keep my eye on him.'

'I have only met Mrs. Warbury once,' said Mrs. Birkett, 'at Mrs. Keith's at Northbridge Manor, and Mrs. Keith told me afterwards that she hardly knew her and she had literally pushed her way into the working party. Poor Mrs. Keith.'

Various other members of the party were about to express their dislike or their dark suspicion of the Warburys when the door-bell rang. The Admiral went to the door, visitors were heard making muffled sounds from among the folds of the curtains, and the Warburys came in. Mrs. Warbury we have already met. Of Mr. Warbury we need only say that any caricaturist wanting to draw a film producer would have been enchanted to see him, so exactly did his face, his hands and his cigar fit the type the public expects.

'How sweet of the Admiral to let us in himself,' said Mrs. Warbury.

Mr. Warbury said 'Good evening, all,' and began ploughing his way towards the drinks.

'Our maid goes home at six, because of the blackout,' said Mrs. Phelps. 'She lives at Elmtree Corner and her mother likes her to get home in plenty of time.'

'You ought to have an Austrian like mine,' said Mrs. Warbury. 'She works from morning to night and loves it. She has no friends nearer than London so she never goes out. She often says to me, "I feel quite English, gnädige Frau." She and your Polish girl ought to meet, Miss Hampton.'

'Don't see how they'd meet if yours never gets a holiday,' said Miss Hampton.

'Now,' said Mrs. Warbury archly, 'you mustn't put that in a book. With you and Mrs. Morland here we shall all find ourselves in print. You must be picking up a lot of character in this quaint nook, Mrs. Morland.'

'People always seem to think that,' said Mrs. Morland plaintively, 'but as a matter of fact I seem to spin things out of my inside like a spider. People have to be much funnier than usual before they penetrate into me as it were, and even then they come out quite different.'

'You don't know how funny Oscar and I can be,' said Mrs. Warbury laughing recklessly. 'You must come to one of our Bohemian evenings.'

'That is right,' said Mr. Warbury suddenly. 'You will all come, yes?'

This was the last thing anyone present wanted to do and there was a moment's uncomfortable silence, which the Admiral despairingly broke by asking the Vicar what they were going to do about God Save the King in church, as they ought to have it settled before the Church Council met. The Vicar, who was very shy and had been longing to get away for some time, said it was a question whether our National Anthem should be treated as a prayer, in which case it should be sung kneeling, or as an act of National Expression, outside the scope of the regular service if he made himself understood, and so sung standing. In his own opinion, he said it would be more reverent to kneel. He said this with some trepidation, for his churchwarden, having been used for many years to read the service himself, looked upon his vicar as a kind of chaplain under his orders and was apt to treat him as such.

The Admiral said there was of course only one way of looking at it, and the whole of the naval contingent supported him.

'Kneeling? Nonsense, Vicar,' said Miss Hampton. 'If my father were alive he would write to *The Times* about it to-morrow.'

Miss Bent said in a congregation composed chiefly of women, she did not include, she said, Hampton and herself in this statement, there was a natural tendency to kneel, which could be explained psychologically in Catholic countries as a Mother Complex, but in Protestant countries was less easy to analyse, as the female element in the act of worship was less pronounced. The Vicar who was terrified of Miss Bent and Miss Hampton, though deeply grateful for their generosity and kindness in the parish, got up and said his wife would be expecting him.

'I cannot see that it is of vital importance,' said Mrs. Warbury, 'but then Oscar and I are not Church of England.'

'Are you Catholic?' said Mrs. Morland with deep interest. 'I have quite a lot of friends who are Catholics and they are really very nice and we never mention anything unpleasant and get on very well.'

'Oh, dear no,' said Mrs. Warbury, showing no interest in Mrs. Morland's apologia for the Catholic faith, 'Oscar and I go much deeper. We are British Israelites.'

If any of the eight other people now present, all of whom disliked the Warburys more and more, had tried to express politely what they thought of them, they could not have hit upon a better description. Tubby choked into his drink and tried to pretend he was only drinking. Mrs. Birkett said it was very late and they must be going as she had forgotten to bring a torch and there was no moon. Bill at once offered his torch, which Mrs. Birkett gratefully accepted, saying that she would send it back that evening by the odd man when he went home.

'By the way,' she added, 'you were talking about an ocarina. I have one if you'd care to have it. It belongs to my daughter who is in Las Palombas with her husband and I know she won't want it.'

'I say, that's awfully jolly of you,' said Bill. 'Funny thing. I know a chap in Las Palombas called Fairweather. I wonder if your daughter knows him. His wife is a peach. I saw her at the Barchester Palais de Danse with Fairweather last time I was on leave.'

Mrs. Birkett's intense pleasure at hearing Rose so described may be imagined, as may the joy of Bill (whose name and rank are for ever unknown) on hearing that Mrs. Birkett who had been sent from heaven to give him an ocarina was also the mother of the peach. All the guests then left in a lump, much hampered by the Admiral's light-lock.

'We have our car,' said Mrs. Warbury, flashing a very large torch full on to a kind of super Daimler-Rolls about ten yards long, and describing circles of light in the air all round it to show off its magnificence.

'Put out that torch, Mrs. Warbury,' said the Admiral in his precise voice.

'I am really not so conceited,' said Mrs. Warbury, extinguishing the light however, 'as to think that hostile aircraft is looking for little me. Does anyone want a lift? Oscar has heaps of petrol. He has been storing it ever since Munich, but not a word to the police.'

There was a dead silence, for everyone present would have walked home with bare and bleeding feet, or on stilts, sooner than accept Mrs. Warbury's offer. So Mr. Warbury got into the driver's seat, lit his cigar with a petrol lighter that illuminated half the village, and drove fatly away.

'High time Bent and I were at the Red Lion,' said Miss Hampton. 'Let me come and see you some day, Mrs. Birkett.'

Mrs. Birkett said she would love it and Miss Hampton walked off with Miss Bent into the darkness.

Mrs. Morland and Mrs. Birkett walked home in silence, turning on the torch as little as possible because of not using up the batteries, though as Mrs. Morland very truly said batteries seemed to run down just as much when you didn't use them as when you did use them, to which Mrs. Birkett replied that the mysterious thing about electric irons was that they went on getting hotter after you had turned them off.

Dinner was rather quiet except for Geraldine, who was now on day duty at Barchester Hospital and so able to entertain her parents and their guest in the evening by telling them what Matron said and drawing very trenchant comparisons between that lady and Miss Pettinger. While she talked the grown-ups were able to enjoy the good food and try not to listen. Mr. Birkett was deep in his report for the School Governors which had to be presented next week and the ladies were still ruminating on the events of the afternoon. Mrs. Birkett and Mrs. Morland were still partially stunned by all they had gone through since tea-time, and it was not till Geraldine was brought to a stop by a very good coffee pudding that they began to revive. Mrs. Morland, as a successful author, was experiencing the hopeless feeling which besets writers when life gets the better of them with one hand tied behind its back. She felt that she might have invented the Admiral and Mrs. Phelps, who were the novelist's dream of what retired Admirals and their wives should be, and might even have managed the Warburys, though British Israelitism was, she freely admitted, quite beyond her. But at Maria Cottage she had been shaken from her bearings in a way she would have thought impossible. Mr. Bissell she had met, liked and could more or less deal with, but Mrs. Bissell had left her perfectly addled. If Mrs. Bissell had been, as she described herself, a mere home bird, or on the other hand an ordinary sample of a teacher, she could have coped with it. But she burst out in such unexpected places. Her obvious though unspoken devotion to Mr. Bissell, her firm yet tender treatment of the dreadful Edna, her terrifying and businesslike grasp of Income Tax, Psychology, the question of the married teacher, the case of Miss Hampton and Miss Bent; all these filled Mrs. Morland's humble mind with slightly envious admiration. She felt perfectly certain that as soon as the door of Maria Cottage had closed behind them Mrs. Bissell had first tabulated them all neatly in her own mind and then forgotten all about them till next time. That Mrs. Bissell thought poorly of her she had no doubt and did not in the least resent it, for before real goodness, and that absolutely shone from Mrs. Bissell, she was silent and abashed. Then, thinking of little Edna, the happy thought swept over her that she had four sons, and thus was infinitely superior to anyone who had no children, not to speak of those that had only daughters. For this feeling she occasionally blamed herself, but it was rooted somewhere in her very deeply. People might know psychology till they were black in the face, thought Mrs. Morland, and be able to take in a business-like spirit all the sinister implications of Adelina Cottage which would never have occurred to her at all. But although such people existed they had not got four sons. And Mrs. Morland's mind began to sketch out the scene for her next story in which Madame Koska should engage two ladies like Miss Hampton and Miss Bent to be mannequins for her tailored costumes and dinner-jacket suits (with skirt), how the Gestapo agent should try his wiles on one of them while planning to abduct the heroine, and the whole should be brought to confusion by a customer, no longer young, not remarkably good-looking yet distinguished, who could only afford one good costume a year, but who had a woman's intuition and the heart of a lion, all because she had four sons.

'What is it, Laura?' said Mr. Birkett, looking up from his savoury as he heard a slight noise.

'I was only thinking about a book,' said Mrs. Morland gulping, for the thought of the middle-aged customer (herself in fact) had been too much for her. 'Do you think, Bill,' she added with one of her snipe-flights, 'that I ought to be doing propaganda?'

'Certainly not,' said Mr. Birkett. 'You haven't the faintest qualifications, my dear Laura. Go on amusing us for God's sake with your books, and saving my life by being my secretary.'

'Fritz Warbury is bringing out a book with the Anti-Imperial Book Club,' said Geraldine, who was now at a loose end owing to not liking cheese canapés. 'It's called *The Lion Turns Tail*. It's all about how rotten the Government are.'

Her parents said nothing, knowing well that their approval or disapproval of this remark would meet with equal disfavour from their daughter.

'I told him I thought it was an awfully silly name,' said Geraldine dispassionately, 'and he's going to take me over the Film Studios.'

'But where did you meet him?' said Mrs. Birkett, breaking the most sacred rule of a parent's conduct, which is never to ask anything about anything where her children are concerned.

But Geraldine was in a favourable mood, so instead of glaring at her mother, or losing her temper, she said 'Oh, places; I must go and telephone,' and left the room.

'And I know what will happen,' said Mrs. Birkett despairingly to Mrs. Morland as the door slammed; not we must say in justice to Geraldine with the slam of passion, but the slam of finding it less trouble to slam a door than to shut it quietly, 'Geraldine will want to ask all the Warburys here.'

'Well, I must go and get on with that report,' said Mr. Birkett. 'Why can't Geraldine shut the door without slamming it? Everard is coming over to go through it with me. We shall be late, so don't sit up.'

'Oh, Bill, one thing before you go,' said Mrs. Morland. 'Who was it that had a casket with nothing but hope at the bottom of it? Not Prometheus, but you know whom I mean.'

'I suppose you mean Pandora,' said Mr. Birkett. 'Why?'

'I only wanted to be sure,' said Mrs. Morland meekly.

IX

SHERRY AT THE BIRKETTS

THE most beautiful autumn that anyone could remember now spread its mantle over Barsetshire and the rest of England. The evacuated children, who were by now all dressed by the hand of charity in coloured woollen frocks arted up at the neck, and coloured woollen coats of no particular shape or cut, not to speak of nightgowns and dressing-gowns and underclothes, looked fatter and pinker every day. Owing to the vigorous efforts of volunteer workers there was now not a lice-infested head among them, except when one of them was taken back to London by its parents for a week, cried all the time, and was returned to start the whole thing all over again. The primitive Wessex speech of the country children was being rapidly overlaid with a fine veneer of Cockney. As far as bad words went neither side had the advantage and the grosser names of Barsetshire were bartered against the more up-to-date obscenities of the evacuated areas. In writing, however, the London children had a distinct advantage. Maturing more early than the children of the soil, quicker if shallower witted, more bad language was written on the walls of Southbridge owing to their efforts in ten weeks than had been seen since Roman soldiers inscribed facetiae on the clay tiles of the Roman villa whose foundations had lately been excavated near Northbridge.

Various voluntary committees had by now got well into their stride. Mrs. and Miss Phelps had collected money for a cottage hospital for the London children, forced a very rich friend to let them use an empty house, furnished it by borrowing from all their not so rich friends and bullied all the girls in the neighbourhood into nursing and cooking in shifts under a professional matron; while the Admiral, who never knew when he was beaten, had so badgered the Ministry concerned both by letter and through every influential friend he possessed that the necessary permits were obtained in less than a month. Upon this all the working parties had fallen to again with zeal and provided a supply of pyjamas guaranteed not to fit any age of child, red monkey jackets, and knitted coverlets that would have kept Florence Nightingale quiet for months.

Another committee, also headed by Mrs. and Miss Phelps, had descended upon the Women's Institute and commandeered its hall as a canteen for London parents when they came down on Sundays to see their offspring. Some of the committee had wished to supply free cups of tea, but Mrs. Phelps was adamant, and Miss Hampton, who was a liberal subscriber to all Mrs. Phelps's activities, came to the meeting in her fiercest tailor-made and putting a monocle into her right eye had looked them all up and down, saying that as the parents, as far as she could see, need never spend another penny on their children's clothes and general welfare as long as they left them in the country, they could afford to pay for cups of tea and buns.

'I do think,' said Mrs. Warbury, who had somehow got on to the Committee, 'that the State ought to do everything for those poor women. In Germany, the State has a far better conception of its duties where children are concerned.'

To which Miss Hampton had replied that if it came to that Russia had a better conception still and they were both wrong. And Mrs. Phelps had said: Were they all agreed then that the canteen was to be self-supporting, would all those in favour signify it in the usual way by holding up their hands, thank you, yes; so quickly that Mrs. Warbury put up her hand without meaning to and was so flurried that she gave half a crown towards the initial expenses before she knew where she was.

Admiral Phelps carried a gas-mask everywhere as an example and worked himself to the bone collecting volunteer casualties for his A.R.P. practice. In the evenings, now beginning far too early, he would patrol the village for illegal lights and twice had the pleasure of knocking up the Warburys and making them turn out the light in their garage.

Miss Hampton and Miss Bent who were very strong and did not know what it was to be tired, took an allotment and dug for victory in a way that compelled the admiration of the sexton, who as an amateur of spadework spent hours of his time watching them and was nearly late with old Mrs. Trouncer's grave, which he had to finish at six in the morning owing to Miss Hampton's kind offer to give him a hand with it. They also collaborated with Miss Phelps in looking after the goats, hens and rabbits who lived in the field behind Jutland Cottage. The hens were no particular trouble except that they had to be fed, watered and put to bed at such various inconvenient hours that Margot Phelps had almost to give up social life. The rabbits were more especially Miss Bent's care, as she had a loom on which she was occasionally moved to weave pieces of gaily striped material that sagged violently at the knees and elbows if made up into coats and skirts, and had visions of spinning the rabbits' fur and weaving it into even looser and more sagging material. The goats therefore fell into the hands of Miss Hampton who, adding a pair of very well-made leggings to her tweed costume, so harassed those odious animals that their spirits were quite broken. Her strength was such that the strongest Billy was outmatched if he tried to pull in the wrong direction. Every time a Nanny trod on her feet while being milked, she gave her a resounding whack with a stick. Mrs. Phelps was at first inclined to question the humanity of these methods, but when Miss Hampton explained that goats had an unfair advantage owing to their hoofs being so small and precipitous that you couldn't tread back, she saw the point.

The real difficulty about the goats was what to do with their milk. The Phelps's who had become acclimatized to goats at Malta didn't mind the taste and in any case didn't take milk with their tea, but everyone else expressed their just abhorrence of it in no measured terms, till there seemed to be nothing for it but to throw the milk away, thus, as Mrs. Phelps said almost in tears, playing directly into the enemy's hands. But very luckily an immensely rich family who had taken a house outside Southbridge for the duration believed that goats' milk was Life for their six young children, so Mrs. Phelps was able to sell it at a good price, and Miss Phelps delivered it once a day on her bicycle. It seemed probable to everyone that the milk would arrive churned to death, but the children throve on it just as if it were nice cows' milk, so all was well.

Southbridge School, with the Hosiers' Boys, did not take a large part in the village life. It had always been a self-contained establishment and under present conditions everyone was too busy to look aside. Geraldine, as her father had predicted, made herself such a trouble to her parents over the Warburys that they almost wished they had Rose back again.

Mr. Birkett said to his wife, for he dared not say it to his daughter, it was difficult enough to keep the school going at present, and make the older boys stick to their scholarship work, and arbitrate on the question of whether the window in the squash court had been broken by his boys or Bissell's, and bear with that man Hopkins's Communism, and take the Classical Sixth himself till he could get a really first-class man to replace Philip Winter, without having impossible outsiders in his house. Mrs. Birkett said to her husband, for she also did not like to say it to Geraldine, that she had never seen anyone she disliked so much as the Warburys and she was sure that the son was even worse, but if Geraldine could not ask her friends to her parents' house where could she ask them.

Geraldine, relying on a war of attrition, merely went on bothering her parents whenever she was not at the hospital till they gave in, which they might just as well have done in the first place. The only stipulation Mrs. Birkett made was that the Warburys should be asked to sherry. She had for some time wished to have a party for the pleasure of seeing people, for what with the petrol rationing, and everyone being busy, and the black-out, she had rather lost touch with her friends of late. In a gathering of this kind she hoped the Warburys might be if not drowned at least so watered down as to be fairly harmless. Accordingly, choosing a day when there would be some moonlight after darkness had set in, though with the firm conviction that there would also be clouds and heavy rain, she sent out her invitations. In case Heaven should disapprove of people enjoying themselves during a period of mingled unhappiness, anxiety and boredom which, as far as she could see, it had done nothing whatsoever to prevent, she threw it a sop in the shape of some very hideous embroidery done by the Mixo-Lydian refugees who were housed about two miles from Southbridge. These embroideries she decided to put in the dining-room, so that people needn't look at them unless they really wanted to.

On the morning of the party the two head refugees, M. and Mme. Brownscu, appeared in person, carrying the embroideries in a basket. Their real titles, which might be the equivalent of Count and Countess or Mr. and Mrs., but no one liked to ask, were Prodshk and Prodshka, but the local Committee for Mixo-Lydia, recognizing that such names must fill any self-respecting foreigner with shame, had given them brevet rank as Monsieur and Madame, so that a great many people thought they were Poles; though they would have been hard put to it to explain the mode of reasoning that led them to this conclusion. There were even unbelievers who said that Brownscu was not a Mixo-Lydian name, nor indeed a name at all, but Miss Phelps, who happened to have recently added that particular committee to her collection, said everyone knew there was somebody called Jonescu in Romania or somewhere, so why not Brownscu in Mixo-Lydia; by which remark she was considered to have scored pretty heavily.

How the Mixo-Lydians lived, no one, not even their Committee, knew. While they had all fled from their country at an hour's notice leaving the dinner cooking in the oven and the beds unmade, they all lived in considerable if unhygienic comfort and even luxury, and some of them went up to town every day by the 8.10 returning to dinner. No English servant would stay, partly because of not liking foreigners and partly because they didn't hold with mucking up the food like that, so three or four inferior Mixo-Lydians were imported somehow from France, where a good many of them had got stuck. And, as Mrs. Phelps bitterly remarked, if *she* had wanted a foreign servant it would have taken her six months to get a permit and then she wouldn't have got it.

M. and Mme Brownscu, being if possible even more disagreeable, selfish and ungrateful than any of their compatriots, had assumed a kind of royal dignity at what the village called Mixerlydian House, and undertook all embassies between it and the outer world. Mme Brownscu was a small wiry woman with a mop of frizzled dark hair and a leopard-skin coat, and by the hideous shape of her legs it was generally thought that she had been a dancer. M. Brownscu, yellow faced and melancholy, wore a skin-tight béret which he never removed, and was permanently huddled in a sheepskin coat.

Mrs. Birkett received them in the dining-room where the exhibition was to be.

'It is not very big, your room,' said Mme Brownscu by way of greeting. 'The Pagnaskaya in Lydianopolis as you call it, though its true name is Lvdpòv, is very much larger. That is where we have our Expositions d'Arts Néo-paysans, what you would call new peasants arts. Have you no bigger room?'

'The drawing-room is bigger,' said Mrs. Birkett, 'but that is where I am having my friends. I think your embroideries will look very nice here.'

'They will ollways look nice,' said Mme Brownscu, 'but the ambiance is not paysanne at all. God wills it so. On this table I shall put them, yes? I shall arrange them for you.'

'Well, I'm afraid we are going to have lunch on this table first,' said Mrs. Birkett. 'But if you will leave them there, I will myself put them out after lunch as attractively as possible.'

Even as she spoke Mrs. Birkett found herself insensibly slipping into her visitor's style of English and wondered why it was so difficult to talk naturally to foreigners who had an idiomatic command of English.

'I shall myself come back and arrange them and change your furniture a little which is not right,' said Mme Brownscu. 'You would not understand. At six o'clock your party, yes? Then I shall come at five o'clock and arrange everything and put the prices very plainly. They will be rich, your friends, yes?'

Mrs. Birkett said she was afraid not.

'Then we shall chaffer,' said Mme Brownscu. 'There is a market in Lvdpòv every Tuesday and there I chaffer with the peasants and hit them down. Nothing will I buy till I have well examined it.'

Mrs. Birkett didn't think her friends would be much good at chaffering, but held her peace.

'And Gradko shall bring his poems and read to you,' Mme Brownscu continued. 'Nòv pvarno orlskjok chjlèm zy chokra?' she added to her husband.

M. Brownscu huddled even more into his sheepskin coat and said, 'Czy pròvka, pròvka, pròvka.'

'He says, "No, never, never, never," ' said Mme Brownscu, and to Mrs. Birkett's great relief did not press the matter any further. In fact she was just going when, much to Mrs. Birkett's annoyance, Mrs. Morland appeared at the door.

'Oh, I thought you were here,' said Mrs. Morland to her friend.

There was nothing for it but to introduce Mrs. Morland. Mrs. Birkett very meanly revenged herself by telling the Brownscus that Mrs. Morland was a celebrated writer.

'Ah-ha!' said Mme Brownscu. 'Then my husband must tell you his poem. It is a great poem, epopic, about our great national hero, Gradko, for which my husband is baptised.'

'Is he a Catholic then?' said Mrs. Morland, who had been writing all the morning and as usual was only just coming out of her bardic frenzy and more than usually vague, and thought the Brownscus might be something to do with the Warburys.

'Czy, pròvka, pròvka, pròvka,' said M. Brownscu energetically.

'He expresses, "No, never, never, never",' said his wife. 'The word Catholic, to us it is like a red rug to a bull. We are Orthodox,' and she crossed herself violently in what Mrs. Morland afterwards described as a very upside-down and un-Christian kind of way. 'But I shall tell you,' she continued. 'Gradko is a son of a peasant girl which has been violée, you would say raped, by a nobleman, so his mother is pleased and lays three grains of millet on his cradle.'

'Why?' said Mrs. Morland.

'It is a custom,' said Mme Brownscu. 'So Gradko grows up and becomes a famous warrior. One day he hears a shriek. He approaches. He sees a lovely maiden being séduite, seduced you say, by a Turk. Mixo-Lydia hates Turks, therefore he kills him. The maiden has run away in terror. He pursues her till night. He hears a shriek and redoubles his pace. The maiden is being forcée, taken in English, by a Bulgar. All Bulgars are enemies of Mixo-Lydia, therefore he kills him. The maiden has again run away in terror. At dawn he hears a shriek. It is the maiden who is being éventrée, eventuated you would say, by a Russian. Russia and Mixo-Lydia are enemies, so he kills the Russian. Thus the prophecy is fulfilled and he is crowned King.'

'And what happened to the maiden?' said Mrs. Morland, wishing she could think of as many incidents, though not quite of that kind, for her new book.

'Par suite de ses relations avec Gradko elle devient mère et accouche de quatre fils,' said Mme Brownscu, getting tired of English. 'Le premier s'appelle Achmet, parcequ'il est Turc, le second Boris parcequ'il est Bulgare, le troisième, qui est Russe, Ivan, et le quatrième qui est le plus beau de tous et fait assassiner son père, sa mère et ses trois frères aînés s'appelle Gradko, comme son père. Every child in Mixo-Lydia knows that story.'

Before her hearers could think of the obvious retort that they were not Mixo-Lydian children, Mme Brownscu had taken her husband away, promising again to return at five o'clock with her embroideries.

The next few hours were spent, as usually happens with a sherry party, in people who had accepted ringing up to say they were so sorry they couldn't come because the petrol had given out, or Betty or Tommy was suddenly home on leave and wanted to go to the Barchester Odeon, and people who had refused ringing up to say might they come after all as Captain King who was staying with them had gallons of petrol from the War Office if Mrs. Birkett didn't mind them bringing him too. With all of these Simnet and Mrs. Birkett dealt. The last to ring up was Mrs. Crawley who asked if she might bring Captain Merton who was staying with them, to which Mrs. Birkett said please do, though the name at the moment meant nothing to her.

At five o'clock the Brownscus arrived with the embroideries, but Mrs. Birkett basely pretended she was lying down and left Simnet to deal with them and give them some tea. That perfect butler, who had been in France from 1915 to 1917, stood no nonsense from Mme Brownscu, and by taking up a position in front of any piece of furniture that she wanted to move and saying 'No bon, madam,' made her confine her activities to laying out her wares on the dining-room table, after which he gave her a very good tea of which she and her husband greedily partook.

By a quarter past six the drawing-room was already seething with people, all delighted to have a treat and talk to each other about the future rationing of butter. Mrs. Birkett was informed in a quarter of an hour by four different friends who all happened to *know* they were speaking the truth that (a) the Government had immense reserves of butter at Leamington and rationing would only be for forms' sake, (b) there were only three days' supplies of butter in the country, (c) that there was plenty of butter but it all had to go to Egypt, and (d) that margarine had all the vitamins of butter and you couldn't tell the difference. None of these statements did Mrs. Birkett particularly believe, and the last she knew to be a downright lie.

'People are so prejudiced,' said Mrs. Warbury, who was the last speaker. 'Now that all margarine has vitamins P. and Q., there is no difference at all.'

'Only the filthy taste,' said Miss Phelps who had just come from an A.R.P. practice in a very belligerent frame of mind.

'I always give it to my Austrian maid, and she says nothing at all,' said Mrs. Warbury.

'Well, if I were Mitzi I'd say a mouthful,' said Miss Phelps aloud to herself.

'But what I think so dreadful,' said Mrs. Warbury, persuading herself that she had not heard Miss Phelps, 'is that the price of butter is so high. Oscar and Fritz have to eat it, because they are delicate, so I eat a little myself, or they would be wretched. But even our little bill for butter is appalling and how the *real* poor live I cannot think. The Government ought to take over all the butter and let the poor have it. When I think of all the homes in England that can't afford butter now I am almost a Communist. All these poor wretched evacuee children should be having pounds of butter.'

'But Mrs. Warbury,' said Kate Carter, whose housewifely mind could not keep away from a conversation in which butter took a part, 'the cottage people in Southbridge really prefer margarine and so do the evacuees. It is just the same at Northbridge where my parents live. People are *so* kind about saying they would be better nourished if they ate nettles and dandelions and butter, but what they really want is meat and margarine.'

Mrs. Birkett said the servants were the difficulty with margarine in the last war, because they thought it was nothing but their employers being mean.

'In the last war,' said Mr. Warbury who had been listening attentively, 'we bought butter and margarine and exchanged the wrappers. Then my wife said to the servants, "You can have the butter and Mr. Warbury and I shall eat margarine". So they were pleased to have the butter as they thought, and stayed on with us till they were interned.'

'Why were they interned?' asked Miss Phelps.

'They were enemy aliens,' said Mr. Warbury simply. 'So then Rachel and I moved into a service flat where we were very comfortable till we had to come down here with my business. Comfort is my motto.'

No one quite knew what to say and Mrs. Birkett was glad of the excuse to greet some newcomers. At the same moment there was a slight commotion near the door and she saw her daughter Geraldine, who had managed to get the afternoon off, leading a young man by the hand, just as her sister Rose had artlessly been wont to lead her many adoring swains. The young man was of middle height, with an elegant supple figure, a handsome if Oriental countenance, dark hyacinthine hair and gazelle-like eyes. Every man in the room wondered who that little bounder was. Most of the women were interested against their better selves, and the Vicar's wife, who had just been reading one of the perennial re-hashes of Byron's life (*The Truth about Byron* by Lilian Tuckwell, author of the *Truth about Shelley, Keats, The Brownings,* and many other popular works) said to her next door neighbour who happened to be Mrs. Phelps, 'Mad, bad and dangerous to know.'

'Who?' said Mrs. Phelps, following the direction of the Vicar's wife's eyes. 'Fritz Warbury? He's a rank outsider, but that's all. No danger there. I'd let Margot go anywhere with him if she wanted to, but she doesn't. He ought to be in the Army. I told the Admiral he ought to be interned.'

The Vicar's wife, with admirable good sense, said that he couldn't very well be both and she knew for a fact, because Mrs. Warbury had told her, that the boy was twenty-four.

Mrs. Phelps said Oh, was that all, in a way that expressed her poor opinion of people that were still too old to be called up, but comforted herself with the reflection that young Warbury would soon be drawn into the jaws of the Army.

Meanwhile Geraldine had dragged her prey up to her mother saying, 'Mummy, here's Fritz. He has simply dashed in for a moment and has to go back to the studio almost at once so I'll get him a drink.'

Young Mr. Warbury said he could do with one, but on being offered a glass of sherry said God, wasn't there any gin.

'Hi, Kate,' said Geraldine to Mrs. Everard Carter, 'this is Fritz. Hang on to him while I get him a drink.'

Kate, who had no clue as to who Fritz might be, but was always kind, thought from his name and appearance that he must be a refugee, probably one of the Mixo-Lydians who were showing their distressed work in the dining-room, so she asked him if he did embroidery.

'Of course I do,' said young Mr. Warbury, 'when I'm not working. How can a man do anything else? I always have my embroidery in the studio with me and work away at it.'

Kate said she supposed he had some with him to-day and she looked forward to seeing it so much, upon which young Mr. Warbury obligingly opened a soft leather portfolio that he was carrying under his arm and took out a piece of *petit point.* Kate's admiration was unfeigned and they were deep in talk about stitches and shading when Geraldine came back.

'I say,' said Geraldine, 'Daddy, won't let me have the gin. Something about war-time. I'm frightfully sorry, Fritz.'

'Gin's a filthy drink anyway,' said young Mr. Warbury. 'What about some sherry?'

Geraldine obediently went to get some and Kate thought how nice it was that Geraldine, usually so offhand to everyone, should take such trouble for a refugee and was pleased to see this change of spirit. When the sherry came young Mr. Warbury drank it and said to Kate that he must be going.

'But you've only just come, Fritz,' said Geraldine.

'Well, come and see the studio one day,' said her young friend. 'Ring up my secretary,' and without any further formality he wormed his way towards the door.

'Do you suppose his embroidery is very expensive?' asked Kate, which led to an explanation that young Mr. Warbury was not a refugee but on very important work in the film world.

'You couldn't possibly take him for a refugee,' said Geraldine indignantly. 'You only have to look at him.'

As this was precisely what Kate had done, she was not convinced, but she felt rather anxious about Geraldine whose manly heart was evidently touched by young Mr. Warbury. Kate could not see him as a son-in-law to the Birketts, but neither had she seen him show much interest in Geraldine and she wished that Geraldine had chosen better.

And now Miss Hampton and Miss Bent hove down upon Kate. Miss Hampton, looking incredibly smart in a black coat and skirt, a black tricorne and a white shirt with onyx links, was carrying the elephant-faced dog in her arms. She explained to Kate that he didn't like being on the floor at parties, owing to being sensitive about his height.

'Poor old Smigly-Rydz,' said Kate, patting his head.

'That's just the trouble,' said Miss Hampton, taking a glass of sherry from a tray that came by. 'Must have a sherry. Bent and I had one before we started, but we haven't been to the Red Lion yet. Go there on the way back. Where's Mrs. Morland?'

Kate pointed her out, doing her best with the doctor's wife.

'Get her, Bent,' said Miss Hampton. 'She'll know. Rydz, you'll have to go down, you're too heavy.'

She put him on the floor where he sat, apparently quite free from any form of inferiority complex about his height, gently slapping the floor with his stumpy tail.

Miss Bent now returned with Mrs. Morland and at the same moment Mrs. and Miss Phelps, who had the greatest admiration for authors and belonged to practically every Book Club or Society, regardless of race or creed, joined the circle to hear the two writers talk.

The literary symposium was begun by both ladies giving an elaborate account, the one of her four sons, the other of her four nephews, all of whom, we are glad to say, were at the moment well, though Mrs. Morland had reservations in favour of her eldest boy, for, as she truly said, if one is in central America and expects to be out of touch with civilization for six months, really anything might happen, except that natives had wonderful ways of knowing things before they could possibly know, but of course that was no use unless they could get into touch with someone and it would be so difficult to know which dialect it was.

Kate said she was sure Rose Fairweather would do something about it if she knew, but no one shared her optimism as to Rose's power of getting news about an exploring party a thousand miles from her neighbourhood, and those who knew her best felt that even if people were exploring in her garden she wouldn't take any interest in them unless they invited her to a night club or a cinema.

'But that's not the point,' said Miss Hampton. 'Point is, what am I to do about Rydz?'

Mrs. Morland asked if he were ill.

'Ill?' said Miss Hampton. 'Never better. Bent gave him a couple of worm powders last week and he's as fit as a fiddle. News isn't at all good. Looks as if we'd have to change his name.'

'Won't he answer to it?' said Miss Phelps. 'Perhaps he's getting deaf.'

'Not a bit deaf,' said Miss Hampton. 'But if Finland is invaded, and it looks like it, what can we call him? Must call him something. Gallant little Finland.'

Mrs. Morland said that without being superstitious it seemed unlucky to call people gallant, because the moment they were gallant they got conquered by somebody.

Miss Bent, making one of her rare incursions into the conversation, said what about Estonia and Latvia and Lithuania. Nobody had called them gallant, not for a single moment, but there they were.

'But aren't they the same?' said Mrs. Morland. 'I mean isn't Latvia how the Lithuanians pronounce Lithuania, like the Italians pronouncing Florence Firenze?'

'It was no good thinking of a name for Rydz in them,' said Miss Hampton, 'because there is simply nobody there.'

Kate thought there must be somebody.

'No one with a name,' said Miss Bent. 'We studied the question, but there was no one.'

'Same trouble with Finland,' said Miss Hampton. 'Must do our best for them. But who is there in Finland, I mean with a name?'

There was a short silence, broken by Kate, who said hadn't somebody once got a Nobel prize or was she thinking of someone else.

'There is Sibelius,' said Mrs. Morland with the air of one making a concession.

'Bent thought of that,' said Miss Hampton, 'but it wouldn't do. If England were in trouble it wouldn't do any good to call a dog Elgar. Isn't there anyone else?'

Miss Phelps said she once went to a concert at Queen's Hall where there was a piece called the Return of Somebody. She wasn't musical, she added, but there was something in the piece that got her though she couldn't explain why.

'The awful thing is,' said Mrs. Morland, in her tragedy voice, 'that I am even worse off than you are, Miss Hampton. You know my heroine that I told you about; and now she may have to be Finnish. I couldn't make her an Esthonian or a Latvian, because they haven't enough appeal. My publisher wants to have my typescript by the end of January at the very latest. Are there any women's names in Finland? And then it will probably be Jugo-Slavia after all.'

But before these important questions could be threshed out, Geraldine, looking very sulky, said Mother said would they go and look at the embroideries in the dining-room, because if no one went Mme Brownscu would be so disappointed. Miss Hampton, stopping Simnet and his tray, said they must all have another sherry and then they'd go.

'Well, here's fun,' said Miss Phelps. 'And don't forget that you are going to help us to move the Billy to the other end of the field to-morrow, Miss Hampton. He's too strong for Mother and me.

'That's because you wear those ridiculous trousers,' said Miss Hampton, who was in high good humour about the billy goat and had long been meaning to speak her mind about the trousers.

'I can't think why you don't wear them,' said Miss Phelps. 'They're a wonderful economy. Two pairs last me a year, except for the few weeks of summer.'

'Well, I know exactly what I'd look like,' said Miss Hampton, 'neither a man nor a woman.'

And she stuck her monocle into one eye defiantly.

'Well, that's exactly what you look like now,' said Mrs. Phelps, pot-valiant with sherry.

Everyone held her breath expecting a first-class row, but Miss Hampton, taking the remark in very good part, laughed uproariously and told Miss Bent that Mrs. Phelps had put one over on them this time. Kate, who in the absence of Rose, and the thundercloud presence of Geraldine, had constituted herself a temporary daughter to Mrs. Birkett, then gently and firmly shepherded a section of the party across into the dining-room. Here a number of pieces of rather dirty embroidery on very inferior material were disposed on the dining-room table. They were all of unusual shapes and no one quite knew what they were meant for, or if they were meant to be something else. M. Brownscu was installed behind a table near the door with a pile of small change spread out before him, evidently ready to receive customers, while his wife, smoking cigarettes whose stubs Kate's eye at once detected all over the carpet and furniture, stood ready to chaffer. Mrs. Phelps, who had decided to spend five shillings, picked up something that might have been a rather hideous collar and looked at it. On the collar was pinned a piece of paper bearing the inscription £15,000. She thought this must be a mistake, so she showed it to her daughter, who was equally puzzled.

'I say, Miss Hampton,' said Miss Phelps, 'do look at this. Mme Whoeveritis must be mad.'

'That's all right,' said Miss Hampton, examining the paper. 'Fifteen thousand Lydions – that's the currency in Mixo-Lydia. About five shillings. But you'd better offer four.'

Mrs. Phelps, who had bargained in every port where the British Navy is known, took the collar over to Mme Brownscu and said firmly, 'Three and sixpence.'

'You wish us to starve then?' said Mme Brownscu throwing her cigarette on to the polished sideboard from which the anxious Kate rescued it. 'It is not for amusing themselves that my compatriots work, it is for their bread. Fifteen thousand Lydions, that is to say five shillings sixpence or nearabouts.'

'Three and ninepence,' said Mrs. Phelps.

Mme Brownscu, at last in her element, launched an attack on English hospitality which would so abuse penniless exiles as to make them sacrifice a piece of work, the fruit of months of patient toil, for five shillings and threepence. But Mrs. Phelps was as keen an amateur of chaffering as Mme Brownscu herself and for several minutes the battle hung suspended. Miss Hampton, who was prepared to buy with her usual generosity, came over to the chafferers, carrying a traycloth which looked a little less hideous and amateur than the other articles. Both buyer and seller had stuck for the moment, the one at four and threepence, the other at four and ninepence.

'Time you settled a price,' said Miss Hampton. 'I drove a Red Cross Ambulance all over Mixo-Lydia in 1918. Know them all well. Give me the embroidery.'

Mrs. Phelps, hypnotized, handed the collar to Miss Hampton, who slapping it down on the table said a few words in Mixo-Lydian. Mme Brownscu answered volubly in her native language and thrust the collar into Miss Hampton's hands, adding to it a small square piece of embroidery in a primitive cross-stitch.

'There you are,' said Miss Hampton, handing the goods to Mrs. Phelps. 'Four and sixpence and she is giving you the other bit for luck because you are the first purchaser. Czjrejok it is called.'

Further incursions of guests now came into the room and under the influence of Mr. Birkett's good sherry the horrid embroideries were snapped up at sums varying from 5,000 to 25,000 Lydions. Mme Brownscu kept a suspicious eye on purchasers and from time to time went to see that her husband was giving the right change. Miss Hampton, who had been back to the drawing-room and collected some more sherry, approached M. Brownscu and said a few jovial words in Mixo-Lydian.

'Czy, pròvka, pròvka, pròvka,' said M. Brownscu, huddling his sheepskin coat more tightly round him and looking at Miss Hampton with terror.

'He expresses "No, never, never, never",' said his wife, kindly satisfying the curiosity of those present. 'I shall tell you he was having frost-bitten feet in the Red Cross Ambulance and these English ladies were so good to him and give him a bath, mais ce n'est pas l'habitude du pays et cela lui a porté sur le foie. Il a une santé qu'il faut ménager et depuis lors il a pris les infirmières anglaises en horreur. C'est un tic, mais que voulez-vous? C'est comme ça chez nous. We 'ate what we do not like.'

'Was anything wrong with the tea?' asked kind Kate, anxiously.

'HATE!' said Mme Brownscu, so vehemently that Kate wished Everard were there to look after her.

But Everard, who had come on later, was safely in the drawing-room, having a refreshing talk with Mr. Birkett and Mr. Bissell about the School Certificate examination, during which he and Mr. Birkett honestly tried to see why it was more important than birth, death, or marriage, while Mr. Bissell on his side did his very best to make allowance for the Capittleist point of view that if you had been at a private school (by which name he thought of what his fellow-talkers called Public Schools) exams mysteriously didn't matter, whereas every right-thinking person knew they were the whole end of education. But they got on very well and none of them were pleased when Mr. Hopkins, the Hosiers' Boys Science Master, joined their party.

'Have some sherry, Hopkins,' said Mr. Birkett.

Mr. Hopkins said sherry was for those who could afford it.

'Well, I can afford it,' said Mr. Birkett, 'so have a glass. It's quite dry.'

Mr. Hopkins accepted a glass and drank it venomously.

The Dean of Barchester, who had just arrived, came up to speak to Mr. Birkett, and Mr. Hopkins gave his gaiters a look of class hatred that should have burst all their buttons.

'News looks bad, I'm afraid,' said the Dean. 'We can but hope in these dark days.'

Mr. Birkett offered him some sherry.

'Hope and trust,' said the Dean, accepting it. 'Finland is a small nation, but she will not lightly give up a freedom won at such cost from her powerful neighbour. I had forgotten how good your sherry is, Birkett. Yes; these are dark days and will be darker yet.'

Everyone felt that this remark, though doubtless true, was not of a nature suited to a sherry party, for hope and trust, though admirable in themselves, are damping to the spirit. When we say everyone, we are only thinking of people we like, for Mr. Hopkins, the Adam's apple in his skinny throat working violently with hatred of nearly everything, said hope and trust were all very well, but we should have made a pact with Moscow two years ago. He hoped, he said, to see the Red Army at Helsingfors within a week and the Hammer and Sickle floating over the whole of Finland.

Everard Carter with deplorable levity said what a very good name the Hammer and Sickle would be for a pub.

Mr. Needham who had driven the Dean and family over said, looking very hard at Mr. Hopkins, that if he saw a pub called the Hammer and Sickle he would give it a wide berth as the beer would probably be poisoned. He then blushed bright scarlet up to the roots of his fair hair and wondered if the Dean would be offended.

'My dear Needham!' said the Dean with a deprecating but on the whole not disapproving smile, 'speaking as one who — —'

The doctor's wife said she thought the Russians drank vodka.

'That, we are given to understand, is so,' said the Dean, thus imparting a kind of benediction and at the same time showing the doctor's wife that she had spoken out of place. 'Speaking, as I was about to say, as one who knows well that beautiful country of forest and lakes,' the Dean continued, 'and has taken a deep interest in its language and culture, I feel we should all use the time-honoured if to our ears less euphonious name of Helsinki, in which I am sure Mr. — — ?'

He paused. His secretary, who was admirable at getting to know who everyone was, murmured, 'Mr. Hopkins, science master of the Hosier's Boys Foundation School.'

'Quite, quite,' said the Dean. 'I am sure that Mr. Hopkins, I think I have the name rightly, learned as he is in the exact sciences,' and into these words the Dean rather unkindly managed to throw the whole contempt of a classical man for a subject that even Cambridge must be slightly ashamed of encouraging, 'would agree with me that where philology leads, we must follow. I had myself the privilege of attending a Conference in Finland last summer and it was a privilege indeed. Our arrival at Helsinki, as I think,' he added with a smile, 'we have agreed to call it, on a fine June morning was an experience I shall never forget. Neither, though here I may be accused of very materialistic views shall I forget the first meal we had on landing. When I tell you, Birkett — —'

It was by now evident that what the Dean really wanted to do was to described his six days in Finland. As respect for his cloth made it difficult to interrupt him, he was able to carry his hearers, by train and steamer, over the southern part of the country, and those who had not heard it before felt that it was so dull that they would almost prefer to hear yet once again how he went to Portugal the summer before.

As for Mr. Hopkins, his rage cannot be expressed. Just when he had seen a chance of telling a group of influential, though of course absolutely uneducated and wrong-thinking men what they ought to think about Russia, a man who was no better than a Roman (for Mr. Hopkins was a loyal son of the brand of Undenominationalism peculiar to his birthplace in Glamorganshire) was allowed to get away with the whole of the talk, simply because he wore gaiters. What was worse, he

himself had been publicly convicted of using the bourgeois word Helsingfors, when heaven knew he had been saying Helsinki to himself for
a considerable time. And Mr. Hopkins, on whom Mr. Birkett's sherry
had had an inflaming effect, expressed upon his features a scorn that
should have withered everyone present. He would have gnashed his
teeth with rage, but that his uppers were a bit loose and he didn't like
to spend any more money on the dentist. So he went into the hall where
Simnet, who despised him, helped him into his coat with a deference
that made Mr. Hopkins wish more than ever that England had made a
Trade Pact with Russia, in which case (so he fondly thought) the
Hosiers' Boys would never have had to be evacuated to Southbridge
and he would not have been thrown into a world where people read
The Times as a matter of course and were bigoted, ignorant and stuck-up.
He was about to shake any dust that Mrs. Birkett's excellent head-
housemaid had not taken up with the Hoover that morning from his
feet when Miss Phelps, zealous as always in any cause that presented
itself to her, saw him go past the dining-room door and advancing upon
him in trousered majesty took him in tow and hauled him into the
dining-room where we shall at present leave him.

It must be stated with regret that no one in the drawing-room
noticed his absence. The Dean, having got his audience back to Helsinki and on board the S.S. *Porphyria*, moved away and came face to
face with Lydia Keith, who had only just arrived.

'Hullo, Dr. Crawley,' said Lydia, giving him one of her friendly and
painful handshakes. 'Let's go and talk to Admiral Phelps and the
Vicar. It's about God Save the King and I know they'll get it all
wrong.'

The Dean, who was very fond of Lydia and often felt as if she were
one of his own daughters, though not so dull as some of them, was quite
willing to do as she asked and following her stalwart lead came down
like a shepherd on the fold upon the corner where the Vicar and his
churchwarden were discussing for the third or fourth time the question
whether God Save the King was to be sung standing or kneeling. The
Vicar would willingly have discussed subjects of more general or less
doctrinal interest, but the Admiral was determined to win his pastor
over to his way of thinking before the Church Council met, in which
case he knew he could manage the rest of the members.

If Lydia had hoped—and she probably had—that the Dean would
suddenly burst in with bell, book and candle and settle the whole
matter, she was not to be gratified. Dr. Crawley had no illusions as to
the power of a dean and while willing to listen to the arguments on both
sides was not going to commit himself. But Lydia herself had no such
scruples.

'If you want to sing God Save the King, you want to *sing* it,' she
announced, 'and if you kneel down your diaphragm is all squashed

together and that's where your voice comes from, at least your breath control does. And I think it's disloyal not to stand up, don't you, Admiral Phelps? If anyone didn't stand up to sing God Save the King I'd think they were a Traitor,' said Lydia defiantly.

The Vicar, who did not know Lydia well and was rather terrified by her, said he was certain that nothing was further from any thought of disloyalty than the attitude of those who felt it incumbent upon them to kneel, but he must in all such matters be guided by his own conscience and the ruling of those set in authority over him.

'If you mean the Bishop, you might as well say so,' said Admiral Phelps. 'We all know *his* views.'

'I wasn't thinking of the Bishop at all,' said Lydia indignantly. 'If you had read the Thirty-Nine Articles you would know that the Supreme Governor of the Church of England is the King, because it says so. At any rate it says so in the Preface. And it says it again near the end, doesn't it, Mr. Danby?'

The Vicar, thus appealed to, had to admit that Lydia's premises were correct.

'Very well then. The King says people ought to stand up to sing God Save the King,' said Lydia, 'at least they always do stand up, so it comes to the same thing. I wouldn't feel I was singing God Save the King at all if I knelt down.'

'The Bishop of Barchester, while feeling that everyone should act according to his conscience, prefers it to be sung kneeling,' said the Dean. 'In the Cathedral we stand,' he added in an unimportant voice.

The Admiral, who knew, as did the Dean, that the Vicar of Southbridge hated his Bishop's views on nearly every point (though not half so much as did his fellow-Vicar at Pomfret Madrigal), felt that everything was shaping as he would wish it and said no more. A voice behind Lydia said, 'I didn't know you knew the Thirty-Nine Articles, Lydia.'

Lydia turned and saw her friend Noel Merton.

'Where on earth did you come from, Noel?' she asked.

'In general,' said Noel, 'from I mayn't say where, but in particular from the Deanery. I would have come to Northbridge,' he added hastily, seeing a faint cloud of disappointment on Lydia's face, 'but I only knew late last night that I would be getting leave and I thought it might upset your mother. How is she?'

Lydia said she was pretty well.

'You wouldn't care to have me for lunch to-morrow, would you?' Noel asked.

Lydia lifted troubled eyes to him.

'Of course I'd care,' she said, 'but to-morrow's my day at the evacuated children's Communal Kitchen, and if one once begins changing — —'

'I know,' said Noel. 'What time is your Kitchen over?'

Lydia said one o'clock for the children, but the helpers usually hadn't finished washing up till after half past.

'Very well,' said Noel. 'At a quarter to two I shall fetch you with some illegal petrol and take you for a drive. Would that do?'

Lydia nodded violently.

'The Communal Kitchen is in Northbridge High Street, in that empty house next to The Laurels,' she said. 'You'll know it by the smell of rabbit and onions to-morrow.'

Mrs. Crawley then descended upon Noel to take him to look at the delightful Mixo-Lydian embroidery in the dining-room, so after exchanging a handshake with Lydia which stopped all his circulation for thirty seconds he followed his hostess. Lydia, feeling a little lost, went in search of other company and found Geraldine with Octavia Crawley and Mr. Needham, all eating potato crisps.

'Hullo, Lydia,' said Geraldine. 'Isn't it a shame Fritz Warbury couldn't stay? He's going to take me round the studio one day, though.'

Octavia Crawley, her utterance rather impeded by a mouthful of potato crisps that crackled like fireworks, said they had a man in from the film studios last week with the most ghastly burns on his arms, but that beast Matron had put him in D ward. Delia Brandon, she added, said they were the most splendid burns she'd ever seen. Tommy, she continued, a little more distinctly, had been in to read to him and thought he'd probably die soon.

'We've never had a funeral from the Hospital since I was there,' said Geraldine. 'It would be rather fun, but I wish it was a military one. Fritz could film it.'

Geraldine and Octavia then continued their artless talk, each on the subject that most interested her virgin heart, while Lydia gravely listened. On any other occasion she would have given her own views in no uncertain manner, but this evening, or more correctly since the last few minutes, she was conscious of an unusual want of interest in her young friends' conversation. Mr. Needham, who had felt a certain awe of her on the day she drove him to lunch with Mrs. Brandon, suddenly had a peculiar sensation of being sorry for her, he couldn't tell why. Her quiet manner seemed to him rather touching after the overbearing ways he had previously witnessed, and he could not help contrasting her with Geraldine and Octavia, who were still eating potato crisps and enlarging in a rather boring way upon films and funerals. Lydia's handsome face in pensive repose suddenly seemed to him much more pleasing than Octavia's plain thought animated countenance; even Mrs. Brandon's more mature charms were forgotten; and it must be confessed that Mr. Needham fell in love for the third time since the beginning of September, which was pretty good going.

The party was now thinning rapidly and Mrs. Birkett begged such guests as were still in the drawing-room to come across and look at the embroideries before they went. Accordingly Lydia and her friends who were still eating potato crisps and accompanied by Mr. Needham, followed the rest of the party into the dining-room from which Mr. Hopkins had been trying for at least half an hour to escape without success, till at last, to his horror, he found himself almost in the arms of Mme Brownscu, who was determined to get rid of the remains of her merchandise.

'You will buy this,' said Mme Brownscu. 'I will abandon it to you for three thousand Lydions, that is one shilling and you will tell all your friends to buy more. You will bring them to see me and I shall sell them much better embroideries which also cost more dear. One shilling, yes.'

But Mr. Hopkins, who was very avaricious, had no wish to part with a shilling. Indeed he had more than once thought of resigning his membership of the B.S.R.S.C.S. or Brotherly (and) Scientific Relations (with our) Soviet Comrades Society, because of the yearly subscription which with the poundage on a postal order and the postage amounted to nearly five shillings and sixpence. So he tried to slip past Mme Brownscu, but was brought up short in the doorway by Mrs. Bissell.

'Good evening, Mr. Hopkins,' said his Headmaster's wife with her usual calm. 'Here you see me a latecomer. Poor little Edna had one of her fits, so I said to Mr. Bissell not to wait for me. But the poor little thing got off to sleep nicely and Mrs. Dingle is sitting with her and here I am. Now you must show me the exhibits. What a pretty piece of work that is.'

'One shilling,' said Mme Brownscu. 'That is as much as giving him a present of it. I shall lose on this bargain but God wills it so. If you have no change it does not matter. It will benefit my compatriots.'

'No thanks, no thanks,' said Mr. Hopkins, angry and afraid. 'Very nice. Quite like the Russian work, but I don't want it to-day.'

He could not have made a more unfortunate remark. Mme Brownscu's eyes flashed, she stubbed her half-smoked cigarette out among the small change on the table with the action of one ridding the world of a loathsome viper.

'Russian, you said?' she inquired. 'You were in Russia, hein?'

Mr. Hopkins, wishing more and more that he had never accepted Capittleist sherry, said he had been in Moscow and must be getting back.

'Ha! Getting back to Moscow, doubtless!' said Mme Brownscu. 'Tu entends, mon ami,' she continued to her husband, 'ce type est ami de Moscou, de ces sales Russes.'

Poor M. Brownscu pulled his sheepskin coat so far up round his face that only his large miserable eyes were visible between the collar and his béret and shrinking away from Mr. Hopkins said in an agonized voice, 'Czy, pròvka, pròvka, pròvka.'

By this time all such guests as were left had gathered round in pleasurable excitement and those that were just going came back and looked over each other's shoulders in the dining-room door. Mrs. Birkett, who did not at all want her party to finish with a row, came up and begged Mme Brownscu to allow her to buy that delightful piece of embroidery which she had so much admired. But Mme Brownscu paid no attention to her at all.

'You do not know what that means,' she said, addressing Mr. Hopkins but gathering the whole assembly in her eye. 'He says "No, never, never, never. Non, jamais, jamais, jamais". Et savez-vous pourquoi il dit cela? It is because of the Russians, c'est à cause des Russes, pouah! quels sales types, which have destroyed his piano and his gramophone, lui qui est musicien par-dessus tout, and driven away, enlevé, all his stallions and mares, lui qui est cavalier accompli, et qui d'ailleurs ont violé sa mère, ses quatre soeurs, sa cuisinière, lui qui adore la bonne chère, et sa femme. And when he sees this dirty type of which I do not know the name which says "Moscou," cela lui tourne les sangs. N'est-ce pas, mon petit Gogo, ça te porte sur le foie? Take your embroidery, Mr. Russian, et allez-vous en à Moscou. C'est un schilling que vous me devez.'

So saying she thrust the embroidery into Mr. Hopkins's hands.

That unfortunate gentleman who had little or no acquaintance with French had not understood what Mme Brownscu was saying, but most of those present had been delightfully shocked and horrified. Among the exceptions was Mrs. Bissell who told Miss Hampton afterwards that she had given up French as a girl, but she saw that Mr. Hopkins, whom she had never liked, was interfering with the amenities of that nice Mrs. Birkett's party.

'Give the Russian lady her shilling, Mr. Hopkins,' she said in her gentle, authoritative voice.

Mr. Hopkins, against his better self, pulled out of his trousers pocket one of those leather purses of rather horseshoe shape, tilted some loose coins into the cover and held out a shilling. Mme Brownscu took it, threw it contemptuously into the plate of small change and then with a sudden effort snatched the embroidery from its purchaser, tore it in two and threw it on the floor. She then lighted another cigarette and hummed a national air very loudly. Mrs. Bissell, with the same imperturbable serenity, took Mr. Hopkins by the arm, led him into the hall, said Good-night to him and returned to the dining-room where Mme Brownscu was putting the money she had collected into a bag and preparing to go home. Everyone was longing to question her about her appalling experiences at the hands of the Russians, but felt a certain delicacy in beginning. Just as despair was seizing upon all hearts Octavia Crawley, whose interest in anything to do with hospitals we already know, earned the everlasting gratitude of her mother's friends by asking Mme Brownscu if the cook had got over it.

'Over which?' asked Mme Brownscu.

'The Russians. I mean what you said about the way they treated her,' said Octavia, suddenly finding it more difficult to talk about the facts of life in her mother's dining-room than she did with her V.A.D. friends.

'Oh, celle-là. Elle n'était pas mécontente. C'était d'ailleurs son amant, ce Russe,' said Mme Brownscu carelessly. 'Viens, Gogo; tu es prêt?'

But Octavia was of the breed of Bruce's spider and did not know the word defeat.

'And were you all right?' she asked.

'Yes, I am oll right,' said Mme Brownscu.

'But I mean then; the Russians,' said Octavia.

'Octavia!' said Mrs. Crawley, much to everyone's annoyance.

'Les Russes? I am not in Lydpòv then. C'est la femme de Gogo qu'ils ont violée; mais enfin c'était le colonel russe, qui était son amant. God wills it so.'

She then swept up the wretched M. Brownscu and took her leave, urging those present to send all their rich friends to buy embroideries. Mrs. Bissell thanked Mrs. Birkett for a most pleasant social gathering and saying how sorry she was for the poor Russian lady having to do all that embroidery went away with her husband, to release Mrs. Dingle from watching over little Edna.

The Dean then said one must not judge uncharitably of anyone, especially of those who were dependent for their bread on the charity of strangers. With this to encourage them the Birketts and Mrs. Morland together with the Deanery party and Lydia skirted with delicacy round the interesting question: If M. Brownscu's wife was not Mme Brownscu, who was Mme Brownscu. And to this question they regretfully saw no chance of ever getting an answer.

'Well, we must be getting home,' said Mrs. Crawley, who had decided not to speak to Octavia about her behaviour, though chiefly, it is to be feared, because she did not dare to. 'Josiah, are you ready?'

The Dean, who often wished that with all due respect to the Bible he had not been called after his grandfather, rallied to his wife and good-byes were said. Noel repeated his promise to Lydia to come and fetch her from her Communal Kitchen on the following day. Geraldine who was on night duty was to go back with the Crawleys. Mr. Needham, who was driving them, was suddenly struck with the thought of Lydia, alone, driving herself home through the black-out, and asked her earnestly if she would be all right. Lydia, seeing nothing not to be all right about, said of course she would.

'I have to be over at Northbridge to-morrow about a football match between the Boy Scouts there and our Choir School,' said Mr. Needham. 'I was thinking I might perhaps come and see you about tea-time if

you are in and your mother is well enough, unless perhaps you are
going to be busy or anything. I thought you might perhaps be kind
enough to help me about something, if it wouldn't be a bother.'

Lydia said of course. As she drove home she faintly wished that Mr.
Needham, whom she did not in her mind call Tommy, as she had never
thought of him since the day they lunched with Mrs. Brandon, weren't
coming on the same afternoon as Noel Merton; but if Mr. Needham
needed helping about something, that was not the way for her to think
so she didn't; or if she did, she tucked it away into the back of her mind,
and gave her parents an amusing account of the sherry party.

Mrs. Birkett and Mrs. Morland agreed at dinner that the party had
on the whole been a great success.

'Why did you ask those pestilent Warburys, Amy?' said Mr. Birkett.
'If I had any time to dislike people, which heaven knows I haven't
just now with chicken pox bursting out in all the Houses, I would dislike those people as much as I have ever disliked anyone. And as for the
boy — —'

'After all,' said Mrs. Birkett, 'Geraldine has nowhere else to see her
friends.'

'Friends!' said Mr. Birkett angrily. 'Rose's friends were bad enough,
but Geraldine's are insupportable. I really wish Rose were back
sometimes.'

He looked very tired. Chicken pox and a sherry party and the
Warburys. Mrs. Morland could not decide whether his remark was less
in favour of Rose or of Geraldine, so for once she held her tongue.

X

THE PATH OF DUTY

On the following day Lydia Keith, after a single-handed fight with
Palmer about tea-cloths in which she scored heavily, went off on foot
to Northbridge village with a large flowered overall in a bag. As most
of the neighbourhood was Cathedral property, and the firm of Keith
and Keith had for many years done much of their legal business, Mr.
Keith had been able to put gentle spokes in the way of building development, and even bully the Barsetshire County Council into building
quite presentable houses for the working classes well away from the
delightful village street, of which no fewer than fourteen different views,
including the church, the brick and stone houses of the gentry and the
remaining plaster and thatch houses of the cottagers can be got at any

picture postcard shop in Barchester. Next to The Hollies, a pleasant Georgian house standing back behind its shrubbery, was a plain-faced stone house that had been vacant for some time owing to a death and an entangled will. As soon as the threat of evacuee children had become a near menace, the Women's Institute, headed by Mrs. Turner who lived at The Hollies and her two nieces who lived with her, had given an entertainment followed by a whist drive and dance by which they earned enough money to start a Communal Kitchen. The trustees had consented to the use of the large kitchen quarters of the empty house, the money from the entertainment had been used to instal a new gas cooker and buy a quantity of cheap tables and forms, some very cheap cutlery and various cleaning materials. Volunteers had supplied cooking utensils, dish cloths, crockery, and other necessaries. The possessors of vegetable gardens and hens had promised weekly supplies according to their means. Mrs. Turner from her own purse bought a part share in a pig whose owner was on the dole and had no intention of coming off it, and supplied a pig bucket, on the understanding that the pig's owner would fetch the bucket daily and make over certain portions of the pig to the Women's Institute when it was killed.

With a great burst of gladness and relief nearly all the hostesses of the evacuated boys and girls sent them up to the Kitchen, paying threepence a head for an excellent and substantial meal. It is true that almost in the same breath they said threepence was too much, but Mrs. Turner took no notice at all. Under her truculent despotism a number of ladies undertook to do the cooking, the serving, and the washing-up in rotation, and it must be said to the credit of Northbridge that very few had defaulted. What with her mother and the house and the Red Cross and the estate and working parties, Lydia had not much time to spare, but she helped to serve the lunches one day a week and, as we have seen, did not allow anything to interfere with it.

The church clock was striking twelve as Lydia went into the house by the side door and down a long stone-flagged passage to what were called by the estate agent the commodious offices. Here Mrs. Turner was hard at work superintending the preparation of great saucepans of rabbit stew and potatoes. She had been at the Kitchen since ten o'clock that morning and would be there till the last helper had gone, and this she did every day except Saturdays and Sundays. By her instructions the gas cooker had been installed in the scullery, so that the washing-up could go on under her eye. The kitchen itself with its wasteful range and huge dresser was not used, and the servants' hall had been turned into a dining-room. In it Mrs. Turner's nieces were laying a knife and fork and a spoon and fork and a china cup fifty times over on the bare deal tables. Lydia put on her overall and seizing two large tin loaves cut them up into small hunks, two plates of which she put on each table. She then filled a large jug with water and poured some into each cup, repeating these actions till all the cups were half-full; for if they were any fuller the children always slopped them at once.

'That's right,' said Mrs. Turner, as she prodded a large saucepan of potatoes to see if they were done. 'How is your mother, Lydia?'

'Pretty all right,' said Lydia. 'What's the pudding?'

'Stewed pears and synthetic custard, and plain cake baked in meat pans,' said Mrs. Turner. 'Where's my colander, Betty?'

'Ackcherly,' said Betty, who was Mrs. Turner's elder niece, 'it's on the hook. I'll get it.'

Mrs. Turner took the colander and began turning out her potatoes, of which a dozen large dishes were put on a long table near the door of the servants' hall, together with piles of plates. At the same moment the younger niece opened the door into the stable yard and fifty children, rushing, clumping into their dining-room, formed up in a rough, pushing, gabbling queue. The well-known smell of children and stew filled the air and Lydia wished for a moment everyone were dead. The other helpers, who though extremely good and conscientious are too dull to mention, lifted great fish kettles of stew from the stove on to the serving-table and the ritual began.

'Who's doing the veg?' asked Lydia, getting behind the table.

'Well ackcherly it's me,' said Betty, 'but you can if you like. I'll do the rabbit. I hope they didn't leave any eyes in.'

Betty stationed herself behind a kettle of rabbit and with an iron ladle half filled a plate with a luscious stew. To this Lydia added potatoes and handed the plate to the child at the head of the queue. The other helpers served in the same way and each child carried its plate to its own seat. No sooner were they all served than a dozen or more came back, carrying their plates, with expressions of fastidiousness and insolence that Lydia tried hard not to see.

'Miss, I don't like rabbit.'

'Miss, there's something nasty on my plate. Dorrie says it's kidneys.'

'Miss, the lady didn't give me any gravy.'

'Miss, Gracie's got a bigger bit than me.'

'Miss, mother wrote to me not to touch rabbit.'

'Miss, can't I have some more rabbit? I don't like potatoes.'

'Miss, Jimmy Barker took three bits of bread and I ain't got none.'

'Miss, I don't like rabbit. I want fish and chips.'

Gradually the plaints subsided. Lydia went round the dining-room with the jug of water replenishing mugs. Already the tables were slopped with water, gravy, rabbit bones and splashings of potato. The smell of children and stew became thicker. The children themselves looked remarkably healthy and were well and warmly dressed. Lydia recognized some of the arted-up frocks from her working party and a couple of boys' jerseys that had belonged to her brother Robert's little boy Henry. The children filed back with their plates which the helpers rapidly emptied into the pig bucket. What with those who didn't like rabbit and those who didn't like potatoes and those who didn't like gravy and those who had taken three pieces of bread and only messed it about, and those who had eaten so many sweets already, bought with postal orders sent to them by their starving parents, that they could not eat at all, the bucket did very well.

The helpers now stationed themselves behind the serving table and dealt out stewed pears and custard, with a strip of cake to each. A number of children raised plaintive cries for or against these different articles of food, but the plaints, owing to fullness, were less violent. As soon as they had finished they rushed shrieking into the stable yard and so out into the street, and quiet fell.

Mrs. Turner and her aides took off the stove the kettles and saucepans of water that had been boiling and did the wash-up. The lay helpers, by which we mean the dull and nameless ones, then said they were sorry they must go home, as their husbands didn't like it if they were late. Mrs. Turner, Lydia, Betty and the other niece washed the tables, swept the floor and washed out all the drying cloths, which the other niece hung up in the yard to dry, after which they sat down and made their own lunch off some stew and potatoes that Mrs. Turner had kept back.

'I wish it was summer and we were having a picnic at the Wishing Well,' said Betty suddenly. 'Ackcherly we couldn't because they've got an anti-aircraft post up there, but I wish we could.'

'If those kind of things really happened like what people write about, about everything really happening at the same time only nobody knows exactly what it is,' said the younger niece, 'we could, but I think that's all rot.'

A pensive silence fell, while the four helpers thought of Time.

'I wonder,' said Mrs. Turner, 'how long it will take to get this place clean again when we stop, if we ever do.'

'It took us days at home,' said Lydia, 'and that was only six children. And *coats* of whitewash.'

'Why they all smell so much I can't think,' said Mrs. Turner. 'They all get one bath a week and most of them get two, and we've dressed them from top to toe and from the inside to the outside. Peculiar. I suppose the whole of the Middle Ages smelt like that. Come along, girls, we'll just wash up our own dishes and then we've done.'

'Ackcherly,' said Betty, 'we ought to be at the A.R.P. practice now.'

Lydia said they had better go and she would wash up with Mrs. Turner. She was just hanging up the saucepan lid on its nail when Noel Merton walked in, announcing that he had tracked her by the smell of rabbit stew from as far off as the Post Office.

'It's filthy,' said Mrs. Turner, with great frankness, 'but the children smell much worse, bless them. I believe the whole of England will smell

of children and stew before we've done. Good-bye. I've got a Polish
Relief working party at two.'

She turned the gas off at the meter and went away.

Lydia sat down on a wooden chair, while she folded her overall.
For a moment her hands lay slack on the flowered bundle and she
looked down. Then she raised her head and looked at Noel.

'You've done it again, Noel,' she said. 'I knew there was something
wrong with you the minute you came into the kitchen.'

'It wasn't my fault,' said Noel apologetically. 'Being of a crabbed and
studious disposition I did rather well in my exams and they made me
a captain. I now have blood lust and would like to be a major. One
crown is an agreeable badge.'

'I suppose promotion means going abroad somewhere,' said Lydia.

'Not yet, so far as I know,' said Noel, 'but you shall be the very first
person to know if I do. Oath of a captain.'

Lydia got up and shook herself with her usual vigour.

'I feel as if I'd never get this rabbit-evacuee smell off me,' she said
vehemently. 'Come on.'

She led the way down the flagged passage to where Noel's car was
standing by the kerb and got in. Noel went round and got in on the
other side.

'Look here, my girl,' he said, 'do you know what you did just now?
You sat still with your hands in front of you. I've never seen you do that
before. Is your mother worse?'

'Not really,' said Lydia. 'Only up and down. Luckily we've got loads
of coal, because she can't stand the cold. I'm thinking of shutting up the
drawing-room and using the library. Father and I do the estate work
there, but that won't worry Mother. Sometimes, Noel, one gets a bit
down, if you know the feeling.'

Noel said he did, and in his experience it always came right again,
and where would Lydia like to go for a drive, as he had vast stores of
petrol.

'Do you know it's a most extraordinary thing,' said Lydia, 'but I
actually – oh bother that word, I didn't mean to say it but Mrs. Turner's
niece says it all the time so I suppose I caught it from her – I mean as
a matter of fact I don't feel much like driving. You wouldn't care to
come for a walk down the water meadows, would you?'

Noel said it was what he would like of all things and turned his car
towards Northbridge Manor. When they got there Lydia said she
would just hurl her overall into the house and wash some of the rabbit
off her if Noel would wait, so he went out on to the little flagged terrace
behind the house and sat on a white seat.

Against this southern wall one could still bask in a mild way. The
trees were dripping their golden autumn coats on to the grass and
everything breathed an undisturbed peace. Noel thought of how many

pleasant visits he had paid to the hospitable Keiths, beginning with the
night he had to spend there unexpectedly, four or five years ago when
Mr. Keith had made him miss a train. He smiled as he remembered the
large, awkward, violent, good-humoured untidy schoolgirl that Lydia
was then. Looking back on their early acquaintance he came to the conclusion that if he had not stood up to Lydia at once she would have
knocked him down and trampled on him morally in her stride. By the
greatest good fortune he had stood up to her bludgeoning and so earned
her favour, and a highly unsentimental comradeship had sprung up
between them. While Noel became more and more successful at the bar
and was increasingly in demand among hostesses, he could always rely
on Lydia to look piercingly through him with her alarmingly honest
eyes and take him down a peg whenever she felt it necessary. In his mind
he compared the Lydia he had first known and the Lydia he knew to-day
and found very little change except for the good. True she did not
appear at river picnics any longer in a shapeless garment with her bright
red face, neck, arms and legs sticking out of it, but her mind still moved
with a good deal of the brusqueness of those days and she was almost as
ready to lay down the law as when she had preached about Horace and
Shakespeare and Browning at sixteen.

Now for the first time he was conscious that his ridiculous Lydia was
in earnest. Only by chance references had he gathered from her all
she was doing, but her father had spoken about her, and so had the
Crawleys, and his admiration for her had grown. With her sister Kate
away at Southbridge busy with her own children and the duties of a
housemaster's wife, and her special brother Colin in the Army, Lydia
had constituted herself the guardian of her father and her ailing mother,
a lonely life when all her friends were enjoying themselves with hospitals
and ambulances. Noel reflected upon his own job, an uprooting it is
true, but in interesting places and among interesting people, and
wondered idly if he could have done what Lydia was doing: a question
that he didn't like to press too far.

And now also he was conscious for the first time that his vital, tireless
Lydia could feel fatigue or strain. When he came down the long flagged
passage into the Communal Kitchen and saw her hanging up a saucepan lid, he had seen her as he always saw her, doing something. But
when she sat so still for a moment, her hands idle on the folded overall
in her lap, he had seen what he had never seen before, a Lydia putting
down her burden before she shouldered it again. The remembrance
pierced him. Then Lydia came out, announcing that if they were going
down the water meadows they might as well tidy the boat-house, a fact
which she evidently considered sufficient explanation for the very
shapeless grey flannel skirt and untidy short-sleeved jumper she was
wearing. Noel suddenly saw his old Lydia again and got up to accompany her.

They walked down the lawn and through the little gate into the meadows, which had already been flooded once and gleamed greyly where the waters had remained standing. The winding course of the river was marked by a fringe of alders, willows, and mountain ashes, now almost leafless, while above it rose the line of the downs with the beech clump showing its tracery against the sky.

'I do like all this,' said Lydia, making a vigorous sweep with her right arm that Noel with difficulty avoided.

She said no more till they got to the boat-house.

Here she made Noel take off his tunic, though the old Lydia would not have stood over him while he folded it neatly and hung it over a fence, and for nearly an hour they worked hard. The boat and the canoe had to be emptied of the leaves that had blown in from the river bank, the oars were put into their winter quarters on the wall, the cushions and mats were heaped on a bench outside for one of the gardeners to bring up to the house. Lydia, with some solemnity, closed and locked the river doors. Then after taking a last look at the green gloom behind her she locked the outer door.

'End of the boating season,' she announced. 'Colin usually does the Grand Closing with me, but last time he wrote he said he didn't know when he'd be getting leave, so I'd better do it.'

Noel put his tunic on again and they walked up to the house. There was a great deal that he wanted to say to her, but he couldn't find the words or the occasion. To praise her would probably only earn her good-humoured scorn; to tell her that he was anxious for her with all her burdens might annoy her; to try to explain what had pierced him in her momentary lassitude might trouble her mind. So he left everything unsaid and discussed the question of buying more pigs for the farm, or rather listened to Lydia's monologue on the subject.

In the drawing-room they found Mrs. Keith, who was pleased to see Noel.

'A friend of yours is coming to tea,' she said, 'Lavinia Brandon. She rang up after you had gone to the Kitchen, Lydia, and said she had a bit of petrol to spare and would like to come.'

Lydia was glad her mother was to have so charming a visitor but her own heart unaccountably sank a little. She blamed herself inwardly for this feeling which she put down to the rabbit stew and the evacuees.

'Oh, and Tommy said he wanted to come to tea, Mother,' she said. 'He's doing something about a football match over here.'

'These young people,' said Mrs. Keith to Noel Merton, in what he felt to be an unnecessarily grown-up to grown-up kind of voice, 'will not use surnames. Which Tommy is it, Lydia? Tommy Gresham, or that girl over at Little Misfit that has the bull terrier?'

Lydia explained that it was the Dean's secretary.

'I can't think,' said Mrs. Keith with great dignity, 'why the Bishop should have a chaplain and the Dean only a secretary. Considering how very Low Church the Bishop is I should have thought a secretary would be quite good enough for him. Whenever I hear of anyone having a chaplain I always think of the *Ingoldsby Legends*.'

Neither her guest nor her daughter felt equal to coping with this particular thought. Noel vaguely wished that this Tommy were not coming and Lydia, who was not as a rule given to such delicacies, suddenly felt that Noel was dissatisfied, which increased her depression and made her concentrate on the rabbit stew as the cause of all evil.

While Mrs. Keith was telling Noel about her elder son Robert's children, Palmer announced Mrs. Brandon.

'You had better do the black-out in the drawing-room now, Palmer,' said Mrs. Keith.

Palmer said she was sure she was sorry, but she had thought it was a pity to shut the light out so soon.

Noel could see in Mrs. Keith's eye that she was going to risk a domiciliary visit from the A.R.P. sooner than offend Palmer, but Lydia said, 'Now please, Palmer,' and Palmer grudgingly closed the shutters and drew the curtains.

'How nice and cosy it is. Just like old days,' said Mrs. Brandon, looking round at the room with its shaded lamps and its bright fire.

It occurred to all three hearers that in the old days it had been pleasant to have the room lighted at tea-time on a late autumn afternoon, leave the curtains undrawn and watch the fading light across the water meadows: but this did not seem worth saying. Lydia poured out the tea with a combination of the ruthlessness of a Sunday School Treat and the kindness of a very good nurse on the invalid's first day up. Mrs. Keith was able to begin the saga of Robert's children all over again, to which Mrs. Brandon listened with not quite her usual deceptive appearance of attention. She was looking as charming as ever, but there was something new about her that the others could not quite place. She was dressed in black, with touches of some filmy purple at her neck and had an air of gently sad abstraction from this world and of mourning for beauty vanished which were most becoming, but rather perplexing. News travels fast in the country and Mrs. Keith read the Social columns of her *Times* very carefully every day, but from neither had she gathered that any loss had befallen the Brandon family. A question about Francis Brandon brought the assurance that he was very well and waiting with ardour for his class to be called up; if anything had been wrong with Delia it would have reached them from the hospital via the Crawleys or the Birketts. Even Noel, who did not take his charming friend too seriously, wondered if she was in black for a purpose and bravely hiding a wounded heart. At last Mrs. Keith could bear it no longer.

'One gets so anxious in these sad times,' she said, 'and I can't help being a little worried about you, Lavinia.'

Mrs. Brandon very beautifully said that no one must worry about her.

'Your black,' said Mrs. Keith, touching Mrs. Brandon's dress. 'It isn't for anyone, is it?'

Mrs. Brandon with an exquisite air of discomposure said No, no; no one she knew was dead. No actual person at least.

'Is it an animal?' said Lydia. 'I wore a black hat ribbon for a dormouse once when I was little.'

Mrs. Brandon said she felt animals were so happy that one need not mourn for them. 'At least,' she added reflectively, 'English animals. That very wearing woman, my cousin Hilary Grant's mother, tells me that animals are still dreadfully treated in Italy, but then she is that kind of woman who would find them being badly treated anywhere. In fact she will not be happy in heaven unless she can find a horse with its ribs sticking out or a pig having its ears punched. Do you think, Mr. Merton, that heaven can really please everybody? Their tastes are all so different. And though we are told we shall see our friends again, there are several that I would so much rather not see, if it weren't too difficult to manage.'

Noel said the law didn't make provision for that particular case, but the Dean's secretary was coming and they might ask him. Upon which Mr. Needham very conveniently arrived, and finding himself in the same room with the most saint-like woman and the most delightful and touching girl he had lately met, became a prey to silence.

'I know you can tell us, Mr. Needham,' said Mrs. Brandon, looking devoutly at the Dean's secretary, 'Does one *have* to know people in heaven or not?'

'Mrs. Brandon is a little exercised,' Noel kindly explained, seeing Mr. Needham's embarrassment, 'because she is so kind to such of her friends as are a little dull and boring, and wonders if she is likely to see much of them in heaven. The Inner Temple is not a good preparation for that kind of special knowledge, so we appeal to you.'

Mr. Needham, after some embarrassing stutters, said he was sure no one could ever be dull with Mrs. Brandon.

'You've got it all wrong,' said Lydia. 'You couldn't be dull with her, but she could be dull with you.'

'Oh, but I could,' said Mrs. Brandon plaintively, 'I could be dull with anyone.'

'What Tommy meant,' said Lydia, 'was that no one could be dull with you. I mean there are two sorts of being dull with a person. One is when you are so dull that *they* feel dull, and the other when they are so dull that *you* feel dull; like Miss Pettinger,' she added reflectively, 'though with her it is really a kind of active horribleness as well.'

Mrs. Brandon said she knew she was very stupid and gave a fleeting glance at her own black dress in a way that wrung Mr. Needham's withers.

'I hope —' he stuttered again, looking at the black clothes which Mrs. Brandon was wearing like weeds.

'It has been rather upsetting,' said Mrs. Brandon, who had now got all her audience well in hand. 'You see I saw that a steamer had been sunk and it was the same name as mine and though one doesn't believe that things like that mean anything, it is a kind of shock.'

'If I may say so,' said Noel, 'you take shocks more becomingly than anyone I have ever known.'

Mrs. Brandon caught his eye, knew that he saw through her completely and couldn't help laughing in a very pleasant way, for her illusions about herself were not really deep and it amused her when Noel pricked them. Mr. Needham, who did not know her well, thought that a woman who could laugh, almost in the face of death, was more like a saint than ever.

Mrs. Brandon, having made her effect, suddenly became very businesslike with Mrs. Keith about some clothes that she was having made for her nursery school and borrowed some patterns of frocks and coats, promising in return to send Lydia a roll of material for Mrs. Keith's working party.

'I really do feel quite wicked sometimes,' she said earnestly to Mrs. Keith, 'at not overworking myself and having a breakdown, but somehow I cannot, and if I broke down the babies would have to go. I am having ten more next week. I have had the old stables made into dormitories and put in fixed basins and a bath and central heating, and Sir Edmund says he can get me enough coal if I don't ask how. But it all seems so wretchedly little when I see Delia at the Hospital and Mr. Merton in uniform and the Vicar and Mrs. Miller with those *dreadful* evacuee children.'

'At least, Lavinia, you are helping all those children,' said Mrs. Keith. 'And all I have done is to be so unwell that my husband had to get rid of our evacuees, and take up all Lydia's time, when she would like to be nursing. She is being more comfort than I can tell you.'

Noel Merton now began to get up.

'I shall see you again whenever I can,' he said to Lydia. 'And let me tell you that when I see all that you do and what a good girl you are being to stick to this place and do the dull jobs, you make me and my uniform feel like three pennyworth of ha'pence.'

Lydia looked at him.

'Well, what else could I do?' she said. 'I'm sorry about not going for a drive to-day, but it was great fun to clean out the boat house with you. If only Colin had been here too — I'll see you out. It's a bit dark on the front door step. Tommy wants to tell me something or other that he wants; more committees I suppose. Anyway I'd better get it over.'

Noel said good-bye to his hostess and Mrs. Brandon and shook hands with Mr. Needham. Lydia took him to the front door with a torch, to light him into his car.

'You are a good, *good* girl,' he said when he had buttoned himself into his British Warm. And he put an arm across Lydia's shoulders for a moment as they stood in the darkness. Lydia turned her torch on. Noel got into the car and drove away, rather wishing that young Needham didn't want Lydia's help about anything. She gave far too much to everyone and though he admitted that she gave very freely to himself, he suddenly had a feeling that she oughtn't to be so kind to young men of nearer her own age. 'Middle-aged fool,' he remarked aloud to himself and then had to give his mind to avoiding a car with far too powerful lights — the Warburys' had he known it — which was crashing along with its wheels well over the white line, causing him to change his note to 'Blasted fools.' But the thought of young Mr. Needham remained too near the surface for his pleasure.

Lydia snapped her torch off and stood in the cold for a moment. She told herself stoutly that Noel must have lots of friends nearer his own age, grown-up in a way that she could never hope to be. There was a freemasonry of age and associations between him and Mrs. Brandon that she could never hope to share. She was too humble to resent it and indeed liked Mrs. Brandon as much as ever, but she wished quite desperately that she were over fifty and a woman of the world. She always thought of Noel as about her own age, but every now and then it was borne in upon her that he must find her rather a green girl. She gave herself one of her impatient shakes. Tommy wanted something and must be attended to. And perhaps she would be able to prop up his feelings for Octavia, which seemed to be melting again under Mrs. Brandon's unconscious influence. Mrs. Brandon then appeared, kissed Lydia very affectionately and was in her turn driven away. Lydia went back to the drawing-room where Mr. Needham still lingered.

'It does make one feel a worm,' said Mr. Needham, 'to see men of Mr. Merton's age in uniform. I mean I know I am doing my duty in a kind of way, but it doesn't seem enough.'

Mrs. Keith looked so tired that Lydia said she had better go up and rest before dinner.

'I expect I'm rather a nuisance,' said Mr. Needham, 'but if you had a few moments to spare — —'

'All right,' said Lydia. 'Have a cigarette and I'll ring for some sherry and I'll come back when I've settled Mother.'

Mr. Needham was then left to face Palmer who brought in the drinks with a manner implying that every drop of sherry consumed in the house was directly taken from her and Cook's wages and that this was the kind of thing that led to a general uprising of the workers. He very basely pretended to be looking at some books in a far corner till he could feel in his back that she had gone, after which he was overcome with a sense of his own selfishness and was just going to slink away when Lydia came back.

'Are you going?' said Lydia. 'I thought you wanted to talk to me.'

'Well, I did,' said Mr. Needham, 'but I expect you'd rather I didn't.'

'Don't be an ass,' said Lydia good-humouredly, 'it's no good coming all the way here and going away again. Only hurry up, because Father will be back and I've got to see him about some business.'

Thus hurried and adjured poor Mr. Needham began to stutter again till Lydia's patience nearly gave way.

'It's often easier for people who stammer to sing than to talk,' said Lydia. 'You couldn't say what you want all on one note, could you? I mean like intoning, only that goes up and down. Is it about the Dean or anything?'

Mr. Needham was heard to mutter the words 'Mr. Merton' and 'uniform.'

'Well, I simply cannot understand you if you don't say something,' said Lydia, very reasonably. 'Just try.'

Thus exhorted Mr. Needham began again, and managed to explain that he had been much exercised in his mind as to his duty in the present series of crises. If only, he said, he could do something really horrible he would feel much better. Being a secretary was like funking everything. If he could be a curate in a very poor, atheistic, East End slum and never see a blade of green grass and be hooted in the streets and work for twenty-four hours on end and have the church open for down-and-outs all night and be in charge of a plague-stricken district and fast a great deal; or if they would send him to convert cannibals, or preach to lepers, or have his hands and feet frozen off in the Hudson Bay country, he would feel much better. As it was he thought he would go mad. Or to be a chaplain in France, though that was asking far too much. It was the older men who got all those jobs and there didn't seem to be any place for a young man at all. His speech then petered miserably out and he said he supposed he had better get back to the Deanery.

'Look here,' said Lydia. 'It's perfectly foul for *anyone* to be themselves just now, but it's about all one can be. I expect the Dean feels frightfully rotten too and would much rather be killed like St. Thomas à Becket, but he can't, so he has to do without. I feel pretty sick myself at doing nothing when Delia and Octavia are on night duty for weeks at a time and Mrs. Brandon is having a houseful of children and Noel doing something secret in uniform and Colin, that's my brother, training artillery in camp like anything – oh and *everyone* doing something. You really aren't the only one, Tommy. Anyway the Dean must have a secretary. And it's an awful help for Octavia to have you about. Buck up.'

'Do you think it really is a help to Octavia?' said Mr. Needham.

'Of course it is,' said Lydia. 'If you didn't take her for a walk when she comes off duty or before she goes on, she'd never go out at all, she's so lazy, and then she'd get fat and bloated and not be able to nurse anyone. Of course you're a lot of use.'

Mr. Needham, who having unloaded all his troubles on to someone else felt quite light-hearted, said he was frightfully ashamed and she was most frightfully decent to have helped him so much and he supposed he'd better go. On his way out he crossed Mr. Keith, who had just returned from Barchester, said how do you do and good-bye to him in a breath and went back to the Deanery, his mind in a confused jumble of adorations: of Mrs. Brandon because she had that effect on nearly everyone, of Lydia because she was a girl one could tell anything to without upsetting her in the least and perhaps the nicest girl he had ever met, of Octavia because it is wonderful to feel that you are really being a help to someone and almost consoles you for not being murdered by East-Enders, cannibals or lepers. But he determined to speak to his employer again about the chance of getting to the front.

'Tiring day at the office,' said Mr. Keith, sitting down heavily in the drawing-room. 'You know, Lydia, it's no fun being old and out of things. It isn't only the young clerks who have been called up, but I find myself actually envying Robert, because he is in the thick of everything. He is helping with every important county activity and I must say doing it all admirably, and so is Edith. And all I can do is what any junior clerk could do, routine work at the office and my usual committees, hospital and so on. It takes the whole heart out of one. There isn't any place for the old men now.'

'Rot, Father,' said Lydia, kissing the top of his head. 'If you didn't keep the office going, Robert would have to stop being useful in the county, and then there's the place, and Mother. And I wanted to talk to you about the third sluice in the water meadows. Something's got to be done about it.'

So they talked about the sluice. And then Lydia went up to dress for dinner. As she pulled her stocking on to her right leg, there was a faint sensation on her knee and she felt the well-known feeling of a ladder rushing head-downwards from knee to toe-tip. It was not a very favourite pair of stockings, and one heel had a small darn, but suddenly it was more than Lydia could bear. She hurled herself on to her bed and there cried uncontrollably, as she had hardly done since she was a child. She would have given anything to cry herself to sleep and forget everything, but it was impossible, so with the last spasm of sobbing she got up, blew her nose several times, washed her face violently and determined to be starting a stye in her eye if anyone asked questions.

'If only Noel were here,' she said aloud to her reflection. But at these words her reflection showed such unequivocal signs of beginning to cry again that she went quickly downstairs, where her father and mother would at least give her every reason for keeping up her courage.

XI

THE CHRISTMAS TREAT

As term drew to a close, the agitating question of Christmas holidays began to press upon everyone. The Hosiers' Boys were almost without exception to go home, as their parents thought it would be nice to have them back for the holidays. The few boys that for one reason or another their parents could not have were billeted on the Carters, where Matron most nobly gave up her usual visit to her married sister, whose boy in the wireless in the Merchant Service had been torpedoed twice and was about to join his third ship with undiminished spirits, and was rewarded by one broken leg and a mastoid, who had to be taken off to Barchester Hospital at half an hour's notice. The married masters relapsed into obscurity with their wives; some of the unmarried ones went back to wherever they lived and others were invited by friends they had made in the neighbourhood to spend Christmas with them. Mr. and Mrs. Bissell with little Edna remained at Maria Cottage and their friendship with Miss Hampton and Miss Bent grew and flourished. Mr. Hopkins, you will be glad to hear, got a very good job at Monmouth and left at the end of the term, unregretted by a single soul.

As for the evacuee children all over the county, their loving and starving parents, having had nearly four happy months of freedom, and seeing no reason why their children shouldn't be lodged, fed, clothed, educated and amused at other people's expense for ever, saw no reason to do anything more about them and hoped that the same fate would overtake the new baby whom most of them had had or were expecting. So all the hostesses buckled to afresh. Mrs. Birkett offered the school gymnasium for a great Christmas party with a tree, the sewing parties vied in running up party frocks for the girls, a levy on jerseys and cardigans for the boys was made in the neighbourhood. A house-to-house collection of small sums of money was made and Mrs. Phelps went to London on the cheap day return and came back with three dozen pairs of very cheap soiled white satin slippers which she and Miss Phelps dyed pink and blue and green, and two pounds' worth of toys, paper tablecloths and napkins, silver ribbons, and sparkling glass ornaments from Woolworths. Cakes were promised by all the hostesses and their friends, fish paste, tin loaves and margarine were bought wholesale, lemonade was laid in by the gallon. In fact every possible preparation that good-will could suggest was made for an afternoon of noise, mess, over-excitement, tears and sickness.

The actual preparations were put in the hands of Kate Carter, whose gentle soul revelled in the prospect of a total upsetting of her life for a week or more and the subsequent clearing up. Under her benign and unruffled sway the Hosiers' Boys who were staying at Everard's House cleared away the gymnastic apparatus, swept the floor, brought in from under the pavilion the trestle tables that were stored for the school sports and big cricket matches, helped to unload with only three breakages the chairs that came like bony sardines in a van from Barchester, rushed down to the village for drawing-pins and string, borrowed the Scouts' trek-cart and collected all the cups and plates that were being lent, carried up the two big tea-urns from the British Legion, and brought in coke for the big stove that more or less heated the building. It was really a crowning mercy that Mason, the School drill sergeant who had come up with Mr. Birkett from the Lower School, was in Manchester with his mother, or he would have infallibly gone mad at the desecration of his temple and the sight of the parallel bars shivering in the cold in the bicycle shed.

The question of invitations was not an easy one. It had gradually dawned upon the promoters of the party that it would be impossible to invite all the evacuated children in the neighbourhood. Mrs. Bissell, who was invaluable throughout the proceedings, suggested that the head teacher of each school represented in or near Southbridge should be given twenty-five invitations, with a request to distribute them among those of his or her scholars who were the least likely to let down the general tone. These schools were St. Bathos (C. of E.), Pocklington Road School (rigidly Baptist), St. Quantock (Catholic) and the Hiram Road School (aggressively non-sectarian not to speak of pink). The invitations were issued three weeks before the party so that the children might be chosen with care and deliberation. At first all went well; indeed too well, for on hearing of the ordeal by behaviour, every child behaved so unnaturally well that their teachers considered drawing lots. As time went on, however, the old Adam, and in a great many cases the old Eve, triumphed over virtuous resolves, and by the end of a week it seemed doubtful whether a single child would be eligible. The tickets were then distributed in a despairing kind of way and when they had all been given out it appeared that every child had several brothers and sisters who were crying all the time because they couldn't go to the Ladies' Party. It then became evident that to control a nominal twenty-five children at least one teacher per head would be needed, and failing this at least four teachers to each party. Sister Mary Joseph, who presided like a devout white pouter pigeon over St. Quantock, sent in a petition that all her teaching nuns might come, as a party would be such a treat for them, a request that could not well be refused to anyone so charming and so used to getting her own way. Urged by professional jealousy Mr. Simon of the Pocklington Road (Baptist) School asked to be allowed to bring his whole staff, saying darkly that he was responsible for his children, by which he was understood to mean that he must guard them against the Scarlet Woman in the shape of Sister Mary Joseph, who had quite enough to do and never thought of his children at all. Mr. Simon's application was rapidly followed by one from Miss Carmichael of St. Bathos (C. of E.) School who wished to bring her entire staff on no grounds at all and was insanely jealous because she was not on the Committee. The rear was brought up by Mr. Hedge-bottom of the Hiram Road School, who had at first decided to refuse to allow his children to attend a Capittleist function, but after wrestling with his conscience forced it to tell him that they ought to see how the so-called Upper Classes lived, that their teeth might be sharpened for the Class War in joyful hopes of which he lived.

By adding to these a number of evacuated mothers who wished their children under school age to participate in any over-excitement and over-eating that might be going on, Kate Carter and Mrs. Bissell, who sat as a kind of permanent Committee of Public Safety, found that they might easily have from a hundred and fifty to two hundred guests, but pinning their faith on the number of colds that were about they prepared for a maximum of a hundred and fifty.

To Kate's great pleasure Philip Winter came back at about this time on ten days' leave, asking if he might bring Captain Geoffrey Fairweather who happened to be quartered near him. Not only was Kate delighted to have two extra in the house, but in her kindly way she thought it would be nice for Mrs. Birkett to see her son-in-law's brother who might have news from Las Palombas. This was quite a mistake, for the Fairweathers, though devoted brothers, never wrote to each other, relying on chance or their various clubs to bring them into touch from time to time.

The only real blot on the entertainment was that Mrs. Warbury had invited herself and her son, choosing a moment when she could not very well be publicly refused. On hearing this Geraldine managed to get leave from Matron for twenty-four hours, as the only casualty under her care was an A.R.P. warden who had stumbled over some sandbags belonging to a rival section in the black-out and sprained his ankle, also having his nose broken by two zealous A.R.P. helpers who hearing the noise had rushed to his assistance, collided in the dark, and fallen heavily across his face. Although Geraldine had rung up young Mr. Warbury's secretary several times, she had not yet seen the film studios and her mother hoped she had got over her ill-judged affection for him, but such appeared to be far from the case. It was distinctly annoying for Mrs. Birkett to think of Geraldine wearing her heart on her sleeve for young Mr. Warbury to peck at, and she could only hope, though without much confidence, that among the crowd her virginal pursuit would not attract much attention.

*

By ten o'clock on the morning of the Treat the Committee were actively engaged. The Hosiers' Boys had stoked the stove till it was almost red hot and gave out such alarming cracklings that Edward the invaluable odd-man had to be sent for at full speed from the school allotments where he was repairing some fencing, to deal with the dampers which none but he had ever understood. Kate, to whose mind conflagrations from one cause or another were always an imminent danger, expressed her fear that the iron chimney of the stove might cause some adjacent woodwork to begin smouldering with slow combustion, which, growing to a head at about five o'clock, would suddenly burst into flame, lick up the Christmas tree and the trestle tables, cause the roof, which was supported by strong steel girders resting on brick walls, to fall in with a crash in five minutes and the whole party, who would have fled shrieking in wild disorder towards the three large exits whose doors opened outwards, to be incinerated in the horrid mass which the firemen from Barchester (for of the Southbridge Fire Brigade she had no opinion at all owing to knowing most of the members personally when off duty) would not be able to approach for three days, if indeed they had not themselves been overwhelmed to a man by avalanches of red-hot masonry and jets of white flame twenty feet long. Just as she was trying to decide whether she had better share the fate of the children, nuns, teachers, mothers, children under school age and other members of the School staff, or make her escape for her children's sake, to be despised by mankind for evermore, Edward, answering her spoken question which had merely been, 'Oh, Edward, don't you think the stove is rather hot?' had suggested that it should be allowed to rage unchecked until lunch time and then be allowed to die down, after which the accumulated heat plus the heat from far too many people crowded together in one room would make a delightful atmosphere. Kate felt much happier, and though at intervals her imagination still toyed with the idea of the slowly smouldering beam, we are happy to inform our readers that owing to the chimney having no beam anywhere near it, nothing of the sort happened.

The great question of the stove being settled, Kate was able to give her full attention to the arrangement of the room. The Hosiers' Boys, with a great deal of pleasurable and unnecessary shouting and shoving were getting the trestle tables up and placing the chairs. On the tables the Vicar's wife, the doctor's wife and Mrs. Birkett were fastening large gay paper tablecloths with drawing-pins and putting a cup and plate to each chair. Paper table napkins with borders of bright red and green holly were also provided, though with but little hope of their being used. By each cup were two straws, and this was a stroke of genius on the part of the Vicar's wife who had noticed from many years' experience that tea for children meant fuss, mess and a great expense of sugar, whereas lemonade needed no adjuncts of sugar or milk, did not stain their clothes so badly, and if drunk through a straw became a treat of the highest order. It was therefore decided that the tea urns should be used only for the grown-ups, who would refresh themselves after the children had been served.

On a spare table, in front of the urns, Eileen from the Red Lion (co-opted to the Committee as a compliment to Mr. Brown who had lent a quantity of cups and spoons), Miss Hampton and Miss Bent were cutting the loaves into slices and covering them with liberal applications of margarine and fish paste. All three ladies smoked incessantly and kept up a conversation about local affairs which to only the initiates of the Red Lion bar had any clue.

Mrs. Morland, who was not much good with her hands, had given herself the job of tidying, by which means she was able to infuriate all the helpers in turn, sometimes by folding up and putting away in a corner the paper and boxes that they particularly wanted, sometimes by sweeping dust and breadcrumbs into little heaps which were trodden upon or scattered before she could come back with a dustpan.

A large Christmas tree, sent by Lord Pomfret through his agent Roddy Wicklow, had already been planted in a tub of earth, the tub being lent by Mr. Brown and the earth by McBean, the head gardener of Southbridge School, who grudged it bitterly but could not resist Kate Carter's gentle insistence. Boxes and bags of toys and ornaments lay about ready for decorating its branches. This important part of the work was under the supervision of Mrs. Phelps who had decorated Christmas trees in every part of the globe since her early married days, and usually in those parts of our Empire or other people's empires where Christmas comes in the middle of the summer. Under her were Miss Phelps as Flag Lieutenant and Mrs. Birkett and Kate as warrant officers.

'The tub looks a bit bare,' said Mrs. Phelps, who looked very majestic with a brightly flowered overall over her zip lumber jacket and blue serge trousers. 'Do you remember, Margot, the year Irons was at Flinders and we had that gum-tree in a huge block of ice for the wives and children of the *Gridiron* and the *Andiron*?'

Kate wanted to know if it didn't melt very quickly as in Australia it was summer time in winter.

'Ice doesn't melt if you have enough of it,' said Mrs. Phelps, who was unpacking the toys with great dispatch. 'Irons got a shallow tank from

the Naval Barracks and we stood the ice in it with some freezing salt.
It looked very well. Margot put paper Union Jacks all over it. We
ought to have something to drape round the tub. Do you remember,
Margot, the year we were at Trincomalee and that nice Khansamah
draped the box our tree stood in with yards of coloured muslin. Now,
what could we use? You haven't a few flags, have you, anyone?'

But at this moment Matron, who had given herself a roving commission to help in all fields of service, suddenly appeared in her white
overall, followed by the biggest Hosiers' Boy who was carrying a large
bulky parcel.

'What a busy hive!' said Matron, looking admiringly at the scene.
'And what do you think, Mrs. Carter? I was just giving Jessie a hand
to turn out that cupboard in the maids' sitting-room, because, I said,
Jessie, it is just as well to see exactly what we have in the cupboard
while we are about it, for you know the way things get put away and
you cannot lay your hand on them just when you most want them,
when lo! and behold what did Jessie find on the top shelf which I had
absolutely forgotten about? So I asked Manners to carry it down like
a good lad, saying to myself, "Now that is exactly the thing." '

Upon which simple explanation Matron proudly undid the parcel
and revealed a huge roll of green baize.

'There!' said Matron with some pride. 'The very piece of green
baize, Mrs. Carter, that Mr. Carter bought for the doors between the
House and the servants' quarters on the first and second floors, but
owing to a slight misunderstanding the Governors had them re-done
with red baize, so there it has been all this time. Of course you wouldn't
have known about it,' said Matron, who though she was devoted to Kate,
liked to remind herself that she had known Mr. Carter before his
marriage. 'And I said to Jessie, Well, Jessie, I said, that will be exactly
the thing, so Manners carried it down and quite a weight, wasn't it,
Manners?'

Manners, who was one of the Hosiers' most brilliant Boys and had
just been elected to an open scholarship at Cambridge, was quite used
to being treated as a bright imbecile by Matron whose class feeling was
very strong, and smiled engagingly, saying that he'd often carried
heavier parcels for Dad on his rounds. As everyone knew that Manners's
father was a greengrocer and furniture remover in those districts beyond
the East End from which the Hosiers' Boys Foundation School drew
most of its pupils, they all liked him the more for this statement and
Kate suggested that he should go and help Mrs. Brown of the Red Lion
to cut up the great slabs of currant and cherry cake and eat all the bits
that fell off, which he most willingly did.

Mrs. Phelps explained aloud with pleasure over the green baize
which she said would give just the touch of Old England that she
wanted. She and Miss Phelps then draped it in folds and billows round

the tub and when Kate had sprinkled a shilling's worth of artificial frost over it, the effect was pronounced quite fairy-like. Then Miss Phelps, mounting a step-ladder, hung festoons of silver tinsel among the boughs and began to fasten the gold, silver, red and blue glass ornaments on to the higher branches.

'What shall I put on the top, Mother?' said Miss Phelps. 'One of the silver stars?'

Matron, who had had a mysterious air of one biding her time, suddenly produced a cardboard box and said she couldn't resist bringing a little contribution. The contribution was a china-faced doll with a yellow wig, dressed by Matron's skilful hands in cloth of silver, with short full skirts, a silver star on the top of her head and a silver wand in her right hand. Mrs. Phelps said it reminded her of the doll their Number One Boy had dressed for the tree at Hong Kong, Miss Phelps tied it firmly by the waist to the topmost twig, and Matron was enchanted.

'Well, that's about enough,' said Miss Hampton, strolling over from the sandwich table. 'Eileen must get back to the Red Lion at twelve. Bent and I must show up too. Doesn't do to let people down. Where's Mannerheim?'

'Do you mean Manners?' said Kate. 'He's helping Mrs. Brown with the cake.'

'Manners?' said Miss Hampton, casting a monocled glanced in the direction of the cake table. 'Don't know the lad. No, no, Mannerheim. Oh, Bent has got him.'

Miss Bent came up, leading the elephant-faced dog.

'He knows his name, you see,' said Miss Hampton proudly. 'Changed it last week. Must do something for gallant little Finland. Thought of Kalevala but no one knew how to pronounce it. Sounds Indian too. Fine fellows the Indians, but can't call them gallant. Not yet at least.'

Kate said she thought our Indian troops were very, very brave.

'Brave as tigers,' said Miss Hampton. 'Lithe as panthers, too. But can't call people gallant till they have their backs to the wall. Hope India will never have her back to the wall.'

'Come along, Hampton,' said Miss Bent. 'I can't hold Mannherheim much longer. He knows it's twelve o'clock as well as I do. Ready, Eileen?'

Eileen, who had just had a new platinum bleach and looked more beautiful than ever, said it had been quite a treat to cut up the sandwiches for the kiddies, but she must say ta-ta now as the lads would be waiting, and so departed with Miss Hampton and Miss Bent, the ci-devant Smigly-Rydz in tow.

They had only been gone a few moments when Philip Winter and Captain Fairweather came in, having, as they explained with a wealth of apology, just had breakfast. Kate and Matron, who liked nothing better than to see men overeat and oversleep themselves, beamed approval, and as the work was now finished they all went back to lunch, leaving Edward the odd-man, to put the final touches by winding yards of electric flex with coloured lights strung on it about the tree.

*

In the middle of lunch Geraldine arrived, having previously said that she wouldn't be home till two-thirty. Three people rang up for Mr. Birkett, wouldn't give their names when Simnet asked them, and took offence. Mrs. Warbury rang up Mrs. Birkett, saying that it was urgent. Mr. Birkett growled, but Mrs. Birkett said she supposed she had better go in case it was about the party.

'Well, what did *she* want?' said Mr. Birkett when his wife came back.

'What to wear,' said Mrs. Birkett. 'She seems to think it is a fancy-dress party and wanted to know if she is to come as a Red Cross nurse or as a visiting royalty.'

On hearing the name Warbury, Geraldine became aloof and ill-tempered, which her parents rightly diagnosed as the effects of love. Mrs. Morland, who was dramatising the stirring nature of the day by taking even less trouble than usual about her hair, dropped two tortoiseshell hairpins on the floor during pudding and as her host bent rather stiffly to pick them up, he felt that for twopence he would go to bed till after Christmas and stay there.

The party was to begin at four and end at six. By three o'clock the helpers were in their places, and just as well, for at three-fifteen precisely Sister Mary Joseph and her flying squadron of white-robed nuns arrived with thirty-six children spotlessly clean though unprepossessing, saying that the children had all been ready since two o'clock and it was eating their hearts out they were and sure we could be young but once. Her lambs, who having eaten their hearts out now had a hearty appetite, began to storm the tables and had to be kept at bay by a strong cordon of nuns and Hosiers' Boys, until the Hiram Road School poured in, when the two schools had so much to do in eyeing each other suspiciously and giggling that the cordon was able to relax. They were quickly followed by St. Bathos and the Pocklington Road School and a crowd of mothers and children, so that by the hour at which the party was supposed to begin the gymnasium was quite full of humanity.

'I think,' said Mrs. Bissell to Kate, 'that they had better have tea at once. When they see food they get restive.'

'Don't they have enough to eat then?' asked Kate, in some distress.

'Quite enough,' said Mrs. Bissell, 'but they are greedy and selfish and have no manners.'

'Oh, Mrs. Bissell; the *poor* little things!' said Kate.

'You see, Mrs. Carter,' said Mrs. Bissell calmly, 'I know them. I taught until my marriage. Come here, Janice, and let Mrs. Bissell put your ribbon straight. You can't really love them, Mrs. Carter, but you can do your duty by them. If I hadn't married Mr. Bissell I'd be teaching still. That's right, Janice, run along now. The worst of our profession, Mrs. Carter, is that you cannot really like your colleagues or your pupils, but it is a privilege to be able to devote oneself to the children and Mr. Bissell and I, being all in all to each other, do not see much of our colleagues except during working hours, which is I can assure you a great relief. I think tea immediately, Mrs. Carter. Sister Mary Joseph is losing control and if she does, all the others will.'

Acting on this advice, Kate told the four principals that tea was now ready. Sister Mary Joseph with the utmost dexterity at once whisked her flock into their places while the rest of the schools played a kind of musical chairs at the end of which some twenty children still remained standing. By the united efforts of the Hosiers' Boys and the helpers a few extra forms were brought in, some supplementary teas were spread, and in a few moments the air was thick with the bolting of paste sandwiches, chocolate biscuits and slabs of cake, while cup after cup of lemonade was upset straw and all as the young scholars grabbed for more food. With the rapidity of a flock of locusts they stripped every plate of its contents, looking at each other with suspicious eyes as they crammed their flushed and shining faces with food. The helpers rushed backwards and forwards replenishing plates till the last crumb of their reserves had been used. Meanwhile the crackers which had been provided were torn open, for a large number of children did not know about pulling them and the even larger number who did, both despised and feared the method, preferring to disembowel the crackers without delay. Mrs. Phelps had ordered nothing but caps and musical instruments. The clamour became deafening. All the children got up and banged into each other deliberately, while they puffed and blew crumbs into the whistles, mouth organs and other wind instruments provided for them. The Hosiers' Boys, who were really invaluable, cleared away the crockery and took down the tables thus giving the evacuees plenty of room to fight, as well as bang and bump and puff. Mrs. Morland, looking on from the door of the gymnasium changing-room, where she was helping to wash up, thought she had never seen a more revolting sight than so many hot children, the girls with their party frocks already crumpled and stained, the boys smeared with food from ear to ear, their unprepossessing faces full of the almost bestial look of satiety that cake and lemonade can produce even in the most gently nurtured young; so she went back to the washing up.

The helpers now got the tea-urns into action and fed the mothers and teachers, who were to have a slightly more refined tea of paste sandwiches and mixed biscuits. By the time this second tea was over a great many of the children were in tears with excitement and it was evident to any motherly eye that a number of them would probably be sick before bedtime. But such is pleasure. Kate asked Mrs. Bissell, who was entirely unperturbed by the scene, to say that the presents would now be given from the Christmas tree.

'Now, children' said Mrs. Bissell; and a hush fell on the room. 'Come up quietly, each school together, and no pushing. Anyone who pushes will go to the back.'

The schools were rapidly organized. Mr. Hedgebottom managed to get the Hiram Road School into the front of the queue, hoping that his un-priestridden charges would get the pick of the presents, though in this he was disappointed for Mrs. and Miss Phelps who were responsible for the gifts were the soul of impartiality and Miss Hampton and Miss Bent who actually presented them, with Mrs. Bissell and Kate as a bodyguard, did not know one child or one present from another. When every boy had received something considered suitable for a boy, and every girl something considered suitable for a girl, they all tried to take each other's presents away, and the noise was worse than ever. In the middle of it, Geraldine, who had really been working very hard all day and was feeling tired, for there had actually been six cases in her ward on the previous day and Matron had let her go on real night duty for a treat, suddenly saw young Mr. Warbury, accompanied by his mother who was roped with silver foxes and pearls.

'Hullo, Fritz,' she said; and her heart would let her say no more.

Young Mr. Warbury, who really has very little to do with this story except to show how easy it is for anyone to fall in love with a totally unworthy object, said God, what a smell and was there a drink anywhere. Geraldine, who had secretly been exercized about this all day, and would have brought some gin with her but that (a) her father had not opened the new bottle and might ask questions and (b) she felt that she had no genius for smuggling at all, exhausted herself in apologies.

'Your *lovely* furs!' said Kate to Mrs. Warbury, with a woman's real admiration for silver foxes. 'You really oughtn't to have brought them. Do be careful not to get anything on them. I'm afraid everything is very sticky.'

Mrs. Warbury, smiling a queenly smile, said to Sister Mary Joseph who was standing near, that she thought one should always wear one's prettiest things when one went among poor children; it was, she said, a kind of duty to give pleasure.

To these beautiful words, Sister Mary Joseph's answer was that the children had had a very pleasant afternoon, accompanied by a calm look which conveyed to Mrs. Warbury that she, Sister Mary Joseph, could give pleasure to anyone at any moment by simply existing and that, being always dressed in an extremely becoming uniform, she never needed to think of what effect she was making. She then gently moved a step aside and replaced a pink bow in one of her children's hair. Mrs. Warbury, for whom one may be a little sorry, then tried to talk to Mrs. Bissell, and to Miss Carmichael of St. Bathos School, but finding it somehow impossible to condescend to either of them gave it up as a bad job and floated graciously towards her son and Geraldine. Geraldine, hoping to propitiate her soul's idol, said how lovely it would be if he could make a film of the entertainment to which young Mr. Warbury crushingly replied that there was enough junk on the market as it was.

As if the Warburys were not bad enough, Mme Brownscu chose this moment to force her way through the crowd, carrying a large wooden box. As she had not been invited no one was surprized or pleased to see her, but Kate, who simply could not help being kind, received her beside the Christmas tree and said what a pity she hadn't come before to see the children at tea.

'I do not come because I am bringing something for you,' said Mme Brownscu. 'You English do not understand Christmas, which is a strongly religious festival. In Mixo-Lydia our peasants each slaughter a goose, which is eaten by all, and then they go to church.'

Kate said in England we usually went to church in the morning and had a goose, or more often a turkey, for lunch, so it was very nice to think that the Mixo-Lydians did the same sort of thing.

'But I shall show you what it is to make a real Christmas,' said Mme Brownscu, ignoring Kate. And thereupon she opened the box and placed it on a chair. It contained a small crèche with brightly painted paper figures of the Virgin and Child, Joseph, kings, shepherds and angels. On each side of it was a fat candle stump. These Mme Brownscu lighted.

Even the cheapest crèche at Christmas 'ime sends a prickle up and down one's spine and into one's throat. Kate and her helpers found themselves almost gulping at the sight of the two flames illuminating the pretty, touching toy.

'So. Now is the devil driven away,' said Mme Brownscu with great complacency.

Such of the children as were near crowded round to look.

'Oh, Mrs. Bissell,' said Kate. 'The doll on the top of the Christmas tree.'

Mrs. Bissell, again calming the tumult by her extraordinary power, announced that the youngest girl present was to have the doll, which Miss Phelps got down from the tree. To avoid complications Mrs. Bissell had made previous inquiries in all four schools and ascertained that Patricia O'Rourke of St. Quantock's was the youngest girl at the party. Sister Mary Joseph, who had been primed by Mrs. Bissell, drew forward a little girl in a stiff pink organdie frock with an enchanting face, guiltless of all expression except greed and bewilderment, and a mop of fair curls. Miss Phelps put the doll into her arms and Sister Mary Joseph said thank you for her, as she was too shy to speak. The little girl stood by the crèche hugging her silver-clothed doll with its uninteresting china face and its crown and star.

'What is it, Patricia?' said Sister Mary Joseph, who saw her rather than heard her say something. She stooped and listened.

'She wants to know if it is the Holy Virgin,' said Sister Mary Joseph, smiling kindly down at her charge.

Mr. Hedgebottom, who was not looking at the crèche, as he afterwards explained to one of his assistant masters, but just happened to be there, heard the remark and looked at Sister Mary Joseph with all the gall of which his communist face was capable, and could barely control himself before such a hideous example of Mariolatry. At that moment one of his young scholars, a promising lad of nine or ten, pointed a very dirty sticky finger at the crèche and said in a loud voice, 'What's that?'

Sister Mary Joseph was human, but she behaved very well. She merely cast on the questioner a look of such compassion that Mr. Hedgebottom nearly burst. For the first time in his painstaking and unpleasant life he saw that entire ignorance of what he called fetishism had publicly humiliated him in the person of one of his most promising scholars and he clashed his uppers and unders together with rage, resolving to put his whole school through a course of religious teaching, of course from a purely economic and anti-Christian point of view, so that they should not let him down again in public. To add to his humiliation, Mr. Simon of the Pocklington Road School and Miss Carmichael of St. Bathos had been close by and witnessed his discomfiture, the one from a Baptist, the other from a C. of E. point of view, and though Mr. Hedgebottom bitterly despised them both, he would have liked them to be somewhere else.

Mrs. Warbury who was just about to go as no one paid any attention to her, saw two officers come into the gymnasium and postponed her departure, not knowing that they were nothing more romantic than Philip Winter and Captain Fairweather who had basely gone for a long walk instead of helping with the treat and were now making a belated appearance hoping to acquire merit. Geraldine, who was desperately trying to entertain young Mr. Warbury, and had almost given up any hope of having a few kind words from him, pounced on her old friends and offered them up to her idol.

'Oh, Fritz,' she said, 'this is Philip Winter and Geoff Fairweather. Fritz makes the most marvellous films.'

'I suppose I ought to salute your friends,' said Mr. Warbury in a horrid way.

Philip and Captain Fairweather said in a general way what a ripping show it was.

'Stinking, if you ask me, and in every sense of the word,' said young Mr. Warbury, laughing at his own wit.

Philip, who had learnt a great deal about controlling his temper since the days when he was Junior Classics Master and rather a nuisance to his colleagues, said to Geraldine that all the children seemed very happy.

'Happy!' said young Mr. Warbury. 'The whole thing is revolting. A lot of women working themselves up and playing at being Lady Bountifuls. Come and have a drink whatever your names are.'

'No thanks,' said Philip.

'Have it your own way,' said young Mr. Warbury. 'Are you coming to see the studio, Geraldine, or won't Matron let you?'

Poor Geraldine, with the earth rocking under her feet, said she'd love to come, but every time she rang up he was out or busy.

'Ring again next week,' said Mr. Warbury. 'I should say I was busy. Some of you girls have an easy time running about the hospitals. My God, this is a rotten war. I'm getting a permit to go to America and I'll have something to say about England when I get there.'

Anyone less silly than Geraldine would have realized that young Mr. Warbury must have had a drink or two before he came, which was at once apparent to Philip and Captain Fairweather. Geraldine went very pale and her eyes filled with tears, because she suddenly saw young Mr. Warbury exactly as he was and wished she could die at that very moment and be buried anonymously. Captain Fairweather, who had known her for a long time, in fact since he was in the Junior School, did not understand all her feelings, but her face and Mr. Warbury's revolting manners were enough for him. He had always been a good boxer and nothing would have given him more pleasure than to land Mr. Warbury one on the chin, but a Christmas treat for children, nuns, mothers, teachers and children below school age did not seem the right place to do it. He gripped Mr. Warbury powerfully by the arm and led him in ominous silence towards the exit.

'Don't do that,' said young Mr. Warbury shrilly.

'Don't open your filthy little mouth again,' said Captain Fairweather. 'Show me your car.'

'Mother!' said Mr. Warbury.

'I'll find your mother,' said Philip Winter, who was acting as escort on the other side. 'Put him in the car, Geoff, and keep him there and I'll tell Mrs. Warbury he's sick. It's all right, Geraldine,' he added, seeing her expression of misery and fright. 'Geoff won't hurt him.'

He then made his way to where Mrs. Warbury was boring Mrs. Birkett and Mrs. Morland dreadfully and told her that her son did not feel very well and was waiting for her in the car.

'You will forgive me then if I fly,' said Mrs. Warbury. 'And it may be a kind of good-bye. I believe we are off to America almost at once. Oscar and Fritz are so sensitive and really England is *no* place to live in now. But you must come and have a drink before we go. Come on Friday, just a few old friends.'

Mrs. Birkett said she was afraid she and her husband were engaged. 'Then you must come, Mrs. Morland,' said Mrs. Warbury graciously. 'There are some men coming that it would be useful for you to meet. Klaus Klawhammer is one of New York's brightest literary agents and he would do quite a lot for you if you got on well with him.'

Mrs. Morland had no pride at all, but she had a violent prejudice against agents, whom she had once described as being paid to make bad blood between authors and publishers, a point of view that had enchanted her own publisher Adrian Coates. Also she disliked Mrs. Warbury very much, and had indeed already cast her in her mind as the she-villain for one of her short stories that people liked so much. And all these feelings combined made her go very pink and talk with more vagueness than ever as she said,

'Thank you so much, but I am *really* engaged that day, because of Mrs. Keith's working party. And of course one can't help being English and I do think England is nicer, even when it is awful, than anywhere else. And as a matter of fact I deal directly with my American publisher who seems very nice, so thank you so much but I must say no thank you.'

She then pushed some hairpins madly into her head and retired again to the washing up.

Mrs. Warbury, quite unabashed, gathered up her furs and her pearls and floated languidly after Philip to the exit. Here her escort produced a small torch and lighted her to the enormous car, in one corner of which young Mr. Warbury was sitting very cross and rather afraid, while Captain Fairweather and the chauffeur, who turned out to be an ex-corporal in the Barsetshires, talked about the difficulty of getting to America in safety, not without reference to the chauffeur's young master who could have been seen going visibly greener if there had been any light to see him by.

'Is it one of your heads again, my poor lamb?' said Mrs. Warbury to the corner in which her son was huddled. 'How nice of you boys to look after him. Come along and have a drink and then I'll run you home. There's always enough petrol for little me.'

Young Mr. Warbury could have killed his mother for this, but Captain Fairweather, answering rather untruthfully for himself and Philip, said they had to get back to camp.

'You poor boys,' said Mrs. Warbury, from the depth of the car and a fur rug. 'What a pity you didn't go to America before all this trouble, or get into a reserved occupation like Fritz. Are you sure you won't come and have a short one?'

But both officers declined her offer. Under cover of the darkness Captain Fairweather slipped half a crown into the chauffeur's hand, who speaking out of the side of his mouth expressed his opinion of what was inside the car and hoped the Captain would get a good smack at

Jerry, adding that he was going into munitions himself that day fortnight and hoped the new chauffeur would drive all the family into a ditch. Upon which hope he drove away and Philip and Captain Fairweather returned to the gymnasium.

Here the party was rapidly thinning. Sister Mary Joseph with her flock had already gone, after thanking all the hostesses in a way that made them feel that they had on the whole been kindly and impartially weighed and found wanting. Mr. Hedgebottom and Mr. Simon were shepherding the last of their boys away from the Christmas tree. Miss Carmichael, though tired, remembered that C. of E. gives one social status and was slightly outstaying her welcome.

'Did you hear that poor little lad from the Hiram Road School?' she said to Mme Brownscu, who was packing up the crèche. 'Fancy not knowing what a crèche was. It does seem shocking to bring up all those lads like little heathen. It hardly seems feasible in a Christian country.'

'To us,' said Mme Brownscu, hitching her leopard-skin coat round her preparatory to her departure, 'England is not Christian. Mixo-Lydia which is a strongly dévot — devoted country you would say — says Pouf of this religion which is all wrong. As well might you all be Yews. Grzány provk hadjda.'

Her last words were all the more terrifying as neither Miss Carmichael nor any of the helpers who were near had the faintest idea what they meant, nor indeed have we ourselves. Mrs. Bissell, who having once placed Mme Brownscu in her mind could not be troubled to reconsider her, said good-bye and hoped that all the poor Russians were well, at which and by Mrs. Bissell's attitude of calm certitude, Mme Brownscu was so flabbergasted that she was for once deprived of the power of speech and went back to Mixo-Lydian House where she picked a frightful quarrel with the unhappy M. Brownscu that raged far into the night, with enthusiastic support on both sides from all her compatriots.

Miss Carmichael, who was not very quick in the uptake, suddenly realized that Mme Brownscu had compared the C. of E. with the Jewish faith and hurriedly collecting her scholars and teachers went off in a huff.

The helpers all looked at each other.

'I think, Mrs. Carter,' said Mrs. Bissell, 'that we had better clear up at once. The longer you put anything off the longer it takes, and I must be back by half-past seven as Mrs. Dingle has to go and get her husband's supper.'

Accordingly the whole band, including Philip Winter, Captain Fairweather and the Hosiers' Boys, set to and by ten minutes past seven the débris had all been removed, the decorations taken down, the chairs stacked ready for removal, the Christmas tree undressed and the floor swept clean. Mrs. and Miss Phelps took the tea-urns back to the British Legion in their little car. Miss Hampton and Miss Bent with

Mannerheim escorted Mrs. Bissell to Maria Cottage, stopping on the way at the Red Lion for a short one, of which Mrs. Bissell with inalterable placidity also partook.

By previous arrangement the Carters and their guests were to come up to the Headmaster's House for dinner, leaving Everard's House free for a gigantic feast with which Matron proposed to regale the Hosiers' Boys as a tribute of gratitude for their help. Mrs. Birkett had said no one must think of dressing, so they all walked up to the School together.

XII

NEWS OF THE FLEET

AT first everyone was rather tired, but under the influence of Mrs. Birkett's good food and Mr. Birkett's good drink they began to recover and by half-past nine, when they were comfortably in the drawing-room, they had all forgotten the major horrors of war as exemplified in the afternoon's treat. All but Geraldine. First love is an astounding experience and if the object happens to be totally unworthy and the love not really love at all, it makes little difference to the intensity or the pain. Geraldine, owing to seeing so much of her sister Rose, had long despised the tender passion. Her thoughts had been more of things of the intellect, such as being fairly good at maths and the horribleness of Miss Pettinger and the odiousness of Matron, and how one's parents would ask questions and expect answers. Then suddenly young Mr. Warbury had come into her life, with his cheap assurance and his flashy good looks, and all was up with her. It must in fairness be said that young Mr. Warbury had given her no encouragement at all beyond being rather rude and offhand, but passion is self-nourished. Geraldine was not so silly as her sister, but far less dashing. Where Rose would have forced her way, quite unconscious that anyone could be busy, into the film studios and made Mr. Warbury take her out to dinner and dancing, and then forgotten him after a week for a newer swain, Geraldine was too timid in her love to assert herself at all. And as Mr. Warbury was not in the least interested in her it is not surprizing that she got no further. She might have gone on like this for months, making a dejected doormat of herself before the man of her choice and blighting her home by moods of gloom, but for the events of the afternoon. She had seen young Mr. Warbury beside Philip and Geoff, who were such old friends that she never thought about them, and suddenly she had seen that he was rude and no gentleman. At the sight her whole upbringing asserted itself and with violent revulsion she hated first him, and then far, far more bitterly, herself. How deeply did she wish that Matron had not given her twenty-four hours' leave and that she could rush back to the hospital and there busy herself in swabs and bandages, but her parents expected her to stay the night and if she tried to alter her plans they would Ask Questions. And with these bitter thoughts it was all she could do to keep from crying. Her mother did notice her dejection and would dearly have liked to comfort her, but she knew her position too well and had to content herself with an occasional anxious glance in her daughter's direction which made that unhappy creature wish that Mummy had never been born or that she herself were dead. The only piece of luck in the whole evening was that she sat at dinner between Philip and Captain Fairweather, who both had a fair idea of what had been happening and kept up a conversation under cover of which Geraldine could gulp almost unnoticed.

As was but natural Mrs. Birkett talked a good deal about Rose and her letters. As was also but natural, Captain Fairweather had heard nothing from his brother since the wedding, had every confidence in his well-being, and was pleased to hear that he and Rose were enjoying Las Palombas.

'We had a letter from Rose,' said Mrs. Birkett, 'all about the naval battle. Would you like to see it, Geoff?'

Captain Fairweather said old John must have been pretty sick not to be in it and he'd love to hear. Mr. Birkett looked as if he did not particularly want to hear it, but said nothing. Mrs. Birkett went to her writing-table and brought back a letter in Rose's well-known dashing handwriting, twenty-five words of which filled the largest sheet of paper.

'If I read it aloud, everyone could hear it,' she said, already a little nervous about its effect and perhaps feeling that her elder daughter's idiosyncrasies of spelling would be less noticeable if orally transmitted. Captain Fairweather said that would be splendid.

'Darling,' (Mrs. Birkett read.) 'I hope you and Daddy are frightfully well. It is marvelous here and Juan Robinson the one I said about is going to take me to Asturias Point to bathe. There is a marvelous hairdresser in Las Palombas and I am having my hair done in quite a new way. I went to have it set this morning and Pedro which is the one that does it wasn't there so I had to wait and when he did come he was so late that I couldn't stay. He said he had been looking at the ships which John says was too marvelous but I must say it was fouly dispiriting and I am going again to-morrow. John says he knows two officers on the Aciles and a lot of other ones so I hope they will come ashore. There is lovely dancing at a club called Mickey Mouse which seems to be the same word here. Give my love to Geraldine and Phillip and anyone else except the Pettinger.

'With heaps of love from

'ROSE.'

We must say, in justice to Mrs. Birkett, that although she thought her daughter's letter slightly foolish when she read it to herself, she had quite underestimated its effect when read aloud and only her great courage bore her up to the end.

'It isn't very much,' she said nervously, and no one had ever heard her speak nervously before, 'but it does seem so interesting to know that Rose was at Las Palombas when that marvellous battle was going on and really might have seen it.'

Her brief apology had given her guests time to recover themselves and they were all loud in their gratitude for this stirring account of one of England's most heroic sea fights. Captain Fairweather said John must have been absolutely sick not to be in it and if it weren't for the Barsetshires he wished he had gone into the Navy himself. Kate said it was dreadful to think of the mothers and families of the men that had been killed, because even if people were one's enemies it was dreadful to think how unhappy they must be and she knew exactly what she would feel like if it was Bobbie. Everard blanched visibly at this vision of his son aged fifteen months gloriously killed in action. Captain Fairweather said By Jove, yes, Bobbie, and fell respectfully silent, so that Mrs. Morland, who had been rapidly visualizing her explorer son transported by magic from a thousand miles in the interior of South America to the scene of the naval battle and there dying a hero's death, her naval son who was on the China Station circling half the globe in a few days only to perish among shot and flame, her third son having unknown to her become a Secret Service Agent and arrived at Las Palombas in time to foil an enemy plot at the expense of his life, not to speak of Tony, now well known to be with friends in Gloucestershire for part of the Christmas vacation, having got into the Trans-Atlantic Air Services and so to Las Palombas and a heroic if unspecified end, surprized herself and made everyone else very uncomfortable by beginning to blow her nose violently.

'I'm so sorry,' she said weakly as, her eyes dimmed with tears, she groped on the floor for a hairpin, 'but it's all the glory and the misery mixed up together on the top of the treat. I think I'd better go to bed.'

At that moment Simnet came in to say that Miss Geraldine was to report at the hospital as soon as possible because a number of German measles had come in. The message, he added, had just come on the phone. He then waited to ride the whirlwind if necessary, but Mr. Birkett said, 'Thanks, Simnet,' so he had to retire, baulked.

'Oh, Mummy, there isn't a train to-night,' said Geraldine. 'Could I have the car?'

'You'll have to ask Daddy,' said Mrs. Birkett. 'I know we're rather low on petrol till the end of the month. I wish Matron had let you know sooner and you could have got the 9.43.'

'You *could* have the car,' said Mr. Birkett doubtfully, 'but there'll have to be someone to bring it back. I might send down to Mason — no, he is away till Monday.'

'I'll run Geraldine over, sir,' said Captain Fairweather. 'I've got all the petrol in the Army. I'll have her at the door in a moment, Geraldine, if you get your whatnots together. Coming too, Philip?'

Philip said he would and in a few minutes the three went off. Everard and Kate left almost at once, as the thought of a naval battle fought thousands of miles away and nearly a fortnight ago had filled them both with vague fears, which neither of them would have acknowledged to the other, as to the safety of Bobbie Carter, now asleep like a rose-petal jelly in his warm cot. Mrs. Morland retired to sublimate her feelings in her novel before she went to bed and the Birketts were able to sit and read in peace, a luxury in which they rarely indulged.

*

'Look here, Geraldine,' said Captain Fairweather as they were nearing Barchester, Geraldine beside him and Philip in the back seat, 'don't worry about things.'

Geraldine sniffed loudly and gratefully.

'That's all right,' said Captain Fairweather, apparently quite satisfied with her response. 'And if you need anyone, I mean someone that isn't your own family, to do anything for you, I can always wangle some leave as long as I'm in England.'

Geraldine made a kind of mumbling noise, choked with her handkerchief.

'After all,' continued Captain Fairweather, conversationally, 'damn that fellow, the police ought to arrest him with headlights like that, we've known each other quite a long time and John being married to Rose makes me your next of kin, or as near as. So if anyone bothers you, just write to me and I'll turn up and lay him out. Do I go by Foregate or by Challoner Street?'

'Challoner Street and then round by the Plough,' said Geraldine, 'and it's *angelic* of you, Geoff, and I have been so *miserable*.'

'Of course you have,' said Captain Fairweather. 'That's why I mentioned it. Here we are. Get out, Philip.'

Philip got out and strolled round to inspect the rear light of the car.

'Listen,' said Captain Fairweather. 'Do you care for anyone? I don't mean that little sweep — that was only a mistake. I mean anyone real?'

Geraldine shook her head violently.

'That's all right,' said Captain Fairweather. 'Then you'd better get used to liking me. You are too silly to go about alone. Not even as much sense as Rose,' he added as an afterthought.

'It's *angelic* of you, Geoff,' said Geraldine.

'That's all right,' said Captain Fairweather, giving her a hearty hug with his left arm. 'We'll probably get married, come the peace; or before that if it doesn't. Now you go on nursing and let me know anything you want. Is that fixed?'

'Thank you a million times,' said Geraldine earnestly, as she got out of the car. 'And I will try to be good.'

'You'll be good all right,' said Captain Fairweather very kindly.

Geraldine ran up the steps to the nurses' entrance and was engulfed by the hospital. Philip came back and took his seat beside Captain Fairweather, who drove back at excessive speed, singing a cheerful song and vouchsafing no explanation to Philip, who did not need any. When they got to the Carters' House Captain Fairweather told Philip that he was going over to the Birketts for a few moments and vanished into the darkness.

The Birketts were surprized by the return of Geraldine's escort and at once jumped to the conclusion that there had been an accident and Geraldine was dead and Captain Fairweather had come, singularly calm and unscathed, to tell them so.

'Sorry to barge in, sir,' said Captain Fairweather, 'but I thought you'd like to know I landed Geraldine at the hospital all right. She's got my address and if she wants me I'll manage to get over at almost any time.'

'That's very good of you, Geoff,' said Mrs. Birkett, wondering.

'Being almost one of the family, with John and Rose married,' said Captain Fairweather, 'I don't think it would be a bad plan if Geraldine and I got married. I just thought I'd break it to you.'

As his future parents-in-law appeared to be struck all of a heap, he continued, standing over them with a pleasant impression of self-reliance and kindness,

'She needs someone to look after her. That little blighter Warbury won't bother her again. I'm not as well off as John, because Aunt Emma didn't leave me anything, but I'll have a bit when Uncle Henry dies and the doctors have been saying for four years that it wouldn't be long. So if you don't want to turn me down, we might take that as settled.'

The Birketts were so taken aback by this totally unexpected development that they were bereft of speech, till Mrs. Birkett recovered herself enough to ask weakly if Geraldine knew.

'She knows all right,' said Captain Fairweather. 'I gave her the idea and it'll soak in all right. She can get married whenever she likes. I should say before I get sent abroad would be better than after, because one never knows if one will come back.'

By this time his shock tactics had reduced Mr. and Mrs. Birkett to such a state of imbecility that they would have agreed equally to marriage by special licence on the following morning or an engagement lasting ten years. When they compared notes afterwards they found that nothing better than tags from Victorian novels had floated into their minds, Mr. Birkett having with difficulty subdued his inclination to say, 'Bless you, my boy; and may she make you happy,' and Mrs. Birkett having an almost irresistible impulse to say that she felt she was not losing a daughter, but gaining a son. Both were a little ashamed to discover that cliché can be the best expression of emotion and both secretly regretted that they had not had the fun of giving vent to it.

Mrs. Birkett was the first to pull herself together.

'It seems so sudden, Geoff,' she said, reflecting even as the words left her mouth that it was rather the affianced than the affianced's mother who ought to use those time-consecrated words, 'but I'm sure Geraldine will be very happy with you and I can really think of nothing nicer.'

'Well, it surprized me as much as it surprized you,' said Captain Fairweather with great candour, 'but when I saw that little swine frightening Geraldine I thought the Barsetshires ought to do something about it. Anyway I've known her since I was a kid – and she was a pretty ghastly kid herself,' said the gallant Captain meditatively, 'so we ought to make a do of it. John will be pleased. He likes Geraldine.'

'Oh!' said Mrs. Birkett, determined to offer all she had to give, 'there is something in Rose's letter that you'd like to hear, Geoff, but I didn't read it aloud. Wait a minute.'

She went to her writing-table, found Rose's letter and handed it to Captain Fairweather, pointing to the last paragraph. Captain Fairweather read the following words.

'P.S. I don't remember if I said in my last letter, but I'm going to have a baby in August. It seemed a bit dispiriting at first but now I think it's absolutely marvelous and he is to be William after Daddy Gefrey after Geff or if it's twins Amy after you Kate because of Kate. The Dr. which is Juan Robinson's father I said about says be sensible but have a good time isn't it marvelous With heaps of love from Rose.

Captain Fairweather grinned from ear to ear and handed the letter back to Mrs. Birkett.

'Jolly good,' he remarked, 'I didn't quite get it all the first time, but I see what she means. We'll call ours Rose, or if he's a boy John. Well, I must be getting along. Thanks most awfully for the Christmas treat and dinner and everything, Mrs. Birkett. Good night, sir.'

He departed, leaving the Birketts shattered, but on the whole content. Though neither of them would have said it for worlds, the prospect of their younger daughter being married filled them with a sense of relief, only comparable to that which they had felt when Rose was safely off their hands. They were good parents and would rather have gone on putting up with Geraldine than seen her married to the Warbury of her choice, though they knew that if she had wanted it they

were powerless to prevent her. But to think of her in the reliable keeping of Fairweather Senior, who (and though one should not think of
such things they are of the utmost importance) would not be badly off,
was as good as having a hot bath and a large tea after a long walk in
the rain. As for the possibilities, the probabilities, of some quick tragedy
cutting across Geoff and Geraldine's life, on these it was worse than
useless to brood and from them they resolutely turned their minds.

*

On his return to Mr. Carter's House, Captain Fairweather found his
host and hostess and Philip Winter very comfortable in the study, with
a large fire and pipes and drinks. From what Philip had told them the
Carters were not unprepared for Captain Fairweather's news, but they
managed to receive it as a complete surprise and with far more outward
manifestations of joy than the Birketts had shown. When Kate went to
bed the two soldiers fell into army talk, of which Everard took advantage to finished the House reports. At a quarter to twelve he had signed
the last and when he had put them into their envelopes he got up and
stretched himself.

'I *am* sorry, Everard,' said Philip, conscience-stricken. 'I had forgotten you were alive.'

'But I am,' said Everard, sitting down in a large chair by the fire. 'It
was pleasantly like old days to hear you talking, Philip.'

'I don't know,' said Philip, whose conscience appeared to be rearing
its head in more directions than one, 'why you didn't kick me out of the
House, Everard. I haven't a great opinion of myself now, but when I
think what a frightful, blethering, Communist nuisance I was, with
every antenna, if that word has a singular, out to find offence and take
it, I feel I ought to be condemned to live in the London School of
Economics for the rest of my life.'

'You weren't too bad,' said Everard. 'Do you remember when you
accused Swan of looking at you through his spectacles?'

'That boy had a devilish and subtle mind,' said Philip. 'I still believe
that he forced his mother to buy those spectacles so that he could look
at me through them. Where is he?'

'Cambridge,' said Everard, 'my old college. He gets called up next
month.'

'I think, sir,' said Captain Fairweather, 'it's almost rottener for
schoolmasters than anyone. I mean all these youngsters getting called up.'

'That's nice of you, Geoff,' said Everard. 'It takes the heart out of
one sometimes. But it isn't one's own body that is going to be blown up
or drowned, and one has no right to such damned sensibility about
things. It doesn't help. One can't help envying Swan and all the others.
If only there were something to do. Anything but schoolmastering;
keeping safe.'

Philip, in all his experience of Everard had never heard him speak with such impatience and realized, with the sensitiveness that had formerly made him such a nuisance to himself and his colleagues, how much Everard, and thousands of men of his age, in his position, might be suffering; but found nothing to say.

Captain Fairweather with the patience that the good professional fighter has for the civilian said:

'It's rotten for you, sir. That's where fellows that aren't brainy like John and me are so lucky. I expect you brood a lot. I've noticed that pretty well everyone wants to be doing something different. If you don't mind my saying so, sir, I think it's a jolly good job. I mean looking after all these kids. Lots of our fellows have got brothers or nephews or cousins and they're all glad to think of the kids having a good time. That's thank to you and old Pa Birky and the rest, sir. I admit we get more of the fun, but that's our job. And we don't have all your troubles with rationing and evacuees. I can tell you one sometimes feels a bit ashamed with nothing to worry about and all you people sweating away teaching and running the games and the exams. It's really a frightfully decent show, sir.'

He was then afraid that he had talked too much, shook hands violently and went off to bed, where he fell asleep at once and to Kate's intense pleasure did not come down to breakfast till ten o'clock.

Everard and Philip left alone looked at each other.

'That's a good boy,' said Philip. 'Geraldine's in luck. He sees straight, which is more than the brainy ones as he calls them can always do. I suppose I'm a bit of a giddy harumfrodite, myself; soldier and schoolmaster too. You know, Everard, you're an extraordinarily good fellow yourself, though severely handicapped by brains.'

'To think that I should live to hear my Junior Housemaster talk like that to me,' said Everard. 'Signs of the times. You go up and I'll put out the lights.'

XIII

BRIEF WINTER INTERLUDE

Two days after Christmas it began to snow in Barsetshire. By the end of the next week the whole county was one vast skating rink on which men, women, horses, motors, lorries and bicycles slipped and slithered and swore. The Hosiers' Boys, who had never seen a country winter before, went about with grateful hearts for benefits conferred. The river rose and flooded the cricket ground a foot deep, so that the Hosiers' Boys had the supreme bliss of rowing on it on a Friday and skating on it on a Saturday. Mr. Birkett had holes punched in an old boiler and turned it into a brazier which the Hosiers' Boys kept supplied with wood from Thumble Coppice. The skaters, who came in dozens from the neighbourhood, warmed their hands and feet at its glow and gratefully drank hot soup which Mrs. Birkett and Mrs. Morland brought down in fish kettles and heated. Mrs. Phelps suddenly showed herself a first-class skater and for once justifying her trousers and lumber jacket performed the most dazzling evolutions with Everard Carter. Kate brought Bobbie down in his perambulator, and as he slept the whole time he was considered to have enjoyed himself very much and shown great intelligence. All the evacuees slid in one corner, threw snowballs at each other with uncertain aim, got wet through twice a day, were smacked, dried and put to bed by their foster mothers and returned next day as full of zeal as ever. Manners, the nicest of the Hosiers' Boys, made with the assistance of Edward the odd-man a wooden sledge, upon which he gave rides to the children below school age.

At Everard Carter's House the bathroom cistern froze and a pipe burst, reminding Matron of the time that Hackett left the hot tap running and nearly flooded the lower dormitory. The Birketts' supply of coal and coke was held up by the state of the roads and for three days there was no central heating, which made Mr. Birkett go to London and spend two nights at his club, where he had some incredibly dull conversations with the older members who were all waiting to pounce on any fresh face and tell it their valueless views on things in general.

Adelina and Maria Cottage spent all their evenings together at Maria partly to save fuel and partly because Mrs. Bissell could not go out at night as Mrs. Dingle couldn't stay and keep an eye on little Edna with the roads in that state.

At the Barchester Hospital such a crop of road accidents came in that the German measlers were despised by the nurses, nearly all of whom had chilblains, and Geraldine was so cheered by compound fractures that she almost forgot the mortification she had received at young Mr. Warbury's hands and wrote long letters to Captain Fairweather about the horribleness of Matron who had put the most attractively maimed patients into D ward.

The water main in the Close burst and the Bishop's cellar was flooded, which had last occurred in 1936, and gave intense joy to nearly all the inferior clergy, Mr. Miller at Pomfret Madrigal going so far as to refer to it, in conversation with Mrs. Brandon, as a crowning mercy. Ribald rumour had it that the Bishop's second best gaiters had been washed onto the front door steps of Canon Thorne, a peaceful elderly bachelor with High Church leanings, whom the Bishop had accused of being a Mariolater and having no soul, but it was universally recognized that this was too good to be true.

In the middle of all this Noel Merton came down for a night to the Deanery and rang up Lydia Keith, which was just as well, for next day two miles of telephone wires came down, and Sir Edmund Pridham said any fool would have known they could never stand the strain between Grumper's End and Tidcombe Halt and wrote a long letter to the *Barchester Chronicle* which printed it with a number of cuts that made nonsense of it.

'I'd love to see you, Noel, but I'm most frightfully busy,' said Lydia's voice on the telephone. 'Wait a minute. I've got to go and see about some pig food and there's a Red Cross thing here and it's the day I do the Communal Kitchen — look here, could you possibly come here directly after lunch, about two o'clock. I could fit you in then. If you want a bath, our hot water's all right.'

Noel thanked her and said the Deanery water was luckily all right so far and he would come at two o'clock unless the chains fell off his car, or the road at Tidcombe Halt was flooded. When Lydia had rung off he felt for a moment unreasonably depressed. It was not like his Lydia to say she would try to fit him in. Then he gave himself a mental shake and reminded himself that Lydia was a very busy person and that so far she had done very much more useful work than he had. He returned to the library and was writing some letters when the Dean's secretary came in.

'Oh, good morning,' said Mr. Needham, with a well-simulated start of surprise. 'I hope I'm not disturbing you.'

'Not a bit,' said Noel. 'If anyone is doing any disturbing, I am, writing my letters here.'

'I expect you are frightfully busy,' said Mr. Needham.

One is not a distinguished barrister for nothing and Noel's ear at once detected the voice of someone who wanted to talk, probably about himself. So he licked up an envelope, put his fountain pen in his pocket, and said he had just finished.

'Come and keep me company,' said Noel. 'How is everyone? I got here late last night and came down disgracefully late to breakfast and I've hardly had a word with Mrs. Crawley.'

Mr. Needham said the Dean was very well and very busy; *very* busy and *very* well, he added, with an earnestness which he hoped might cover the idiocy of his reply.

'And how is Octavia?' asked Noel Merton. 'Still at the hospital?'

Mr. Needham's ingenuous face assumed a reverent expression.

'Octavia is quite magnificent,' he said. 'She simply lives for the hospital. Even when she is at home she talks about nothing else. It makes me feel so useless.'

'Oh, come, come,' said Noel. 'Think how much the Dean needs your help.'

'Anyone could do a secretary job,' said Mr. Needham dejectedly. 'I'm frightfully fit and strong and it seems such waste to be writing letters when all my football friends are doing their bit. There are heaps of people with flat feet or something who could do my job; or even women. I mean it's a great privilege to be working for the Dean, but it's pretty awful, especially when I think of Octavia.'

'I suppose you won't believe me,' said Noel, 'but I often feel exactly like that myself.'

Mr. Needham stared.

'But you're a soldier, I mean an officer,' he said.

'As a matter of fact I'm a secretary like you,' said Noel. 'Secretary in uniform. I have hopes of being blown to bits or rotting in an enemy dungeon some day, but for the moment I chiefly fill up forms and do odd jobs of interviewing people. And if it is any comfort to you, when I look at Lydia Keith and see how much she is doing, I think it's pretty awful myself.'

Mr. Needham almost gaped. That Mr. Merton, that ex-man-of-the-world, now practically a Death's Head Hussar, or at least a Secret Service Agent of high degree, should feel as out of things as a Dean's secretary, was extremely upsetting to all his ideas. And yet comforting.

'The fact is,' said Noel, partly to reassure Mr. Needham, partly following his own thoughts, 'everyone wants to be doing something different since the war began; except the people who are actually in the thick of it. I don't suppose either of us are particularly afraid of the idea of danger or discomfort, but we feel we are wasting our time. As a matter of fact I don't believe we are. Lydia and Octavia make one feel rather ashamed,' said Noel, basely pandering to Mr. Needham by throwing in Octavia of whom he had no very great opinion though quite in a friendly way, 'but they have had the luck to find their jobs made to their hand, and the great self-control to stick to them. I know Lydia is pining to nurse, but her mother needs her and so does the estate, and all the local things. Octavia always wanted to nurse, didn't she?'

This slight denigration of Octavia could not pass without a protest.

'She loves her work, especially head wounds,' said Mr. Needham, 'but she did once tell me when we were talking about things that she thought it would be splendid to train as a medical missionary,' said Mr. Needham.

Noel nearly said he would be sorry for the savages, but restraining himself said it was a very fine ambition.

Mr. Needham said a missionary's life was of course in many ways the highest calling one could imagine, but of course if one could possibly be a Chaplain at the Front — He stopped, diffident at having betrayed a secret, mumbled something about meeting a train and went away, leaving Noel to finish his letters with a divided mind.

After an odious drive along the by-roads, which a fall of snow the day before and a fresh attack of freezing had made into one long pitfall, Noel got to Northbridge Manor, where he found Lydia angrily strewing sand on the front door steps.

'Hullo,' said Lydia. 'Our idiot kitchen maid washed the steps with hot water this morning to melt the ice and Father nearly broke his leg when he went out to get the car. Come round on to the terrace, and help me to carry some things indoors. I'll have to take those two bay-trees in tubs into the hall, or we'll lose them. I did put straw round them, but it won't be enough.'

Noel accompanied her to the terrace, where though the air was cold there was shelter from the wind, and a pale sunlight gave a faint illusion of warmth. He and Lydia were able to lift the two trees and carry them through the garden door into the hall, where they looked very well, though lumpy.

'I'll take the straw off afterwards,' said Lydia, surveying their trussed shapes. 'Come outside for a moment. I feel so stuffy after that Communal Kitchen.'

'Was it rabbit stew?' asked Noel, falling into step with her on the stone flags, where the frozen snow had been partly scraped away.

'Shin of beef and dumplings, and tapioca pudding,' said Lydia, 'and we had to bring all the water in pails because the pump froze. I'm *pleased* to see you, Noel.'

'So am I,' said Noel; which Lydia quite understood.

Lydia then put Noel through a searching examination about his physical welfare and the general state of things at the Deanery. It did not pass unnoticed by Noel that she never asked about his work. He was able to report that he felt disgustingly well and the food in the mess was good. He then gave her a fairly faithful narration of his conversation with Mr. Needham.

'He and Octavia don't seem to get down to it,' said Lydia, with a touch of her old intolerance for any methods but the most direct and bludgeoning. 'I must speak to Tommy. He's really a bit too stupid for Octavia but she is pretty stupid too. I think they ought to get engaged and then Tommy ought to be a Military Chaplain and they could get married after the war. Octavia won't want to stop being a nurse, but if Matron gets any more horrible she might go to France and then if Tommy were there she might see him sometimes.'

Having thus disposed of her young friends she stopped and they took another turn.

'You don't think I ought to be nursing, do you, Noel?' she asked with what for Lydia was almost diffidence.

'No,' said Noel. 'You are a good girl; a *very* good girl. And you are
doing everything you ought to do.'

Lydia turned on him a look of such gratitude that he was abashed to
receive so much for so little. They continued to pace the terrace in
silence, very comfortably.

'I wish Mother would get better,' said Lydia, with such a forlorn note
that Noel's heart was wrenched.

'So do I,' he said. 'And if you need me you will let me know, won't
you. I could probably manage to get over at any time if you needed a
bit of comforting.'

'I'd like it more than anything in the world,' said Lydia, 'but I
wouldn't ever, ever ask you, however much I wanted it. Thank you
most awfully though.'

She slipped her hand into Noel's as they walked. He, surprised and
touched by her mute appeal, so unlike the Lydia he knew, gave her
hand the slightest pressure and then let it lie in his, anxious not to
presume in any way upon her confidence. If a kind but ferocious hawk
had suddenly perched on his hand in a friendly way he would not have
been more surprized. Glancing at her profile as she walked beside him
in the pale afternoon sunshine he noticed a faint shadow under her
cheek bones that again strangely wrung his heart. It occurred to him
that ever since he had known her Lydia had been shouldering other
people's burdens, sometimes it is true in a very rumbustious and almost interfering way, but always with the best of intentions; and of late
and in a quieter, more self-effacing way, she had taken responsibility
more and more upon her, till her father, her mother, the house, the
little estate and much of the local war work seemed to depend very
largely upon her. Noel thought of his own life, among men of his own
sort, doing work that was more interesting than he was allowed to say,
full of food for his mind, with no particular troubles except such as the
world in general had to share. There was his Lydia, doing work
beyond her years, often alone, tied by an ailing mother, the long evenings spent with parents whose life and interests, much as they loved her
and she them, were far away from hers. It seemed to him that his Lydia
needed a friend. Not needed perhaps, for she seemed to be unconscious
that anything was wanting; but a friend she ought to have, someone
older than herself who could give her help and support, someone not
so much older that he could not see things as she saw them with her
younger eyes. What Lydia needed, in fact, he decided, was someone
rather like himself, very fond of her, loving her for her very faults, her
brusqueness, her occasional overbearing ways; loving her too for her
courage, her newly-learnt patience, her capable ways and above all for
the rare moments when she let herself bend a little under her burdens.
Such a moment was upon her now and Noel cherished it. Deep peace
lay on the downs, the water meadows and the Manor. A white

unfamiliar landscape, quiet as midnight, untouched by the world's trouble.

'It is all very solitaire et glacé,' said Lydia, half to herself.

'If we are spectres évoquer-ing le passé,' said Noel, 'it is a very nice past. What fun we have had here. Do you remember the picnic on Parsley Island and how dreadful Rose Birkett was?'

'She was ghastly,' said Lydia, withdrawing her hand from Noel's as if the spell were broken, but so kind a withdrawal that Noel felt it almost as a caress. 'And the day Tony and Eric and I cleaned out the pond and Rose threw her engagement ring at Philip.'

'And you had on that dreadful short frock with no sleeves and all your arms and legs were the colour of a beetroot,' said Noel.

'And then Philip dropped the ring into the pool below the pond. I wonder if it is there still. Rose got engaged about twelve times before she married John. If I got engaged, I'd *get* engaged,' said Lydia with a flash of her old arrogance.

'I think you would,' said Noel. 'And mind, you promised to mention it to me when you do, so that I can see if he is good enough.'

'Of course I'll tell you,' said Lydia. 'But I don't think I will at present, because unless it was someone like you I wouldn't like them enough.'

Then Noel knew that it was not as a friend that he wanted Lydia to need him. The blow to his heart made it impossible for him to speak for a moment. Divided between a wish to tell Lydia that she was the core of his life and a fear of disturbing her peace, wrenched suddenly by the violence of his own feelings, his self-possession lay shattered. For the first time in his life he was entirely at a loss. They had come to the end of the terrace.

'Lydia,' he said, as they turned. And on that his foot slipped on the frozen snow and he would have fallen if Lydia had not supported him with her powerful grasp.

'Hold up!' said Lydia reprovingly. 'You ought to have nails in your shoes for this weather like me,' and she turned up the sole of one of her heavy country brogues to show him serried rows of nails.

The moment had fled. Lydia said she was frightlly sorry but she must go to a meeting in the village and would walk, as it was so slippery to bicycle. Noel offered to drop her there on his way back to Barchester.

'It's Mrs. Knowles's, that stone house with the blue door,' said Lydia as they slithered down the village street. 'Thanks awfully, Noel. Give Octavia my love.'

'Take care of yourself,' said Noel, for banalities seemed the only thing to say. 'I'm more than likely to be at the Deanery when I get any leave and I'll always let you know.'

Lydia crushed his hand to a jelly and strode up Mrs. Knowles's garden path to the front door, her heart very heavy. The unwonted

load lay upon her all that day and for many days and she found herself
entirely unable to account for it.

XIV

DINNER AT THE DEANERY

THE long winter of everyone's discontent like a very unpleasant snake
dragged its slow length along. Pipes continued to freeze, burst and
thaw with wearisome regularity. Southbridge School and the Hosiers'
Boys went back to work. Men in their early twenties were summoned
away and men a little older registered. More than half the evacuated
children were taken back to London whence they wrote long letters to
their country hostesses expressing a determination to come back and
live with them for ever as soon as they were old enough. Those children
who remained became stouter of body and redder of face every day,
and with wearisome regularity had to return to the clinic to have their
heads cleaned. Party feeling raged high over this question, the London
teachers saying that their children were infected by the cottagers; the
local committees asserting that the cottage children were free from any
infection until the London children brought it back from town on their
visits to their parents. Mrs. and Miss Phelps, taking no notice of either
side, cleaned all heads with violent impartiality. The Admiral had the
intense pleasure of welcoming Bill and Tubby again as his guests when
they returned from a cheerful violation of Norway's highly un-neutral
waters, with their rescued fellow-seamen; and when Mrs. Birkett heard
that Bill had had the ocarina with him on that glorious occasion she felt
that she had in no small measure contributed to the victory and the
rescue and became quite bloated with pride.

Two outstanding events are to be mentioned in that long depressing
season before early Summer Time came in again.

The first was the end of the Warburys, preceded by a crop of rumours
which were a perfect godsend to the county. Many people who ought to
have known better announced as gospel truth the following perfectly
unfounded reports:

(*a*) That Mr. Warbury was in the Tower. Origin unknown and
firmly believed by everyone until the birth of

(*b*) that Mr. Warbury was under arrest in the film studios with an
armed guard at the door and only allowed to eat boiled eggs into which
it is practically impossible to smuggle notes, files, prussic acid, or bombs.
Origin: Mrs. Dingle, who cleaned at the studios once a week and saw

some sandwiches going in and a sham soldier waiting to go on the set for a faked propaganda film, who playfully presented a dummy bayonet at her.

(c) that Mrs. Warbury was under observation by the Secret Service for Luring Officers to tell her Things (unspecified). Origin: Mrs. Phelps who had been to town for a day's shopping, for once in a coat and skirt, and was taken to lunch at the Café Royal by one of her many naval friends, where she had seen Mrs. Warbury, more dripping with foxes and pearls than ever, drinking Pernod with two dark men who looked like soldiers in civilian dress. The Admiral had rounded upon his wife, reminding her that soldiers did not go to the Café Royal in mufti and she ought to know better. But Mrs. Phelps, who hated Mrs. Warbury without reserve for herself alone, refused to be checked.

(d) that all the Warburys had been shot. Origin: Mr. Brown of the Red Lion, who after young Mr. Warbury had been throwing his weight about more than usual in the Red Lion, said he wished they were all put up against a wall. This rumour gained immense credence among all the patrons of the Red Lion, whose faith was untouched by the fact that all the Warburys were seen in the village on the following day. But as Eileen said, patting her new bubble curls into place with her well-manicured hand, it was easy to dress up like some people and it stood to reason that the Government would do things on the quiet; which convinced all but the most hardened unbelievers.

(e) that young Mr. Warbury had been caught red-handed spying on the railway and was to be deported. Origin: the station-master at Tidcombe Halt, who had found young Mr. Warbury travelling to Barchester with a very suspicious tin case which might have been a bomb if it hadn't been film negatives. Young Mr. Warbury had refused to open it and produced his identity card, upon which the station-master had said he didn't hold with them things and they didn't prove nothing and hauled young Mr. Warbury out of his first-class smoking carriage and locked him into the porters' room while he rang up the police, to whom young Mr. Warbury had been so rude, obstructing him in the execution of his duty and threatening actions at law, that his father had had to go and make a quite grovelling explanation and apology.

After two months of such delightful hopes and fears it was a distinct disappointment to everyone that the Warbury family all went to America and were not even torpedoed on the way over. When Geraldine heard that they were going she was afraid that she might mind, but to her great relief she found that she didn't, which made her write several very long dull letters to Captain Fairweather about a trepanning case and a dislocated pelvis. Captain Fairweather rightly interpreted these letters as a proof of love and confidence and carried on with his military duties.

The second event, perhaps of less general interest, but deeply exciting to our immediate circle at Southbridge, was the publication of Miss Hampton's new novel, *Temptation at St. Anthony's*, which was chosen as the Anti-Sex Immorality Society Book of the Month in U.S.A., and the *Daily Dustbin* First Pick for April in England, besides having in a more intellectual daily a slashing review which sent its sales up by thousands. Miss Hampton had wished to dedicate her book to Mr. and Mrs. Bissell, from whom, she said, she had learnt many interesting facts hitherto unknown to her, especially from Mrs. Bissell, whose studies in the psychology of educational establishments were as profound as her mind was innocent. But the Bissells, though immensely flattered by the idea, felt that such notoriety might be prejudicial to them in their profession, in which, they said, one must always consider the weaker members, so Miss Hampton dedicated it to All Brave Spirits who have been my Friends. The Bissells, whose social education had advanced by leaps and bounds during a winter's association with Adelina Cottage, burst into a small sherry party to celebrate the event, particularly inviting Mrs. Morland as a literary light.

'It is always,' said Mrs. Morland, shaking hands warmly with Miss Hampton, 'so difficult when you want to congratulate someone, because you are never sure if they want to be congratulated, but I can't tell you how pleased I am about *Temptation at St. Anthony's*. I haven't exactly read it, but I'm just as pleased as if I had and of course I shall.'

'I wouldn't if I were you,' said Miss Hampton. 'Strongmeat. Not for people with your sensitive outlook.'

This surprised Mrs. Morland very much, for though she knew that she was no good at being coarse, she had never thought of herself as sensitive, having been for many years far too busy to consider such things.

'No, no,' continued Miss Hampton. 'You and I needn't read each other's books. We write for Our Public, not for our friends. Mercenaries, you and I. Must say though we work for our pay.'

'Well, that is a great relief,' said Mrs. Morland, picking up her gloves which she had dropped, 'because I never expect people – I mean real people – to read my books, and I must say I have never read any of yours, though I'm sure they're frightfully good. It is funny about one's friends. Sometimes one likes the book and not the friend and sometimes the friend and not the book; and sometimes both, or neither. You know George Knox, don't you, who lives near me at High Rising? I am very fond of him and I admire his books though one would never guess they were the same person. But with Mrs. Rivers I feel exactly the opposite, not that she is a friend, because I only met her once, years ago, at a lunch party. I don't mean that I admire her and am fond of her books, which would be the exact opposite; but I find them both very unsympathetic. Then there is Mrs. Barton whose books about Borgias and things are entrancing, but somehow we've never quite hit it off. And I do really like you so much, but I know I wouldn't like your books, so that is perfect.'

'You're a pretty good sort yourself,' said Miss Hampton, giving her tie a jerk. 'You had some kind of Book of the Month once, hadn't you?'

'I couldn't really help it,' said Mrs. Morland apologetically, 'and it pleased my publisher frightfully. I call it my Child of Shame.'

At this simple piece of wit Miss Hampton laughed uproariously and said she wished she had thought of that.

'I'll give it you,' said Mrs. Morland. 'I haven't used it much.'

Mrs. Phelps, who had been listening with deep interest, said she simply couldn't understand how people could write books, but she was always telling Irons he ought to write his life, as he had been pretty well everywhere. She had, she said, found a splendid title for him: Irons in the Fire, because his friends called him Irons and the Fire part would mean partly that he had been under fire and partly that he had a lot of irons in the fire in every sense of the word.

Mrs. Morland and Miss Hampton, who had a pretty good idea of what the book would be like, looked at each other with eyes of despair and said in a jumble of simultaneous speech that it would be perfectly splendid. The Admiral, pleased though modest, said he was only a rough sailor and all his diaries were lost in that fire at the Pantechnicon while he was at Simonstown, but he would like to try his hand at it.

'You ought to collaborate with Bent, Admiral,' said Miss Hampton. 'Tell him your idea, Bent.'

'You know I make a special study of Vice, Admiral,' said Miss Bent.

Miss Phelps said Father was a Rear-Admiral.

'Tut, tut,' said Miss Bent, to the great admiration of her audience, who had never known those words used outside a printed book before. 'Vice. Unnatural Vice. Now, Admiral, I would like to pick your brains about the lower deck.'

This reasonable and scientific request frightened the Admiral so much that only the intervention of Mrs. Bissell kept him from summong his wife and daughter and going home at once.

'Pardon me, Miss Bent,' said Mrs. Bissell, 'but you have the stick by quite the wrong end as the saying is. It would be quite useless to ask Admiral Phelps, because his protective or escapist complex would not allow him to open his eyes to social evil. You would do much better to read the chapter on the Libido-Involuntary in *A Concept of Neo-Phallic Thought* by Spurge-Mackworth. He used to lecture at the Training College and is a lucid and courageous thinker.'

'It's very good of you,' said Miss Bent, who was sincerely fond of Mrs. Bissell, 'but you know my motto: One Crowded Hour of Glorious Vice. The Admiral could tell me more in ten minutes than your friend could in ten books.'

But the Admiral could bear it no longer and took his wife and daughter away to meet some young naval friends who were arriving by the 6.40.

'It's a pity,' said Miss Bent sadly. 'When I think of the side lights you and Mrs. Bissell have given us on school psychology — —'

'But you must remember, Miss Bent,' said Mr. Bissell, 'that Mrs. Bissell has made a study of psychology. Of course she can't write fiction like you ladies, though I often say to her, You never know till you've tried, but her knowledge of the subject is very thorough. I assure you the County Libery simply cannot keep pace with the books she asks for. In February alone she had out seventeen books, didn't you, Mother?'

'Mr. Bissell has omitted to state,' said Mrs. Bissell, looking affectionately at her husband, 'that two of them were for Mrs. Dingle. Her husband is apt to be troublesome, and I thought she might get some help.'

'What kind of psychology did you get for her?' asked Mrs. Morland with much interest.

'Oh, not psychology,' said Mrs. Bissell pityingly. 'That would be quite useless without previous training. I got her a book on curing alcoholism without the patient's knowledge and another one on elementary ju-jitsu. She is a well-developed woman in intelligence and physique and I gather their home life has been quite a different thing.'

Mrs. Morland then said good-bye, leaving Miss Hampton and Miss Bent to make a night of it with the Bissells, which they did till nearly half-past eight, when Miss Bent said they ought to go down to the Red Lion and see who was there, so she and Miss Hampton departed, with Mannerheim in tow.

*

As April came on, life altered a little. Oxford came down and Mrs. Morland left the Birketts for her own house at High Rising. By an amicable arrangement her publisher's wife Sibyl Coates had transferred herself and her nurse and children to her grandmother at Bournemouth for the East Vacation, so that Mrs. Morland would have her youngest son Tony at home with her. Mrs. Morland's new book of short stories came out and all the reviewers said 'Another vintage Morland', or 'Mrs. Morland can be relied upon to give her readers exactly what they expect, and in her new book has given them generous measure, pressed down and overflowing', or 'A laugh and a thrill on every page'. Mrs. Morland, who never read press notices, was pleased to get her advance on royalties and felt that Tony's education and the pocket money of her other boys were safe for the present. Her books made no great noise, but her publisher Adrian Coates rejoiced in their steady sale and had the great pleasure of finding out, through underground channels, that a loudly boomed novel called *My Burning Flesh*, translated from the Mixo-Lydian by a young woman on the staff of the *Daily Dustbin*, and described by his friends and rival publishers, Johns and Fairfield, as a stark and gripping piece of realism, had only sold half as many copies as Mrs. Morland's.

Various people in Southbridge, and indeed all over England, were embarrassed by parcels of food from friends or relations in Canada, Australia, the United States, Kenya and other more or less English-speaking countries. While deeply grateful for the kindness that prompted the dispatch of such parcels to a starvation-haunted England, they were much annoyed by the excessive duty they had to pay, and in several cases wrote to *The Times*, whose *défaitiste* attitude towards the Crossword had by now alienated many of its staunchest supporters.

Miss Hampton and Miss Bent had the first serious difference of opinion in a companionship which had lasted for some twenty years. The cause of this rift was the invasion of two small and defenceless northern kingdoms, which were thus automatically added to their list of gallant little nations. Not that they differed by a hairsbreadth in their hatred and condemnation of the invaders, but the question of moral support from Mannerheim drove them into separate camps. On the chief premise, namely that there was nobody one had ever heard of in Norway or Denmark except Hans Andersen, they were united, but Miss Bent, less impetuous than Miss Hampton, insisted that Norway's claims should be further examined, and to that end took the temporary Mannerheim round to the Bissells one Saturday morning, followed by the protesting Miss Hampton.

Mr. and Mrs. Bissell, always delighted by an intellectual discussion, were quickly put in possession of the facts and brought their minds to bear on the question.

'I quite see what you mean about Norway,' said Mr. Bissell. 'One might of course mention Nansen.'

'No!' said Miss Bent, quite violently. 'Look at the trouble the League of Nations has got us into. Besides, Nansen is *no* name for a dog.'

With such conviction did she speak that all her hearers felt that if they called a dog Nansen she would hate it.

'Of course there is Longfellow,' said Mrs. Bissell.

'Long Tooth, you mean,' said Miss Bent.

'No; Longfellow,' said Mrs. Bissell, placidly. 'His beautiful rendering of that fine old saga about King Olaf. I learned many a canto of it by heart when I was a girl, and I used to teach it to the girls in the Fourth Standard.

'Eienar then the arrow taking from the loosened string,
Answered: That is Noway breaking 'neath thy hand, O King!'

This quotation was felt by her audience to be vaguely and uncomfortably too near the present state of things and a depressed silence fell, broken by Mr. Bissell, who said:

'Hayken.'

'Harken, Daddy,' said Mrs. Bissell.

'Hawkon, I think,' said Miss Hampton.

Miss Bent said she knew one pronounced it Marterlinck, but that was perhaps different.

'Call him Haakon if you like, Bent,' said Miss Hampton, going rather white and sounding suspiciously as if she were going to cry. 'You know I only want to please you.'

At this sudden collapse of Miss Hampton, whom her friends had always taken for the strong and gentlemanly spirit of the pair, the Bissells stood amazed. Mr. Bissell wished he were safely in the Masters' Common Room, but Mrs. Bissell, a psychologist first and foremost, quickly recovered her poise and looked on with kind detachment at this interesting practical demonstration of all she had learnt in theory, and suggested a nice cup of tea. Miss Hampton and Miss Bent suddenly knew, as Aurora Freemantle had once discovered, that a nice cup of tea was the one thing in the world worth while, and though the Red Lion had been gaping for them for the last half-hour, they were glad to accept Mrs. Bissell's offer. Miss Hampton blew her nose violently, Miss Bent said 'Sorry' in a gruff voice, and after a great deal more discussion, on the most amicable terms, it was decided that pending further political moves Mannerheim should be called Andersen, Mrs. Bissell pointing out with her usual excellent common sense that he would probably not hear the difference between the two names and so answer to his new name more readily.

The ladies then left, happy and reconciled. As they walked down Maria's little front path a car drove past.

'There's Lydia Keith,' said Miss Hampton. 'Nice girl. She looks thin lately. Wonder if anything's wrong.'

'Miss Keith is a very peculiar and I might say almost abnormal type,' said Mrs. Bissell.

'How?' said Miss Bent, hoping that Lydia might afford her some side lights on Vice.

'She is perfectly normal,' said Mrs. Bissell. 'Good-bye, Miss Bent. Good-bye, Miss Hampton. Good-bye Andersen, old fellow.'

*

Now that the days were longer, or as the Dean said, the hours of daylight were perhaps a more correct expression, Mrs. Crawley decided to give a dinner party, nominally in honour of a retired Colonial Bishop who was going to do locum work in Little Misfit whose vicar, Mr. Tompion, had managed to get abroad as a Chaplain with the Barsetshires, but really because she felt that she would die unless she for once got into proper evening dress and knew that many of her friends shared her feelings. It was to be a slap-up party of eighteen, with all the leaves but one put into the dining-room table, which when fully extended could take twenty-four, but Mrs. Crawley made a concession to the troubled times by inviting people who were either staying in Barchester or could come in the same car and save petrol. Under the first heading were the retired Bishop, who was staying at the Deanery till the Vicarage at Little Misfit was ready, Noel Merton who was again down for a night's leave and Miss Pettinger who of course lived near the High School in a charming Georgian house which was far too good for her. Under the second were Mrs. Brandon, Delia Brandon, and the Millers from Pomfret Madrigal who were coming with Sir Edmund Pridham in his car, and the Archdeacon from Plumstead and his daughter who would pick up the Birketts on their way. Mr. and Mrs. Keith had been asked, but Mrs. Keith was not well enough to come, so Mrs. Crawley had asked Lydia instead, knowing that Noel would be pleased to see her.

The party from Pomfret Madrigal were the first to arrive. Mrs. Brandon with a charming and quite illusory air of fragility wafted herself into the drawing-room in a chiffon cloud of every soft colour of sweet pea, followed by Mrs. Miller in a dark blue lace dress with a dark blue velvet jacket and Delia in green.

The Colonial Bishop was introduced to Mrs. Brandon and being unmarried at once felt thankful that Little Misfit and Pomfret Madrigal were only three miles apart. True, petrol was rationed, but he was a confirmed bicyclist, having covered on that exhausting machine many hundred miles of his sub-Equatorial diocese where he was known to his flock as Mbanga Ngango, or roughly in English Roly-poly Witch Doctor.

'I am delighted to hear that you are coming to Little Misfit,' said Mrs. Brandon. 'Mr. Tompion is quite delightful and so is his wife, but of course as he is an Army Chaplain he is not there.'

The Colonial Bishop, by now almost demented with admiration, said No, of course, one could quite see that.

'And his wife, who is very nice indeed,' Mrs. Brandon continued, looking pensively at her left hand on which shone the diamond ring, legacy of her husband's rich aunt Miss Brandon, 'has gone back to Leamington for the duration to her parents who are a very charming retired Colonel and his wife called Parkinson. I wished she could have stayed on at the Vicarage because she is splendid with children owing to having none of her own and was such a help with my nursery, but with you coming I suppose she couldn't.'

The Colonial Bishop longed to explain to Mrs. Brandon that though a joint household of Mrs. Tompion and himself might have presented difficulties Mrs. Tompion would have been scrupulously respected by him; but finding this not easy to put into words, he asked if Mrs. Brandon had a large family.

'Only two,' said Mrs. Brandon, with an exquisitely melancholy inflection as of a Niobe to whom Apollo had spared the last of her brood.

'But luckily in the nursery,' said the Colonial Bishop, glad that his new friend was not likely to suffer through her children.

'Well, not often,' said Mrs. Brandon. 'Delia really likes children very much, but of course as she is mostly at the hospital she has to go to bed a good deal when she is at home, and Francis is at work all day and the children are in bed when he gets back, but he will have to register next month and then he will feel much better.'

At this point Mrs. Birkett most luckily intervened and took away the Colonial Bishop, who would otherwise have gone mad, to introduce him to the Archdeacon, who was burning for a new audience to whom he could repeat himself about the difficulties of the West Barsetshire pack in war-time.

Noel Merton now claimed Mrs. Brandon, who said it was a long time since she had seen him, implying by her voice and look the epithet 'deceiver'.

Noel said with proper gallantry, Not half so long as it was since he had seen Mrs. Brandon, and they both laughed, for they were excellent friends and voyaged about the Pays du Tendre in great comfort, with return tickets.

'Listen, Lavinia,' said Noel, serious for a moment. 'Mrs. Crawley has put me between Mrs. Birkett and Miss Pettinger. I love the one and have every intention of hating the other, but what I really want is to have a talk to you. Will you league with me after dinner?'

'Of course I will,' said Mrs. Brandon. 'This dress fluffles out very nicely and if I sit on the little green settee, there won't be room for anyone unless I choose to make it.'

And then the party from Plumstead and Southbridge School came in, the Archdeacon's daughter apologizing for their being late, but she had been working the tractor at Starveacre till the last moment and was so stiff she could hardly get her breeches off.

The Keiths and Lydia followed hard upon, and then the whole party had to wait for Miss Pettinger. Lydia, Octavia and Delia said loudly that the Pettinger had done it on purpose, and it was just like her horribleness. Mr. Needham came in and said someone had rung up to say that Miss Pettinger had been delayed, but was just starting and hoped they wouldn't wait.

Dinner was therefore put back ten minutes, at the end of which time Miss Pettinger was announced. Her gracious entry was marked by a black lace dress, a white rabbit-skin coatee, and a very large white, shiny handbag.

'I must really apologize for keeping everyone waiting,' said Miss Pettinger, 'but my secretary had mislaid my gas-mask. How are you,

Mrs. Crawley? And the Dean? And Lydia and Delia and Octavia? It is nice to see so many old High School Girls.'

Mrs. Crawley introduced such of the party as were not known to Miss Pettinger, who had just had a very tight new permanent wave (for she believed in setting a standard of personal care to her girls), which made her hair, as Delia said to Lydia, look as false as her teeth.

'You may wonder where I put my gas-mask,' said Miss Pettinger, while the parlourmaid vainly tried to announce dinner. 'I carry it in my evening bag at night and I had asked my secretary to transfer it for me, but she had forgotten and so it could not at first be found, till I looked on my writing-table and there it was. So I put it into my bag, took my torch and braved the terrors of the black-out and here I am.'

Octavia said, rather too loudly, that it was bright moonshine to-night and received an admonishing look from her mother.

'Never take my gas-mask out to dinner,' said Sir Edmund, who had had more than one tussle with Miss Pettinger on committees and had no fear of her, nor indeed any opinion. 'Can't eat with a mask on. Bad manners, too.'

'There's only one person that can, Pridham,' said the Archdeacon, who hated Miss Pettinger because she used the word blood-sports and in a deprecatory sense, 'and that's a fox.'

Mrs. Birkett herded her guests downstairs, hoping that Miss Pettinger had not heard the Archdeacon, as indeed she had not, for she was already explaining to the Dean, who took her down, how useful it was to have a white, shiny bag for one's gas-mask in the black-out, and how hers also held her torch, her identity card, and her name and address on a visiting card contained in a talc-fronted case, besides, she added laughingly, her make-up and other feminine trifles.

'Much as I like sitting next to you,' said Noel, who was between Miss Pettinger and Mrs. Birkett, to this latter lady, 'I am looking forward with rapture to the moment when half the heads will turn to the left and half to the right, instead of half to the right and half to the left as at present. I am longing to hear my neighbour's views on make-up. Tell me, how is the School?'

Mrs. Birkett needed little pressing to give Noel an account of the activities of Southbridge School and the Hosiers' Boys during the current term and as she knew a good many of the characters concerned, he was properly interested.

'Talking of the Bissells, Miss Hampton was there not long ago,' said Mrs. Birkett, 'and she saw Lydia Keith as she was coming away and thought she looked thin. I haven't seen her till to-night for some time and I think so too. I think she worries about her mother, poor child.'

It is one thing to think your nicest friend is thin yourself, but quite another to hear a third person say so, and Noel almost disliked kind Mrs. Birkett for taking so much interest in Lydia. He would have liked to look at Lydia again and satisfy himself about her, but unfortunately she was on the same side of the table, next but one to Mrs. Birkett, and heavily involved with Mr. Miller on the question of a Communal Kitchen, which Pomfret Madrigal had not yet instituted. So he had to content himself, which indeed he found it easy to do, with Mrs. Birkett's agreeable company, until such time as the heads should turn.

Beyond Lydia, Mr. Needham and Delia were prattling away very harmlessly, and beyond Delia the Archdeacon discussed with Mrs. Crawley on his right the opening of the new buildings at Hiram's Hospital, a charitable institution that was one of the prides of Barchester. The reparations and additions to Hiram's Hospital had been carried out by Mr. Barton, an architect who did much of the cathedral work and about whose wife's books we have heard Mrs. Morland's opinion. The ceremony of opening them was to be performed by the Earl of Pomfret, the Lord Lieutenant of the county.

'I was talking to Foster at the Red Cross Committee to-day,' said the Archdeacon, alluding to Lord Pomfret's cousin and heir who had for some years been taking an active part in county work. 'He tells me that Pomfret is not at all well. He has never really been the same since Lady Pomfret died. What a beautiful woman she used to be. I remember her when I was a boy, driving in a victoria and pair under the archway of the Close to a garden party at the Palace.'

Mrs. Crawley, who was fond of Lord Pomfret in spite of his sometimes terrifying manner, expressed her sorrow at this news.

'There's no doubt Foster will do well,' said the Archdeacon, 'but Pomfret would be very much missed. He stands for a great deal that we need at the present moment.'

'Sally will do very well too,' said Mrs. Crawley, for Mr. Foster's wife, who had been Sally Wicklow, was a great friend and ally of hers.

'They are a good lot, the Wicklows,' said the Archdeacon. 'You know her brother, Roddy, Pomfret's agent?'

Mrs. Crawley said she did and was very fond of little Mrs. Roddy Wicklow, daughter of Mr. Barton, the architect.

'That all brings me round to what I wanted to tell you,' said the Archdeacon. 'I don't know if you remember Mrs. Roddy's brother, Guy Barton. He and my girl have known each other for a long time and the engagement will be announced in a few days, but I wanted you and the Dean to know before it is public. He left his father's office last September and is in the R.A.F. and they want to get married before he is sent abroad, which might be fairly soon.'

Mrs. Crawley expressed sincere pleasure, but her thoughts were more with Lord Pomfret than with the young couple. She and her husband had known him for a good many years and his passing would mean the passing of an old order, far too much of which was already engulfed. Mrs. Crawley did her best to be broadminded about social changes and managed to have faith that the next generation would make the world a little better, but all her broadmindedness could not make her think that it would be so happy for the people of her own age who had seen the golden Edwardian prime. Whatever happened it would mean eating other people's mental bread and treading strange stairs, and Mrs. Crawley sometimes felt that she would like to shut herself up in the Deanery, stop her ears, and there decay gently in a corner, living in a dream of the past. Pomfret Towers had for many years been a friendly house to her and her husband. When Lord Pomfret died the new Earl and his wife would bring to their duties the same admirable devotion that old Lord Pomfret had always shown and would if possible bring up their children in the same spirit. But with death duties and war taxes the estate would be grievously crippled. The Towers would probably be shut, or the new owners would live in part of one wing, economizing; a small runabout instead of the three large cars and the chauffeurs; vegetables, fruit and flowers sold instead of being used in the house or given away on the estate, shooting let to a syndicate, horses put down, nasturtiums sown in the Italian garden whose bedding-out had been the head gardener's joy. The tenants, she knew, would be the last to suffer, as the new Lord Pomfret, and his wife would roof a cottage or mend a gate before they would give themselves a new bathroom; and that was as it should be. But when those days came Mrs. Crawley knew that she and her contemporaries would find themselves in a world where their chief use would be to oil the wheels where they could and to die in decent time so that the young might inherit a world whose most enchanting pleasures they had not known and would not miss.

Mrs. Crawley looked down the long table at the end of which she was sitting with the Archdeacon. Who among her guests were to inherit this new world? Lydia, Delia, Octavia, the Archdeacon's daughter; Mr. Needham. Noel Merton perhaps, though his life and thought lay more with the older generation. Four nice, ordinary girls and a young man of no very particular ability. That they would all behave well in any given circumstances Mrs. Crawley did not doubt, but what standard of life were they going to keep? Then she blamed herself for harsh judgment of a generation that had not yet been tried. She remembered that Delia and Octavia were diligent at the hospital and never tried to change their hours for the sake of a treat, that the Archdeacon's daughter was training land girls with efficient zeal, that Lydia Keith, who she thought looked more subdued than was her wont, was managing the little estate and both her parents, besides her many other activities, that Mr. Needham was a painstaking secretary though his spirit longed for more active work. 'Good, good children,' she said to herself.

And marriage. Would those girls care to marry? How many would lose a lover, a friend that might have been a lover. If Octavia would only show the faintest interest in men, thought her mother almost angrily, for she herself had married young and had all her large family by the time she was thirty-five, partly owing to the twins, and metaphorically speaking had the decks cleared for action by the time she was forty and full of energy. Were Octavia, Delia, Lydia to go on being nice useful girls for ever. She almost champed with rage at the thought.

And all this went through her mind while the Archdeacon was talking about Hiram's Hospital and repeating his anxieties about Lord Pomfret's health, so that he got a very long innings, by which means the Colonial Bishop, whose name does not matter and who indeed only comes into this book as an excuse for a dinner party, was able to immolate himself thoroughly at Mrs. Brandon's shrine, who like an exquisite and tender Juggernaut was rolling over him, talking delightful nonsense all the time. While she thus carried out her mission, Mr. Birkett on her right was able to get from the Archdeacon's daughter some excellent advice about putting in winter greens, to which end he had just had a new piece of ground dug up. This professional talk threw Sir Edmund and Octavia together; not that Octavia minded, for one audience was to her as good as another and she had an abdominal on her mind that she required to get off it. But Sir Edmund, who liked girls to be pretty and ready to flirt, and wanted to talk to the Archdeacon's daughter about the vixen at Tolson's corner, did not enjoy himself at all until, Octavia stopping to take breath, he told her about the wound in his leg that he got at the Battle of the Marne and found for once a thoroughly sympathetic listener.

Beyond Octavia, Mr. Keith talked quietly to Mrs. Miller about some new books and the fate of Brandon Abbey which had been left by old Miss Brandon as a kind of Home of Rest for veterans of her brother's regiment.

But owing to trustees and things, Mrs. Miller said, it had not yet been properly organized, for a great deal of alteration and new plumbing had to be done and there was a good deal of red tape with various Ministries. Now, however, the Government had taken it over, plumbing and all, as a military hospital, so it was just as well, and she was sure old Miss Brandon would have been pleased. Looking across the table at Lydia, she said she was so glad to see Miss Keith again, and how delightful she looked, but a little tired. She could not admire the girls enough and the way they tackled everything.

Mr. Keith also looked at Lydia and wondered if seeing his daughter every day made him not realize how much thinner she had grown. But as she was almost perfect in his eyes, he decided that Mrs. Miller was not only wrong, but slightly interfering, and became rather reserved, which Mrs. Miller did not notice in the least, though she found him so heavy in hand that she was relieved when the Dean, who was sitting beside her at the opposite end from Mrs. Crawley and the Archdeacon, took advantage of a moment's pause in Miss Pettinger's monologue to ask her advice about a giant assemblage of Mothers' Unions which was to be held in the Cathedral in the following month. At this Mrs. Miller said, Ha-ha! inside herself, for daughter of a vicarage and wife of a vicarage, Mothers' Unions were in her blood and she knew she could organize for ten thousand women if necessary without the slightest difficulty.

'Our chief stumbling block,' said the Dean, 'in the Cathedral Service, will be the gas-masks. They have all been told to bring them, but I know, I *know* that they won't, and I have had, however reluctantly, to rule that no mother will be allowed into the Cathedral without showing her mask.'

'I know what I would do,' said Mrs. Miller quietly, 'though it would be quite wrong. I would collect as many cardboard containers as possible and have them at the various points of assembly. Then each mother who has not brought her mask could first be spoken to severely about her negligence and then given an empty box to carry. My dear father would, I fear, have condemned this as mere expediency, but there are moments when expediency becomes a necessity, and this seems to me the moment.'

The Dean thanked her warmly and said he would privately make this suggestion to those responsible for convening the various branches.

Mrs. Miller said that gas-masks in the Cathedral, though showing a sense of public duty, would be entirely useless. Last time she went to Evensong, she said, her mind wandered, as one's mind is, alas, too apt to do, and she could not help reflecting that if a single bomb fell any-where in the neighbourhood, the rose window, the monument to Lord Pomfret's grandfather, Vice-Admiral Thorne's Trafalgar monument with Neptune and a mourning Britannia, besides the draped statue of the Honourable Augustus de Courcy, the last representative of old Barum before it was disfranchized as a Rotten Borough, would at once have fallen in glass splinters and masses of masonry on her head, not to speak of the whole of the roof of the North Transept where it was being repaired.

'I know, I know,' said the Dean. 'We should of course try to get every-one out as quickly as possible. But I must confess, though I could not say this to everyone, that I always hope I may be in the Cathedral if there is an air-raid, just to observe some of our clergy and elder choristers leaving the building as they are officially commanded to do, with all reverent speed. I feel that the speed would, in so many cases, get the upper hand. But I oughtn't to talk like this.'

Mrs. Miller, however, being of the inner circle, took the remark in very good part and they laughed so much in a quiet way that Mr. Keith, grappling with Octavia, felt very depressed and wished he could share the fun. Sir Edmund, having exhausted the story of his wound, from which he still suffered though he never complained, was thus enabled to turn with relief to the Archdeacon's daughter and from her got the most valuable support about the vixen, who had been much harassed by the ploughing of a field that she regarded as her own and had practically implored Sir Edmund's protection.

Mr. Birkett, having done his duty by winter greens, had a very pleasant chat with Mrs. Brandon, as indeed everyone always did.

'I do want you and your wife to know,' said Mrs. Brandon, 'before it is in *The Times*, that Delia is going to marry our nice cousin, Hilary Grant. When I say cousin, he is really no relation at all, only a connection which makes it all right though in any case they wouldn't be first cousins which is, I believe, where the bad blood comes in.'

Mr. Birkett said he was delighted and he knew his wife would be, and asked if Hilary was in the Army, as nearly all the young men he knew now were.

'Well, not *exactly*,' said Mrs. Brandon, 'because his eyes are not good enough, but he speaks Italian very well and has been taken on for a temporary job in a Government office which I am not supposed to mention though everyone knows about it and exactly where it is. I know it is wicked,' said Mrs. Brandon plaintively, 'but I cannot help being glad that Hilary won't be killed at once. Of course if there is a bomb or anything he will do his best, but it is so *very* nice to feel that Delia won't be a widow for the present. If he is sent abroad she will go back to the Hospital unless of course she is going to have a baby which I do hope she will, or Nurse will never forgive me, and then she would come home.'

Mr. Birkett, disentangling Mrs. Brandon's various emotions, said a suitable word for each, adding that he saw nothing wrong in being glad that one's daughter was not likely to be a widow at once.

'You know,' he said, 'that Geraldine is engaged to Geoff Fairweather of the Barsetshires, whose brother married Rose. They are a very undemonstrative couple but they have known each other for years and we are very happy about it. And Rose is to have a baby in August.'

Mrs. Brandon was enchanted and they plunged together into an orgy of grandmothering and grandfathering that lasted them till dessert.

The Colonial Bishop had meanwhile been taken over by Mrs. Crawley and cautiously sounded as to his views about the Bishop of Barchester. With great disloyalty to a colleague he said he already saw eye to eye with the Dean, so he and his hostess got on very well.

Delia being now claimed by the Archdeacon, Lydia found herself at liberty to deal with Mr. Needham, tucked up her wristbands and came into the ring, asking her neighbour how he had been getting on. Mr. Needham said quite well thank you and how charming Miss Brandon, whom he hadn't met before, was.

'Oh, Delia,' said Lydia. 'She's awfully nice, but I shouldn't have thought you'd have noticed it. I thought it was her mother you were gone on. Most people are.'

'Of course I do admire Mrs. Brandon frightfully,' said Mr. Needham, casting a sheep's eye across the table to where Mrs. Brandon was enjoying herself with Mr. Birkett. 'But there is something so very nice about Miss Brandon. She is so very pretty.'

'That's why she's engaged,' said Lydia, determined that Mr. Needham should not be distracted from the one suitable object. 'She told me before dinner.'

'Oh,' said Mr. Needham, a little dashed.

'I should have thought you might have noticed her ring,' said Lydia severely, 'considering which finger it's on. How's Octavia? I mean is Matron being horrible? I didn't have time to ask before dinner.'

'I think Matron is being very unfair,' said Mr. Needham chivalrously. 'She has put the worst abdominal in D Ward and Octavia was just going in for abdominals, because she says she has enough head wounds and wants more general experience. Octavia was marvellous about it. I wish I thought about my work as much as she does. But then she's doing real work and I'm — —'

'That's enough, Tommy,' said Lydia. 'I told you before that you were doing jolly good work. I think Octavia looks ripping to-night.'

She looked firmly across at Octavia, who was certainly not looking any less uninteresting than usual and finding Mr. Keith curiously unsympathetic to her account of a patient who had had a heart attack.

'She makes me think of some heroine,' said Mr. Needham, 'and I feel so ashamed of myself. I know I couldn't be a hero, but — —'

'Oh, shut *up*, Tommy,' said Lydia, exasperated. 'I'd hit you on the back if it weren't a dinner party. What about you being a military chaplain? Then if you got wounded Octavia could nurse you.'

Mr. Needham's eyes gleamed.

'And now tell me about the Choir School football team,' said Lydia, feeling that she had done enough for Mr. Needham's love affairs.

He needed no encouragement to tell her all she didn't want to know and she was able to listen in a kind of dream, her thoughts in the past, on a cold winter's day, walking on the terrace at Northbridge Manor.

All this time Mr. Miller had been comparing notes with Mrs. Birkett about evacuees and Mrs. Birkett had secretly come to the conclusion, as she always did, that Mr. Miller was that nicest of things, a really good person who was wholly unconscious of being good, and felt that only a devil would have disliked most of the Southbridge evacuees as much as she did, so that it was quite a comfort to her when Mr. Miller confessed that he had harboured un-Christian thoughts against the worst of their boys who had drowned six chickens and kicked the hen and broken her leg.

'What did you do, Mr. Miller?' Mrs. Birkett asked.

'The old Adam rose in me and I beat him,' said Mr. Miller. 'Not even after reflexion, I fear, but in anger.'

'Then I am certain that you did him a great deal of good,' said Mrs. Birkett firmly, 'and probably saved him from the gallows later.'

'That is what my dear wife said,' said Mr. Miller, casting an adoring look at Mrs. Miller who was in the middle of the Mothers' Union with the Dean, 'and indeed, indeed I hope that it may be so, though I fear the gallows are still gaping for that boy. He has been trying to dig to Australia among the lettuces, thus causing considerable loss of good food. But my wife is the greatest comfort in these trials and her influence over the boys is astounding.'

By now Noel was well in possession of Miss Pettinger, but much to his annoyance the game of Pettinger-baiting which he had promised himself had lost its savour. It was not that Miss Pettinger had lost hers, for her horribleness was more pronounced than ever, but instead of being amused Noel found her simply boring. Dinner seemed to him quite interminable. After what felt like hours of the Pettinger's voice he suddenly heard the words 'Lydia Keith' and came to attention with a jerk.

'Lydia Keith and Delia Brandon and the dear Dean's Octavia and so many more of our Old Barcastrianas are doing excellent work,' Miss Pettinger was saying, 'worthy of the very best traditions of Barchester High School. I was very much gratified to have a letter this morning from Miss Wixett, our first head mistress and still among us at Lyme Regis I am glad to say, bidding us all God-speed in our work. I read her letter aloud to My Girls after prayers.'

'How like you,' said Noel admiringly. 'I am sure it is largely due to your influence that Octavia and the others are doing such good work.'

This appalling lie was, as Noel fully realized, merely a bait to Miss Pettinger to go on talking about Lydia, though for some reason Noel found it impossible to mention her name at the moment and had to include her among others.

'I do my best to carry on the wonderful traditions of our old school,' said Miss Pettinger bridling, 'and I think I can say that no girl passes the School Certificate from Barchester High School without being in some way moulded or even changed for the good.'

'I am sure Octavia was,' said Noel generously.

'Dear Octavia is just the type that we wish to turn out,' said Miss Pettinger, looking with an almost human look at her ex-pupil's dull but self-satisfied face.

'I know I would feel exactly the same about her,' said Noel in the pleasant certainty that Miss Pettinger would not understand.

'As for dear Lydia,' said Miss Pettinger, 'she is a warm-hearted girl, but I could wish she had had the Honour of the School more at heart.

She never seemed to realize the importance of attending to every rule in the School's Code of Honour. I remember that in her last summer term I had to give her four Red Marks and one Black Mark for repeatedly hanging her shoe bag on the wrong peg in the Senior Cloakroom. Now her elder sister Kate was quite different; so conscientious. And her sister-in-law, Mrs. Robert Keith, who was Edith Fairweather, was a wonderful influence among the girls, so good at hockey and cricket and keenly interested in *The Barcastriana*, our school magazine. It is a pity that Lydia has not kept up with us more. She has only come to one Old Girls' Reunion since she left. She does not look to me so fit as I like to see our Old Girls. I wish she would take up nursing, or land work, or some healthy form of war activity, but one cannot well interfere.'

'No, indeed,' said Noel, who, having gained his wish and heard Miss Pettinger speak of Lydia, would now have liked to strangle her.

But at this moment Mrs. Crawley collected her ladies' eyes and rose.

The conversation of women is on the whole so much more interesting than that of gentlemen that we will leave the Dean and his guests to discuss local and world affairs and waft outselves up to the drawing-room. Here Mrs. Brandon, true to her promise, seated herself on the little green settee, but did not fluffle out her dress, because she wanted to talk to Mrs. Crawley.

'Come and sit with me,' she said to her hostess. 'I want to tell you about Delia before it is in *The Times*. She is going to marry our nice cousin Hilary Grant. I am telling everyone, so really *The Times* will almost be a war extravagance, but one cannot quite get engaged without it.'

Mrs. Crawley expressed warm congratulations and was glad to hear that Hilary would not at present be in danger.

'We are *all* in danger,' said Mrs. Brandon stoutly, not wishing anyone to think that Delia would be too comfortable. Mrs. Crawley said it was in a way a comfort.

'No, I really can't agree with you,' said Mrs. Brandon with one of her devastating attacks of truthfulness. 'It would be much nicer if we weren't, only one doesn't quite know where to draw the line. If all the children and everyone under about thirty was safe it would be much more comfortable and it wouldn't matter so much about us, except for all the ones that are being *really* useful like your husband and Sir Edmund and the Birketts and practically everybody one knows. But what is really annoying, because though it may not be dangerous it is very worrying for her friends, or at least the people that know her, is Hilary's mother.'

'What has happened to her?' asked Mrs. Crawley.

'Nothing,' said Mrs. Brandon, 'which is just what I complain of, because she *will* not leave Calabria where she lodges with a very short, stout chemist and his wife who is often a bandit in a small way, at least he is, called Marco Aurelio, and is writing a book about Calabrian folk-lore which she knows far too intimately. And I am so afraid Hilary will feel he ought to go out and bring her home, which she certainly would not do and would be a very great trial to everyone when she got here owing to having no settled home. She spent a few weeks at the Cow and Sickle in the village when she was last in England and owing to her trying to teach Mrs. Spindler to cook macaroni in the Calabrian way with goat's cheese, which of course one luckily cannot get, Mrs. Spindler has hated me ever since, though all I did was to go and call on Mrs. Grant once or twice.'

'I think I met her at Lady Norton's,' said Mrs. Crawley. 'All home-spun and sensible shoes.'

'And hung with distressed jewellery,' said Mrs. Brandon. 'And do tell me about all your family.'

This Mrs. Crawley was not averse to doing and when duty compelled her to move on to Miss Pettinger, who was being held at bay valiantly by Mrs. Miller who made her promise to lend the School Hall for a summer meeting of G.F.S. branches before she could think of an excuse, Mrs. Brandon fluffled her dressed and sat all over the little green settee looking like a delicious double sweet-pea, so that the Archdeacon's daughter, who wanted to tell her about her engagement to Guy Barton, had to bring up a little stool.

'I am very fond of Guy,' said the Archdeacon's daughter, clasping her competent, workman's hands round her knees. 'He used to be a bit of an ass, but we've always got on well and the R.A.F. will do him all the good in the world. I don't think we'll get married yet, because I've got all the Land Girls to organize for West Barsetshire. Either after the war, or when he is invalided out, if he crashes.'

Mrs. Brandon, not quite sure how much of this detachment was real, how much a mask, said she didn't know Mr. Barton, but she had heard how very nice he was.

'A bit too nice if you ask me,' said the Archdeacon's daughter dis-passionately. 'He didn't behave frightfully well to Phoebe Rivers when he was engaged to her, but he won't do that again.'

'Wasn't she a cousin of Lord Pomfret's; a good-looking girl, very smart?' said Mrs. Brandon.

'Jolly good-looking,' said the Archdeacon's daughter. 'She married Humberton, Lord Platfield's eldest son, down in Shropshire. I was a bridesmaid and Lord Humberton can't stand Phoebe's mother, so that's all right. It was a nasty slap in the eye for Guy and I had to take him in hand.'

And now the men came in and Noel advanced upon Mrs. Brandon, who suddenly shrank to half her former size and smiled to him to sit down beside her.

'Need I say how exquisite you are looking?' said Noel.

'Of course you need,' said Mrs. Brandon. 'It is only women who trouble to tell other women that they look nice, so coming from a man it has great value. But this dress is a rag.'

'You are not only the most charming, but the most untruthful woman I know,' said Noel, so that they both laughed.

'And now,' said Mrs. Brandon, who would undoubtedly have tapped him with her fan if she had one, 'what is it you want to say? And pray be quick, for I see the Dean's eye on me.'

'It's difficult to be quick,' said Noel, 'because you see I've never fallen in love before, and I am a little shamefaced about it.'

Mrs. Brandon's enchanting face assumed the expression of a child who sees a very large ice-pudding.

'Do you mean you want to tell me about it?' she said.

'I do, Lavinia,' said Noel. 'And nobody else.'

'Is it Lydia?' said Mrs. Brandon, pretending as she spoke to assure the fastening of one of her diamond earrings, so that her face was half concealed from the room by her arm.

'How did you know?' said Noel, utterly taken aback.

'Because I've seen it coming ever since the Vicarage fête at Pomfret Madrigal two years ago,' said Mrs. Brandon placidly. 'And I must say I have been an extremely good warming-pan for your attentions, though to call it chandelier as the French do is much more elegant and I hope you are grateful.'

'Devil!' said Noel, looking so affectionately at Mrs. Brandon that Lydia Keith, who happened to be looking that way, couldn't help noticing it and almost wishing she were Mrs. Brandon.

In a less sophisticated age, Mrs. Brandon would automatically have said: 'Oh, you naughty man,' but though she was quite capable of such an anachronism she merely smiled one of her most bewitching smiles and asked if she could help.

'I don't know,' said Noel. 'You see I never knew it till all that cold weather we had. And now I can't help reflecting that I am a great deal older than she is and might lose a perfect friend by trying to gain a wife. Do you think she would consider my application?'

'Of all the nincompoops!' said Mrs. Brandon, which made Noel, who although considerably her junior had always felt like her contemporary, suddenly realize that she looked upon him as a young man, not belonging to the real world of grown-up people.

'You think I could, then?' he said.

'How long are you on leave?' said Mrs. Brandon.

Noel said he had to go back to town by the night train in about an hour.

'Well, you *might* manage it to-night, though it would be difficult,' said Mrs. Brandon. 'If you can't, you must do it the very next time you get leave.'

'Thank you, Lavinia. You are an angel,' said Noel.

'And if you don't, you need never come to Stories again,' said Mrs. Brandon. 'Oh! Dr. Crawley, I *did* so want to talk to you. What do you think the Bishop's wife said at Lady Norton's the other day?'

Noel took this *congé* and the Dean, saying that whatever that woman said would be in keeping with the Palace traditions, sat down beside her to gossip. Noel looked towards Lydia, but she was conversing so earnestly with Mr. Needham in a corner that he suddenly felt old and fell into talk with the Colonial Bishop.

It was not altogether of Lydia's own will that she was talking again to Mr. Needham, but that young gentleman had waylaid her, to explain to her all over again his efforts to be a military chaplain.

'I believe I could get to France now,' said Mr. Needham, 'because two or three of the people who deal with that are old Internationals but I can't decide if it is my duty or if I am only being selfish. After all I am a priest.'

'A clergyman, you mean,' said Lydia severely. 'Priest sounds like a monk. Look here, Tommy, have you read the Thirty-Nine Articles?'

'Do you mean *The Thirty-Nine Steps*?' said Mr. Needham who could not believe his ears.

A year or two earlier Lydia would have said: 'Of course not, you great fool,' but that arrogant Lydia was far away, and Miss Lydia Keith said to Mr. Needham that she meant Articles and supposed he was a Christian.

Thus challenged, Mr. Needham said rather huffily that he saw no point in such a question.

'I'm only trying to help you,' said Lydia patiently. 'I've been reading it myself and I must say I think it's a frightfully good bit of work; I mean, there's room for everyone in it. And it says that it is lawful for Christian men to wear weapons and serve in the wars, so there you are. And if you want a Magistrate to commend you, I know Sir Edmund would, or Mr. Keith. They're both J.P.s.'

At this jumbled and earnest piece of special pleading, the scales fell from Mr. Needham's eyes and to his intense joy and relief he suddenly saw the paths of duty and desire for once coinciding. With real gratitude and humility he thanked Lydia.

'That's all right, Tommy,' said Lydia, 'only don't ask anyone's advice again. You just go ahead.'

'Do you think I ought to tell Octavia?' said Mr. Needham.

'Of course,' said Lydia. 'And I'd tell her at once if I were you.'

'If I had anything to offer,' said Mr. Needham, 'do you think she would wait for me till I came back? Or perhaps it wouldn't be fair to ask her.'

'Don't be an ass,' said Lydia, with a flash of her old impatience. 'Take her for a walk when she comes off duty to-morrow and tell her everything.'

Then Sir Edmund, who was very fond of Lydia, came limping down upon her and she exerted herself to be the kind of girl Sir Edmund liked and gave him an amusing evening. The party broke up early and by half-past ten the guests had said good-bye to Mrs. Crawley and assembled in the hall for their last glimpse of light before plunging into the black-out. Lydia, waiting for her father to get his coat and hat on, found Mr. Needham at her elbow.

'I asked Octavia if she would have a walk with me to-morrow,' he said in a voice of subdued excitement, 'and she was going to an extra lecture on peritonitis, but she is going to cut it for me. You are an *angel*, Lydia,' he said vehemently.

'Write to me at once, won't you,' said Lydia. 'I can't tell you how happy I am.'

And she slipped her arm through Mr. Needham's and gave it a friendly and encouraging squeeze.

'Sorry, Noel,' she said, as she bumped her elbow against Mr. Merton, who had been jammed between Sir Edmund and the Archdeacon and so had very unwillingly heard Mr. Needham call Lydia an angel and Lydia beg Mr. Needham to write, besides seeing her take that young gentleman's arm. He was used to his Lydia's ebullient ways but he found himself hating Mr. Needham in a most unseemly way for being so much younger than himself.

'Good-bye, Noel,' said Mrs. Brandon, all furred and cloaked (for these phrases come naturally to one's mind when speaking of her). 'Don't forget.'

'You may command me in anything,' said Noel. 'Bless you,' and he lifted her hand to his lips for she was one of the few women he knew who could take such homage with grace.

Owing to the squash Lydia could not disentangle her arm from Mr. Needham's in time not to see what she saw, hear what she heard.

'Good-bye, Lydia,' said Noel. 'Shall I see you when I get my next leave?'

'Of course,' said Lydia, wondering, as they shook hands.

Their eyes met, asking questions that this was no time, no place to answer. Lydia drove home with her father and Noel caught the night train to London, each thinking, just like people in novels, that the other's heart was not so warm, not so near, each determined to die sooner than infringe by a hair's breadth the freedom of the other.

XV

STORY WITHOUT AN END

THE loveliest spring that England could remember had emerged from the long hard winter and went flashing by in luxuriant riot into early summer, at cinema speed. And with the quick and profuse blossoming of almond, wild cherry, hawthorn red white and pink, buttercups, lilac, laburnum; with the onward rush of the trees from a mist of tender green to a heavy and sullen leafage, the rush of events came thundering down from the Arctic Circle across the Low Countries, marshalled by the Powers of Darkness.

The Earl of Pomfret died quietly in the small hours of the morning, early in May. I do not think he had any fears or regrets. His heir, whom he had at first mistrusted and gradually come to value, would carry on, under changed conditions, work for which he knew he would soon have been unfit, and had already two sons. His heir's wife he liked and respected, for she had the best hands in the county and good common sense. They were both by his bed when his eyes failed to see the sunlight flooding his room. He held a hand of each and spoke the name of his dead wife and the son who had been killed a lifetime ago in a frontier skirmish. The eighth Earl of Pomfret looked down on the seventh Earl and took up his burden.

Old Lord Pomfret was buried quietly in the parish church-yard. There was a Memorial Service at St. Margaret's, Westminster, for the outer world. Then there was a Memorial Service in Barchester Cathedral, attended by the whole county, high and low; the last time that many of those in the great congregation were to see each other.

Lydia Keith and her father were among those present. Lydia had half hoped that she might see Noel Merton in the Deanery pew, but when he was not there, she knew that her thoughts had been self-delusion. She went home by train alone, for her father was to stay on in Barchester for a committee and dine with his son Robert to discuss some business of the firm. Mrs. Keith had not been so well and depended more and more on Lydia, who handled her mother with firm and unaltering kindness. Lydia and her father knew that Mrs. Keith's heart was less satisfactory each month, and they both felt a chill shadow of private grief among the shadow of general sadness and apprehension, and both bore the shadow with courage and worked all the harder.

But the shadow was not to touch Mr. Keith. When he left Robert's house that evening he walked down to the County Club where he had left his car in the morning. In the uncertain light he stepped into the road in front of a stationary car, was hit by a lorry and taken unconscious to the Barchester Hospital. He had only done what thousands of people do every day, and paid the penalty. The lorry driver was in no way to blame, rather to be pitied for the sense of guilt that Mr. Keith's carelessness must have caused him. Lydia was fetched by her brother Robert early next morning. As Mrs. Keith was used to her husband and daughter being out and about before she came down, she felt no alarm. Mr. Keith lingered, always unconscious, for two days and then died without recognizing Robert or Lydia.

It had been necessary to tell Mrs. Keith that her husband was injured and this Robert and Lydia had managed with such kindness that she was not made ill, as they had feared. When she had to be told that her husband was dead she was more stunned than unhappy. Luckily Nurse Chiffinch, an excellent nurse who had been with old Lord Pomfret and was known to Mrs. Morland, could be secured, and was installed to look after Mrs. Keith for the present.

Lydia, who had prepared herself for her mother's possible death, was shaken to the core by this turn of fate, but held valiantly to her post. Robert's wife offered to come and stay with her, as did her own sister Kate, but with many thanks Lydia said she could manage it better alone. Robert took over all business matters for her. Northbridge Manor was left to him. As he and his wife had no wish to live there at present it was agreed that part of the house should be shut up and Mrs. Keith go on living there for the present under Nurse Chiffinch's care, while Lydia would do her capable best with the estate and all Mr. Keith's local activities.

To Lydia's intense joy her brother Colin was able to get twenty-four hours' leave on the day when Mr. Keith was buried. He was well and fit and absorbed in his soldier's life and for a moment Lydia's burden was lifted. Of his future movements he gave Lydia no information, for he had none. Lydia asked if he had heard of Noel, but he had dropped out of touch with many old friends, Noel among them. There could be no Grand Opening of the boating season this year, so they took the punt up to Parsley Island and laughed at remembering the picnic there when Rose Birkett had taken Noel's and Everard's coats to shelter her pink dress from the thunderstorm and Philip had been so unpleasant and Communist about flowers in churches.

Colin had to go back the same evening. Lydia sat with her mother till Nurse Chiffinch announced that her patient ought to be thinking of Bedfordshire now, which she did with a brightness that only Mrs. Keith's apathy and Lydia's restrained grief kept them from resenting, though she was so good and kind and conscientious that they were really grateful to her. Lydia sat up till late answering letters of condolence for her mother and went to bed so tired that being young she was able to go to sleep at once.

Next day, in the full loveliness of spring, the world was told of the betrayal of a little army, sent in answer to a stricken country's cry for help. Every heart was stunned by the thought of what might come, every heart was steeled to bear the very worst, and darkness covered the sun. England held her breath and was silent, waiting, while the author of the betrayal slipped into black oblivion, beyond human blame, beyond human compassion.

Lydia, wisely considering activity the best remedy for most ills, after seeing her mother and Nurse Chiffinch had a few words with Palmer about the silver. It had been arranged that most of it was to go to the bank for the present, a step which Palmer chose to take as a direct personal insult. Lydia accepted Palmer's notice with complete equanimity and even relief, and after putting on an overall began to turn out things in the drawing-room, for it had been decided to shut it up and use the small study or library. For a couple of hours she rolled up rugs, took the washing covers off chairs and sofas, dust-sheeted much of the furniture, wrapped china in tissue paper and put it in a hamper to be stored in the garage. Then she turned her attention to the books. Some she proposed to put in the study, the rest she began to pack in empty cases supplied by the gardener. As always happens when one begins to finger books she opened first one and then another, read snatches, rebuked herself and went on with her work. And all the time sunshine was flooding the room and the scent of wistaria came piercingly on the light breeze through the open french window.

Presently she found an old volume of Grimm's *Household Tales* which had belonged to Mrs. Keith's childhood and had been read aloud to all the young Keiths in turn. Turning its rather battered pages, many of them loose with age and hard use, she fell completely into its charm and was reading earnestly, perched on the uncomfortable edge of a packing case, when a shadow fell on the book. She looked up and saw Noel Merton who had come in by the french window. Lydia laid down her book, got up, and went straight to Noel's arms. Noel, hardly able to believe that his proud Lydia could lay her head so on his shoulder in peace, held her very lightly and said nothing. Then, sensitive to a faint withdrawal on her part, he let her go.

'Lydia; I didn't know,' he said, speaking as if nothing had happened between them. 'I hadn't seen a paper for days, or only the cheap rags, and I never knew about your father. I ran into Roddy Wicklow in town last night and he told me.'

'It was pretty bad for Mother,' said Lydia. 'But Robert and Edith and Everard and Kate have been angels and we have a splendid nurse. And Colin did get down for the funeral and we went on the river. I am *pleased* to see you, Noel.'

Noel asked a few questions about the future of Northbridge Manor and satisfied himself that Lydia and her mother were being well looked after. Then he did not quite know what to say. His Lydia looked well though her eyes were shadowed, but his missed her uncaring arrogance and wondered with a pang if he had bad news for her. But it had better be told.

'I came down to the Deanery to-day,' he said, not adding that he had come solely to see Lydia and give any help he could, 'and found Crawley and Mrs. Crawley transported with joy, though a duller thing to be joyful about have I never seen. Had you heard about Octavia?'

'She isn't engaged to Tommy, is she?' said Lydia, suddenly alive with pleasure and interest.

Noel nodded, with such a revulsion of relief that he could not speak.

'I don't want to boast,' said Lydia, 'but I practically did it. I gave Tommy a most *awful* talking to that night at the Deanery and he promised he'd take Octavia for a walk next day when she came off duty. Good old Tommy. When are they to be married?'

'That part is even duller, if possible,' said Noel. 'Needham has just heard that he can go abroad, and he and Octavia have decided that it is their duty not to get married, though for no reason at all as far as I can see except that it makes them both feel heroic and Daisy-Chain-ish. I think the Crawleys would have liked to see Octavia married; in fact I know they would because Mrs. Crawley told me so, but of course they can't thrust their child into matrimony if she and her bridegroom don't want it. However, Octavia proposes to go abroad with the Red Cross and her eyes are glistening at the thought of meeting Needham in a hospital one mass of head wounds and abdominals.'

And at this they both laughed in a very un-serious way till Lydia suddenly stopped.

'Gosh!' she said. 'If I loved anyone I'd marry them at once.'

Then to Noel's intense surprise her face went bright pink and she looked at him as if imploring forgiveness.

'You couldn't think of me in that light, I suppose,' said Noel. 'Because if you did I would be more than willing. Much more.'

For the first time since he had known his Lydia her gaze dropped before his.

'I thought perhaps I wasn't grown-up enough for you,' she said in a small, desolate voice. 'I mean Mrs. Brandon and people are the sort I thought you really liked.'

'Listen to me, my girl,' said Noel; 'and let me tell you that I thought perhaps I was too old for you. I am ashamed to say that I thought you might like Needham.'

'*Tommy?*' said Lydia, lifting her eyes in wonder at Noel's stupidity.

And upon that she gave such a very credible imitation of a small fit of hysterics that Noel had to hold her until her voice and body were steady again; which did not take long, for she had herself well in hand.

'I've always thought you were the nicest girl I knew,' said Noel. 'And when you said in that voice that you would marry anyone you loved at once, I couldn't bear it any longer.'

'Of course I will,' said Lydia. 'I'll have to go on living here and looking after Mother and the place of course, but then you'll probably be busy and you can always come here when you get leave. We couldn't get married to-day, could we?'

'I'm afraid not,' said Noel. 'But I think we could manage it to-morrow if you like. And as for leave, I think I'll be sent abroad at any moment.'

'That's all right,' said the old Lydia. 'I mean, I expect you'll be much happier abroad. We'd better tell Robert and Kate. Oh, and Colin.'

Without wasting any more time over sentiment Lydia rang up her sister Kate who was enchanted, and very untruthfully said she had always known it. Kate said she would get Robert and his wife to dinner and Lydia must bring Noel. A telegram was sent to Colin who answered with the longest and most expensive Golden Telegram ever sent of love, approval and regrets that he couldn't get away. Kate had undertaken to tell the Birketts and a few old friends. Then Palmer grudgingly came in to ask if Mr. Merton was staying for lunch.

'It's Captain Merton,' said Lydia. 'Yes, he is. And we are going to be married to-morrow, so you'd better tell Cook and everyone. Come on, Noel.'

Mrs. Keith was staying in bed till the afternoon, so they only had Nurse Chiffinch for lunch. That excellent creature was delighted by the news and eagerly entered into the discussion as to when they should tell Mrs. Keith. It was finally decided that Lydia, who as she pointed out was twenty-one, should say nothing to her mother till the marriage had taken place. Noel wondered if it was rather deceitful, but Nurse Chiffinch said so firmly that her patient would only worry if she heard of the engagement that she got her way.

Noel then had to go back to Barchester.

'I'll come and fetch you this evening,' he said from the inside of the car, 'and take you to Kate's. I do like your Chiffinch.'

'She's an awfully good sort,' said Lydia, 'and an angel with Mother, even if she is a bit nurse-ish. I know she will count on her fingers from the moment we are married and take offence if I don't engage her almost at once.'

'I hadn't really considered that question yet,' said Noel, wondering if he were blushing, and thankful for the years of comradeship with Lydia that made her unabashed frankness so easy a thing.

'Babies, you mean,' said Lydia, with all her old severity. 'Well, I really hadn't much either,' she added frankly. 'I should think I'm more a wife than a mother, but you never know. Anyway, we'll not bother and see what happens.'

Noel found nothing to say. He pressed Lydia's capable hand that lay on the door of the car and was answered by such a look of mute adoration as seriously disturbed his driving.

At the Carters' house the millennium appeared to have set in, in spite of every discouragement. Noel, who had spent the afternoon over various matters of business, some at his father's office (a solicitor as it may be remembered in Barchester), some with other authorities, was able to report that he and Lydia would be married to-morrow and the Dean insisted on performing the ceremony himself and Mr. Needham was to be allowed to help. With Robert he had a short talk which showed Robert that his young sister's material interests would be well cared for.

Kate, who was joyfully in her element of kind fussing, then said that she knew the sight of Bobbie would do Mrs. Keith more good than anything and that she proposed to bring him and his nurse over to Northbridge on the following day and stay there as long as Noel could get leave, so that he and Lydia would be free to go where they liked.

Mrs. Brandon then rang up to say that she had to go to London for a few days to get some clothes for Delia and would be deeply offended if Noel and Lydia didn't use Stories for their honeymoon.

'You are an angel, Lavinia,' said Noel, who had taken over the call.

'Of course I am,' said Mrs. Brandon. 'That is all an old woman like myself is fit for.'

'I refuse to make any comment on that remark,' said Noel.

'Nincompoop. Bless you a thousand times,' said Mrs. Brandon and rang off.

Then Mr. and Mrs. Birkett came over full of congratulations. Mr. Birkett was preoccupied with the School measles which were wavering between German and plain, but extremely cordial. Mrs. Birkett not unnaturally felt that the engagement was a peg on which to hang conversation about Geraldine, who was to be married at the end of May all being well and had been allowed to assist at a blood transfusion; but she was warm in her congratulations.

'Is there any news of Philip?' said Noel.

'None, since he went abroad,' said Everard.

But for the moment the shadow of the little army fighting its way stubbornly back from treachery to the friendly sea was not allowed to intrude.

When Noel and Lydia left, Everard caught Noel for a moment.

'Have you any idea of what your movements are likely to be?' he asked. 'I'm not being Fifth Columnist, but we'd like to know what Lydia can count on.'

'It is three days' leave,' said Noel.

'That means,' said Everard, 'that you have to go back the day after to-morrow. We'll take care of Lydia.'

Noel left Lydia at the door of Northbridge Manor.

'Noel,' she said out of the darkness. 'I suppose you will have to go abroad fairly soon.'

'The day after to-morrow,' said Noel.

'That's all right,' said Lydia, and vanished into the house.

*

Kate was as good as her word and not only brought Bobbie over, but managed so to insinuate into her mother's mind the horrible idea of

Lydia's being an old maid that Mrs. Keith said she had always been afraid when Lydia did so badly in her exams that she would never get married, and what a pity it was that Noel Merton, who was so very nice, wasn't a little younger as he might have taken an interest in Lydia. With this to work on Kate managed to break the news that Lydia and Noel, properly married by the Dean, would be back to lunch, and by this time Mrs. Keith was so sure that she had foreseen and arranged the whole thing herself that her greatest anxiety was having mislaid a very hideous set of garnets belonging to her grandmother that she wanted Lydia to have. By dint of Kate and Nurse Chiffinch's united efforts in looking in all the places where Mrs. Keith was sure the garnets were, they were at last discovered in the one place where she knew that they weren't, and she was able to welcome the married couple and was reported by Nurse Chiffinch to be standing it splendidly.

*

'I must say,' said Lydia, as she and Noel, after an astoundingly good dinner, sat under the Spanish chestnut in the garden at Stories, 'that being married feels much the same.'

'Only nicer,' said Noel. 'You are much the nicest girl I ever met in my life, Lydia. In fact, perfect.'

'It is all so nice and comfortable,' said Lydia, 'because I know you so well. I mean it must be rather a bore to marry someone you don't know. They mightn't be as nice as you think. Where shall we live, do you think, when you come back? I mean when you really come back for ever.'

'We'll have to consider it,' said Noel.

'Will you ring up or send me a telegram as soon as you get back to England,' said Lydia. 'I should be so glad to know.'

Noel said he would.

'Of course it might be a telegram to say you were dead,' said Lydia, facing facts with her usual firmness. 'But I'd go on loving you just the same.'

*

On the next day Noel went. Lydia came back to Northbridge Manor and took up her old way of life. Kind Kate stayed on for a time and kept Mrs. Keith from asking Lydia more than once a day if there was any news from Noel. Full spring merged into early summer with incredible riot of blossom and leaf, while the sea before Dunkirk was covered with a thousand ships. Philip Winter returned to the Carters' house, looking aged by many years, and spent most of his time sleeping. On a hot afternoon he bicycled over to Northbridge Manor to see Kate and Lydia.

Kate was sitting on the terrace by her mother who was better that day. Bobbie was on the grass, being headed off from the flower beds by his nurse. Lydia, in a garden apron, was weeding at the other end of the terrace, for the warm days and a reduced garden staff had made weeds spring up everywhere and it was not easy to pull them up from the sun-hardened earth. Philip sat and talked with Mrs. Keith and Kate for a little and admired Bobbie's peculiar manner of speech, unintelligible to all, but considered a masterpiece of elocution by those best qualified to judge.

'Everard sent you his love, Kate,' said Philip, 'and he has some good news. Mr. Bissell told him that Mr. Hopkins has been rounded up as a Fifth Columnist and interned.'

Kate, who simply had to be kind to someone, said it would be very horrid for the people Mr. Hopkins was interned with, which is perhaps the most unkind thing we have ever known her say.

Presently Palmer, who had withdrawn her notice after the gentle Kate had spoken words of fire to her, and been allowed to stay on, came out into the garden, carrying a salver.

'It's a telegram for Miss Lydia, madam,' she said.

Kate and Philip exchanged glances.

'Please remember to say Mrs. Merton, Palmer,' said Kate in her best housemaster's wife's voice.

Palmer meekly said she was sorry she was sure.

'I'll take it to her,' said Philip as carelessly as he could, while Kate headed her mother's thoughts towards the enormity of Palmer calling Lydia 'Miss Lydia'.

Philip walked along the terrace to where Lydia was weeding.

'It's a wire for you, Lydia,' he said.

Lydia looked up and her face was white, but she got to her feet and took off her gardening gloves.

'Shall I open it?' said Philip, his heart beating furiously with his anxiety.

'No, thank you,' said Lydia. 'I think I ought to open my own telegrams. And whatever it was I'd love Noel just the same.'